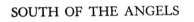

SOUTH OF THE ANGELS

Other books by Jessamyn West

THE FRIENDLY PERSUASION

A MIRROR FOR THE SKY

THE WITCH DIGGERS

CRESS DELAHANTY

LOVE, DEATH, AND THE LADIES' DRILL TEAM

TO SEE THE DREAM

LOVE IS NOT WHAT YOU THINK

# SOUTH OF THE ANGELS

BY JESSAMYN

# WEST

NEW YORK ⬚ *Harcourt, Brace & Company*

PS3545
E8315
S6

© 1960 by Jessamyn West

All rights reserved. No part of this book may be reproduced
in any form or by any mechanical means, including mimeo-
graph and tape recorder, without permission in writing from
the publisher.

first edition

Library of Congress Catalog Card Number: 60-6714
Printed in the United States of America

36787

SOUTH OF THE ANGELS

STRAHORN LIBRARY
THE COLLEGE OF IDAHO
Caldwell, Idaho

# BOOK I

1    In los angeles, Mrs. Sylvester Perkins was dressing. She and Perk were going out to the Tract for the meeting at seven-thirty. It was not much after three, but Perk wanted to get an early start.

In Los Angeles in 1916 you had only to open your windows and pull up your blinds on a summer afternoon and you could rest on your bed in light as warm and sweet as that enjoyed by any hiker stretched out on the faded grass along the Hollywood hills. The lace of a drooping pepper tree, the frond of a palm, might put a shadow here and there in the bedroom which the hiker would not get; otherwise, for country air and August brilliance you were his equal: if country air and August brilliance were what you wanted.

They were not what Louella Perkins wanted. She had the blinds all pulled down and was ready, except for putting on her dress and hat, for the trip to the Tract. Stepping outdoors was as unnatural an act to her as stepping into a pond of water. She could and did do it; but she always returned to her substantially built, densely furnished home with the passion luckier women have for persons. She would sit in the center of a room content as any webbed spider, feeling as the spider does about his web, that the room and its furnishings were a part of her being. She had, without knowing it, a touch of claustrophobia, and to sit as she did now in a room as thoroughly closed as hers and Perk's added just that touch of painful apprehension needed to keep her nerves pleasantly a-jingle. Except for this exacerbating quality, the room might have gone flat for her.

She waited without impatience for Perk, who was in the bathroom

3

down the hall shaving. It was his second shave of the day; but he had said, looking at himself in the glass, "I don't intend to let so much as a whisker stand between me and success tonight."

The colors of the room were rose and beige, with a touch of blue here and there for contrast. They were her colors exactly, and the ratio of blue to rose to beige was a duplication of their ratio in her: large blue eyes, small pink cheeks, and a lot of beige skin and hair.

Perk came in clad in pants and B.V.D.s. His cheeks were pink, glazed with the shine of the newly shaved. Perk had a hard time shaving. He fought his whiskers the way another man might fight a rival or a horse, and he liked to report the ups and downs of his struggle to her. He was patting his face with a hand into which he now and then splashed lotion from a bottle he carried.

"Glycerin and rose water," he said. "The glycerin softens and lubricates, the rose water contracts. I've been using it since last Saturday and I think I can tell the difference already."

"That's good," said Louella. She did not in the least credit Perk's struggles with his whiskers. She thought they were perfectly ordinary whiskers that any other man would have removed as casually as he spit. She recognized the fact that she might be wrong about Perk's whiskers, but she was willing to gamble on her own intuitions. She and Perk never had a cross word; they occupied a double bed every night; she had borne Perk a son; and it was nature, not herself or Perk, who had let childbearing stop there. But Perk never moved her as much as any pretty room, well-placed chair, or nicely starched curtain; not as much, that is, as any object; though in fact she regarded him as an object; unfortunately, however, not one that she had selected.

Perk had selected her; and by the time she had discovered that he was, as far as she was concerned, an unpleasing object, she was married and pregnant. She was not in the least bitter or unhappy or discontented. She sat at the center of her marriage as if it were a room, and regarded *its* central furnishing, Perk, with the same kind of entranced disapproval she had for objects she approved. It was extraordinary, unbelievable, too—she didn't know the word ironic—to find her marriage, which was supposed to be a woman's end-all and be-all, centered upon a person like Perk: this man, whose every outline her eye corrected, every word she contradicted, every act she endured. The story of the frog turned to fairy prince, which was what you had a right to expect in marriage, was in her case the other way around. But that it should

4

be so and Perk never guess it—or anyone else, so far as she knew —made her a little queasy with pride of power. It was godlike to know, in the face of so general an ignorance, all the facts. And she did feel godlike sometimes with Perk—she, knowledgeable and self-contained, and Perk never questioning or doubting.

And there was this further fact that capped it all: she might be wrong. She alone—of the world's population—seemed to know these facts about Perk and to have these feelings for him. Was it possible for her to be right and the whole world wrong? Perk had the gift of succeeding. And by succeeding she was not thinking only of money; though if that was the test of success, there were not many in Southern California who had passed it as well as Perk. But, money aside, Perk was liked. The face that did not impress her struck others as handsome. Perk's secretaries remembered his birthday with affectionate notes and hand-crocheted neckties. At parties he was always the hub of a wheel of women. The widows of old friends doted on him. She, in fact, was the only woman in the world, evidently, who believed a man, before setting up in business as a male, should have visible eyebrows and sizable ears and mouth. Perk's little ankles evidently looked dapper to some women, his big middle dignified, and his slender neck refined. And maybe they were. It almost seemed they had to be; still, she held onto her own ideas of Perk, did not condemn him for his failure to please her, and waited to see how their story would turn out. The world fooled about Perk? Or she fooled? She watched events unfold the way a scientist watches an experiment; only, she was a part of this experiment, the metal the acid would eat—or vice versa, if vice versa should prove finally to *be* their story.

Perk, rubbing the rose water and glycerin into his face, said, "I want you to listen to my speech before we start."

"All right, I'm ready. That's what I'm waiting for."

"I can't make a speech to somebody undressed," Perk objected. "This is a serious speech. A lot depends on it. I want to feel like you're my audience. Put on your dress, Louella."

"Shall I put on my hat, too?" Louella asked, not sarcastically, because Perk would not have recognized sarcasm from her, but nevertheless enjoying her little joke.

"You do as you like about that," Perk said. "But I want to keep my mind on what I'm saying, not be thinking about your pretty little boobies." Perk came over, and, as far as he was able, hampered by her starched camisole and petticoat, and he in a hurry and still holding

5

his bottle of lotion, gave each, at its supposititious center, a snappy little tweak.

Perk's idea of himself, Louella knew, was that he was a man of strong passions, and perhaps, for all she knew of such men, or any other man at all, he was. But something told her he was not. He was a man of steady appetites and had the same passion for her he had for his morning coffee—was irritable without it or her, and in the habit of both; but neither she nor his coffee had a place in his imagination where she supposed the passions centered. Still, she could be wrong here, too, and she hung evenly balanced in her speculations on the subject, amused to think how much the joke was on her if she actually was the object of a superior man's lifelong passion. Whatever the name was for what Perk felt, she *was* its lifelong center. And far from having gratitude for this devotion, she blamed Perk for his lack of venturesomeness. She had the power to turn all his virtues wrong side out, to discover the rough side of any softness. For if a man never thought about other women, if he could not build up stories around the sight of a strange face, or did not need to clench his fists to keep from following that particular walk, then his lifelong choice was nothing but habit and lack of imagination, wasn't it? Nothing she needed to feel personal about? She was that habit's chance and that lack of imagination's victim, wasn't she?

She had her dress on by the time Perk was ready to practice his speech.

"Sit over there," Perk said, pointing to the rocker on the other side of the room. "Ladies and gentlemen," he began, holding his chin up and looking in her direction, but taking in the rows behind and in front of her, too. Then he relaxed from his oratorical pose, went across to the chair where his coat was, put it on, and returned to the spot he was using as platform. But he stayed relaxed, looked at Louella as though she were a wife instead of an audience, and said, "Louella, do you ever think what the Tract is?"

Perk had a number of ways of thinking of the Tract, Louella knew: as a sign of his own enterprise; as a chance for him to make a mint of money; as the last frontier; as a golden opportunity for its settlers; as the location, if the settlers wanted it that way, for a kind of latter-day paradise. A good deal of the time he thought of it in all these ways at once, but there was no use her hazarding a guess as to what he was thinking now, getting it wrong, and somehow hurting Perk by not knowing what was in his mind.

6

"I don't suppose I do," she said.

"Well," he said, "as I see it, it's a God-given opportunity for folks, especially young folks who haven't been able to get a toehold elsewhere, to start afresh in as beautiful and fertile a piece of country as there is on this planet. There's that. Just the land and the people. Just to move in there, between the foothills and the sea, on land that's not been worked over. I don't know what family could ask for more. Do you?"

Louella thought, Yes, we ask for more. But Perk, she remembered, had taken care of that. He'd said "folks who haven't been able to get a toehold elsewhere," so she replied, "It's an opportunity."

"It's not just an opportunity to make a living in a good land," he corrected her. "It's more than that. The settlers coming in there are all fresh to each other and fresh to the land. No church, no school, no chamber of commerce. There's nothing to keep them from building up there on the Tract something as fresh and sweet as hasn't been seen since the Garden of Eden. They've got a chance to start over, to build from the ground up and to build good. That's what the people on the Tract are getting."

Perk had tears in his eyes. They were real tears; he was ashamed of them and tried to blink them away before she could see them. Perk's tears were another source of doubt to Louella. The Perk she thought she knew should not have had them. They weighed in the balance against her judgment of him, just as did his apparent successes. "A boy riding his bicycle in the rain!" Perk had once exclaimed, seeing a boy doing that, and had turned away from her then also, to blink away his tears. In many ways this remained for her the most moving and exciting sentence she had ever heard Perk speak. Perhaps it was a sentimental thought that had prompted Perk's tears, but her imagination had been pleased by the source of the sentimentalism. She had since spent a good deal of time wondering about rain and boys and bicycles, and why the combination brought tears to Perk's eyes; but she would not for the world have asked him, for fear he would have given her an answer that would have tended to settle the balance of doubt she needed to have about him.

Perk paused, and she said, "I think that's a very good speech."

"Speech!" Perk exclaimed. "That's not my speech. I was just talking to you. I haven't started it yet."

She had not the least objection to listening to Perk rehearse his speeches. She was usually bored with them, knew where his sentences

7

and paragraphs were going before they were well started, and had generally, as the result of the experience, the same feeling of power and resolution an Indian fakir must have upon arising from his bed of nails: the feeling of having been able to take it. But she helped Perk as much as she could, without hurting his feelings; and she had a semi-conviction that she should say nothing. Rearrange the speeches to suit her, and they would perhaps lose their effectiveness for the audiences to whom he spoke. She often sat in those audiences of prospective buyers of his property, conclaves of real-estate agents, chambers of commerce, and she knew Perk spoke to them effectively. This difference between her response and the audience's augmented the enchantment of her life. Who was crazy? She or everyone else? There she sat (she knew it) looking more like the audience than the audience itself: tan hair marcelled evenly; beige silk dress with sprigs of blue and rose flowers; gloved hands folded—the speaker's wife, attentive as could be. But (and she knew this, too) she was fully as mysterious as everyone else.

She had no objections to hearing Perk's speech, but he had told her they must be on their way not later than four. She asked him what the time was.

Perk went over to the bureau where he had put his watch and loose change and looked at his watch. "You're right, Louella. I'll have to say it to you as we drive."

But once in their new black Overland, which Perk had picked as much as any reason because he liked its name, he appeared to lose interest in his speech. Instead, he talked to her of the reasons for the meeting, the unfairness of the settlers' demands for immediate water, and how he planned to handle both. The motion of riding bemused Louella. She could travel an entire day without feeling any need for speech, and since Perk did not expect any response from her, she only half heard what he was saying.

They traveled east out of town, passing the gas tanks on the right and Bishop's cooky factory, with its saliva-starting smells of warm chocolate and vaporizing vanilla, on the left. They passed through the shadow of the Catholic orphanage, perched bleak as death itself on a hilltop; drove between the two graveyards at the city's edge, as pretty under the low-hanging peppers as make-believe cities made by children; and were finally in the open country of the San Gabriel Valley, a long swale of river-watered grassland, sloping gently southward to the ocean. There had been no rain since mid-May, and nature's grass, except for a little at the river edge, was as dead and brown as coco matting; only the alfalfa of man's planting and irrigating stood up juicy and green from the water of the canals and reservoirs. The afternoon was warm, but there was in it that balanced delicacy of arrival and departure which makes early fall a time so touching to humans—a known good departing, and something else, hard to remember, arriving.

The landscape went past Louella like sections of a picture. She had never been mixed up with any of it. She did not know the feel of milkweed, silk or sap, had never chewed an alfalfa strand or gone to bed tired with the pull of a slope of the Sierra Madres in the calves of her legs. She gazed at all they passed with something of the same wonder that she accorded Perk, as mysteries she could not fathom and did not care to. People with some knowledge of milkweed and mountains were not so haunted by them; they had a little reality to chew on; mountains, they knew, were nothing but dirt and rubble piled high; milkweeds, nothing but a tall sticky growth.

By the time they had crossed the San Gabriel River, sparkling in its sunlit shallows, the Sierra Madres were blueing off toward evening and old Pio Pico's mansion, east of the river, sent up from a back chimney a spiral of sweet-smelling supper smoke. Beyond the governor's mansion, they came to Los Nietos, a Mexican town where children spilled over from the packed dirt yards into the road, and Perk had to slow down for fear of hitting them. After he had ten-miled his careful way through them, Perk said, "Those are the people who'll be ruling us once again if the Germans have their way."

"Again?" asked Louella, aware of the children, but old Pio Pico already out of her mind.

"They did once," Perk reminded her. "Whose house do you think we just passed?"

Louella, remembering, said, "There's not much chance of that happening, is there?"

"There's a good chance of Germany winning, if you want my opinion. And the Mexicans don't have any reason to love us. This was their land till we took it away from them."

Louella did not want to talk about the war but did not want to say so either.

"Have there been many new settlers recently?" she asked.

"New ones every day," Perk said. "I don't try to keep pace with them any more."

Louella asked no more questions. If Perk wanted to talk about them, that was the best of his talk. If he did not, she would not feel put out. Perk's descriptions of people gave her about the same glimpses she got from driving past trees and mountains, appearances she could speculate about, with this bounty added: from what Perk had told her, his conclusions seemed wrong. When she looked at a tree or a mountain, she accepted it as such: she never said to herself, "You think you're a mountain? All right. I won't dispute you. You've got a right to your own opinion. But in twenty years' time we'll see who's right."

Perk stopped talking Tract because they had reached the west boundaries of the Tract itself. He always pulled up at a certain hilltop to marvel, and he always wanted Louella to marvel with him. Getting out of the car jarred Louella loose from her inner soliloquy, but an argument with Perk jarred her still more, so she always alighted and faced with him the five thousand acres of which he was the proprietor.

"Well, there it is," Perk said. "The Tract."

Louella recognized perfectly well Perk's right to pause and congratulate himself. While others had overlooked it, he had seen that these barley hills were suited to citrus fruit and had seen also that the situation was one that would appeal to settlers. And behind this knowledge was the money he had made and saved and without which the whole enterprise would have been impossible. And behind the money was the luck, the luck Perk always had, which convinced Louella that forces of nature she knew nothing about were on Perk's side. Even the war, everyone else's tragedy, was Perk's luck. It had made every square foot of tillable ground valuable and was bringing new settlers to the Tract every day. It took a kind of reverse faith to doubt Perk in the face of his luck; to have seen and yet not to believe. She held herself to this faith, though. She did not let events come between her and her belief that Perk was somehow fooling everyone—except herself.

"It's not given to many men," Perk said, "to look over a stretch of land of this size and be able to call it his own. And be willing to do what I'm doing. Open it up for a lot of families, who without my help would never be able to own a square foot of earth."

Perkins then faced the Tract without further talk. The quiet land always made him quiet. There was not much growth where they stood for the wind to touch and not much wind to touch what growth there was. An elderberry bush, whose branches rose above the top of the little arroyo that circled the base of the rise onto which they had climbed, moved slightly; but the wind had no part in it. A red-winged blackbird had alighted and was picking a supper of dust-covered berries. A lizard taking the sun on a warm rock lifted himself up and down on his forelegs. Louella watched him, wondering why, but would have resisted being told.

The gray green of the sage and cactus land and the bleached stubble of the big barley fields were increasingly broken into by plowed ten- and twenty-acre rectangles. Several hills were now topped with new houses, and these, still unpainted, threw back from the shine of undressed yellow boards the slanting sunlight. Off in mid-Tract a moving automobile carried its pillar of dust above it, an omen of the future.

2    TELL me what the Lewises look like," Rosa asked her husband. She was cooking supper for them and it was natural to want to know something about the people for whom she was taking all this trouble. She had planned the meal to suit them, not the Mexican food she and Pete ate but bland soapy American food: fried chicken, mashed potatoes, gravy, sliced peaches with cream and sugar. Pete worked for Shel Lewis, and she had spent the afternoon cooking in order that Shel could welcome his family with a little food. She was doing this out of pure neighborliness and love; the love being for her husband.

"Shel's the only one I've ever seen," Pete said. He was standing in the doorway of the Lewis tent, looking westward over hills gray green with sage and cactus or honey-colored where the barley stubble caught the slanting light. He was keeping an eye out for the dust that would tell him that Shel's spring wagon had arrived on the Tract. So far, the August air was as clear as if dropped straight from the sky onto water or grass. Nothing rose up into it to testify for earth. Ten miles away across stubble and uncleared land, the Olinda oil rigs were black ladders against the sky. Sometimes Pete thought he could hear the stomp of the pumps, but he was never sure that it was not the thud of his own heart. The Tract had once been the least valuable part of his own grandfather's mountain-to-sea acres. Another man, he supposed, would have been bitter about the subdivision of those barley fields into ten-acre ranches and the arrival of these would-be orange growers. The newcomers bothered him no more than passing coyotes. The stakes pounded into the earth by the Perkins Investment Company impressed him no more than yesterday's clouds. He worked for Shel

Lewis and liked him; he did not particularly like grubbing out cactus and castor beans, but since he had never discovered any way of living without work, he considered Shel a providential means of providing it.

"What's Shel Lewis look like then?" Rosa persisted.

If she had asked him what a woman looked like, he could have told her, but he had worked with Shel Lewis for three months and had never given his looks a thought.

"He's a fine man," he said.

The clatter of Rosa's spoon told him what she thought of such a description. She was interested in color of hair, length of nose, weight, height, dress, manner of speech. She wanted something she could see and hear. Pete, though it had never occurred to him before, had a sudden intuition about Shel Lewis. "We look something alike," he told Rosa.

"He is a good-looking man then," Rosa said. She turned down the fire under her skillet and faced him. "Isn't he?"

"You're the one that said that, not me."

"You know it; why won't you ever admit it?"

"You'd stop telling me, then."

"No, I wouldn't."

"Why risk it?"

"I wish they'd come."

"I told you, you're starting too early. Shel's going to be showing them every trap-door spider and horned toad he passes. He's going to be kissing stones. This is the first thing he's ever owned."

"How do you feel, Pete, somebody owning land that belonged to your family? And you working for him?"

"Feel? I feel fine. I don't have any envy for Shel Lewis."

"I have some envy," Rosa said. "This furniture."

Pete looked about the room. The canvas walls made the furniture appear more solid than it really was. He shrugged his shoulders: he let a claw-footed dining-room table, a sideboard with a mirror, a mission rocker, a taboret with a fern, and six straight-backed oak chairs, slide off him with the gesture.

"You wouldn't take this if he gave it to you?" Rosa looked shocked.

"I will take the bed. If Shel will bring it to me."

This was proper talk, and it made Rosa smile. The bed was brass, fancier in its curves and colors than the altar at St. Joseph's; she went to it and stroked the satiny tubing.

"Is this new?"

12

"It'll be new to Shel's family. Shel bought it a month back."

Rosa bent to straighten the top quilt, and Pete watched, admiring his wife's beauty. They were childless, and Rosa's beauty, if it was not made for motherhood, was as contradictory as spring water unfit to drink. She was as smooth as a petal. She carried her arms curved, as if she had just set a baby down. She walked lightly, so as not to disturb a baby's sleep. She lived practicing for a baby. But the baby never came.

Rosa straightened up and looked at Pete. Pete saw that she knew what he had been thinking and was already calculating how she could make use of her knowledge. If Rosa had not been beautiful and had not been able to joke about their childlessness, her constant harping on having a baby might have been tiresome. After all, she was not the only one failing in that enterprise; though she assumed all the blame, there were plenty of women who looked at him reproachfully when Rosa cuddled their babies. Too bad poor Rosa didn't have a good man of her own.

Since there seemed no reason in their own healthy bodies for their childlessness, Rosa had begun to seek explanations in circumstances outside themselves: in what they ate or did not eat; what they wore or did not wear; whether they were in bed or out of bed, confessed or unconfessed, praying or laughing. The hour of the day or night, the state of the moon, the direction of the wind, the slant of the rain—there was nothing Rosa did not examine to determine its influence upon her getting a baby.

The whole world had become important to Rosa only as she thought it would be lucky or unlucky for this enterprise. But she did not wait passively upon the moon and the rain and the wind. She experimented; she tried every help recommended to her by her women friends; she ate garlic till Pete had to be crazy for a baby to go near her. She did what she had been told would never fail, said ten Ave Marias without missing a word during love-making. When this was not successful, she reversed the formula and tried to keep her mind at such times entirely off God. The ten Ave Marias she could manage; but it was not possible for her to forget God—even then. Especially not then. Praying came as naturally to her as breathing, and she could never refrain from saying, "O Blessed Mary who loved Thy little Son help us to have a baby," or "O Sacred Heart of Jesus, I thank Thee for my beautiful husband and his strong body and pray Thee put it in him to give me a baby."

Pete was accustomed to this kind of prayer being whispered while he clasped Rosa, and far from being troubled by it, liked it. It made a nice sound. Rosa was the troubled one. She thought God could put up with a married couple's making love—after all, it was His own idea for providing babies—but she supposed He considered worship one thing and love-making another. She did, certainly. Nevertheless, she was continually getting them mixed up.

"I never love God more," she would tell Pete contritely, "than you know when."

"It would certainly be wrong to hate Him then," Pete had tried to reason with her. "Wouldn't it?"

"Not hate. Just keep separate. The day I do that, God will say, 'Rosa, you have learned the difference between loving your husband and worshiping Me and I will reward you with a little baby.'"

Pete, though he had no sense of any such close superintendence of his love-making by God, or of babies as rewards for any particular kind of thinking, never attempted to change Rosa's convictions.

Now he watched Rosa move from the bed, whose headboard she had been stroking, to the table on which she had placed a fruit jar filled with black-eyed Susans. These she rearranged, and, as she did so, she reached one hand to Pete. Rosa had a tiny-wristed, plump-palmed hand. Pete admired it. He did not care for long narrow hands, nothing but an arm split five ways for fingers. Rosa's hand was a separate and specially made part of her. He took it the way he would kiss her mouth. It was a special act. While he held her hand, Rosa looked about the tent.

"It's nice being here, isn't it?" she said. "Like camping."

"We can't camp here long."

"It's nice to listen to someone else's stove, isn't it?"

The oil stove, turned low, made small bubbling sounds as it burned.

"It sounds like a baby nursing," Rosa suggested. "In somebody else's house I feel like somebody else."

About the baby nursing, Pete had no opinion. But the new surroundings did take hold of the familiar edges of their acts and stretch them out into unfamiliar forms. A tent so filled with furniture, and the furniture, with the tent flap tied open, half outdoors, and the sun putting down a second yellow square on top of the square of flowered yellow carpet added to the excitement. Where were they? Indoors or out? Who were they? Pete Ramos and wife? Or Shelby Lewis and wife? What were they doing? Keeping house or playing house?

Rosa turned her hand, which was incapable of much folding, inside

Pete's palm like a small warm apple; fingers and nails were folded inward and Pete held it like a fruit he had picked. Then he felt a gentle steady pull which he could have ended by opening his fingers. He kept his hand closed and followed Rosa to the bed.

"I have heard," Rosa whispered to him, "that in a new bed it is sure."

There was a surety there he knew of, baby or not. He was a lucky man. "My wife is at me night and day," his cronies said, "for this and that"; this and that being washing machines, new Congoleum, mission-style tables, Bissell sweepers, ivory crucifixes, gocarts with shirred silk lining.

Oh, Rosa, who wanted only this and God's blessing and her little baby! She was turning down the spread she had earlier smoothed straight, she was turning down the sheet.

"We will have their luck," she said.

She was brown as a sweet potato, sunny and warm, mealy and sweet. She had given up the garlic. The tops of her breasts were cool, as if the blood to warm them had tired of traveling all that distance upward. He warmed them with his lips. He did not feel the need of Shel Lewis's luck. Or anybody's. He could make his own.

3    IF THIS was not Paradise, Shelby Lewis did not care to see it. He stood outside the moment and in it; knew this was the hour and place his life had been working toward since he was six years old and had told his father, "I aim to own my own place some day." Kentucky to California was a considerable journey, and it had taken him thirty years to make it; but not only had he made it, he had arrived at the time of day he had selected, midafternoon, with the sun slanting down onto his white tent and the ones he had chosen by his side.

His wife he had certainly chosen; and while there was no way to choose children beforehand, now that his three were here he doubted if given the pick of the entire world he would take any other three. He did not claim them to be the brightest or prettiest: he sometimes doubted if Chad had his fair share of wits; Ellen was plain—the best heart in the world wouldn't make up for turkey-egg freckles and straw hair; and Zoomy, if he kept heading the way he was going at nine, would end up in the pen. He did not care to think of himself as a man who loved whatever was his just for that reason, and decided that his children, for all their drawbacks, as obvious to him as to anyone else, were somehow unusual. Otherwise, why would he love them? Shelby Lewis considered himself a cut above the common run and so far nobody had disputed him.

First, to the three children on the back seat of the spring wagon, then to his wife, Joicey, who was beside him, he presented the Tract.

"There," he said, including with a wave of his hand not only their own tent, but Old Saddle Back, the brown foothills, the Santa Ana River, and, far off, the blue afternoon glitter of the Pacific, "is your new home."

He scanned their faces to see how they accepted his gift. He had kept them away from it on purpose, not wanting to give them paradise piecemeal, a feast of chips and whetstones. He wanted to stun them with it; though stunning was nothing they themselves had asked for. Joicey, not a woman to keep things from him, had threatened to walk the twenty miles from where they had been living to see the Tract if he did not take her out to it. But he had pleaded with her to wait until the place was in order for their moving out.

"Don't you trust me?" he had asked her.

"No," she had answered him with that flash he loved, "I sure don't." But she accepted him. If he was untrustworthy, she took that; he had forced it on her once in the worst way possible and it had not daunted her. Didn't trust him, but didn't blame him either, and was, with him, likely as he was with the children, not fooled but not wanting any change. He watched her look at the Tract. Was she going to hate bareness and brownness? Want clover and timothy instead of cactus and sagebrush? Want gray squirrels instead of ground squirrels, bumblebees instead of trap-door spiders, bobolinks instead of buzzards? Was she going to want a made place instead of a place to be made? Was she set on the world's being one color and that color green? And as crowded with growth as an old lady's dooryard garden? Everything showed in Joicey's face. It did away with the need of talk, which was a pity. Lose your hearing and you'd never miss it with Joicey; lose your eyesight and no one could show you the way to where Joicey was. Now she was gazing and gazing. This would be home, and it took some exploring. Just because you were there, you didn't ram the flag into the snow like Admiral Peary and say in a quick voice, "I claim this for the Shelby Lewis family."

Shel asked just three things of a woman; which doesn't mean, he thought, that I don't appreciate more. But if a woman was little and curly-haired and had a red mouth, that was all he *asked* of her. A woman could give him more but he would not ask for more. Big, straight-haired women with colorless mouths belonged more to the cow or horse breed, and he looked at men married to these creatures with about the same astonishment he would have for a man he caught out in the barn kissing Old Dobbin. Maybe there were men who felt about these big bloodless ones the way he did about Joicey. He thought not. He thought they just hadn't known what they wanted, had got stuck with what they didn't want and found out about it too late; never did understand why the sight of those big shoulders with that straight hair falling down over them like loose hay across a barn floor didn't seem the prettiest sight in the world. Joicey's hair curled in little ringlets at the back of her neck where her Psyche knot did not catch them all. Made him tremble in his finger points just to look at them.

Well, it was all in her face, it was mirrored there. She had been sitting with her hand on his thigh and she took it off. Joicey was the reverse of those small boys who cannot pound a nail without the help of their tongues. She could not use her tongue to speak without the help of her hands. She made a picture with her hands, then hunted with her tongue and red lips for a title for her picture. Sometimes he helped, told her what her title was, sometimes he let her draw untitled picture after picture. The kids were in on the struggle. Shel, turned to face Joicey, could also see the kids. Every one of them had their words for the Tract but they were waiting for Mama. Sometimes they could not wait for her but burst forth and left her fanning the air like a beached fish. But sometimes Mama was funny, or, if they waited long enough, downright uncanny. Said something that didn't fit and didn't have to, because it wasn't made for that.

Now, she said, "Why, it's a ship of land and our tent's the sail."

Shel, who had looked so many times at the Tract and their tent, white up there on the east ridge, had never before seen that this was true. If he had not loved Joicey as much as he did, he would have resented her noting something at first sight that he, in three months' looking, had not figured out. She saw it because her hands had drawn the picture. The Tract rose above the stretched Pacific, floated at the edge of the foothills, was as bare and undecorated as a ship, and did not have trees any more than a ship does. It was the color of weathered wood, with tumbleweeds blowing across it the way spray breaks across a deck. It was a ship of land all right, unmanned, uncaptained, unnamed, lying there waiting to be boarded and sailed. Oh, he could see it plain as day now Joicey had pictured it.

"Did you hear what your mother said?" he asked the children. Some parents praise their children to each other, but Shel praised his wife to the children. "Ellen," he shouted.

Ellen, whose eyes were not very big to begin with, squinted them when she was thinking, so that they disappeared into her face and she looked like some broad-cheeked old Chinaman. All she needed at these times, Shel thought, were chopsticks and an opium pipe; he could not bear this in his peerless daughter. He tried to remember at least once every day to startle her into really opening her eyes. When she opened them up, they were big enough and alive enough to fit her high cheekbones. She would thank him for it later.

"What, Papa?" Ellen asked.

"Open your eyes," Shel said, which was not what he had intended at all. He did not want her self-conscious, opening and shutting her eyes like fans. He hastened on. "Look at your new home, daughter."

Though he had been coming out to the Tract for three months, had cleared his twenty acres, laid the foundation for his house, fixed a tent as snug and neat as a kitchen cabinet, this seemed to Shel the real entering, the official taking over. But he did not want to ride into the promised land in a spring wagon. He wanted to walk in, he and his family and his horses and his flocks, like the Bible times. He no more believed in the Bible as the word of God than he believed in Sears, Roebuck as ditto, but it did provide him with a few acts he wouldn't mind imitating.

"I'm going to walk for a ways," he said, unwilling, even to these, to bare his heart completely.

"Me too," Zoomy said.

Shel wanted to say something to the kids. In California they took blue skies and property and oranges growing on trees as much for granted as their toes. Did they know they had stopped being renters? Did they know they had stopped moving around? Did they know they had begun working for themselves? Did they know he had been coming toward this spot for thirty years?

"From the time I commenced remembering," he said, "around three or four, I'd judge, to the time I married your mother at eighteen, my folks had moved fifteen times."

"That's more than once a year," Zoomy said.

18

"It was more likely twice a year. But fifteen I can account for."

"Why did they move so much?" Ellen asked.

"They moved to make a living. They hunted work and a roof over their heads and somebody who'd pay them for setting tobacco, or picking peas, or shocking corn."

"Wasn't Grandpa a steady worker?"

"Oh Jesus," Shel said, "you are Californians already. Native sons every one of you. Pa was steady enough. It was the work wasn't steady. Or the pay. I was dropping corn at six myself."

"Dropping?" asked Zoomy, as if his father had been some kind of tree shedding leaves.

"Planting. Planting corn. Three to grow and one for the crow." He forestalled Zoomy. "One for the crow to eat. I turned over tobacco leaves hunting worms. I picked up windfalls. I carried water by the bucket to cabbages."

"When did you go to school, Papa?" It was a good thing Ellen asked this.

"I didn't," he answered.

"You can read and write and figure."

"Oh, I shadowed the door once in a while. And Pa was a reader. Oh, I learned like Honest Abe," he said scornfully. Then, not wanting to set himself up as a boy wonder and rail splitter doing sums on a fire shovel and reading borrowed books, he said, "But I'm ignorant as a polecat. If America was discovered by a Turk, I don't know it. Or the other way round. Or who fought the Declaration or wrote the Civil War. Or why. But you kids are going to learn. You are going to go to school, and as much as your heads'll hold I'm going to see's shoved in. And we are going to live in one house and on one spot and with no moving around for the rest of my days, at least. That place," he said pointing to their tent, "will be known as the Lewis place. We'll be the old settlers here, the pioneers. And the pea-pickers and the worm-hunters will work for us."

"Things'll be just the same then, won't they?" Chad asked.

The question was like Chad, and Shel looked at his son. His son, at nineteen, was thought good looking by most people; but he himself could have wished for something more pulled together, flesh-colored, and stubby-haired. Chad was actually strong and wiry, more so than Ellen, who, though she looked a picture of health, was always coming down with something; but Chad, with his white face, gaunt eyes, big pinched nose, and hair so long he looked like he had been too weakly lately to chance the shock of a shearing, appeared just up from a siege of lung fever or cholera morbus.

"You help them other pea-pickers and worm-hunters if you're a mind to, Chad," he said. "I got my hands full with this little bunch of five. I've got our noses out of the landlord's pocket and I'm the owner of a bona fide mortgage. I'm working for the Lewises. You choose. It's your right."

Joicey was building some kind of a picture with her hands. The picture was "You do not understand your son." Well, if he was a picture-maker, he'd build another saying, "The son does not understand the father." The shoe was more on that foot, and naturally, too. He had lived with Chad since before Chad was; he knew how he had leapt in Joicey's womb—a weak leaper compared with Ellen—but Chad did not know a thing about being a mover and renter back in the hills of six Kentucky counties, a tobacco suckerer and worm-picker, a born no-good with people pitying his bleeding feet on frosty mornings. He wanted Chad to understand that past and the need to get away from it—but by taking Chad away from it he had blinded him to it. He could tell Chad about it from now to doomsday and it would mean nothing. First, because he said it—and kids were inoculated against what their folks said the way they were against smallpox—and second, because the only way to understand bleeding feet was to watch your own tracks and see blood.

Joicey said nothing. They had got to the place where some arguments were not necessary. He gave her a hand out of the wagon. Zoomy and Ellen were already out. The road was dusty, but not the deep dust of a rain country where wet and dry alternate, first the earth water-soaked to make ready for a dust harvest when the sun comes out again. It was a thin sweet dust, smelling like the sage and cactus and greasewood that grew in the uncleared land beside the road. He breathed it in like balsam and felt the air enriched by having a little earth in it. He put his arm around Joicey, and with his free hand pointed out the landmarks all over again. The Copes' house, biggest and best so far on the Tract. The Raunces'; LeRoy Raunce was a preacher.

"What kind?" Joicey asked.

"He just got the call recently. So far as I know, it didn't come labeled. He's waiting to see if God wants him Baptist, Hard- or Soft-Shell; Methodist, South or North; United Brethren, sprinkle or dip."

"Shhh," said Joicey.

"Maybe he will be a priest," said Ellen.

"It's a little late for that, Sis. He's married and got a houseful of kids."

Her father and mother led the way, as was right, Ellen thought; she and Zoomy and, finally, the spring wagon, with Chad driving, followed. Ellen was better looking than her father thought, though large, straight-haired, and with lips only moderately pink. She suited the landscape she walked through better than did her mother, who looked like fox grapes or bramble berries, some growth intended to flourish by a riverside in a green land. Ellen's half-shut eyes were made for sunshine; dust did not show on her blondness, and in a landscape broken up by nothing smaller than mountains and foothills, a good-sized girl did not stick out like a sore thumb, the way she had back East. Shel marched into the Tract out of his past, a man beginning again. But so did his kids. They marched in, and out of all the past they had, turning new leaves as fast as he did; fewer leaves, cleaner, was the sole difference.

Ellen wished her father would take his arm from around her mother and *lead*. If they were going to march into the promised land on foot like Aaron and his band, she was in favor of something more soldierly than hugging.

Then she forgot her parents. She was seventeen, and all she saw and heard, touched and smelled, was filled with her own mystery, the mystery of her own body and identity—whatever they were, whatever they would be. She marched—let the others walk—through the dust, Zoomy by her side. She heard the cicadas with their dry rattlesnake alarm, heard a road runner's cry, heard the sound of the scarcely moving wind as it slid past her face. She smelled cactus apples oozing sweet juice and elderberries ripening in the dry washes and bleached grasses fragrant with a summer-long seasoning. And they were all mixed together, so that she heard what she smelled and saw what she felt, and she herself, down to the very dust under her feet, was a part of the Tract she was entering.

Either no one spoke or she did not hear them. They were on a ridge, walking on the level, about to drop downward along a zigzag road. She could still see their tent, a puny sail for such a scope of land. Shel planned big, he planned bigger than anything he had known so far, but that lean-to in the Kentucky hollows did not give him the strongest foundations in the world to work on. Ellen's foundations were nothing but herself and the Tract, both unknown and growing. She was on her way into it, not claiming it the way Shel did, as something earned and to which he had a right. *Being* it, she did not feel the need of claiming.

Zoomy was the first to notice the car coming toward them, climbing the grade below.

"An automobile," he yelled.

Ellen had never been in a car, but it was not the car's strangeness to her but its strangeness there, under the buzzards and in the dust, that stopped her. The car was red, and the sun, reflected from its metalwork, flashed them heliograph signals.

"Pull off the road," her father yelled back to Chad, as if without his warning Chad might sit still and be run over. Chad was already pulling off.

Zoomy called to his father, "Will he miss us?" He seemed to think the auto had been aimed like a cannon ball and the driver had nothing to do with the direction it took.

"It's Tom Mount," Shel told his family. "He's a carpenter."

The red car reached them and stopped. Ellen had expected its driver to wear goggles and puttees. Instead, he was bareheaded, and dressed like her father except that in place of blue overalls he wore khaki-colored pants pressed as neatly as if they belonged to a suit. He did not sit back, lounging in his car, but got out and surveyed them, smiling. He took her father's hand, shook it between both of his. "Well, Shel," he said, "I see you did it just the way you planned. Led the family in like Moses."

"Aaron," Ellen said before she had thought.

Tom Mount let go her father's hand and turned toward her. "You've been reading the Bible since I have," he said.

He was a bigger man than her father, not taller or wider, but thicker through. He was her definition of beautiful, but she had talked with enough girls about ideals in looks to know this possibly meant that there was something a little queer about Mr. Mount's appearance. Not that she cared. It was not her intention to follow signboards. It hurt her pride to do so. Her definition of beautiful was black to begin with, then large, then sharp. Her definition of ugly was blond and small and round: man or woman, it did not matter.

"I hope you never meet the devil," her mother had once told her, "for your description of your ideal man sounds like Old Nick to a T."

"Why, I hate wickedness," Ellen had answered. "I know you do," her mother admitted, "and when you meet wickedness I hope it *looks* like what you hate, too."

Mr. Mount's goodness was as plain to the eye as his size, black hair, and big face. Her father was a feisty, fault-finding man beside him. Mr. Mount's voice was quiet, but with a kind of accusing chuckle in it. "Haven't you?" he asked, smiling at her as if her Bible reading had been something she should have reported to him. He did not turn back to the rest of the family, but waited for her answer.

"Yes," she said, unconsciously matching her voice to the secret in his, "I have." Then he released her and turned again to the family.

When her father introduced Tom Mount, Ellen saw his pride. "My friend, Tom Mount," he said, and Mr. Mount was as attentive to Zoomy as he had been to her.

"Where you carpentering now?" her father asked.

"No place," Tom Mount said, "if I don't get the church job."

"Church? Why, we don't have a church here yet. Who's talking of building?"

"Raunce, the preacher, for one. I'm on my way to see him now."

"Raunce never struck me as a man with enough money to be able to run up a church at will."

"He's not paying for it. There've been donations."

"Donations," Shel said. "There's not enough people on the Tract to get him very far with donations."

"There's ninety-five," Mount told him. "Seventeen families, five bachelors, two spinsters, one widow, a total of forty-two grownups plus fifty-four children."

"Ninety-six," Zoomy, who was fast at figures, told him.

Tom Mount moved his big shoulders. "A few one way or another don't make much difference."

They made a difference to Shel. Tom Mount's figures made him mad, first of all at Mount himself. What did the fellow mean, here on the Tract a day or two and already an authority?

"You had time to count them all?" Shel asked.

"I was estimating," Mount answered with a smile that admitted that estimating was not his long suit.

"There's not half that many," Shel insisted. He faced back the way they had come. Behind them lay nine-tenths of the Tract, and Shel, with a sweep of his hand, showed Mount its emptiness. "Where're you going to put your ninety-seven people?" he asked. There were two roof tops not far away, and farther west, close to the townsite, the sun-struck gleam of a couple of tents was visible. "People don't live in squirrel holes," Shel said. "They ain't sheltering in the cactus patches. Where are they, then? These spinsters and widows you got counted?"

Mount said nothing, as he might have done, about the houses and tents out of their sight behind the hilltops. He only smiled and shrugged. "Kids, too," he said. "Give me credit for counting the kids, too, Shel."

But Shel would not joke about it. "Where are they?" he insisted. "These folks you've counted?"

Mount shook his head. "I'm no census taker. You know a lot more about the place than I do. If you say it's empty, it's empty."

The minute Shel heard the word "empty," he understood his anger. It was not Mount he was mad at, but Mount's figures, with their threat to the emptiness he loved. He had never been a man to hate the earth, even back in Kentucky, where if a leaf did not move at the time you were looking, you might never catch sight of the earth at all—so wooded, so vined, grassed, flowered, bushed, creepered, and thicketed it all was. Shel, on the Tract, was like a man seeing for the first time the naked body of the woman he loves; seeing what before he has only guessed, the long, clean lines, the sun-flushed simplicity, the grave starkness. The sight had turned his love to worship. Here was a nobility he had never imagined back in the Kentucky hollows, bedizened as they were with all their little flowers and ferns, tinkling with summer showers, gurgling with spring branches, and smelling at all times like store-bought Florida Water. Here was silence; here, what the air was sweet with was all outdoors. The man who would change this emptiness for the smothering push of Eastern growth would be the one to hustle his naked love back into her corsets and drawers. And when Tom Mount had dumped his ninety-seven settlers down on the Tract, that was exactly, to Shel's mind, what he had been doing.

Shel opened his arms to the emptiness he loved. There was an autumn spareness in the dry heat of the August afternoon. The air touched his body with pin points of static electricity. The faraway horizons gave his mind room to stretch. No hungry creeping greenness endangered the earth's butternut colors. Nothing hid the long naked lift and fall of the hills. Nothing yet, anyway, and he would not have Tom Mount rushing things.

"By my count," Shel said, "there's not half that many people here."

It was all one to Tom Mount, fifty or a hundred. He had been asked

24

a question and had given an answer. If that answer did not suit, he would find another.

"I expect I was carried away by Sylvester Perkins's promises," Mount said. "All the stuff he's written about 'the city of the future' we've got here on the Tract."

Shel laughed then. "That's no promise Syl's making, that's a threat. And when you know him better, you'll think twice before you bank on any of his promises. Even his good ones."

"You planning to attend the meeting tonight?" Mount asked.

"I don't want to miss it, if we can get settled in time," Shel said.

"I'll see you there, then," Mount told him.

He waved to them; they watched his car until it disappeared behind a hill.

Then Joicey asked, "What meeting, Shel?"

"A meeting about water, mostly. The Investment Company's way behind on delivering it."

But he would say no more about that, though they all asked questions; all except Ellen. Ellen knew what he wanted. He wanted to forget the interruption and resume the march.

Her mother, understanding this too, took her French harp from her pocket and began blowing some tune; first, it sounded like "Tenting Tonight," then "Old Folks at Home," but it settled down to neither, something her mother was making up as she marched ahead of them, something with the war in it and Kentucky left behind and their ship of land ready to sail.

Ellen ran back to the wagon. "Get down," she said to Chad, "and walk in. Don't ride. The horses will follow." But Chad, who thought he was being ordered, would not, and she walked alone, following in the road the print of Tom Mount's automobile wheels and keeping time to the unknown tune her mother was playing.

4    TOM MOUNT, a one-day resident of the Tract, had never met the man he was on his way to see. Lute Cope had told him that Raunce was looking for someone to help him build a church. Raunce at present was holding services in a tent, but the Santa Ana winds had already uprooted the tent a couple of times and the winter rains were

liable to float it away. Raunce had been able to collect some money from his congregation, and, with what he could contribute himself from his wages as a driller in the oil fields, he was prepared to start building. Drillers were the prima donnas of the oil fields. A man said, "I'm a driller," and thought that told the story: a man of money, courage, and skill. Riggers and pumpers were not in it. As for farmers, school-teachers, storekeepers: they were needed but, the drillers wondered, were they really men? About themselves the drillers had not the least doubt.

Raunce, the Reverend LeRoy Raunce since his being recorded as a minister, had ten acres adjoining the townsite. The townsite, still ninety-nine per cent site and one per cent town, was situated on the flat land that lay at the center of the Tract. Tom Mount, driving west from his meeting with the Lewis family, had a mile of dusty uphill and downdale driving before, from the top of the last hill, the town-site, with its half-dozen buildings, came into view. He slowed to look at it, thinking he was seeing what might be the beginning of a great city; but he could not raise up in his mind's eye the New York or Chicago of the future there in the midst of the sagebrush. It was eas-ier to think the townsite bare of its half-dozen buildings, think it back to the hills a white man had never trod on. Mount enjoyed the sensa-tion of being thus suspended between the past and the future, of commanding time. He drove on like a king, the sun warm on his face and glinting off the polished brass of his car. He had a moment of double vision. He saw himself, white-shirted and black-haired, a trail of golden dust behind him, rolling forward into the little nucleus of the city to be, diving into it like a fertilizing pollen-flecked bee into a flower.

The emptiness of the landscape, the transparent yellow air of the late August afternoon, emphasized the few objects which were visible and gave Mount the illusion of being able to see the impossible, the hidden eye of a ground squirrel poised in profile, the far side of a fac-ing building. He drove into the blueprint town, past the brown frame building that was the office of the Perkins Investment Company, past the tent of Asa Brice, past the Reverend Raunce's church tent. He saw the Raunce cow, tied to a stake in Raunces' back yard and surrounded by straw like a prospective martyr. He saw a girl dart from the back door, run halfway to the cow, fling a pan of greenness toward it, and run back. On a ladder, painting the house, he saw a man, the Reverend

LeRoy Raunce himself, he supposed. He slowed down, stopped his car in front of a bare yard, and walked up a path neatly outlined with white and gray pebbles.

"Are you the Reverend Raunce?" he asked the painter.

The painter swiveled about and looked down at him. "That's my name," he said.

Raunce was a big man, heavy in shoulders, arms, and thighs, but flat-bellied. He had a head of red hair, raying out in spikes like the hair of Apollo in old pictures of the sun god. He gave the same impression of ruddy effulgence. His neck, too, was godlike, fluted with temple-column muscles. At the base of his Adam's apple was a knuckle-sized rosy pocket big enough to hold a half-cup of rain water. While Mount looked Raunce over, Raunce put his brush in the bucket of paint, which hung by bailing wire from the ladder, and descended.

"What can I do for you?" he asked when he reached the ground.

Face to face, the Reverend LeRoy's godlikeness disappeared. He had the frame, and the fire; but he had also a big lumpy face like a potato that has had to shape itself in stony ground. There were two bony knobs above his eyes, and his cheekbones, even in his well-fleshed face, were prominent. Between these two promontories, his eyes had no more than the required space for peeping. His nose began large and ended the same way. The lips, full and muscled as biceps, had the minutest scroll-like upturn at the corners.

Mount, postponing his answer to Raunce's question, said, "You don't look like a preacher."

"I'm a new one. Maybe it don't show on me yet."

"You want it to show?"

Mount had made the discovery a few years back of being personal. He had hit upon the pleasure to others and the power to himself—which was a pleasure, too—of engaging people at their centers. Hence, personal questions were his policy. He knew that most people prided themselves on "never getting personal." He prided himself on never getting anything else. His pride sometimes outstripped his performance; sometimes he was tired or his interest flagged or he could see nothing to be gained by keeping himself so concentrated. But this evening he was not tired, he was interested, and he had a job at stake.

"I don't know as it matters," Raunce answered, "what I look like. Unless there's people who wouldn't want to listen to me unless I looked like a preacher. I'm satisfied God don't care what I look like.

27

And I can't bring myself to believe He ever gave a thought to Jesus Christ's looks. I don't think He ever asked himself, 'Does that Boy look like a Son of God?' Do you?"

Mount was stopped in his tracks. Raunce was more personal than he was, and on a subject that had never entered his head. But new ideas interested him, so he turned this one over in his mind.

"I don't suppose God would've enjoyed it if His Son had looked like a rascal."

"How do you know He didn't?"

"Didn't look like a rascal?"

"Yes."

"You don't *sound* like a preacher either."

"Yes, I do. A man's looks don't figure with me, and they oughtn't, me being a preacher. And I give God at least as much credit as I do myself."

A man's looks, everybody's looks, figured with Mount. He was a handsome man himself, knew it, and counted on the fact weighing in his favor. He supposed it weighed in his favor with Raunce. He gave Raunce his hand. "My name's Tom Mount. I'm a carpenter. Luther Cope told me you needed help building your new church."

"I do," Raunce said. "I need help bad. I can run up a house myself but a church is a more particular job."

Mount nodded understandingly. "Spires and pews and pulpits."

"There won't be any of that. This is going to be a Quaker church."

"You a Quaker?" If Raunce did not look like a preacher, he looked still less like a Quaker.

"Surprised?"

Mount did not particularly care for facts that outstripped his imaginings, but he stayed truthful as well as personal and said he was.

"It surprises me, too. I never expected to find myself a Son of God, let alone a Quaker."

This was one of the plainest-speaking Sons of God Mount had ever encountered. Being personal seemed wasted on Raunce. He appeared to be living where his own personality was not in any need of outside bolstering.

"What surprises you about it?" Mount asked, out of habit rather than real interest.

Raunce motioned Mount over to a pair of sawhorses, gave him the one with even legs, and there, to the tune of the cow's munching and

28

under a sky blued out with the intense light of the yellow sun, he let him have the tale that it still surprised Raunce to tell. He told it for that purpose, for the purpose of being himself awe-struck by the fate of LeRoy Raunce, early oil driller and lately Son of God.

He was thirty-six years old, the year all this had happened. Up to his thirty-sixth year, he had felt like a man going to pieces, a man breaking up. He had felt like an uncapped gusher, all his riches wasting away. He had been tormented with a sense of loss he knew neither how to name nor how to take care of.

One hot Sunday, he and his family had headed for Long Beach. The car had broken down on the outskirts of Rose Park, a small town down in the flat cow and alfalfa belt, halfway between the Tract and the sea. While they waited for a new timer to be sent out from Los Angeles, LeRoy had dropped in on the Rose Park Quaker Meeting. He had visited the Meeting in the same way he would have gone to a Sunday ball game, to kill time and pass the time of day, and with no intention whatsoever of getting into the game himself.

"I went into that Meeting one man and I came out another," he told Mount. "I experienced conversion."

Raunce had experienced nothing of the kind; he was born what the revivalists called converted; but he had found in that Meeting names for himself: Christian and Quaker. It was as satisfying for him to be able to thus identify himself as for a boy brought up by wolves to discover that his lack of fur is not the sign of being an incomplete wolf but is a mark of being human, to have finally a name to account for his difference from his pack mates.

"I went into that Meeting a son of the Old Adam and I came out a Child of Light. I tell you that preacher reached right down into my vitals and lifted the sin out of me the way a poultice lifts out a carbuncle."

"Preacher?" Mount asked. "I thought Quakers didn't hold with preaching."

"I'd heard that myself. I understand that's the order of things back East. But us Quakers here in Southern California don't bow to anybody when it comes to preaching. We've got the gift of tongues as strong as any Baptist or United Brethren."

Being personal, Mount thought, occasionally gets me more than I've bargained for. He was accustomed to having men and women shine the whole beam of their lives onto him; and he was a moon that asked for that kind of heat and lighting, that had to have it. But once in a while, being personal let loose a blaze whose warmth went deeper than his reflecting surface could comfortably handle. Raunce sat there on his sawhorse, preaching a sermon calculated to set his listener on fire. Raunce had had the kind of experience a man can make a life-work of repeating. Fall in love, kill a mountain lion, strike oil: these are tales that lovers, hunters, and wildcatters can and do retell. But they cannot make a profession of telling these stories the way a preacher makes the retelling of his. They cannot stand in a pulpit and tell their story three times a week for pay. Discovering God: that's the kind of hunting, loving, and wildcatting that strikes oil every time, Mount thought, the well that never runs dry.

"Redemption was the last thing I had in mind. I was as innocent of the Second Birth as a newborn babe when I went in that Meeting. I walked out of it two hours later, reborn. Mr. Mount, I can never sin again."

Mount scanned the big craggy face, lifted as calmly as though the man sat there passing the time of day. He had an impulse to test Raunce's Second Birth, give him a blow on his big cheekbone and see if he would turn the other for a second smack.

"Raunce," he said, "you're a married man. Do you mean to say that since that Meeting you've never seen a woman you'd like to go to bed with?"

"Never," Raunce answered.

Mount did not ask Raunce how he had stood on these matters before the Second Birth and did not know that even when inhabited by the Old Adam, Raunce had never hankered after anyone but his wife. Nor had Raunce been able to inform the Rose Park Quakers, delighting as they were in his Second Birth, of these things, or let them know that he had always been deficient in a sense of sin, this being a fact he did not know himself. He had sat through that Meeting, listened to the preaching of a hell-and-brimstone revivalist, and found what he had always lacked before, a name to give his natural goodness and, before it was over, a use for his natural eloquence.

"Before that Meeting," he told Mount, "my heart was heavy with thankfulness. It was a real burden to me. Who could I thank?"

"Thank for what?" Mount asked.

"Life," LeRoy said.

This was a more general statement than Raunce intended, and he provided specific examples later. But he did have a faculty very rare in the human race—he was born with a sense of gratitude. Thankfulness flowed out from him, washed over pine planks, crude oil, Jersey cows, applesauce, daybreak, nightfall, the marriage bed, the Acts of the Apostles, and everything between, behind, before, after, under, and above these items. He relished the Santa Ana dust in his hair and the hauled water with which he washed it out. He had not, before the Rose Park Meeting, been able to flex a muscle without being sorrowful with praise unuttered, to take a step without wishing for someone to thank for providing something so suitable as the earth for walking on.

"I'll praise my Maker all my days," he told Mount. "I used to feel like a fool. Dolly and the children got embarrassed when I tried to tell them. Down at the oil field, a kick in the teeth is easier understood than thankfulness."

"I take it you find preaching comes natural?" Mount's irony never reached Raunce.

"Why, friend, I take to it like a freed bird to the air. I say the same things now I used to, and instead of hearing 'What in hell are you talking about?' I hear 'Amen.'"

Mount knew he was facing a man who had found his vocation. The fact filled him with a nervous sorrow. He reminded himself he had come to build a church, not listen to a sermon. He tried to throw the forward drive of the personal into reverse and get back to business, though, to tell the truth, Raunce's religion was too natural to be called personal. It was about as personal as his breathing.

"Who's this church going to belong to after it's built?"

"The congregation."

"Luther Cope told me you were putting your own money into the building. Do you plan to collect from the congregation?"

"No."

"Have you been officially appointed to the ministry?"

"The Yearly Meeting recorded me."

"I don't mean that. Have you got a contract with this church?"

"There isn't any church yet. I go down to the tent and preach and people come to hear me. They can hire anyone they want to when they get organized. I hope it'll be me, but they'll have the say."

"I understand there's another preacher in town."

"Twining? He ain't preached in some time."

31

"Why?"

"I never asked him. The gift comes to you. I reckon it can leave you."

"You preach the straight Quaker doctrine?" Mount did not know what this was and he supposed Raunce to be even more ignorant, as innocent of theology as a woodchuck of grammar.

"As fast I learn it."

"How much do you figure on paying a carpenter?"

"Five a day be about right?"

That was the sum Mount had in mind, but before he could answer, Raunce had called to his wife, who had come out of the back door with a milk pail on her arm.

"Dolly, I want to make you acquainted with Mr. Thomas Mount. He's going to carpenter on our new church."

If Raunce looked like the sun, Dolly looked like a woman the sun had shone on, brown and smooth, colored and shaped like a pecan shell. She had on a faded cotton dress. Mount looked down at her feet, half expecting to find her barefooted. She was firmly and trimly shod. He lifted his eyes to her face, disappointed.

"Pleased to meet you, I'm sure," she said.

If Mount was a man and she was a woman, nothing in Dolly Raunce's voice recognized it. Mount was accustomed to this recognition. He looked into her eyes to see if she was hiding it from him. She was not. She recognized him as her husband's acquaintance and as possible carpenter for the church.

"The pleasure is mutual," Mount said. He stopped the conversation, but she went on politely, without his help.

"The cow is drying up. I'll be glad when she freshens."

She walked away from them, her uncorseted, pear-shaped buttocks moving, he could tell, without the least consciousness that he was watching. Her going left the evening empty behind her. It was like walking into an illusory stream for Mount, water there for the eyes beforehand but the limbs undampened after entry. He felt a desperate need for the response he had not found. LeRoy Raunce's tale of his conversion had been no response to *him*. He told that story three times a week to anyone who would come into his tent and listen. It seemed a long time to Mount since he had driven into the sunlit town, trailing his comet tail of pollen. He felt the sun going down on all his happiness. At this minute, a girl came out of the back door carrying refreshments to the visitor—as a preacher's daughter should.

32

Raunce, with his back to the house, facing the scaffolding of distant oil derricks, black now against the setting sun, did not see her. Mount, as the girl hesitated, not wanting to break in uninvited upon their conversation, called to her, "A thirst quencher?"

She came to them with her pitcher and glasses, and Raunce introduced her with the same words he had used for his wife.

"I want to make you acquainted with my daughter Crystal."

"Crystal?" Mount repeated, not sure he had the name right.

"Sometimes we call her Crissie," Raunce said.

Mount drank his glass of lemonade. "How do you make it so cold without ice?"

"We keep our water in an olla."

"Here we stand," Mount said, "in the midst of sagebrush, drinking cold lemonade. A new kind of pioneer. Did you ever think you'd be a pioneer, Crystal?"

"No."

The three of them, heads thrown back drinking, watched a big sooty bird as it drifted overhead.

"See that, Crystal? It's a hawk hunting its supper. It can drop a hundred feet a second. Wonder what it thinks of us, taking over hawk land, the way we have?"

She was not a pretty girl, but the attention he was bending upon her lit her up. Her eyes, beneath a brow knobbed like her father's, reflected every word he said. He went on about the habits of hawks. He saw her frame answers her shyness did not permit her to speak.

Raunce, during this talk, kept his face lifted to the sky. Flight alone was enough for him, without facts and figures on the bird's habits of eating and flying.

"Eyes and something to use them on," he exulted. "That's the combination my blessed Lord has given us."

Mount saw that the girl suffered because of the peculiarities of her father. His understanding of what the girl was feeling brought him closer to Raunce than had any of Raunce's explanations of himself. A man, misunderstood by his daughter, was more lovable to Mount than a creature praising his Maker. The situation was more human. Praising was a cold act for an outsider to witness; complete in itself, no more place for a third party there than between a mother and her sucking child. One to give and one to take, and both content in the simple teeter-totter of the self-rewarding movement.

"Raunce," he asked suddenly, "what're you trying to do?"

33

"Why, praise my Lord and Master. Bless His holy name."

They were back where they had started. Mount did not want any more of that. He concluded his visit. "I'll come to work Monday at seven," he said, "if that's all right with you."

Raunce and his daughter watched the red car drive away.

"That was a buzzard," Crystal told her father, "not a hawk."

"Beautiful bird," her father answered. "God's beautiful bird."

God had made it, and that, for her father, was enough. For all he cared, it might have been a high-flying bug. She moved away from him. It seemed unfair to stand so close, misleading him with her nearness, when her thoughts were so condemning. It was fair, it seemed to her, to love and not tell; in fact, this was required; but to hate and not tell was weak.

Her mother had finished the milking while her father praised God's birds. She stopped to show them the contents of the pail.

"Just about liquid cow," Crystal said, looking at the thick yellow fluid.

Her mother, puzzled, showed the milk to her father. There, in the back yard, in the sight of anyone who cared to look, her father lifted the bucket and, unsanitary and big-necked as a horse, had a smacking gulp or two. Then he set the pail down and licked the cream from the stubble on his upper lip.

Let him not praise God, Crystal thought, for milk. She was the opposite of her father. She did not thank God for a thing, blamed Him for a lot, and petitioned Him never. Her present wish was granted. Her father, without a word of praise to anyone, God or the cow, put his arms about her mother. Crystal would not have been surprised to see him carry her to the straw pile, undress her, and make a baby in her. He praised God for things like that, too; she had heard him. It was one of the reasons she was soured on praise and God and her father.

After her father and mother had gone into the house, she lingered outside in the lessening light hating him, hating her own quince-colored eyes, the two bony bumps on her forehead, her sandy eyelashes, her big thin mouth; hating, in fact, every single thing about herself —except her ability to hate. She intended to hang on to that.

All she asked in life was reasonableness, the one thing she would have supposed human beings were born to be. Love was too much to

34

ask, she knew that, and she did not ask it; but to act reasonable, what else were we given reason for?

But I don't care, she told herself. I can get along without love, or reasonableness either, if I have to. I am Crystal J. Raunce and I don't need a soul on this earth. I am alone and I hate everybody and am beholden to nobody.

Tom Mount's bird, or its friend or brother, passed overhead, bound for his roost in some distant eucalyptus trees. "Hawk," she hooted. "Hawk, hawk!" The buzzard, careless of names, sloped homeward; Crystal, watching, smelled potatoes frying and the sweet-sour scent of dried beef being frizzled for gravy. In spite of the fact that her father was singing "Oh that will be glory for me" loud enough to be heard in the next county, she let the smell of food draw her inside, thus betraying, as always, her latest oaths and deepest feelings.

5    Eunice fry and Opal Tetford, the widow with whom she made her home, had gone, as had all the residents of the Tract, to the lake for their weekly barrel of drinking water. They were driving home slowly, both to keep the water from slopping out of the barrel and to enjoy the scenery—which was still a middling novelty to them.

Eunice, who was twenty-four, felt older than Opal, who was forty-two. Eunice carried her spinsterhood like a personal blight, while Opal considered her widowhood a mere accident, something that had happened to her husband really rather than to herself. That Charlie had passed on did not mean that she was not in the full tide of life. This conviction was expressed in the energetic way she drove. Opal was a small woman, round-eyed, roundheaded, with short curly hair which showed the curve of her skull. She sat on the seat of the wagon as responsively and alertly as a dandelion on the brow of a hill.

A road runner, feeding in the August stubble, took their progress as a challenge and set out to distance them. He was so low spread by his big stride and so elongated by his outstretched neck and tail that he reminded Opal of the little autumn streams of her childhood, half water and half brown leaves. She slapped the reins across the haunches of the team, not in any hope of winning the race, but too kindhearted to disappoint the bird, if a contest was what he had in mind.

"For a woman who won't drive, you do all right once you get the reins in your hands," Eunice said, as Opal slowed up.

Opal agreed. "It's the truth. But I've got to be hit in the head with a thing to know it's so. I like driving. Why don't I drive more?"

"Search me," Eunice said. "It's not that I don't ask you."

"Oh, I know that, Eunice. The real trouble is I'm a stick-in-the-mud."

And there I've put my finger on it, Opal thought, whether Eunice knows it or not. When Eunice drove, Opal could not think of anything pleasanter than sitting, hands folded, watching clouds dapple the hills with shadows and listening to the sand pour off the wheels. Then by chance she would pick up the reins and everything else immediately became a skim-milk story. She had invented driving and horses and wanted never to be mixed up with anything that did not have harness or trot. Though she knew she was not actually the kind to have invented anything. Left to her, the horse would still be undomesticated, the wheel still undiscovered. And except that she had had to make the move to California for Eunice's sake, Millstone, Colorado, would still be her home.

But for her own sake she was glad to be here. She slowed the team still more. The day was changing, going from afternoon to evening, and she liked to watch changes, they were so foreign to her nature. She viewed them the way a fish surfacing views the banks of his stream: real, but too strange to believe. The brown hills were beginning to turn pink. The meadow larks were singing their last songs, songs perhaps not really more beautiful than those sung earlier in the day, but seeming so because they were the last. In the dry arroyo beside the road, the blue-green leaves of the wild tobacco trees were beginning to flutter in the wind that blew inland off the Pacific a little before sundown each day.

The Tract, though the Investment Company hoped eventually for thousands of settlers, was still empty and silent. Sounds were a luxury to the ear, something to be gathered and treasured like other scarcities in that barren land—elderberries or cactus apples or water. The two women looked and listened. They took their pleasure and made their comments with smiles and gestures as if the meadow lark were Madame Schumann-Heink singing and the leaves Madame Helena

36

Modjeska reciting, and any talk of theirs, in these circumstances, a rude interruption.

Eunice said, "You're missing the turn."

"Oh, I'm not missing it," Opal answered. "I'm not taking it on purpose."

"Nobody lives up this way except Lute Cope."

"I know that. I thought it would be nice to see how Lute is getting on with his house."

"Lute Cope is a married man."

"Well, I've got no designs on him. Have you?"

"I don't care for Lute Cope," Eunice answered, ignoring the question.

"Care for him? You don't have to care for him. You don't have to care for a man to be neighborly."

"There's something wrong with him," Eunice insisted.

"There's something wrong with most of us," Opal said. "I'm no kettle myself to start calling the pot black. You can if you want to."

"He's married," Eunice said, ignoring this. "His daughter told me so. His wife ran away from him."

"With another man?" Opal asked. She had to pry such information from Eunice nowadays.

"No," Eunice said. "She's visiting her own folks."

"I don't hold it against Lute," Opal said, "that his wife runs home to mama."

"I do," Eunice said. "A handsome man like that. What makes her do it if there isn't something wrong with him?"

"Maybe there's something wrong with her."

"No woman wants to run away from a man," Eunice said. "She won't do it unless she's forced."

"You can't judge everybody by yourself, Eunice," Opal said. When Eunice did not answer, Opal said, "Well, I'm going to call on him. I feel neighborly. He's not going to eat us alive, even if his wife did run off from him. And I don't aim to be shut off from the human race just because God called Charlie home. Or because He created half of us male and half of us female."

"It was a mistake," Eunice said somberly.

"It's not a mistake I'm responsible for. If there are consequences, I'm not responsible for them either."

She was such a feisty little talker because she did not act. Things happened to her, and people remembering her aggressive speech misconstrued these happenings as acts of her own. It was not so, and Opal Tetford knew it. Her words were no more than sails put out to catch the wind. She had said to Eunice, "Let's go to California," but if Eunice had not acted, she could have repeated those words every day of her life without feeling that the saying ought to be illustrated by any pulling up of stakes in Millstone. She held all possibilities in her mind, and whatever direction she was pushed, she was not surprised.

Eunice had chosen the Tract from advertisements she had read after they reached Los Angeles. The advertisements in the newspapers said the same things as the big tin billboards that dotted the Tract. "Terra Buena: City of the future. Five acres and independence. Abundant water. Sunshine 355 days of the year. Frost free. Ideal for oranges, lemons, and pomelos. Beautiful homesites. Easy terms. Let your fruit pay for your ranch. Perkins Investment Co., 315 So. Spring St., Los Angeles, California."

The tin billboards, put up to be read, were not often read; but they were a welcome source of sound on the silent Tract: they uttered a small tin whine as the wind split itself around their sharp edges, or an occasional metallic pop as the tin, having bellied momentarily outward, snapped back into place. Eunice, as they neared one at the top of the last rise before they dipped downward toward Lute Cope's place, read the words "Abundant water" and laughed. "Abundant in the Pacific Ocean." But everything else was true: the homesites were beautiful; the sunshine was as promised; the climate to the end of August, at least, was frostless, and the land, so far as anyone knew, would be ideally suited to the growth of citrus fruit—as soon as irrigated.

Eunice and Opal expected to plant their five acres, but they were less impatient than the men to get at it. They were content for a while to have escaped from Millstone. It seemed remarkable to both of them that the mere traversing of a thousand miles should have been capable of so changing their lives. They had underestimated, like all people with considerable inward life, the effect of the exterior world; and now, taking themselves to be new persons in the new environment, they wondered why so simple a remedy was not tried more often by people in trouble; too simple to know how often it had been tried and how often it had failed.

38

Opal, especially, believing she had invented starting over again, awakened each morning smiling, thinking of the secret she knew and others did not: "Pick up and move." And though the whole Tract was filled with people who had done just that, they had come, in Opal's opinion, because of the advertised climate or the magnet of easy money; people who only wanted something more to be added; not people who, by leaving something behind, had become, as she and Eunice had, new beings altogether.

6   M o u n t, heading back toward the Copes', decided on impulse to stop at Asa Brice's tent and ask Asa when he planned to start building. A man at the end of summer would surely be thinking of some covering more substantial than canvas. Asa's tent was set on the edge of the arroyo that was the boundary line between the townsite and Reservoir Hill—which resembled the townsite in being, so far, more site than reservoir. The main road petered out into a single track a hundred yards or so before Mount reached the tent. A motorcycle, as up to date as the tent was backwoodsy, explained the single track to Mount, but not the contradiction. A burro would have surprised him less. As he stopped his car, a man came to the opening of the tent and stared out. Mount hailed him, and it was possible that Brice responded to his "Howdy" with a nod. If he did, it was so slight as to be arguable.

Asa was annoyed at this interruption. He had two meals a day, a breakfast and an early supper. After supper he read, wrote, and tested, after a day in the open, the nature of time in an enclosure. From his slant-topped desk he could look out through the opened tent flaps onto a kingdom that included not only the arroyo which he had recently bought, but the sky and the hills, his possessions since boyhood. He lived on the edge of his arroyo as another man might live by a stream or pond. The arroyo was as filled with life as any river. It was visited by skunks, bobcats, jack rabbits, cottontails; coyotes with their icy cry of times vanished from the earth; flocks of red-winged blackbirds flashing through the thickets of wild sunflowers. It had a constant population of ground squirrels, horned toads, lizards, trapdoor spiders, field mice, pack rats, centipedes, and one cat turned wild, who was that arid jungle's tiger. The life in the arroyo was more easily observed than the life of a river or pond.

When interrupted by Mount's arrival, Asa had been writing up a fight between two tarantulas, which he had spent the afternoon watching. Of what value an account of a tarantula fight in an unknown Western arroyo would be to himself or anyone else, he did not know. Nor did he know what passion drove him first to observe, then to record: but to do so was his obsession. He was as lonely without them as another man might be without women or alcohol. Because of this, he watched Mount's approach with a double anger: because he was being interrupted and because he was the kind of a man who minded interruptions. He nodded curtly to Mount. The dry sand at the bottom of the arroyo and the flash and parry of those furry legs seemed to have infected him until he, too, was dry and combative.

Mount recognized the lack of cordiality in the spare gesture—recognized, accepted, and liked. Resistance completed him. Resentment and antagonism at the beginning of an encounter did not daunt him. They provided him a gauge for measuring his effectiveness. Indifference was something else.

"Howdy, sir," he called out again halfway up the path.

Asa said, "Good evening."

Mount, when he reached the tent, faced a short-legged, long-waisted young fellow, probably ten years younger than himself. He was ruddy-complexioned, lank-haired, long-jawed, and large-headed. But his features were big enough to command the skull they rode. His remarkable eyes, blue or gray or green, doubted every aspect of Mount's appearance. Feature by feature, the eyes interrogated him. After a day with insects, a human face comes as a remarkably unconcentrated surprise.

Mount said, "I'm sorry if I'm interrupting you." Asa still held pen and notebook, as if waiting for his visitor to be gone. When Asa made no reply to this, Mount went on. "I'm looking for work."

This was the one sentence with which it was possible to win Asa's attention. A man looking for work was semiholy and deserved to be heard. He put pen and notebook down on his desk.

"Won't you step in?"

Mount stepped in. The tent was as neat and spare as a Western graveyard, as composed as a picture. The room was warm, but airy. The sharp austere light, strained through canvas, had been softened.

The floor was pine, sanded and scrubbed. The furniture, in addition to the slant-topped desk, was a cot, plank-thin and plank-wide, a two-burner oil stove, a deal table and two sets of shelves, one holding groceries and cooking utensils, the other books.

Mount, who could arrive at an encounter all calculation, had the faculty of forgetting what his calculation had been, of becoming absorbed. He recognized the faculty in himself. I am like a medium, he thought, a man pretending visions for profit, and in the midst of a pretended vision I begin to bark like Napoleon's little dog. No profit in it, nobody giving a damn about Napoleon's little dog, but I *am* that dog and what else can I do? The intent false as hell, but the performance pure. It was a sickening bit of irony for a man like Mount.

Asa Brice appeared, in his living, to emerge from that pine-board floor like a deep-rooted growth. The idea of separating him from it, of suggesting that he prepare for the winter by building himself a bungalow or a Swiss chalet, left Mount's mind. Still, he had to explain himself and his visit.

"I stopped in because I thought you might have some work for me."

The idea of employing a man was as foreign to Asa Brice as buying one. He made a gesture that took in his place. The room obviously would not provide an industrious child with thirty minutes' work a day.

"I'm a carpenter," Mount explained further. "I had thought you might be planning to build before winter. But I can see you're not."

Asa hated explaining. There was no possibility of friendship, to his mind, between those for whom explanations were necessary. Mount's recognition, without explanation, that he had no intention of building pleased him.

"Sit down, won't you?" he asked. He pulled the tent's second chair opposite his own, and Mount sat facing him.

"I have a feeling we look like two Civil War generals met for a field conference," Mount said.

Asa Brice laughed. "Which side do you represent, Mr. Mount?"

"The losing," Mount said with assurance.

"I'm on your side in that case," Asa answered. "But I plan to keep on fighting."

"Are you a writer?" Mount motioned toward the notebook and pen.

"No, I'm a farmer."

41

"Farmer? I thought everybody in California was a rancher."

"You can't very well call a thousand-foot stretch of sandy arroyo bottom a ranch."

Then, because Mount did not ask, Asa told him. The arroyo bottom was an ideal place for growing sweet potatoes and peanuts. Neither crop needed irrigation. Later, he intended planting a few strawberries and tomatoes. For these he would terrace the edge of the arroyo and water by hand. The Tract, as a whole, was so wrapped up in citrus fruits there probably would not be any garden truck planted. There would be a good market for his produce, and caring for it would take very little of his time.

For some months, Asa Brice had been searching for a companion, someone he could speak to or, better still, not speak to. He was nourished by Tom Mount's attention. He had a friend who was disappointing him, Ben Jessup. Often now when he was in the midst of observing, head upflung to the sky or bent low to the earth, the act of observation would become meaningless; despair, black and cold as winter ice, would fill his chest. "For whom, for whom?" he would cry. And shock himself, since it had always been his belief that there did not have to be a "for whom." For the sake of the object, for the sake of Asa Brice, for the sake of truth.

But he turned now to Mount. "I figure I can make all the money I need by working three hours a day."

Ben would have said, "What will you do with the hours you save?" Mount said nothing. He sat there imagining the life Asa would live. He would work the three hours, weeding the sweet potatoes and peanuts, watering the tomatoes and strawberries; then he would come back to the tent and write, God knew what, in that notebook.

"That's a nice crop you plan on," he said. "Two yellow and beneath ground, two red and above."

Asa had thought of this himself. He had not supposed it would occur to anyone else. The two men sat in the door of the tent immersed in time, like water, buoyed up and refreshed by it. Birds, black and slow, flew overhead.

"Buzzards," said Asa. "Something's dead around here."

Mount, looking upward, recognized his late hawks.

"I thought they were hawks," he said. "I just finished calling them hawks. I described the habits of hawks."

"Hawks!" Asa exclaimed, startled. He attempted no explanation of the differences between hawks and buzzards, any more than he would have explained the differences between cows and horses. He considered it an aberration of eyesight. He could not believe in such ignorance.

"I don't know one bird from another," Mount admitted.

This, the truth, was the most palatable substance he had had in his mouth for months. My God, he thought, those damned women with all their talk of how big . . . how handsome, how they lead me on to being what they want, and not what I am. Teach me to tell the truth, Asa. I'm sick of women. A man can lead a decent life only with another man. And suddenly the spareness, cleanness, hardness of Asa's tent was dearer to him than a thousand petticoats, corset covers, and frilled drawers.

Asa Brice, as if aware of these thoughts, got to his feet.

"I'm going to the meeting tonight," he said. "I'm sorry to have to say that I haven't any work for you. Good luck. And drop in again some time."

The two men parted without shaking hands.


7    The Cope girls—Pressley was seventeen and Hannah was nine—had helped their father transfer their water (they got three barrels at a time) to the cement weir box where they stored it. Lute was still back in the shed where he kept his barrels, but the girls had walked to the south edge of the little knoll on which the Cope house was built and stood looking off toward the invisible lake of their afternoon's adventure.

Hauling water was an adventure only for the young. Everyone else hated it. The men hated it because of the time it took—a good half-day, when all the time in the world was not enough for the clearing and planting to be done; though no one was going to be so foolhardy as to plant before there was water in the pipes. Rain was due not later than November; but to set out citrus stock at a dollar and fifty cents a tree on the chance that the rainfall would be heavy enough to carry the trees through the winter without irrigation was a bigger gamble than any sensible man was willing to take.

The women did not hate the actual hauling—they did not have to make these trips, but went, if at all, for the outing. What they hated was: first, the lack of water itself; next, the Perkins Investment Company; and finally, and most strongly, their husbands for being such poor sticks as to let the Investment Company bamboozle them with its everlasting promises of "next month," "by fall," or "spring, at the latest." "Do something," they stormed, trying to take baths in teacups of secondhand water.

There were many jokes among the women, all bitter, about the best way to get the full use of a pail of water. The method most advocated was to begin by using the water to boil potatoes and to end with foot-washing and chamber-rinsing. But the children, and even Pressley, who, at seventeen, was no child, went to the lake like travelers to a foreign land. The lake was actually a reservoir; but unlike the Tract reservoir, which, when completed, would be all cement and obviously man-made, the lake, except for an earthen dam placed a little too exactly to be God's handiwork, appeared no more unnatural than any oasis or geyser; something unexpected to be sure, but perhaps made so by God on purpose to teach mortals that He was not to be limited by their expectations.

Press, wet from helping her father empty the barrels, smoothed her dress over her thighs with a swimming motion. She was still bemused by the trip. The lake was no more than a big pond, shallow, fringed with reeds like a thick-lashed, muddy eye; but any water amidst the dry hills was so unexpected she would not have been surprised to find other unexpected things there: a mermaid breaking the afternoon shimmer of the water to speak to her.

She lifted her hands, which still smelled green and weedy, to her face. The seepage of water through the earthwork dam nourished a rich growth of willows and acacia, of mullein and mint, fennel and dock. Press had taken off her shoes and stood with Hannah and the other children, barefooted on the wet spongy earth. She had stretched out in the midst of mint and bryony to watch the hummingbirds explore the wild-tobacco blossoms. She had heard the Mexicans, who lived on a straggling street above the lake, laughing and talking. She was home now and had supper planned in her mind; still, she was home in the way of a returned traveler whose memory is all of foreign ports and phrases, of faraway smells and sounds. She made more of the trip than it really was because it had to take the place of love affairs and dances and trips to town and new dresses—and even a mother. She was getting an imagination so practiced it did not matter much what happened to her; she could transform it in her mind to

44

suit her needs. Or anyway, her wishes. She smoothed her dress with the hands of the admirer she did not have and noted with his eyes the outward curve of her long thighs.

Hannah, who was beside her, called, "Father, Father, company's coming!"

Press, who had seen Opal's and Eunice's spring wagon for some time, thought, there's not one second's delay between Hannah's getting an idea and her expression of it. If Hannah was not eating, she was not hungry. When she did not have anything to say, she kept silent. Hannah did not leave much to the imagination, and Press, with imagination to spare, was foiled in her company. Hannah always knew her own mind and gave Press little opportunity to interpret Hannah to Hannah. I had as lief have a speaking stone for a sister, Press thought. Hannah went right through, from rind to core, one hundred per cent the same material and utterly content with that material. Press knew that her father found Hannah "restful"; and while she would not care to have that adjective applied to herself, still, if rest was what her father needed, she wanted him to find his rest in her. But Hannah no more made Press feel restful than a cliff makes the sea feel restful. Hannah stirred her up. Stirred her up to lies and taunts and neglectfulness; and then, to counterbalance all this, to wild sacrifices and a motherliness so loving it could only be practiced by a nonmother with plenty of time for imagining roles of farfetched devotion. Most of the time, Press would have felt better if she could have slapped or kicked Hannah. Once she had bit her—but she was brought up not to do these things and felt too miserable afterward to make the momentary pleasure worth while.

Press was born to affect people and had a feeling of physical sickness when she met no response. She leaned forward at an angle to meet others, and if she did not encounter a stance of like eagerness, she felt awkward and had to fight for her balance. But when she met the same stance, and each in supporting the other felt himself weightless, she was as calm as a waltzer.

Press gave her sister a shake which set Hannah's braids to swinging. Not that Hannah minded. She only swung her braids a little more.

"Father's busy," Press rebuked her. "Let him alone."

"He's just putting away the barrels. He can do that any time."

"The ladies are calling on us."

"Why don't you want Father to see them? You're not his guardian angel."

45

Sometimes the stone spoke as if it had fallen to the bottom of that well where truth is. Press *was* her father's guardian angel. She thought of herself so. How Hannah could know these things was beyond her. If a person was going to be uncanny, it would be fairer if his face gave more warning than Hannah's.

"I want him to decide for himself," Press said, but she went with Hannah to meet the two women when they drove into the yard. Eunice, she welcomed openly; but Opal, who she supposed was her father's age, she ignored. Opal, attributing Press's quietness to "the queer way girls are nowadays," paid no attention to her lack of courtesy. Instead, she talked to Hannah, "who hasn't," as she told Eunice, "reached her sister's stage yet, thank goodness."

"Is your father here, Hannah?"

"He's putting the barrels in the shed. I called him when I saw you coming."

"You been getting water, too?" Opal asked. She wrapped the reins round the whip and prepared to make a real visit.

Hannah had never seen Miss Fry in anything but white; today she had on a white Indian Head skirt and a white voile blouse. Her white camisole could be seen very easily because Miss Fry's skin was golden brown. It was Hannah's intention to be as much like Miss Fry as possible when she grew up. She hoped she would have down on her arms, a mole near her left ear, and heavy brows, all like Miss Fry's.

When Opal stepped down from the wagon, she gave Hannah a hug, and Hannah, who was solid, co-operated by making herself as compressible as possible. The fun in squeezing was, she knew, that something gave.

Catching sight of Lute down at the shed, Opal called out, "Lute, you've got visitors."

Luther Cope was forty years old and as handsome as Eunice thought him. No one in the past minutes' speculations about him had, in fact, erred: good-looking, a grass widower, far from blameless, finding Hannah restful, grateful to be protected from widows by Press. If either woman had been alone, he would have beat a retreat, leaving Press to explain his absence as best she could. Two of them were another matter. "There's safety in numbers," as his mother used to say. His mother's sayings, when he lived next door to her, had often irked him. Now, with five hundred miles separating them, they were frequently in his mind.

"Safety in numbers." Why did he feel that? Because he wanted to be a faithful husband to his absent wife? No, his retreat would have had nothing to do with being faithful to Indy, only with himself and his own ease and security. Women by twos, by threes, by tens he enjoyed. It was not that he was shy; most shy people found crowds alarming, but were able to converse with one other human being without undue suffering. With him it was the reverse. He enjoyed a crowd, but hated to be confronted by one person alone. He had no name for this preference and neither did Indy, though they often spoke of it. Often quarreled about it, in fact.

Indy was always taking up with strangers, a single stranger, that was. She got tangled up with their personal lives. Oh, not men, or not men as men, anyway. Interest in men as men was no more a weakness of Indy's than interest in women as women was a weakness of his. But Indy would listen to some poor derelict, some man or woman obviously half crazy, get in over her head, and have to be rescued by him. While from sensible persons of the kind with whom they had naturally associated in their home up north, the friends of a newspaper editor whose family had been landowners since before the Bear Flag Raising, Indy had run away. From them, actually, far more than from him, he believed. After an evening of such company, everything light and pleasant, his mother taking half the labor of providing refreshments off Indy's hands, Indy, who had been mum for hours, would complain to him, "But Lute, no one spoke a single word of truth to me."

Truth! A single word of truth! What did she want? The weather was the truth and politics were the truth and the crops were the truth and dying and being born were the truth. He ran a paper and made a living out of such truths. Other wives didn't complain to their husbands after a pleasant evening of whist or seven-up that they hadn't heard a word of truth. He liked a house full of people. Indy liked one person—"speaking the truth," whatever that meant. "We're enough truth for each other," he would tell her when she brought up that tired old complaint. Or he would ignore the disputed word altogether and say, "Indy, what you need is the cure," and lead her upstairs to bed.

But Indy was capable of no permanent cure. She had got the idea that if they moved away from the people he had known all of his life, away from the community his grandfather had settled, away from his mother next door, he would, amidst strangers, be unable to live as he did with those known so well they had become nothing, so Indy

47

said, but labels and occupations and names. He would have to live freshly, without any pattern of living to protect him. And he and Indy, too, in the new community, would live freshly together, Indy had argued.

When he had refused, as any man in his right senses was bound to, she had left him, gone back home to her own folks in Indiana. Now here he was, as Indy had wanted. A newer place could not be found in California; but the feelings he had had in the old town of Marysville were still with him. He still did not care for the company of a woman alone. Except Indy, of course. How many wives would object to that? A man alone, he could talk to; they had a dozen subjects in common. But a woman? What did they have in common? Nothing but what he felt more comfortable to keep his mind away from.

Two women, four actually, with Press and Hannah, were not so bad. Were good, in fact. They could have a party. He loved company, hated to be alone, and found in the chatter and banter of a group, if not happiness, his greatest protection from melancholy.

He moved forward to greet his guests with that extra heartiness which the host who has had some inhospitable qualms always assumes.

"Howdy, Opal, Eunice," he said. "It's nice of you to take pity on a poor lone man."

"We just stopped in for a drink of your water, Lute," Opal said. "We thought we'd drink yours and save ours."

"Anything I got is yours," Lute said, "though I serve water in small glasses."

They all went into the sitting room, prickly as cactus apples because of Press, who was up to something, no one could say what.

"Would you care for tea?" Press asked Opal. She looked at her bitterly, with a glance that imputed greediness if Opal accepted, discourtesy if she refused.

"Water's fine," said Opal.

"Make some tea," said Lute Cope. Daughters were fine but conversation with them soon ran up against a dead end; they were too young for ideas and too well known to provide him many surprises in themselves.

"You going to the meeting tonight?" He addressed his question to Opal. Eunice Fry looked as if it would hurt her to talk.

"Truth to tell," Opal said, "I can't get much stirred up about a meeting to organize the community."

48

"It'll stir you up if you have to go on hauling water, won't it?"

"I like the trip; though I reckon I *could* make it without a barrel. But why do we have to organize for that? That's the Investment Company's business, not ours."

"The Investment Company needs reminding."

"That's up to you men."

"It's up to us landowners—and you're one of us."

"I was planning on coming," Opal said. "To meet folks though, I admit, not to fight for water."

"You can kill two birds with one stone tonight," Lute said. "No better way of getting acquainted than fighting."

"Against or with?" Eunice Fry asked, unexpectedly.

"Don't matter much. No, I take that back. In some ways you get better acquainted with your enemies than your friends. You got to know your enemies. If you don't know them, they'll wipe you out."

Press brought in the tea. Opal supposed it wasn't poison, otherwise the girl would have had to hand it round more pleasantly. She watched Lute take his cup and saw he esteemed the giver, thought he had raised up a jewel. His face, as he lowered it over the hand-painted violets, was manly. It occurred to her that a newcomer on earth, a man from Mars who didn't know anything about sex, could tell from the difference between Luther Cope's face and Queen Victoria's, that more separated them than the fact that one was short and round and the other tall and spare. More joined them, too; though she didn't suppose the man from Mars, ignorant as she was supposing him to be, could guess that.

It was in the midst of these thoughts, as if the word "sex" in her mind had called him up, that she saw Tom Mount come to the doorway. His hand was raised to knock, but seeing her he arrested the force of the knock so that it was soundless, and smiled. However things fell out, with sound or without, was all one to Tom Mount. He would land on his feet like a big cat, clean his whiskers, and prepare to relish whatever lay nearest to hand. Though his appearance in that doorway was the last thing Opal had expected on earth, she was somehow not surprised; or surprised only in the way she would have been if a Colorado thunderstorm had blown up; hardly to be expected in Southern California, but the wonder being only that they had been spared so long. Her one thought was to protect Eunice, say something before Eunice *saw*. The ears, she believed, took surprises easier than the eyes. Let Eunice hear his name before she saw his face.

49

"Tom Mount!" she exclaimed loudly. "It *is* Tom Mount, isn't it? Mr. Thomas S. Mount? Late of Millstone, Colorado?"

"Howdy, Opal," he said, relaxed as a husband or a home-coming child.

Eunice, who had a teacup in mid-air, continued to lift it. At mouth level she tipped it, as one would, drinking; but she forgot, or was unable, to open her lips. The tea, poured in a thin stream down onto her white shirtwaist, disappeared under her camisole in the natural runway between her breasts. Either her tea was lukewarm or Eunice was beyond feeling the difference between hot and cold. She did not wince.

Opal could not make up her mind whether to run to Eunice or to keep up her talk with Tom Mount. Tom Mount decided for her. He came in, not waiting for a word from Lute, righted Eunice's cup, and said to her playfully, "That little shouting woman's still at it, I see." He used his handkerchief on the tea stains, and the looks he bent upon Eunice were tender. In the midst of his tea-sopping, he apologized to Lute. "Since I caused the damage I figure I ought to repair it."

Lute, who had met the man only once before and had then asked him to come over, was pleased to see him again. Things were livening up. This grows to be a real party, he thought. Friends dropping in, tea being poured, if not all of it in exactly the right places. He went over to Tom.

"Who's going to make the introductions here?" he asked. "Me, or you, Opal?"

"You," Opal said. "Let the blood be on your head, Lute."

"You know these two ladies, Mr. Mount?" Lute asked.

"Know them?" Tom asked. "Except for them I'd never be here."

Opal bristled at once; but before she could say a word, Tom Mount continued. "They lived in a town in Colorado I used to pass through. I heard they'd settled here, so when I was casting around for a place to light, I thought what's good enough for Opal and Eunice'll be good enough for me."

Opal noticed he said her name first. She supposed Eunice had noted the same thing. Chronologically, it was her due, but Tom would have been smarter to have forgotten that.

Lute said, "Mr. Mount, I want you to meet my daughters. This is Hannah. She's nine. Pressley's seventeen."

"Shall I bring in some Nabiscos, Father?" Pressley asked.

Lute turned to Tom. "You want a Nabisco, Mr. Mount?"

"Kind of a thin shingle with a sugar coating?"

"That's it."

"That's what I've been hungering for."

"Besides us," Opal asked, when Press left the room, "besides Eunice and me, what other magnets bring you to California?"

"Sit down, Mr. Mount," Lute said.

Tom stretched out in the proffered chair. "I've changed my work, Eunice," he answered. "I was a salesman for Swift when I was in Colorado," he explained to Lute. "But I decided I didn't want to spend the best part of my life in butcher shops. I'm carpentering now."

"Don't that kind of change require some training?"

"I was a carpenter before I was a salesman."

He was the center of the party now, extended in the rocking chair, managing Nabiscos, tea, conversation, and even the rocking chair, with ease. Opal watched him. He was as far away from her as Moses. He was a man she had heard about. He was a man the others were listening to. Nothing, except Eunice's spilled tea, had been anything she would have expected, yet nothing surprised her.

"We had better be getting on," she suggested to Eunice.

But Lute Cope, Opal saw, was in love with his party. He acted like it was a rare bloom, too pretty to pick. He asked for more tea, more Nabiscos. "You don't want to go, do you, Miss Fry?"

"No," Eunice said. "I'm in no hurry."

8    Though Press Cope had lit the lamps before Eunice and Opal left, she had lit them unnecessarily early. There was still a streak of yellow in the western sky. Press had brought in the lamps to tell the ladies how late they were staying. She had put them down as much as to say, "Shall I make up a bed, too? Would you like a postcard to send the folks at home?"

Press's lack of hospitality had been a godsend to Opal, an excuse for getting Eunice out of the house and away from Tom Mount. When Eunice, after climbing into the wagon, sat there staring straight ahead, Opal unwound the reins herself and clucked up the horses.

"What man has done, man can do," she said.

She was speaking of herself and driving, but it came to her

that Eunice might think she was referring to Tom Mount. If Eunice did, that was just too bad, because she did not want to speak Mount's name now. She could think it, was thinking it, but she didn't want to shape her mouth around it. Instead, she looked at the sky and said, "Hard to remember it was ever blue." Eunice remained mum. That was all right with Opal. She would like Eunice to remember why they had left Colorado in the first place.

Eunice Fry had been a teacher in Millstone, Colorado. Eunice had liked the town, but since she had never been anyplace else, she had nothing with which to compare it. All of her critical faculties were exercised on the seasons and sights of Millstone; she compared Millstone in summer to Millstone in winter; she contrasted Millstone with rain falling to Millstone with snow falling. She knew that she liked the river road more than the road over the mesa, and she knew why. She thought that winter, with the rimrocks blazing white in the midday sunshine, and the stars visible under the dark spruces by the time school was out, was the best of the seasons. She constantly discriminated about the quality of experiences in Millstone; but, since joy came easily to her, she discriminated about varieties of easy pleasure. The truth of the matter was that on every count but one she was easily satisfied. That count was the fact of her spinsterhood. She was an old maid and she was probably going to remain one. She didn't like it and she didn't know what she could do about it.

She had never had any other ambition than to marry. She had admired boys from the very beginning. She had admired them so much that, as a young girl, she had imitated them. It was the sincerest kind of flattery, but the boys had not recognized it as such. She had walked stiff-legged, swinging along from the hips, because boys walked this way. For the same reason, she had scorned pocket handkerchiefs, worked her cheek muscles, and scrubbed her face with her hands as men do. Such tactics, when practiced with the intention of attracting the opposite sex, are always bound to fail. No boy wants an imitation boy, though he may be well suited with an imitation girl. Eunice never learned this. She gave up imitating boys because she thought she did not imitate them well enough. The boys laughed at her failures; on the other hand, they did not applaud her successes. In fact, they seemed to resent them. From sixteen on, she tried hard to be a girl.

This was a late start on a complex job. Having spent ten years imitating boys, she had to imitate girls for three or four years before *their*

52

ways became natural to her. Boys were actually easier to imitate. It was far easier to twitch cheek muscles, swim naked, and lift billy goats than to put her hair up in curlers, take small bites, and wear corsets. She thought that both boys and girls were farfetched in their actions; she wished that she didn't have to fit into a pattern of one or the other, but could be herself, Eunice Fern Fry. Eunice Fern Fry was quieter and more gentle than most boys; on the other hand, she was less silly than most girls. But from sixteen to twenty, she gave silliness a good try. Silliness did not seem to be the answer either.

She was almost twenty when she decided that the real trouble was her looks. She was getting warmer in her suppositions. She was no fool, so it was perfectly plain to her that half the married women in Millstone were a good deal uglier than she was; alongside some of them, it was perfectly obvious, she was Lillian Russell herself. The flaw in her looks was something that went deeper than the size of her nose or the color of her eyes, something that didn't "appeal" to men. That something, though she never discovered it, was a certain matronliness, which kept her, even in the cradle, from being chucked under the chin as much as most babies. And with the matronliness went some intimation of seriousness and even of passion which the Millstone young men found rather frightening. She gave the impression of meaning every word she said. Her acts, they felt, would be final, not done for exterior reasons, because she wanted to make an impression. Women of this appearance and temperament often marry men who carry boyish faces to the grave; but the men in Millstone with boyish faces found other matrons to marry, and at twenty Eunice was moving about Millstone, large, dark, calm, good-looking —and alone. Always alone.

She had been in love more times than she could remember. Since she made none of the usual signs of being in love, the only way these tumults could have been guessed was by watching the men and boys she avoided, was tongue-tied with, refused to sit next to or even to look at. These were the objects of her love. These were the men and boys she adored.

Eunice's emotions were always too strong to be expressed by any coquetry or fiddle-faddle. She scorned the surreptitious pawings and pattings with which other girls courted young men. She sat alone at the winter box-supper parties and the summer baseball games, if not perfectly happy, at least without jealousy for those who came partnered. How could she be jealous of that which she had never possessed and of whose very nature she was ignorant? And how could she be unhappy, deeply in love as she was sure to be, with the summer catcher or the winter auctioneer?

Loving in this way, mystically united with the beloved, and ignorant of any other union, she stood a good chance never to marry—or even to be kissed. Her one chance lay in the appearance of a man with whom she could fall in love and who would in turn be drawn to her; a man who would pursue her in spite of her disappearances and who would not be put off by her direct ways when, finally, he did catch up with her. This man had at last come to Millstone. His name was Thomas S. Mount. Most people called him Tom, though Eunice, partly because she did not want to be classified with "most people" when it came to Tom, and partly because she could not bear to reject so much as three letters of his name, when she first knew him, called him Thomas.

Eunice, after the death of her parents, had made her home with Opal Tetford, then recently widowed. Opal had never had a child, had always wanted one, and while Eunice was a little old for a daughter, yet Eunice's virginal state made her acceptable as such. Her straightforward, manly manner, partly a leftover from her days of imitating boys, partly natural, qualified her also as a husband substitute; and, finally, her knowledge of community goings on, picked up from her students, equipped her as a female companion capable of producing enough small talk to last out an after-school chat.

Opal was completely aware of this threefold combination of satisfactions. She often called Eunice, copying the trade name of the oil she used to lubricate her sewing machine, "My little three-in-one girl." Eunice gave her most of the pleasures of having a man in the house and none of the drawbacks. She brought in money, had a good appetite at the table, and was more appreciative of special culinary efforts than Charlie had ever been. Eunice needed the services of a needlewoman and laundress as much as any husband, and she relished affection more. More than Charlie, anyway.

Opal liked to shock her friends by saying, "If Eunice would use a mustache cup and hang a razor strop by the sink, I'd forget I was a widow." This struck the Millstone ladies as being a perhaps truthful, but tasteless, epitaph for Charlie. When they recovered from this sally, Opal would come at them from another direction. "If Eunice occasionally needed her ears washed and her hair combed, I could forget I was childless."

54

All in all, and all joking aside, Opal had never been happier and never more surprised. Who could have guessed that, if asked "What days of your life have been the happiest?" she would have had to answer, "Now, boarding an old-maid schoolteacher." Of course, this was before Tom Mount came to Millstone. But this answer was typical of Opal; it illustrated her ability to learn from the past, and also her inability to imagine a different future.

Before Tom Mount's appearance in Millstone, Opal had gone about her work singing as she had not done since she was fourteen. She was a woman who liked to please others—and to do so, as often as possible, by surprising them. Charlie had been a hard man to surprise. Opal had tried both good surprises and bad on Charlie, in an effort to liven him up a little, but he was as calm in disaster as in good fortune. She had almost killed him one night, taking the two middle slats out from under their feather bed. Charlie had hopped into bed with his usual dispatch and jackknifed through the opening with the feather ticking wrapped round his throat like a garrote. All this had happened quickly and quietly while Opal was in the bathroom, and, except that she had forgotten her comb, Charlie might have died without speaking a word. He had recovered in the same way; Opal pulled him out, and Charlie, without either complaining or laughing, rubbed his throat, replaced the two missing slats, and was asleep before she left the room. Opal went back to the bathroom convinced that she was missing something in marriage. Either what I did was funny or it was mean, she thought. If it wasn't funny, Charlie might at least have taken a slat to me.

Eunice knew how to respond to a surprise. She knew that a surprise was a two-handed game and had to be played that way. When Opal made blancmange, colored it purple, molded it in a berry-shaped pan, covered it with black raspberries, and served it surrounded by a wreath of grape leaves, Eunice exclaimed. She had feelings and she took the pains to say what those feelings were. After Charlie, this was a treat.

Eunice made no bones to Opal about her desire for a husband. Though she shied away from men, at least those she was attracted to, she could talk to women with perfect good humor on the subject. Opal, who had never found Charlie anything to write home about, respected Eunice's illusions about marriage. If Eunice thought a husband would be such a treat, Opal, who had had one for twenty years without ever discovering what the treat was, didn't want to tell her that, matrimonially speaking, there was no Santa Claus. Opal's ignorance, in a way, was far deeper than Eunice's. Eunice's imaginings were truer than Opal's knowledge. Eunice could imagine many men. Poor Opal, who had experienced only Charlie, was unable, with him as a model, to make any generalization fair to marriage.

It was Opal's love for Eunice that drew Opal to Tom Mount. If a husband was what Eunice wanted, Opal would find her one. He would be a bigger surprise for Eunice than any she had yet been able to supply. Opal decided to do this, knowing perfectly well how lonely she was going to be if the big girl, with her smell of orris root, chalk dust, and rose water, should find a husband and leave her. Though for all of her appreciation of Eunice as child and husband substitute, Opal did not know that Eunice was providing her with the first human companionship she had had since she left her parents' home twenty years ago. Eunice's gifts to her were greater than Friday's to Crusoe. Opal had been on a desert island all of her adult life; Charlie had been a track made by a man, and for a while Opal had been hopeful; but the man himself had never materialized. Until Eunice came, Opal had never talked, planned, laughed, worked with another human being. It was more exciting than a honeymoon; more exciting than hers, anyway.

Opal had never been shy with men. There had been no qualities in Charlie suggesting that there was much difference between men and women. Men were stronger, sleepier, quieter, duller; really, so far as she could make out, not much more than a breed of uninteresting women. So when she was introduced to Tom Mount in Mayhew's market, she was not the least bashful about asking him over. She treated him like a visiting matron who would undoubtedly enjoy, in a strange town, the domestic comforts of another woman's home.

Opal was not a woman's idea of the kind of woman who appealed to men, and since most of Opal's ideas were picked up from women, and since Charlie had never said or done anything to make her value herself as a woman, she accepted as a fact this estimate of herself. Charlie, she figured, had chosen her more or less by chance. Discovering that she was a good housekeeper with an even disposition, he had decided that he might go further and do worse. So he had stuck by her and, unattractive to men as she was, she was lucky to have held him.

The truth, unbeknownst to Opal and her women friends, was that men found her very attractive, though her matter-of-fact camaraderie was almost as disconcerting as Eunice's disappearances. Men made

56

eyes at Opal, and Opal did not know enough about men to know what they were up to. For years, the ticket agent down at the Denver and Rio Grande depot had been trying to make her wake up to the fact that he was a man. He was still just the ticket agent to Opal.

Opal went in occasionally to buy a ticket to Denver or Fort Collins, and Basil Updyke—that was the ticket agent's name, though Opal never troubled to remember it—would spend forty-five minutes on a ten-minute job, singing, whistling, moving about in time to his music and stamping the forms with all the slap-dash of a Dixieland drum player. Opal occasionally noticed the old fellow's antics (he was eight years older than she), and she thought him an energetic, sunny-tempered old codger. It never crossed her mind that his energy and his sunniness flashed on automatically when she entered the door. Or that all his prancing and banging was aimed at impressing her with his robust virility.

And it certainly never occurred to her that he liked the looks of the short round woman who stood before him, a woman who reminded him of a sego lily, shape, color and scent; nor that there wasn't a man alive, Basil Updyke supposed, who wouldn't like to bury his nose in that sweetness.

Certainly not Tom Mount. He had had an eye on her long before Gus Mayhew, leaning across his cutting block, told Opal who Tom was. A bachelor, a lonely traveling man.

"Just the ticket for you or Eunice," Gus said.

"You sure he's a bachelor?" Opal had asked. She was looking for the real thing for Eunice. She did not want any surprises that back-fired.

"What's your guess?" Gus asked.

He looked like a bachelor all right, a man interested in women but not in the way of a married man, who can't keep a look of smugness off his face, appreciating as he does what he's putting over on his wife.

"I'd like to know," Opal said. "Not guess."

Gus, a bloodless man, whose white face above a poor cut of meat made even that, by contrast, look rosy, stopped pounding a circle of round steak.

"You've got to be a real prowly widow all of a sudden, Opal. What's come over you?"

Opal had no intention of giving Eunice away. "I get lonesome once in a while, Gus."

Gus, who was as aware of Opal's sego-lily qualities as anyone, felt

57

himself being admitted right down into the heart of her sweetness.

"Sure you do, Opal. I guess we all get so locked up in ourselves we don't think about anyone else. Now you don't give the appearance of ever having had a lonesome minute in your life."

"The lonesomer we are, the more we try to hide it," Opal said, a fact she believed to be true but had never actually experienced.

Gus had a sudden piercing vision of a contradictory world and of himself and Opal penetrating to the core of it. He put down his mallet and lifted his white face. Here, on a fall afternoon, a butcher and a widow had, between them, hit upon a truth: Things are not what they seem. The glory of seeing that this was a fact transfigured the bunch grass across the street, the specks of blood on his straw cuffs, the sunbeams filling the spaces between the particles of sawdust on the floor.

Opal didn't know what had struck the poor butcher. Got a cramp in his arm? Took a sudden loathing, as why not, after dealing in it day after day, to dead flesh? So the source, to Gus, of the idea that had transfixed him—"Things are not what they seem"—was unaware that Gus was illustrating his own discovery.

"Opal," Gus said, tenderly, "I ain't got papers on Tom Mount. I ain't seen his registered bachelor's license. But he's a bachelor—or living single—that's my opinion. He's not a close-mouthed man, likes to chew the fat better'n most, and he's never let a word fall about wife or child. I know where he was born: Red Wing, Minnesota. I know his sister threw a pair of scissors at him when he was a boy. See that scar on his face? I know he's the oldest of four. But no word of a wife. Or any other woman, for that matter. He's a clean-speaking man. As men go," Gus added, not wanting to spoil this hour of revelations with untruths. "I've knowed him for two—three years; I wonder you ain't seen him before. I know he's taken notice of you more than once. I'd enjoy making you acquainted."

Gus called Tom Mount over, and Opal was as free with him as could be, double bolstered as she now was against self-consciousness: unattractive to men and working for Eunice.

"You going to be in town this evening?" Opal asked.

"I'd like to be," Tom Mount said, "though at the minute I haven't any reason for lingering."

"I'll give you a reason. Come to have supper with me and my friend."

58

"Lady friend," Gus explained, not wanting to have the evening die a-borning.

"I'm having Swiss steak. I'll order another pound if you'll come."

"Order it," Tom Mount said.

Gus was already cutting it.

Opal lived in her house like an egg in a shoe box, curves enhancing corners. It was the West, 1914, and small town to a T. A brown, shingle-covered bungalow with brown mission furniture, white scrim curtains, cretonne drapes, and a round dining-room table. The dining room and living room were semiseparated by shoulder-high glass-doored cupboards. There were a thousand dishes on the dining-room side of the cupboards and six books on the living-room side. In addition to the books, there was a palm fan, decorated with a painting of red poppies, a large piece of wood from the Petrified Forest, seventeen cock pheasant feathers, and a Siamese duck egg. The effect was lovely. Opal loved her house, and perhaps this was what was enjoyed rather than the objects themselves. Or, more likely still, it was the cleanliness and the order. Or, most likely of all, what one responded to was Opal's domination of the place. She ran a happy bungalow—as they say of captains and ships.

Opal was of two minds as to whether she should announce to Eunice the fact that there would be a guest for supper. She decided finally to save Tom Mount as a partial surprise. She told Eunice there would be company for supper, but not who the company was, a man who looked like a younger, happier Abe Lincoln.

Tom Mount was a very orderly man, and his orderliness extended to time. He was patient with the tardiness of other people but almost never tardy himself. He arrived at Opal's on the dot of the hour.

Opal saw to it that Eunice answered his knock. Tom Mount was the best surprise she had been able, so far, to provide. She watched her guest's arrival from inside the kitchen. Tom Mount looked large, dark, calm, and this evening, in addition, pale and well-scrubbed.

Eunice, because she thought Tom was Opal's guest, was able to be spontaneous; Opal, always spontaneous, tonight was unusually warmhearted as well because her intentions were so unselfish. Tom Mount, supposing that he was being courted by Opal, felt perfectly at home. Thus misled, all three were happy and at ease.

59

The only action proceeding out of understanding, though he had his facts wrong, was Mount's. Some of the women he knew had, in the beginning, been the friend of a woman friend. He did not know why, but two women, instead of being separated by having to share a man, were often drawn closer together. They were separated, of course, if the man repudiated one for the other. But if he did not, and he never did, the knowledge, when it reached the first woman, often seemed to enhance him in her eyes. Acting out of this insight about women, Tom quietly, lazily, smilingly directed some of his attention to Eunice. The more he did so, the more Opal seemed pleased. Tom understood that there was something in the situation not quite open to him, but he was in no hurry to find out what it was.

Opal, no drinker herself, but determined to make the evening appealing to her guest, had got hold of a bottle of whisky. When she brought this, with glasses and a pitcher of water, into the living room, Tom said, "What does alcohol mean to you, Opal?"

He was really interested, really wanted to know. This interest, together with his immediate use of the women's first names, startled and pleased both Opal and Eunice, and started the evening off in an immediately frank and, for them, exciting way.

"Alcohol doesn't mean a thing to me," she said truthfully. "I bought it for you. I thought it the thing to offer a gentleman."

"How about you, Eunice? What does alcohol mean to you?"

"I've never tasted any."

"Well, this *is* a celebration. Why not?"

"No one ever offered me any before."

"You can't live like that, you know. Taking what's offered to you and nothing more."

"I have lived like that."

"Maybe you just think you're living."

"Oh no, I'm really alive. . . . I know I am."

"How do you know?"

Eunice was silent for a moment. "I suffer," she said to her own great surprise. Not because it was not true. It was the truest thing in the world, but she had never admitted it before to another human being.

Tom Mount received the information gravely and seriously. "You're alive all right, Eunice." He lifted his glass. "Here's to the three of us."

The two women were excited enough to respond pleasantly to the sedation of the drink. Their nerve ends stopped quivering. A wind began to blow down off the already white mountains, thin as a butcher

60

knife. They heard it go round the corners of the brown bungalow and they all looked about the room and saw how they were protected from it, shut away from it with afghans, with piano keys, with plump footstools, with red coals in the grate. And they might just as well have been out in that wind. Fate might have handed them that. None of the three could say by what chance they had landed inside those walls, or any walls whatever, instead of outside in the windy dark. Here they were, in need of shelter, and fully provided with what they needed.

"I am beginning to like whisky," Opal said, two full tablespoonsful inside her.

Tom Mount went to the window, parted the scrim curtains, let the blind up. The moonlight was on the faraway wall of white mountains, on the black spruces by the river, on the dried grass across the driveway. The two women joined him. He put a hand on the shoulder of each. His touch felt comfortable to them and without desire.

"Are we here? Or there?" he asked.

"I don't understand you," Eunice said.

"When I looked at that snow I was up in those mountains."

"But I felt your hand," Eunice said.

"Me, too," said Opal.

Tom pulled the blind. He put the curtains together. "I have never argued with a woman and I don't plan to start tonight. But you must admit that when I'm looking at those mountains and thinking myself in the snow, I'm not so much here as when I close my eyes."

He closed his eyes and once more put a hand on each woman's shoulder. "Now I am one hundred per cent present."

"Me, too," said Opal, before she could think. Then, thinking, she said, "Let's eat."

After supper, Opal saw no way, when Tom Mount was ready to leave, to make Eunice go to the door with him. Opal held back and gave Eunice meaningful glances, and still Eunice sat like a bump on a log. So Opal went out onto the porch with him, daring the wind and the mountains.

For three days after Tom Mount's visit, Eunice was unusually well and cheerful. She taught school with one hand and with the other re-papered Opal's bedroom, made thirty-six pints of quince honey, and reread the whole of Elizabeth Barrett Browning's "Aurora Leigh." She ran up- and downstairs, smiled continuously, and was loving and compassionate toward all. She knew not why.

Then the fourth day, Thursday, the kitchen filled with jars of quince honey, "Aurora Leigh" finished, and her lesson plans for Friday complete, Eunice went out into the side yard after supper. The cold wind, which had swept down off the mountains the night Tom Mount had come to supper, had let up. There had been a warm sun all day, and the evening air was mild. Eunice stood under an enormous old Baldwin apple tree and looked up at the sky through the cage of its half-bare limbs. A few stars were out, and above the curve of the tree was the matching larger curve of the sky. For a minute Eunice was completely content, delighting in the fit of sky and tree, in the smell of the warm evening air; the next minute she was lifting her arms and crying out, "What can I do with it all?" By "all" she meant the energy, the good will, the love, the Baldwin apple tree, the stars, the balmy air. But especially the love. It was odd that she should have at the same time a feeling of great emptiness and of an armful of gifts. Emptiness, she would have thought, would be the result of lack. And here she was feeling empty because of riches she could not share; and tormented, and wasted, so that she wanted, and felt she had the strength, to tear the apple tree from the earth and sweep the starry sky with its branches.

When this image passed, she knew she was in love with Tom Mount. She was no beginner at being in love, but up to this time all of her pleasure had been in keeping the knowledge of her loving secret, in relishing the irony that no one, least of all the man or boy she loved, knew it. She had walked about in a perpetual disguise. Self-knowledge, not shared, gave her a great sense of power. She had been able before this to stand in front of some dark-browed garage owner and think, "I love you, I love you, I love you," and not only be satisfied by that unspoken declaration, but walk away giddy with the power of restraint, of knowing and not divulging.

That was all over. She was plunged downward into the ordinary human state of wanting the fact of her loving known. She walked about under the tree, her mind lively with ways and means. It never occurred to her to wait until Tom Mount returned to Millstone on another selling trip; or that she should not speak out until he himself had made some declaration. Nor did it occur to her that up to this time she had considered Tom Mount Opal's friend. She did have two reservations. She did not want anyone except Tom to know what she felt and she intended to write him in such a way that if he did not love her he could say so without embarrassment. She did not consider the possibility of any halfway ground. She went upstairs at once and began to write.

Dear Mr. Mount [she began]. Since you were here four nights ago, I have been thinking about many of the things you said. I thought about them at first as if I had read them. This evening, as I was standing in the yard under Opal's big apple tree, it came to me that I was chiefly interested in your opinions because they were yours and that I would like to talk to you again.

I could invite you to have supper here. Opal asked you in the first place and I know she enjoyed your visit. This is my invitation, though, and I'm not as unselfish as Opal: so I wonder if you would like to meet me in Fort Collins and have lunch or supper with me, alone.

I will ask your friend Gus Mayhew where to mail this.

Whether I see you again or not, may I send you my sincerest best wishes,

Eunice Fry

The minute she had sealed the envelope, she unsealed it. The words were a bond which tied her to Tom Mount and she did not want them shut away from her.

The next thing she did was to get out all her old pictures, programs with her name on them, letters to her which she had saved, and a scrapbook of poems and pictures she had kept. She did not understand the impulse that made her stare at all the pictures and reread all the words. In so far as she had any existence outside her own body, it lay in these pieces of paper. It was as if, since Tom Mount lived in her mind, she wanted to be able to couple him there with her own image, and could not, without the help of the pictures and words, really imagine who she was. Or perhaps she was saying good-by to the big dark girl in these pictures, the girl who had collected the poems and the pithy sayings, who had made lesson plans and pleased Opal with her play acting over strange hooked rugs and odd-shaped puddings.

Opal, herself, came into her room while Eunice was propped up in her bed, pictures and writings spread about her. She put her letter to Tom Mount under her pillow the minute she heard Opal's knock.

"What're you doing?" Opal asked. Opal acted like a woman who has something urgent to say; but out of fear that once she starts to speak, she will not give anyone else a chance, keeps resolutely silent until the floor is undoubtedly hers.

"I'm looking at these old pictures and letters."

"Why?"

"I'm not sure, Opal."

This was as long as Opal could hold her tongue. "Eunice," she asked, "would you like me to ask Tom Mount over here again?"

"No," said Eunice instantly.

"Why not?"

Eunice did not want to say. "Have him, if you want to, Opal, but not for my sake."

"Didn't you like him?"

"Oh yes."

"Then why?"

"Ask him for yourself, Opal, but not for me."

"All right," Opal said. "I will."

9    SHEL LEWIS was determined to get to the meeting on time if he had to curl his wife's hair himself. He had not traveled these years and miles to miss his say about the running of his own town. Joicey stood by a lighted lamp, frizzing lovelocks in no need of frizzing, the curling iron so hot he smelled burning hair. He was not himself dressed, for he tried to keep step with Joicey in her dressing. It made him less impatient, waiting for her, if he did so in his shirttail. Once he had put on his coat and pants, he wanted to go. He tried in this way to fool himself into thinking that he was the tardy one. But try as he would, waiting gave him a glaze of angry impatience. He had a watch in his pulses, a timetable in his head. He saw, when he got up in the morning, the accomplishments the day might hold; tardiness and postponement wasted all that calculated richness. If he could plan for all, and be assured that all would follow his plans, what distances they would travel!

He finished shaving, rinsed his face, cleaned his razor, and wastefully tossed once-used water out the back flap of the tent. He followed it, without intending to do so, outside. The bleached barley stubble still held a lot of daylight. The dry air touched and warmed his face. Ellen was running up and down with Zoomy as if they were both nine years old. He drummed a sundown tune on the galvanized wash pan in his hand. It sounded as if it might be—a wonder, since he could not carry a tune—"Old Black Joe." He tried it again and it wasn't. His im-

64

patience left him. He lived where he was, began to enjoy the moment he was in, instead of fuming about the moment of departure which should have, and had not, arrived. These were his life's beatitudes, times when his own nature did not separate him from his life; when the needle of his being held steady at the very moment and place of his existence. It was his ambition to live his whole life in this way; though he had schemes and plans for everything else, he knew no way to scheme himself into such moments. But, by God, he thought, I am in one now.

Behind him, he heard the sizzle of Joicey's spit on her hot iron; the birds, which he was sometimes in a fever to name, were chirping in elder clump and cactus thicket, and their namelessness did not trouble him. An owl went by, extinguishing sound, absorbing the trill of cricket and locust in its soft feathers.

Ellen ran up to him, got behind him, spread his shirttails to hide her. "We're playing run sheep run," she whispered. She exposed him in the front, but what did it matter, in the deepening dark and only his sons to see?

"Oh, Papa," Ellen whispered, "I'm so happy."

"Why?" he whispered back.

"I don't know. Something has happened to me."

"Shel," Joicey called. "Are you about ready?"

The further behind Joicey was in her dressing, the more she made a point of urging him to hurry. He could pretty well gauge how late they would be by the frequency with which Joicey ordered him to hasten. He figured they would about make it tonight. Ellen darted away, leaving his behind suddenly cool in the evening air.

He had heard it said that some men are born for the sea, some for the mountains. And that they feel this destiny in their bones from the very beginning and fight their way toward their rightful places. All he had wanted was his own place, his own land, a chance to make his own living and be beholden to no one. He would have headed for Alaska or Mexico if they had been as full of promises of easy money as California; and hunting money, he had landed in these brown tree-less hills, for which, it seemed to him now, he had always been honing; moving west since I was born, toward my rightful home. Westering home, I been doing nothing else, and now I've arrived. He felt strangled, remembering all that greenery back East, like a man held down by weeds under water who suddenly breaks free and rises to the surface. He breathed in the air like life itself, sweeter than any food or drink he had ever tasted. He held his hands out into it; he would like to gather up a fistful of it, do more than breathe it.

"Shel," Joicey called. "Shel, hurry and get dressed. You'll be late."

He went inside. Joicey was in corset cover and petticoat, her arms up, curling iron now wound in a forelock. A faint line of blue rose from the iron.

"You're burning," he said.

"Hurry," Joicey told him.

If Joicey was not pretty, she had spoiled his taste for prettiness. She knew he was watching her, and the strutting he would have loved to see as a sign of her awareness did not happen. Instead, she moved like a turtle a little deeper into her corset and corset cover.

"You'll be late," she warned.

He laughed at her. He did not have a thing to do but step into his pants. She turned her back on him. Joicey could talk to him with her back; he knew its language from A to Z. A to D anyway, asking to disdaining. Now she was disdaining, but at the same time saying, Make something up to me.

"Joicey?"

No answer.

"You still bothered about what we saw here?"

"I don't care about its happening."

"The kids didn't see."

"I know that."

"What then?"

She held the curling iron as if she would like to burn him with it. "Our bed. The bed I've never slept in. She was in it first. I'll never forgive her."

"He was there, too."

"I don't care about him."

"Why not?"

"Because you don't. But that woman. I'll always feel her there."

Shel went over to the bed and began to strip the covers off it. Joicey turned on him. "What are you doing?"

"I'm going to throw this bed away."

"Don't be a crazy fool."

"I can't sleep with two women at once. If that woman's going to always be in this bed, I'll throw it away."

Shel threw bedcovers left and right, the tails of his unbuttoned shirt

66

flying as he worked. Back in Kentucky, Shel had been called slab-sided. He was plank-shaped, wide and flat, no thickness through him and hardly enough tail to hold his pants up. His hair, which had been tow, was going butternut. He still kept a kind of bashfulness in his eyes, a lit-up laughing bashfulness, like a boy who mingles new knowledge with natural delicacy. It was there with almost every woman he talked to, but held in. Joicey saw it; but she saw the held-inness, too; something was in his eyes that said, We know and do not act. That was to the others, not to her. Most eyes get worn down. They do not go dancing that way, tickled with the knowledge of knowing and not acting. The silliness of it, in a way. But the sense, too. If Shel had not had that look and what lay behind that look, why would she want him? She got two gifts with Shel: the go-by he gave other women, and the seeking-out he gave her.

Joicey went to him and began to help him remake the bed.

"I do feel that way about her. But I'll try to swallow it. I'll try to be reasonable."

Joicey, trying to be reasonable, always melted Shel's heart—like a bird trying to plow, a baby wanting to pitch hay. He put his arms around her. She rose up now out of her corset and starched flounces and reached for him with all of her softness. He smelled her burned hair and felt its broken ends with his face. There were some things about her he noted afresh each time he clasped her. They went out of his mind when he left her and waited to surprise him when he returned. Thick-lobed ears, nose with a dent, teeth in-curved.

The children swept near the tent in their game, and Joicey drew back. He let her make the choice. She came back to him.

"How anybody with one kid ever finds a chance to get another beats me," he said. "I never laid down with you in my life but some kid comes busting in. Can't you learn them better. Say, when Papa wants to . . ."

"Shhhh."

"What'd you think I was going to say?"

"I know."

"What were you going to say?"

"You'll be late to the meeting."

"Meeting? What meeting?"

They lay on the half-made bed. "Do you feel her here now?"

"Who?"

"That woman?"

"What woman?"

He laughed with his face against her hair. It was like a music with words at first, then they were finished with words.

10    I T  W A S  Chad who put an end to their playing. "How about a little exploring before dark?" he asked.

Ellen and Zoomy were running back and forth in front of the tent where their folks were dressing for the meeting.

"I haven't done the dishes," Ellen told him.

"Tonight, you don't have to."

Ellen did not know how Chad knew this, but she trusted him. She took his word for many things without explanation.

They headed away from the tent north toward the foothills. Zoomy and Old Silver, his hound, led the way. Ellen walked along thinking, Now we are really Out West. Now I am here. But it was hard to believe. They had talked about it too long. But there was plenty they had never spoken of or even imagined, which remained fresh as a dream: rocks sending off heat after the sun had gone down; a carpet of gray, hairy plants smelling like turpentine; insects buzzing like rattlesnakes and leaving, when that sound let up, a silence so deep they could hear the soundless wind blowing in the soft dry grass at their feet.

The three were not of an age or temperament to enjoy each other's company very often, though Ellen did not like to admit this. She flourished in amity like a leaf in light and tried to interest her brothers in work and pleasures they could share. And any work she did with them was for her a pleasure. "Come," she would urge, "let's scrub the entire house as a surprise for Papa and Mama." It was not actually the surprise for Papa and Mama that excited her, but working together. When that happened, she was sick with happiness. She did not have to suffer from this sickness often. Work was work to Chad and Zoomy. Sharing it made it quicker but not, except for that, more joyful.

Their walk, which at the beginning had not been a walk together, was becoming so. Their first steps taken had been on Chad's suggestion and to get away from the tent; their next, to see what Old Silver was barking at; finally, they had tried to catch a road runner. Then their

68

real walk began, the walk of the Lewis children, exploring their home in the virgin Tract.

Not virgin, Ellen reminded herself. She had asked her father. Her father had thought a while before answering.

"It's raw land," he had said. "Mighty raw. But not virgin."

"What's the difference?" Zoomy had asked.

Her father had thought again. "Raw is used—some; virgin is not used at all."

"I am virgin," Chad had said in his hard still voice.

Her father had turned on Chad, to hit him she thought, but he had stayed his hand. "Haven't you got any sense of decency?"

"I reckon not," Chad had answered indifferently.

Her father and Chad didn't get on together. Chad had started this walk probably more to get away from their father than anything else. Nothing Chad did suited Father—and this seemed worse because there was nothing she could do that did not suit him. She didn't go out of her way to please her father; she didn't court his favor, and she hoped Chad knew this. When she defended Chad, her father would turn on her brother. "Chad, be man enough to fight your own battles. Don't make your baby sister fight them for you." As if Chad would ever ask a favor of anyone. And, "baby sister!" But Chad was really with them now, perhaps telling himself, "Remember this happy hour"; though if he was, you wouldn't know it by his face, white, hard, and sullen as usual. These were the right words, this was the way Chad looked; but she always believed that Chad wore white, hard, and sullen as a mask to hide the loving brother underneath. Chad had straight black hair, not one lock of which would stick to another. The fashion was for pompadours. Chad's hair would not even go backward, let alone stay there, let alone mound upward as a pompadour should. It collapsed, hung downward. He was always shaking his head to get the hair out of his eyes. He scorned to use his hands or a comb. He would conquer it by power of the neck alone. All that his head-shaking ever did was to move his hair a little so that one gray eye could be seen peering through the angle he opened up. He was stoop-shouldered, had a scrawny neck, and a big Adam's apple like a rivet holding head and body together. When he walked, the separate parts of his body moved, each in its own direction. It was a wonder that the whole of him arrived anyplace at the same time. "Moves like a damn hillbilly," her father, watching him, would say. And, on watching more, "Looks like a damn hillbilly, too."

She loved Chad in spite of the fact that he never showed any signs of doting on her. She believed her looks affected Chad the way his affected her father. Chad appeared never to look at her any longer than was necessary. But he was kind to her, and though he could be side-splittingly funny and had a tongue that could skin you alive, he always spared her.

Chad pretended to hate books. He appeared to be ashamed to be caught with one. He read over other people's shoulders and moved on if noticed. But he knew better than she did what had happened and would happen in the novel she was reading. A few words told him the whole story.

He always had money in his pockets. He could always find jobs, and once he made money, he could hang on to it. Night or day seemed all one to him. He was never sleepy, but if there was nothing better to do, he slept. He sat down, stretched out his long thin legs, threw his head back until his sharp Adam's apple threatened to cut his skin, and that done, he was asleep. When something better than sleep turned up, he opened his eyes and, without any yawning or head-shaking, began to do that instead. He was as inscrutable as the wind to her. She followed him about, watching for signs that would give him away.

Zoomy was inscrutable, too, but because he was younger than she was, she never supposed he had any secrets worth ferreting out. What could nine tell seventeen? Nothing but an old story, and one better forgotten. Zoomy was almost a son to her. She had changed too many of his diapers to be impressed with Zoomy as a thinker and mystery man. Once, when he was still a nursing baby, she had held his lips to her pinhead nipples, imagining motherhood. There were times when she feared that Zoomy remembered. One day he had laid a hand upon her bosom and asked, "What makes you so fat here?"

"Womanhood," Chad, passing by, had answered, and Zoomy, his mind diverted, had trailed after Chad. "Chad, what's womanhood?" he had asked; but Chad, if he knew, would not tell him.

Zoomy was as hidden as Chad, but it was talk, not silence, that hid him. Amidst all his words, who could tell which one had the secret in it? Her father could never call Zoomy a hillbilly. He was born a city man, a little, round-eyed, round-stomached storekeeper. He already had a good trade in marbles, pocket knives, whetstones, top strings, old belt buckles, colored pill bottles, teeth of dead animals, and live toads. But he did not care about storekeeping. He could do that with one hand tied behind him. What Zoomy wanted to be was funny, like Chad. It was pitiful. Nothing ever came of it. But Zoomy never gave up. The more he failed, the more he was convinced, like a gambler, that next time he would have to win. Fate could not always be against him. But determination did not help at all with funniness; either you were born with the gift or you were not. She often left the supper table, hoarse from pretending to laugh at Zoomy's sorrowful jokes. Chad never made the effort. He chewed silently, staring at his plate, bleak as a crow. The bleaker Chad looked, the harder Zoomy tried. Then Chad would say two sour words out of the corner of his sour mouth, funniness the last thing he had in mind, and they would all laugh so hard they would have to rest their jaws before they could chew again.

She was happy now watching Zoomy with Old Silver at his heels, the burdens of attempted funniness forgotten. Zoomy knew buzzards were buzzards and harmless but he liked to pretend that they were eagles, a menace at dusk to him and especially to Silver.

"Come, boy," he called protectively to the old hound. "Stay close to me."

Old Silver was Zoomy's heart laid bare. One reason Zoomy was always so cheerful, in spite of his failures at funniness, was that Old Silver's troubles did not leave him much time to worry about himself. If Chad looked like a hillbilly, Old Silver looked a thousand times more like a hillbilly's hound. He was not underfed, kicked around, or mangy, but he looked all three. Bitches gave him the go-by, porcupines shot him full of quills, polecats did worse. Fox terriers no bigger than one of his own down-drooping ears beat him in battle. The animal world despised him; all human beings, except Zoomy, endured him. But Zoomy and Old Silver were both optimistic. Old Silver still expected success in battle as much as Zoomy expected someday to say something funny.

The sun went down with Zoomy dreaming eagles. The sky became immediately larger, like a room emptied of all its furniture. The insects stopped their humming as if the disappearance of the sun was something they were seeing for the first time. In the valley beneath them, Ellen watched a distant column of dust—dust following *his* car, she believed; and she imagined Tom Mount driving with all that shirt-sleeved, tender, commanding grace toward someone who longed for his coming.

Zoomy, as the twilight thickened, came closer to her and Chad. Their walk together was almost finished. When they started home, they would once again be separate. The Lewis children, who had been together discovering their home, and who might never be so close again. Zoomy held a small white bone and a faded green shotgun shell in his hand. He had not entirely ceased, even while exploring, to be a trader. Chad was reading the valley the way he read a book, only half looking at it, his white face turned partly away. Ellen wanted to pull her brothers closer to her, to say, "Let us clasp hands, make a vow, promise to be blood brothers all our lives." They who were born blood brothers! But she wanted them to decide on it then and there before the separating journey began, not leave it up to something in the past and chancey.

While she postponed speaking what was in her mind, Chad said, "Look, a coyote." There, where he pointed, on the top of a hill, a little foxy dog watched them. Old Silver gave him stare for stare. Then the coyote lifted his pretty prick-eared head and surprised Ellen with a sound the wind might have made. The skin at the back of her neck tightened and her cheekbones grew cold. But it was to Old Silver the coyote really spoke. The sparse hair along Old Silver's spine bristled and his warning growl changed to baying. While they watched, unbelieving, he launched himself up the hill. It was as unexpected as having the set sun rise again.

Except to Zoomy. He had been waiting confidently all of his life for the hero in Old Silver to show itself. "Eat him up, Silver," he yelled, as Silver, still baying, followed the coyote over the rim of the hill and out of sight.

"What did I tell you?" he shouted to Chad and Ellen.

Ellen rejoiced with Zoomy. At last Zoomy had a joke on everybody, Old Silver chasing a wild animal.

"Poor coyote," Zoomy said.

"Do not shed any tears for the coyote," Chad advised.

"Why?" asked Zoomy. "Silver will kill him."

"Do not count your coyotes before they are killed," Chad told him.

There were no longer any sounds—of eating or being eaten. The insects began to chirr again; the wind they could not hear moved the grass at their feet. And there was nothing to be seen when they climbed to the top of the rim, and though Zoomy wanted to wait, he could not admit it. Old Silver did not need anyone's protection: that was his story and he had to stick to it. They started homeward, Zoomy far behind Chad and Ellen and looking over his shoulder as often as he could without betraying his doubts of Silver.

Each was alone now, as Ellen had known they would be; the walk had been an adventure they had gone toward together, but going home was different. You did that by yourself. They could not possibly have stayed up in the hills; she loved her home, but she was sorry when she saw the tent, rosy with lamplight, below them. They went quietly and somberly, sliding on the slippery dried grass of the final slope. They were halfway down that slope when from behind them they heard a well-known sound, the cry of Old Silver panicky with conviction of mortal danger. Zoomy turned, then stood stricken. Old Silver, with the coyote behind him, came over the top of the hill, his tail between his legs and his unashamed voice crying, "Save me, Save me." The coyote was taking it easy, loping along, tongue out, a white-toothed grin splitting his sharp little muzzle. His grin and his gait said plainly that chasing Old Silver was scarcely worth the trouble. One nip at the old hound's flanks and the dog would drop dead with fear. So he chased him carefully, like a cat with a delicate mouse, sparing him in order to prolong the play.

Chad, at the sight, bent backward, laughing in his silent exhausted way.

"Save me, save me," he cried in a thin voice which mocked Old Silver's, exactly.

Zoomy turned and gave Chad a blow in the crotch; a spot her mother had warned Ellen, in her early fights with Chad, to avoid because men were especially sensitive there. This knowledge had made it doubly hard for Ellen to refrain from landing just such blows, and Zoomy had certainly gotten quick results with his. Chad bent over groaning.

Zoomy, uninterested in Chad, sped after the dog and the coyote, alternately trying to shoo the coyote away and encourage Old Silver. Ellen did not know who was in the worst fix, Zoomy or Silver or Chad. Chad, she believed. Chad was still bent over, sweat on his face, and breathing hard, like someone finishing a long bout of sobbing.

"Are you all right?" she asked.

Chad did not answer.

"Will the coyote kill Silver?"

"I hope so," Chad said.

Then she knew that Chad would recover, and she ran without him after Zoomy, who was running after the coyote and the dog. Halfway home she saw the coyote, his job finished, loping back into the hills, untired and still grinning. Long before she reached their tent, she heard Old Silver's voice. Perhaps the coyote had caught up with him after all, had given him a mortal bite; such sounds surely could only be made by an animal who was dying. When she reached the tent, there under the wagon was Old Silver and, stretched out beside him on the ground Zoomy, with one arm across his dog. Both were howling; though until you were close, Zoomy's part in the racket could not be heard. Old Silver cried high and Zoomy low, but Zoomy's noise was just as unending as the hound's. Beside the wagon, leaning over to have a good look at what was underneath, was a young man. He did not appear to be worried, only amazed. He straightened up when Ellen arrived.

"What's going on here?" he asked.

Ellen was too out of breath to answer—if she had wanted to. And she did not want to. In the first place, the man knew more about it than she did since he had been there longer. Why was he asking her questions? In the second place, she did not care for anyone who looked at Zoomy as if he were simple-minded.

Zoomy gave over howling long enough to bawl, "Is he dead? Is he dead?"

"Dead? Dead?" the young man repeated as if Zoomy were speaking a foreign language.

Ellen got enough breath back to answer him. "Dying," she explained coldly. "His dog is dying." No one could make fun of Zoomy while she was around.

"Dying," the young man repeated again. "Don't be silly. Nothing that noisy can be dying."

It was hard to hear over the combined howling. "What do you know about dying?" she screamed.

The young man stopped looking under the wagon, faced her squarely and seriously, and said something she could not understand.

"I can't hear you," she told him.

He outyelled Zoomy and Old Silver. "It's true. I don't know a thing about dying."

Appeased, she told him what had happened. "He was attacked by a coyote, defending us."

"The boy or the dog?" the stranger bellowed.

Before she could answer this, Chad, still kinked in a knot from Zoomy's blow, came loping in sidewise.

When he saw the stranger, he straightened up momentarily.

"What's going on here?" he asked, using the stranger's own words, but his suspicions were directed toward *him*, not Zoomy and Silver.

Zoomy still knew the answer to that. "Old Silver's dying."

But Chad had the answer to everything. He reached under the wagon, got Zoomy by the shirt collar, hauled him out and set him on his feet. Then he gave him a half-dozen teeth-rattling shakes, partly for his own good and partly to repay him for that earlier blow. "Stop being crazy," he told Zoomy. That, with the shaking, took care of Zoomy.

"Quiet," he yelled at Old Silver, and Old Silver, as if he had been waiting for permission, shut his mouth and stretched out like a man after a hard day's work.

Then Chad turned to the stranger. "Anything I can do for you?"

The young man looked as if he was not sure he wanted any help from Chad. "I was looking for your father. My name's Jessup. My car broke down and I was hoping to catch a ride in to town with your folks. I suppose they're going to the meeting?"

"They're going," Chad said.

"Where is your father?"

"Napping, maybe."

"In all this racket?"

"Gone for a walk," Chad suggested.

The stranger looked skeptical. "Do you mind if I wait?"

"You won't have to wait, Ben." Shel Lewis, looking as if he might actually have been napping, hair rumpled, and still pushing his shirt-tails into his pants, came to the opening of the tent.

"Howdy, Shel," Ben said.

"Did I hear a commotion?" Shel asked.

"I guess you could call it that," Ben said.

"Are you getting deaf?" Chad asked his father.

Ordinarily, Shel would have snapped Chad up for this kind of impertinence, but tonight he only smiled and said, "It might be, son."

Agreeing or disagreeing, Chad and Shel did not get along. After Chad's sauciness, Shel's words were kind, but Chad went doubling off with an injured look.

"Shel," Ben began, but Shel stopped him. "You don't have to tell me. It broke down again."

"Fell completely apart. Lights failed, to boot. Got room for me to ride in to town with you?"

"Sure. We're going as soon as Joicey dresses. Ben, this is my daughter, Ellen. The two under the wagon"—for Zoomy was back with old Silver, both resting together—"are my youngest and his dog."

Shel went back into the tent, and Ellen, alone with Ben Jessup, tried to think of something to say. She knew at once, and for the first time in her life, that the young man who was looking at her liked her. She would have thought that this kind of mind reading would take practice, that it wouldn't come to you all at once. But evidently not. She might have been reading men's minds all of her life, she felt so sure. She remembered an old phrase, perhaps from the Bible, "she found favor in his eyes." She knew—and it did not make her vain, but responsible—that this was what she was finding in Ben Jessup's eyes. He was pleased with her. She had come in steaming and panting from her run, had been ready to kill him if he picked on Zoomy, and Ben Jessup liked these things in her. If someone had asked her how she knew, she could not have said. There was nothing flirtatious about Ben; he scarcely smiled, but he bent upon her a fathoming regard, a look that took her in and welcomed her. She need not extend herself to please him, try to entertain him, or pretend to any high-flown feelings. Once, she had fainted and come to with just such a sense of ease as she had now, as if, without knowing it, she had never before been quite at home in the world.

"You've just arrived on the Tract, haven't you?" he asked.

"This afternoon."

"You haven't had a chance to meet anyone yet, I suppose."

"Oh, yes," she said, "I have. I met Mr. Thomas Mount. Do you know him?"

"No," Ben told her. "He must be a newcomer."

"You can't miss him," Ellen said. "He's a big black-haired man and drives a red car. I'll point him out to you tonight. He's going to the meeting."

She could talk to Ben as if he was her oldest friend. "Now I must get ready to go. Excuse me, please."

She ran into the tent with the knowledge that the way she ran was observed and approved. She basked in the knowledge of this approval. It added to her value. It was an extra gift to offer Mr. Thomas Mount.

II    THE LAMPS, burning in a room still lighted by the sun, were an embarrassment. They were unnatural and unneeded. But Press did not know how, without reminding everyone that she had lighted them in the first place, to blow them out. Getting rid of Opal had made her feel triumphant; but she had expended so much energy and emotion on that job that the situation now before her was paltry. She was tensed for something more exciting than getting supper. She had protected Papa, and been true to Mama; she had done what she willed. She had triumphed and was now unhappy. Her father, Hannah, and Mr. Mount sat unspeaking, like people recovering from a robbery. She, no doubt, was the thief. She had robbed them of a party. Mr. Mount looked calmly at her, not seeing her, his face dreamy, she supposed, with remembrance of his two old friends. Hannah, hunched like a toad on a footstool, was mesmerizing herself with lamplight. Her father, head flung back, had his evening look. By another act of will, she determined to make up their loss to them, to fill in the vacancy made by the departure of the ladies; she herself would be a party, she alone provide the noise and movement she had lost them.

She began to bustle with the work of clearing away the teacups and the leftover Nabiscos, to clink cups and imitate the movements of someone anticipating merriment. She walked around Mr. Mount's outstretched legs. Though his face was still sleepy and masked, his eyes caught hers, then followed her as she worked. She was unperturbed. He was a man who would be company for her father.

She paused before him with her stacked tray and said, "Mr. Mount, I hope you'll like what I've fixed for supper."

Mr. Mount smiled. "I'll like it."

"But you don't even know what it is."

"It isn't canned salmon, is it?"

"No."

"Then I'll like it."

Hannah looked up from her footstool, her eyes out of focus from lamp-gazing.

"Don't you like salmon?"

"Too much, maybe. I've been living on it."

"Why?" asked Hannah.

"Darned if I know." Then Mr. Mount pulled in his legs, sat up in his chair, shed his sleepiness, and turned his wide-awake gaze on Hannah. "Well, I suppose there are reasons. If you're interested in them."

"Yes, sir," said Hannah, who stayed with a subject once she had started on it and was delighted to find someone equally serious-minded. "I'm interested."

"I was a meat salesman for a while. That might explain why I'd like fish for a change. Do you suppose?"

Hannah nodded.

"All right, that explains the fish part. But why salmon?"

Hannah considered this, rejecting easy answers.

"Pink is your favorite color?"

Tom Mount laughed. "As a matter of fact, it is. I'd never thought about that. Maybe that's the real answer. Are we having something pink for supper?" He turned to Press, but she, released by the question from her trance of listening, shook her head and carried the tray to the kitchen.

But pink did not satisfy Hannah. She got up and went to stand beside Mount.

"What else," she asked, "besides pink?"

Without the least appearance of reluctance, Mount turned his attention to her. "Fish is a brain food."

"Is that true?" Hannah asked. This was the kind of talk she liked; at the end of it you had learned something.

"Darned if I know," Mr. Mount said again. "I eat an awful lot of salmon but I don't seem to be getting much brainier."

Lute Cope smiled a little. He, who experienced at each twilight the worst hour of his day, was beginning to emerge from its bitterness. At the end of each afternoon, his throat closed, his chest clenched as if around a stone instead of a heart. He was too sick at heart to live, yet he did not die. He was amazed when the people with him at such times noticed no change in him. For the last hour, he had been gripped by this misery. Home, health, daughters, a friend, the exquisite light of evening: he had said the words; they might have been in a foreign language. He was false to them all in that hour; he pretended interest; he faked love; the knowledge of his falseness increased his sorrow.

When it began to be dark, he was always given a reprieve from his misery. Some judge, as the last of daylight faded, said, "That's all. No more punishment for today." He was saved for tomorrow. He was never pushed beyond what he could endure. He never dreamed of suicide. He went to bed calm, and awakened each morning hopeful. When the pain let up, he was delivered from any clear memory of it. In the midst of it, a part of its terror was that it seemed to him interminable. The edges of his two worlds did not fit; he was either wholly despairing or wholly forgetful of despairing. And there was no cause for it. Indy was gone; but he had suffered in the same way when she was present.

Thirty minutes made the difference between agony and ease. Nothing had changed: same home, daughters, health, friends. The light had yellowed and softened; that was all the difference. In the moment of transition, he longed to make some extreme sound or movement. Sometimes he did so. It convinced people that in spite of his unusual dignity, he was human. Tonight he did no more than suddenly stand and stretch. Then he resettled himself in his chair. Tom Mount, noticing the smile, began to direct some of his conversation away from Hannah and to her father.

At the supper table, Lute spoke to Mount of the work he wanted done on the house: a screened-in dining porch off the dining room; a bay window in his bedroom; a drainboard on each side of the sink; window boxes under all of the windows at the front of the house.

Press, as she listened to these jobs being outlined, thought, Mama is coming home! She wanted to ask her father if this was true, but knew better than to do so. She tried to read his face, but its good humor revealed nothing.

She made a calculating statement. "Mama always loved bay windows and window boxes." She looked at her father, daring him to say, "Your mother's preferences for bay windows and window boxes has nothing to do with this."

Instead, he agreed with her. "Her home never means as much to my wife as some little shed or balcony she rigs up herself."

"Means as much," Press thought, "means as much," not "meant as much." She rushed on. "Mama loves to eat outdoors." She said this because they were themselves sitting on a mild, golden evening inside a steamy room that smelled of creamed cabbage, boiled potatoes, and fried sausage. "Don't judge her by us," she implored Mount, "or, if you do, think of somebody who is our opposite."

"I'm not much of a hand to judge," Mount said, "but I'd hate to think she was your opposite, Press."

79

"If you're talking about looks," Lute Cope said, "you don't have to. Press is the picture of her mother at her age."

"Did you know Mama when she was Press's age?" asked Hannah.

"We were engaged to be married at Press's age."

"I'm not like Mama in the least," Press insisted. "Mama is beautiful."

Mount didn't argue the point with her. "At least you have her name," he said.

"I have her last name, Pressley. Mama has a beautiful first name. Indiana Rose." Press spoke the words like a great poem's greatest line.

"Do you call her all of that?"

Tom Mount did not look at her father, but his question, Press knew, was addressed to him. She thought her father might not answer, but after a pause he said, "Her friends call her Indy."

"And so does Papa," said Press.

Something came over Press when she spoke to others of her mother. She did not tell untruths, but what she told was not the truth. She had no notion why this was so. But she knew that if Hannah were to describe their mother, the woman Hannah spoke of would not be enough like the woman Press described to be a second cousin. Hannah never corrected or contradicted her when she talked about their mother; but Press knew that Hannah listened like a person hearing the report of a foreign country, strange and enthralling—and nothing to contradict, because so completely unknown.

Her father, when she spoke of her mother, never corrected or interfered either. But in his mind, Press knew, he speculated—and perhaps contradicted. He asked himself questions: Is this Indy? Is this her daughter speaking of her in this way? And why does she do so?

Even so, he often appeared, as tonight, to listen intently as she talked. There was some bond between them as she spoke. In a way, she was competing with him, saying "I love Mama more than you do." In a way, she was endearing herself to him, saying "Look, you have company. I know how you feel about Mama."

"I expect you miss your wife," said Mount, who knew none of the circumstances of Mrs. Cope's absence from home.

"Miss her? It's like being dead around here when she's gone," Press said.

Press looked at her father. He was waiting for her to say more, to speak for him.

This girl, Mount decided, is a real beauty, this seventeen-year-old. But no word he could say to her would equal in power what her mirror told her every day. He had no wish for any such competition. This girl was complete. He admired her, but was unmoved.

"Do you know what?" Press asked in her breathless rushing way. "Sometimes I used to think that it would be nice if Mama would go on a little visit so I could be the housekeeper and take care of Hannah and Papa by myself. But by the second day I always longed for her to be back."

"Housekeeping isn't as easy as it looks from the outside," Mount agreed.

"Housekeeping!" Press was scornful. "It wasn't that. I can keep house with one hand. It was the quietness. Hannah and Papa and I are too calm. We sit here dead as doorknobs. Without Mama, we haven't one word to say to each other."

"You are doing all right without Mama tonight," Mount said.

"Hannah," Press asked, "do you remember the first time we went to the beach?"

"I thought people in California went to the beach every Sunday," Mount said.

"Not if they live a hundred miles from the ocean, they don't," said Lute Cope. "The way we did."

"We went to the ocean for the first time," Press said, "in a wagon. It took us three days. Mama dressed to suit the occasion. Mama said this was a gypsy adventure, so she dressed that way. Mama has pierced ears and she wore her biggest bangles for this trip. And a red blouse. And pants."

"Pants! I never saw a lady gypsy in pants."

"That's what we all said, and Mama said, 'I'm not imitating gypsies. I'm being one.' And she was."

"Indy gave the countryside a real treat," Lute said dryly.

"We camped out," Press went on. "The night before we got to the ocean, we stopped early just outside the town in a eucalyptus grove, and people came to watch us put up our tents and our beds. It was like a covered wagon stopping with Indians crowding around. Wasn't it, Hannah?"

"You didn't think so then," Hannah said.

"Well, this isn't about me. It's about Mama. You should've seen her. Cooking supper while those people watched and talked about her pants and her earrings. When she finished cooking and dished up, she said, 'Folks, this is just to give you a taste of what is to come tonight. The real show begins at eight p.m. Then we have Luthero Copo, the great lion tamer; Miss Hannah, who can walk on her hands as well as on her feet; and last, but not least, Miss Pressley, the tattooed girl.' "

"Well, did you take a bow then, Miss Pressley?"

"Take a bow?" Hannah exclaimed. "What she did was take a spanking."

"Spanking? How old were you?"

"She was thirteen," Hannah said.

"Hannah, shut up. I'm talking about Mama."

"So your gypsy Mama spanked you?"

"She did not. Mama never spanked me in her life. She never laid a hand on me. It was Papa." There was pride rather than accusation in her voice. "I'm not going to tell you what I did, but it was wrong and I deserved what I got. All Mama did"—Press turned to Hannah—"was to say, 'Lute, this is your daughter.' And Papa did the rest. And what happened then was my own fault, too. I jumped over the wagon tongue, fell down, and cut a gash on my forehead."

Mount looked at Luther Cope. He thought, This is about enough confession, I should think; but Lute's face was calm.

"Press," her father said, "since you've told this much, you'd better tell the rest of the story."

Press smiled at her father. "That was the last time I ever was spanked." She paused, like a girl speaking of her last doll or her last day at school, and refused to let Hannah break in. "No, Hannah, I'm talking about Mama, not me." She turned to Mount. "What I wanted to tell you was about Mama and the ocean, how daring she was and how she scared me. Do you remember the first time you ever saw the ocean, Mr. Mount?"

"I sure do. It was about six weeks ago."

Suddenly Press knew that she didn't want to tell Mr. Mount about her mother and the ocean. The ocean was too near him and too ordinary. Or if that wasn't the reason, there was some secret in what had happened, which, if she put the happening into words, might become clear to her. She had thought about what had happened again and again, because in the center of it was something hidden, some mystery. It was like a package you were always touching or shaking but wouldn't for anything open.

"I'll tell you about the ocean some other time, Mr. Mount," she said, and went to the kitchen to get the dessert.

After supper, while Press and Hannah washed the dishes, the two men walked out into the twilight. They leaned silently against Mount's car for a while, then began to talk about automobiles. Mount's car, a Duro, was the first he had owned, and Lute, now on his fourth, a Maxwell, advised Mount to get shut of it. "Unless you just naturally like to tinker on a car." Then the conversation ceased. Mount knew why. Cope was not really interested in anything or anyone but his wife. The whole house was infected with this Indiana Rose.

Cope, he knew, had been the owner and editor of a paper in a good-sized town in Northern California. Then, because of some misunderstanding with his wife, or over his wife, Mount was not sure which, he had sold out, sacrificed friends and business, to start over again here in these empty hills, though so far he had done nothing about starting over. He was not interested in ranching, and the Tract could not support a paper yet. All he thought of, as far as Mount could make out, was this absent Indiana Rose. His building plans were nothing more than a trick by which he kept himself, in his imagination, in touch with his wife. As long as he was doing something for her, he held onto her, proved to himself that he had not given up hope.

Mount could not fathom men who made women so much the center of their lives. And he had tried to; he had made a real effort to jump into their shoes, especially into the shoes of men who felt an unswerving attachment to one woman. Here was Cope, who had had eighteen or nineteen years of this runaway Rose, and yet had no better plan in his head than to get her back and experience more of the same. Though he didn't understand such men, he envied them in a way. It was, except when you got mixed up with a woman like this Indy, an easy life. As simple sexually as settling on a diet of bread and milk in the beginning and wiping out with that one decision, nine-tenths of the eating problem, and a lot of the earning problem as well. He looked closely at Lute Cope in the half-light. There was nothing unnatural in the man's appearance. A little of the widower's plumpness was distributed over his big frame and some of the politician's blandness blurred his handsome face.

The men faced the kitchen window, where a hanging lamp lit up the two girls: Press washing, and Hannah drying, the supper dishes. Press, moving much faster than Hannah, finished first and left the room. As she did so, Cope turned to Mount. "There's a thing I haven't told the girls yet," he said. "Their mother's coming home."

Mount said, "That's good news, I'm sure."

"Yes, it is. I had a letter from Indy. I'm satisfied she's coming, but I'm old enough not to bank on anything any more, and I wouldn't want to get the girls' hopes up for nothing."

"When do you expect her?" Mount asked.

"Any time. Indy doesn't like to be bound down by dates. It's her coming makes me want to rush the building here."

"I'll do what I can. But I've got the church job on my hands, too, now."

"Stay here while you're working on the house. It'll save time. When Indy gets back . . ."

He broke off, fearing, Mount thought, that if he got started again on Indy, he might talk all night. "I'll hustle the girls out. It's time we're started."

Press, who must have been watching, came out as soon as her father went inside. "Mama's coming back, isn't she?" she asked Mount.

"What makes you think so?"

"Don't try to fool me. I've known for a week."

"Are you glad?"

"Glad? Of course I'm glad. I worship my mother. And it's time she's coming home. All these widows making eyes at Papa."

"Mrs. Tetford?" Mount asked, delighted.

"Didn't you notice her?"

"I noticed you. So that's what you were up to?"

"Up to?"

"Freezing her out."

"Well, I succeeded."

"You sure did, sister."

It's an amazing thing, Mount thought. Here I am talking to this beautiful girl as if she were an old woman. He was consciously reserved with pretty young women as a matter of self-protection; they were takers, every one of them; but he did expect to feel something in their presence. With Press Cope—nothing—except admiration for her looks and the utmost ease in talking. Where was her lack? Or was it in him? Was she talking to him the way she would to any old man?

"You know that trip to the ocean I was telling you about before supper?" she asked. "It was then I knew I'd die if anything happened to Mama."

Mount said, "Do you always talk to strangers like this?"

"Like this? Like what?"

"Tell them your secrets."

"I'm not telling you any secrets, Mr. Mount. Everybody knows how I feel about Mama."

"I've been put in my place," he said, smiling.

84

"Put in your place? I didn't know you were out of it. It doesn't matter what I tell you, secret or no secret."

"Why doesn't it?"

"Because what I say doesn't matter to you. It goes in one ear and out the other. I could tell you that I was half Negro—or a murderess. You wouldn't care a whit."

"Why wouldn't I care? At least I care to know that."

"Of course. That has something to do with you."

"Don't you care more about yourself than other people?" Mount knew he was defending himself and didn't like the feeling. It was a thing he never did. If a woman attacked him, he agreed with her. If she accused him, he admitted the accusation.

"No, not when Mama's concerned."

"All right. What happened to you and Mama on that trip to the beach?" Mount did not care what happened on that trip and he knew she knew it. She did not excuse him, because of this, from listening.

"Nothing very much, really. I'd never seen the ocean, and I heard it roaring the whole night before we got there. We camped out, slept on the ground, only I couldn't sleep. I thought I could feel the ocean shaking the ground. That scared me. Then when I saw it, I was still more scared. It moved so much. It wasn't going anyplace, like a river or the wind. It was there, forever, but it tossed itself around—like a person. I can understand water running downhill, that's gravity. It has to. But this water, perfectly level—and moving, like a person in a bed!"

Mount said, "That's gravity, too, you know. The tide coming in."

"Oh, you mean the moon? I know that. But with no moon in sight it's not very easy to remember. Or even believe. Oh, I do believe it," she assured him. "The earth is round, the earth goes round the sun, and all that. But you don't think of that, the first time you see the ocean tossing and heaving. The waves were reaching for us. That's the way it seemed. I couldn't bear to go near them. But Mama couldn't wait. She put on her bathing suit, and I watched her walk down toward the water. I knew she was walking down there to her death. She'd be drowned. I knew that, but I didn't warn her. I just watched her, scared and angry because of what she was doing, taking such chances, frightening me. And being such a big hero in Papa's eyes, too. I knew exactly what would happen. One of those waves, like a big claw, would pick her up, carry her out to sea, and she would never again be seen. I saw us going home without her, and me having to run the house for Papa. But I hardened my heart. You don't care about me and I don't

85

care about you, I thought. Go on, drown yourself. But the minute the water touched her ankles, I began to scream. And it was my screaming saved her. Exactly what I had imagined, happened. One big wave knocked her down and another dragged her under. Except for my screaming, Papa, who was undressing behind the wagon, wouldn't have known a thing about what was happening. He heard me and ran to her. He pulled her out just in time. Ever since then, I've known that Mama was the center of my life, and I have been trying to make it up to her for almost killing her."

Mount felt tired. The stars had come out and a big butter-colored moon had suddenly floated free of the mountain. The dry, clear air was cooling fast. Winter was in that moon, and the end of growth. The metal of the car, against which he had been leaning, had gone from warm to chilly. He pulled himself away from it.

"That must be quite a burden to bear," he said.

"Don't worry about me," Press told him. "Not for a minute."

"I'm not worrying."

"One thing is true. I never have told this to anyone else."

"I still don't count—is that it?"

She smiled at him in the moonlight. The smile agreed with him, and he was glad of it. He had a vision of himself, as Press had had of her mother, carried beyond his depth in an undertow of vitality greater than his, battered against a flintier hardness than any he could muster.

"What if I told your mother?" he asked.

"What makes you think I haven't?"

"I don't know what makes me think so."

"Tell her if you want to. I'm not the center of her life," Press said indifferently.

Mount's mind wandered off to Eunice and Opal. It made him happy to think of them. "You better get a wrap of some kind," he told Press, smiling. "It'll be chilly coming home."

12    AFTER her meeting at the Copes' with Tom Mount, Eunice got out of the wagon and went to the house without so much as offering to help Opal with the unhitching. She entered the kitchen with a dreamer's memories of it. The peach pie, baked and put on the table

86

to cool before they went for water, might have been something left over from her childhood. It was that far away in time. She stopped in the kitchen, wanting the objects she looked at to hold her attention as long as possible. She gazed at the scrubbed Congoleum, the newly blackened stove, the full wood box, the pitcher of blue dust flowers: they had the power of all good things out of a vanished past to arouse feeling. Here she had lived before Mount's reappearance.

Opal came in and stood in the doorway as if she wanted to size up the situation before getting any closer to it. Behind Opal, Eunice could see the sallow western sky. Opal closed the door quietly, but still did not speak. A fly, caught on the tanglefoot they kept spread in their screenless rooms, began a sudden buzzing.

"Do you want to wash up before supper?" Opal asked.

Eunice did not answer. A new understanding was coming to her. He was here.

"Opal," she said, "he has come all the way here from Colorado to see me, to be near me."

Opal did not reply.

"I can't believe it. I can't believe he came. I can't believe I saw him. And I can't believe that I feel the way I do. I thought I had put him out of my mind."

"I knew you hadn't."

"If he was still in my mind after we got here, it wasn't in the way he used to be. I didn't fool myself about him any more."

"No?"

"I could call him by his right names."

"Like what?" Opal asked.

If Opal thought that the sight of him, once more, had blinded her to that, she would disprove it.

"Like liar," she said, "like woman-chaser."

"That's a start," Opal said.

"But I don't hate him."

"Neither do I," said Opal.

"*You* hate him?" Eunice flared up. "What grounds do you have for hating him?"

Opal did not answer for a minute. "I can hate anybody I want to, Eunice, without asking your permission."

"Forgive me, Opal."

"I don't have a thing to forgive you for, Eunice."

But Eunice's thoughts were not on Opal.

"What you know in your mind hasn't got a thing to do with the real facts, has it?" she asked.

"I don't know what you mean, Eunice."

"I mean, thinking about it, I would've sworn everything between me and Tom Mount was over. But it was only over in my mind. I would have sworn before God, my hand on a Bible, that the last thing I wanted in this world was to see Tom Mount again, but I have only to see him to know that nothing is over, that I want to see him more than anything in this world. That nothing about him and me can ever change. Those are the facts."

"Something has changed. You didn't used to call him names like those you just gave him."

"I'm talking about feelings. They haven't changed. And those names —they belonged to him all the time. I didn't know it, that's all. I loved him before, when he was those things. I still do. They make no difference."

"Let's go back to Millstone," Opal said.

"And leave him here?"

"Try to. Though I wouldn't want to bank on our being able to do it."

Eunice laughed. Expectancy filled her. She was not the woman she had been yesterday. And the world had changed with her, had become, in the interval of her leaning against a kitchen wall, charged with promises.

"I will never leave him again," she told Opal.

"In that case, we'd better hustle up supper and get to the meeting. You'll want to get the word to him."

Opal spoke dryly, not caring whether she hurt or not; and not flattering herself that with Tom Mount in town, Eunice was capable of taking a hurt from any other hand but his.

Tom had answered Eunice's first letter promptly and matter-of-factly. It had made her feel, in so far as a letter could, that there was nothing unusual in a young schoolteacher's traveling sixty miles by train in order to meet a man for supper. She had no way of judging the expertness which had gone into his writing, but she responded to it. His "home," he wrote, was a room at the Western Hotel. The hotel served very good food. He hoped she'd be his guest at dinner.

She had two weeks to wait before the date he had set, a date she would never forget, January 13, 1915. The knowledge that what she was planning was done quite naturally by other young women had no power to calm her. She was twenty-two years old; she had lived, since she could remember, in a dream of love. Now the pent-up, unspoken emotions of that long dreaming were all turned toward Tom Mount. She did not even have Opal, who was at La Grande, nursing a sick sister-in-law, to talk with. She read and reread Tom's letter. If she had read anything else a tenth that many times, she would have known it by heart. Something, perhaps simply the desire that the letter remain fresh to her, prevented this. She always carried it with her; she would be seized in the middle of teaching a class with a desire to read it once more and would retire with it to the cloakroom. Her feeling about the letter was too strong and too personal for her to risk reading it in public.

Her reply to his letter had been three words: "I am coming."

There had been no further communication between them. This was what she wanted. They were going to meet. Silence recognized that no word was equal to dealing with the event. She felt that with him words might be given up: looks and touch would be sufficient.

Her real life became unreal. She taught school, fed Opal's buff Orpingtons, and watered the Boston ferns as an angel might, by emanations of will. She was not physically present; her whole being was expressing itself to a man she had to imagine. She was too tremulous to eat or sleep, but she had no desire to eat or sleep. Eating and sleeping interrupted her dream.

The dream of her meeting with Tom Mount, and she knew it, was made up of novels read, words overheard, gestures seen. And whatever firsthand stories her ignorant body told her. This dream, so richly furnished with particulars, was interrupted by long periods of enchantment when she was only her pulse, her breath, her curved mouth, her extended hands.

The painful, the ridiculous, the disturbing thing was that she could not remember Tom Mount's face. Here she was, all of her waking hours spent with a man whose face did not exist for her. Oh, certainly, if someone had asked her, she would have been able to say large, dark. But saying those words did not make a face, any more than saying "Nile" and "pyramids" made Egypt. She struggled toward his face as a drowning man struggles toward land. I must see it, she told herself. But she could not. And the failure was worse because there would rise, unbidden before her, every freckle and missing tooth and cowlick of her classroom. And Tom Mount, whom she loved, she could not see.

Was it a sign of some disaster ahead? She was finally able to decide that it was a sign only of a limitation of her own. She had felt so much when she was with Tom Mount that her eyes had been unable to do the eyes' usual work of putting features together to get faces. She became proud of her failure to see Tom's face, since it now indicated the strength of her feeling for him. She called this feeling "love." What other name was there for it? She had never heard of any.

Opal, on the evening of Tom's first visit, had come back into the house after seeing him off and had said, "Do you know who he looks like, Eunice?"

"Mr. Mount?" Eunice had answered abstractedly.

"Oh, for heaven's sake, Eunice! Who do you think I'm talking about? Woodrow Wilson?"

Eunice, riding high on incipient love, had answered with unusual jocularity. "I wouldn't like to think so."

"That's more like it," Opal had said. She had no patience with cat-and-mouse games. She dearly loved Eunice, but she never soft-soaped her, told her her dowdy dress was becoming or her scorched stew tasty. "All right," Opal went on, "now that you know who we're talking about, who he looks like is Antonio Moreno."

At that time, Eunice had made no reply. But later, when she was struggling to recall Tom Mount's face, she remembered what Opal had said and went to see Moreno in "The Island of Regeneration." If there had been an iota of likeness between the actor and Tom Mount, she would have been lifted out of her seat with a cry of recognition. She knew that. So Antonio Moreno's dark and dreaming face was nothing like Tom Mount's.

When she told Opal this, Opal, with her usual good humor, said, "Maybe you're right, Eunice." Eunice had not been fool enough to try to track down Tom Mount's face through every dark-haired movie star who crossed Opal's mind. The truth of it, as she finally understood, was that there was some of Tom Mount in every face a woman dreamed about.

Opal came home from La Grande four days before Eunice was to leave for Fort Collins. Eunice was not too lost in her dreams to notice that Opal, who would usually have joked and pampered her out of her abstractions, was pretty quiet herself. Quiet, but apparently happy.

Eunice was determined to meet Tom Mount, though she knew that by doing so she was endangering her calm world of schoolteaching and book reading. Mrs. Browning's poetry, long solitary walks in the snow, afternoon chats with Opal—these were good things, and she knew it. But already they had begun to appear unsubstantial and unnourishing.

She was to leave Friday after school let out. The night before, a wind had come up with the raw smell of snow in it. She had listened to it, snug under Opal's down comforter, and for a minute she had thought of missing the Fort Collins train. The wind, with its sound of what was alien and wild and comfortless, said, "Stay where you are." But she had elected the journey and whatever lay at the end of the journey and did not think she could turn back with honor. Honor? she asked herself. What has honor to do with it? This much: she could not with honor turn back because of fear.

When she awakened, the wind had died down, and a gray sky, heavy and cold, had moved close to the earth. She dressed and went to breakfast, where Opal greeted her with "Well, this is the big day."

"Big day?" Eunice asked, horrified, forgetting that a trip to Denver also constituted a big day.

"Your Denver trip. Don't tell me it's slipped your mind?"

Eunice relaxed, though at the same time she experienced a sickening ache in her chest. This was the first time she had ever lied and had to live out that lie. The pity of it was that this unaccustomed lying had to be to Opal. Something sweet was going out of her life. She was tempted to regain it by telling Opal everything. She teetered on the brink of confession, of saying, "Opal, I lied to you." But she believed that a confession would make it impossible for her to go. Not because Opal would try to dissuade her (as she surely would), but because once her plan was in the open, she herself would see its folly. And she was determined not to see it.

Opal, with unselfish interest, discussed the Denver shopping trip with her, gave her advice about buying winter coats and woolen underwear. But as Eunice discussed these fictions, she discovered that there had been hidden in her, during her years of truth-telling, a real talent for lying. Her wonder at this unexpected gift somewhat lightened her pain. She spun out lies like any hardened old deceiver.

And Opal, oh God, Opal continued to respond with her usual enthusiasm and openness; she debated the practicality of blue rather than gray, or hundred-per-cent wool rather than a mixture of wool and cotton. Ordinarily, this kind of interest delighted Eunice. Now she sat listening, first with wonder, then with some scorn. Was Opal so easily taken in? Had she always been, without Eunice's perceiving it, something of a fool? Ready to take anybody's word for anything? How strange that the lies she was telling, which should have diminished her, seemed instead to be cutting Opal down to a lesser size. Did you spoil the person you lied to as well as yourself? Eunice lingered over her coffee, not drinking, until the cream covered its cooled surface with a murky film. Opal finally hurried her away from the table, into her coat, and out onto the porch.

"What's got into you?" Opal asked. "Don't you care about getting to school on time any more?"

Feathery curls of snow had begun to fall; though "fall" was hardly the word for their drifting movement, as nearly horizontal as vertical.

"You'll be home early?" Opal asked.

"Yes."

"I'll have something hot for you. There's no diner on that train. And no use spending a weekend in Denver with pneumonia."

She fanned at the whirling snowflakes, treating them as a curtain to be parted. This gesture, humorous, futile, brought tears to Eunice's eyes. There were forces that human beings could not deal with. She knew that and Opal didn't.

"Cheer up," Opal said, "we're not parting forever."

They were; that was just the point. "Opal," she began, but Opal shooed her off the porch. "A trip to Denver is nothing to spend a morning over, saying farewell in a snowstorm." She went inside the house, slamming the door behind her.

It was sleeting when Eunice left for the depot at three. She was dressed for the weather, but no more than that. Nevertheless, Opal's friend, the jaunty ticket agent, pretended to see in her outfit something unusual.

"Where you headed for, Eunice? The North Pole? It can't be any ordinary trip you're making. I swear I've never seen such a rig-out, or smelled anything half as sweet. With all them furs, you look like a honey bear. What d'ya say, Eunice? Let's us two find a nice little cave and hole up for the winter?"

They were both surprised and taken aback. Do my intentions show so plainly, Eunice thought. And he thought, By God, I better watch myself, starting to make passes at old-maid schoolteachers. But he took another look at her. This girl was no old-maid schoolteacher, and why he hadn't seen it before, he didn't understand.

92

"We get smarter every day," he confided to Eunice. "Only pity is the learning comes so late."

Eunice reached Fort Collins at six and walked into the Western Hotel fifteen minutes later. The clerk at the desk, a mournful liver-colored man, told her that Mr. Mount was out momentarily but had left his key and had asked that she go to his room and wait for him. Eunice was greatly disappointed. She had collected herself, poised herself, for this minute, the minute of stepping into the hotel. From there on, she had expected Tom to take charge. What was she to do now? Going to a man's room in this public way seemed a doubtful business to her. She scanned the clerk's face for some knowingness, some leer. There was nothing in his face. He had used up a long time ago his entire stock of feeling about other people. He had very little left even for himself. He examined his fingernails as indifferently as he would bark on a tree. Whether she went to Tom Mount's room—or any man's room—mattered about as much to him as whether the cockroach, which had distracted his attention from his nails, had a safe journey across the floor of the alcove behind his desk. He was free to crush it. He would not extend a foot to do so.

Eunice took the key and, without the sustaining reassurance of defying anybody, climbed the stairs. Puffs of dust rose from the faded carpeting. This was no idyl of love in a rose-covered cottage. This was a raw town, an ugly hotel, a November night of rain and sleet. This was her war. She went right on up the steps, unlocked the door, and entered Tom Mount's room.

Here was something nearer the imagined idyl. Not many men, or women either, could have made of this high-ceilinged, drab-papered, bed-sitting room anything half as inviting. Opal couldn't have. The couch was covered with an Indian rug. There were two pots of red geraniums on the window sill, and on the fumed oak mission table there was a gray glass jug of dried grasses and seed pods, wispy and insubstantial as smoke. There was a bowl of goldfish on one taboret, and, balancing it at the other end of the bay window, on a twin taboret, was a flourishing Boston fern. On the mission table, beside the dried grasses, was the November *Scribner's,* and a plate of red apples. A scrap of paper on the plate of apples said, "Help yourself, Eve!" A fumed-oak bookcase held the collected works of Rudyard Kipling, O. Henry, and Wilkie Collins.

93

What if she never had had the courage to climb those stairs? If qualms about dust and cockroaches and cynical clerks had overcome her? A room could not consciously have been made more reassuring to a woman. She had always heard that rooms reflected people. If so, this room reflected a good man.

There was another note on the table. "Dear Eunice: Sit down, watch the goldfish, and wait for me. I'll be back in a trice. A trice? What does that mean? Tom."

If it meant in three moments, as she had always supposed it did, it was not true. A half hour went by. She could not possibly eat an apple or lose herself in reading. The movement of the goldfish made her feel nauseated. She had noticed a snapshot album on the under part of the library table. She longed to look into it, to see one picture of Tom Mount—at twelve was the age she would choose. But she didn't want to pry—and still less to be caught prying. She told herself she would look at just one picture. The picture she opened to was of a family group, a tall, dark-haired, rawboned mother and four children. The largest, a boy of fourteen or so, was plainly Tom. He stood, defiantly erect, an arm laid protectively about his mother's shoulders. Beneath the picture, in Tom Mount's handwriting, were the words "Just us."

The words wrung her heart. Why were they so much more affecting than "Mother and us children" or "Last Thanksgiving at home"? She began to cry. She put the album down, went to the window, and pressed her cheek against the cold glass. In the street beneath her, late shoppers were hurrying homeward through the sleety drizzle. Here lived a man who had been part of a home, who had loved his mother, who had followed a snow-cleared path to a lamplit room. Now they were all separated, they lived God knew where, their only home was in this man's room and in her mind. "Tom Mount," she said, "I will always love you and always be true to you."

She stood there waiting for the sound of his footsteps. She waited for him with her finger tips, her cheekbones, her dry aching mouth.

He opened the door with no previous sound having announced his coming. "Eunice," he said.

She turned, but could not move toward him. He, too, stood where he was, smiling quizzically. His hat and overcoat were beaded with moisture. He took off his hat, and a strand of black hair fell across his forehead. Quietly, still smiling, he came to her, held her close, and pressed his cool rain-smelling face to hers. Then he kissed her, long

94

and fondly but without desperation. His tongue in her mouth was the most natural thing in the world, though she had never imagined such a kiss. He kissed her only once, though that once seemed forever. She never expected to be clear of that moment. Then he pressed his cheek once again to hers, hugged her and, as he did so, groaned, the sound that of a man who has found something too delightful for words. Then he let her go, stood away from her, and gave his wet hat a blow against his thigh.

"Have you got any closets in this place where a man can hang his coat and hat?"

With those words he made her the one at home, the one doing the welcoming, the sought-after rather than the seeker.

"Oh, of course," she answered. "What kind of a place do you think this is?" She helped him out of his coat, and, opening the most likely door, found a closet with hangers.

With the coat and hat taken care of, she had nothing to do but wait to be touched again. Her entire life seemed to have been lived for the purpose of preparing for this touch, a ripening toward this moment. Everything that had preceded or would follow would be inconsequential. She stood still, almost deaf and blind, all of her senses concentrated in touch. She could not ask, nor move toward, nor initiate. She could only wait.

Tom Mount smiled at her. He seemed to understand her state, but humorously and affectionately.

"What a big, dark-eyed, passionate girl you are," he said.

Passionate? She? This was not a word one heard used in Millstone, especially about its big tomboyish schoolmarm, Eunice, the lonely walker and skater. She attempted to repeat the word, to ask him to explain. But her tongue in her dry mouth moved croakingly around it. "Passionate?"

"Even the way you say the word." He continued to look at her. "Why, when I came into this room and saw your blazing eyes, I said to myself, 'This girl has more passion in her little finger than most women have in their entire bodies.'"

She had never imagined such talk between a man and a woman, a talk about facts. But she was at once at home in it. She could not reply because her throat was too filled with emotion to hold words. But as soon as feeling let up a little, she knew that she could take part in such a conversation with an ease she had never been able to bring to the usual exchanges between men and women. Usual, at least, as far as she had known them, the trivialities of "Think it's going to clear up?," "How long do you figure we can stay out of the war, Eunice?," "Behaving yourself, girlie?"

The minute all pretense was gone, she was comfortable. Between leaving childhood, where no one had pretended, and reaching Tom Mount's bedroom, she had marked time. Now she began to live again as she had in her childhood, no reservations separating words from acts. This was real, too real, almost, to bear. What she felt she said. A wound was healed, or healing. It was strange that what she had always thought of as being romantic was not romantic at all, but extremely homey and natural, like washing her face or lighting a fire. The romantic, the exotic life would be to avoid this, to stay away from a man's room, a man's life. Even her trembling—the tremors in her body were so extreme she had the sensation that the upper half of her body was insecurely balanced on the lower half, a feeling that a quick movement might separate the two—even her trembling was perfectly natural and unromantic.

Tom Mount said, "First, we are going to have something to eat."

That "first" let her relax. Eating would not be possible for her, but she could sit across a table from him, use her eyes and ears once more, see him and hear him. He put his arms about her again, and, though he again groaned with pleasure, he held her lightly and did not kiss her. Then he stepped back and said, "I ordered, without consulting you, a standard meal."

She wondered what a standard meal would be. She need not have. When the waiter brought it, it was exactly that—roast beef, gravy, mashed potatoes, creamed peas, lemon meringue pie. She could not swallow a bite, and he did not try to persuade her to do so. Nor did he let her own lack of appetite affect his. Accustomed as she was with other women to being pushed into eating with or without appetite— the ladies did not care about your hunger or lack of it, but only about the comment your eating or failing to eat made upon their cooking— Eunice found this masculine indifference pleasant. Tom ate with relish and large appetite. When he had finished his own roast beef, he helped himself to half of hers.

"You see how smart I am? I pick a dainty eater and get most of the food."

"I'm not really a dainty eater."

"I know that."

"How?"

96

He stopped eating and looked at her. "Those curves. They weren't fed on air."

"Curves." That was another word not often heard in Millstone. And curves weren't fashionable either. She wanted to repudiate them. "I'm a good skater and hiker."

"I know that."

She wanted once again to ask him how he knew, but felt the conversation was centering too much on her.

"Ask me how I know that," he bade her.

"How do you know that?"

"I've had you in my arms. I felt those skating muscles."

She believed that nothing she had, curves or muscles, was good enough for him. An appealing woman did not, surely, remind a man of a skater when he held her in his arms.

"I wish I were more feminine," she murmured.

"No," he said. "My God, no."

She had no answer to this. He cut two more bites of roast beef and, when he had disposed of them, asked her, "What do you mean when you say you wish you were more feminine?"

"Small. Fragile. Blond. Flirtatious."

"A definition like that would put a lot of women out of the running."

She had no answer to that either.

"What do you mean by flirtatious?"

"You know."

"I don't know what you mean by it."

"I mean—being able to talk like this—and being able to breathe at the same time."

"That's one of the most flirtatious things I ever heard a woman say."

She shook her head in denial.

"You're breathing."

In the silence they both heard the sound of her sharply indrawn breath, like the last in a series of sobs.

"What do you call that? Isn't that breathing?"

"No. That's hurting."

"Where?" he asked. He put down his fork as he asked this question and looked at her intently.

She put her hand at the base of her throat. "Here," she said. "It hurts so much here."

"And you're not flirtatious? No, I expect you're right. You don't know what you're doing, do you?"

"I'm trying to tell the truth."

"Poor baby." He had not touched her during the meal, but now, beneath the table, he caught her knee between his legs. This pressure, like his hug, was firm but not frantic. "Poor baby."

No one, not even her mother, had ever called her this. She had an impulse to throw herself out of the window. She could not feel so much at once and survive.

He took his legs from her knee and smiled. "Baby, I kneed you," he said.

She heard the word as "need." Then something in his eyes suggested the pun to her. He ate another onion ring and said, "I'll be blowing onion rings all night."

It was not so deadly serious after all. It was possible to laugh with a man, though she could not really laugh, the muscles across her diaphragm were too tight. But she knew it was possible. She could not make the sound of laughter, but she felt inside her its warmth. The impulse to laugh, which she could not satisfy, put her onto her feet to extend and exercise those skating muscles with room-pacing, a substitute for the long gliding push across Goose Lake's gray steel. Tom Mount ate and let her walk. He did not ask her why or jump up to be with her; but he gave her permission and with his eyes admired her use of it. He put down his knife and fork, sat back from the table, and watched her.

"Going somewhere, baby?" he asked. Baby, oh baby! A sweet and fondling name, a name that so subtracted inches, lightened swarthiness, and added merriment. She walked across the room, under his eyes, as another woman might have danced or sung or played a harp or posed naked or displayed a thousand-dollar dress. For him, she was, she existed, in that walk. Nothing that she had ever thought or felt, been or wished, acted or refrained from acting was held back. She felt him accept it all, felt his capability of accepting it all. She circled him as a planet circles a sun. But the direction of light and heat was reversed, and this was what they both wanted. At the moment when the pacing needed to be terminated, she remembered that she had put a bottle of brandy in her suitcase. Opal's provision of whisky had struck her as so elegant and worldly that she had thought that she could not do better than to imitate her.

Tom Mount laughed at her brandy. "You two women," he said.

"You ought to be barkeepers, the way you enjoy handing out the liquor. Though you'd go broke, giving it away the way you do." He looked at the bottle admiringly but made no move to open it.

"I'm not interested in making money," Eunice said.

"Tell me, Eunice, what are you interested in?"

"I am interested in you."

Now she had said it, declared herself, made the pursuit which she had always understood was, for the man, half the pleasure, unnecessary. And words, she supposed, were the real means of declaration. Nothing was finally true without words. Words made marriages and declared wars, and, with the words unsaid, nothing was irreparable; with the word she had committed herself. The word somehow went beyond the flesh. It gave her away beyond any giving of arms or lips. It endorsed with consciousness the movements and longings of the flesh, subscribed to them, stamped them as official. There was nothing to do now but wait.

Tom Mount came to relieve her waiting. He pushed the chair from the table and stood before her, matching seriousness with seriousness. She had never imagined being more equally met. He touched her, without tempest, put an arm about her waist, and led her to the window. Beneath them, though the sleet had let up, the pavement was still streaked with white and the passers-by had lost their home-going briskness. They were on the street now only because the street was better than home; their shoulders sloped earthward.

"Living on the lower floor of sadness," Tom said.

She supposed he spoke of those passing below, but was not sure. And she had no idea what he meant by "living on the lower floor of sadness."

He took his arm from her waist, crossed the room to the dresser, and, facing into the mirror which also reflected her, he began to undress. She needed advice, or help. She was given none. She could not simply imitate him, play some game of follow-the-leader, penalties for a false move. He undressed like a tired man; he exposed his body slowly. She did not see him as a naked man, but as Tom Mount—all of him. He lay down upon the bed, which came down when he opened a door, his body on the white counterpane not white, his hair black on the pillow. She had had no practice, in her imagination, in feeling emotion for a man's naked body. If she was passionate, as Tom had said she was, it was for glances, touches of the hand, tones of the voice. But her tenderness, her pity, even, were enough to cause her to walk toward him. What she was experiencing at the minute was nearer the passion of a mother than of a sweetheart. She could not look at the whole of his body, physically could not. She had seen him, then her eyes had of themselves turned away. Every instinct, feminine as well as virgin, repudiated this swiftness, cried out for initiatory steps, for postponement, for time. His eyes were closed. By this act he shut her away from everything she knew about him, everything she had made a journey to join. This body, this great marble body, stretched like a corpse the length of the bed, what had she to do with it? Yes, she had to do with it. Though she had never expected it to be presented to her like this, and did not now want it, still she took another step nearer the bed. This war was stranger than anything she had ever dreamed, still it was her war.

"Tom?" she asked.

"Yes, dear," he answered, eyelids unmoving, his voice kind and emotionless.

She took one more step. A floor board creaked under her foot. Down on the street, open ended to hills and sky, the wind swept around the solid masonry of the hotel with its long anguished cry of emptiness. Oh, nothing, nothing but the wind; and this building, a fake, to fool the wind, with its semblance of a human habitation, but it, too, empty, deserted, filled with transients as separated as though it had never been built, and the persons its walls hid faced each other on a dark mesa, the wind off the mountains blowing strong and icy between them. The wind in its long sweep, how many cabins, rooms, beds, men, women, did it sweep around? How many lamps did it smoke? How many candles gutter? How many shirttails, left overnight on careless lines, did it tatter? How many cattle, shivering, turned their rumps to it? The sound of the wind tied her to all of these objects at a moment when she needed ties: its currents washed them all. By what chance was she islanded here in a room full of apples and dry grasses and goldfish with a great strange unmoving statue? The smoking lamps, the lonely cabins, the forgotten clothes, the huddled cattle— all these she knew: with any of these she would have been at home. By choice, by determination, by lying, she had made her home with strangeness. There was a sandy spatter of sleet against the window; the wind, fair-minded in its lonely destructiveness, was willing to give other elements a chance. She went to the window and pushed it up. Let something happen, she asked. If we are to be frozen in this room, let us be truly frozen. The wind that blew the curtains aside brought sleet with it. The street below was now empty. Those living on the lower floors of sorrow had gone home to experience sorrow at higher levels. She was pierced by the wind; the sleet salted the leftovers of the standard meal. She turned to face the man on the bed. If he felt the wind or the sleet, he gave no sign. He lay unmoving, stretched out to it, willing to accept whatever came to him.

She did not shut the window, but she did begin slowly to take off her own clothes. The wind offered her the touch she had lacked. She took her clothes off *to* something, *for* something, because of something, in spite of something. She was helped by it, buffeted by it, stung by it. She began once again to tremble. The wind took away her self-consciousness. Naked with the wind was more modest than clothed with a statue. With it she was a tree or a wheel. The lights in the room still burned as bright as when Tom Mount had entered, days and years ago, smelling of this very wind and sleet. She stood in front of the window, and if anyone across the street wanted to look, let him. She faced the mirror. She had no fault to find with her body, except to have it of an entirely different kind. If a woman was to be tall and dark, broad-shouldered, big-bosomed, long-waisted, her way was likely as good as any to be these wrong things. She undressed, and seeing herself in the mirror, let down her hair. Not for modesty's sake, though her hair was heavy enough and warm enough to be useful for both. She let her hair down because it went with her nakedness. She let it down the way a painter adds something to the corner of his picture. I am not so miserable as I thought, she told herself, as she pulled out the pins, able to see that nakedness and hair skewered up in a knot do not go together. But she was miserable enough. She held her breath with the cold; there was a sucked-in place the size of a washbasin under her ribs. Her bones were as naked to the cold as if her flesh had been burned away by a fire. But the worst of all was her separateness and her consciousness. She had not come here to be alone, to be left out in the cold. She wanted to forget herself and to remember only Tom Mount.

He spoke to her from the bed. "Pull down the window." There was no hint in his voice of the fifteen-minute silence he had kept.

She pulled it down, though she missed the wind. A quiet cold was worse than a noisy one, stealthier, deadlier.

"Shall I pull the blind, too?"

"No, not the blind."

"The lights? Shall I turn out the lights?"

STRAHORN LIBRARY
THE COLLEGE OF IDAHO
Caldwell, Idaho

"Not unless there's something in this room you don't want to see."

There was something. His body and hers.

"Come here, baby."

She went to the bedside.

"You have frozen us both."

"Yes."

"What good did you do by that?"

"No good." She dropped to her knees by the bed. His eyes were closed again, and she thought, When he is dead he'll look like this, blue under the eyes, big sharp beak, lips with the shape of teeth behind them. She leaned forward and laid her cold cheek against the big cold box of his chest.

"Dear love."

"Help me, baby."

Help him? Help him what? She was the one who needed help. "I will help you," she said firmly, promising she knew not what. Warmth was the first help she knew how to give, and she extended her arms, mantled him with her flesh and her hair.

"Help me," he said again.

"I will, I will," she declared. He was asking her what she felt capable of providing. His request was a child's to a mother, a pupil's to a teacher. With those words, he returned her to a world she knew, to lamps in the wind, cabins at the mouth of the draw, a wash forgotten on the line. Help? Help was her whole stock in trade. She clasped him more closely, warmed him, cradled him, rocked him. She closed her own eyes, as they say of those dying, calmly, and there was nothing in the feel of his encircled body she did not feel born for.

"Help me, baby." Then he showed her what he meant by help.

She hung for one moment equal, poised between running and staying. If thought could have transported her, she would have been instantly back under the eaves at Millstone, under Opal's comforter, dreaming some more familiar dream. Her mind went there. Her imagination denying where she was and what she did made it possible for her to stay. She embarked upon the fatal division. In her mind she spoke words that repudiated what she did, and words were what counted, weren't they? And beyond this justifying division lay the help of her mulishness. She would finish this, spend the rest of her life living it down if necessary, recovering from it, forgetting it, but she would not run away from it. This was her war, and if it was a foolish or wicked or forbidding war, well, all right, it was hers and she would die in it. Only she wished the window were open and that the wind swept round her and cried with the sounds she could not make.

Opal, who had finished her supper, looked across at Eunice. "That's the first time I've heard you do that since we came to the Tract."

"Do what?"

"Groan that way."

"I was thinking of something else."

"I know you were." When Eunice did not answer, Opal said, "Why do you want to get mixed up again with something that makes you groan and cry? Why do you want to start it all up again? All that suffering?"

"Opal, it was the only happiness I ever knew."

"Why did we leave Colorado then?"

"It was a whim."

"I gave up my home for a whim, then?"

"I didn't know it then. Opal, I'll explain this to you if I can. I think I owe it to you."

"You don't owe me anything—least of all explanations of how you feel about Tom Mount."

"I want to explain. I don't think you and Charlie . . ."

"You're right about me and Charlie. But I know a few things I never picked up from Charlie. I've been to a few beauty parlors and quilting bees in my day. I've heard a little talk in my lifetime. I don't suppose anything you could tell me would come as a surprise."

"I didn't intend to tell you anything surprising . . . only that afterward . . ."

"Afterward? Oh yes, afterward. How about before and during?"

"Before?"

"Afterward is anything you make up to tell yourself to take the place of what wasn't. You've got a little time then. I know all about afterward."

"You don't. You can't."

Don't I though, Opal thought. She watched the big dark girl remember and search for words. She let her struggle. She let the brown eyes go black and the skin tighten over the cheekbones and the mouth despair. Let her try to tell it and find out what words would do to that story. Let her cut afterward, and before and during, too, down to size with words and hear with her own ears what she plans to throw away her life on. There weren't any words for that crazy man's woman-like power of gentleness and his woman-like power of lasting and his woman-like interest in every remembered how-it-was or might-have-been, and all this tied, till it broke your heart with contradictoriness, to what rose from him so unwoman-like it took an increase of woman-liness to contain and no going away but an oncoming which it took a night to kill and you dying, too, and learning in the afterward the truth of dying into life, the truth that living in the morning, after death in the night, was a resurrection, oh, Jesus, to lilies in the valley, to a room where fly song was sweetest music and a chair shadow the shape of thrones, and all around you hummed a silence that had at its center the two of you and you not caring about anything any more because what more was needed, once you were a fact? There were no words for that. Try to put it into words, tell somebody how it was, and it's gone, gone. Tell me, Eunice. Hear for yourself and wake up. Spit it out. Make it no bigger than a sentence. Then eat your peach pie and drink your coffee and live with things we got words for.

"Tell me, Eunice," she said. "Tell me all about it. I admit I'm ignorant."

"I don't know that I can. Or ought to."

"Ought to?"

"Some things are sacred."

"We oughtn't have run away from something sacred, had we, Eunice? Tell me. Maybe it's not as sacred as you think."

She wouldn't, Opal saw, take a chance on discovering that. She had to be there at the center of the humming, not standing outside of it, listening and reporting.

"You'll have to change your clothes before we go to the meeting," Opal said finally. "You can't go with that tea stain on you."

Eunice looked down at the stain, brushed it a few times with her hand as if she hoped to rid herself of it that easily. The outside doors —the house had two, one in the sitting room, one in the kitchen— were both open, and through them and the opened windows came the nighttime's warm sleepy harvest sound of insects. As long as they chirped, summer lasted. They felt the earth still warm beneath them. They were making the wrong music, though, for sorrow; and the big moon, rising, was giving the wrong light; and the soft wind was providing the wrong touch. But these things existed not even for themselves, let alone human suitability.

"Eunice," Opal said, "we ought to be happy. We've come a long way for that purpose."

"I am happy," Eunice said. "Oh, Opal, what makes you think I'm unhappy—on a night like this? He's come a long way, too, and I'll see him again soon."

"Have you forgotten why we left Colorado?" Opal asked again.

"No. I haven't forgotten. But I've learned something, too. If you love anybody—it doesn't matter what they do. You keep on loving them."

"Baby-strangling, bank robbery?"

"I expect so. You never did love what they did. You loved them. It isn't stopped by acts."

Opal pushed back her chair. "You get ready," she said. "I'll clear up. We're going to be late as it is."

13    Asa Brice was the first man to arrive at the meeting. He was punctual by nature, and with no wife to make love to, no car to break down, no dog to be chased by coyotes, no sweetheart to turn up out of the past, there was little to interfere with his punctuality. He left his motorcycle at home and walked from his tent to Raunce's church tent on his own reliable legs. He listened to the wind, blowing punctually inland at this hour. But in his heart he believed that he and the wind alike were both essentially wild.

But where is my wild act, he asked himself? Where? Where? My wild act, not of defiance, but of being and doing? I break away from the shingled bungalows, the seven-to-five jobs, the snuggeries of marriage and churches and fraternal orders, but what do I do? My savage heart, my rage to be: but what do I do with them? I live calm under canvas. I peel myself down to the nubbin of an eye that observes and a hand that records. I turn up punctually at meetings for community betterment.

He stuck his head inside the tent when he arrived there and called, "Ben." Ben Jessup had promised to come early to the meeting; since his car wasn't in sight, he surely hadn't arrived; still, Asa wanted to make sure.

"You looking for someone?" Up front, LeRoy Raunce was arranging yellow field daisies in a big crockery churn.

"I was looking for Ben Jessup."

"Ben's car's probably had another breakdown."

In the stale warmth of the tent, Raunce, or maybe it was the daisies, had a rank smell, not bad, but strong and penetrating.

"How do you like the way I've dressed the place up?" Raunce asked, indicating a galvanized pail of blue dust flowers on the opposite side of the pulpit. "I brought them in first. Then the place cried out for something to balance them. Looks better evened up with these daisies, don't it?"

When Asa hesitated, Raunce said, "I'm no hand for decorating, but I can spot lopsidedness all right."

"You pick these as well as fix them?" Asa asked.

"I had a little time after I got home from work."

Raunce's energy was a byword on the Tract. Asa himself was no slouch when it came to work, but he knew he could not hold a candle to Raunce. Raunce worked nine hours at the oil field; came home and carpentered or painted for a couple of hours; then he wound up his day reading the books prescribed by the Rose Park Elders. They did not have to urge LeRoy. If God had spoken in burning bushes, opened up seas, ordered plagues, produced doves, provided chariots, brought water from rocks, LeRoy wanted to know about it. Asa thought, He's like any other man in love. He can't hear too much about God.

LeRoy read the Bible six nights a week; twice on Sunday and once on Wednesday he preached, sharing what he had learned from his reading with his neighbors. "Oh, friends," he would call out, leaning in his eagerness over the little homemade pulpit, "God sent a chariot down to pick up Elisha. He will do as much for any one of us."

Asa had gone three or four times to hear LeRoy preach. He gave Raunce and his sermons the same attention he would have given any other natural phenomenon. Raunce wrestling with the word of God was as interesting as a tarantula fight any day. There was the same life-and-death determination in the performance. The word of God usually won, a sign, no doubt, that Raunce fought fair. Asa had no stomach for what the man preached, but the man preaching, that was another story: the man committed, illuminated, transfigured. By what? By something invisible, beyond the skies. There was a wild poetic act! That believing and declaring. Asa regarded Raunce with the same envy he had for Indians and eagles, for all creatures unseparated from themselves.

"Are you going to have some part in the performance tonight, LeRoy?" he asked.

"Perkins asked me to sit up on the platform with him and Wendlin

Jessup, and open and close the meeting with prayer. I'm willing to pray, but I'm not going to do it from this platform. I'm not going to lend the pulpit to the Perkins Investment Company. Anything I'd say from up here would sound like an amen to Syl's excuses for not delivering us the water he's promised."

LeRoy, as soon as he had his flowers evened up to suit him, left the tent. "Hate to waste the water," he said, "but I got to do a little washing up before the meeting. I appoint you the reception committee till Syl gets here. I don't want to see him. He'll be at me again to pray from the pulpit, and since I don't intend to do it, there's no use our going through all that again."

LeRoy didn't make his escape any too soon. Asa heard Raunce's screen door slam a few seconds after he heard the approaching car. LeRoy probably sprinted that last fifty yards, Asa thought, and he wished he could have seen him.

When he went outside, Syl had already turned off his engine. Asa was glad to see that Syl was not pretending to be a rancher among ranchers.

Asa's first meeting with Sylvester Perkins had taken place in the Los Angeles office of the Perkins Investment Company. A salesman on the Tract had told Asa, when he tried to buy the arroyo, that it was not for sale.

"Nonsense," Asa told him. "Everything out here's for sale. They'd sell the coyotes if they thought anyone would pay for them. I want the arroyo."

The arroyo, technically, was a part of the reservoir land. No price had been set on it, and the salesman, whose inclinations were all toward picking up as many commissions as he could, nevertheless had no choice but to send Asa in to see Perkins himself.

Asa made the trip into Los Angeles on his motorcycle. On the Tract, Asa wore bib overalls, an article of clothing other young unmarried men left to middle-aged heads of families. They thought bib overalls about on a par, for men, with Mother Hubbards for women: something you put on when your shape was better guessed at than revealed. Asa was slim-hipped and gaunt-tailed enough to be in no need of any disguise. But he was extremely logical, and logic led him to bib overalls. They were practical: the bib protected the shirt; healthful: no belt to stop the circulation; economical: they lasted longer than Levis. So he wore bib overalls. Los Angeles, however, Asa recognized, was not the Tract. He was not one to court attention, so he put on what he considered a city costume: well-pressed khaki-colored cotton pants and shirt, and a matching khaki-colored cap. The cap had goggles attached by Asa himself, with the help of elastic carried by stores for girls' bloomers. Asa rode into Los Angeles on his red, well-polished Indian motorcycle, feeling as conventionally dressed as a banker.

The outfit was conventional, but the convention it suggested to Sylvester Perkins's secretary was that of a delivery man of some kind, and it was thus she reported him to Mr. Perkins. Sylvester Perkins had nothing against such men. He was democratic for the soundest reasons—it made him money; but he was also busy, and it was not until Asa sent the secretary scurrying back with the magic words "Tract" and "buy," that Syl said, "Show him in."

"Tract" and "buy" meant that Asa was one of "Syl's people," and Syl felt like a father to "his people." Asa had no inkling of this; and he had never set eyes on a man for whom he felt less filial response. The interview thus started off with one of the performers ignorant of the part he was expected to play. Asa thought of himself as a land buyer and of Perkins as a man with land to sell. Perkins thought of himself as a combination pioneer and Father Christmas and of Asa as a boy whose stocking he might fill. It took them both a little time to get their parts straightened out.

Syl's first desire was to let Asa know that selling real estate was far from being his primary interest. He did so, of course; and he made money at it, of course; he had to live, like anyone else. But it was not by chance that he was making ranches available to buyers on terms that made it possible for men who had never owned property before to do so. It was his business; he was a subdivider in the same way another man was a grocer or a lawyer; but it was also his mission.

After he had made this clear to Asa, he pointed, without saying anything, to the view from his windows: twenty miles away across the Los Angeles Valley, the purple saw teeth of the Sierra Madres bit upward into the blue sky.

"Now you see where I get my trade-mark, don't you? When I moved into this office, there they were, waiting for me: Mount Lowe, Mount Wilson, Old Baldy, an entire unused mountain range. I thought to myself, If fate can be for me, the least I can do is to be for fate. I deal in top values in land, and here are the tops in land. Nothing I could have arranged and paid for could have been half as effective as these natural reminders of this fact. All it took on my part was a willingness to see. That, fortunately, I have. I had the silhouette of those mountaintops used at once in all of our advertising and on all of our stationery. You've seen how the Prudential Insurance Company uses the Rock of Gibraltar? That's British territory, half around the world from us. This is pure California, used to remind us that when it comes to ranch land, California and the Perkins Investment Company top all rivals. The words underneath, 'Where the snow-crowned golden Sierras keep their watch o'er the Valley's bloom,' are from our state song. I bet you didn't know that, Asa."

Asa confessed he didn't.

"All free, all native California, all good things to keep in mind. The height of our mountains, the words of our songs, the opportunities offered by the Perkins Investment Company."

"Those aren't actually the Sierras, are they?" Asa, who knew they were not, asked.

"A mountain's a mountain," Syl said.

"What about the Valley's bloom? There's not much of that yet on the Tract."

"Time," Syl said, "time, time. That's all we need for bloom."

"And water," Asa reminded him.

Syl admitted this. "Time and water."

"God will take care of time," Asa said, "but you will have to produce the water."

"I accept that responsibility, I accept it fully," Syl said. He looked out the window. "I can't credit my eyes when I look out there. Our trade-mark right across the sky."

Asa smiled. He believed Sylvester Perkins was convinced that the trade-mark had come first and that the mountains were an imitation.

"We have a little ceremony here in the office at this time of the day," Syl said. "We call it 'the changing of the colors.' We drop all work and watch those peaks as the colors change on them."

Asa knew those transitions from blue to rose to mauve to gray by heart, and he certainly had not lost a half-day's time and ridden twenty-five miles on a motorcycle in order to look at them through a fly-specked office window. He wanted to buy an arroyo, and he did not need any sunset thrown in as a premium. If what Mr. Perkins wanted was silence at this hour, he should not be in his office. An office was a place of business, and Asa had business to transact. He had no more stomach for mumbo jumbo with mountains and sunsets in a real-estate office than he would have had for them in a grocery store. Without even bothering to face the mountains at which Sylvester Perkins and his secretary were gazing, he said, "I want to buy the arroyo on the southwest corner of the townsite, the one that circles the bottom of Reservoir Hill—at that point."

Without moving his eyes from his trade-mark in the sky, Syl said, "It isn't for sale."

"Why not? It's not worth anything to you."

"By the same token, it oughtn't to be worth anything to you."

"We don't use the same tokens, Mr. Perkins."

Sylvester Perkins had been taken aback by this, but impressed. He did not discover that Asa's plans for his arroyo were as sound commercially as those of the citrus planters until after he had sold him the arroyo for next to nothing as unusable land. When he did find out, the fact tickled him. He thought Asa was an eccentric; but any eccentric who could best Sylvester Perkins had Syl's complete respect.

The minute Syl was out of the car, he called out, "How's life at the bottom of the gully, Asa? Any peanuts ripe yet?"

Syl introduced his wife to Asa, and Asa was pleased with her appearance. Louella appeared, with her carefully selected colors, her unnaturally waved hair, her unmoving face, unreal to him, something fabricated and requiring study.

"I can't make a speech unless I see Louella in the front row encouraging me," Syl boasted.

"The truth about me doesn't matter a whit to Perk," Louella said, without any tone of complaint. "He makes up whatever suits the story he's telling at the moment."

Asa had never heard Sylvester Perkins called anything but Syl, and without thinking, he said, "Perk?"

"That's my wife's pet name for me."

Louella made no comment. On their honeymoon her husband had asked her to call him Perk; she did not know why then and had never since inquired the reason; but she had never from that day called him anything else, and this difference between his public name and his private name suited her very well. The public thought he was Syl while she knew that he was Perk.

"What kind of a turnout do you think we'll have tonight?" Syl asked.

"If everybody who's dissatisfied with the water situation shows up," Asa said, "the whole Tract'll be here."

"They don't think I'm handling it right?" Syl asked good-humoredly.

"That's what they intend to find out tonight."

"Good," Sylvester Perkins said. "I'm glad to hear it. That's exactly what I hoped for. Asa, I want every man, woman, and child on this Tract out fighting for this Tract. Fighting me, if necessary. That's the way I planned it. They're wrong in this case—but that don't matter. It's the principle that matters. As long as they're for the Tract, first, last, and always, why, I tell you, Asa, the sky's the limit out here. We can have a paradise out here, an organized, well-run paradise."

"Irrigated, too, I hope."

Syl laughed. "Yes, siree, bob. An irrigated paradise."

Louella was always amazed at the way Perk could take the wind out of his opponent's sails. A man could come to Perk with what appeared to her to be a genuine grievance, find himself in the wrong in ten minutes and struggling to justify his actions. Perk had the power, just by being quiet and asking a question or two, of letting a man get in bad. To do so, he must have logic and reason on his side from the beginning. But it was a logic and a reason that, at the beginning, Louella never saw. She was always a fool and victim with the man to whom Perk was giving enough rope to hang himself. And usually she, too, was given enough rope for a good throttling, if not a complete hanging.

"Have you seen Wendlin Jessup?" Syl asked. "He's going to preside tonight. I've got a few things I want to talk over with him before the meeting starts."

"I haven't seen him, but I'll tell him you're looking for him if I do," Asa said.

"Fine. You do that, Asa," Syl said, and moved on to greet other settlers who were now beginning to arrive.


14　THE NIGHT was warm and the moon was full. This was a meeting for grievances, and the settlers planned to get down to the brass tacks of complaining and demanding in due time; but meanwhile it was a social occasion, the first of its kind on the Tract: the first chance the women had had to put on a dress a little more flashy than was suitable for church; to survey and to size up; to begin to play the parts that might be theirs for the rest of their lives. Nothing was settled yet. To whom did they feel superior, to whom might they have to truckle? They came filled with emotions they wanted to use, and were searching for suitable objects on which to use them. They had a store of love, scorn, hatred, reverence, pity. They wanted to laugh, cry, anticipate, be surprised, excited, transported. They wanted to feel others moved by their glances, by the mere shape of their cheekbones; they hoped there would be significance for someone in the particular breast pin they wore, in the tremulous breath with which they framed a hesitating sentence.

Asa, still on the lookout for Ben, stood at one side of the tent opening, watching the arrival of his neighbors. He knew most of them by name. Ben's father and mother pulled up in a buggy, open to the night air and the stars. Asa went over to greet them and to ask about Ben.

Ben's father, Wendlin Jessup, was sixty; Ben's mother, Mary, was somewhat younger. Asa believed Wendlin Jessup had, not the finest or handsomest face he had ever seen, but the clearest. It was not a matter either of color or of features, though the man did have, with his high color and silvery thatch, a kind of old farmer's handsomeness. Asa, who could watch a ground squirrel with pleasure, relished Wendlin's assortment of colors and planes as such. But they were less than half of Wendlin Jessup's story, were not, in fact, the story at all, but only the page on which the story was written. Asa plagued himself wondering what that story was. The man was religious, an old-line Quaker; but Asa had looked into the face of many a religious man without being able to detect a thing there except a lifelong satisfaction in eating fried chicken and talking about sin.

He was not sure that goodness was what accounted for the clarity in Wendlin's face; perhaps it was singleness of purpose. The same purity might perhaps be seen in the face of a cannibal chief whose good it was to pursue, catch, and eat his enemies—if he had been wholehearted about the pursuit of this good. Wendlin's face was as innocent of contradictoriness as a pond. There was nothing in it, minute by minute, to figure out. You would look at it once in a while, the way you did any pleasing natural phenomenon, but there was no need to do so in order to keep track of Wendlin. He was what he had always been and would be. He had taken his stand.

Wendlin jumped out of the buggy with an old farmer's stiff jauntiness and went around to help his wife down. Mary Jessup was no one's idea of a Quakeress and not many people's idea of a lady. She was a big tawny old thing, one of those women who should have subsided some years back into a graying quietness. Instead, while her yellow hair had faded and her skin had developed a slackness it had not had at sixteen—or even forty—this old Quakeress, or old lady, or old tigress—whatever she was—did not take to age any more noticeably than the ocean. Ancient of days, if you wanted to count the days; but who, at the seaside amidst wave and spray, wanted to concentrate on that aspect of his holiday?

Asa knew no one, male or female, religious or irreligious, more likely than Mary Jessup to call a spade a spade. He was a spade-caller himself, but there were some matters from which he habitually turned his eyes. Not Mary. She was in some ways an unlikely partner for Wendlin and an even more unlikely mother for Ben. Asa cared more for her than for any other woman he had ever known. When he went to the Jessups', he went there, as much as anything, to talk to Mary.

Wendlin was not much of a talker, though he was a great jokester. Asa was not sure why, but Wendlin's joking made him suspicious of the old saint. Joking was a means of bearing things that probably ought not to be borne. It was a device for avoiding suspicion. Say something true, but in such a way that men laughed, and they would forgive you for it. By God, Asa thought, I don't want to be forgiven for a thing.

Mary was full of good humor, an easy laugher, but no more capable of a joke than the sun. She got out of the buggy with none of Wendlin's jaunty bounce, but flowed, all feminine flounces of striped blue and white, over the step and so down to the dusty earth.

She turned to Asa without any salutation. "Is that preacher here?"

"You mean Raunce?"

"Don't tell me this Tract's blossomed any others? There's going to be more shepherds than sheep here soon. Ben getting the craze and Twining an ex of some kind."

"Raunce was here a while back. He went home to clean up. Do you want to see him?"

"Not him, especially. But I brought some cookies and a couple of pounds of coffee. If the Raunces will let me use a kettle—or a big Suetene can—I'm fixed to provide the crowd with some refreshments."

"That's quite an undertaking, isn't it?"

"Maybe so. But it seemed a pity on our first get-together that there shouldn't be something to eat."

"By the time this meeting's over," Wendlin told her, "you may not be able to find any two people willing to break bread with each other."

"Bread, maybe. But they're not going to be able to turn down hot coffee and ginger drops."

"You women don't know anything about us men and our principles, Mary."

"Maybe not your principles. They're kind've hard to make out at times, I admit. But your appetites, that's a different story, and crystal clear to every woman. Hand me that coffee bag."

Wendlin fished the bag out of the back of the buggy. "Mary puts the Bible to shame," he told Asa. "She undertakes to feed the multitudes without benefit of miracles."

Mary hurumphed, but was not shocked. The Quakers treated the Bible like an almanac, a book helpful for daily living but not so holy you could not put it and a joke in the same sentence.

Asa had no stomach for professional do-gooders: ladies in favor of teetotalism or men trying to cleanse the world by doing without meat. Missionaries and reformers had the sour smell of a root cellar toward spring. He hated to get to the windward side of them. Mary Jessup was an exception. She was full of good deeds, but she was as sweet as running water. She did her good deeds, and once they were over, she was as finished with them as she was with her past minute's breath. She enjoyed making ginger drops and coffee for others the way most people enjoy making money for themselves. Asa forgave Mary Jessup her goodness with his whole heart, and smiled, watching her set off toward the Raunces' place, as bountiful and unpremeditated as a harvest.

The crowd, while Asa had talked to the Jessups, had been growing. The moon, which had floated free of Old Saddle Back, dimmed the illumination provided by Sylvester Perkins's lanterns. Syl himself stood near the tent opening, greeting settlers like a father at a holiday home-coming. Some appeared to relish his greeting; others gave him a wide berth. He was rich, and they all owed him money. This was enough to make some resentful and suspicious. Tala Camp, an old lady whose single interest in life, as far as Asa knew, was china-painting, chatted with Syl for several minutes; the Irby Wagners, Mrs. Wagner twice the size of her husband, sailed past him; Nard Fitzgerald, the Tract's earliest settler, and his brood of towheads, which included a second wife who looked as if she had been picked to suit an already established color scheme, went by nodding and smiling, but too diffident, until Syl laid a hand on Nard's arm, to take up the Tract owner's time.

The Mexicans, Pete and Rosa Ramos and Julian Ortiz, stood some distance from the others, quiet and watching. Asa wondered why they had come. Just for the party of it, he supposed, since they owned no Tract land and had no water troubles. Asa raised his hand in salute, and the two men responded with smiles. Pete Ramos had the spread-legged stance of a man with heavy shoulders and narrow hips. And there was a fullness in the firm-muscled flesh at the corners of his mouth which Asa associated with power, though, as far as he knew, Pete had none and wanted none. Ortiz was another make of Mexican: a young man with a silky mustache and a brow wrinkling upward under a head of hair so big and black it dwarfed and lightened his fine-boned face.

While Asa watched the Mexicans, the Basil Cudlips arrived, gave the Mexicans a wide berth and paused in an uneasy cluster, like hornets fixing to swarm. They were as black as the Fitzgeralds were blond. The young Cudlips scattered to lark around with the other children, playing ante-over over the tent with wild gourds and rolling tumbleweeds like hoops. Base Cudlip scanned the crowd as if looking for someone. Asa had always been of two minds about the story a man's appearance told. He didn't believe a low brow showed a lack of brains or a small jaw a lack of will power. Still, he had observed too many animals not to know that there was some connection between character and appearance, though animals hadn't man's power to disguise character by changing their appearance: black hearts hidden by big smiles, and shyness covered up with booming voices. If those were the signs, Base Cudlip was neither blackhearted nor shy. He neither smiled nor boomed. Silent and scowling, he came up to Wendlin, unhinged his beard-shadowed jaw enough to say howdy and to ask Wendlin who was in charge of the meeting.

"What do you mean, in charge?" Wendlin asked. "I'm going to preside, if that's what you mean."

"I don't mean that. Who has the say-so about who comes?"

Raunce, scrubbed clean, but still smelling of paint and the turpentine he had used to remove the paint, joined the group, and Cudlip turned to him. "It's your tent. You got the say-so, Reverend?"

"Anybody can come to my tent," LeRoy said. "It's open to all."

"What's the trouble, Base?" Wendlin asked. "Won't they let you Cudlips in?"

115

It was one of Wendlin's jokes, and it tickled Asa, but Basil Cudlip did not crack a smile.

"We're in, all right. The question is, do we want to stay?"

Wendlin, who knew perfectly well what troubled Base Cudlip, was not going to make things easy for him. He would have to come out with the dirty facts himself. "That's something you're the only one can decide, Basil," he said, and showed he had dismissed the whole subject by starting a conversation with LeRoy. "I hear you're ready to begin work on the new church, LeRoy? That right?"

But Cudlip, though one of Raunce's faithful listeners, was not going to be sidetracked by church talk.

"What I want to know is, who asked those greasers here?"

Asa listened to hear the reply to that. There was none. LeRoy and Wendlin could not have looked blanker if the question had been put to them in Hindustani. Cudlip saw the blankness, too, and changed his word.

"What are those Mexicans doing here?"

"Pete and Julian?" LeRoy asked.

"I don't know what their names are."

"They got names just like us, Basil," Wendlin said. "Though not so fancy as yours and mine, I grant you."

"I don't give a damn about their names. All I'm interested in is— who asked them to this meeting?"

Raunce said, "They've got a right to be here. This meeting is open to everyone."

"Now we're getting somewheres. Who said it was?"

"Sylvester Perkins is the man who called the meeting."

"Perkins don't care who he sells land to."

"I hope that's true," Wendlin said.

"Oh, it's true all right. I know for a fact he's sold land to a Jap. The chief reason I pulled up stakes to come West was to get shut of niggers. Look at that fellow." He pointed to Pete Ramos. "I've seen plenty of niggers lighter skinned than him. I didn't travel three thousand miles to run into a bunch of watered-down blacks. If I want niggers, I want the real article, all wool and a yard wide."

"Looks like you better be heading back then," Raunce said.

"I'm not heading back. But I'm not taking things laying down either. Where's Perkins? If you fellows don't accept the responsibility for them being here, I want to find somebody who will."

"Oh, we accept the responsibility all right, Base," Wendlin said. "We accept it fully."

"He speak for you, too, Asa?" Base asked. And Asa, realizing that he alone of the three men had said nothing, felt the need to say something stronger than the others to make up for his silence.

"He speaks for me. I don't go to any meeting where they're not welcome."

"Well, that lets me know where you three stand. That makes it all clear. I'll speak to Perkins on my own hook. I'll fight my own fight without help."

He walked away, a fine figure of a man, as black-haired as Pete and Julian.

"LeRoy," Asa said, "tell me how you figure on making a Christian out of a man like that?"

LeRoy's fleshy big-boned face was troubled. Basil Cudlip was a faithful, paying, praying member of his congregation. Saved and sanctified.

"I don't know," he said. Then he added, "Except treat him like a Christian. There ain't no other way, is there?" he asked Wendlin.

"No. Not so long as we treat Pete and Julian the same way."

"Oh, I know that. And it don't bother me any, turning the other cheek to Basil Cudlip. But I don't cotton to Pete and Julian having to turn theirs."

Wendlin put a hand on LeRoy's arm. "It's their Christian privilege, LeRoy," he said, "as much as yours. If they want it."

"I know that, Wendlin," he said humbly. "Every man's got a right to his own holiness."



15  At the tent church, Chad Lewis, with no building to lean against, leaned against a wheel of the Lewis's wagon, listened to the horses, Diamond and Chinopsee, munching away in their feed bags, and watched the settlers arriving for the meeting. They all irritated him, and he endured the misery of feeling that his irritation was unjustified. The other young people were playing games with the kids, trying to bridge the space between strangeness and acquaintanceship

with running, loud noises, collisions; with the artificiality of choosing up sides, of pretending animosity for pretended enemies.

The grownups' bridge was talk. "So you're from Ohio? My husband was born just outside Wilmington." "How many barrels of water do you use a week?" "You're located over on the west side of the Tract, aren't you?" "What do you think of Sylvester Perkins?" That was the kind of talk they had, and Chad thought it empty.

Talk didn't please him, screaming didn't please him, his own silence didn't please him. I'm a born kill-joy, he thought. They had driven over together, Ben Jessup and the rest of his family, tender and cooing as doves. But not silly, nothing he had any right to hold against them. They were just happy, that was all. He had listened to them like a rock that longs to be human, but doesn't know how. His mother had ridden with one arm across his father's shoulders, the other snuggling Zoomy. Zoomy was still full of Old Silver. He had been able to figure him out a hero in spite of everything.

Chad himself had sat on the back seat between Ellen and Ben Jessup. For all of those two, he could have been a stone. He didn't know what Ellen had to be so happy about. Her own words appeared to delight her. She lingered over them as if parting with them was almost more than she could bear. She talked automobiles with Jessup. What Ellen knew about automobiles wouldn't fill the eyetooth of a bird. But she had seen one recently, and with that to go on, she was an expert. Ben Jessup had encouraged her. He had taken her ignorance like a jewel, polished and examined it; it would take some plain talk from big brother to get her straightened out again.

Women didn't care whether there was any truth in what they said; if a man listened to them, that was all they asked. "A ship of land," his mother had said, and because that struck his father's fancy, she didn't examine the idea for truth. The first fact about a ship was that it was made for travel and capable of motion. The fact was, he hated himself and the life he was leading. He hated himself because by wanting much he got so little of what he wanted. He defeated himself and all his resolutions, day by day and night by night.

He saw his mother making for him with a girl in tow. Short of jumping into the wagon and slashing up the horses, he didn't know any way of escape. Even by moonlight, the girl wasn't pretty. And she was as far from springing toward him as he was from springing toward her; but with his mother's arm through hers, she didn't have much chance to balk.

"Chad," his mother said, "here's somebody else who doesn't like games."

"I like games all right," he said, nipping that bond in the bud.

"Here's somebody who isn't playing games."

He didn't see any way to contradict that, so he kept his mouth shut.

"Chad, this is the Reverend Raunce's daughter, Crystal."

Crystal. Oh God, he thought. Crystal Chandelier Raunce. Seventeen crystal water goblets. Oh, my precious watch crystal, let's break the glass and buy a new timepiece. "Howdy," he said.

"Chad," his mother said, "I'd like to speak to you in private. Excuse us, please," she said to the preacher's crystal daughter, and she put a strong thumb and forefinger between the muscles of his arm and led him up to the heads of the horses and whispered over their munching and the yells of the ante-over kids, "She was alone and crying, Chad. Now you be nice to her."

He didn't ask her, Why don't you take her to Ellen? They both knew why. First, Ellen didn't need anybody; second, misery loves company; and third, whenever possible, kill two birds with one stone.

His mother did not take any chances on his escaping, but marched him right back to the girl. And the girl, who had had her fair chance to escape, had not taken it. She was still there. It meant something to him, though he would never have admitted it, least of all to her.

His mother said, as if they were four-year-olds, "There'll be refreshments later, I understand."

Neither replied. They were somewhat united by their shared silence and discourtesy. His mother started to leave, then hesitated, like somebody at a sickbed, fearful lest, the minute her back is turned, the patient will die. But she had to chance it, trust them to stay alive together.

The girl Crystal began by accusing him.

"I suppose you feel sorry for me."

The one he felt sorry for was himself. He hadn't wasted an iota of pity on her. "Nope," he said. "Why should I feel sorry for you?"

"Didn't your mother tell you I was crying?"

"That's what she said. But my mother's a well-known liar," he added indifferently.

"There were tears on my face," she admitted.

"But that's not crying. My poor old mother, she sees tears and thinks that means crying."

"You're not crying if you don't make any sounds."

"What you're talking about is sobbing. Nobody said you was sobbing. What you were doing is crying. If you shed tears, you are crying. You go around giving different names to things than other people do and what they'll think you are is crazy, not crying. And they'll be right."

"They're the ones who are crazy."

"That's what crazy people always say."

"How do you know?"

He laughed, in spite of himself. He didn't like her but he was glad to laugh. He was always handing out laughs to other people, and nobody ever thought to hand him one back. He took another look at her. If asked what was wrong with her, he didn't know what he could say. They had run out of conversation and needed someone to help them part as much as they had needed someone to bring them together. They faced outward from the wagon, watching the talking grownups and the playing children. There was one girl neither playing nor talking.

"There's one pretty girl on the Tract anyway!" Chad exclaimed, looking at this self-possessed nonplayer, and was ready immediately afterward to bite his tongue out. "Even if you aren't" was what this had said, and while it was the truth, he knew plenty of truths he intended to keep to himself, particularly the mean ones. He was too mixed up with a lot of mean truths himself.

The preacher's daughter did not flinch. "There are two pretty girls on the Tract. The one you're looking at is Medora Cudlip."

Medora Cudlip, like themselves, was neither playing with the kids nor talking with the grownups; but unlike them, she had not slunk off to hide her aloneness. She stood out in the open, calm and visible as a lighthouse, and let the ante-over players who swept around her figure out for themselves how to avoid a collision.

He tried to make amends to Crystal. "Pretty, if you like them dark," he said, which was fifty per cent of the truth. The other fifty per cent was that he did.

The preacher's daughter—he could no more think of her as Crystal than he could think of her as china or cast iron—was evidently used to playing second fiddle.

"I expect *you*'d like her. Most people don't."

The minute they had something to talk about, Crystal proved herself just as contrary as he had guessed she was. She left him for Medora, but instead of bringing Medora over to him, as he had expected, she linked arms with her, and together the two girls walked into the tent.

16   S H E L   L E W I S   entered the tent with three of the five he had driven over to the meeting. Chad had disappeared the minute they had arrived without so much as a by-your-leave; Ben Jessup had stayed long enough to say, "Thanks for the lift," then he, too, had left.

Once inside the tent, Shel made the place they would sit a subject of study. He had an inclination to take a back seat, but overcame it. He was finished with living like that, with hovering on the edges and hoping for the longed-for. It was his intention to claim the longed-for.

The tent was as seething with movement as a can full of worms. There was a smell of people who obviously had no water to waste on bathing; but there was a smell, too, of stubble fields and of sage hills and of dusty, sun-soaked, roadside flowers. Shel felt like a man going to a show of some kind: he half expected to see minstrels in blackface or Chautauqua ladies in sailor hats singing a boating song. Or maybe, he thought, I feel like old Ben Franklin, getting ready to draw up the bylaws for his country. Some country, he smiled to himself, recalling the Tract's brown hills; some Franklin, too, for that matter. But he remembered Ben with the loaf under his arm; so though Ben had traveled faster and farther than he had, their start hadn't been so different.

He guided his family out into the aisle, letting them see and be seen. Zoomy and Ellen were red-cheeked with excitement. There was a big heavy pulse at the base of Ellen's throat, and Zoomy held his mouth open, the better to take the wonder in. Shel guided Joicey with a light finger on her arm. He felt so tender toward her, he had a hard time not making a show of his feelings. But that was another of the things he was against: men fondling their wives in public, like pets bought and paid for; huddling up against them in church like old rams hunting warmth on a day of pinching cold. Joicey understood; he'd been at pains to see that she did, so that she wouldn't think, seeing others at their hand games, that the inclination wasn't in him. It was in him,

121

all right, but he'd honor this woman in public in a courting way, nothing his by rights. Every touch would ask, not take.

He stopped to make his family acquainted here and there. He wasn't sure how Joicey would take her second sight of Rosa and Pete; or how Rosa and Pete, now clothed and upright, would greet them after that earlier, embarrassing meeting. That earlier meeting could have been a funeral or a wedding, something public and ceremonial, for all the self-consciousness anybody showed. Even Joicey, her feelings now tempered by knowledge of what they all shared, was gracious as a wedding guest.

He made Joicey acquainted with Mrs. Wendlin Jessup. Wendlin himself was up front with Sylvester Perkins and LeRoy Raunce, arranging procedures. Mary Jessup reached up and took Joicey's hands in both of hers.

"I've got a daughter who looks a sight like you," she said. "I'm glad you've come. You'll make me less homesick for Paula."

"Where is your daughter?" Joicey asked politely.

"China. Away in China. She's a missionary. I'm so proud of her. Help me with the refreshments tonight, will you? I need somebody I can rely on."

Shel was as proud of Joicey as could be, recognized as reliable the minute she set foot on the Tract. It was his intention to take his family right down to the front rows, but Joicey, after they left Mary Jessup, whispered to him, "Shel, let's sit where we can see people in front of us." So he began to hunt for four seats together and maybe near someone he knew, so Joicey could get a start in her neighboring.

It was Ellen, not he, who saw the people they could sit with. "There's Mr. Mount, Papa. We can sit behind him."

Mount was with Lute Cope.

"Where's your girls?" Shel asked Lute, after the introductions were over. "Your oldest and my girl here must be about of an age."

"Press is seventeen," Lute said, "and at home I get to thinking of her as a young lady. But get her out with a bunch of kids and she starts rioting around like the youngest. That's where she is now. What're you doing, sitting in here with us old folks?" he asked Ellen.

Shel held his tongue, hoping Ellen would find hers, and, for a wonder, she did. "I can play ante-over any time, Mr. Cope."

Lute laughed. "You got a real politician here, Shel. Or coquette, I'm not sure which. Preferring our company to ante-over."

122

"And saying so," Tom Mount said, turning around to smile at Ellen. "That's what counts."

"You better run her for the school board or something, Shel," Lute said.

"She'd be my only chance to make it. My oldest boy'd rather bite a nail in two than be caught saying a nice word to anybody."

"He playing ante-over, too?"

"Not Chad. I don't know where he is."

"How old's he?"

"Nineteen."

"He interested in the water situation here?"

"He don't know there is a water situation."

"Me either," Joicey put in, killing two birds with one stone: defending Chad and proving she wasn't tongue-tied.

"Wait till you start hauling water, Mrs. Lewis. Then you'll know it."

But Shel was not going to let her off that easy, pretending she didn't know there was a water situation. "It's like this, Joicey," he said, not that he hadn't said it before, but this was one time she'd have to listen, or pretend to, "everybody on the Tract got a share of water stock with each share of land he bought." He waited to let this sink in. "That clear?"

"Yes," Joicey said. Then, as an afterthought, she asked, "What's a share of water stock?"

Lute Cope laughed. "What's your answer to that, Shel?"

"It's a promise, Joicey, to deliver to each acre of land a fifth of a miner's inch of water."

"What's a miner's inch?" Joicey asked.

"You sure make me homesick for my wife, Mrs. Lewis," Lute said. "I didn't know how lonesome I was for talk like this."

"It's enough water per acre to irrigate citrus stock. That's all you need to know. We bought it and we paid for it and we haven't got it."

"Maybe Perkins fooled you, outright," Tom Mount said. "Maybe you've been sold a gold brick."

Shel bridled. "There's water, all right. We didn't buy blind. We know what the water levels are, down by the Santa Ana where the wells are being sunk."

"What's holding them up, then?"

"Workers are hard to get, steel's hard to get. The rainfall's been the lightest in years, so the pumps have got to go deeper than was planned."

"Perkins'd better get you up there on the platform with him. To help excuse him."

"I'm not excusing him, but I'm not fooling myself about facts either. Water won't come out of any made-up story—on our side or his. The fact is, we bought land and water, and the land without water is just about as useless as the other way around. Maybe more so. I'd rather eat fish than ground squirrels."

"You found that out?" Lute asked.

"Two chaws is enough to learn you that, Lute."

"So you plan to be reasonable?"

Tom Mount had swung around in his chair, and Shel examined his face. It was a big tired face tonight, and Shel noticed for the first time that the eyes, which in daylight appeared deep blue, were hooded with a film of white. Mount's question was in order. He was asking for information. But there was some slight in it. A man on the outside, nothing at stake, drinking the water somebody else hauled, didn't have the right to come by information so easy or to care so little which way the answer went. Don't he know he's asking us about how we plan to live and die? Don't he know that when he says 'reasonable' that way, he's like a man watching a fight and egging the fighters on? Shel had no idea what was in his own face, but some of his thoughts must have shown, for Tom Mount's face pinked up a little and his eyes met Shel's finally unveiled.

While Shel was unraveling his own thoughts about Tom Mount, Lute Cope gave Mount his answer. "You got any better plan, Tom?"

"How about fighting?"

If there was going to be a fight, Lute Cope was the man, in Shel's opinion, who ought to head it up. He was the right age—Shel supposed him to be ten years his senior—he was better educated than most of them, his newspaper years had taught him the ins and outs of people, and he had his own land, which meant he had his own money and his own future to think about, too. Shel didn't intend to take a back seat—unless he saw a man clearly marked to be up front. He thought Cope was that man, and he was ready to enlist under him.

There were other men on the Tract he admired. Raunce was a hard worker, but crazy as a grasshopper and spitting Bible texts like tobacco juice. Asa Brice was in some ways another oddity; though what was odd about minding your own business, growing sweet potatoes

124

instead of oranges, and watching birds instead of courting girls, he couldn't say. It was this last that made him wonder. Any man past twenty not married or trying to marry struck him as a halfway suicide. That man either had been scamped in his make-up or he lacked imagination. Either way Shel didn't fathom him.

He wondered some about Tom Mount, no bird-lover, he'd lay his bottom dollar. Anyway, he didn't strike him as a bachelor.

There were plenty of people who took Wendlin Jessup to be the Tract's leading citizen, but Wendlin was too calm and easygoing; he'd make a joke of anything. If you had to lose, be on Wendlin's side; he'd teach you how to smile while eating crow. I don't plan on needing that knowledge, Shel thought. Base Cudlip, on the other hand, didn't have a calm, easygoing bone in his body. Shel looked across the tent to where Base sat, reared up amidst his younguns like a crested cock. The man had rubbed him the wrong way. They were from the same state, and Shel worked against his instincts to give the man his due. What's the matter with you? he asked himself. You want to be the only Kaintuck crowing on the dung heap? Ben Jessup was maybe the best man he'd ever known. Shel had a lot of respect for goodness, but it was Ben's present purpose to model himself on Jesus Christ, which might fit him for the pulpit but not for leading a fight for water; his model, being One who had turned water into wine, might give Ben the idea a miracle would serve here. Shel didn't think they could afford to bank on it.

No, Lute Cope was the man, and Shel, having elected him, was on the point of giving him the news and giving him his hand, too, saying, Captain, I'm Lieutenant Shelby Lewis reporting for duty. In his own struggle toward self-reliance, Shel could still use a model. He had a bump of veneration on his skull. He had a yearning for nobility. He could accept—he'd had to—the meanness and nastiness of the human race, but, by God, what he hankered for was a man who could rise up, steadfast in the face of it, and conquer it. He was still hurt, admit it or not, by that old drifter he'd left back there in the Kentucky hollows; he was still hunting examples to refute him, men whose lives would say to him, Shel, you don't have to be a man like your pappy. Shel made a halfway motion of his hand to touch Lute, get his attention, and say plainly what was on his mind, "I'm behind you, Lute, I'm backing you up. You can depend on me."

But by the time he'd steeled himself to be so outspoken, Lute was busy with two ladies who were asking him if the seats on the other side of Tom Mount were being saved. Shel looked up into the faces of Eunice Fry and Opal Tetford.

"I was saving them for Press and Hannah," Lute, reluctant to seem discourteous, said hesitantly.

Opal was equally reluctant to have Lute blaming himself. "There's lots of other seats, Lute. Don't you worry."

The meeting had obviously excited these ladies; the chance for a little party had gone to their heads. Eunice Fry, usually so calm she was not much more noticeable than a tree or an outcropping of stone, was all ablaze, a tree on fire or an outcropping blasted open to show a vein of gold. Shel stared at her, forgetting to introduce his family. He was abashed before so open a display of feeling. He felt he should warn her that the occasion was not up to it, that starting out at this pitch, she was in for a disappointment. She had her excuses, he knew; those two ladies had been living a hard lonely life, doing a man's work in getting their land cleared and their house raised. Still, this was a meeting for water: it wasn't Christmas, the Fourth of July, or a June wedding. And he didn't overlook, either, the fact that the two seats they'd picked were, just by chance, next to the only two unaccompanied men of a suitable age in the tent. In their shoes, living a womanless life, he reckoned he'd be breathing hot and heavy, too. But able still to breathe through my nose, I hope, he thought, looking at Eunice's opened mouth.

He introduced Joicey and the kids. Eunice gazed at Joicey; no, she gazed at the two of them, at him *and* Joicey, as if entranced. He didn't know what was so remarkable about them; they were neither one beauties, a mill-run married couple, perhaps a little happier than usual tonight. Eunice continued to stare at them in smiling satisfaction, as if they were Exhibit A at a zoo, as if she could now go home and say "I told you so" to somebody.

Joicey, since the ladies made no motion to leave, said, "If you'd like to sit with us, I'll ask the children to move up front. There's still plenty of chairs up there."

Opal wouldn't hear to it, but Eunice would. She thought it would be very nice to get acquainted with Joicey and said so. Ellen wasn't happy about moving, but she was too nice a girl to let it show much. Zoomy was willing to move anywhere and the oftener the better. Shel and Joicey stood up, the children squeezed out, the ladies squeezed in. Shel had conscious flesh tonight, and, without looking, he saw Eunice Fry steady herself with a lingering hand on Tom Mount's shoulder as she passed behind him. Tom Mount, evidently thinking someone wanted to speak to him, turned around. The tired hooded eyes of the water discussion had completely disappeared; color burned in his cheeks, and under the surface blue of his eyes were layers of purple and violet. Seeing that it was only the Fry woman, he turned back without speaking or changing expression. But Shel was so impressed by the change in the man he wondered whether it was actually there, or whether his own eyes earlier had mistaken what they saw.

The meeting was about to come to order. Raunce had joined his wife in the front row. On the platform, Wendlin and Sylvester Perkins, with glances that said, "Be quick" and "Be quiet," were eying the stragglers. Ben Jessup and his friend Asa Brice also made a bid for the seats Lute was saving and were sent on up front to look further. They settled for the two beside Ellen and Zoomy, and Shel was glad. He knew Ellen was of an age when her pride—he thought it was her pride—made her enjoy the attentions of a young man in public.

17    AFTER Crystal left him, Chad felt lonesomer than ever. If he had been nice to Crystal, he could now be talking to the prettiest girl, or, at the very least, the second prettiest girl, on the Tract. He leaned back against the wagon wheel, shut his eyes, and wondered what he could do with his life here in the hills. He wasn't a born farmer, like his father, and so far he didn't have the education for anything else. He would have to help his father through the clearing and planting stages. After that, he intended to break away: where and to what, he didn't know. His father was content to own his own land, to make a living. There was a step beyond that, and he intended to take it: not just make a living; starve, if necessary, but be himself, do what he alone could do. Whatever that was. In his eagerness to repudiate the old life and begin the new, he took a step, eyes still closed, forward.

By God, he thought, I won't be stuck here.

As he moved forward, he was crashed into, and, except that he was still anchored by one hand to the carriage, would have been knocked down. He opened his eyes, but he couldn't see—and whoever had run into him was now using him as a prop to lean against. His head rang,

127

his lip was split, his teeth felt loose in their sockets. The minute he got breath and sight back, he intended to give the blind careless fool as good as he had received. Before his sight cleared, it came to him that he was being leaned on by a girl. He opened his eyes, and because the girl still had her eyes closed, he had a good chance to look at her.

What he saw caused him to swallow as much blood as he could and to try to lick his lips clean. His anger disappeared automatically. So this was the way a girl looked when she was beautiful! Immediately, he felt that with this girl looks didn't matter. She was the soul of beauty, and with the homeliest face in the world would still have been irresistible. The girl opened her eyes, and what looked out from her eyes and trembled on her lips would, he knew, transform any face in the world. He had never in his life felt such tenderness.

She put her hand to her forehead. The blow that had split his lip had been delivered by her forehead; a knot like a clenched muscle was forming there. She shut her eyes again and swayed away from him.

He, whose hands had ached so many times to touch a girl, any girl whatsoever, now had, through necessity, to touch this beautiful one. It was his duty to steady her, support her, hold her upright. She was as alive and soft as any small animal, any rabbit or squirrel or kitten. He had misjudged the way a girl would feel. Their clothes were misleading. He would never have guessed that you could feel *them* so much beneath all their layers of clothing. She could have been naked, for all he was aware of cloth. She sank against him, limp as a stunned bird, and rested her head in the hollow between his neck and shoulder, a hollow he deepened for her comfort by rounding his shoulders. He put his arms clear around her, but very lightly. He could feel the lift and fall of her bosom against him.

Over the shoulder of the girl he held, he saw Crystal, who had come to the door of the tent, looking straight at him. He didn't mind if she considered him a fast worker. He didn't mind the other way either.

The girl in his arms lifted her face from his shoulder. "I think I am going to be sick to my stomach," she said.

There was nothing he knew more about. Zoomy threw up as easily as he swallowed, which was easy. The first thing needed for puking was privacy. Even Zoomy, not very shy about some things most people did in private, didn't like to puke in full sight of anyone. Chad led the girl gently behind the wagon, put one of her hands on a wagon wheel for support, and then turned away, prepared, for her sake, to be deaf and blind. He couldn't help hearing, and she sounded so pitiful in her misery that he went to her and put a steadying hand against her cold damp forehead. She leaned against his hand, far too sick to worry about his being a young man. When she was better, he got their canteen from the carriage, so that she could rinse her mouth; after her mouth was rinsed, he gave her his handkerchief for a towel. She wiped her face and hands and stopped her swaying. His entire body ached for the return of her touch, but short of another accident, he didn't know whether he would ever be able to touch her again. There was some bond, though. He could feel it and he could feel her reluctance to leave.

She said, "I won't give you back your handkerchief. I'll take it home and wash it and iron it."

Those were the sweetest and wisest words he had ever heard in his life. Now they would meet again, and she had figured out a way. That they would meet again seemed, for a second, all he wanted in this world; but as soon as he had that, he wanted more. He wanted her to stay; but his fear that she would leave paralyzed his mind so that he could not think of a single word that would detain her. She had no intention of leaving him.

"Your lip is bleeding," she said.

"Oh, no," he said, "no, it's not. It's nothing." But when he saw she intended to wipe away the blood with his handkerchief, he willed himself to bleed again. She was very gentle. "I ought to be shot for being so awkward," she said. "Crashing into you like a streetcar."

"Oh, you weren't awkward. It was all my fault. I had my eyes shut or I could've sidestepped you. I might've killed you. How do you feel now?"

"Empty," she said.

He laughed for the second time in an hour. Poor Zoomy, he thought, he tries so hard, and any girl evidently can tickle my funny bone without half trying.

"What's so funny?" she asked.

"You," he said daringly, and was shut up at once by his own daring.

But she was not defeated by his silence or his awkwardness. He began to relax, to trust her. She was not going to leave him and she would make things easy for them while she stayed. He waited on her now; he let her alone without any help; she would bring them a subject to talk about. She brought the horses. She walked to their heads, looked them over, and said, "This is the most unmatched team of horses I ever saw."

He laughed again, in the way his father didn't like, silently. He took the feed bags off the horses so she could see the full extent of their unmatchedness.

"What are their names?" she asked.

"This one," he said, putting his hand on the black's muzzle, "is Chinopsee."

She echoed the name, as he had hoped she would. "Chinopsee? What a funny name for a horse." She tried it out, experimented with the word in her mouth. "Get up, Chinopsee." The black pricked his ears in her direction.

"It's an Indian name. It means blackbird."

"Does he skim along? Does he fly?"

"He skims and he flies."

"We wouldn't call a black horse 'Blackbird,' would we?"

"We?" He repeated the word, for a second breathless with its intimacy, with her linking of the two of them.

"White people," she explained.

"Oh. No, we'd call him Nigger or Blackie."

"What's the name of the other one?"

"Diamond." Diamond was a dapple gray, flashier than the black, a horse to pull the lord mayor's coach.

"Which one do you like best?"

Even her questions show how unusual she is, he thought. He had often speculated about Diamond and Chinopsee, about their differences and what caused them. So far as he knew, there wasn't another person in the world interested either in these differences or in his speculations about them. As he began to answer her question (and it was because she had asked it, or because she was listening), he was filled with a profound knowledge of horses and their habits, a knowledge he had never had before. As he spoke and she listened, the sounds of people talking, of children playing, became faint. The girl and he were alone under the great sailing moon. The two horses by their side were quiet, except for an occasional jingle of harness; the crickets and katydids at their feet chirred in the nighttime warmth and light. He told a story he was amazed to hear. What he had to say about horses seemed to have meanings pertinent to the whole world. He was clearing up mysteries for himself as he went along.

If you got to the bottom of one subject, did the truth about all other subjects lie there, too? If you knew one thing fully, did you, in a way, know all? Was that the reason old farmers and coon hunters were so wise?

Once before in his life he had been drunk. At the age of sixteen, he had sampled a jug of raw corn whisky. He had felt a kind of power at the time: as if he had transcended himself, were suspended above himself. This enabled him to see a lot of the world ordinarily not visible; he saw also his own smallness in this world.

Now he was drunk again, but in an entirely different way. He was more himself than he had ever been before; and this was happening at the very minute when he was also more aware of another person than he had ever been before. How could this be? It contradicted all the rules of arithmetic. To give himself away and to have more left. He felt like saying his own name over and over again: Chadwick Lewis, Chadwick Lewis. That was who he had been, but might never be again; for this girl was making him over by listening to him.

Though it was not a one-sided conversation. He was not delivering a lecture on horses. He could never have done it without her. She taught him all his powers, showed him all his meanings. Until she asked her questions, he didn't know his answers. He had never in his life felt so radiant. She looked at him, she asked. He spoke. Something towered upward out of the interchange; together they opened up meanings he had never glimpsed before. About horses? That was the subject, but the night and the clear dry Western stars, the world and the Tract, her soft body and his supporting one were not excluded.

When he gave his attention to the words they spoke, he was amazed all over again. There was nothing in them.

"We were fooled with Chinopsee. He's a saddle horse."

"Won't he work?"

"In his own way. He wants to lope."

"I like to lope."

"Horseback, it's all right. It's not right with a carriage. Or with another horse. Or plowing."

"Doesn't Diamond like it?"

"Diamond doesn't want to be part of a team, even. Diamond wants to do everything alone. He pulls nine-tenths of every load. This old blackbird lopes along for the fun of it."

"What does Diamond think of that?"

"Sometimes he balks. Feel here."

He took her hand and guided it under Diamond's belly to the hairless welts. "Feel those?"

He felt her shudder all along her arm. "What are they?"

"Scars where a fire was built under him to make him move."

"Who did that?"

"My father. But he put out the fire."

He still had her hand, which he had guided to the scars. The sounds which earlier had dimmed had now ceased altogether. The people had gone inside. The meeting had begun. She swayed in his direction as she had done when she was beginning to be sick. In the clear moonlight he could see her face distinctly. It was lifted to him serenely. He leaned to her, and they kissed, very gravely and quietly, as though taking an oath. They drew apart, though he still held her hand, and looked at each other. Girls had been much in his mind lately. He had spent entire nights, it seemed to him, thinking of them: not only thinking of them as flesh, but as flesh separated into distinct and hidden parts. He had felt dirty a good deal of the time. How could he have guessed that he could be cleansed of this feeling by holding a flesh-and-blood girl in his arms? For she was in his arms now. It was nothing whatsoever like his imaginings. She was not arms, legs, breasts, but a person. Tears came to his eyes. The only act he could think of now that would be worthy of her and of his own feelings would be to die for her without her ever knowing it.

They did not kiss again. She put her cheek to his very softly and gently, then drew away from him.

"My father will be worried about me," she said, "if I don't come."

He watched her run toward the tent. She ran with the same headlong speed that had carried her crashing into him. She has not learned a thing, he thought, smiling. And he didn't want her to.

He decided not to go into the meeting. The proceedings would interfere with his thinking about her. After a few minutes, it came to him that she was at the meeting and that inside the tent he could look at her as well as think about her.

Crystal Raunce, an usher for the meeting, met him when he entered the tent.

"What's her name?" he demanded.

"Whose name?"

"Whose name?" He didn't understand how anyone could be so dense. "The girl I was with, of course."

"Why didn't you say so? Pressley Cope."

"Pressley Cope." He could not say her name without smiling. Smiling hurt his lip, and he put his hand to it.

"What's the matter with you?" Crystal asked. "Did you get in a fight?"

He was already trying to locate Pressley Cope. "A fight? No, I had an accident." He could not help smiling again, even though it hurt his lip. "A lucky accident."

Crystal watched him going slowly down the aisle. Four hours ago, she had said, "I am Crystal J. Raunce. I don't need another person in the world." Now she felt as if her evening had ended as he walked away from her.

When Press joined her father, as breathless and excited as Eunice had been, Shel was convinced that there really must be something queer about him and Joicey. Press Cope also stared at them, turning around in her seat to do so. She was white-faced, her eyes looked feverish, and she had a knot on her forehead the size of a turkey egg.

Tom Mount, who sat next to her, spoke to her. Either Press did not hear him or decided to ignore him.

Eunice Fry leaned forward and touched her shoulder.

"Mr. Mount is speaking to you, Press."

Press said, "I'm sorry," but did not speak to Mount. Instead, she said to Shel, "Do you have a son?"

"Yes," Shel said, not bothering to mention Zoomy.

"I've been talking to him."

Shel said, "I'm glad to hear it. It looks more like you might have been fighting him."

"Oh, no," Press began, but her father shushed her.

Wendlin Jessup was on his feet, waiting for the crowd to quiet down.

Asa Brice's heart sank as he saw Wendlin get to his feet. Up to this time, the Tract had been a certain section of rolling hill land in Southern California and no more. Its people were individuals, individual families, individual men and women, all looking out for themselves. Men had stood on barley-stubble hilltops and planted the acres below them with their eyes and picked oranges with their imaginations. Men saying, "I'll make out. Me against wind, weather, and the Perkins Investment Company." Now they were going to band together, every man willing to be a little less in order to get a little more. Now they were going to adopt rules and frame regulations. Now they were going to elect officers and appoint committees. Now they would extend the right hand of fellowship—but only on official occasions: in lodge halls and chamber of commerce meetings and at church suppers.

Asa felt as if he were attending a funeral. Farewell to the wild land: the land open to road runners and trap-door spiders, to winds and fogs, to cactus and greasewood. The land that had been free to voyage silently under the stars, subject to nothing but its own laws, was going to be made to earn its keep like any yoked oxen.

If it wasn't a funeral, then it was a wedding, and something sweet was going to be wed to something coarse. The union was going to be blessed by Raunce, who, at a motion from Wendlin, had risen to his feet. Now is the time, Asa thought, for me to stand up and give my reasons for believing that these two should not be united in holy matrimony. Speak now or forever after hold my peace. He held his peace. He knew the reasons and he held his peace.

Raunce's prayer was short. Thanks to God for these gifts, and a petition that His gifts be used for man's good and God's glory; which, Raunce said, were one and the same. Amen. He sat down, taking the audience, prepared for something much more long-winded, by surprise. All of the audience, that is, except Base Cudlip, who was on his feet the minute Raunce sat down.

"Mr. Chairman," he called out in his lingering Southern voice, a tart little "ah," like a pendant crab apple dangling at the close of each of his words, "I'd like to have the flo-ah."

Old Wendlin smiled. He could not have looked more benign, but the flo-ah was nothing he intended to relinquish to Base Cudlip. He had a surprisingly strong voice when he wanted to unleash it, and Cudlip's tenor was smothered under its big rumble.

"Mr. Cudlip, motions from the floor are not now in order. Ladies and gentlemen, let us all stand and unite in singing 'My Country 'tis of thee.'"

Cudlip, who was already standing, appeared, as he was joined by the others, to be a leader instead of a dissenter. He could not, under the circumstances, sit down, but he was far from happy joining in. Asa, with pleasure, watched him scowling and squirming. Wendlin had him boxed in for the time being, anyway. Either Cudlip'll keep his mouth shut or mingle his singing voice with those of the dark skins present.

Asa, himself no singer, turned about to watch those who were. Ellen

Lewis sang "Land of the Pilgrims' pride" as if she had herself set foot on Plymouth Rock. "Sweet land of liberty," her father sang.

You are met here to sing away your liberties, Asa thought: farewell, sweet land of springtime flowers and autumn fallow. Farewell, sweet land of coyotes and road runners, of Mariposa lilies and soapweed and yellow violets.

But who are you for, Brice, he asked himself, the land or the people? What would you give to be able to trade your arroyo for Ellen's tears or Shel's belief? He opened his mouth to sing. He couldn't do it. He hadn't joined in anything like that for too long a time.

Two men stayed on their feet as the singing finished and the others sat down: Sylvester Perkins and Base Cudlip. Before Cudlip could get in a word, Perkins said, "Mr. Cudlip, your question as to who's invited to this meeting has been passed on to me. The answer is: One and all. This isn't my answer alone. It's Reverend Raunce's answer. He owns this tent. He's the chairman of this meeting. You're welcome and so is every other resident of the county. Or the state, for that matter. We're pleased to see the widespread interest this Tract is arousing in men and women from all walks of life and to have as many as are interested in attendance. Does that answer your question, Mr. Cudlip?"

"It does," said Mr. Cudlip, and without more ado he got his wife and children onto their feet. With them standing, he added, "And this is my answer." Then, walking behind his family like a drover behind cattle, he nudged his little herd outside.

Wendlin Jessup, as they left, said, "It's the second Secession, folks."

The crowd laughed, but they noticed, too, that the Secession was not complete. Medora Cudlip had stayed in the tent. In spite of Wendlin's joke, Cudlip's leaving was embarrassing. This was secession before a union had been established. If they could not even get started together, how were they going to carry on together?

If Sylvester Perkins felt any uneasiness, he did not show it. He let the Cudlips file out. He let his audience wait. He stood up there, his very lack of any marked superiority reassuring them, and let them wait on him. He was their reason for being here, on these hills and under this tent. Without him, they would be in other states and under other roofs. Then, with his first sentence he surprised everyone.

"How many of you today have thought of the war in Europe? I don't mean worried about it or prayed over it or shed tears over it. I mean given it one small thought."

He threw this out at them, and Asa saw the sudden indwelling-

n the faces around him as men and women, thinking back, held
elves accountable for their forgetfulness and accused themselves
...ishness.

"Last month, on a single day the British lost sixty thousand men on
the Somme."

The faces, as Asa watched them, said, We could've spared them a
thought. We could've taken our minds off weir boxes and standpipes
for the space of a minute. We could've remembered that blood is
thicker than water. Perkins's listeners went that far with him. But only
that far. Already Asa saw other questions forming in their minds:
How's our going without water going to help them? They won't die
any easier because we're thirsty. Perkins may be a humanitarian, but
he's not selling the Tract for humanitarian purposes. He's here to
make money. That's all right. We're all here to do that. But if Perkins
is planning to make his at our expense, he can't blind us to it by reminding us of our shortcomings. They waited for his next words, but
they were wary now.

His next words were, "I have thought about it today. It's been on my
mind most of the day. But I'm not standing up here taking credit for
that. In my shoes, you'd all be thinking of it. This is something I've
never mentioned. It wasn't in my mind to mention it tonight. But
we're all mixed up here together. You've told me, a lot of you have,
anyway, about your problems and your troubles. This isn't a problem,
though it troubles me. I have . . . we have a son in Europe. An
only child. He's twenty. He joined the Canadian army a year ago. The
Canadian artillery. There's a big push on all along the Somme battle
front. That's where our son is."

Asa was disgusted. He had the sensation of having watched a man
pursued by wolves throw his only son to them.

"As I said," Perkins went on, "perhaps I shouldn't have mentioned
the boy. But why not? I'm proud of him. And it's a fact that some of
our setbacks here on the Tract don't bulk as large in my mind as they
ought to in the face of what he—and other boys like him—are
up against Over There. I mean, here we have this and that difficulty
we hadn't figured on. At the moment, we don't have enough water—
and it's a real drawback. I grant you that. I'm not trying to make a
molehill out of a mountain. But we aren't standing up to our knees
in water in a trench. We're not living on cold rations. We're not separated from our families. We're not listening for the shell that's got
our number on it. Instead—here we are. A peaceful moon overhead.

The sweet flowers at our feet." Perkins indicated Raunce's galvanized pail and churn. "Here we are, living in one of the richest, most picturesque sections of the State of California—and that means the world. Against the bigger background, the world background I'm suggesting, we look pretty lucky. Pretty lucky."

There was not a sound in the audience.

"Pretty lucky. Not one-hundred-per-cent lucky. I understand some of you are getting kind of tired hauling water. That right?"

Now he got his answer. "You bet." "That's right!" "What's holding it up?"

It was too bad about his boy, it was too bad about the war, it was too bad they were all such low-down cusses they'd let a day go by thinking of nothing but their own troubles. But they hadn't come here tonight to win the war for anybody; all they wanted tonight was to make sure they'd get their one-fifth inch per acre—and get it soon.

When the crowd had quieted, Perkins said, "I think the best way to handle this situation is for you to ask questions and for me to answer them. I understand some of you have got some questions?"

They had questions, all right, and they laughed a little at Perkins's question. Nobody was anxious to be the first man on his feet, putting himself forward as a mouthpiece for his neighbors. They weren't anxious, either, that it should appear to Perkins that there were no questions. A half-dozen men stood at once. Perkins recognized Shel Lewis.

It galled Shel to be speaking with Sylvester Perkins's permission, like a good schoolboy. And it offended his idea of how the matter should be handled, his taking the lead instead of Cope. But on his feet and recognized, he had no choice but to open his mouth.

"Mr. Perkins," he said, "there ain't but two questions here tonight. The first may take some time for you to answer. You take your time to it. The second you can answer in three or four words. The first question is: Why hasn't the Perkins Investment Company delivered water as scheduled? The second is: What's the date of delivery?"

Before Shel had seated himself and before Sylvester Perkins could open his mouth to reply, there was a disturbance at the back of the tent. A man's voice called out, "Is there a Mr. Luther Cope present?"

Shel turned with the rest of the crowd to see who was speaking. A young man in a collarless white shirt and wearing a peak-brimmed cap stood in the doorway. Lute lifted his hand to show his presence, and the stranger said, "Excuse me for interrupting, but you're wanted outside, Mr. Cope."

137

18  INDY COPE arrived in Los Angeles at three o'clock on the afternoon of the meeting. No one met her because she had told no one when she was coming. Being met would emphasize, she felt, that she had gone away, had left. If she simply arrived, suddenly and unexpectedly, hung up her hat and coat, unpacked her suitcase and began to peel the potatoes and set the table, her absence might appear almost dreamlike, something that would in time fade from all their memories. Or so she hoped.

She had come by Santa Fe from Chicago, sitting up in the coach all the way. There was no need for such economy. Lute had bought her a round-trip ticket when she left, with Pullman accommodations included. And her father had given her, as he put her on the train, $250 in cash. Lute was not hard-pressed for money, but a berth was a luxury she wanted to forego, as a sign to Lute that she was wholly with him in whatever sacrifices they must face in starting over again.

She stepped off the train immaculate, wide-awake, untired. There was nothing she could not do when excited and challenged. Amidst the hot, harried, bedraggled crowd at the station, she was noticed and she knew it. Because she was naturally shy, the knowledge that she was being looked at made her uncomfortable. She felt like a woman on a stage, but without any reassuring lines to tell her what part she was playing. She dug her fingernails into her palms to hold herself steady under observation. The more she was looked at, the more her color deepened, her back straightened, her gait became elegant and defiant. And the more she was looked at.

"She's on a mighty high horse. Be fun to take her off it." Thus, the men. The women thought only, How does she do it? How does she keep clean amidst the dust and soot of travel? Energetic in the heat? Calm in the confusion?

She was clean and she was energetic, but she was far from calm. Too self-conscious to walk slowly or look carefully, she missed the sign telling her where to claim her baggage. She felt like crying. She had left one life behind her there in her parents' home on the banks of the Ohio; she was ready to begin a new one on the Tract; but in this interval, midway between the two, she was miserable. She sat down on a grimy bench, unclenched her hands, breathed deeply, and refused to cry.

Indy was not prettier than Press, but she seemed to have been deprived of more and was hence more appealing. A stranger in a strange place, she threw her heart, as was her nature, into the enterprise of being strange. She was not putting on an act, though as a person she was in some ways deeply and inherently an act. She had never been taken out of herself. Without this corrective, she found no relief to her feelings except in trying imaginatively to realize herself in each passing emotion.

The dress she wore was responsible for some of the attention she was getting. It was a becoming and fashionable dress, but too close-fitting and of a color inappropriate for travel. She had not worn it on the trip west, but had put it on after lunch in a washroom filled with women bathing and changing their squalling babies. She would not have owned such a dress, lavender summer wool, cut on princess lines which outlined her high-busted, slender-waisted figure, or have bothered to change in such trying circumstances, except for a shock her mother had given her that summer.

Indy was thirty-five years old, the mother herself of a nearly grown daughter. But between Lute, Lute's mother, and the conventional protective pattern of the small town where they all lived, she had not been permitted much experience. She had returned to her home a curiously girlish-hearted thirty-five, ready to be a daughter again to her father and mother. If she had been widowed, her father and mother would have humored this girlish illusion of hers; but she was a grown woman and fugitive wife, and they believed she belonged in her own home, not theirs. Indy made no complaints to them about Lute; and Mrs. Pressley, coming to her own conclusions, had urged pretty dresses, new hairdos, summer colognes, and frilly underwear upon her daughter. She had herself bought two dainty Philippine hand-embroidered nightgowns for Indy. "A man, even the most devoted husband," she said, "is affected by such things." She gave Indy a package of Golden Glint shampoo. "Your hair used to have a lot of high lights in it," her mother explained. "It needs brightening up."

Indy had believed at first that her mother was trying to cheer her up, trying to keep her from being homesick for her girls. When her mother gave her the nightgowns and the hair lightener, she understood that she was being made attractive to Lute; that her mother was in fact trying to make sure that she should not remain a daughter at home. This knowledge, though it had shocked her, had had nothing to do with her decision to return to Lute. That decision was based on Lute's willingness to move away from the town they had lived in and on her own inability to remember when she was away from Lute what it was that she held against him. There were no beatings, infidelities, squandering of money, gambling, drunkenness, indecent sexual demands. There was not even any untidiness about the house. Lute was free as a girl of the usual masculine faults. Away from him, calm, content, even joyous, Indy would think, It is I who must be wrong. If I would be this way at home with Lute, all would be well. So she would leave Lute because of the intolerable empty heavyhearted life they led together, and return to him, ironically, because away from him she became another person.

And this other person, in her determination to lead a better life with Lute, had hearkened to her mother. It was true that she had made no effort to captivate Lute with bright colors, sweet colognes, and lacy underwear. In the first place, Lute was already thoroughly captivated, and in the second, he either never noticed what she wore or how she was scented, or did not think such subjects suitable for talk between husband and wife. But Lute had been willing to start over again, and so would she. The lavender summer wool was the first indication of her intentions. She was also scented with White Lilac, and shampooed with Golden Glint—and whatever the effect on Lute might prove to be, her efforts were not wasted on the patrons of the Santa Fe railway.

She had never before been in Southern California, let alone Los Angeles, and was uncertain as to the best way to get to the Tract. The Pacific Electric Railway, Lute had written her, ran southeast from Los Angeles as far as Whittier, and Whittier was only ten or fifteen miles from the Tract. She would take the Pacific Electric to Whittier, and, once there, she could perhaps hire someone to drive her to the Tract. But, first of all, she had to find her luggage. She got up and made herself walk slowly and calmly through the station, carefully reading every sign. Almost immediately, the "Claim Luggage Here" sign stared her in the face.

She had, besides the grip she had used en route, a small trunk, a box, and two suitcases. While she was wondering what to do, a young man in a peculiar cap, something between a railroad engineer's and a golfer's, stopped beside her. "Ma'am," he said, "are you looking for transportation for your bags?"

She was reassured by both his youth and his cap. His cap indicated that he had a right to speak to her as some kind of a bag-mover, and his youth, even if his cap meant nothing, gave her confidence.

Indy was truly comfortable only with men considerably older or considerably younger than herself. She knew how to be a daughter and she knew how to be a mother. These roles she could play with pleasure. But faced with a man of Lute's age, a man with whom she could be neither filially innocent nor maternally wise, she did not know who to be: she did not know how to be a woman the age of a wife. This was the role she was once again asking Lute to teach her.

The peaked-cap fellow was no problem. He was young and he was trying to be helpful, in the way of young men with older women. She could see he was not anyone officially connected with the station, and this also gave her confidence. She was easily daunted by officials.

"You weren't planning on coping with this stuff yourself, were you?" he asked.

Indy could not resist the pun. "Even with help I'll have to cope with it. That's my name."

The minute she spoke, she was sorry. Here was one place she and Lute saw eye to eye. "It plagues me to death," Lute used to tell her, "this smart-alecky talk of yours to strangers. You'll sit mum as death in a roomful of neighbors, then to someone you don't know from Adam's off ox, you'll make some intimate remark. I know you're not trying to show off or get attention, but that's how it sounds."

She agreed with Lute; and she did not understand, herself. For two days and nights, she had ridden on a train without speaking to anyone. Then the minute she stepped off the train, she began by telling some passing stranger her name.

The stranger said, "We ought to trade jobs. My name is Waite."

"Let's change names instead," Indy said. "You cope and I'll wait." Some breeze of merriment and liveliness stirred in her; she felt suddenly thoroughly awake and expectant.

"Where are you going, Mrs. Cope?"

"To the Tract, Mr. Waite," Indy said.

"The Tract?" Waite asked. "Where's that?"

"It's a new development," Indy told him, "about twenty-five miles southeast of here. The Pacific Electric will take me the first fifteen miles. Can you take me and my things to the depot?"

"That'll be easy," Waite said. "It's not far from here."

Her luggage filled the back of his battered car, and he apologized both for placing her in the front seat and for the condition of the car. "I about live in it," he said.

He missed a turn on the way to the depot, which she would not have known anything about, except that he told her.

"I don't know Los Angeles as well yet as I ought to," he explained.

"Are you a newcomer?" Indy asked.

"We've been in California three months."

Indy wondered about the "we," but said nothing, trying to make up by present restraint for her earlier openness.

It was late afternoon, and light fell down upon them from a cloudless sky like pellucid drops from some towering and hidden waterfall. After the green gloom of the East, Indy was newly aware of light and understood as never before the pioneer's joy in a clearing.

"California is the clearing of the nation," she burst out, forgetful of her resolution to be Lute's ideal woman, silent with strangers. Waite did not understand her and said so. "Clearinghouse?" he asked.

"No. The open space. Open to the sun. Clear of trees."

Waite, busy with his driving, nodded but did not reply. When he pulled up in front of the depot, he turned to her. "Is someone meeting you in Whittier?" he asked.

"No," Indy said, and explained, since it hurt her vanity for him to think that no one cared whether she came or went, that her arrival was to be a surprise.

"How're you planning to get from Whittier to the place you live?"

"I'll have to hire a car, I suppose."

Waite was silent for a second or two, then he said, "I'll drive you to the Tract for whatever your fare on the Pacific Electric would be plus the hire of a car from Whittier."

When Indy did not answer, he said, "I don't think you're going to be able to take all this stuff on a streetcar anyway. Why don't I go in, ask about the fare to Whittier, the charges for carrying baggage, and so forth? Then you'll know exactly where you stand."

Indy had dreaded the inquiring and negotiating that lay ahead of her. If she hired Waite, all that would be taken care of. He stood on the sidewalk, his peak-brimmed cap on the back of his head, awaiting her decision. He looked tired and underfed to Indy, and as if he needed the job. And if he charged her only the Pacific Electric fare to Whittier plus what she would have to pay to get to the Tract, she would not be out any more than if she chose the more difficult trip by streetcar. It was necessary for her to sum up all these advantages to herself and add to them the additional fact that she would undoubtedly be helping a deserving young man before she could say yes. Otherwise, she might have to believe that she was hiring a driver because he was attractive and she liked to talk to him.

"If the charges are the same, I'll be glad to have you drive me."

The young man was just as businesslike as she. "I'll let you know the cost both ways down to the last nickel."

Waite's forthright talk about money pleased her. Lute would never speak of money. It was one of the subjects he did not consider nice. He would overpay rather than ask any questions about a bill. He would never inquire beforehand about prices. He insisted, when they dined out with others, on always being the one who treated. When Indy protested, Lute's face would harden. "Let's not talk about it," he'd say. And to make sure they wouldn't, he would walk off and leave her.

When Waite came back, he said, "You should never have let me go in there. I'm going to have to charge you two dollars more. It would cost you that much to send your trunk out by freight—and you wouldn't get it until two or three days, either. I hope you don't think I'm talking too much about money, but I'm not in this business for my health."

"No, no," Indy told him. "I don't think you're talking too much about money." She thought she could talk money all afternoon with Mr. Waite. The very word "money" struck her as both daring and flattering. And intimate. She felt like a girl who has heard the word "sex" used in public for the first time. A fresh, heady breeze of reality swept across her. Waite respected her common sense, that was the flattering part; and he spoke to her of matters usually hidden, that was the daring part. She was exhilarated. This was no cat-and-mouse conversation on a subject neither cared about.

"Money decides our life," she declared earnestly. "If people won't talk about it, I don't know what they will talk about. Money is important."

"It's sure important to me," Mr. Waite agreed in a flat voice, which, nevertheless, conveyed some surprise.

Indy thought she had perhaps been once again more carried away in her speech with a stranger than was seemly. She kept quiet until they were out toward the end of Seventh Street, where the city smells gave way to the smell of the summer-dried crops of wild mustard and volunteer oats that grew on the vacant lots.

Then, still excited by that word "money," she burst out, "But

143

wouldn't you have made more money staying in town and getting a lot of passengers?"

"I might not've got a lot of passengers. Besides, you're going to the Tract."

"The Tract?" Indy felt suspicious. "I thought you said you didn't know where the Tract was?"

"I didn't. But it's in the right direction."

"The right direction for what?" Indy asked.

Mr. Waite turned to her and smiled. "The right direction to get to Banning."

"Is that where you live?" Indy asked.

"No. But my wife lives there."

Indy said nothing, but her picture of Mr. Waite was changing. What was he, a kind of grass widower, gallivanting around picking up strange women?

"My wife's in Banning for her health," Mr. Waite said.

"I'm sorry," Indy said.

"Sorry for my wife, or for the things you've been thinking?"

"Both," Indy admitted in a low voice. She wanted to tell the truth but she was not often permitted to.

"You like things pretty cut and dried, don't you?" Mr. Waite asked. "You don't care for any surprises."

"That's not what I've always thought about myself."

"You don't like surprises in yourself either, do you?"

Indy changed the subject. She had not the courage for such intimacy. It meant too much to her. She took it as another woman might have taken a kiss. But she had not the strength of character to leave it alone either. She did not change the subject so much as shift it. They, she and Waite, were still the subject, but she shifted the emphasis to him.

"Where is Banning, exactly?"

"It's about seventy-five miles southeast of here, on the edge of the desert. The dry air there has done wonders for other people with lung trouble. I sure hope it helps Rosalie."

"Rosalie?" Indy said, drawn back to herself in spite of her resolution. "My name's Rose. Though I'm not called that."

"You look something like my wife. That's how I first came to notice you. You look like she did when she was younger."

"Younger? I must be a lot older than your wife."

"Rosalie's thirty. Two years younger than me. But consumption ages a person. It wears you down. You've got to live old, with it, whether you are or not."

"It must be terrible for both of you."

"It's hell," Waite said. "For her and for me. And for the kids, too."

"Kids?" Indy asked.

"Two boys. We left them back in Nebraska with their grandmother."

"Why don't you live in Banning?"

"No work. Too many fellows there like me, willing to do anything."

"Your wife must look forward to your visits."

"She does. And when I get there she can't talk."

"Can't talk?"

"She can whisper a little. But she oughtn't to do that. The disease has settled in her throat, and talking keeps her throat from healing. I tell her things. But it's hard to talk when there isn't any answer."

"Yes," Indy said, "it is."

"There's no blame to her, God knows. But that's probably why I'm running on to you. You can talk back."

They had to stop in Whittier for gas, and Waite apologized, both for the stop and for the fact that he had to get an advance from Indy to pay for the gas.

"I've been kind of living from hand to mouth lately," he said.

Indy, who had had to get out of the car while gas was put in, walked about admiring the garage owner's flowers. Across the street, she noticed an eating place called "The Kitchen Café." The building was half hidden under drooping pepper boughs and had waist-high geraniums covering the weathered, unpainted boards, which were met, a little above the geraniums, by screen. The food smelled good, and when Mr. Waite had settled for the gas, she asked him to have supper with her. She felt nervous and daring about issuing such an invitation, but his "living from hand to mouth" had decided her.

"If you're not in too much of a hurry, would you mind stopping to have supper here?" she asked.

"I'm not in too much of a hurry, but I'm too broke," Waite said.

"I've got more than enough money for both of us."

Waite hesitated, then said, "You're the judge of that, I guess. All I'm required to judge is whether or not I'm hungry. And I am."

The Kitchen Café, the minute she stepped inside, pleased Indy. The floor, splintery and unpainted, was well scrubbed. There were ten tables covered with flowered oilcloth. The napkins were in the water glasses, and the cutlery was covered by upturned plates. On each table a round, hard-packed bouquet of oleanders, geraniums, and nasturtiums blazed like a small sun. Pepper boughs dragged their lacy fronds across the roof with the sound of wind. The hard little pepper berries pattered on the dry shingles in cool rainlike flurries. A Mexican boy was irrigating the lemon grove behind the café. He mended the ditches with light clean strokes of his hoe, keeping time to the tune he whistled. Doves, suppering on the pepper berries, wheeled and called about the building. In the palm trees, mockingbirds sang their own songs, though with an undercurrent of the sound of the doves which they could not resist imitating.

The food was cooked by a large Mexican woman and served by a small white man, perhaps her husband. They had no choice about the food, which was a pot roast cooked in some spicy Mexican way, but it was good, and Indy found that after train sandwiches, she, too, was hungry. Except for a family with small children, eating at the other end of the café, they were alone. The waiter, when he had tended to his customers, sat in the kitchen talking to the cook. Perhaps she was not his wife. She laughed a lot at what he said.

"They sound nice, don't they?" Indy asked.

"Yes, they do. I like to hear a woman laugh."

He spoke sadly, Indy thought. She supposed he was thinking of Rosalie, who could no longer laugh.

"I wish Rosalie could be here," she said.

"I do, too. But she can't, so I'll have to enjoy it for both of us. And I do. I don't usually have such luck. Good meal, no expense, somebody beautiful to talk to me."

"Mr. Waite," Indy said immediately and reprovingly.

"What's the matter?" Mr. Waite asked.

She did not know how to answer that question and was sorry she had spoken. There was nothing wrong with it. She wished she could speak as openly as Mr. Waite, could say, Mr. Waite, there is something about your face that makes me very happy. I don't know whether or not it is beauty, but it makes me want to talk to you honestly.

When she did not answer his question, Mr. Waite said, "You're a full-grown woman, a married woman, I see by your rings, though for some reason you haven't told me so. Why beat around the bush about such things? You ought to be glad I think you're beautiful."

Indy was, but the old habits held. "We don't have to say everything we think."

146

"Not if we've got ugly thoughts. Or if they won't do any good. That wasn't an ugly thought."

"Will you tell your wife you told a woman she was good-looking?"

"Beautiful," Mr. Waite said. "No, I won't. Rosalie's prettiness is gone now. And there's no point hurting her bringing back reports of something she's lost. I'd no more tell her that than I'd tell her I met a mighty healthy woman. But I hope some stranger in the days when Rosalie was well and pretty told her so. I was too busy grubbing away in those days to say it. I sure hope some stranger said it for me. I hope she can remember that. Why not? We're men and women. We look at each other. We've got our ideas about what we see. If we see something good, why not say so?"

"I don't know why," Indy answered.

"Well, I know why," young Mr. Waite said, "and I'll tell you. We're so damned starved for some honesty and some hint somebody's really looked at us and seen us and sized us up that when we do hear a word like that we get dizzy. We're so starved for it, it hits us like alcohol. It goes to our heads. Or to places less mentionable. We think someone wants to make love to us. Nothing so terrible about that either, though it's not always the case."

"Who are you?" Indy half whispered.

"You mean, what do I do, don't you? That's how you judge people, isn't it?"

"Yes," Indy said. "That's what I mean, I suppose."

"I've been a dozen things, including farmer, teacher, cook, ditch-digger. Now I'm a taxi driver. Does that answer your question?"

"I don't know. I'm not sure what my question is."

"You needn't act so shocked about my saying you were beautiful. You told me you liked my looks when you let me take care of your luggage instead of getting some redcap."

"What I thought about your looks," Indy said, "was that you were a poor, tired, hungry young man."

"Well, you must like the looks of poor, tired, hungry young men, then."

Up to this moment, Indy had truly not looked at Mr. Waite's face beyond the youthfulness, which had proved false, beyond the hunger, which had vanished, beyond the tiredness, which was no longer visible. Now she looked, and time, in the moment of observing, fell away from him, and she saw across the table from her a man of her own age, a human being of a different sex, but equally eager to speak and to listen. Time, falling also away from her, made the moment timeless—and true—and she faced, across the packed bouquet of blazing flowers, not only a man's face, but an enduring symbol, bronze or marble, out of the past and somehow out of the future, too.

"Talk to me," he said. "If we spend thirty more minutes here and it takes thirty to get to the Tract, that's only an hour. Let's not waste it. There's no sense in wasting it, is there?"

"No," Indy said. But she remained silent.

The pepper boughs and pepper berries continued to simulate the sound of wind and rain. The Mexican boy had put up his hoe and was watering the garden flowers. The air was sweet with the rich scents of a summer night's blooming: phlox and petunias, roses and Nicotiana.

"Don't you think and feel?" Mr. Waite asked.

"I feel," Indy said, and added, not wanting to be vain, "I don't know about think."

"Talk to me," he said again. "Don't you believe in saying what you feel? Are you out of the habit of speech? Or don't you believe in it?"

"I believe in it. And am out of the habit."

"You've got to start sometime. I've told you about Rosalie. Now you tell me about someone you love."

"I'll tell you about Press," Indy said. "I'll tell you about my seventeen-year-old daughter."

They sat at the table later than they had intended. Day was long finished when they went outside. A great star the size of a lantern, luminous with the watery splashed yellow of lantern light reflected from a wet road, hung low in the west. In the east, there was the white light of a moon not yet risen.

On the way to the Tract they talked less. They left the watered groves and the scents of fruits and flowers behind them. The dry, tangy air of the barley-stubble fields, of baked earth and sun-dried grasses flowed across them. The bleached moon was ahead of them now, leading like a polestar. Indy spoke less because she was shaken by the experience of speaking at all, and anguished by the knowledge that in a few more minutes she could speak no more. If only each day for half an hour I might talk to him, no matter what else happened, I would be happy, she thought. I wouldn't care how many other people would be in the same room, or whether or not they listened. Whatever happened to me, sickness or poverty, wouldn't be important, because we would talk about their meanings. And it's the meanings that are important.

She felt a desire to tell Waite how much she had liked his talk, how wise and good she believed him to be to reveal himself to her as he had. She wanted to match his forthrightness and honesty in telling her what he had thought of her looks, by telling him her opinion of his talk. She couldn't tell him all—if she did so, he would think she was crazy. She could remember only one other time when she had been filled with such joy: that was the night of her conversion at the age of twelve, at the Sand Creek Baptist Church. This evening she felt as if she had been converted again. Converted to what, she didn't know. To the life men and women can lead when they speak to each other truly? Was this Mr. Waite's message of redemption?

"I wish I could talk to you every day," Indy said, speaking with effort. "I feel as if I'd climbed a mountain and had seen something beautiful I'd never seen before. Or only once before. I'll think of you and Rosalie often. I want to live the way we've talked. I thank you for it. You are a beautiful talker."

Mr. Waite laughed. "You are beautiful and I'm a beautiful talker. We're quite a pair."

"Talk is very important," Indy said. "Talk is the soul."

"Talk is more than that. It's the whole man," Waite said. "If there is a whole man."

Indy understood what this meant. When you liked the talk, you liked the man. She had come far enough in three hours to understand that this might be so, but she was not ready to accept it. She wanted to go on separating the two. She wanted to be able to dislike and disagree with the words, and love the man. She wanted to be able to revere the words, be shaken by the words, have the heart sucked out of her chest and the blood out of her veins by the words, and say a calm good-by to the speaker.

She was able to do so. She got out of the car, paid Mr. Waite, thanked him, and asked him to stack her luggage in front of the tent.

"I know my husband's in there," she said. "He's a newspaperman and goes to all public meetings."

"I'll go in and see," Waite said. "I won't drive off and leave you here in this godforsaken place alone. You wait here, Rose, till I get back."

It was the first time he had used her name. "You called me 'Rose,'" she said.

"You have any objections?"

"No."

149

"You never asked me what my name *was,* even!"

"I thought about doing it."

"I know you did. Why didn't you?"

"I thought it would be pretty personal."

"Yes, it would have been," Waite agreed. "It really would have been."

He pushed his cap to the back of his head, smiled, and said, "So long, Rose. I'll find your husband for you."

Indy stood still until he was inside the tent. Then, running, she followed him inside, calling, "Lute, Lute!"

Indy and Lute met about midway to the door.

There wasn't any question of Sylvester Perkins discussing water while that meeting took place. Lute's lone state, permanent or temporary, had been discussed by all, and since Lute had never made any bones about being lonesome, this was like a play with a happy ending.

If Perkins at that minute had said, "There'll be water in all standpipes tomorrow at seven a.m.," no one would have heard him. Love meant more to them than war—or water. Perkins's son, dying, for all they knew, on the Western Front, had not diverted their attention, but a woman in a man's arms made them forget their irrigation problems.

We're lovers before we're killers, Asa thought; but he knew it wasn't a fair test. The dying had been nothing but words and statistics. The loving was going on right there before their eyes. Though Lute Cope was far too mannerly a man to be carried away, even by his own wife, in full public view. It was apparent that he was saying, "Let's go. Let's get out of here. " But his wife would have none of that. She would not hear to taking him away from his duty and his meeting. So this time Press was the one who got up to provide another seat.

Shel watched Press slide past Tom Mount and into the aisle. He could not tell by her expression whether happiness was what she felt at her mother's return or not. But she felt something intensely. She did not kiss her mother, but grabbed her hand, pressed it to her cheek in a theatrical way, then turned toward the back of the tent.

When Lute seated his wife between himself and Tom Mount, Shel took a closer look. Indiana Rose Cope was no raving beauty; she was no one you could size up that fast. But she had a troublesome face, one that kept you looking at it. It asked some question. You didn't want to turn away from it until you'd found the answer. It was no simple question like "Will you go to bed with me?" which any man of the right age could answer. It was a question for which maybe you alone in the entire world had the proper answer. Turning away from her, with her question left unanswered, gave you a guilty feeling. And the feeling of guilt made you resolve to try to make it up to her some way in the future.

The arrival of Lute Cope's wife lost Shel what hope he'd had of Lute's leadership. It was perfectly evident that, with her by his side, Lute didn't care whether he ever again had as much as a swallow of water, let alone the legal amount of miners' inches. And she had lost all of them their concentration; they were not as prepared as they had been to bear down on Perkins, wring, if not water, at least promises out of him. But her arrival robbed Sylvester Perkins of more than it robbed anyone else. She had stolen his thunder.

Perkins paused; he let them wait again, but they would not hang on his words twice. "I am going to skip Shel Lewis's first question," he said, "and turn my attention to the second. In answer to it, it gives me pleasure to tell you this. I'll have water in all standpipes on the morning of November 17, 1916."

If he had expected cheers and hand clappings, he did not get them. He got silence, an accusing silence. Why had he put them all in the wrong, with the news about his son, making them think he was trying to pull the wool over their eyes? And now he was taking the wind out of their sails, making a gift of what they had been prepared to fight for.

Shel Lewis got to his feet. "Mr. Perkins, your promises haven't all held water in the past. But I'm going to gamble on this one. We've all gambled coming here, buying unimproved land. A little more don't make a hell of a lot of difference. But I want you to know one man believes you and is gambling on your word. I'm going ahead setting out my trees. I'm not going to dibble along, bucket at a time. So far, you don't have anything to answer for but our hardships. Our time's wasted, our kids go dirty, our wives have got short tempers. I grant you these things are no life-and-death matter. Our kids have been dirty before, we've wasted our time before, our wives have been mad at us before. But you make another mistake—you misfigure dates again—and you've got something more to answer for."

Nobody clapped for Shel either. He sat down feeling that he had been crazy to risk, for some damn-fool reason not clear to himself, his

151

whole future on this man's word. But he was tired of postponing. If he had to fail here, let it be sudden instead of inchmeal.

He expected Sylvester Perkins to make some reply. Sylvester Perkins nodded, as if fully accepting this responsibility, then he, too, sat down.

19    TWELVE people sat around the center table in the Jessups' sitting room. Two others, Mary Jessup and Asa Brice, who was helping Mary hand around the ginger drops (held back from the meeting for just such an eventuality), stood in the doorway to the kitchen, looking to see if anyone's cup needed refilling. It had been the most natural thing in the world for Mary to ask a few people home with them after the meeting. The two ladies, Opal and Eunice, had felt obliged to refuse; but Reverend Raunce and his family, the Lewises, and Ben's friend Asa Brice had snapped up her invitation before it was fairly out of her mouth.

The Jessups' sitting room had been imported, down to the last peacock feather in a vase on the secretary, direct from Emporia, Kansas. No one else on the Tract, with the exception of Lute Cope—and his stuff came only from Northern California, not from back East—had anything like it. Against the plain pine walls, the furniture looked a little as if it were camping out; but there was not a person in the room who did not feel enhanced by the red plush sofa, the secretary full of books, the center table lighted by a hanging lamp, the piano spread with hymn books. Everybody had worked hard all day, had had his feelings wrought up by Perkins's oratory, and was now prepared to smile and luxuriate in the presence of something which promised that life finally rewarded hard work with a little ease.

Mary Jessup had spent thirty years choosing, helping to buy, and arranging the objects that gave her guests so much pleasure. The room was her handiwork, in some ways her life; to have it used, because it was herself, was like being a mother to babies all over again. Men, she thought, never have a chance to see what they've lived for used in this way. Oh, a man with a farm or a factory sees it used, she supposed, but not by lamplight, not by people he loves. And love, to tell the truth, was what she was feeling for everyone in the room: for the women whose hands smoothed the plush sofa; for the men who, chewing ginger drops, caught her eye, and gave their heads quick little turns of satisfaction to show her that her cooking had hit the spot.

At the moment, love was what she felt even for old Wendlin, for whom ordinarily she entertained only the dearest affection, admiration, and tolerance. She did not fool herself into thinking that this moment was going to last forever: that the knuckle-headed Raunce, his nonentity of a wife and their snip of a daughter wouldn't get on her nerves again someday; but at the minute, there wasn't a foot in the room she wouldn't wash, and, washing finished, dry with her hair. Lovableness was as real as knuckle-headedness, and she didn't ask herself to experience everything at once.

The four men, Raunce, Wendlin, Ben Jessup, and Shel Lewis, held the center of the room; their talk rolled out from them and lapped around their wives and children. Chad Lewis, who might have been counted a man, paid no attention to this talk. He sat bemused, as if he had suffered a sunstroke and was just coming to. His father shot him a glance now and then to see if the boy was behaving all right. He was. The Raunce girl sat beside him, and he answered all her questions and even, now and then, put in his own oar. Usually, he tossed his head like a horse fighting the bit; tonight, he not only kept his head still, but had possibly run a comb through his hair as well.

When Crystal said, "What are your plans for the future?" Chad felt like telling her, "My plan is to marry Press Cope." He knew this was his plan, though he didn't yet know he was in love. Love was a part of him, like the blood in his veins. But marriage was an act; it was something that had to be planned for and accomplished, like barn-raisings and cornhuskings. Feeling by itself, he knew well enough, wouldn't get him anywhere when it came to a practical affair like a wedding. And he was going to wed that girl. Oh, nothing else, none of that woods-colting around that had sullied his father. He was silent for so long, so busy with the practical details of arranging his marriage, that Crystal gave him up and listened, in spite of herself, to her father. She preferred not to hear him; she waited apprehensively for him to say something ridiculous. But at the minute he was as sensible as could be, nothing but citrus fruit, water, and the Perkins Investment Company. You wouldn't know God existed (praise God), to hear him talking now.

"Why'd you want to get yourself out on a limb like that for, Shel?" he asked.

"To tell the truth, I don't know," Shel Lewis answered. "Except I wanted to pin Perkins down. He might worry more about ruining one man—when everybody knew he was doing it—than he would about stringing us all along and ruining us all, finally."

The minute he said that, Shel was sorry. It sounded like he was ready to die for the good of others, and when Wendlin said, "Shel, you don't look to me like a man cut out to be a scapegoat," Shel had a chance to set them all right.

"I'm not, Wendlin, and I don't aim to be one either. First of all, I got carried away because I was sore at Perkins. Then I figured that he's going to have the water ready when he said he was. I don't mind a gamble—if I think the chances are I'll win. But the main reason I spoke up was all that war talk, sprung on us to make us think we're nothing but mean little scrabblers, while bighearted Perkins is living and dying with the soldiers."

"Say, Wendlin," Raunce asked, "what would you've done if Perkins'd turned the meeting into one big hurrah for us to get into the war?"

"Why, same as you, LeRoy. Got down off that platform."

"LeRoy wouldn't have to get down," Ben Jessup said. "He could stay up there and recruit for war. LeRoy can't sin. Can you, LeRoy?"

Even though the discussion, with her as well as Ben and Wendlin talking, would turn into a Jessup round robin, Mary Jessup spoke up from the doorway. It wasn't that she objected to sin as a subject of conversation. What else, except goodness, was there in the world? It wasn't that she was overly tender toward Raunce. But Ben was no preacher yet, and she hated to see him setting himself up as a judge of others so early.

"Ben," she called out, "LeRoy's sinning's his own private affair."

LeRoy himself contradicted her.

"No, it's not, Mrs. Jessup. A man can't sin to himself. No man and especially no preacher. If I sin, it's Ben's affair and I'll thank him never to forget it."

"If you start forging checks . . ." Mary began her hypothetical case, but LeRoy interrupted her.

"It'd be too late then, Mrs. Jessup. Besides, Ben's right. I can't sin."

LeRoy did not announce this boastfully or sorrowfully; he did not seem proud of it or worried about it. He said it the same way another man would say, "I can't play the piano." But it shut down the conversation in the room. It was no new doctrine to the Jessups or to Asa

Brice; but to the Lewises it was about on a par with hearing a man say, "I'll live forever" or "I've got a couple of little wings under my coat"; except that such declarations did not have to be proved minute by minute, the way LeRoy's would have to be proved.

When Shel got over his shock, he said, "LeRoy, is that what they're learning you over at Rose Park?"

"They believe it over there, but it's nothing a man could be learned. It's no credit to me. I'm not boasting about my own goodness. If you're born again, you're dead to sin. Once it's happened to you, you can't misdoubt it."

He was as open-faced about his state as a boy with the mumps. He made sinlessness sound like cross-eyes or big Adam's apples; nothing you could boast about, but nothing to contradict either.

"Joined to Christ, where's the room for sin?"

Raunce sounded to Chad as if he was talking about marriage. To Crystal, it was all scalding nonsense. Asa heard it as backwoods theology. It was the simple truth to Dolly Raunce. She had a sinless husband. Shel Lewis gloried in the novelty. He had never heard the like. By God, the world turned up something fresh every day. Old Wendlin thought, History repeats itself. LeRoy and Rose Park had worked their way back to where Quakerism started.

"Fox would subscribe to that, LeRoy," he said.

"George Fox?" asked LeRoy. He was learning about Fox over at the Park, but what Fox thought about sin was a mystery to him. And what Fox thought didn't matter. LeRoy wasn't living out of any book, not even the Bible. The Bible writers got their inspiration from the same place he got his.

"You and Fox, maybe," Ben said. "But not me. I can sin."

"That's your opinion," Raunce told him.

Ben was startled but admitted it. "But I don't know who's got a better right to that opinion."

"Maybe you can and maybe you can't," Raunce said. "Maybe you've lost the power."

Ben gave a start, like a man suddenly told he's lost his manhood; he looked around the room wondering if such a thing could happen and a man be unaware.

"It's your pride, boy," LeRoy told him. "I've struck at your pride. You don't want to give God the credit. You want to take credit for every little victory yourself. You don't hone after your neighbor's wife. Or mine," LeRoy said, giving his Dolly, who sat beside him, a big hug and kiss, and almost forgetting, in the pleasure of that act, to carry on his argument. "So you want to think that you deserve the credit. You don't look on your neighbor's wife to lust after her. Why, Ben, you couldn't."

Ben contemplated giving some proof of his ability to sin, if no more than a solid blow to the chin of Brother Raunce. But though his fist clenched, his arm did not rise up to deliver the blow; and he didn't know any other way to refute Raunce. He certainly, with Ellen Lewis sitting there looking up at him dewy as apple blossoms, wasn't going to refute Raunce by saying he was as lustful as the next man and that he owed his restraint to cold baths and cross-country running. Sometimes he doubted that he had ever received a true call to the ministry; and the ironic part of his doubt was that no one was surer to plant this doubt in his mind than another minister. He himself, as a person incapable of sin, was incredible; but what worried him about this conviction was that a world in which sin wasn't possible seemed to him lackluster, tepid. Where was the triumph in a world like that? But was Raunce right? Did he want goodness, not as a gift from God, but as a sign of his own strength?

Raunce, who had seen Ben look at Ellen, hugged her as heartily as he had Dolly. "You don't think this young fellow's any sinner, do you, honey?"

The word "sin" abashed Ellen. They didn't talk about sin at home. People did things that were wrong, and she did herself, but she didn't say to her mother and father afterward, "I have sinned." She wanted to be polite to the Reverend Raunce but she also wanted to change the subject, to get away from talking about sin.

"How do you drill for oil, Reverend Raunce?" She spoke, in her embarrassment, with the intensity of a wildcatter heading at once for the fields. Everyone laughed; they were through with sin for that evening.

Mary Jessup started to make the rounds with her coffeepot, but Asa took it from her.

"Mary, you haven't had a bite yet yourself. You sit down and eat and let me take care of the company."

"Coffee's turned against me lately, Asa."

"How about some cookies?"

"Cookies, too."

"Well, what can you eat? Let me get it for you."

"I never was much of a piecer between meals, Asa. I'm not hungry."

156

Asa looked his friend in the face; he tried to see if there were signs of a sickness she wasn't admitting there. She knew what he was doing. She returned his look with a knowledgeable and accusing smile.

"There's nothing wrong with me a little baking soda won't cure. Don't you ever get heartburn, Asa?"

"Heartburn? Why, Mary, I'm slowly dying of it," he said.

Lizzie Cudlip had been as fully prepared as Mary Jessup to ask some of their new neighbors home for refreshments after the meeting; more fully prepared, if elaborateness of food counts. When she and Basil lit the lamps, there on the dining-room table were the hand-painted plates, the cupcakes iced with coconut, the big glass bowl full of floating island, the silver, newly polished. The sight made her momentarily sad. It reminded her of the frequency with which her hopes of hospitality were disappointed. Basil's, too, for that matter. He was as anxious as she to give parties and to go to them, to be neighborly, to set a good table and to share the goodness with others. They wanted to do that, but they didn't want to do it at the cost of backing down about what was right. First of all, they must take a stand, and after that, if no one wanted to visit with them, well, that was the sacrifice they would have to make for their convictions.

A room prepared for a party, and partyless, Lizzie thought, is like a tree in spring that fails to leaf; though she knew that her house was sad only because of the absence of what she had imagined. In itself, with no party in her mind, the house would appear cheerful, clean, and orderly, bright with black-eyed daisies and some late-blooming monkey flowers she had found in an unexpectedly damp spot at the bottom of an arroyo.

Sylvester Perkins had had something other than this house in mind when he had told Louella that the Cudlips would bring a little tone to the Tract. Syl, always optimistic about the Tract, had convinced himself that the Cudlips would establish an outpost of the Old South on their twenty acres. Syl's ideas about the Old South were sketchy. He had seen a movie called "The Clansman" and read the second half of a Civil War story called "Cease Firing," and he had in his possession a ring carved from a bone button by a great-uncle while imprisoned at Andersonville. The great-uncle had died at Andersonville, and that button should, in all logic, have done nothing to make Syl sentimental about the Old South. But All Logic is a realm as fanciful as the Old South, and Syl had never even seen a movie about *it*.

The Old South meant to Syl white columns, fanlights, bluegrass meadows, fast horses, open stairs, grandfather clocks, silver candlesticks, and mahogany drop-leaf tables laden with mint juleps, beaten biscuit, and Southern fried chicken. There wasn't a single item of Syl's imagining inside or outside the Cudlip house. Nevertheless, the place did have a certain tone. This tone was wholly the result of an effect in furnishing and arrangement achieved by Lizzie as the result of the impression made on her mind by Basil's accounts of his grandfather's home. Such was the tenacity of Basil's memory and the strength of Lizzie's love for him that with no help, except poverty, she had been able to give to her home a certain perpendicular elegance and patrician spareness.

The image of his grandfather's home in Tennessee was as fresh in Basil's mind as anything on the Tract. In and about *it* had been everything Sylvester Perkins imagined, when Basil spoke to him of the South. And no wonder. Without once mentioning bluegrass or beaten biscuits, Base, as he spoke, saw his grandfather's home with the concentrated despairing intensity that we have for objects we have lost— and have lost unfairly. All of it would, except for his father's lack of rectitude, have been his. Chairs, carpets, clocks that he would never have noticed if he owned them were pictured for him by his deprivation down to the last rung, extreme fringe, and final numeral. His mind clotted around them; they were obstructions preventing the free flow of his blood. He would awaken in the night and see some globed lamp hung about with teardrop pendants, long since, no doubt, so shattered as to have vanished completely; and he would long for it with the unquenchable bitterness and desire men have for loved women who have been unfaithful; though those noble acres and gracious buildings had never been unfaithful. They lived in his mind as more than themselves, as symbols of the rectitude that had built and adorned them; and as symbols, too, of the looseness that had lost them. Since he did not have the objects stolen from him by a lack of rectitude, he concentrated on the quality he believed was responsible for them: rectitude, aggressive, unyielding, fighting rectitude. That much of his grandfather's life he could have. His grandfather would have done what he did tonight—and every person at the meeting would have followed his grandfather from the tent, though in his grandfather's day there would have been no occasion for the protest he had had to make.

Lizzie put the food on the center table in the sitting room, and the two of them sat down and ate as formally as though guests were present. Whatever else Basil was, he wasn't two-faced. He did not care about appearances, only about what was right. He had no dainty manner which he put on in public but dropped with his family. He was, in fact, often more surly and contentious in public than at home.

If Lizzie had a fault as a wife, it lay in her adoration of Basil. Nothing she did or said asked him to be other than he was. There was nothing slavish or calculated in Lizzie's approval. She could not help herself. By chance, Basil was the man she had always imagined marrying. And having been honestly and naturally brought up, she had not imagined someone against her own nature. Most women either imagine against their natures and marry men who fit their false imaginings, only to find such men disappointing, if not unendurable; or, imagining truly but failing to encounter the imagined man, they marry whom they can. In either case, there is heartsickness (often well hidden) at the discrepancy. These wives wake up each morning with a little knot of sorrow at the base of their throats. But not Lizzie. She awakened happy, knew she was lucky, and thanked God for her luck. She never wondered whether or not it was lucky for Basil to have a wife so incapable of imagining a better man than Basil.

Lizzie, as a poor girl living first in one rented house and then another, with a father who was shiftless and put-upon, especially by his wife, had always dreamed of a strong man, a man older than she, dark, hard-muscled, commanding, righteous. Basil was all of this—and more. The more was that he was continuously able to keep her imagination alive by his life of action in the world outside their home. In that world, she did not live; there, to follow him, she had to keep him in mind. He had a life she had to imagine, and because she did so, Basil was never to her the unwanted interruption some women find their husbands. He was the comforting materialization of what had been tantalizing her imagination. He came home to a woman prepared for him by her dreams. And she never dreamed of wanting him any different.

Only Medora in the Cudlip family did this. Her parents, partaking decorously of the refreshments they had planned for the evening, were waiting up for her. Basil had left the meeting in too much anger, shame, and disappointment (for his fellow citizens) to notice that one of his five was missing. Lizzie, who did miss Medora, supposed that Basil knew that he was leaving her behind and had his reasons for doing so. They were halfway home before it came to Basil that Medora was not with them. He pulled up his team, sat silent for a while, then clucked up the horses and headed on toward home. The walk home, a couple of miles, was nothing; but Lizzie had been surprised that Basil did not drive back to the meeting to get Medora. Time was when he would have done so; not only because he did not want Medora out alone, but to protect her from the debasing mingling of white and colored.

When they had finished eating, Basil said, "You go on to bed, Lizzie. I'll wait up for Medora."

Lizzie was glad to go. She had been up since four, cleaning and cooking—but she believed also that Basil was the one who should talk to Medora. She herself was no match for the girl.

It was fifteen after eleven when Medora came into the house. She had told herself she would be home by midnight, but had made it earlier because she had accepted a ride with the Ramos family and their friend Julian. She had accepted the ride with misgivings, but out of principle. She *believed* that all men were created equal, but it had taken some courage to put the matter to a test after dark and with strangers. Equal! She, who usually felt her powers to be far beyond any call made upon them by persons or circumstances, had felt lumpish and tongue-tied with the Mexicans; but she had enjoyed the three pleasant-mannered, gay, exaggerating, flattering young people.

She came into the house so full of her discovery and happiness that she had forgotten her father and his certain anger—as he had forgotten her. He was in the rocking chair by the center table in the sitting room, lamp turned up and light full on his sleeping face. His head was neither tilted against the back of the rocker nor was it resting on his chest. He slept in the position of a man awake. Medora stood directly in front of him and explored his face as she had never been able to do before. Sleep was a sign of desired privacy, like a pulled blind or a closed door. She gazed at her father like a keyhole peeker, and felt the peeker's guilt and triumph. There was in her father's strong, composed features a sadness never visible when he was awake. She was sorry to see it, because he was her enemy and she did not want to soften toward him. She did not hate him, she supposed, any more than the man in one trench hates the enemy he is shooting at in the other trench. Later, they might even be friends. But now, he stood in her way.

She was still staring down at him when he opened his eyes. He had no need to rearrange his face, close his mouth, straighten his hair. The

160

same in private as in public, he was also the same sleeping as waking —except for that hint of sadness which he lost when he opened his eyes. It was this consistency in her father that made fighting him a comfortable business for Medora. He was always wrong, always strong, always attacking.

"Sit down, Medora," he said, not like an outraged father, but like a Southern gentleman. He never sat while ladies stood.

When Medora had seated herself, Basil said, "Why did you stay at the meeting, Medora, after we left?"

"Because we're going to live here and I want to know somebody. There were girls there my own age."

"Did you talk to those girls?"

"Yes, I did."

"Do you know why I left?"

"Of course I know why."

"You don't have any respect for your father's convictions?"

"I respect your convictions, all right. I don't try to make you do something you think is wrong, the way you do me."

"Don't you recognize any differences between parents and children?"

"Of course I do. Parents are old-fashioned. They try to live by what's over and done with."

"Right is right," her father said. "Year in and year out. Right is never over and done with, I hope."

"Wrong's wrong, year in and year out, too."

"Medora," Basil said, "you know I can't whip you any more. Tell me, how can I teach you something without it?"

"You can whip me if you want to," Medora said indifferently. She ran her left hand over the crook in her right elbow.

"You know that was an accident," Basil said.

"It doesn't make any difference one way or the other to me."

"You know I have no wish in this world except to make it a good place for my children to live."

Medora didn't answer. "You know that, don't you?" her father persisted.

"I know it. I don't agree with you about what's good is all."

Her father said nothing. "May I go to bed now?" Medora asked.

Her father still didn't answer. After a long time, he got to his feet. "Medora, we'll wait and see who's right, and who's wrong. You keep on headed the way you are, and in the end, you ask yourself if you don't wish you'd listened to me. Don't think I'm washing my hands of you. Don't think for a minute I won't try to head you off from the trouble you're bent on getting into." He stood staring at her, and Medora returned his gaze. "I'm right, Medora, and you can't fight what's right," he said. "Don't try to. There've been others in our family did it and they went to their graves in sorrow."

He turned and went up the stairs without a good night.

As she bent over to blow out the lamp, Medora saw the spare formality of the sitting room from an unusual perspective. Colorless and rigid, it seemed a part of a different world from that of which she had been a laughing part before she came into the house.

20    THE Nabiscos were out again, the lamp lighted again; in the kitchen, the kerosene stove was bubbling again, and the night wind blowing around the corners of the house smelled like nonexistent red roses. Press could smell them. Mother was home. The returned wife sat in a rocking chair, not rocking. Her husband faced her in a straight-backed chair, a Nabisco in his hand, not eating. Press, who had been watching them from the kitchen door, went outside. She wanted to include in her picture of her parents the house and the night. Under what kind of a sky, in what kind of weather, did her newly united parents meet? Under a cloudless sky, under a yellow moon, under stars paled by moonlight. If her mother would only rock a little, if her father would only eat his Nabisco! Her mother wore a high-necked white shirtwaist with rows of ruching and a new gold breastpin. It made her look like a visitor. Her father leaned toward her, smiling as if remembering a past happening, past but happy. The eye couldn't see it, but something was missing; something was held back; somebody said "maybe," "perhaps," "I hope so," but not "always." It was surely not her father. Press had a sense more delicate than sight or hearing, which waited to be reassured. She had made it her religion to anticipate her mother's wishes. It was a hard religion, since her mother did not always know her own wishes.

The tea Press brought, her mother wanted; but any further hanging around, as if at the sickbed of an invalid, she did not want. Press knew that. Hannah had gone to sleep on the way home from the meeting, and her mother had walked her straight into bed. Mr. Mount had been sent upstairs to his bed in the attic in the middle of a sentence. Now her mother waited for her to be gone; but Press felt a need to make up to her mother, by some act of unusual devotion, her half hour of infidelity with the black-haired boy. Her mother knew nothing of the boy, would care less; but for the time she had been with him, Press had forgotten the existence of her absent mother. So, not wanted, and knowing it, she still lingered on; and in a minute, her mother would break through the held tenderness of the home-coming with some sharp word. Press was willing to be hurt. She owed her mother, at the very least, a little gift of suffering. She asked for it, to help even up the score.

"Do you want some more tea?"

Her mother flared up, her voice breaking with impatience. "If we do, I can make it."

"Go to bed, Press," her father said. He was always on her mother's side in any contest between the two of them. It was where he should be, of course. She wouldn't respect him otherwise.

When Press left the room, Lute clenched his Nabisco to crumbs, put the crumbs on the plate on the center table, and looked at his wife. "Indy, I've lived for this hour."

She didn't doubt it. His happiness was in his face. She was home, resolved never to leave it again, and not deserving any welcome. Oh, not a *man,* no real reason for staying away so long, and her absence less excusable because of that. Lute's words under these circumstances should have been music in her ears. Why weren't they? What did she want to hear? "I've finished with you"? "You've gone off once too often"? "I've found me another woman"? Or even "I'm going to horsewhip you within an inch of your life"? Imagining these answers from Lute, she began to think how, in such circumstances, she would outwit Lute, win him over, once again. She imagined desperate acts; she imagined herself pushed to the end of her tether, struggling with all of her powers. This man, this handsome man, this man women liked, would be moved by her, find her irresistible. She would win him back in spite of his better judgment. As she lived for a minute through these trials and triumphs, her mouth relaxed and the blood warmed her face.

"Indy, you look better every minute," Lute said.

She smiled at him, a made-up smile, but Lute could never tell the difference. He deserved a smile, and she knew how to make one. She made it, and he was delighted. This man who could edit newspapers, write pieces other papers copied, understand politicians, influence elections, make money, had a blind spot when it came to his wife. She, who could turn on a hundred moods, had them at hand ready to use, and needed to use them as much as a man with muscles needs to flex them, found herself with a husband to whom they were all one because he loved her so much. She was Indy, and whatever she did was all right. He would accommodate himself to her and out of devotion refuse to differentiate. Where was her opponent? How could she take her measure? Who conquer? No wonder she lashed out at Press once in a while, would give her, with tongue or hand, an unwarranted backhanded slap. But Press, too, robbed her of all victory. She was forced to be her own opponent, to fight herself; to bring home again the Indy who ran away, captor and captive all in one; a civil war won, where every victory was half defeat.

She held the teacup in both hands, lowered her face to it so the steam touched her tired eyes.

The action was familiar and homey to Lute, Indy with her eyes in her teacup. "Are you glad to be home, Indy?"

She had come home; he should take the gladness, if she did not put it into words, for granted. Oh, how he trains me up to be a liar! No woman not a fiend could bear to say anything but yes to such a question; but true answers should well up, not have to be pumped. He should think that what he requires of me for his pleasure I may someday learn well enough to use for my own pleasure. Still, for all the practice, lying did not come easy.

"Oh, Lute," she said. Then she added, "I counted the days."

That was the truth. Once decided to return, she was impatient to have her body and her mind in the same place. When she was absent from Lute, she was always able to dream their future life together into any shape she chose. There was some break in her mind between the past and the future. She was never able to see that the past extended into the future. Never, until she rejoined Lute, did the future she had dreamed become nothing more than an extension of the past from which she had run away.

"Do you like the house, Indy?"

"Yes." She didn't have to lie about that.

"There're going to be other improvements. Mount's a carpenter."

"Lute, you'll get him out of the house, won't you?" Lute had some streak of sociability which, except for her, would keep the house filled with visitors.

"He'll leave tomorrow. I couldn't very well put him out tonight after having asked him."

She set down her cup, stood and blew out the lamp. She went to Lute, abruptly, as a boy jumps into a pond of cold water. She leaned against him, and Lute, with a shuddering sigh, took her onto his lap. She was small enough to sit there comfortably, her head on his shoulder. Except for the continuous breathing of the wind, there was complete silence. They might be the last man and woman on earth.

She remembered the past, the unchanging past of their boyhood and girlhood. She began to speak of it. She wanted to lose herself in something. Lute loved this kind of remembering talk, and she herself found pleasure recalling those two young people about whom they knew so many facts but so little truth. "Why do you suppose we did that?" they would ask each other, held by a mystery to which they had clues —but no complete answers. It was like trying to piece together a story, only a part of which they knew—and each knew different parts. They found a bedtime bewitchment in this storytelling. There was pain in it, sorrow and misunderstanding, but time and repetition had ennobled the mishaps; pain and sorrow were a part now of the story, and without them the story would have been as flat as Romeo and Juliet without the tombs. Though there was this difference: she and Lute altered as they went along; memory would return to them some forgotten word or incident, and an understanding was added that afterward became a part of their story—and of themselves.

Indy drowsed deeper into Lute's shoulder, knowing the game they were going to play and wondering who would start it. The beginning had to be delicate, something half remembered, about which they could both muse for a minute, something inconsequential and pleasant. Indy put her hand down to Lute's feet.

"Before I saw you, I saw your feet. I remember your shoes. You were crossing that little bridge in front of the dorm, and the oleander bushes hid your face."

"It was a footbridge," Lute said.

"Your shoes had cloth tops."

"I remember them."

Now they were in the past landscape, students at the one-horse college, where at sixteen and twenty they met and at seventeen and twenty-one married.

"I saw you the first day you came to school," Lute said. "You were two weeks late. When you got there, you were the 'new girl.' I was looking out of the window of the mathematics room. It was the first of October, about five-thirty, and no one else was in sight. You went right under the window, with that high-kneed walk of yours, like a horse on miry ground. You had on a hair ribbon. You got rid of that in a hurry. I never saw you with a ribbon on again. You had your head up, your eye on the horizon. You were seeing the future of I. R. Pressley. Then you looked up, saw me, knew you'd been seen acting out your future, and you smiled. You smiled right into my eyes admitting everything. That was the end of me."

"The end?"

"Or the beginning."

"You were the first boy I ever went with."

"Why did you say yes when I phoned?"

"The girls said you were nice."

"Was I?"

"Yes. I remember the first time you put your arm around me. We drove over a chuckhole, and you said, 'I saw that bump coming.' I thought you really had."

"The first kiss? Do you remember that?"

"Under the arbor in the rain. You were my first everything, Lute. I used to get so excited I'd be sick after our dates."

"Be sick?"

"Come sick, I mean."

There was a pause. She had endangered the mood of their remembering. Lute did not like to speak of such things—or to hear her speak of them.

"We never did anything but spoon."

"I know."

"I was brought up to respect girls."

"Your mother told me."

"Was it because of that night?"

"Maybe."

"You surprised me that night. I thought you'd made a mistake about the bedrooms."

"How could I?"

"What else could I think? You in my bed? I thought you were mixed up about the rooms."

"I wasn't mixed up. I thought, We'll be married in ten days, and it's crazy to wait. It's not a race. We don't have to wait until somebody fires a gun."

166

"You're glad we did wait, though, aren't you?"

"Things like that don't matter to women. I didn't know it then."

They were near a spot where the web of remembering might let them fall through into the present; let them awaken to pain unennobled by being past. Indy went on quickly, practicing with Lute a bedtime trick of her own when sleepless.

"Do you remember our first house?"

"First shack. Three rooms."

"It faced the river and the mountains."

"I remember painting that living room white."

"The curtains were cream chintz with yellow-and-brown flowers."

"Were you the happiest you've been . . . there?"

Careful, careful, this was another weak spot.

"The curtains made the room gold-colored."

She pressed her face more closely into his shoulder.

"When the wind came through the windows, the curtains lifted and fell as if the room was breathing."

He rocked her a little in his arms. "Are you sleepy?"

Oh, she was. She was half drowned in sleep. They had come a long way together, been boy and girl, husband and wife, father and mother. The hour was late, the room was deep in moonlight, the first of all their possessions still surrounded them, even the easily breakable lamp was a first; and the center table on which it rested, and the chair on which they sat. Nothing was discarded, nothing mattered, the power of the first still held her; and when Lute rose to carry her to bed, she went as unresisting as Hannah had.

She didn't understand yet the need to go slow with water. She had gone to bed without washing and knew that she would never sleep until she had bathed. The grime of the whole train trip burned her face; her fingers were dry as pieces of kindling wood. It must be near morning. There was still no morning light, but far off, roosters had begun their crowing. She got out of bed, stealthy as a thief, robbing Lute of her presence. He did not stir. The air had freshened; it flowed under her nightgown like the beginnings of a bath. She got the dishpan from under the sink and went out to where Lute had showed her the barrels of water. She filled the dishpan and took off her nightgown. Mist marked the windings of the distant river; the foothills were sharp and sad in the moonlight. This was her home: the Tract, empty, unplanted, no houses visible; there were no sounds except for the katydids, remembering yesterday's sun, and the roosters getting ready for today's.

As she washed, she shed tears. She made no effort to stop. She accepted sorrow and loneliness as her lot and began to figure what she could do in spite of them, how to make herself so busy building little balconies and having outdoor suppers and teaching Hannah to recite poetry that she'd never have time to indulge them. Finally, she stood in the pan and rinsed herself with dippersful of water; the air striking her wet body was cold enough to make her hold her breath, and holding her breath she stopped crying.

Two men saw her as she stood in the dishpan pouring dippersful of water over her shoulders. Both, after the first sight of her, turned away.

Tom Mount, hearing from his attic room the unaccountable splash of water, went to his window for a look. There beneath him, naked as a jay bird in the dishpan, was Indiana Rose Cope, wasting water by the bucketful. Her husband would give her a good talking-to tomorrow. She was a well-built woman, and if she had any lack, the moonlight hid it. But he was not particularly interested in women's bodies. They were natural objects, sometimes pretty, as this one was, sometimes not, and in this respect on a level with trees, horses, hydrangea bushes, and the like. What interested him in a woman was what he became with her. None of this being ascertainable, at this distance and at this hour, with Mrs. Cope, he went back to bed, hoping she'd leave him enough water for tomorrow morning's coffee.

Asa Brice, heading south toward the river for his usual dawn survey, also saw Mrs. Cope. Taking short cuts and ignoring the road, he came up over the rise on which the Cope house was built and saw her as she lifted a dipperful above her head. He stopped in his tracks. All beauty was holy, and this was beauty, pure and timeless as marble; in this respect impersonal; but beauty belonging also to a particular woman, and she should have the choice of revealing or hiding. He turned for this reason instantly away; grateful as he would have been to see a falling star or hear a dove call; deprived by his choice, but wanting nothing here that was not a gift. He began to whistle so that she would believe, if she caught sight of him, that she had been unobserved.

She did hear him, saw him go over the hill with his easy Indian stride, whistling softly. The night was ending. She emptied the dish-

168

pan, put her nightgown back on, and re-entered the house. Calmly, without awakening him, she got back into bed with Lute. His body, after the cold water and the tears, was warm and comforting. She turned sidewise to fit her body to his, put an arm across him, and fell asleep.

21    THE CLOCK began to strike as Opal and Eunice entered the house after the meeting. They stood still and counted eleven. They might have missed a note, but when Opal lit the lamp it was eleven all right.

"It's been quite a day," she said.

Eunice's lips parted, but she said nothing. She seemed to be uncertain as to what she wanted to do next: sit or stand, go to bed or stay up, speak or be silent. She had taken special pains with her dressing, but in so far as Opal could judge, all her pains had come to nothing.

Everything could be explained; that was the trouble. What else, in the circumstances, Eunice had asked, could Tom have done? Well, he could have grabbed Eunice, thrown his arms about her, announced their engagement, kissed her, pressed her hand, given her a note, asked to see her again soon, recalled old times, kept his eyes off other women. He had done none of these things. Yet, in these circumstances, Eunice could and did say, "He did what was sensible. He was protecting me as well as himself."

If Eunice had met Tom alone and he had been that undemonstrative, she would now know how things stood between them. As it is, Opal thought, she can keep on hoping; believe that when they are alone, when Tom doesn't have to be polite to Indiana Rose Cope, or when he's made a little more money, he can reveal his true feelings.

"I'm going to bed," Opal told Eunice. "Seeing Tom Mount again, on top of hauling water and going to the meeting and being reminded of the war, has worn me out."

The house had four rooms, a kitchen-dining room, a sitting room, and two bedrooms. In warm weather it was their custom to leave the two outside doors open. They had done this not so much for ventilation as to experience fully the freedom of the Tract, its openness and safety. It was a part of their new life to lie in their beds and hear and feel the night-long movement of the wind through the house and to smell the dry sweet scents of greasewood and elder and sagebrush. Now, without thinking, Opal closed the kitchen door.

"Why did you do that?" Eunice asked suspiciously.

Opal didn't know why, until she was asked. Then she knew it had been a gesture of protection toward Eunice; not of protection from Tom Mount—there was nothing she could do about that—but the protection of some tender useless act.

"I wasn't thinking," she said, and reopened the door.

After Opal had gone to bed, Eunice slowly took down her hair and let the wind lift it and blow through it. She was not discouraged. She did not feel that she had been repulsed, as in her early, all-or-nothing life she would have felt. All-or-nothing was only the shape she had tried to impose upon life; life was not really like that at all.

In the first days of her loving and being loved by Tom, she had been free of thought. She had dreamed, and remembered; she had planned what she could do for him. It was odd. What had happened then to her body had freed her of her body. She had been tireless, sunny as sunshine, swift as wind. By being a woman in love, she had gone back to being a child again, to the time when there is no separation between self and body. No one, feeling what she had, could have dreamed of heaven or feared death or declared a war. Each day, beginning with sunup and ending with sundown, was enough. Each morning she awakened smiling, not in anticipation of anything. What more could come? She smiled because she was smiling, because she and Tom were alive.

The state was nothing she imagined. It was apparent to others. People turned to look at her and Tom when they were together with the same open approving pleasure they showed for happy children. And she and Tom didn't care. They knew they were looked at, but they hid nothing. After what happened later, she might have believed that Tom had faked all that early glory. She wanted to believe he had. If he had, then she had lost nothing. You can't lose what has never existed. But she had no such comfort. It had all been real. She had seen it reflected in other people's faces and heard it echoed in their voices. People, complete strangers, were compelled to speak to them on a subject usually avoided even by friends. Strangers came up to them and spoke to them of their love.

There was a restaurant where she and Tom ate sometimes, called, in honor of Theodore Roosevelt, "The Teddy Bear." It was not an especially cozy place, though she was never able to judge what the places where she and Tom ate were really like. The minute they entered any hotel or eating place, it enfolded them like a home. Waitresses and bellboys stayed near them, as if they provided some comforting warmth. Food she ate with Tom was the best she had ever put in her mouth.

There was a waitress at "The Teddy Bear" whose name was Bessie Sweeney. She and Tom always called her "Sweet Bessie" because when they first knew her, she continuously sang the praises of sweet basil as a seasoning. Tom also called her the "Irish Gypsy" because, though her name was Irish, she had a gypsy's black bramble hair and big hoop earrings. Sweet Bessie used to hover over them, eating them up with her sad, shining eyes. Eunice and Tom were both aware of her, but nothing in those days troubled them. Nothing made them self-conscious or pushed them into any unnatural act or nonact. Sweet Bessie would hurry back from her other tables to be near them. They seemed to satisfy some longing in her, to prove something to her. One evening, while Tom was getting their coats, Sweet Bessie leaned over the table to speak to Eunice, watching out of the corner of her eye to keep track of Tom. "If I had a man who treated me like that, I would turn myself inside out for him." She whispered, her voice trembling with feeling.

The words touched Eunice and troubled her. Didn't she value Tom enough?

When they left the restaurant, she told Tom what Sweet Bessie had said. Tom was unimpressed. "That's what she told me," he said indifferently. At once, questions came into her mind: When? Where? But the rush of their conversation, the closeness of their bodies in the bite of the bitter mountain air, put the questions out of her mind. And only afterward did it come back to her. "When, oh when? Where?"

Whatever the answers to these questions were, Sweet Bessie proved that other people had believed that Tom loved her. The two of them had been a magnet; and even with Tom as handsome as he was, they weren't so extraordinary a couple as to turn, by their looks alone, the heads they had turned. Something, when they were together, came into being, and it was this people saw and believed in and wanted to become a part of. It was like a religious revival, but stronger. Revivalists had to drum up trade, to ask people to come up front and say they believed. She and Tom had done none of this and yet people believed

171

and came up front and said so. Observers found some saving grace in them. This was nothing Tom could have made up to fool her, because other people saw it and believed it.

One other time, in this same restaurant, there was a woman whose looks Eunice despised, forty, at least, her hair colored with something artificial, her mouth painted, a scraggly fox fur wrapped around her long yellow neck. "How cheap!" Eunice had said. And Tom, for the first time since she had known him, had flatly contradicted her.

"Cheap?" he asked. "What's cheap about trying to be as young and attractive as you can? That woman hasn't given up; she's still living. She's a woman, not a housekeeper or a teacher."

At the word "teacher," Eunice flinched, not for herself, but for Tom. He had forgotten that she was a teacher.

"What's wrong with not giving up?" he demanded when she remained silent.

Then in a single flash it was revealed to Eunice that men didn't look at these cheap women in the same way another woman did. Everything this woman did praised men. Men wanted women (didn't they?) young, bright-colored, vivacious. That was what this woman was trying to be. Beside her, Eunice knew (for all she was so mad about Tom), she didn't praise men. What she praised was some old ladies' idea of neatness and propriety. This dyed and painted woman had come, like Sweet Bessie, to their table. She had a bunch of battered imitation violets pinned to her fur. She unpinned these and put them, without a word, in Eunice's hand. And for an instant, Eunice saw, under the paint, back of the lines of her face, dragged down by disappointments and hatreds, a glance as clear as water, as fresh as real violets. The look was for Eunice, but it was because of Tom. Alone, Eunice would never have been given it or the violets. After that one clear look, the woman sank back out of sight, behind the years and the hatreds. It was a real death, and right there before their eyes. Eunice left the restaurant crying. She was living inside a mystery visible to others, she felt, but invisible to her. What seemed the most natural thing in the world to her and Tom, their deep mutual love, seemed unnatural, or at least unusual, to others. Was love so much a miracle in the world?

She never spoke of marriage; nor did she often think of it. If Tom wanted it and spoke of it, she would listen. It was her delight to want nothing but what he wanted. She was happy without hope. The future for her was never further away than the date of her next meeting with Tom.

The nearest they had come to anything resembling marriage had been during an Easter vacation, when Tom got the loan of a cabin belonging to a friend. The cabin was a one-room affair made of logs, a bed at one end, a cookstove at the other. They didn't pay much attention to the cookstove. She didn't suppose marriages could really be lived the way she and Tom had lived their week of marriage. Children and work would get in the way. But children and work were God's punishment to Adam and Eve, weren't they? And there was no use pretending, was there, that a marriage was better because the man and woman had to be separated most of the time? Separation could only make a marriage better if the man and woman didn't love each other—and she and Tom did, and they were almost never separated during that week.

There had been a heavy snow on Good Friday, a wet, clinging snow that whispered down about them, walling them in with whiteness and silence. They heard the snow fall, they saw it, and they smelled it, too. It had a raw, sweet fragrance like the scent of something green, blown across water; they would stand in the doorway of the cabin inhaling deeply and trying to say what the smell was. Buckwheat blossoms, Tom suggested, or greasewood in bloom, or the scent of greasewood burning? They never had enough of that sweet snow and of guessing where its fragrance came from. And for Eunice, there had been something bridal about all that Easter whiteness.

Soon they were like the snow: untimely, unseasonable, paying no attention to clock or calendar. They lived on their pulses and by their appetites; though these imposed an orderliness of their own upon them. They did not eat or get up at any which time; there was a pattern, but it had their own shape, not the shape of someone who had to be back at the store or behind the teacher's desk at a set hour. Eunice felt guilty for a day or two. She missed her prison. She wanted to hear the school bell ring and to salute the flag on the stroke of nine. Then she stopped thinking about her past life. If she had been happy without hope before, she now became happy without memory. She lived in the center of the snow, in the center of a bed, at the mid-point of her life's being. There was no division in her life, and this concentration, like a magnifying glass, revealed the world to her with a sharpness she had never known before.

173

On my deathbed, the world I remember, she thought, if one remembers, dying, will be the world of that snowy Easter. And on the wind tonight, the dry, barley-stubble Tract wind blowing off the desert, I can still smell the wet honeyed fragrance of that snow.

She could smell, too, the pinewood scent of the fire in their cabin cookstove; she could smell the coffee Tom made and brought to their bed each morning. He was more womanly in many ways than any woman. He had a woman's handiness and pleasure in household tasks. The contradictoriness of his body and his temperament astonished her. From what she had heard of men, she had believed that, in spite of all their assets as husbands, they were a trial to live with. Women spoke of waiting for their husbands to get out of the house in the morning. They prepared for their return at night with all the wariness of a householder fearing an invasion. Tom was no trial to live with.

They awakened each morning in their timeless world, in their room, milky-white with sunshine reflected off snow. Neither said, "I wonder what time it is?" It was now. They smiled at each other and sometimes went back to sleep again; more often opened their arms to each other and started their day with the love-making with which the night had ended. He was a long, fondling, silent lover, partly from preference, partly from policy. Talk, he said, might distract him. She practiced whatever he preached. He was womanly in that he loved to be loved; clasp or be clasped was all one to him. In the beginning, she had believed that such transports as she experienced would, if continued, kill her. No one could feel so much and live. Tom laughed at her. She found she was hardier than she had imagined. She developed another worry. Had nature intended her for a brothel or harem? Tom laughed some more—at that idea and at her words. "You're all right where you are."

The feeling she had with Tom was as strong as any other natural wonder, stronger than many. What she felt with him put out the sun and the stars; stopped the wind from blowing, the snow from falling. In the timeless moment it seemed impossible that time would return, or that the earth, which had ceased, could take shape again. She puzzled her head about it. How could the eternal cease? Would she not always live in the power of that transcendent moment?

No, time returned, and with it the world, more real than ever before. When they went into town at four in the afternoon, the streets and the people on them were as entrancing as if she had returned to the earth after a long sojourn on the moon. People, people, she wanted to cry, oh how beautiful, oh how touching! A woman sweeping her porch; what a grandma she was: there was love and clean cupboards and rice puddings in every stroke. A man reading the afternoon papers, one foot on the bottom stair of his front porch; he could not move until he had the war news for the day. A ten-year-old signing the snow on a vacant lot with his tracks. In the timelessness of their cabin, she had forgotten signboards and sidewalks; piles of new potatoes and old apples; earmuffs and runny noses. In the emptiness of eternity, in the aridity of passion, she had, without knowing it, grown homesick for something domestic and passing.

Though their days were not altogether undomestic. They ate brown bread and strawberry jam with the coffee Tom made in the morning. They played catch with a baseball left by some summer visitor. Tom had brought a *Literary Digest* with him and he sat her down and gave her an examination in current events. She taught current events to eighth-graders and knew more about Black Jack Pershing and Papa Joffre than he did. He was proud of her. "You are quite a woman," he said.

In the last week in June, after their Easter miracle of strawberries in the snow, Eunice phoned Tom to tell him she could come to Fort Collins on Friday. They chatted for a minute or two, then Tom asked her if she had forgotten that this was the weekend of the annual get-together of Swift men in Denver? She had, she had. Tom had shown her the leaflet announcing the affair, and they had laughed together at the packing company's attempt to combine business and pleasure: sack races and instructions to push mutton and pork; homemade ice cream and sermons on the nutritiousness of kidneys and hearts. Tom hated the prospect of going. "There's not a man on earth who can tell me a thing about livers and lights. And I've won the sack race three years hand running."

"That's winning it the hard way," Eunice said.

"Sister, are you telling me?"

"There's the homemade ice cream."

"That's all I'm going for."

They arranged to meet the next weekend, and Eunice, though disappointed, accepted the postponement cheerfully. She was prepared to live Tom's life; if it was livers and lights and sack races for him, why, she asked for nothing better for herself. She knew that if he wanted to, he could take her with him to the Denver meeting. She didn't for a minute consider this neglect, or hold it against him. Instead, she worried about the lies she caused him to tell—even without such complications. To her, Tom was a real Lincoln, a man of such deep probity that she had tried to invest herself with earlier lovers to ease Tom of any concern he might feel as the despoiler of a virgin.

"Most women," he had told her, "want to convince me I am the first man they ever kissed. Why are you working so hard to do the opposite?"

She couldn't very well tell him her reason: that she wanted to take his burden of guilt from him. And since she couldn't tell him, Tom believed she was trying to impress him with the number of former admirers she had had. He didn't understand that her picture of herself, as an already fallen woman, was to keep him from feeling any responsibility for her fall. She thought there was sin in their lovemaking; and she supposed, rightly, that most people would believe that Tom, an experienced man, fifteen years older than she, was the greater sinner. She didn't want this idea ever to occur to Tom. She was determined to be his equal in sin and to spare him all remorse.

When she discovered the mistake she had made about the date of the Denver meeting, she decided on a thorough cleaning out and refurbishing of her room. It would help pass the time until she could see Tom. The first step in her cleaning was to sort through the year's accumulation of lesson plans, hectographed maps, notes from parents, Valentines and Christmas cards from pupils, pictures cut out of magazines for class use, graduation programs, and the like. Before she knew Tom, she had kept such things. But now? She would as soon think of saving each year's fallen leaves. They had served their purpose; they were a sign of something that had passed.

It was in the midst of this discarding and sorting that she came upon the Swift and Company leaflet and saw that the date of the Denver meeting was not this weekend, but the next. She was sitting on the floor, two desk drawers beside her, when she made the discovery. How that piece of paper had got in with the school stuff, she didn't know; but she blessed the industriousness that had led her to find it. Now they needn't wait for a week. She kissed the leaflet like any schoolgirl, jumped over the drawers, and was halfway down the stairs to phone Tom when she had a better idea. Instead of phoning him, she would go at once to Fort Collins. Tom himself would have discovered his mistake by the time she got there, and they could have a meeting of the kind she had often longed for, spontaneous, unplanned. Her mind, as she packed, was filled with images of this meeting. She would open the door to Tom's room, Tom would look up, doubt his eyes, then stand, arms opened to her. And he would groan as he always did in that sweet suffering way when he clasped her.

Tom was not in his room when she reached Fort Collins, and the clerk did not know, or at least wouldn't say, when he would be back. After their Easter in the snow, Tom had given her a key to his room. Not because either of them expected that she would ever have occasion to use it. But he gave the key to her as another man might give a woman a ring or a breastpin. It was a sign that he had opened his life to her. She kept it with her always. When the clerk told her that Mr. Mount was not in, her first thought had been to wait his return in the lobby; then she remembered her key and went up the dust-smelling stairs to his room. There were some letters half under his door, and she picked them up without looking at them and took them in with her.

The room's emptiness was not the emptiness left by a man who has just stepped out. Yesterday's paper, still folded, lay on the table. A vase of drooping roses was circled with fallen petals. Two empty beer bottles stood on the window sill. The air was warm and stale. She pushed up the windows and heard the sounds and smelled the scents she had imagined back in Millstone; but what she had not imagined was that she would stand alone at the window, that Tom might never have discovered his mistake.

She went to the closet where Tom kept his clothes and saw that his Gladstone bag and best suit were gone. She felt desolate and leaned her face against the sleeve of his winter overcoat, the one he'd worn when he'd come in out of the rain on the night she'd first seen this room. Why had she believed that by power of the imagination alone she could have him waiting here for her? Why had she refused to act like any sensible woman, and phone him? Did she think her love was miraculous enough to convey messages without benefit of phones? That she had only to want Tom and he would be *where* she wanted him? For a while she would not admit defeat; she would go to Denver, where he had mistakenly gone, find him, and regain the happiness she had thrown away by her foolishness. She went again to the window, and there in the last light looked down at the letters that she still held in her hand. She read the address on the top letter as a person in pain reads a newspaper, hoping to find some distraction. The top letter was addressed in a woman's hand and was postmarked in Denver two days ago.

Without making any decision, her hands operating mechanically, she opened the letter and saw in a glance, without knowledge of individual words, its meaning. Its meaning was: I love you, I wait for you. I remember. The woman's name was Clara. Eunice wanted to believe the letter silly, stupid, wicked. It was exactly as silly, stupid, and wicked as every letter she had ever written Tom. He was with Clara at this very moment, she supposed. The letter had been intended to reach him before he left, to bring him, as Eunice liked her own letters to do, a welcome before they met.

She leaned against the window sill and looked out into a world that had become an assortment of meaningless shapes. She stood at the center of it, still alive, but alive to no purpose. She had lost every reason for action; move or stand still, close her eyes or open them, it was all one to her now. An image came to her, the only comforting one, of some far-off mesa where she could lie face down, unseen, blind as a stone, never again speaking or spoken to. She was as dry of tears as a handful of dust. And though the world she saw with Clara's letter in her hand appeared unreal, the true unreality was in the world she had believed in before reading it. If Tom didn't love her, she had been living in a mirage.

She slowly opened the next two letters. The first was typed without dates, or names of any kind, Tom's or the writer's. It was written in the third person, the writer calling herself "your correspondent." It was written deep in the night after Tom had left the woman. Eunice could not bear to look at it, let alone read it. It was a mirror in which the face she saw was her own. The third letter, painstakingly written on lined tablet paper, was signed, "Your Irish gypsy."

The situation now appeared to Eunice to be laughable; but she was as far from laughter as she had been from tears. She had begun by hating Clara. But Clara was as much betrayed as she. It was completely dark, the middle of the night for all she knew, when she left the window. She had stood for so long in one place that she moved creakingly, like an old woman. She had suffered a lifetime at that window, the hours had worn her like years. She was very hungry. She went to Tom's kitchenette, opened a can of salmon, and ate it, using her fingers; she let the salmon juices dribble where they would.

She pulled Tom's fold-away bed out of the closet and, with the three letters in her hand, lay down fully dressed. Sometimes she slept. It was hard to tell sleeping from waking. When she slept, the pain of what had happened did not leave her. When she was awake, it seemed that it must be a bad dream. Even in her sleep she touched the letters constantly, as if trying to prove to herself that they were real.

As soon as it was light, she got up and washed thoroughly. After she had made and drunk a pot of black coffee, the torpor of the night left her. She sat down and wrote Tom a letter.

She could not write "Dear," or even his name, only: "I add my letter to the three which I found here. I am leaving my key. I will never see you again. Eunice Fry."

She put the four letters on the library table, tidied the two rooms and herself; then she stood in the doorway looking back at the scene of her life's beginning and ending. Would she have walked into this room on that January afternoon if she could have seen how she would be leaving it? But what had changed? Was Tom now any different from the man who had come to her, who brought her alive? No, he was the same man. Nothing at all had really changed, except an idea in her head. Did she want to live with an idea in her head or with Tom? With Tom, of course. She went to the table, took her letter and tore it into pieces.

Tom was some other kind of man than she had believed him; that was all. No, that wasn't true. All that was true was that he did not, when away from her, live as she had believed he did. Did that change anything? Make untrue what was true when they were together? No, it was all still true. Nothing, in so far as she was concerned, had changed. She loved a man, didn't she? She might be unable to love all that man did, but she loved him and she did not want to be separated from him. She spent the rest of the day discovering more about this man she loved. She did it quite deliberately. She did not want ever again to be surprised as she had been. She went through his apartment carefully and brokenheartedly. The truths he had told her, the hundred little absolute truths he had told her! These hurt her more than the lies. The truth about fig bars and Old Farmer's coffee and vegetables stored in a churn and eighty-nine dollars in the bank and an insurance policy with the Provident Mutual and two suits to his name and brown eggs and a push broom to sweep with. These truths were the bounty he had freely given her. She went about, sick with gratitude, like an old mother who thinks, as she dies of a blow from her son, how sweet he has been to spare her the pain of strangling.

She found a notebook in which Tom kept track of everything, expenses, towns visited—and especially women. She was there, given no more space and no less than the others. The notebook told the truth about her; she supposed it told the truth about the others. I love a Mormon, she thought, that's the way it is; though there was a difference she would not look at: the Mormons married their women and took care of them.

She had no intention of staying another night. She asked herself why she was staying at all and found no answer. She stayed because staying was easier than leaving. She shrank from showing her face on the street; she had the self-consciousness of a person just out of a prison or a hospital; she believed that what had happened had marked her. She stayed because she was tired, because a crushing apathy and sleepiness weighed upon her. She walked from one square of the kitchen linoleum to the next, counting squares like a man counting fence palings or railway ties. She had become very clean all of a sudden, and took her second bath of the day, scrubbing carefully. She slept without awakening, but heavily and miserably.

At ten o'clock on Sunday morning, she was dressed and ready to leave. What she had experienced had made Fort Collins a foreign country. She sat by the window watching passers-by, bound for church. Families together; men and women together; married, nothing to hide, their love as respectable as their churchgoing; the women in pretty summer dresses; the roast cooking in the oven at home. How had she cut herself off from them?

As she sat looking, a car stopped in front of the hotel. It was one thing, she saw at once, to tell her mind to accept the facts and another for her body to experience them. Tom was in shirt sleeves with suspenders. The woman beside him was about his age, small and dark-haired; she wore a pink ruched shirtwaist, and on the arm, which she stretched with easy familiarity across Tom's shoulders were two heavy gold bracelets. Where was that animosity that made it possible for a woman to kick and scratch her rival? She would like to experience it. She felt no animosity, only a deep throbbing hurt. Tom got out, looked up and saw Eunice, or at least a woman (he made no sign of recognition), in the window above him. He motioned to his companion, who was already on her feet, to stay where she was. He talked with her for a few minutes, then he entered the hotel.

Eunice remained exactly where she was, the letters in her hand. When Tom entered the room, she said, "Hello, Tom."

Tom closed the door behind him and stood with one hand on the doorknob looking at her.

"What are you doing, sitting here watching me out the window?"

180

"I wasn't sitting here watching you, Tom. I was sitting here reading your mail," Eunice said.

Tom stared at her and the letters she held up; then he laughed like a man who finds that the joke is on himself; and who, in the long run, has never really expected anything else.

"What would you have done if I had brought her up?" he asked.

Eunice was grateful that he said "her." If this was Clara, she didn't want to know it. "Nothing," Eunice answered. "You can bring her up now if you want to."

"I don't want to," he said. "You stay here."

When he came back, he said, "So you scuttled up here to spy on me?" He spoke matter-of-factly.

It was the word "scuttle" that hurt her. "I didn't scuttle," she said. "I walked up, happily. No, I ran up. I thought you would be here."

"How could you think that? After what I told you?"

"I thought you had made a mistake about the date. That you would find it out and still be here."

"I told you that to save you from being hurt." The key lay on the table beside her, and he looked at it. "I had no idea when I gave this to you that you would use it for spying."

"Neither did I."

He walked over to her; if he intends to kiss me, she thought, it is too soon. But a kiss was not in his mind. What he wanted was the letters. She handed them to him; he looked at the two handwritten letters indifferently, but the third, the typed letter, he held in his hands, turned it over and over as if afraid to read it. Red spots burned on his cheekbones, and the corners of his upper lip lifted in the spasmodic way that characterized him when he was troubled. Finally, he took out the typed page, and, as he glanced at it, his hands began to tremble. With a sudden desperate motion, without putting the letter back into its envelope, he rammed both into his pants pocket and went quickly to the kitchen. Because he looked so sick, Eunice followed him. There was nothing in the typed letter, though she had only looked at it, not really read it, different from what was in the others. The only difference, in so far as she could see, was that the typist had been at greater pains to hide her identity. Did the letter have nothing at all to do with Tom's sickness? Did he tremble for the two of them, instead? For their love, which he had endangered?

He had got himself a glass of water and was trying to drink it. The glass, in spite of his efforts to hold it steady, tapped against his teeth.

She reached up, took the glass, and held it firmly for him. He drank all the water, then she put an arm around him and helped him to the chair by the window. He lay back in it, the trembling lessening; there was perspiration at the edge of his hair, and the sudden burning had left his face white and made the blueness under his eyes more apparent.

"Don't worry, Tom," she said, "don't be upset. Everything will be just the same."

He looked at her curiously. "You think so?"

"Nothing can harm us."

He reached out and touched her hair, then let his hand drop back into his lap. He looked at the key again.

"I didn't intend it to bring you so much trouble."

She took the key and pressed it to her lips. "It told me more about you. It gave me more of you. I don't want to love just a part of you. Whatever, whoever you are, I want to love all of you."

"Poor Eunice," he said.

"I am not poor. I am lucky."

"Not from where I sit," he said. "From where I sit you look way out in left field."

She was not sure what that meant, and in any case she did not want to talk about it any more. If they did not speak of the letters, the enchantment of their being together would take hold of her; of him, too, she believed. She was already beginning to feel the familiar bemusement and delight. There was nothing she need do, nothing she need say. She need not even have faith; she could doubt all she pleased, deny or renounce; his presence was strong enough to overcome her. A quietness fell upon her; she became whole. It was summer, it was midday; light and warmth from an unclouded sun filled the room. She fed on the summery fragrances. The voices of the churchgoers, homeward bound, were cheerful. The scrim curtains lifted and fell.

He closed his eyes, reached down, pushed her slipper from her foot, and, with his hand about her instep, held her foot firmly.

"You are the only woman whose foot I can hold."

It was a ludicrous statement and perhaps a lie as well. Yet it was perfect for the moment and for them. It was the one touch she could at the minute tolerate; it had a certain objectiveness about it which suited their condition; a certain pitiful silliness. In every act involving touch he was infallible.

"What are you thinking about?" he asked.

182

She did not know until he asked; then she knew, but it was a secret she could not share. It was something she was born for and he wasn't. What she was doing was marrying him. She was espousing him, Thomas S. Mount, this recently trembling man, this man with the letters from three women in his pocket and the sweat from his fright still visible on his forehead; she was taking him for better or for worse, in sickness and in health, to be her wedded husband. In a way, she was not so much marrying him as recognizing that in the months of their loving, a marriage had taken place. All she was doing now was accepting the obligations of her wifehood. She saw that marriage had nothing to do with licensing and orange blossoms, old shoes and double-ring ceremonies. Church and state had been mixed up with Opal's and Charlie's marriage, but she doubted that Opal had ever felt herself half as much wife as she did now. Marriage was a sacrament, she had always been told, a mystery. If there was to be a mystery, something had to be mysterious, unfathomable. This big, dark man, her husband, with his tender susceptible mouth and tired eyes, was her mystery; he was able to meet all that rose in her, asking for the unknown, the unexplainable; she went into the darkness with him, where the mysteries were; he took the measure of her powers; she struggled to apprehend and to endure him. He was her opposite; he fulfilled the Biblical requirements, he was created male; but, happily, time and his own inclinations had domesticated him. She longed for a witness; since Tom could not be her witness, she called out to God. Oh, God, she said in her heart, hear me. I am this man's wife. I will always be true to him.

Tom opened his eyes. Something of what she felt must have shown in her face, and he smiled.

"Tom," she said, "do something for me."

She took the key, which she still held, and extended it toward him. "Kiss it for me."

He looked at her questioningly. Another man might have said, "Don't be silly." Or, "What's this mumbo-jumbo?" Or thrown it out of the window. Not Tom. There was a good deal he could not do for her. But he did not jibe at what she wanted and he could do, on grounds of silliness or lack of meaning to him. He took her word for what mattered to her. He also accepted some mysteriousness from her. He leaned forward, grasped her hand, and kissed the key.

That was the whole of her marriage ceremony with Thomas Mount. It took place in her head on Sunday, June 28, 1915 at one p.m. At the

183

time, at the moment Tom bent his head over her hand and kissed the key, she felt that marriage was like dying: one made one's peace with the world. Later, she saw that she had been mistaken, at least about marriage.

Opal awakened with her nightgown twisted uncomfortably about her. As she lifted herself on heels and shoulders to pull it straight, she heard sounds she had heard before: Eunice crying, or Eunice "carrying on," if those were better words for it. Nothing noisy; worse to hear because Eunice was taking pains to be quiet. There was still a light under the door to the kitchen, but Opal had the feeling that it was very nearly morning. She got out of bed, and the night air flowing under her gown was sweet as water.

Eunice was at the kitchen table, face down, her hair spread about her on the flowered oilcloth. At the sound of the door opening, she sat up, and Opal had been right. She was not crying. Eyes and cheeks were perfectly dry.

"Look at the clock," Opal scolded her. "It'll be light in a couple of hours, Eunice. Come on to bed."

"I can't sleep. There's no use going to bed."

"You could rest, anyway."

"No."

"Look, Eunice, you can't spend the rest of your life longing for Tom Mount."

"It looks like I can."

"Yes, I suppose you can. There's more than one way of committing suicide."

"Suicide? I'm not killing myself. I may not be happy, but I can tell you one thing—I'm more alive than most people."

"You mean you're suffering more."

"That's one of the ways of being alive."

"Cut off your nose, too," Opal told her, "to spite your face. Put salt in the wound. Starve yourself. Why, you haven't half come up to all the ways people can suffer. You're sitting here taking your suffering pretty comfortable: nice kitchen for it, bothering nobody but me— and maybe Tom Mount, with your sheep's eyes and letters."

"I haven't been writing him. How could I? I haven't known where he was."

"Eunice, where's your pride? A man runs off, don't tell you where he is, and all he has to do is turn up again and you're waiting with open arms. And legs."

"Don't be dirty, Opal."

"I'm not dirty. I'm just truthful."

"Tom never did cast me off. He never did give me the go-by."

"He never will cast you off. He hoards women. He can't bear to part with a one. They might come in handy sometime. Cause him some real trouble sometime and see how long you last."

"I don't want to cause him trouble. I want to help him. I'm married to him."

"Look, Eunice, you can tell me that and I know it's just a way you have of talking. But you start talking that way to other people and you'll end up in the asylum."

"I know that."

"When I think what that man has done to you in two years' time! You sit there with your hair streaming down, your skin yellow, and your eyes big as saucers, and I declare I can't even remember the girl you were when you first came to my house. She's lost, that girl. Sunk, gone. Nothing left but . . . I don't know what to call you. He's no good. Can't you face that?"

"I face it. But I don't stop loving him. Any more than God does."

"Any more than God does!" Opal repeated. "Any more than God does! Now you are really going out of your mind. You're not called upon to play God to Tom Mount—or anyone else. All God asks of you is to act like a decent reasonable girl. God's enough God for the lot of us. We don't need any imitations from girls out of their minds from running after men."

"I don't run after men."

"You run after Tom Mount. I should think you'd be ashamed to make such a nuisance of yourself."

"Oh, Opal, love *is* a nuisance. It's a nuisance to me. But it is, it is. I can't change it. It isn't like schoolteaching. I can't pull down the flag and go home at three o'clock. It goes on all the time. It aches all the time, it hurts all the time. But I'm not going to try to make love any littler, or change it. I'm going to change myself. I'm going to be strong enough to stand it."

"And that's what you call love? Something you have to be able to stand? Something you have to steel yourself for?"

Opal felt herself getting hot with anger and she was glad. She

185

needed to be mad to say what she had to say. Perhaps the best thing she could do for Eunice would be to say, Leave this house. You've wasted all your money on Tom Mount. See how much you love him when you have to start packing oranges or scrubbing floors to keep yourself alive. See how much he loves you. See if you're strong enough for that. For Eunice's sake, she ought to send her away. For her own sake, she wanted to keep her, the one good companion she'd ever had. When Eunice didn't answer her question, she said, "Love isn't a nuisance if it's the right kind of love. It's a comfort."

"You don't know what you're talking about."

"Why don't I? You tell me why I don't know what I'm talking about, Eunice." The clock struck half past three. Opal pulled her gown closer about her. The air that had felt so fresh and sweet when she first got out of bed was giving her goose pimples. "Go on, Eunice, why don't I know what I'm talking about?"

"You've told me you didn't love Charlie."

"Charlie isn't the only man I've known."

Eunice lifted her head, with all the interest and sympathy, Opal thought, of an invalid who learns you've suffered from the same disease.

"I didn't know you'd been in love, Opal."

"It didn't last long."

"I'm sorry. I wish you could've known someone like Tom."

Opal knew she had come to the end of her postponements. There was nothing in her life she wanted less to tell: what she had to say might help Eunice. It might not, too: it might do nothing more than make Eunice hate her. She knew what a poor figure she cut, standing there, hair on end, her nightgown showing how much she needed a corset. And she was glad of it. Let Eunice take it all in. If she had been an eighteen-year-old raving beauty, Eunice would think, Oh, she is irresistible, I understand exactly how it happened.

Well, let her understand this, if she could, she who wanted to be deprived of none of Tom Mount; here was another cubit to add to his stature. She looked about the room, still postponing. It came to her that she and Eunice had left Colorado, come to California, built this house, furnished this room, cleaned it this morning, all in preparation for this conversation. This was what it had been made for and was now waiting to hear. She walked over and closed the door. She felt the need of all the privacy she could get.

"Maybe you're right. Maybe I don't know about love. Charlie sure

186

didn't teach me. Nor Tom Mount either. But I don't think love's limited by my bad luck. I got enough imagination and spunk to see there's maybe some other yardstick for measuring love than my bad luck."

There was quite a long silence. The clock ticked. The wind blew around the house with its ceaseless sighing. The lamp, low on oil, went tup, tup, like a carp surfacing.

"Tom Mount?" Eunice asked. "Did you fall in love with him, too?"

"For a day or two, I think I called it that. Anyway, I went to bed with him."

Eunice, already perfectly still, became even quieter. It seemed to Opal that all the life ordinarily used for breathing or the circulating of the blood was concentrated wholly in Eunice's eyes. They deepened and at the same time brightened. Opal could imagine a man facing a firing squad like that, everything in his eyes in his one last minute of living. Eunice hung on to life; though dead, her eyes blazed. Drop, drop, Opal thought. You've been shot. Don't make me keep on killing you.

"He made love to me," she said deliberately, "kissed me, held me. Everything he did with you he did with me. Called me the same names, said I was an Irish gypsy . . ."

"He never called me that."

"Well, you're the only one, probably. And if that's enough of something special for you, in the man you say you're married to, why, you're welcome to it. Dear Tom, he never called me 'Irish gypsy.' How I love him for his faithfulness."

"Don't cry for me, Opal."

"I'm not crying for you. Or me. I'm just festering. I'm just getting rid of the corruption. And don't think I'm crying for Tom Mount either. I'm crying because I have to tell you all this."

"You don't have to."

"Now look here, Eunice. You be the authority on love if you want to. But don't start telling me you're the authority on friendship, too. You and God and Tom Mount! I'll tell you who Tom Mount is in that combination. He's the wholly ghost, spelled w h o l l y. He's not there. You love him, all you're loving is yourself. He's whatever you think he is—and if you stop thinking, he don't exist."

"I can't stop thinking."

"You've got something new to think about now anyway."

"Yes, I have."

All that bonfire of life that had flared in Eunice's eyes when Opal first spoke had died down. Opal saw that Eunice was now back in the past, where this pain began.

"When?" Eunice asked. "When was it?"

"When? I'm not like Tom. I don't keep a date book."

"I mean . . . before . . . me?"

"Before. And during."

"Not . . . after?"

"Not after."

"Oh, Opal!"

"Don't 'Oh-Opal' me. You were very careful to keep everything well hidden, Eunice. You turned out to be a pretty nifty liar once you got started. And you were the last girl I would ever have suspected of such a thing."

"Why, Opal?" she asked the question like a child hoping in the midst of disaster for a trade-last.

"I thought you were too nice a girl—for that kind of thing."

"But you weren't?"

"I'd been married for twenty years, Eunice. That takes some of the niceness out of you."

"Did you go to his apartment?"

"Eunice, I'll answer every question you want to ask me. I made up my mind to that before I ever began to talk to you. Now you make up your mind if you want to hear. Charlie was a kind of dirty talker. I've got just the right kind of words to tell you all about Tom and me. The answer to your first question is yes. I went to his apartment. Now what's your next question?"

The beginnings of daylight were already in the room. Not enough to do any good, but enough to spoil the lamplight, to take the warmth and sparkle from it. It was the hour when lamps were blown out too early and householders either stumble around for a quarter of an hour in the dark or, admitting they have made a mistake, burn their fingers on hot chimneys and light up all over again. Opal resisted the desire to have it all one thing or another and waited for sunup to put out the lamp. She would have given a pretty to stand outside and look in at the two of them, gaunt-eyed and draggle-tailed from worry and want of sleep; and, off a mile or so to the south, Tom Mount, she would bet her bottom dollar, was sleeping like a baby.

"What's your next question, Eunice?"

"There aren't any more. I don't want to hear anything about Tom from you. A long time ago, when the worst thing had happened to

188

me and Tom, I tried to help myself by thinking I was no worse off than a Mormon woman. They share one man, and it's even a part of their religion to do that. But they share a man they love. It might be like having Tom around, in some ways, to be with another woman who loved him. Then we could talk about him, maybe; I love to talk about Tom. But I can't listen to you. You don't love him."

"No," Opal said, "I sure don't love him. What's lovable about him?"

Eunice said, "You want me to say he's honest, industrious, a good provider, don't you? That's what lovable means to you, isn't it?"

"No," Opal said. "I know better than that. I had twenty years of learning that's not the answer. But the opposite's not the answer either."

Eunice said, "I'm going outside, Opal. I'm going to take a walk."

"You're not going off hunting Tom Mount, are you?"

"No. But I can't go to bed and I can't sit still. And I can't be where you are either, for a while."

"I was afraid of that. I knew you might feel that way."

Eunice stood up and shoved her hair into some kind of order with her fingers. "If only he had meant something to you. You could have had some excuse for killing me, then."

"Killing you?"

"Don't you think it kills me for you to have been with him . . . you . . . I don't mean just the word, Opal. But you, that body . . . maybe that nightgown even. On some night when I loved and missed him so. Don't you think that kills me? And he means nothing to you."

"I've told you, Eunice, I didn't know about you. And I wanted Tom Mount to mean something to me. God knows, I wanted him to."

The two women faced each other, Eunice so much taller and younger and wrapped all about with the pride of her suffering. She had the strength for it and she flaunted it in Opal's face. "Opal, I pity you from the bottom of my heart."

Opal took that kindly. "I deserve pity," she said. "I wouldn't want to think you didn't pity me."

Eunice, the wind taken from her sails, said, "Well, don't waste any pity on me. I don't want any pity from you or anyone else."

"I don't waste pity on you," Opal said. "I envy you."

Eunice turned—she had started for the door—but she went on, without another word.

"Leave the door open, please," Opal said.

After Eunice left, Opal blew out the lamp. It was not yet sunup, but there was plenty of light to see by, light without shadows or warmth. She was alone and at the worst hour of the day, the hour when the light disguised nothing. It was an hour either to be sleeping or up to some purpose, plunged out of bed to get an early wash on the line or to pack a lunch for an all-day picnic. But to be up at this hour, wide awake in a spotless house that needed not a hand's turn of cleaning, nothing to prepare for, no one to straighten up after; no reason for being! She went to the door and saw Eunice already a quarter of a mile down the road. She wasn't sure that she was doing the right thing, trying to help Eunice to get over Tom Mount. Let her chase him, waste her money on him, break her heart over him. What was a woman's heart for? If Eunice had vowed herself to Tom, maybe the only happiness she ever could have would be to keep that vow. She might not ever land Tom, but land him or lose him, she'd be pretty sure always to have her pain for company.

22    THE THREE of them saw each other coming, and unless they chose to turn tail and run, or to sit down on a stone and proceed no farther, were going to have to meet. Or one of them, hitting up a fast pace, might be able to outdistance the other two, reach the ridge they were all headed for, and be on his way down before the other two arrived. It would be an obvious action and look either discourteous or suspicious—and maybe both—but it was possible.

Asa Brice was the only one to whom this idea occurred, and he was the one capable of carrying it out. He couldn't recognize, at the distance he was from them, the other hikers, but he didn't want to meet anyone. He'd had enough talk last night, and if he still craved something human, he'd had it in that white body balanced in her dishpan like Aphrodite in her seashell. That was enough humanity to get him through the day without any good-morning hellos to hikers.

Spiders had had a night of weaving, and he destroyed webs with every footstep. Meadow larks and blackbirds were already fluting, and the hot day to come was heralded by the chirping of katydids. Big white butterflies fluttered around the milkweed pods. He trod on a wild gourd vine and stooped to breathe deep of the rank smell, the way another man might bend to drink of a spring. Stooping, he saw a snake's imprint in the sandy dust and paused for a better look. The wind from the east, still fresh, blew over him as he touched the snake print with a finger. He squinted to follow the barely visible print of that scaly sliding, and what he had come out for came back to him: rapture.

Chad, already enraptured, hadn't come out to hunt it; and he hadn't lost it either. He was filled to bursting with it and with speech. He had been talking to himself, talking to birds, talking to lizards, talking to God; and everything he said was for Press to hear. Present or nonpresent, existent or nonexistent, cut no ice with him. He had the gift of tongues this morning and could converse with stones and read the meanings of clouds. He saw the two hikers coming, and as for him, let them come. He could pass them unspeaking, or make them stop and tell them his life's story, including last night's installment and this morning's promises. He was completely surrounded by magic, and there was not one thing that could break the spell.

He hadn't been able to sleep for thinking of Press, and before daylight the idea had come to him to go have a look at her house, see where she slept, stand where her feet had been, breathe in some of the air she had breathed out. By God, he was a born fool and lover, and the suitability of his action delighted him. It was proof of what he'd sometimes doubted: he was as human as the next one. Looking askance at others came so natural to him he'd often feared he'd been left standing behind the door when the humanness had been handed out. He could size up things too well; and he took the time to size them up. Ellen went around with her heart on her sleeve; heart and soul both. She was the original inside-out girl. Give Ellen the smallest tap and you'd hit a vital organ. All he wore on his sleeve was his brains and his doubts; and the smallest tap hit them, too.

He had dreamed sometimes, daydreamed, that is, that there was a key, some secret key, he'd discover that would let him into the world where others lived and free him from looking before he leaped. Well, he had found that key, he was leaping, and all his looks were for Press, not for where he'd land. Press was the key; she had unlocked him, let him out of himself. He had lost his mind; or at least he'd lost the coat with his mind on the sleeve, and it was the happiest mislaying of his life.

The sun had come up as he walked toward the Cope house and that was all right with him but not necessary. It made a fine light, resting in clouds like a cinnamon apple in a bed of pink cotton candy; birds flashed across the sky; the stubble was cobwebbed, and the cobwebs were bedewed; a coyote gave him a familiar look, perhaps a leer left over from last night's triumph. He gave him a wave in return; the coyote grinned but didn't wave back. He didn't care. He had the key that let him in. He could take the sweet away from the spines of a cactus apple, think a joke into Zoomy's jokeless mind, and maybe even learn to like his father. He had the key.

The Cope house was an ordinary house, not a thing more, and he could digest that, too. *He'd* been transformed; that was enough of a gift. But to him that hath shall be given. Under the first window, where he planted himself to imagine Press sleeping, he had no need for his imagination. She came to her window, pulled there by his presence, for he made no sound. She came as if awakened from a dream to find that her dream was real. She smiled with her eyes and her lips; she moved her hands toward him. She had on a white nightgown, deep-necked and sleeveless; and at first, waking up so fast, this didn't trouble her. Later, it did. He had heard that women, when they first woke up, were often a sight to behold. Press was, but not in the way the saying suggested. She was a sight to behold in her beauty. His knees had a tendency to buckle, not from weakness but from a desire to kneel before her. By will power he kept them straight; a time for kneeling might come, but this wasn't it. They did nothing but look, and as far as he was concerned, there was nothing else he wanted to do. She was the key that opened him to the rest of the world, but between them there was no need for keys. They were open to each other. It was a strange thing that a girl in the flesh, a girl he loved, a girl whose breasts were more visible than the breasts of any of his imagined girls, should make him want to kneel. When he imagined girls, his knees were never what he wanted to be on, and though he saw all Press's beauty, it was her sweetness and her goodness, he thought, that really moved him. He believed that he would have loved her for these qualities, no matter what she looked like; he believed that he was filled with true wisdom to be able to see, beneath the disguise of all her curves and colors, her soul. He loved her in spite of her beauty and was carried away by her quick movements, by the trembling of her eyelids and by her mouth's courageous, shamefaced smiling. These were not chancy, like beauty, but Press herself making herself known to him.

192

He had no idea how long they had stayed, gazing at each other. If she had not left, he might still be there. But she came to herself, suddenly, pulled her gown closely about her, and without a single good-by for him went out of sight into her room. It was sudden and it hurt him, but he understood it. All at once, the way she was dressed and the time of day it was had come to her. He hadn't hung around hoping for any reappearance, but had lit out across the hills. He knew when he'd had a gift; and when he'd had it, he didn't spoil it by asking for more.

Eunice knew that she was walking through a fine morning because she could remember that this was the name she had given to such mornings at other times in her life. Asked what kind of a morning it was, she would have answered, "Fine," in exactly the same way she would have said that two and two make four. It was a fact, but she had no feeling about it. She walked fast, avoided cactus, rocks, squirrel holes, as well as ever; but her body was only a means of transportation and the passing landscape only a means of occasional distraction from pain.

Of the two facts she had learned since the night before, she did not know why the bitter should crowd out the sweet. Tom was here. Why couldn't the sweetness of that fill her mind? He was here; he had come this unbelievable distance. She would probably see him today. There had been sadness in her meeting with him last night, and disappointment. She had expected at the very least that they would walk together in the moonlight, speak of the wonders they had known, and of the wonder of this new coming together. It had not happened; but she had known of whom she said this. She was going to love the man Tom Mount was; she had espoused him in full knowledge. It was a kind of unfaithfulness even to ask him to be different. So Tom's arrival, whether she saw him as much as she would like or not, was her blessing. And it was not her blessing that filled her, but the knowledge, the trivial knowledge, in the face of all she already knew of him, of his having made love to Opal.

She could not blame Opal; Opal had known nothing and owed her nothing. Opal had done to her what she had done to Clara—and to all the others. They were a band of sisters. He was irresistibly lovable. "Take me. I am yours." What else could a woman say to him? Opal had agreed with her in saying "yes" to Tom. If "yes" was what she said. Perhaps she had said "please." She was not jealous of Opal. Tom was a man to cure you of jealousy. You could no more be jealous of him than you could be jealous of the sun. You missed his warmth; but his absence only made you long more desperately for his return. She was jealous of no one, blamed no one, but terrible visions rose before her eyes: Opal, unbuttoning her soft, motherly clothes. . . . She tried to walk her eyes out, or walk some other sight into them.

On the afternoon in Fort Collins when she had first read Tom's letters, she had left his apartment and bought a bottle of D'jer Kiss perfume, the duplicate of the bottle (belonging to Clara?) she had found in his bathroom. She kept it with her; she still had it. She made it a part of her life; no vision of it and what it stood for could rise suddenly to sicken her. She lived with what the vision only pictured.

Chad was the first one on the ridge, Eunice the second. The boy had something on his heart to say; but face to face with Eunice, he became silent. He could talk to a stone but not to a face like a stone. He was in love, something she didn't know anything about; and never would, thrashing about the hills like a wild woman, her hair to her waist, and her white shoes ruined with dirt. He pitied her, but he had a notion to keep right on traveling. She looked like bad luck to him.

Eunice stopped him. It was like meeting herself two years ago, when everything was before her. She spoke to the boy in the tone she would have used for that girl—pitying him for what lay ahead.

"Do you like early-morning walks?"

The question stumped Chad.

"I used to like them a lot back in Colorado," she told him.

"This is the first early-morning walk I ever took in my life," he said. "I liked this one all right."

"You're Shel Lewis's son, aren't you?" she asked. "How do you like it here on the Tract?"

How? He didn't know how. But he knew who. "There seem to be some very nice people here," he said.

"Did you meet some nice young people last night?"

He decided to chance it. "I met Press Cope."

"Press Cope? She's my best friend."

It seemed unlikely to him. Eunice was in his mother's class. But with those words Eunice became a real person, a person who knew Press. He was now prepared to listen to her all day, but he never got

194

to hear a thing. Asa Brice arrived, and Chad could not talk of Press before another man.

"They'll be waiting breakfast for me," he said, and went off down the ridge toward the floor of the valley.

"The Tract's full of walkers this morning," said Asa. "Runners even," he added, as Chad lit into a downhill jog trot.

"He's in love," said Eunice.

"Did he tell you?"

"He didn't have to."

Asa left it at that. He had too high a regard for love to make chit-chat of it.

It was sometimes hard for him to move out of his solitude into conversation, to shift from winds and trees, who asked nothing of him, to persons, who did. Eunice made this shift easy for him. They were both "old settlers"; he had known her for six months. He had never before been so struck by her naturalness. Her hair, hanging loose, and her white dress made her appear timeless. She was not hidden from him by anything passing or fashionable. She did not separate him from nature, because she seemed to be a part of nature. He had expected to do what Chad had done, to pass the time of day and move on. Instead, he stood beside her looking down the ridge to where small heat waves already formed and broke. After a while, he said, "If you're thinking about turning homeward now, I'll walk with you, if you don't mind."

She said she'd be glad for his company, and they started down the ridge together.

# BOOK II

1   In NOVEMBER, the Lewises moved into their new house. Chad still slept outside in the tent, but the rest of the family slept upstairs in the unpartitioned attic.

There was an unused bedroom downstairs, but Joicey loved the idea of a spare room, a room ready on a moment's notice for any visitor who wanted to spend the night. She had been brought up to believe that every nice family had such a room, but this was the first time she and Shel had been able to manage one.

She had put the new bed in it and had outfitted the bed with a coverlet and bolster inherited from her Grandmother Covington. It was a beautiful room, and so far had never been used. In fact, the idea of someone staying in the room, now that she had made it so nice, did not set well with Joicey.

When it got dark, she would light a lamp and put it on the bureau in the spare room. Then, during the evening, if the fancy struck her, she would go stand in the door and admire the perfection she had created.

Sometimes she would be able to persuade Shel to look at it with her.

"Isn't it pretty, Shel?"

"It's pretty, all right. Too bad about that bed, though."

"Too bad about it?"

"It had such a lively start to end up down here. Must feel like it's been put out to grass before its time."

"Oh, Shel!"

In mid-November, during a prolonged spell of unseasonably hot weather, Shel stopped one night before going upstairs to bed to look into the spare room. "Let's sleep down here until the heat wave's over, Joicey."

Joicey said she would as soon think of sleeping in her dress, and Shel did not insist. More was at stake, he saw, than comfort. He took one last sniff of the spare room's coolness and marched upstairs to the hot attic. He had rigged up burlap curtains, hung on baling wire, to separate his and Joicey's end of the attic from Ellen's and Zoomy's. Tonight, trying to coax a little air through the attic, he had pushed them back. The attic's only windows were in the east and west gables, and Shel, undressing in the dark by the west window, said, "With this kind of weather it don't seem possible that Thanksgiving's almost here, does it?"

Joicey was on her knees saying her prayers, and it made her out of sorts to be talked to at such times. And since it seemed to her wrong to get out of sorts while praying, she would be in an unhappy mood when she got into bed. Mad at herself and mad at Shel. Remembering this, Shel kept his thoughts about the weather to himself. A heat wave in November was nothing unusual in Southern California, but it astonished the newcomers. After the long hot days of September, they thought summer had spent itself. Now there had been three days of near-ninety heat and no sign yet of any letup.

When Shel got into bed, he could feel the warmth of Joicey's body added to the heat of the night. Joicey slid over to her own bedrail. "You're just burning up, Shel," she said.

"You're not exactly a snowbank yourself."

They were both a little touchy about a matter in which they held opposite opinions, and in which Shel was getting his way. And the weather didn't help their feelings any. It wasn't just the present heat. Except for a spattering in mid-October which did no more than temporarily lay the dust, there had been no rain since last April. Everything was bone dry. Joicey's skin felt to her as if it was weathering away, flake by flake; and her hair, filled with electricity, rose up off her head like something magnetized, to meet the comb. They were still hauling water, and she never had an extra cupful for cooking or cleaning.

And Shel had all that water stored out there in the weir box and in Jessup's water wagon, to be used for planting trees! Planting trees that would more than likely never live.

It made her mad, and she had been against it and had fought the

198

idea until she saw that she was fighting more than an idea; she was fighting Shel himself. Then she stopped. She was against planting trees for as long as she believed that it was Shel's stubbornness or impatience or pride she was fighting; the minute she saw that what she opposed was Shel himself, the fight went out of her. She couldn't win, if that was the case, without Shel's losing some part of himself. And she wanted Shel Lewis just as he was.

If Shel was determined to plant trees before there was water in the pipes, not because he was mad at the Perkins Investment Company but because he was a man who believed in taking a few chances and wouldn't be himself unless he did, she would keep right on scrubbing the floor with bath water without complaint. In some ways, Shel, who wasn't a believer, was a better Christian than she was. "You have to take some things on trust," he said. "You've got to believe the sun's coming up tomorrow. And that there'll be a normal rainfall. And you've got to believe that some men mean what they say. You've got to live with some faith. You've got to bet on your own luck."

That was the kind of man Shel was. A man who would bet on himself and on his luck. He had some trust in the world. He thought it was on his side; and so far, it had been. But if his luck changed and the world turned against him, Shel was the man she had married.

"Shel," she whispered, "do you know what I wish I had?"

"I sure do. Something we ain't got and can't get. Cold clabber. Or saucer peaches. Or maybe a pawpaw."

"No, I don't. But I do wish I had a nice juicy apple."

"Some special kind, I reckon. Hard to come by."

"I've been thinking about a Russet. They're so juicy."

"How about a Maiden's Blush?"

Joicey gave Shel, already over on his own bedrail, a shove.

"It's a little late for that, I reckon," she said.

"Maybe," Shel said, "but it won't help you any now to push me out of bed."

They drifted off to sleep talking about apples.

At the other end of the attic, Zoomy was wide awake. He was hot and he had a bad conscience. As long as he had been able to hear his parents' voices, he had been able to keep his mind off his own troubles. Now there was nothing to distract him. His throat was dry, his scalp itched with sweat, and his skin crawled as if he had chicken lice.

On the cot against the north wall, Ellen was breathing evenly. He

199

wanted to wake her up. It seemed selfish of her to sleep when he couldn't. He sat up cautiously so that he could look out of the east window. There was a light still burning in Chad's tent. It would be cool down there and it would be fun to talk to Chad in the middle of the night. Still, he postponed getting out of bed. Under the best of circumstances he did not enjoy the prospect of the trip down the dark stairs, across the back yard to Chad's tent. And these were not the best of circumstances. Because of what he was doing, he deserved to come to a bad end: to stumble and break his neck on the stairs, to step on a coiled rattlesnake in the middle of the back yard. And even if he were to escape all these dangers on the way to the tent, Chad was likely to send him upstairs, right back through them again.

He got out of bed. He was dying of thirst and sleeplessness and the itch, anyway. He reached under his mattress and got the tobacco bags that held his money and made his way fearfully down the stairs, through the house, across the yard, and to the tent, his ill-gotten money as safe as if he'd earned it with honest sweat.

Chad had both the tent flaps tied back and was lying naked on top of his covers, reading by the murky light of a lantern. Zoomy hadn't made a sound, but Chad knew somehow that he was there. He put down his book.

"Think you'll know me next time you see me, Bud?"

Zoomy felt a little abashed. "I reckon so."

"What're you doing down here in the middle of the night, anyway?"

"I couldn't go to sleep."

"Keeping me awake's not going to help you any."

Up to this minute, Zoomy had thought that what he wanted was coolness, or somebody to visit with, or maybe a drink. Now he knew he wanted to confess. He swung his moneybags back and forth.

Chad ignored them for a while. Then he said, "You taken up smoking?"

Zoomy shook the bags so that the money clinked.

"That's not tobacco," he said.

"What is it?"

"Money."

"What'd you do? Hold up a bank?"

"There's no bank to hold up."

"Well, one thing I know for certain," Chad said. "You didn't work for it."

200

"I worked for it," Zoomy said. "It was kind of unusual work," he admitted.

Chad bunched his pillows under his head. "I bet it was," he said, and waited.

Zoomy wanted to confess, but he felt the need of some help.

"This isn't half of what I've earned," he said, jingling his Bull Durham bags.

"I reckon you got the rest out at interest."

"It's buried," Zoomy said.

Chad picked up his book again.

"You know the Anaheim irrigation canal?" Zoomy asked. "Where nobody's supposed to swim?"

"Sure."

"You know big, fat Ralph Sanchez, who rides around on the lookout for swimmers?"

"I know what Ralph does. What I'd like to know is what you do."

It was this that Zoomy wanted to confess. Still, he thought Chad might understand it better if he could hear about it gradually.

"Come on, come on," Chad said. "If you haven't got anything to tell me, go on back upstairs to bed."

"I warn kids," Zoomy said.

"Warn them of what?"

"Ralph."

Chad had been keeping his place in his book with his finger. Now he closed his book and put it on the orange box, which served as his bedside table.

"That's your work?"

Zoomy nodded.

"Where does the money come in?"

"I charge."

"Who do you charge?"

"The kids."

"What do you charge them for? And how much?"

"They pay me a nickel to swim all afternoon."

"They can swim without paying you anything."

"Yeh, but Ralph can catch them and fine them. I warn them if Ralph's coming."

"How can you warn them?"

"I got two helpers." Zoomy began, in spite of himself, to let some

of the pride he felt for his business creep into his voice. "If I see Ralph,
I give a kind of signal to the first kid and he gives it to the second kid
and the second kid warns the swimmers."

"What's the signal?"

"It's a secret."

"What do the swimmers do when they get this secret signal?"

"Run. Or hide under a bridge."

"Who's your helpers?"

"Burleigh Raunce and Buddy Cudlip."

"They help you for nothing?"

"Of course not. I pay them a penny apiece."

"For a whole afternoon's work?"

"They don't have to work for me if they don't want to."

"How much do you make in an afternoon?"

"The most, so far, was thirty-three cents. I got $7.35 altogether
now."

Chad whistled. "I didn't know there was that much money on the
Tract."

"If the kids didn't pay me a nickel, their folks might have to pay a
five-dollar fine for them if they got caught. It's better for them to pay
me five cents. Ain't it, Chad?"

"I don't know if it's better. It's cheaper, I reckon."

"That's what I thought."

"Did you ever think why there's rules against swimming in the
ditch? That people drink that water?"

"I got strict rules. We dip up a bucketful of water from the ditch
and every kid's got to clean off good before he goes in. He's got to
promise not to do anything in the water, too."

"Do anything? Oh. You got any way of checking on that?"

"They got to give me their word of honor before they go in."

"And a nickel."

"I told you that."

"Has Ralph caught anybody yet?"

"No, siree. Not any of my kids, anyway."

"If somebody gets caught, won't he want his money back?"

"No. I'll pay his fine."

"A couple of pieces of bad luck would wipe you out, wouldn't it?"

"Well, you can't make money without gambling," Zoomy quoted
his father.

When Chad said nothing, but continued to stare at him, Zoomy said, "We help Ralph, too. We fish out dead cats and drowned squirrels. Stuff he's supposed to get. And we don't let anybody dirty in."

"Well, I reckon you don't have anything to worry about, do you? The Reverend Raunce will have you helping him preach soon."

"Oh, I'm not in the same class as a preacher," Zoomy protested uncomfortably.

"No, I suppose not. You're just helping a little stealing to go on—and making money out of it."

The word "steal" shocked Zoomy. "I don't steal anything."

"Those kids are stealing the use of water that don't belong to them, and you're helping them. And getting paid for it."

Zoomy put his moneybags down beside the lantern and Chad's book. "It would be hard to give the money back, because I don't know what kids paid it."

Chad said nothing.

"Are you going to tell Papa?"

"No, I'm not going to tell him."

Chad picked up his book, found his place, and began to read again, as if he had never been interrupted.

Zoomy felt very lonely. The night was so warm; the katydids were chirping almost as loud and fast as in the daytime. He could see the stars through the opened flap of Chad's tent, and they, too, seemed out of place in the warmth. Stars and coolness went together. Katydids and daylight. Everything was mixed up. He reckoned he knew it was stealing all along.

He began to sidle carefully nearer the bed, ready to stop if Chad looked up from his book. Chad read on. Zoomy settled himself, an ounce at a time, on the edge of the bed. Without stopping his reading, Chad moved over. Something told Zoomy not to remind Chad of this by saying thank you. He intended to stay awake as long as Chad did. He took a last look at his moneybags, and his eyes closed.

Ellen was suddenly wide awake, the dark night empty and towering above her. She began to think of Tom Mount. She did not imagine love scenes, or even a single touch. There was no conversation. She thought of him as something beautiful; she was like a horse-lover remembering a noble animal or a naturalist recalling trees and mountains. She smiled to think that he was alive in the world she was in. She watched him walk, with his big thrown-back head and his soft tigering footsteps; he moved his hands in wide, slow gestures which

203

made her think of water lilies. Oh, she knew very well that she was a girl dreaming of a man. She knew she wasn't thinking of tigers or water lilies or mountains or forests. She knew she was thinking of a man; and she knew that men married women, fondled and kissed them. But her mind didn't go near enough for that; it stayed at a distance and watched him.

All at once, without knowing how the idea came to her, she thought, Zoomy is gone. She held her breath, waiting to hear some sound from Zoomy's cot, but there was none. Her dream of Tom Mount vanished in a flash. She could dream of strangers, but for her family she acted. She tiptoed to Zoomy's cot; he was gone, and the bed cooled off from his body. She put her hand under his mattress: the moneybags were gone, too. Well, he had at least left with all his wits about him. She looked out the east window and saw that Chad's tent was still lighted.

She went downstairs, and with each step entered cooler layers of air. She moved in the air like a swimmer and felt her thighs go goose-pimply with the unexpected coolness. She walked through the house, loving it in a new way, without responsibility, like a visitor.

The sky was pricked like a colander with stars. They were the lights of some other place shining through holes in the sky. The sky was a tent, and starlight leaked through like rain. Her feet had become tender since summer's barefoot days, and she walked on tiptoe to spare them. Snakes never entered her head. Katydids sang, thin and sweet. Was their song, like the light of the stars, part of a bigger sound, leaking through? No, that was silly; they were little animals fiddling.

She entered the tent, and Chad looked at her as if he had expected her. He was wearing a book like a fig leaf. She had a momentary thought of what the book covered, but she knew all about that. She had no more interest in it than in an ear; except that she felt some pity for the ragged unkempt way in which men were made, not neatly finished off like women. She didn't wonder at their always covering up. It was nothing to be really ashamed of, since God had made them that way, but it was nothing to flaunt either.

Lying beside Chad, taking two-thirds of the bed, was Zoomy. "I missed Zoomy," she whispered. There was no need to whisper. Once Zoomy was asleep, he was in some other world; but the night and the lantern light and Chad's grave questioning face made her daytime voice seem unsuitable.

Chad whispered back, which surprised her. When there was no need of a thing, Chad didn't do it. He didn't waste himself pretending. She was halfway playing at not waking Zoomy. Chad was whispering because he felt like it.

"He's been here all night."

"All night? Why, what time is it now?"

Chad's watch was on the orange box beside the lantern. "Five," he said; then, after looking, "Five-ten."

"Are you going to sleep now?"

"There isn't time."

"Let's go for a walk, Chad. Let's see the sun up."

"I see it every morning. All right. Blow out the lantern," he said. "I'll go outside with you."

Bending over to blow out the light, she saw Zoomy's round face, gone back to babyhood in sleep. She turned down the wick and blew. In the darkness, speaking quietly but no longer whispering, she said, "He's a baby."

Chad said, "He'll have to get over that now."

"Why will he?"

"We're going to have a new baby brother or sister."

"I didn't know that. Who told you?"

"Let's go outside," Chad said.

There was no light yet, but the darkness had thinned. Something was going to happen over in the east. The air, though warm, had freshened. Chad had put on pants, but no shirt; and though he didn't want to walk, he didn't want to stand either. He picked out a place for them to sit: the edge of the weir box. It was made of cement, as high as their shoulders. Water for the tree-planting filled it. Chad helped her up, then vaulted up beside her. Ellen put a hand in the warm water. A new baby spoiled her idea of them as a family. She had thought they were perfect as they were.

"I think they're too old for a baby," she said.

"They don't think so," Chad answered.

Weren't we enough for them? What would they think if one of their children said, "We're going to have a new parent." It would hurt them, wouldn't it?

"Maybe you're mistaken," she said. "Did Mama tell you?"

"Nobody told me, except my own eyes."

"I wonder why God let them go for ten years without any."

"What do you know about having babies?"

"Everything."

"Tell me."

"God plants a seed in a woman, a married woman—and it grows inside her until the baby's ready to be born. It takes nine months."

"Why a married woman?"

"A mother needs a man to earn a living."

"Did you figure all this out for yourself?"

"Of course not. Nobody could ever guess that babies grow inside women. For one thing, you wouldn't think anybody could stretch that much. I didn't figure it out. Mama told me. Who told you?"

"I forget."

"Forget? How could you forget a thing like that?"

Chad didn't answer her, and she leaned down again and lifted a double handful of water and let the drops back into the weir box with a rainy sound. It was still too dark to see a thing. Only their familiar voices kept them from being strangers. She spoke as if the night were a river and her words would be carried away on it. She could say anything, and when daylight came, no trace would be left.

She asked a question, as an example of how she would like the conversation to go.

"Are you in love, Chad?"

She didn't expect an answer. Love was nothing Chad talked about, or himself. He would put her off with a funny answer, then say, "How about you, Sis?" Then they would talk of Tom Mount.

Chad said, "Am I in love? Oh, Ellen, I wish I could tell you."

"Tell me," Ellen said. "I won't tell anybody."

"I don't care who knows. It isn't that. I want to talk about it and I don't know how. You're her age. You're a girl. You're not like her though. I mean, I think of you as my little sister. You are my little sister; you're more of a baby than Zoomy. Press is a woman."

"Why, she's no woman any more than I am," Ellen said, forgetting the big thing, Chad loves Press, in the desire to set him right about the little thing.

"She's Press. I'm going to marry her."

"Have you proposed?"

"No. She knows I'm going to marry her though."

"Are you happy?"

"Happy? Oh, God, I could die."

"With happiness?"

"No, not happiness. She won't see me—or if she sees me, all she wants me for is to wait on her mother. You'd think I was a slave she'd bought for her mother. That's the only way I can please Press. Are all girls like that? If you loved a man, would you want him waiting on Mama?"

"No, I wouldn't want him to wait on anybody. I would want to wait on him, hand and foot, myself. You just think she loves you, Chad."

"She loves me. I know she loves me."

"Did she say so?"

"She said so."

Ellen thought of Tom Mount and what she felt for him. She considered herself experienced in love. She spoke with absolute authority. "She doesn't know what love is."

"I will have to learn to like the kind of love she has, because I will never want anyone else's."

Ellen believed this. Chad did not make mistakes. This was the first sad happening of her life. Only yesterday, she had said to her father, "There is not one thing in my life I would change." And even as she had said it, life had been changing about her: a new baby coming; Chad unhappily in love. She could love, and not be loved in return, and she would get over it. She knew that. And not do anything wild or desperate either. But not Chad. He was final and he was desperate, otherwise he wasn't Chad.

"What will you do?" she asked.

"Love her. Keep on loving her. Never stop."

"Oh, Chad, I'm sorry for you."

"Don't be sorry for me. It will come out all right. I will make it come out all right."

She had a woman's pessimism, which men construe as optimism. She could doubt that it would come out all right and still not despair.

"There are other girls," she suggested.

"Not for me."

"If she wasn't so beautiful, it would be easier."

"You'd as well tell me it would be easier to be burned if fire wasn't so hot."

Press *was* her beauty—even Ellen felt that, and felt its power. Medora Cudlip was as beautiful, compare complexion with complexion, eye with eye, mouth with mouth, as Press was. But she didn't live in her beauty as Press lived in hers. Medora had an outside and an inside, and you were never mixed up as to which was which.

Ellen thought, Now I can tell Chad about Tom Mount. But she

couldn't say a word. Compared with Chad's sorrow, her happiness didn't seem real. There was no problem in it; there was nothing to wonder and figure about; there was nothing that needed doing. When happiness came, the story was over. She had no story to tell Chad. She had started happy.

It was going to be light soon. The darkness was breaking up; it was becoming tremulous, wavering like water. Chad's face, which had been masked, now had eyebrows and a mouth. His eyes, as she had guessed, were closed. What she had not guessed, and could scarcely believe, was what the beginning light showed her: Chad had been crying; there was a glaze of tears on his cheeks. He had cried the way he laughed, without a sound. Zoomy could bellow his head off, and often did, and she thought nothing of it. But for Chad, who was above the world, to sit beside her crying! She could not say a word to him, not even touch him. She knew why he was crying, but she was too humble to believe any word or touch of hers could make up his lack to him.

There was a small wind blowing and nothing for it to move, except a wisp of her hair and a feather fallen onto the water. She saw that the beauty of the coming light was not in the east, but in the hills to the northwest, which were changing in color from grape blue, with a dusty bloom, to the blue-pink of faded cabbage roses back in Kentucky. As the sun came up, heat came with it. She leaned over the water and picked up the feather, which had drifted toward her. It was finished with flying and unsuited for swimming. She leaned lower and pushed the water into waves and made them rock against the cement box with a hollow echo of the sea. She turned clear about and lowered her feet into the water. There was nothing wrong in doing that; this water was not intended for drinking. It felt wrong, though, very wicked, like putting her feet into a bucket of new milk.

"Chad?" she asked.

He turned and saw what she was doing, sliding ankle-deep, calf-deep, thigh-deep into the water. She was lifting her gown as she entered the water. Getting that wet was as strange as being in water at all. As she went down, Chad lifted her gown over her head. She was in water to her armpits and as modestly covered as when she wore her nightgown. But being naked in a covering of water did not feel the same as being naked in a covering of muslin. It felt better, to tell the truth: blissful in the steady, cool touch, which both covered her and left her naked.

"Turn around," Chad said, and she faced away from him, then felt the movement of the water as he slid in beside her. They were shy of each other, and each kept to his own side of the weir box, like strangers sharing a bed. The water, like the darkness earlier, made them whisper again.

"Oh, Chad." The sun was still not up, but it would top Old Saddle Back any minute. She remembered stories of the war, of men crouched in trenches waiting for shells to go over. She felt that way about the sun, as though it were a shell about to explode and she was waiting, protected by the water, for it to shoot up over the mountain. What could be more beautiful? And except that she had, without thinking, put first a hand and then a foot into the water, they would not be here at all. It had all come by chance, and this made her angry.

"Chad," she whispered. He looked at her inquiringly. "It's just chance that we are doing this."

"Everything's chance."

"It oughtn't to be. We should've figured this out. We should've planned it. We might've missed it."

"You can plan and miss, too."

"It is better to try."

Chad smiled at her. He had gone clear under the water and there were no longer any signs of tears. "I'm going to try." He hit the water with his fist. "Don't think I'm not going to try."

Forgetting that she had decided it was nothing to say, she said, "I'm so happy." Then she, too, sank down until she was completely covered and held her breath, planning not to come up until something told her the sun was up. They would shoot up together. Under water, clear as a bell, she heard Zoomy's voice calling; more accustomed to obeying it than the sun, she came up and went to the edge of the weir box. Chad was already there, signaling to Zoomy to be quiet. Except for a clump of cottonwoods away off in the distance, Zoomy was the only object in all the space between the weir box and the mountains. He filled it peculiarly, his big-legged homemade B.V.D.s down to his knees and his moneybags in his hand. But he didn't look little or lonely there, just peculiar. She had supposed that finding his brother and sister naked in the weir box would astound him, but what he was exclaiming about was something else.

"Look, Chad," he said, turning his back on them and pointing to the east.

There, in the utterly clear air and a little to the left of Old Saddle

Back, San Gorgonio, the mountain they couldn't usually see at all, rose up enormous, white-domed, a world in itself, towering above their little flat stretch of earth. But it wasn't this mountain, suddenly visible and nearer, that Zoomy was pointing to: it was a gray-green cloud that filled the pass on each side of San Gorgonio and hid the base of the mountain, so that its snow-peaked, blue-shouldered mass seemed supported by it. They had caught glimpses of San Gorgonio before; but never of this gray greenness, which, for all it looked so solid, must be newly made.

"What is it, Chad?" Zoomy asked.

"It's dust," Chad said. "It's dust off the desert. It's a big Santa Ana blowing up. There'll be a bad wind before night. You go tell Father. Maybe he won't want to plant today after all."

The sun came up as Zoomy slammed the back door; it came up fast, red and murky, and they heard Zoomy going through the house slamming doors for every inch the sun climbed.

"You get out first," Chad said, and turned his back, so that she could climb out modestly.

Ellen stood naked for a minute, arms uplifted in the dry warmth. Then she pulled her nightgown over her head and ran after Zoomy into the house.

When Zoomy called at the head of the stairs, "Look out of the window, Papa," his father jumped out of bed. "Which window?" he asked. Zoomy pointed, and his father was there before he was. The cloud, in the few minutes Zoomy had been away from it, had risen higher.

"Chad says there's going to be a big wind."

"Chad's right," his father said. "It's fixing to blow."

Shel thought that all he was deciding that morning was, Plant today or postpone till the wind's over. Afterward, he saw that he'd been deciding more than that. He wasn't at the window more than three or four minutes, watching that green-gray cloud and trying to make up his mind what to do. The safest thing to do, he knew, was to leave the trees right where they were, well-balled and soaked, packed close together out of the sun and the wind on the north side of the shed he called the barn. Yet even that morning, he must have had some forebodings; otherwise, he would never have been able to remember those few minutes so well.

"Time stood still" was a saying he had heard used to describe such moments in a man's life. Time did not stand still. It moved at its regular gait; but occasionally a man's mind, racing, seemed to leave time behind. So it was that morning, as he weighed the reasons for planting or postponing. He decided to plant. The hollows of Kentucky were full of men waiting for suitable weather. He would take the risk. Let the wind blow. He would fight it. Let Sylvester Perkins renege on his promises. He would sue him. Let the rains fail. He would water the trees, bucket by bucket, with his own hands.

He gave Zoomy a slap on his bunched rubbery bottom.

"Get your pants on, boy, we've got a big day ahead of us."

He pulled on his own pants.

Joicey said, "Are you going to plant in spite of the wind, Shel?"

Shel said, "I've decided to, Joicey. I hope I'm not making a mistake."

"Light the fire," Joicey said. "I'll be right down and start breakfast."


2  THAT cloud in the east was both a threat and a promise. To most people on the Tract, since they had never seen one like it before, it was a promise: something was going to happen. Day after day, the skies had been cloudless, the heat intense, the breeze unvarying in its strength and direction of blowing; a buzzard's shadow passing over the plowed fields was enough to cause comment. They were all waiting: waiting for water in the pipes, for the heat to let up, for the church to be finished, for the school to start, for the rains to come. They did not know that they had been waiting for a Santa Ana wind, but the minute they saw that cloud in the east, they knew they had been waiting for it, too. If that cloud had showed any signs of wavering, subsiding, fading, they would, according to their various natures, have wished it, prayed it, willed it, ordered it back into the sky. They began to stake their lives on it; if nothing came of it, they were done for. Not a one of them, except Raunce and the Mexicans, knew what it actually was, or could do. Not a one of them except Asa Brice cared about it as a thing in itself. It was a promise that something was going to happen, and that was enough for them; though unless it blew their houses over, they were not sure what the promise was. They faced the east like Mohammedans that morning, and the cloud was their Mecca. Blow, blow was their prayer.

Except for that one distant smudge, the day was like crystal. Old Saddle Back, fifteen miles away, moved up to the edge of the Tract. The sun could be seen shining through the transparent ears of jack rabbits, feeding on the dry grass of ridges four miles distant. Four miles was what it looked, anyway.

The rains might not come; who cared? They were drowning in light. The clarity of the morning air excited everyone. The Tract, under that light, was a different place. The settlers had made a journey without travel, because the nature of their environment had changed. They felt as wild and irresponsible as tourists. What they did today would not count because they were away from home. Their senses, already worn to the quick by heat and dryness and waiting, were now pricked into still-greater aliveness by having something new to use them on. And the contradictoriness of the omens excited them. Out of this perfect stillness, would a wind come? Out of perfect clarity, dust? Out of perfect familiarity, strangeness?


3    Rosa, like any good Mexican wife, was up before her husband. When she saw the cloud, she came back into their bedroom to tell Pete about it.

"You won't have to go to work today," she said.

"Why not?" Pete asked. He was comfortable; he worked from necessity, not for pleasure, and he hoped Rosa was right. Still, he didn't trust Rosa when her conclusions gave him some unexpected pleasure.

"A big Santa Ana is coming up."

"I am not so weakly," Pete said, stretching himself and flexing his arms, "that I can't work if the wind blows."

"You are strong enough. I know that. But when Mr. Lewis sees that cloud, he will decide not to plant today."

"I told him I'd be there."

"It'll be a trip for nothing."

"Maybe." He wanted to stay. He wasn't like Shel; he wasn't trying to get anyplace. His grandfather had done that for him. All he wanted to do was to hang on to the four rooms that were left him of his grandfather's eighteen. The adobe walls were thick and the window sills wide. Rosa kept pots of flowers on them, and a hummingbird

212

whirred now, above the geraniums. Rosa, in a pink house dress, might easily be mistaken for a flower. Except for what seemed unchangeable in their lives, he didn't know how they could be happier.

He threw back the sheet. "I better have a look at that cloud," he said. "Don't look at me that way."

"I'm not looking at you any way," Rosa said.

"Why not?" Pete asked.

He stepped into his pants, and they walked out into the yard together. The coming Santa Ana did not excite him as it did the people on the Tract. He did not need a wind blowing up out of the east to convince him he was alive. They turned away from the dust cloud on the horizon to look at the village of Ramos, of which their house was the last outpost.

There was no nonsense in the village of trying to make the grass grow in the yards; instead, the earth was packed hard and treated like a floor. Paths and flower beds were outlined with pebbles, shells, pieces of broken china, and colored glass. The flowers were none of them small or faint-colored: big red and yellow zinnias, purple bougainvillaea, red geraniums, hard-blue asters. No Mexican pretended that these flowers had been dropped down from heaven by the hand of God and had no responsibility except to Him. The flowers had a responsibility to their planters, and their planters never let them forget it, training them in ways which would make it impossible for them to be mistaken for any natural growth. The gardens were arranged in raised beds, and these beds themselves were interestingly shaped. Only along the houses where there was not much choice were there dull rectangular beds. Flowers were planted in Mason jars, hanging baskets of clay and willow, coffee cans, Suetene buckets, big seashells, sugar bowls without handles, old churns, and cracked chamberpots. The minute any plant showed a tendency to live a natural life, it was pruned back, lopped off, tied up, or transplanted. The Mexicans did a lot of living in their yards, and they no more cared for wild, unshaped growth there than they cared for it inside their houses; a tree was a nice thing, but it served man best cut up and nailed together in the shape of a table or a bed. It was the same way with flowers.

In addition to the hanging baskets, thick amidst the branches of the pepper and umbrella trees, there was a lot of aerial bloom pendant from trellises and arbors and festooning downward from vines trained to run up trees. Birdcages hung with the flowers, and under this canopy of vines and birds and leaves and blossoms, babies and dogs lived as though in a handmade jungle. Petals and shadows fell on their faces. Water ollas sweated in the shade of jacaranda trees; water dripped from the perforated tin containers placed on the tops of coolers covered with barley sacks; water ran in ditches along the rows of vegetables and filled the basins at the feet of the orange and lemon trees.

The village was already wide awake; there was a smell of greasewood smoke and the sound of singing and wood-chopping.

After long looking, Pete said, "I better eat and be on my way."

"If you go, I am going," Rosa said.

"Why do you want to go?"

Rosa had two reasons. She told Pete one. "I want to help Mrs. Lewis with the cooking."

"She will need it," Pete admitted. She, or more likely Shel, had invited some friends in for a meal to celebrate the first planting on the Tract. "Do you know what she is going to cook?"

"How could I know?"

"Ground squirrels."

Rosa thought for a minute that this was a joke of Pete's to persuade her not to go. "You can't eat squirrels."

"Back in Kentucky, they eat squirrels."

Mexicans were sometimes accused of eating dogs. Rosa herself had never eaten one; but if she had to choose between squirrels and dogs, she would choose a well-fed, fat little dog rather than an animal like a rat, devoured by fleas and living in a hole in the ground.

"Why?" Rosa asked.

"They are cheap," Pete said. "With Shel planting trees and paying so much money to haul water, Mrs. Lewis says to herself, 'Somebody must save money, and squirrels are cheap.'"

"I had better take something along to kill the flavor."

"I don't know what would."

"I can make them so hot no one could taste anything except the chili."

"They won't like that either."

"It will be better than ground squirrel."

"I didn't know you and Mrs. Lewis were such friends."

"We are getting to be," said Rosa. "I want us to be."

While Rosa was getting breakfast, Julian Ortiz, who lived next door, came into the kitchen carrying his youngest brother, a baby of eight months. Most Mexican men liked children and would help take care of them in an aimless, loving way; but Julian was careful and sensible with his younger brothers and sisters. He was Rosa's age, twenty-two, unmarried, though with plenty of admirers.

Rosa wasn't one of them; she wasn't sure why. Perhaps the reason was that she could admire only Pete, or at least a man like Pete, while Julian was Pete's opposite in most ways.

Pete was big, strong, lazy, and wicked. Julian was small, quiet, industrious, pious. He looked precious, like something made by a jeweler. It was a surprise not to hear him tick. There was absolutely no way his perfect features could be bettered except to enlarge and coarsen them. He had beautiful, long-lashed eyes, firmly curled red lips, and a silky black mustache. There was nothing in the least girlish about his small precise features. His nose was a man's beak, and his Adam's apple alone would stamp him a man; and Rosa had seen him too often, bare to the waist and washing, in the back yard next door, to think him soft. He was small, but he was a weapon like any other man.

In addition to everything else, Julian was religious. This certainly should not turn her against him, but a religious man who was not a priest made her feel uncomfortable, as if he were taking over some work or privilege that should belong only to women. If a man was religious, it cut her off from him. Part of her duty to Pete as a wife was to lead him toward God, to urge church and prayers and fasts upon him. It shocked her to admit it, but the truth was, she didn't want Pete a bit holier than he was. She wanted Pete to get to God, but she wanted to be the ladder by which he climbed. If a man made that climb alone, wouldn't his wife feel left out? She would. No, religion was for women and priests. A man who was religious had better become a part of the church. Feeling all this, she was especially polite to Julian.

"Have you had your breakfast yet, Julian?"

"An hour ago. What I came over for," he said, "was to see if I could ride with Pete to the Lewises' this morning."

"I didn't know you were working for Mr. Lewis today."

"I am not working for him."

Rosa slapped a tortilla from hand to hand, trying to think what reason Julian could have, if he wasn't working there, for going to the Lewises'.

"I can drive over myself, if you think Pete won't want me. I have been asked to a picnic," he said, "at the Lewises'."

Rosa woke up. "Of course you can ride over with us. I'm going, too. You'll probably wish you hadn't. Mrs. Lewis is going to cook squirrel for dinner."

"The picnic is not given by Mrs. Lewis. It is given by the girls. I have been invited by Medora Cudlip."

Rosa stopped her work on the tortilla. Mexican men did not go with American girls. The Cudlip girl might not know this, but Julian did.

Julian knew what she was thinking. "It's not a private picnic."

Rosa was silent again. She had seen Medora, a girl who looked like an Indian. It was strange, the shape a person's face takes. Pete, as nearly pure Spanish as there was in California, looked, she knew, like the Americans' idea of a big, dark, easygoing Mexican, a man mostly Indian; and Julian, who had no such claim to pure Spanish blood, was a throwback in looks to some Sepulveda or Yorba, and everyone's idea of a Spanish gentleman. And here was Julian, liking a girl whose face had no Spanish quickness about it, whose face was broad and grave as an Indian's, the skin tight across the cheekbones, the eyes set shallow in the head, and her skin darker than Julian's own.

"How long have you known Medora?" Rosa asked.

"Since the night we went to the water meeting," Julian said. And for all Rosa tried to get more out of him about Medora, he had had his say.


4    L e R o y  R a u n c e, like the Mexicans, knew the meaning of the cloud and, like the Mexicans, was unexcited by it. A bad Santa Ana out on the oil field could be dangerous; otherwise, they were nothing but a nuisance and a hardship: they could ruin half an orange or lemon crop; they filled houses with sand and food with grit; and most housewives complained that for the three days the wind blew they were nervous and blue. Females were evidently more sensitive to them than men. Even the cow was affected. She was near enough calving to be fidgety on that account, without having to figure out something as foreign to her nature as a three-day blow. Thinking of her, LeRoy dressed without waking Dolly and tiptoed down the stairs.

The queer light of a Santa Ana day was already in the house; it sharpened his vision. He saw what was ordinarily invisible. In the Raunce house, this meant an extra layer of disorder. Dolly was a clean housewife. She scrubbed and washed, swept and dusted, as often as anyone else, but that was the whole of her housekeeping. The assemblage of their household articles looked no more permanent than those in the overnight habitation of a hobo beneath a one-span culvert. The pure light of the strange morning coming through Dolly's sparkling windows illuminated all the clotted helter-skelter of misplaced equipment. LeRoy came down the stairs, stepping skillfully among shoes, saucepans, hats, bedding, toys, which usually he did not even see.

LeRoy no more thought of his house as being untidy than a sailor thinks of the sea as untidy. A sailor is a sailor because the sea suits him as it is; he has no wish to set the seaweeds to rights with a fine-tooth comb or to shift barnacles about until they all point in the same direction. Raunce was the same way about his house. He sailed it like a sea; he was at home in its unpredictability.

It took an alert person to find anything in that house; the demands of life were not watered down by deciding once and for all where everything was to be kept. "A place for everything and everything in its place" is a help to the tired and slow-witted. None of the Raunces were. They lived like hunters in a forest, never sure of what they would find behind the next tree. Nothing could be taken for granted; even less so than in hunting, where there are seasonal migrations and the moss always grows on the north side of the trees.

LeRoy had it in mind to shave before he went out to have a look at the cow; to the little triumph of getting the whiskers off, he would first have to add the greater one of finding his razor. The kitchen would be the most likely place for it, and he was headed in that direction when he heard a sound in the dining room. It could only be Crystal.

Crystal had, in the midst of the Raunce jungle, built in the dining room her own little two-by-four world. LeRoy never tired of looking at it; it was as surprising as coming upon a marble P.O. complete with recruiting posters in the midst of a cactus patch. In a way, Crystal's order, successfully maintaining itself under the Raunce rooftree, was a part of its fertile disorder. For a while, Crystal had driven them all crazy by trying to impose her neatness upon them. There was no use looking for an article in the place where you remembered seeing it last. It wouldn't be there. It would be in what Crystal called "some logical place." That meant out of sight. Her intentions were good, and LeRoy knew it and felt sorry for her. She never got a word of thanks for her efforts. All she ever heard was everybody's everlasting "Where did you hide the comb?," "Where did you hide the ironing board?," "Where did you hide the milk bucket?" So she gave up and retreated to the dining room.

When LeRoy built the house, he had seen the dining room being used to entertain visiting Friends at the time of Monthly Meetings and for dinners after Sunday services. It had never occurred to the Raunces to use it very often themselves. They ate in the big east kitchen; and the dining room, with its round fumed-oak table and six matching chairs, was a fine catchall for the overflow from other rooms.

In one corner, with its back to all this, was Crystal's orange-box world, which she had built for herself without the stroke of a hammer. Two orange boxes, upended, with a plank between them, made the desk. Orange boxes were her bookcases; orange boxes at each end of the desk, and at right angles to it, made her fences. Within this symmetrical arrangement, her face to the wall and her back to the Raunces, Crystal sat, surrounded by all she valued most.

LeRoy was delighted to see Crystal seated so seriously amidst the unnatural line-up of all her oddments. He loved her and was proud of her and gave all the glory to God.

Crystal looked up and saw her father in the doorway; she could tell by the look on his face that what he wanted to do was pray. He showed it as clearly as most people show that they need to sneeze, and she thought it was more or less the same kind of impulse. If he could pray without words, make a great snort directed upward toward God, she wouldn't mind; but she didn't care to listen to any "I love, I worship, I adore." This was as bad as having to watch any other kind of love-making. But there was something in her that could not bear to criticize anything so wholly her father as his desire to pray. It would be like stepping on his uncovered heart. She suffered, listening; but some delicacy in herself would suffer more if she spoke. She could hate him, and did, for not seeing that she did not want to listen to him pray, but she could not say a word to stop him.

He stopped himself. She saw him master his impulse. His face and eyes, which had been all aglow, settled back into his ordinary look of good will, and he said, "Crystal, Bess is likely to calf today. Can I count on you to look after her?"

In her relief at missing the prayer, Crystal was willing to promise almost anything.

"Papa," she said, "you know I'm going out with Mr. Cope to the Lewises' to see the tree planting and to write about it for the paper. But all the time I'm here, I'll look after Bessie."

"I'd forgot the planting," LeRoy said. "Anyway, I don't know what you could do for her. All she needs is a bucket of water and some straw for the calf. And this wind's liable to blow that away."

Crystal gave up the protection of her orange boxes and came to the dining-room door. "Let's go look at her," she said.

"I was fixing to shave," LeRoy told her, but it was a job he was always glad to postpone.

Bess, the Jersey, was swollen tight as a drum, and there was already a little dribble to show that inside her things had begun to work. She was switching her tail and moving her head restlessly. "Poor Bess," LeRoy said, patting her, "you got to feel worse before you feel better."

Calving was no mystery to Crystal; this was Bess's third calf. She was interested in it only to the extent of wanting the calf born safely.

"I wish Bess had someplace to be," Crystal said.

"Be?" LeRoy asked. Bessie had the whole of his ten acres and, beyond that, the entire Tract with the exception of a house here and there. A herd of cows wouldn't need more.

"Be out of the wind," Crystal explained.

There was not a building of any kind on the Raunce place except the house and the privy. LeRoy planned on more, later; but so far he had been too busy building a house and a church, preaching, drilling a few wells out on the field, to get them up. He parked his car in front of the house, parked his cow behind it; and except for the slight miscomfort Bess might have from calving in a windstorm, the arrangement was satisfactory to all.

"Oh, once Bess starts having her calf, she won't care anything about the weather. What time will you get back from the Lewises'?"

"I don't know when Mr. Cope's coming back. But I'm going to a picnic Ellen Lewis is having."

"Well, Bess may take a look at the sky and decide to put off her coming-out party for a few days." LeRoy rubbed his chin. "Do you think I need to shave?"

Filled with benevolence, Crystal said, "No."

Crystal went to work early that morning. Her white middy and white pleated skirt were freshly washed, starched, and ironed, and her white sneakers were freshly cleaned with Shu-White. She stepped carefully along the dusty path between the broken stumps of sagebrush, trying to keep clean. There would not be time to change before she went out to the Lewis ranch, and she wanted to look nice there for several reasons; but most of all because she would be seeing Chad. She checked the cloud in the east. It was a threat to her, because if Chad's father decided that he would not plant in a Santa Ana, there would be no point in her interviewing him. And Ellen's picnic in that case would probably be called off, too. She gazed at the cloud commandingly. "Don't blow," she told it, "don't blow!" And having said that, she immediately forgot the cloud and its threat. She stood there for a few minutes, key in hand outside Lute's office building, enjoying a feeling of proprietorship. It was silly, she knew, to call a one-room shack, stained as were most of the buildings on the Tract with a mixture of crude oil and red lead, an office. And it was silly to call herself a newspaper writer. But she did both. This building might not be *much* of an office and she might not be *much* of a newspaper writer, but they were both the best in their respective lines the Tract could yet boast.

The office building was the color of, and not much bigger than, a devil's-food cake; but what it smelled like, in the hot morning sunshine, was a sump hole up in the Olinda Hills, a combination of earth and crude oil and some element that could not be named but was nevertheless present. A smell that made you keep sniffing and sniffing in an effort to name it. One thing was certain, it was a dark, sunless smell out of an underworld of veins and workings, ordinarily kept hidden from man. But it was a smell that was often in the Raunce home, too, for it was her father's smell when he came home, oil-stained, from work.

Inside the office, she felt herself to be in an extension of her orange-box world. Not in outward neatness. Nothing could be outwardly neater than her orange-box world. But in this office Lute put order into each week's happenings. Each week he boiled weddings, funerals, births, visits from back East, parties, accidents, lawsuits, down into neat paragraphs. People screamed, cried, laughed, swore, had fits, swooned for joy; they raved and they caved. They wished they could die, and didn't; wished they wouldn't and did. They ran away from home and then ran back again. They had to get married and they did.

They had to have babies and they did. None of these things could be written about as people really experienced them. It would be too awful. But Lute knew how to let people know what was going on without telling about it in so many words. It was a special way of writing, which made terrible and astounding events appear to have happened long ago in another country and to someone who was only a name, not a flesh-and-blood person capable of bleeding and screaming. He was able, by a reverse process, to make small unimportant happenings, a church social or the visit from someone's aunt, appear important and exciting. He was even able, by some kind of special writing, to make the account of a week lived through by his subscribers read like news to them. "So this is what happened," they said to themselves, forgetting that the happening had been occasioned by themselves. Lute was teaching Crystal to write in this way, which meant first of all that she had to see in a special "newspaper" way.

In the beginning it had been difficult. A young man who had come to Randolph (Lute's paper was not for the Tract only, but for surrounding communities that had no paper) hoping to find a cure for his weak lungs had died. Crystal felt so sorry for him—he was only nineteen and far from home—that she wanted Lute to give him in print some of the life he had missed in reality. She told Lute that she could write forever about this poor invalid and his death far from home. Lute said he didn't doubt this, but that his problem was to find any subscribers who would be willing to read about him forever. They owed a debt to the living, Lute said, as well as to the dead: and the debt to the living, owed by him, was to provide the living with some interesting reading matter. And a paragraph or two about the young man from Iowa coughing his lungs out in Randolph was as much, he was convinced, as his subscribers would find interesting on that subject.

Crystal couldn't help seeing that this debt to the living included the need to put out a paper somebody would pay money to read. She wished Lute had said so. She knew which side his bread, and hers, too, was buttered on; and she didn't enjoy being treated as if she were too young or stupid to recognize such facts.

But in the main, she enjoyed being able to boil down the rich conglomeration of the week's happenings, cut it into neat paragraphs like squares of fudge, and, finally, hand it out to people as "life last week on the Tract."

"The weather continues warm." "Mrs. Jessup confined to home after recent operation." "The Sylvester Perkinses spend a day on the Tract." "Cudlips welcome new baby." "Water-bearing gravel reached at well." "Shelby Lewis determined to plant." "General Pershing promises early success in Mexico." "School to open January 2, 1917." "Church nearing completion." "German submarines continue attacks on American shipping." She wished her father could be finished with things in the way Lute was. Her father kept on praying and praising, nothing ever said once and for all.

She enjoyed being alone, but this morning she missed Lute, too; or at least she missed the sounds he made at work, slapping down the press, lighting a match, sucking in on his pipe with a bubbling sound, then exhaling with a long sigh.

Lute came in late for a day on which they had so much to do. "Good morning, Crystal," he said. "What's Teddy done today?"

Teddy Roosevelt was Crystal's hero, and Lute enjoyed teasing her about him. He hurt her feelings sometimes and afterward swore he would never mention the old Rough Rider to her again. Then the first thing he knew, out the name he had forbidden himself would pop again.

When Crystal did not answer, he said, "Don't tell me you two've had a falling out?"

A teaser is always asking for a response from somebody without having to take any responsibility for it, and Lute was no exception. He continuously asked for something; day in and day out, he asked for something: Press, Indy, Crystal. He did not know it. This was a time in his life when he thought he could not possibly ask for more. Indy back, new home, new business, daughters happy.

"Teddy and I are getting along fine," Crystal said, proud to be able to speak so lightly when her feelings were not light.

Lute hung his hat on a nail and rolled up his sleeves. The man and the girl were aware of each other, pleased with each other, and completely mistaken about each other. Lute supposed Crystal's problems had not yet begun, and Crystal supposed Lute's were long since all over.

Of the two, Lute was the more mistaken, since he shared Crystal's view of himself. He had been brought up not to look at some things; and if, by chance, he did catch sight of them, not to name them. This had been his mother's practice, and because she had started him at it early, it had become more than a practice with him; it had become his life.

222

Lute was a pattern of a man, a pretty good pattern, but one shaped by another hand, as a pattern must be. And no matter who makes it, a pattern, if it is going to survive, needs to consort with another pattern. A live creature threshing about will tear a pattern to shreds.

It was all right with Crystal for Lute to be a pattern. She was at the age when that was what she wanted everyone to be: Lute to be the pattern of an older man and editor. Her father, a pattern of a father. That was what was wrong with her father. He had about as much pattern as a volcano. A new eruption might at any minute change his shape.

One of the things Lute asked for from Crystal and Press alike was admiration. He did not want it put into words; that was the last thing he wanted. Words, except as he used them in his newspaper work, made him uneasy. Both girls admired him; but, forbidden to voice their admiration, each girl felt uneasy about Lute. Press, filled with guilt about her feeling for her father (she valued him so much more than her mother), tried to make it up to her mother with unusual devotion. And Crystal, who also had to have someplace to put her emotions, had found a use for them by falling in love with Chad.

Lute would never have believed any of this. Certain things "couldn't be." He considered himself, in the first place, a very modest, unassuming man; and it would not have been modest for him to admit that two girls, and one of them his daughter, were having their lives shaped because of their feeling for him. He was completely protected by his belief in what "couldn't be," and enabled by it to ask without knowing and to receive without responsibility.

Crystal believed him to be perfect: he had gone to college, he knew grammar, he could edit a newspaper, he was courteous, he never prayed in public, he had a beautiful wife whom he never kissed or hugged when people were watching.

The paper came out on Friday afternoons. This was Saturday, and Lute had not only read the paper thoroughly, he had written most of it. Still, the stack of *Reporters* on the chest-high counter that separated the front, public part of the office from the rear, working part drew him to them as if for a first sight. He picked up the top *Reporter* and looked through it.

"Handsome little paper this new settlement's getting out," he said.

Crystal, seated at a table in the public part of the office, was addressing copies of the paper to a list of persons Mr. Perkins had given Lute.

"Do you know what they say, Crystal? 'The editor couldn't get the paper out without the help of his assistant.' What do you think of that?"

"The report has been exaggerated," she said.

Lute laughed. "I heard a funny story about Teddy Roosevelt yesterday. Want to hear it?"

She didn't want to but she didn't want to say so. Funny stories about Teddy didn't sound funny to her. She had a scrapbook filled with pictures of Teddy Roosevelt: a rancher in the hills of Dakota; a soldier at San Juan; a boxer in a gymnasium; a father with his children on the lawn at the White House; the President of the United States, with the Kaiser of Germany, each man on horseback; a hunter with a dead lion at his feet; the victim of a would-be assassin's shot, bravely saying, "It is nothing."

One of the fantasies with which she occupied the ten minutes between getting into bed and going to sleep had to do with saving Teddy's life. An assassin would strike again. She would be there. Sometimes she disarmed the assassin; sometimes she threw herself between Teddy and the bullet or knife intended for him, and died; but not before Teddy had told her that he owed his life to her.

"Well, what they say is this," Lute went on. "They say that Teddy wants to be the bride at every wedding and the corpse at every funeral."

In spite of her firmest resolves, Crystal felt herself trembling with anger.

"Who's they?" she asked.

"People who've been watching him. Roosevelt doesn't care anything about his party. All he wants is to be president again. He doesn't care who wins the war. All he wants to do is to put on a cowboy hat and go galloping over to the trenches."

Crystal stood up behind her table. This was assassination, too. "It's a lie. Theodore Roosevelt doesn't care a thing about himself. All he thinks about is the United States of America and how he can save it from being run over by the Huns."

Lute looked at Crystal for the first time that morning. By the standards of the women of his own family, she was a plain girl, narrow-faced, with pinkish hair and eyebrows; but he had stirred up a fire in her that made her looks invisible, the way a candle's flame keeps anyone from noticing the candle. Her response to his teasing made him continue. No man can tease a girl about another man, even a former president, without being a little mixed up with her response. His teasing says, in effect, "Do you prefer him to me?"

"Crystal," Lute said, "do you mean to tell me that you don't know who this great hero of yours resembles?"

"The devil, probably, to hear you tell it."

"Well, Crystal, you just about hit the nail on the head. Kaiser Bill. Those two boys are as much alike as peas in a pod. Put Teddy in Germany and he'd act like the Kaiser. Put the Kaiser here and he'd be carrying Teddy's big stick."

Crystal knew she was going to cry, and she raced to get as much said as she could before the spasms that were already shaking her diaphragm gripped her throat. She despised getting mad and crying; she loved coming to the office and working for Lute because, with him, she was a person she herself liked, not the girl of her home angers and hatreds. But now she was proving to herself that the home Crystal was the real one.

"They are the exact opposite," she said, keeping her voice unusually even to compensate for the break in it she knew was about to come. "One orders other men to die so that he can take the land of the French and the Belgians away from them. But Theodore Roosevelt is willing to die himself to save our land and freedom for us. That's the exact opposite, isn't it? And do you know what he said when the Germans sank the *Lusitania*? Do you?"

"I don't remember the exact words," Lute said, the teasing going out of him.

"He said, 'We owe it to humanity' "—but she could get no further. The whole of the world and its sorrows, all the dying and disorder and unloving, and this one man struggling to help the world in spite of his own wounds and frailties and the attacks of others, and she so unworthy, not caring for anything but her own personal troubles, unable in a pinch, when it would do him the most good, to even remember his noble words. She did not want to be seen crying, so she turned, put her arms against the wall, and in the cradle of her arms cried as quietly as possible. This was not very quiet, though she did not bawl like a child. She cried like a woman—deep, shamefaced sobs which she tried to hold back, in spite of the fact that with every sob she felt better; already sacrificing like a woman, in her holding back, giving up something for somebody, giving up her relief to spare Lute's feelings.

225

Lute was ashamed of himself, though less ashamed than he would have been had he known he had asked for these tears from Crystal. All I did, he thought, was tease her a little about the old Rough Rider. It isn't as if I said something about her father or that boy she's stuck on. I would never have done anything like that.

But he had done the same thing. More. Teddy stood for the father she did not like, the beau she did not have, the learning she longed for, the country she was ignorant of. He was all the stories of heroism, all the persons undervalued, and dead young; he was the magnet of martyrdom, the mystery of ambition, the promise of her own hidden talents.

When Lute derided Teddy, he pulled the props out from under her whole world.

Lute came around from behind his counter, feeling sorry for the girl and wondering how he could stop her crying. She stood with her back to him and continued to sob. If this had been Indy, he could have said, "I'll go outside, Indy, until you feel more like yourself." He could not very well go outside the office, walk back and forth waiting for the crying to stop. How would he explain that to a passer-by? He had put a hand on her shoulder when Tom Mount came in.

It was not the position of Lute's hand but the sound of Crystal's sobs that said "sex" to him. Tom Mount heard this word, or saw it illustrated, more often than most people; and without either condemnation or surprise. He was like a painter whose eye composes pictures wherever he looks; or a poet whose ear hearkens to the rhythms wherever he hears words spoken. Tom Mount looked at people or listened to them, and was conscious of the naked male and female responsiveness. He was like a pornographer who does not need to read; a Peeping Tom who needs no keyhole. Sex was everywhere, and everywhere expressing itself; and though he had not the need of searching, which is part of the satisfaction of the pornographer and Peeping Tom, yet, whether he liked it or not, he had many of their responses and satisfactions.

He had heard this sound of sorrows ebbing in women's voices before, and it didn't matter to him that Lute would have said, "Such things can't be," and that Crystal would have been ignorant of the causes of those exquisite subsiding shudders. He had a dowser very sensitive to such matters. Sometimes he told people, as a part of his policy of being personal, what his dowser told him. Sometimes he didn't. Now, because he intended being personal in another way, he didn't.

"Maybe I should've knocked," he said.

Whatever the insinuations were in this, Lute ignored them. "I ought to be horsewhipped," he said.

Tom waited for more. Lute had always interested him, but now that he knew Indiana Rose, the interest had increased. He enjoyed talking to one about the other.

Lute always spoke of Indy to others as "my wife," in the same way as he would speak of "my paper," "my ranch," "my auto," as if he couldn't face, Tom thought, the fact of any existence for Indy apart from himself. Once, to tease Lute, Tom had spoken of "my friend." "Who's that?" Lute asked, and hadn't tumbled to the joke when Tom said, "My friend is your wife."

Talking with a husband or wife about the other was like being with two persons at once. He had some of the same pleasant doubling of feeling when he talked with Eunice or Opal. With a husband and wife, the situation was, of course, somewhat different. But facing Lute now, he could see Indy's round white arms, with their soft dusting of dark gold-tipped hairs, around Lute's neck.

When Lute remained silent, Tom said, "Most men ought to be horsewhipped, I guess, if they got their just deserts. Women, too. We're about an equal match."

Lute never enjoyed discussing men and women and their relationships, and he certainly didn't intend to get into any such discussion now.

"I got to teasing her about Teddy Roosevelt. One word led to another and finally I said too much. I'm ashamed of myself."

Crystal was ashamed of causing all this disturbance. She turned away from the wall, and Tom thought: Love's wet face. Her lips were swollen and her pale skin luminous. She looked contrite, but calm.

"Poor girl," Tom said, "crying over Teddy Roosevelt."

His voice was very kind. This was the first time he had spoken to her since he had told her that buzzards were hawks. "I can't imagine anyone crying over Teddy. Except Teddy himself," he said.

She looked up at Tom, determined not to get that started up all over again. "Teddy can take care of himself," he said, in a way that made her feel he was not attacking Teddy, but protecting her.

227

She went back to her desk, and again Lute retreated behind his counter and the stacks of the *Reporter*.

Tom, between them, looked from one to the other. It was odd the way people ducked any talk about the very thing that made or ruined their lives. Eunice, who was making it the aim of her life to accept him exactly as he was, refused to talk when it came to these simple matters. Accepting Tom Mount, making the acceptance of him the aim of her life, was making the acceptance of sex the aim of her life. But when it came to believing that what was true for her was true for others, she balked. He had got her to the place where she could listen to him without exclaiming "Oh, no, I can't believe that!" or "It isn't true, you're just making that up." She held her tongue, but he could see that she had no real belief. What Eunice did, by refusing to believe these stories about other women—though she of course could never see it—was to claim that she was the only sexy woman in the world. They were all sexy! What gives me the advantage, he thought, is that some men aren't sexy enough to have discovered it.

He turned to his own personal business with Lute.

"What time are you going out to the Lewises', Lute?"

"Right away. If I haven't got Crystal too upset to travel."

"I'm all right," Crystal said. "I hate myself for crying when I get mad."

"Indiana Rose not going?" Tom asked.

"My wife had some work she didn't want to put down this morning."

"I'm coming out later, this afternoon. You got any objections to my bringing her out, if she's finished by then?"

"That's up to my wife. Whatever she wants is fine with me."

Tom saw that he believed it. His pattern of a husband was a man like that.

5    THIS proved to be the Jessups' morning for company. Asa Brice arrived first.

Mary Jessup had experienced hot weather in Kansas and knew what to do about it. Close the house before the morning loses its coolness

228

and pull all the blinds; brush the house out three or four times a day with small twists of dampened newspaper; keep a pitcherful of lemonade on hand.

When Asa arrived, he stepped into a cool dusk, smelling of damp carpets and freshly cut lemons. Mary and Wendlin were in the kitchen, Mary reading the Bible and Wendlin the *Emporia Gazette*. At seven-thirty, breakfast was long past for these two, and Wendlin was already tempering his system against the heat of the day with a glass of lemonade.

Asa paused in the doorway to admire them. They were a handsome couple, and if he were asked to nominate an example of the humanity of the so-called human race, he thought he might put forward this room and its occupants.

"Well, Asa," Wendlin said, "you catch us with our Bibles."

"He thinks that's a joke," Mary said, "but it isn't. William Allen White *is* his Bible. He can't start a day until he knows where Willie White stands. I tell him Willie White is nothing but a short, stout man living in Emporia, Kansas. He's not the voice of God. But Wendlin hearkens to every word he says."

"Hearkening isn't agreeing."

"If a disagreement is what you want, you don't have to pay Willie White for it. I can give it to you gratis."

Wendlin folded his paper and threw it across the room. "If Willie don't stop beating the drums for war, I'll take you up on that."

"I feel like taking a shot at those Germans myself every now and then," Asa confessed.

"Oh, Asa," Mary said. "'Feel like'! What kind of a yardstick's that to live by?"

"Now, Mary," Wendlin began, but Mary turned on her husband.

"Wendlin, don't you have something you could do outside? There's a matter I want to speak to Asa about in private."

"If you want me out of the house, Mary, all you have to do is say so."

Mary's highhandedness with Wendlin always made Asa uncomfortable. With everyone else, Mary was the soul of courtesy; but she often used Wendlin as an instrument by which she could demonstrate her thoughtfulness for others. Wendlin was in a chair someone else would like: "Get up, Wendlin." Wendlin was keeping the sun off someone: "Move, Wendlin." Wendlin was reading a book someone else would enjoy: "You can finish it anytime, Wendlin."

There was never the least friction between the two about such things. And no one ever thought of Wendlin as being henpecked. Why, Asa didn't know. Unless it was that Wendlin had only to move or speak to convince you that he had what he wanted from life. If Wendlin found it suitable for Mary to treat him sometimes as if he were not quite bright, this must be the exact flaw she needed to make her virtues endurable to him.

Though Asa wanted her perfect. He delighted in her and that was all there was to it. There is an unaccountable kinship, he thought, which unites us to some and severs us from others. Little Johnny in a coonskin cap is immediately a son or brother; a faded, tawny woman, wife or sister. Time, time! It has its own gait. It cares nothing that it has carried one who would have been the making of your life beyond you; or that another has been picked up by time's current so late that he hears, when you speak, nothing but Methuselah's voice. And you, gazing forward and backward in time, in an effort to make the two of you, separated by time, equal, spoil yourself for the day's actual minute-by-minute gifts.

Asa was a real ladies' man. Though no one, including himself, had ever discovered it. He delighted in the company of women, even when they were fools. Interested as he was in the sounds of nature, he could listen to the prattle of ladies with the same pleasure he found in the flutings of quail and blackbirds. He himself, though, never pretended in their presence to be either a fluter or a prattler. He hung onto his rationality. And this, added to his bib overalls, his silence, his solitary arroyo life, his indifference to getting ahead, made women a little afraid of him. They gave him the go-by before they got to know him.

So, shut off from the companionship of women, he had embraced the world; he had given his love to the universe: to stars and trees, to the notion of stepping westward, to the sound of the wind through telephone wires, to winter rains and the dusty bloom of fall on elderberry clusters; these were his loves. It was a lonely loving. Continence is a habit more compelling than tomcatting. Enough tomcatting sooner or later acts as its own cure. Continence does not cure continence. There are more reformed rakes than reformed celibates. Don Juan, sooner or later, slows down; but the dried-up old bachelor seldom speeds up; and Asa knew this. He had no ambition to be a Don Juan, but he didn't want a dried-up heart either. Mary was the only human being to whom he could open his heart. He could open his mind to a man—but only to a woman could he open his heart.

230

Mary poured him a glass of lemonade.

"I feel like a tippler, drinking at this time of the morning," he said.

"You're going to need all the liquids you can get before the day's over, Asa."

Asa waited for Mary to pour a glass for herself. When she didn't, he said, "Aren't you having any?"

"It would just come up, Asa."

Asa put down his own glass. Mary's exterior was so jaunty, one accepted it as Mary. Her dresses were always stiffly starched and freshly ironed. She coiled her springy hair into big, defiant, and pretty hairdos. Her white canvas shoes sparkled like snow. She admitted that she washed and ironed her shoelaces. She seemed a person not subject, as others are, to external conditions. She managed Wendlin, rebuked William Allen White, defied the heat, fed the multitudes. And she couldn't drink lemonade.

"Asa, there's something I've been wanting to tell you."

He knew what she was going to say before she said it. She looked up at him without flinching and in and behind her eyes he saw death appear. There was no other word for it. The effect was of an enormous momentary quickening. All the life that she had had, and was going to miss, gathered itself into consciousness and flung itself out into the world in an attempt at one final, all-seeing flash. It was far more sorrowful than real death, which, when it comes, has a conquered kingdom waiting. This look was death in life: the living consciousness taking into its being its own destroyer.

It is against nature, and nature itself asks it of us. But not of Mary, Asa thought. Not of Mary, with her laundered shoelaces, her kitchen smelling of lemons, her Bible with its crocheted bookmark. Not of the one person to whom I can open my heart.

Asa slid, as naturally as when out in the hills hunting yellow violets, to his knees. He took Mary's hand, which lay in her lap, and pressed it to his face. Mary, Mary, Mary . . . He thought he spoke, but the words were in his heart.

Asa's act released Mary from the need to contemplate eternity. It gave her a little particular problem here and now in her hot November kitchen. She looked across Asa's shoulders and remembered at this odd moment that the lemonade pitcher had been a wedding present to her and Wendlin from Willie White's mother. She put a hand on Asa's shaggy head.

"Asa, you need a haircut. You come over here sometime this week and let me give you a trim. It's bad enough, you living like a hermit. But there's no call for you to look like one."

Asa got back onto his chair.

"That's more like it," Mary said. "If you intended getting down on your knees to me, you should've done it sooner."

She had made him smile. Yet a declaration of death and a declaration of love have a lot in common, and she knew it. When she had said, "I love you," to Chester, she had said also, and necessarily, "I die to all others." Loving and dying both require the leaving of a lot of life behind.

"Asa," she said, "it probably seems strange to you that I'm telling you this and not someone else. It's strange to me. I've got a husband and children and brothers and sisters. And then, when it comes to dying, I pick some stranger to tell."

"I'm not a stranger, Mary."

"I know you're not, Asa."

He couldn't bring himself to ask any questions. What did she know? How did she know? A declaration of death differs from a declaration of love in this way. Lovers delight to share their whens and hows and wheres. Death, instead, separates like passion, locks each sufferer inside his own feeling, so that communication is impossible.

"Asa, when I was operated on, I made the doctor promise that if he found anything incurable he wouldn't tell Wendlin."

"Wouldn't Wendlin want to know?"

"Of course he'd want to know. But the least I can do now is spare Wendlin some suffering. That's why I'm telling you instead of Wendlin."

Asa, keeping track of earliest blooms and prevailing winds, observing the habits of centipedes and horned toads, casting up the accounts of one man on a particular earth and in a certain season, sometimes cried out, Was I born for such bookkeeping work? Am I nothing but a rain gauge and a weather vane and a flower press? Now he thought, Perhaps it was this I was born for, to listen to Mary in her hour of trouble. Though he knew instantly that this, also, was not enough. A man was born for his own joy, not for anyone else's sorrow. But there was at least more humanity in this than in peanut-growing and stargazing. And humanity had seemed, recently, what he'd lost. Perhaps he had *not* been born to listen to Mary's trouble. This didn't mean that Mary might not lead him, by way of her suffering, back into the human fold.

232

"You don't like Wendlin's joking, do you, Asa? Blame me for that. When I married him, Wendlin was as sober a fellow as you'll find. The joking all came later. It was likely joke or cry with Wendlin."

Asa was prepared to suffer the pangs of death with Mary. The pangs of life were something else. Was he better fitted to meet death than life?

Mary walked to the window where Asa could see Wendlin, currying an already-curried horse.

"Poor old Wendlin," she said.

Then she faced Asa again. "Asa, do you know that when I left Kansas I thought I was coming to a land of coconut and palm trees? Bananas and pineapples right outside the windows. I declare to goodness, I believe I was ignorant enough to expect monkeys and parrots."

"Just give us time," Asa said, "and we'll probably have them, too."

"That's what I haven't got," Mary said. "Time. That's why I'm telling you."

"Haven't you told Ben?"

"Ben? Why, Asa, you know Ben. The first thing he'd do would be to bring Paula home from China. Paula's the sweetest girl in the world. When a girl's sweet and she's your daughter, there's nothing to equal it," she mused.

"Don't you want to see her?"

"Of course I want to. But she's only been there six months. Asa, do you know what she does? She's teaching Chinese girls to play basketball. Oh, yes, she is. I have pictures. That's what she went all the way from Kansas to China for. Middies and bloomers. And Ben's going to be a preacher. And Wendlin's a jokester. That's not what I expected of life. I made Wendlin a jokester, but I want the children to take their own gait, no matter what I think."

She came away from the window. She was as tall as he, and so far there was no sign of her sickness upon her.

"I'll need medicine. I'll have to depend upon somebody."

What she was asking was, "Help me die." Dying, when you came down to it, was a job. It took planning and attention and energy—like setting up housekeeping or planting corn.

"You can depend on me, Mary."

"I don't think I'll be much trouble. Though I suppose it's hard to tell beforehand."

"Don't worry about the trouble."

"Dying seems to be two things. Getting used to the idea and bearing

233

the pain. I'm already used to the idea and I've always been able to bear pain pretty well. That's all there is to it, isn't it, Asa?"

He didn't know. There was no way to know anything from the outside.

"Mary, I'll help you."

"One thing I can be glad of. Wendlin's still young enough to find himself another wife."

6    EUNICE and Opal drove into the townsite at midmorning: Opal, to give Mary Jessup a hand with her housework, Eunice, to start cleaning the Perkins Investment Company's office. Sylvester Perkins had donated it to the Tract for use as a schoolhouse, and Eunice had agreed to begin teaching at the first of the year.

They had the buggy top up, but the sun came through it, tightening the skin across their cheekbones and drying their already cracked lips. They drove through the clear, quiet air as if through glass. The heat had silenced the birds, but katydids hummed without letup. The sound of sand pouring off the slowly turning wheels made them thirstier and hotter.

Eunice drove, watching the dust cloud in the east. San Georgino was now lost to sight, as the wall of dust moved toward them.

"I wish it would blow and get it over with," she said.

"You won't like the wind either, from all I hear."

Eunice was beginning, once again, to live naturally with Opal, though she didn't like this in herself. She was in the midst of a dilemma that was tearing her apart. It was the most natural thing in the world for her to love whoever and whatever Tom loved. How could she love a man and not follow him in his tastes and inclinations? She told herself over and over again: "You love a man who loves other women." It always seemed to her that anything that could be put so simply ought to be endurable. But it did not get more endurable. She had only to see Tom speak to another woman in that hovering, personal way of his, and all her calmness left her.

But calm or uncalm, rejoicing or enduring, she loved Tom Mount. She had accepted him the way a nun accepts her vocation, never expecting it to be easy.

But the nun, she thought, doesn't have to live, as I do, with some ex-nun like Opal, who is continuously bringing back reports of the sweetness of life outside the cloisters. If Opal was just any woman attacking Tom Mount and lecturing me about my foolishness, I might dismiss it, thinking, "She doesn't know what she's talking about." But Opal knows. She's an ex-nun, she's free now, and glad of it.

When Eunice told Opal that she was determined to accept Tom Mount as her destiny, Opal said, "That's very practical of you."

"Practical?"

"Practical," Opal repeated. "Tom Mount wouldn't put up for a minute with a woman who caused him any trouble. You've chosen the one way you can hang onto him. Eunice, don't you have one shred of pride left?"

"No," said Eunice. "I'm through with pride."

"He's got his foot on your neck."

"I'm where I want to be."

Yet she wasn't sure that she was, that she didn't dream of a time when Tom would be touched by her devotion, would tire of all others and say, "Eunice, there is no one else for me."

When she was conscious of such daydreaming, she would take out the bottle of D'jer Kiss that she had bought in Fort Collins, inhale deeply, so that she would be reminded painfully and clearly of the nature of the man she loved. Love him as he is, she would remind herself. Do not love him for what he is not and never will be.

The Jessup ranch adjoined the townsite on the north. To reach it, unless they made an obvious detour, they had to pass the church where Tom was working. Eunice had not the slightest idea of making any such detour. She wouldn't stop—Tom wouldn't like that—but with luck she might be able at least to see him.

Opal, who was as aware as Eunice of what they were approaching, said, "I think Reverend Raunce is making a big mistake, letting Tom Mount live in the church while he works on it."

"He's not living in the church proper. Just in a kind of porch that's going to be a Sunday school room."

"I don't care what room it is, I'm not going to feel the same about the church after his having lived there."

"The Quakers don't believe God leaves a building just because there's a cot and a kerosene stove on the porch."

"The Quakers don't know Tom Mount."

"They don't judge a man by the world's standards."

"They'd better, as long as they're in the world. They better let God be God, and they better try to be sensible men. Jessup and Raunce are just too gullible."

"Or too good."

"Too good's as bad as not good enough in some cases."

"Well, Tom was working on the church. It was handy . . ."

"Handy, handy. There's a lot of handy things we better keep our hands off. Including Tom Mount. Why didn't he put up a tent? Asa Brice doesn't have a patent on living in a tent."

Eunice said no more until they came in sight of the church; and she *was* lucky. Tom came out of the church with a bundle of shingles and climbed the ladder to the roof, balancing the shingles with one hand on his shoulder.

"He'll just about get them up there in time for the wind to blow them off," Opal said.

Opal couldn't have said anything that would have pleased Eunice more. Nothing Tom can do, including shingling, is right in Opal's eyes, she thought. She's absolutely prejudiced. I'm not required to listen to such talk.

Tom, seeing them coming, stood up, sure-footed against the hard blue glitter of the sky.

"Howdy, girls," he yelled.

Opal didn't reply. Eunice, though she wished he had said her name, was happy to say his. "Hello, Tom," she called. "Watch out, don't slip."

"Don't worry about me, pet."

Afterward, when they pulled up in front of the Jessup house, Opal turned very seriously to Eunice.

"Eunice, I want you to promise me one thing."

"I'm not making any promises."

"I want to ask you one question."

"I can't stop you."

"You wouldn't think of going there to the church to see Tom, would you?"

"Other people do. Wendlin Jessup goes. . . ."

"I'm not talking about other people. And especially not about Wendlin Jessup. I'm talking about you. Would you go there?"

There was one question Opal wouldn't ask her, and Eunice knew it. "Do you still let Tom Mount make love to you?" But Opal would ask all around it.

236

Eunice answered the question Opal did ask. "So far, I have never gone there."

"There are some things you can't play fast and loose with."

Eunice didn't reply to this—though in her mind, she said, "Love's the only thing you can't play fast and loose with."

The church-to-be was about half a dozen blocks, though there were no such divisions yet, up the main street of the townsite from the school-to-be. Eunice, working in the school-to-be, took pleasure in the thought that Tom was near her and that they were both engaged in good work and work of a like nature. She made the most of whatever bonds there were uniting them.

Sometimes, when she told Tom how much she missed him, he reminded her that they were together about as often as most married couples, couples where the husband is a businessman, with conferences and meetings, or a hunter or fisherman, or golfer or cardplayer, with pleasures away from home. And he reminded her further that their meetings, unlike those of married couples, were never perfunctory or dutiful.

She didn't want anything from Tom because he "owed" it to her. At times she did think about children—hers and Tom's. But she believed that women who longed for children weren't very much in love with their husbands. She would love a child of Tom's, but she never thought of Tom as "the father of my children"; she never cut him down to the size of a seed planter, and loved him for what he could do instead of for what he was.

She remembered the nights and days when she had determined, sensibly, never to see Tom again: how barren and reasonable that time had been, empty and arid as a desert. She could hear now the rat-a-tat-tat of Tom's hammer as he nailed shingles to the church roof, and it pleased her to match the swing of her broom to the rhythm he was setting and to think that, though he didn't know it, he controlled the movements of her body.

A musty stink, somehow exciting in its strangeness, filled the Investment Company's office: the smell of men and real-estate transactions. It was odd that beings so like women could give an office a smell so different from a home, where women ruled. Men were supposedly outdoor creatures, but once indoors they never thought to open a window. (Except for Tom, who had a woman's sensibilities about such things.)

237

The Perkins Investment crew had never opened a window, they had all smoked cigars, and they had gone to the chemical toilet every few minutes. Or did men naturally have a stronger smell than women?

Tobacco, dust, urine, spit, sweat. More than likely a man contemplating sinking his life's savings in a risky real-estate deal sweat more than usual and left more of a stench behind him. She opened all the windows and the two doors, one at the front and one at the back of the building. She was standing in the opened front door getting a breath of fresh air when Indiana Rose Cope went by, bound for her husband's office up the street. Eunice waved, Indiana Rose smiled and lifted her hand, and Eunice went back to her work.

Tom was waiting at the back door of the church when Indiana Rose came around the corner of the building. He smiled down at her, and she saw that he understood the heat and dustiness of her walk, her fears, remorses, resolutions. He had a white carpenter's apron on over his khaki pants, his face was browner than when she had last seen it, and he was the only person on the Tract whose hair had not been ruined by the dry heat.

She stood at the bottom of the steps, trembling, unwilling to turn away, unable yet to climb them. Tom didn't say a word. There is something reassuring about a carpenter, she thought. It is difficult to believe that a man who deals with sweet-smelling lumber, works in the open, and builds homes is not the soul of honor. She was there, though, because of a deep-seated intuition that this was not so. But she was grateful for the illusion, for the external appearance. It permitted her to climb the steps. It was the temporary anesthetic she needed.

Inside the Sunday-school-room-to-be, which was now his home, Indy received another needed whiff of ether. Tom's room was one in which a woman at once felt at ease. It told her, intent upon, and frightened by, the differences between men and women, that there were enough likenesses to get them over the interval until they were ready to experience the differences.

"Sit down while I take off my apron," Tom said. He smiled at the way in which his words parodied those of a housewife.

"It was nice of you to be on time," he said.

Did he think she had any choice? For a meeting like this, you were either on time or didn't come at all.

"I spoke to Lute about driving you out to the Lewises'. He said that was fine with him."

238

Of course it was. Lute would hand her over without a word to any asking man rather than endure any discussion. Lute was doing what he had always done. She wasn't. She was doing what she had never done before: she was choosing another man in preference to Lute. If going to the Lewis ranch had been what she wanted, she could have gone with Lute. He had asked her, and she had put him off with an excuse.

"Let's go," Tom said.

She rose and faced him. He made no motion to touch her, but she felt the space that separated them filled with imagined touchings. And they might never happen. This was the first time, though, that she had knowingly placed herself where those touches might become real.

On their way to the Lewis ranch, they passed the Perkins Investment Company's old office. Tom waved, though Indy saw no one.

"Sylvester Perkins's donated the office for use as a school."

"I know," she said.

"Eunice Fry is getting the place cleaned up. Do you know her?"

"I've met her. I saw her as I came in."

"You ought to get acquainted with her. She's a nice girl. You'd like her."

Sometime before Tom and Indy drove past, Eunice had missed the sound of Tom's hammer. The silence at first meant to her only that Tom had gone down from the roof for another bundle of shingles. As the silence continued, as she stopped her own work to listen for the rat-a-tat-tat to begin again, other explanations came to her, and in her heart she felt the familiar contractions of grief. She sat down at Sylvester Perkins's old desk, first resting her face on its ink- and cigar-smelling surface, then later looking out across the road and into the shimmering heat waves that stretched away toward the dusty murk in the east. She was sitting there and looking out when Tom drove by and waved to her.

She knew that he couldn't see her, seated at the back of the poorly lighted room. She believed that his wave said, "If you are looking, remember that I remember you."

It did not say "Forgive me," or "Try to understand," or "It won't happen again," or "Wish you were along."

He didn't wish that she were with him. And it would happen again. His wave said, "You will have to love me as I am." That was the way she did love him. She did not and never would ask him to be her Charlie or her Wendlin or her Lute.

She stayed at the desk until midafternoon. She tried, by remembering the pleasures she had experienced in former autumns preparing for the first day of school, to regain her morning's interest in her work. It was gone. As well talk to a child who has learned to walk of the pleasures it used to have creeping. It will never again creep with pleasure.

At midafternoon, she felt the return of the compulsion that had first seized her in Fort Collins. See! Know! If you cannot be near the man, be near his life: be near the mail, the bills, the presents other women have given him. She needed the relief of a desperate act. She went to the church.

She was trembling when she entered Tom's room. The lilac scent of Indiana Rose's perfume was still in the air. She had never seen this room before, but nothing in it surprised her. It was the room of a man not overwhelmed by life. Nothing he experienced was strong enough to interfere with his keeping track of his encounters, changing the water on his flowers, hanging his pants up so the crease wouldn't be ruined. In the corner, where a piece of canvas on baling wire hid his clothes from the room, she found and embraced the old rain-smelling overcoat of their first meeting.

After a little, she went on with the bitter business of accepting Tom Mount as he was. She was no longer able to read the letters through. She didn't know how Tom could. The letters were all so long, and they all said the same things. He must feel, reading them, like a god worshiped with prayer wheels. There were some new names. For a while she had kept track of the Eleanors, Marys, Graces, Gertrudes, Louises. She had given this up. There were new gifts, some stored unopened in a pasteboard carton. Somewhere, women who had schemed, dreamed, pinched pennies, lied to husbands were solaced by the belief that their testimonials of love were making Tom Mount's Western loneliness more bearable. There was a gift of hers in the carton: a framed enlargement of a picture of the two of them, taken in that long-ago Easter snow. When they were separated, she had lived in that picture. She had supposed he would. The package had been opened, but the picture was still in the tissue paper in which she had wrapped it.

240

She had vowed she would always love Tom Mount, and her trembling sickness convinced her that she was not wavering in her vow. She needed the sight of her own wounds to believe. If the worshiper bleeds, the god is real.

She was bleeding. A woman will feel something. She will have her storms somewhere.

She left Tom's room and went to the front of the church; though it was scarcely a building yet, let alone a church. The roof was going on because it was the season for rain. She sat on a sawhorse and gazed out into a landscape becalmed in light and heat. She reminded herself that she was sitting in what would be a house of God. She tried to regain some of the calm beatitude she had felt as a girl, sitting in church and repeating with the congregation, "The Lord is My Shepherd. I shall not want."

But she did want.

She sat dry eyed, looking out across the parched hills. Basil Cudlip, with his wife and carriageful of young ones, drove by. Base tipped his hat. She could not bring herself to offend her feelings with anything so friendly and hypocritical as a wave.

7　A T  T E N - T H I R T Y , Joicey took a pail of lemonade down to the men who were setting out trees. The minute Joicey left the kitchen, Rosa ran out to the buggy and got the wreath of flowers she had brought with her. She had wrapped the wreath in damp papers, and it hadn't wilted at all. She tiptoed into the spare room with it, placed the wreath on the bolster, and knelt beside the bed. She had made a vow not to tell anyone, even Pete, that the baby was coming, until she could kneel by this bed and give her thanks to God.

No sooner had she thanked God for leading her to the bed and giving her the baby, than the baby, whom she had not before dared to accept, filled her with its presence, flooded her with warmth and light. She was like a saint with a vision, only her vision was a living flesh-and-blood baby, inside her.

She was still on her knees when Joicey came into the room. When she stood, she saw that Joicey knew. She had wanted Pete to be the first.

Pete, at least would be the first one she would tell. Joicey had guessed without any help.

"How did you know?" she asked. She moved her hands over the front of her dress. For all that she had imagined it so many times, curved outward with the visible presence of her baby, she knew as a matter of fact that it still hung straight and flat. "Does it show?"

Joicey smiled. "No, it doesn't show. But something told me. I'm expecting too," she explained.

"When?" Rosa asked.

"The last of May."

"The same with me," Rosa said. She did some calculating. "This is a very fine bed."

Joicey was not accustomed to such frank talk. She had never mixed prayer and love-making as Rosa had. She had kept God and bed separated. She said her prayers on her knees before she got into bed.

Rosa saw this; still, the subject interested her, and though for Joicey's sake she phrased her questions delicately, she couldn't refrain from asking them.

"How old is your littlest boy? You call him Zoomy?"

"Zoomy's nine," Joicey said.

"For nine years, no children?"

Joicey nodded. "Zoomy was the last."

"You try not to have any more babies?"

"No. But no more came."

"Then—in this bed—a baby?"

This was nothing Joicey could be absolutely sure about. But it had seemed likely to her, too.

"In this bed," she agreed.

Rosa was pleased. The bed was miraculous twice over. She touched it, as she had the very first time, with pleasure.

"Now you are keeping it for special?" she asked. "In the special pretty room?"

She was keeping it in the special pretty room, though not for the reasons Rosa believed.

"This bed," Rosa said, "had better not be used by somebody not wanting a baby. It is a baby-bed. That is what I think. Do you?"

"It seems that way," Joicey said.

"When this baby," Rosa said, touching the spot where she now felt the baby to be, "is born, I will come over again. With Pete, if you will let us. I don't want to wait six years again."

Rosa paused, thinking of all that unnecessary garlic and olive oil and moon-watching.

"What will you name yours?"

"Elizabeth," Joicey said, "after my mother."

The idea of planning on a girl was strange to Rosa. Plan on boys and reconcile yourself to girls if necessary. A wife who hoped for a girl did not do her husband much honor. In doing so, she hoped for a copy of herself instead of a copy of him.

"Mine will be a boy," Rosa said, "and he will be named Peter after his father."

They left the room arm in arm. Outside, Rosa sniffed a little, delicately.

"You don't think those squirrels stink a little?" For fear this was untactful, she softened her words by saying, "Perhaps it is my condition."

"They do smell a little strong," Joicey admitted.

"I have brought something to kill the smell and the taste. I came for two reasons," she explained. "First, to thank the bed. And you. And to show my thankfulness, I thought, I will bring a little something to kill the squirrel smell and taste. You want it killed, don't you?"

Joicey looked doubtful. "How can you do it?"

"Chili," Rosa said. "I brought chilies with me. Put enough in, and they will never know but they are eating skunk. Their mouths will burn too much for them to care what it is that stinks."

Before she went into the kitchen, she took Joicey's hand.

"You won't tell Pete?"

"About the chili?"

"The baby," Rosa said, "the baby."

"Doesn't he know?"

"Not yet. For one time I wanted to be sure. 'Baby, baby,' I tell Pete twelve hundred times. And it was never true. This time, I made up my mind to be one-hundred-per-cent true. It will be a great surprise to Pete. He had begun to think he could not do it. Me, too," she added frankly.

Joicey did not know what to say.

"Perhaps without the bed, he could not," Rosa added reflectively. But she cheered up immediately. "With the bed, however, he has no problem."

In the kitchen, she took her sack of little red chilies out of the cupboard and began to stir them into the squirrel pot. "Now," she said, "for all anybody will care, it could be a rattlesnake." She stirred and Joicey watched. "You had better bring in another bucketful of water," she advised, and Joicey went out after it.

Shel wondered if everything always happened a little too late. If someone had interviewed him ten years ago, asking him, "When do you plan to start your cornhusking, Mr. Lewis?" he might have got some glory out of it. But now, with Crystal Raunce at his heels, notebook pages riffling in the wind and licked pencil drying before she could set it to paper, he felt as ridiculous as could be. If Lute wanted information for his paper, why didn't he come down and ask his own questions? Learn something against the time he'd be setting out his own trees? Though Shel had to admit the girl was smart and perhaps Lute knew what he was doing, training her to write.

"Why did you decide to plant orange instead of lemon trees, Mr. Lewis?"

"I am planting some lemons later. Back there on the slope below the house. Lemons ain't as hardy as oranges, and the high ground is more protected."

"What kind of oranges are these?"

"Valencias."

"How long will it be before these bear fruit?"

Shel began to wish that the idea of making a kind of back East barn-raising out of the planting had never come to him. It was bad enough to have made the show he had at the meeting of his intention to plant, without keeping the matter fresh in everybody's mind with all this serving up of stewed squirrel and elderberry pie. He really needed no more than three helpers: Chad, Pete, and Asa Brice; but to look at the place you'd think there was a county fair in progress. He'd lost track of all who had arrived. Pete's wife, Rosa, was helping in the kitchen. Lute Cope had come out because of the paper. And Indiana Rose was here because Lute was, he supposed; and he didn't know why Mount had come. The girls were here because they were Ellen's friends; and Julian had come out with Pete and Rosa.

"Chad is a fast worker, isn't he?" Crystal asked.

The girl was going to have an article on Chad instead of trees if she kept the questions moving in that direction. Chad was a surprisingly fast worker; without flash or fury, he was managing to keep a half-dozen tree holes ahead of him and Pete.

"What do you call what Chad's doing?"

Shel looked at Pete, who was helping him to put the balled trees into the ground, and said, "What would you call it, Pete?"

Pete straightened up, looked at Chad as if sizing up a complicated situation, then said, "I'd call it shoveling."

That was what he was doing, all right, but Shel gave it to the girl in a little better newspaper style. "He's cleaning out the tree holes. They been dug some time, and the sides have got hard and packed. He's loosening up and freshening the dirt so the tree roots'll have something easy to catch hold of."

The girl scribbled hard to get that all down, and he and Pete moved up to the next tree hole. Shel set the notched lath across the hole so that the tree could be centered properly, and Pete put the balled tree down in the earth Chad had stirred up. Then they both filled in the hole and shaped a big shallow basin to hold the water that Asa Brice, who was working behind them, would deliver from the Jessups' tank wagon.

Chad, who was a dozen tree holes up ahead of them, came back and said, "It'll be dinnertime before you catch up with me. I guess I'll go on up to the house."

"You go on," Shel said. "You been turning out as much work as me and Pete together this morning. You got a right to knock off early."

When he was out of earshot, Crystal said, "What Chad wants is to talk to Press Cope."

"That the girl he's soft on?" Shel asked.

If Press Cope was responsible for the change in Chad, Shel was for her; though he didn't care to be always judging his children by the amount of work they turned out. He valued lovingness and cheerfulness as much as the next parent; but sweat somehow seemed to come from even nearer the heart than a smile. He glanced down at Crystal and caught her with her heart in her eyes, gazing after the departing Chad. Her look abashed Shel. He knew Chad had changed in the past two months, but he didn't know the transformation had made a ladies' man out of him. That look of hers makes a grandfather out of me, he thought. And one in no need yet of help from my boys.

He had too much delicacy to let Crystal know what he had seen. "Come on, Pete," he said, "let's catch up with what Chad's done, then go have us a drumstick of squirrel ourselves."

His voice brought Crystal back as a newspaperwoman to herself. "Mr. Lewis, how many trees do you plant to an acre?"

"I'm planting an even hundred myself. They're twenty-two feet apart running this way, twenty-four the other. They cost a dollar apiece. Usually they're more. I got a good buy. This hole is eighteen by eighteen."

Shel centered his tree carefully. You could take all sorts of pains digging your tree holes, then be careless centering your trees and end up with a grove as wobbly as a horse with the staggers. He turned to see how far behind them Asa was working with the water wagon; for the first time, he saw that what they had planted this morning had shaped up like a grove; the trees were already marching in diamonds or squares or rectangles, depending upon how you looked at them.

Planting a grove put corn and tobacco planting out of face. The pattern he was making this morning would last. He would be able to keep track of a tree's bearing the way he could keep track of a cow's or a mare's. This was a crop there'd be time to get acquainted with. These were the facts Lute's reporter should be setting down for his paper, not statistics about inches and feet and dollars. What the hell was that? As well sum up a man by counting his teeth or say a woman was so many eyelashes.

Some teasing exultation, rising out of this first sight of his grove, made him say, "Write this down, girl. Tell Lute this is what I want published. Say that what you write was set down by you in a high wind from a man bent on spitting against it. You got that?"

Crystal's hair was in her eyes, and the wind blew her dress between her legs. "Yes, sir," she said, "I have."

"You write down that if the wind snaps these whip-stem tree trunks, and the heat curls the leaves, and they're all dead by morning, that one man on the Tract, at least, had him a green grove, watered and growing, for some few hours this afternoon. You write down that you seen it with your own eyes. You have, haven't you?"

"Yes, sir," Crystal said, taking a sweep with her eyes, between words, at the green grove, small but watered and growing.

"You write down that there's not a jog in a tree row nor a wobble in a tree, and if the pole star vanishes overnight, you can start directions over again by these tree rows. They've been trued off by the sun and evened up by the stars. You believe me?" Shel asked.

"I believe you," Crystal said.

"You write it down there that the desert's been made to bloom like the rose, and if the rose don't last, why, Mr. Sylvester Perkins is the man to blame. He made us a little speech some time back in which he tried to make us blush for forgetting the war. Well, you tell him for us that we're fighting us a little war of our own right here. A war against wind, heat, dust, and dryness. And maybe against Sylvester Perkins, too. Say, whoever it's against, we're going to win. You got that?"

"I haven't got it all written down yet, but I've got it in my head."

"You write that down, then I'll tell you some more."

Shel stepped into the kitchen at twelve exactly, and said, "Whew!" The kitchen, like the rest of the house, was shut tight against wind, dust, and heat; but what had kept them out had also kept the squirrel steam in.

"You tired out, honey?" Joicey asked, and Shel didn't have the heart to tell her that tiredness wasn't what he was whewing about.

"I won't mind sitting for a spell," he admitted.

"Taste this stew," Joicey said. "Rosa put chili in it, and I'm afraid she's ruined it."

Shel speared an acrobatic-looking hind leg. "If this can hold out a little longer," he said, "it'll be able to make it out of the kettle and back to the barley field on its own."

"Taste it," Joicey said, without smiling.

He managed to tear off a string of gray meat and was working away on it when he crunched down on his tongue, as he was always liable to do when eating. He groaned and put the back of his hand to his mouth.

"Is it that awful?" Joicey asked.

"I bit my tongue," he mumbled.

Joicey, who forgave him everything else, never failed to hold this awkwardness against him. For some reason, it rubbed her the wrong way. She never expressed pride in any feature of hers: eyes or red lips or curls or ankles. But she was proud of having a little pink tongue that she never bit, and she could never resist, when Shel crunched down on his, sticking hers out as an example of what a tongue should be like. She did so now, as she had done on a hundred occasions before. It was pale pink, long, and pointed. Shel stuck out his own, bleeding, to show that he had something else altogether to contend with.

"You got no problem, Joicey."

"I wouldn't have a tongue like that. I never saw anything like it. Put it in," she said. "The company's looking at you."

Shel put it in, swallowed blood, and went into the dining room, a

247

little self-consciously. "Draw up your chairs, folks. We're ready to eat."

At the far end of the sitting room, Lute, Lute's wife, and Tom Mount were talking together. Hannah and Zoomy, sitting on the floor, were helping to keep the rag carpet anchored against the wind, which, blowing under the house, came up through the cracks. The carpet, where people or furniture didn't hold it down, was filled with rolling swells, like a pot of cornmeal mush coming to a boil. Ellen and her three girl friends were clustered against the dining-room windows. Asa was having a serious talk with Julian and Pete.

Shel began to have a holiday feeling. Though the squirrel stew didn't provide a good substitute for the spicy smells of a Christmas tree and popcorn balls stuck together with sorghum molasses and an old hen in the oven, the wind whining around the house put him in mind of sleety Christmases back in Jackson County. He was glad once again that he had decided to celebrate the planting. The man who didn't have a house to ask his friends to, a table to set them at, or the food to put before them missed something in life.

"Come on, folks," he said again. "You can talk *and* eat."

Chad picked up a chair. "Where do you want to sit, Press?" he asked. "This is the best chair in the house. Spring-bottomed," he said, giving it a whack, then blushing at the sound of the word he had used.

"Would you mind asking Mama where she'd like to sit?" Press said in a tone that said also, "Don't you have enough manners to ask her first?"

Shel, overhearing her, thought, If that chair's going to a mother, it can go to Joicey, not Indiana Rose Cope. If that girl don't want it as a gift from Chad, she can't order it delivered elsewhere.

He took the chair out of Chad's hands, stopped with it long enough to say to Press, "If you don't want this chair, it belongs to the lady of the house," then carried it to the head of the table.

He stayed behind it after Joicey and the others had seated themselves.

"What we've got here today may not chew like turkey," he said, "but it's a real Thanksgiving as far as I'm concerned, and the first of many for all of us, I hope, here on this Tract and under this rooftree."

8   At three that afternoon, Mary and Opal sat down in Mary's sitting room to savor their morning's accomplishments. Mary was having one of her good days, and she had been able to join Opal in several little jobs she enjoyed but had been forced to give up since her visit to the hospital. The silverware was all polished; the copper chafing dish, the only one on the Tract, from which Willie White and his Sallie had had many a helping of Welsh rarebit, had been shined to such a state of ruddiness that Mary said it was almost too glary to look at on such a hot day; all the pictures had been taken down, their frames dusted, and their glass coverings cleaned. Opal had washed, starched, and ironed every tidy and headrest in the house. Mary had finished another brushing out with twists of damp paper, and now Opal was sipping cool lemonade and eating oatmeal cookies.

On days like this it seemed to Mary that she had dreamed her operation, the doctor's report, her past pain, her impending death. She felt no pain, no weakness; her spirit was as calm and serene as a summer Sunday. She knew the pain would return and with it the knowledge that she was dying; when she had first experienced such days of ease, she had believed that she ought not to forget death. Now she forgot it. One thing at a time, she now told herself. In the midst of life, we are in death; but since this is true, there is no need to harp on it. True, there were moments when the sorrowful knowledge of ending would suddenly blacken a day of the kind she was now having. She was learning to accept the blackness, also; to say at such times, "Yes, life is ending," "Yes, there won't be many more days like this one"; she was learning not to ruin the time she had by bemoaning the approach of an eternity for which she had always believed, as a Christian, she was living.

So she was living wholly in time, letting eternity take care of itself, when she heard a pounding at the front of the house which made Opal jump out of her chair.

"Somebody must be dead or dying," Opal said.

Somebody is, Mary thought; but this dying was perhaps one something could be done about.

Opal swung open the door to Basil Cudlip.

"Come in," Mary said, "and shut the door behind you. I'm trying to keep out as much of the heat as possible."

Cudlip came in and, as an afterthought, took off his hat. "Where's Wendlin?" he asked.

"At the Lewises'," Mary told him.

"Have you got a tent?"

"I don't think so. Wendlin will be back in a couple of hours. He can tell you."

"I need a tent now. If you don't have one, do you know anybody who does?"

"Eunice and I've got one," Opal said.

"It'd take me too long to get out to your place and back. I need a tent right away."

"What for?" Mary asked. "What's so pressing, in weather like this, about getting a tent up right away?"

"The weather don't have anything to do with it. But Raunce's cow is over there in his back yard visible for twenty miles in every direction."

He paused as if he thought that might be enough; reluctant, even to ladies of Opal's and Mary's age, to come right out with it; but neither gave him any help.

"The Raunce cow is going to calf," he said, "and from the looks of things, it ain't going to be easy. She's going to be some time at it, and it's not a sight for women and children."

Mary was brought up as much as Cudlip in the belief that everything having to do with birth, down to a hen laying an egg, was not a fit subject to talk about, let alone watch. But the scarcity of her days or Cudlip's red face made her feel balky. The world wasn't going to end if a cow, even the preacher's cow, had a calf in public.

"What women and children," she wanted to know, "are around? So far as I know, everybody who isn't over at the Lewises' is inside on a day like this. Who's there to see?"

"My wife and children, for one. They drove into town with me."

"Drive them out again," Mary said.

"Miss Fry is sitting over there in the church. I can't drive her out. A young woman comes into town to sit in church and pray and she has to watch that."

"She can turn her back," Opal said. "And she didn't come to town to sit in church."

"Whatever she came for, the church is where she is. And if she lifts her eyes that's what she'll see."

"I doubt if she'll lift them."

"It don't matter if not a soul sees. That's not the point. A thing don't have to be seen to be wrong. Raunce ought never have left the animal like that out in the open. He ought to've got her out of sight. He's a preacher. He ought at least have the delicacy of an ordinary man. Back in Kentucky, we'd run a man who'd do a thing like that out of town on a fence rail."

For the first time, Mary began to feel the real freedom of dying: first, she wasn't going to have to live with any of the ill will she might stir up by speaking the truth; and second, she seemed, at the end of her life, to be getting nearer the truth.

"We're a step or two ahead of Kentucky, out here in California, Base. You better wake up to it. A cow can have a calf out here and nobody take exception."

"It's not the cow I'm talking about. It's Raunce. A man who don't have decency in one line won't have it in another. A man's got to have an awful lot of animal in him not to take notice of such things."

"Or the other way 'round," Mary declared jauntily.

"You come from Kansas, don't you, Mrs. Jessup? I don't know what the practice is there, but in Kentucky our womenfolk are spared such sights. I aim to get a tent and cover up that cow. Then I intend to bring charges against the Reverend LeRoy Raunce."

"What kind of charges?" Mary asked.

"Indecent exposure of a cow," Base Cudlip said, after a little hesitation.

He bowed to the ladies, to show them that in the South they didn't hold stupidity against their womenfolk, opened the door, letting in a shaft of light and heat, then shut it with a bang.

Mary laughed until her sides hurt. It was the first time that, without forgetting death, she had felt free of it. It was something that was going to happen, in time and in the world, but not especially to her; or not to her any more than to the Raunce cow calving, or Cudlip pawing the earth to hide the fact from women and children. It was going to happen to her sooner was all. They were all in it together.

She wiped the tears from her eyes. "Opal," she said, "it appears we have missed something in life without the protection of a Southern gentleman."

"We'd be spared knowledge of other men, I expect," Opal said, "to say nothing of gentlemen cows."

Mary laughed again. "Let's walk over and see what he does," she said.

"In all this heat?" Opal asked.

Mary kept forgetting that with no health to take care of, she was willing to take chances healthier people, with something to lose, weren't.

"We could take it slow," she said, "and carry parasols."

Elizabeth Cudlip watched her husband bang the Jessup door behind him. She felt herself flush with anger. She had no anger for herself, but let Base or the children be scanted in any way and she turned white with fury. Whiteness showed on her because she was usually so high-colored. It had been hot waiting for Base, though she stood the heat well, having, as Base said, "no lard to melt." She wore her black hair in a tight, smooth knot on top of her head. She had on a black-and-white-patterned high-necked percale shirtwaist and a black poplin skirt. All that blackness and spareness and neatness made her look a little like a beetle; but she was tender to her children and was waiting to be tender to Base—if he would let her. She didn't have any other purpose in life; and didn't want any.

"No tent there?" she asked, as Base climbed into the carriage.

"No tent and no caring either." He sat unspeaking for a minute, and she said, "What do you plan to do, Base?"

It was an unnecessary question. Base didn't change his plans. "I aim to get a tent and cover up that cow. You drive the girls on home."

She saw eye to eye with him. At thirty-four, and after seventeen years, she could not have said whether this was so because their ideas were the same or because she had grown accustomed to looking at the world through Base's eyes. Their only falling-outs were about Base himself: she thought he should eat more, rest more, sleep more. She saw him with all the tenderness of her own sacrifices, her own willlessness before his will. He was as strong as a religion to her. She said, and always had said, to Base, "Thy will be done." She had the satisfaction of knowing here and now, without waiting for reassurance from the skies, that her behavior was pleasing. And since it was God's will that a woman please her husband, she pleased Him, too. She was thinned down to bone and a high-colored skin by hard work; but there wasn't a line in her face. *Things* went wrong now and then—a crop failed; a mean teacher didn't give one of the children his due; Medora turned glum and obstinate—but these were a part of life on earth, and she slammed into each day eager to cope with them.

She thought Base was completely right about that cow and about Reverend Raunce. Even a farmer would have to be careless and ignorant to leave a cow out in full view like that; for a preacher, it seemed downright nasty. She wouldn't for a minute have one of her girls see that sight. It wasn't so much the blood and misery. If the cow was only dying, it wouldn't be so bad. But the cow wasn't dying. It was in the last part of what had started when the cow and bull had come together. That was what came to anybody's mind at calving; the man who wouldn't see anything wrong in the last part's being public probably wouldn't see anything wrong in letting the first part be seen either.

"Do you want me to come back for you, Base?"

"No. I'll walk—or pick up a ride some way."

"I hate to leave you here."

"There's no help for it, Lizzie. Somebody's got to take a stand for what's decent. Otherwise, we're going to have a dirty, mean community, not fit for children to grow up in."

It never occurred to either to say good-by. They scarcely thought of themselves as being parted. Lizzie Cudlip never doubted that Base would find a tent and get that cow covered up. She looked back at him, and, surprisingly enough, he had not moved. When he saw her backward look, he waved.

Tears came to her eyes. Base was not soft like weaker men. "Girls," she said, "you've got a fine father."


Eunice drove home to get their tent. She didn't care about the cow, or decency, or Base Cudlip, or anything like that. She needed action. She needed to be taken out of herself. She needed to be given no room for choice. Base gave her none. He said, "I understand you got a tent at your place?" Eunice said, "We do have." Base said, "Well, get it here as fast as you can. That cow's got to be covered up."

By the time Eunice got back, it was already a little gusty. Mary and Opal had come over, complete with sunshades, to watch the goings-on. Eunice joined them. The Raunce cow was in need of protection for her own sake. The heat and the rising wind were adding to her natural troubles; but Base's mind was set on saving something more precious than a cow: human decency. And saving it never has been an easy job. He knew that.

The tent was bigger by a good deal than was necessary for a cow to calf in, but then, Eunice and Opal had never bought it for a cow shelter. Base struggled for a while with the lifeless hulk before discovering that some of the tent pegs were missing. He supplied this want, and also got a hammer from the church next door. Stretching out the canvas was not much of a job. But getting the center pole up and the stakes into the packed earth was a different story. Particularly in a gusty wind that flounced at you from different directions. He needed help. Mary and Opal were hoping to see him fail. He knew that. They stood there under their sunshades like ladies at a plowing contest; and they were backing, not him, but Raunce and his cow, and the wind. And they were the very ones he was aiming to protect.

Eunice helped. She did not volunteer, but when he told her to hand him a tent stake, she handed it to him. He had no idea, of course, of how much she needed an emergency, how she would welcome a fire or a lynching; but he recognized a strong biddable assistant when he saw one.

"Hold up the center pole," he yelled, "while I get the stakes in."

There, in the midst of the smothering canvas, arms looped around the heavy center pole, which, as soon as the tent got some spread to it, began to buck and veer, Eunice had no time for the past or any need to take vows to be faithful. The present held her.

"Hang on to it. Hold it still," Cudlip yelled.

"I'm trying to," Eunice called back from under the canvas.

The hard earth, which was resistant on top, was powdery beneath the surface, and the tent stakes pulled out easily. The wind would hit the east side of the tent squarely and then, surging underneath, get at the west spread from inside. Eunice clasped the center pole, first with her arms, then with her legs also. If she had to fight canvas, she would have preferred to go to sea and have spray instead of dust to contend with. She could hear Opal and Mary laughing as if they thought what she was going through was funny. The sound made her mad. She had not felt mad for a long time, and she enjoyed the sensation.

From where Opal and Mary stood, it *was* a funny sight. First of all, there was Cudlip, racing around from stake to stake, putting in a new one and resetting an old one. He might have been wired to the tent, a

254

part of it, the way a cuckoo is a part of the clock. The wind blew, the tent rocked, and Base sped around and around, hammer in hand, giving a lick here and tightening a rope there. He was never made for such work. There was no humor in him. That was what made him so funny. He might be a backwoods murderer or the lawyer who saved the murderer from the noose. But running around and around a piece of flapping canvas, trying to get it up and keep it up, in order to provide privacy for a pregnant cow! Mary and Opal held their sides. They had closed their sunshades. It was easier to endure the sun than to battle the rising wind. They used them to lean on while they laughed. They guessed that what Eunice was undergoing inside that tent—in the periods it *was* a tent—wasn't funny. When the tent semicollapsed about her and she called, "Mr. Cudlip, Mr. Cudlip," she sounded half smothered. And when the canvas draped itself about her as she still faithfully clasped the center pole, she looked like some angel in an old-fashioned cemetery, clinging to the cross that saves. Though that pole was obviously nothing to bank on for saving purposes.

"Mr. Cudlip, Mr. Cudlip," she would cry, her voice trembling with fear or perhaps pain, and Mr. Cudlip, flying from peg to peg, would bawl, "Hang on. Hang on. We've just about made it." And Eunice, encouraged by this command, would slowly bring the pole, and herself with it, once again upright.

"I've laughed myself sick," Opal said, wind-dried tears of laughter on her cheeks.

"Me, too," Mary answered, without a thought to what she was saying.

It was Opal who first noticed the cow. Whether it was the rising wind, the heat, the dust, the flapping of canvas, the shouting of Eunice and Cudlip, or her and Mary's squeals of laughter that had helped, Opal didn't know. But the calf had arrived, without regard for human decency.

"Mr. Cudlip, Mr. Cudlip," Opal called. But at this minute, a particularly strong gust of wind hit the canvas, and Eunice, for so long the pole's faithful support, was knocked over. The cow and the calf could have used some help at the minute. They were ignored while Opal, Mary, and Cudlip struggled in the wind to get Eunice free of the smothering folds of canvas.

9    WHILE his father was planting trees, Zoomy was raking in the coin. All the nickels on the Tract seemed to have been saved for just such an afternoon; though if a kid said he had only four cents, and Zoomy's instinct told him this was true, he let the four-center in, too. The kids had come to believe that the ditch had been invented by Zoomy for their pleasure. They had forgotten that protection was all they bought; they thought it was water, with protection thrown in as a gift. They enjoyed the sensations of robbery, not from the Anaheim Water Company and Ralph, but from Zoomy himself, as they floated with dust rinsed off and bladders emptied down the winding canal.

The ditch had never been more appealing. Even Zoomy, accustomed to regard it as merchandise, saw beauties that had nothing to do with salability. Down in its depths, sheltered by its steep banks, it was quiet in the midst of windiness. It was as strange as a mirage, and better: it didn't disappear. Fennel and anise and heavy-headed grasses grew along the banks, and these, reflected in the water, made the water green; at the very center of the ditch—the grasses were not mirrored that far—was a vein of blue where the sky looked back at itself.

Zoomy watched the road following the left bank of the canal for the dust that would announce Ralph in his two-wheeled cart. Ralph's habits made him easy to keep track of. In the mornings, he came from his home in Ramos, on the far side of the lake, and traveled downstream. In the afternoons, after an hour and a half for lunch and a nap, he turned homeward, patrolling upstream. And whatever direction he traveled, on the untraveled Tract, the dust of his two-wheeled cart warned of his coming.

This afternoon, Zoomy was less concerned than usual about Ralph. On hot days, Ralph sometimes prolonged his afternoon siesta until near quitting time at five. And perhaps, Zoomy thought, he won't patrol at all this afternoon, but go over to watch the doings at home. Pete and Rosa and Julian had come over early, and Ralph was one of their friends.

It was dangerous for Zoomy to look at the ditch as water instead of looking at it as a source of income. When he looked at it as water, his dry skin began to imagine how it would feel. He was the owner

256

of a commodity who begins to hanker for what he sells: Mr. Barnum falling in love with one of his own midgets, a saloonkeeper developing a taste for liquor.

Away upstream, he could hear the muted sounds of his customers' pleasure: a world he had created but knew nothing of. He was lonely as God. He stood at a narrow part of the ditch. A tumbleweed, windborne, bounded right across it. His big-legged, homemade pants flapped like frayed sails of some old abandoned ship. The dry wind parted his hair, and it seemed melancholy to be alone and so handled —as if he had no mother or sister to do that job for him. When he licked his teeth, he felt dust. Nobody loved him, and he didn't blame them. He wasn't lovable. This was a big day for his father, and instead of staying home, he was out stealing. His pants would have flapped more, except they were weighed down with money. He emptied his bladder, out of necessity, he thought. Actually, he was getting ready. He could have held in hours longer. The whole ditch began to reach out to him. He heard its small rippling sounds, like birds after rain; he saw its golden sands. Sprigs of licorice bush down next to the water got a touch of the wind, and their moving feathers set the reflected green to wavering.

He undressed slowly, heart-heavy like any other traitor. He wasn't a man for easy pleasures. He stood there, mostly butt and belly, though with a considerable bulge of forehead, too. Eat, sit, and think seemed to be what he was cut out for. Except for floating. He could rest on the water as buoyant as any webfoot. He went in quietly, heavyhearted but determined. In a way, he was showing his father that his unfaithfulness to him wasn't personal: he wasn't against his father; he was a hundred-per-cent bad: a guard who wasn't guarding, a person who took money under false pretenses. What else could his father expect from a son like that?

The water lulled it all. He closed his eyes; he floated half submerged, all sensations, except those of slipping through wetness, touched by coolness, gone. He lost sight of money and customers, father and honor. He let water slip in and out of his mouth; he pee-ed again. He would give something to the ditch which had given him so much. He didn't want to know the difference between who he was and what he was in. Old Zoomy was the ditch and the old ditch was Zoomy. He believed he might stay in the ditch forever; and turn, finally, like a horsehair after long immersion into a water snake.

Ralph, tooling homeward in his two-wheeled cart behind his quick and gentle mare, thought he had sighted a late melon, floating white side up. He intended to let it float. He hated wind and heat and was anxious to get home. He would stop for a dead dog or a dead cat, but he didn't know that he would let anything as small as a dead squirrel stop him. Certainly not a melon. Someone had probably put it in to cool it off and it had gotten away from him. Let it go.

Swimmers he would haul out, because he had had explicit orders to do so if he wanted to hang onto his job; and he did. His job suited him to a T. He wanted no other life than to follow that stream behind his little red mare on his two-wheeled cart. And he understood the feeling of his employers. Why should they, who had long ago built the Anaheim lake and dredged the Anaheim ditch, want to give the use of water free to Sylvester Perkins's settlers? The directors of the Anaheim Water Company had an agreement with Perkins that the settlers could take water by the barrelful from the lake so long as Perkins paid his monthly fee. But to make a public bathtub and swimming pool of the ditch was another matter. It was trespassing. It was dirty. It was illegal. There were fines for those who were caught at it. And Ralph felt a personal anger toward the swimmers, health and legality apart. Before the Perkins Investment Company had brought people to the Tract, he had been able to patrol the ditch in a long, quiet dream: see that those who had the rights to water were getting it; remove the dead and unresisting bodies.

Now there were swimmers, and swimmers were another matter. They were not unresisting. They ran, whooping. They hid under bridges. They called him greaser and chollo and lump of lard and fatty. They scared his mare. They made him exert himself. He could no longer flow along the stream, a part of it. They stifled his love. He hated them, and he hated hating, especially in this weather.

Today, to protect himself from the heat and the wind, he had gone as far inside his three hundred pounds as possible. Some little eye of his mind, not his two physical eyes, for they were closed against the wind and glare which hurt them, was keeping track of the ditch. The red mare kept track of the road. When his little noneye reported the floating melon, he opened his real eyes momentarily to check on this. His real eyes noted something unusual: the melon had a navel.

Ralph carried a long-handled crook with him for fishing the bodies of dead animals out of the water. He stopped his cart and went to the edge of the ditch; with a fat man's feline stealth, he hooked the floater around the neck. He didn't care whether what he got was male or female, dead or alive, though dead was in some ways preferable; it would be less trouble than something alive. It was alive and male.

Zoomy had not left even one little noneye open as he floated. The horsehair-to-water-snake change was about to come over him. He was hauled up, the next thing to a water snake, dragged to the edge of the bank, too choked to yell and too surprised to think. Ralph unhooked him in the knee-deep water at the foot of the bank. The minute Zoomy got a little air in his lungs, he gave his warning whistle. The muscles of his throat were still too constricted to let him do much more than croak. He scrambled like a toad up the bank of the ditch, his whistle clearing as he got to the top.

Ralph, wiser than he used to be in his simple dead-cat days, took as firm a hold as he could manage with his pudgy hands on Zoomy—who did not provide much more of a handhold than a wet rubber ball.

"What's that you're doing?" he asked.

Zoomy did it again. Then he had a bad fit of coughing and hawking.

"I'm trying to get the water out of my lungs," he said.

"You don't have any water in your lungs."

Out of sheer determination, Zoomy brought up or manufactured some water.

Ralph was impressed but still suspicious. "Why do you whistle?"

"You strangled me. You smashed my windpipe." Zoomy breathed hard, mingling whistle and croak. "It's getting better," he said. "Don't worry."

Ralph wasn't. He was feeling pretty good. He had a real lawbreaker, caught in the act, without too much exertion on his part.

"How much do I owe you?" Zoomy asked.

"Owe me?"

"The fine. It's five dollars, ain't it?"

"It's five dollars."

"I've got it."

"Where?"

"In my pants. Back up the ditch aways."

"What's your name?"

"If I give you the five dollars, you could put it in your pocket, couldn't you?"

"What you mean, put it in my pocket?"

"I mean keep it. Not tell the water company."

"You mean steal it?"

The talk was, on the Tract, that the Mexicans were light-fingered. Zoomy thought this question was a thief's recognition of an opportunity.

"Sure," he said.

Ralph had been wanting, ever since he hauled the boy out of the water, to pink his bouncy butt. Ralph was no fighter; he had never hit a man in his life; but having been called a thief, he didn't resist his desire to let Zoomy have it where it would do him the most good. It was pleasant as bouncing a ball. Zoomy let out a howl, which made Ralph jump. He gave Zoomy another whack to pay him for the damage done to his nerves. Zoomy, better prepared this time, let out an even louder bellow. Another slap. A kind of seesaw of bellow and slap was set up. Bellower saying, Stop slapping; and slapper saying, Stop bellowing.

The wind, now blowing strong, carried Zoomy's cries to Cudlip, traveling on foot toward the Lewis ranch. They were exactly the sounds his ears hungered for; sounds of pain and disorder; they confirmed what he believed. The Tract was going to the dogs. He had set out on foot for the Lewis ranch, too furious to waste a minute in getting the report of Raunce's misdeed to those he hoped would be as shocked as he. If there had been anyone at the townsite, except those three women, and two of them against him, he might have been able to stay and speak his mind there. But there was no one, and he was not a man who could endure to hold his peace. He had to act and speak. An unexpressed idea burned him like a fire. His desire to denounce Raunce was so hot in him that he traveled effortlessly, moved against the wind as light as the tumbleweeds that passed him headed in the opposite direction. Zoomy's screeching reached him like bird song: something else had gone wrong!

He hurried in the direction of the screaming. An oversized Mexican whaling a small white boy! He felt great satisfaction. If he had any doubts about his errand, they were silenced. That cow wasn't just a cow and this Mexican wasn't just a Mexican. They were both signs of what would have to be fought on the Tract: dirtiness about sex and uppity greasers, and the two of them more than likely going together.

Neither Zoomy nor Ralph saw him. Ralph was tired, but he hated to admit that Zoomy could yell harder and longer than he could spank. Zoomy's throat was raw and he wished he had never given the first bellow, since he did not know how to give the final one. Cudlip solved both their problems. He wrestled Zoomy away from a more than will-

260

ing Ralph; then he launched himself at Ralph, like a harpoon at a whale. Ralph was not only a greaser: he was Raunce and that shameless cow and the two women who had laughed at him, and all those other troubles, unsolved, back East.

Ralph keeled over at once and lay at Cudlip's feet, before Cudlip had punished him for anything but spanking Zoomy. Cudlip was frustrated by this, and, unusual for him, of two minds as to what to do next. He gave Ralph a couple of kicks, halfhearted, but strong enough to show he meant business. "Never lay a hand on a white boy again, greaser."

But when he looked around for the white boy he had been protecting, he was nowhere to be seen. Though that didn't matter; his real interest was in the culprit, not the victim. He decided to take Ralph with him to the Lewises' as an example of what they all had to fight. The cow they would be able to see for themselves when they went back to the townsite. How to get Ralph to the Lewises' was his problem; Ralph was on his feet now, sulky but undamaged. Cudlip certainly was not going to walk while Ralph drove; and the cart, even if he had been willing to share a seat with the greaser, wouldn't hold both of them. The only possible solution was for Ralph to walk while he rode.

The Lewis ranch was only half a mile away, and except that Ralph was balky, that shouldn't have been much of a trip. When Cudlip tried to hustle Ralph up a bit with a nudge or two from Ralph's own long-handled crook, Ralph obstinately slowed down. A touch from the buggy whip got no better results. So there was nothing for it but to let him take his own gait. They reached the ranch at four-thirty; the low sun was red and dust-covered, and the hot wind, blowing through the pitiful showing of Shel Lewis's new trees, promised to make short shrift of Shel's ambitions as a citrus grower.

Shel was down at the west edge of the ranch, deepening the basins about his newly set trees so that none of the precious water would be lost. He was dog-tired and of two minds about his day's work. It was unreasonable, he supposed, to take the satisfaction he did in it, considering what this wind might do to his trees before the night was over. He leaned on his hoe, gazed east up the slope toward his house, and, reasonable or not, gloried in what he saw. His own orange and lemon grove, not a tree out of line. If by morning every tree had been uprooted and blown fifteen miles west, clear into Los Angeles County, nothing could rob him of this hour's joy. If man on earth, as he had heard say, had to fight the powers of nature, stand up to wind and rain, sun and storm, well, he was fighting. If a poor man had to claim his rights from men like Sylvester Perkins, well, he was claiming. He had said he would plant and he had planted. He had said he was finished with waiting and he wasn't waiting. He might fail. So might those who didn't fight or claim, those who waited for fine weather and water in the pipes. His eyes were bloodshot and his mouth dusty, but, by God, he had something else in his mouth along with the dust: he had the bit in his mouth; he wasn't being driven; he was choosing his own gait and his own direction, and if he failed, he'd have the grim satisfaction of knowing he owed it all to himself.

The trees at this stage could have been round-headed rose bushes. He'd seen them like that in Kentucky gardens he had never walked in, lining a walk or circling a sundial. Citrus leaves had the same hard glossy finish. They looked waxed. The lemons, up on the higher ground where they'd get the benefit of the highest temperatures in any unlikely time of frost, would be yellow green, instead of blue green like the oranges. It took a bunch of them together to show the difference. He had taken pleasure in his own acres, uncleared: the cactus gullies, the flop-eared jack rabbits, every damned little elderberry bush and long-legged road runner. It was nothing to what he felt for his planted acres. For the second time that day, time hollowed out for him and gave him a chance to take in not only his planted grove, but himself, passed beyond his lickspittle days and into a future where these trees, full-grown and globed with what was as good as gold, would set him free of grubbing. Free of grubbing . . . free for what? When he put his hoe down, what then? The wind beat against him, he shoved his chin out into it, and it occurred to him that it was something to lean against as well as fight.

He had gone back to his hoeing when he heard Zoomy calling, "Papa, Papa." He turned to see his youngest, never a world-beater at running, and now making hard going of it against the wind and over plowed ground. Shel put his hoe against a tree and walked down to meet the boy.

Zoomy arrived, white-faced in spite of the heat, and momentarily wordless. "What's the matter, son?"

Shel felt sorry for the chunky little tad in his big-legged britches. "You look kind of tired, Judson." He didn't suppose he had called Zoomy Judson half a dozen times since he'd been born—and he didn't know why he had done so now—except that maybe with the new baby coming he felt it was time for Zoomy to leave off the nicknames of his babyhood.

Zoomy appeared to take no notice of the change in name. Instead, he handed Shel two Bull Durham bags. Shel took them, felt what filled them, and said, "Where'd you find these?"

"I didn't find them." When Shel didn't say anything, Zoomy, staring at the ground, said in a voice so low Shel could hardly catch his words, "I stole it."

At the word "stole," Shel's stomach dropped sickeningly. He had noticed during the past weeks that Zoomy had been troubled about something, but he had been too taken up with his own problems to talk to him. He opened the bags and poked the nickels around. Out here, chin in the wind like some damned hero, begetting more children, and proud of it, while your youngest has taken to thievery.

"Who'd you steal it from?" he asked.

"The Anaheim Water Company."

He asked the least important question, but it was one he *could* ask. "Where'd they ever get such a store of nickels?"

He felt immeasurably better when Zoomy explained the nickels. He supposed it was stealing, as Chad had said; still, as far as he was concerned, it was several cuts above burglary, and in his relief he had to pretend a sternness he felt he ought to feel, but didn't.

"What's the idea, turning the money over to me?"

"I done wrong to get it the way I did."

"Who put that notion in your head?" he asked, a new suspicion coming to him.

Zoomy, who suspected the suspicion, didn't try to beat about the bush. "I got caught."

"Ralph?"

"Yes, sir."

"So he put an end to your little business?"

"No, sir. He don't know about my business."

"What was it you got caught at?"

"Swimming."

"I thought you said you was the lookout?"

"I was swimming," Zoomy said doggedly.

Shel's face felt too tired to smile, but inside, where it took no physical effort, he did feel jocular. "At least there's no jail sentence for that."

"There's a fine."

"With your business going so good, I reckon that won't trouble you much."

Shel could tell by Zoomy's face that he'd been postponing something, maybe the worst yet.

"I tried to pay Ralph."

"I've got an idea he's not the one you pay fines to."

"I didn't try to pay him my fine. I tried to pay him not to tell on me."

"What did Ralph say to that?"

"He didn't say anything. He spanked me."

"Good for Ralph," Shel said. "I didn't reckon he had that much get-up-and-go."

"He don't try very hard, but he's so big if his hand just falls on you, it hurts. He made me yell."

"It don't take much to make you do that."

"No, sir," Zoomy looked at the ground. "While it was going on, Base Cudlip come along. He knocked Ralph down and kicked him."

"Why?" Shel asked.

"Because Ralph's a greaser and I'm a white boy. That's what he said."

"Did you help Ralph?"

"No, sir."

"Did you tell Cudlip the rights of the matter?"

"No, sir. I run."

"It looks like you've got yourself in pretty deep, don't it?"

"Yes, sir. I want to give the money back and tell Ralph I'm sorry."

They both saw Ralph at the same time, though for a second neither recognized him. He was plodding along in front of his cart, which Cudlip was driving. Once, Cudlip reached out and gave him a poke with a stick, as if Ralph had been some kind of a slow-footed animal.

"Telling Ralph you're sorry's not going to turn the trick, now," Shel said. "You'll have to tell Mr. Cudlip what happened."

Zoomy turned and half faced the house, but Shel put his hand on his shoulder and they walked down together to meet Ralph and Cudlip.

264

10    THE CAVE was Ellen's most precious possession, so naturally she offered it to the girls for their picnic. When she loved anyone, her first thought was, What can I give him? What is good enough? The cave had been her secret; not even Zoomy, who had a nose for the secret and the hidden, had been able to ferret its location out of her. She suffered a little at the idea of sharing it; she knew she would miss the pleasure of going to it and thinking, I am the only person in the world who knows about this. She even knew she would blame the girls a little for accepting so easily what was so precious to her. Nevertheless, she was leading them straight toward it.

They had left the Lewises' later than they had intended. The arrival of Medora's father had upset everyone's plans. Ellen would have thought that if anyone had a right to be humiliated it would be Medora, with her father raving and ranting about Reverend Raunce's cow and getting into a fight with a man like Ralph, who was too fat to fight a baby. But Medora didn't seem to care what her father did. Crystal was the one who cared. She agreed with every word Mr. Cudlip said about the nastiness of a preacher who would leave his cow out in full sight of women and children while it had a calf—and she even went Base Cudlip one better. "There is nothing I would put past my father," she said. "Nothing." This shocked the others, even Medora, into silence.

The grownups had tried to persuade them to give up their foolish idea of tramping off into the hills in such weather. "In this wind?" "In all this heat?" they asked.

So the girls had been carried halfway to the cave simply by their scorn for the kind of people who would let weather stop them from doing exactly what they planned.

"Old scaredy-cats," said Medora, who was their oracle.

Ellen didn't disagree out loud, but she knew her father was no old scaredy-cat. He didn't take orders from the weather any more than they did. And he risked more on it. All they risked was a little discomfort. The wind blew their skirts around their legs, half hobbling them, blew dust into their eyes and against their wind-burned cheeks.

"I can hardly wait to get into that cave," said Press, "where it's cool and damp."

The girls had the wrong idea of the cave. They imagined that it was dark and drippy, filled with ferns and perhaps bats. Not very pleasant, but at least cool. Ellen let them think so because she wanted them to have the surprise she had had in discovering it.

She had stumbled upon it on one of her sundown walks. It was the evening of a gloomy, overcast day, and the cave had opened up before her like the mouth of some white flower. She had been walking up the incline of a big north-traveling arroyo, and at the point where it ran into the east-west ridge of the foothills, there was this cave, as if the arroyo, before giving up its forward movement, had rammed its way as far as possible into the hillside. Though of course it had been the sea, not an arroyo, that had scooped out the cave. Otherwise there was no accounting for the little shells and the thick white sand. The cave faced seaward, open to the sea winds, but the slight uptilt of its mouth prevented the wind from blowing directly into it.

From inside the cave, the sea could be seen, like a deep-set, far-off eye, blinking and sparkling in the center of the grasses that grew about the opening of the cave and were the sea eye's lashes. Back in Kentucky, Ellen had never imagined the sea as anything but blue. But the sea was many colors: sometimes it was moonstone-colored, at others the color of a smoky tear. There were times when it looked exactly like an iron skillet covered with a silver film of cold bacon grease. She never tired of staring at it.

As the girls came up the final slope, she thought, Perhaps they'll be disappointed in the cave and think I have taken them on a long walk for nothing.

"This is it," she said apologetically.

They bent their backs and went in. There was a silence, then Press said, "I never saw anything so beautiful."

"I'm sorry it's too dusty to see the ocean today," Ellen told them.

"We don't have time for the ocean anyway," Crystal reminded her, "if we're to get through the initiation by dark."

The girls had formed a club, the first on the Tract, and they had come to the cave for a combined picnic and initiation. Crystal was in charge, and she had hinted that the ceremonies would test them all. They all wanted to be tested. Except for Crystal, who was sixteen, they were all seventeen and felt that the time had come for some boundary to be crossed, some sign to be made. They had been waiting a long

266

time to perform a significant act. Ellen hoped Crystal had devised one. She would be glad to feel herself on the far side of such an act, ready to begin living in earnest.

When they were all seated with picnic and initiation stuff ranged neatly beside them, Press said, "I feel like a part of the Swiss Family Robinson."

"What's that?" Medora asked.

The other three smiled. This was their Medora. Everything that had to be learned by reading was a mystery to her. Everything else was an open book. They were as proud of Medora as though she were a mountain lion. Their mothers warned them against her, and they didn't hold this against their mothers. If their mothers were right, Medora was wrong. Medora was just as dangerous as their mothers suspected. What their mothers didn't know was how capable of handling danger their daughters were.

Medora had the initials of a boy's name, L. B., in raised red welts, high on her left thigh. She had done the job herself with a butcher knife and salt.

"Didn't it hurt?"

"Of course it hurt."

"What did the boy think of it?"

"He never saw it."

"Did you do it because you loved him so much?"

"I did it to spite my father."

Medora had a stiff right arm. Her father, giving her a strapping with his belt, had made the mistake of using the buckle end. Her elbow bone had been cracked and had healed stiff, because Medora wouldn't give her father the satisfaction of letting him know how much he had hurt her. When she threw a ball with her stiff right arm, it looked like a horse casting a shoe.

Medora had a beautiful, stony face. If you can hold your face still while your arm's being broken, there's probably nothing strong enough, after that, to make it move. Her skin and eyes were about the same color, a deep apricot. She had black, shiny hair, which she wore in a washerwoman knot. Of all the girls, she thought the least about her looks.

The girls had given themselves labels. They were self-centered and loved classifications, and labeling themselves served both passions. "Is my nose snub?" "Do I have an hour-glass figure?" "Would you say I'm imaginative?" They could talk about such things for hours. They were getting acquainted with themselves. It is always interesting to meet strangers, and when the stranger is yourself, the meeting is particularly fascinating.

Press was, of course, Beauty. Where did this leave Medora, who was also beautiful? Medora was Personality. Crystal, obviously, was Brains. Ellen had to be content with what was left, which was Character.

Ellen didn't care for this very much; Character seemed a nice place to end but a dull place to start. But then, none of the girls liked their labels: except for Medora, who didn't give a damn what any girl thought of her. Press wanted to have Character; Crystal had long since discovered that it was no help to a girl to be known as brainy, and dreamed of being beautiful; while Ellen herself longed for Personality.

Ellen kept on justifying her label by her actions, though. She was the only one who had cooked something special for their initiation meal, and she was the one, also, who had made the club the gift of a cave. In spite of herself, what Ellen kept demonstrating was Character, not Personality.

Miss Personality was already greedily munching away on one of the marguerites Miss Character had unselfishly baked.

"Have we decided to eat before the initiation?" Miss Intelligence, who knew they hadn't, asked.

"You suit yourselves," Medora said. "I'm hungry."

Too brainy to try to change Medora, Crystal said, "We'll eat first."

The cave, the twilight hour, the vows they were about to take, kept them silent. They chewed their bologna and soda crackers slowly and reflectively. They were soon going to put themselves to a test.

They all felt a degree of faithlessness to their families. If they had listened to their mothers and fathers, they wouldn't have taken this windy hike through the hills, or be sitting now on the sand of a cave they alone knew about. But faithfulness to their families was something they were born to. It might not be nice to hate a father or a brother, but none of them had taken any vows to love fathers or brothers. Families were wished upon you, and you did the best you could with them. You had not chosen them. Not a one of them had by any word yet vowed herself to another human being. But now they were going to choose; they were going to enrich the worlds they lived in with the possibility of infidelity. They were all eager for a test; their muscles ached for lack of a burden. Childhood was running out.

268

The pleasures of defying parents were about used up. What they now needed to learn, their parents could not teach them. They were ready for something that had nothing to do with being daughters. They were going to choose each other as a practice step toward something else. Something unnamed, a peril they feared and longed for, and for which they were going to begin to practice that very evening, was marriage.

When they had finished eating, Medora said, "Let's start the initiation."

"What's the hurry?" Press asked.

"Someone's coming up here to see me."

"Who?" asked Crystal.

Ellen, full of character in spite of herself, said, "It's none of our business, Crystal."

Crystal objected. "It is our business. The cave is the meeting place for the club, and nobody should use it without permission from everyone else."

"Nobody told me I had to have permission," Medora said.

"Is that why you joined?" Crystal asked. "To have a place to meet somebody?"

"No," Medora said. "I joined because I wanted to. The cave had nothing to do with it. I'd of joined if we'd had to meet in the middle of the street."

They all believed her.

"But when I knew about the cave, I planned to use it."

"Who's coming up here to meet you, Medora?" Press asked.

Ellen winced at Press's question, so personal. Because of Chad, she was already beginning to treat Press like a member of the family and to ask more of her than of the other girls.

"Who, Medora?" Press insisted. "You've got to tell the truth. We promised each other we would."

"I'll tell you the truth. I'm not meeting Reverend Raunce. That's the truth."

"Nobody meets married men," said Ellen, defending Press from this teasing.

"Well, Miss Character!" said Medora. "You really know about life, don't you?"

"I wouldn't put it past Papa," Crystal agreed.

Ellen was shocked all over again. "You know that's not true, Crystal."

269

"I didn't say he was meeting anyone. I said I wouldn't put it past him. Look what he did this afternoon."

"Let's not get started on that again," Medora said. "I'll tell you somebody else it's not, Press. It's not Asa Brice."

Press, at one end of the semicircle they sat in, moved like a flash to Medora, who was opposite her, grabbed her by the shoulders, and began to shake her. "You tell me," she cried, "tell me who it is and stop joking."

"Press, Press," Ellen screamed, but there was no need for alarm. Medora was laughing and flapping forward and backward like a rag doll as Press shook her. Press, defeated by this lack of resistance, dropped her hands and doubled over so that her head rested in her lap. "I'm sorry," she said, her voice muffled in her skirt.

Medora stopped her laughing. "It's not Chad. Now are you satisfied?" Then her voice hardened. "But you don't deserve that it's not. Not after the way you treat him."

"How do I treat him?" Press whispered.

"You know how. As if you despised him. Do you?"

"No. I love him," Press said, full and loud for all to hear.

There was a long silence after this word. It was one word none of them had yet spoken aloud about a boy. Everything changed with the saying of that word. They all moved on to someplace from which they could never turn back. They heard, in the quiet, that the wind had died down, and saw that the white sand had been turned rosy by the setting sun. They listened, as if for an echo of the word; then Medora repeated it, on purpose it seemed, so they'd understand the point to which they'd come. "If you love him, you oughtn't to treat him that way."

"What way?" Press asked.

"You know."

"I don't want my mother to think I don't love her."

"Why would she think that?" Medora asked.

Press lifted her head from her lap. For a minute, she looked as if she knew the answer to that question, as if it had just come to her and surprised her. It was in her eyes and almost to her lips. Then she lost it. They all saw that she had truly lost it, that she hunted for it and could not find it.

"I don't know," she said.

"You treat Chad like dirt. He'll find someone else."

270

"Oh, no."

"Yes, he will. You're beautiful, but if that's all he wants, he can look at a picture and not get slapped in the face every time he looks."

"I can't help it," Press said.

Medora accepted this. "It's your funeral," she said. She turned from Press to the other girls. "Julian is coming up here as soon as the initiation is over."

Ellen's first thought was about the cave. "How does he know where the cave is? The cave's my secret."

"You just thought it was your secret."

"Did you know where it was all the time?"

"No, but Julian did."

"Why does he want to meet you here?"

"He doesn't, very much. But I made him promise."

"You asked him to come?"

"Yes, Miss Character," Medora said, "I asked him to come and I begged him to come and finally he gave in, and he is coming."

Ellen and Press and Crystal looked at each other. They were united by shock. They did not know that this could be done, that you could beg a man to meet you, admit it, and still lift your head and look the world in the eye.

"I am going to marry him."

They relaxed a little. They supposed that once marriage intentions were declared, you could begin to treat the man like a husband, tell him when to come and where to go.

"When will the wedding be?" Crystal asked.

"The minute I get him to say yes."

They looked at Medora with still bigger eyes. She might have been a savage they had caught sight of through an opening in the forest.

"Hasn't he proposed?" Ellen asked finally.

"No," Medora said. "I don't suppose he ever will."

"How will you get married then?" Ellen asked.

"The usual way."

"Perhaps he'll say no," Crystal suggested.

Medora nodded. "He might," she said.

The other three thought in silence about the possibility of being turned down by a man. It was more difficult to speak about than death. Not only sad, but embarrassing.

"I'd be ashamed," Crystal said, "to ask somebody to marry me."

"What's there to be ashamed of?"

"Do you have to get married?" Crystal asked, ready to understand all, if this were true.

"Oh, shit," Medora said kindly.

The other three had been brought up not to use this word, even for what it meant, let alone in conversations having nothing to do with the privy. But they were becoming less and less sure that any of their rules applied to Medora.

"I don't have to get married, and I don't know if Julian will marry me. But I'm going to try to get him to. I'd never forgive myself if I didn't try. I love him. I love the way he looks and walks and talks. I even love the way he smells. What are you kids going to do? Sit around and wait until somebody you don't love proposes, and say yes for fear nobody else will? Not me. I love Julian and will try to get him and won't give up easy. I don't, you know," she said matter-of-factly.

Ellen didn't know about the others, but she thought Medora was a heroine, ready to flout all laws for love. She felt uplifted to be with her. She never doubted that this was one of the hours of her life she would never forget.

"Medora," Crystal half whispered, "do you think, if you love somebody, you should always tell him?"

Medora's tact was perfect. If she knew that Crystal was asking a question about herself, she didn't let on. "I don't know about other people. I had to tell Julian."

Crystal said, "I love Chad Lewis." Each word came out like a stone.

Ellen looked at Press, expecting more strangling and shaking. Instead, Press said, "Poor Crystal." This pity was humiliating to Crystal, after the way Press had taken on at the least suspicion of Medora's meeting Chad. But she didn't say a word.

"What are you going to do about it?" Medora asked Crystal.

"Nothing," Crystal said.

"Then you can't complain, can you?"

"I'm not complaining."

"Crystal," Press said, "I'll tell him for you."

"Press Cope," Medora said, "you're crazy as a bedbug. Who do you love, Chad or Crystal?"

"Chad."

"If any of you said you loved Julian, do you know what I'd do? I'd tell you if you ever breathed a word of it, you'd be sorry. The only

272

thing you want to do in this world, Press, is to make Chad miserable."

Ellen, to stop the quarreling, and to stop being Miss Character, said, "I love Tom Mount."

She stopped the quarreling and she stopped all talk. She waited for Medora's advice, for anybody's surprise or sympathy. "I've loved him since the first moment I saw him," she added.

Medora said, "Ellen, that's just wonderful."

Press said, "Does Chad know?"

Crystal said, "I think he probably looks a good deal older than he really is."

Not a one of them takes me seriously, Ellen thought; and she really didn't care. None of the others were happy, and she was. Her heart had been filled with a rich, sweet dreaminess simply by saying the name: Tom Mount.

"Let's start the initiation," she said finally.

They expected a good deal from the initiation. Crystal had planned it like a church service, she said, only more gruesome. Ellen had seriously believed she might lose consciousness. There was the page of the Bible, Psalms 25, to be torn in four pieces, each girl to have a piece and always to keep it with her as a reminder that, separated one from the other, they were incomplete. There was the fire to kindle, and onto which they would squeeze blood from their wounded hands, and the flames carrying the scent and smoke of this sacrifice upward toward the stars would register it in heaven.

That was the way it had been planned, and they did everything just as planned. Inside the cave, the smoke of their ritual fire did not have a chance to rise very high; otherwise, the Psalm was torn, the blood was mingled, and the sacrifice burned according to schedule. But the initiation was an anticlimax. Nothing they could do, after the word "love" had been said, seemed very impressive. That was their initiation; the rest was just duty and stubbornness and a thrifty use of gathered materials.

When they left the cave, the stars were out, brilliant and wind-burnished. The valley below held the dust like a river; but up above, the November stars moved in their clear solemn paths. Medora stood at the mouth of the cave, eager to have them on their way. It seemed lonesome to leave her there, as if she were their sacrifice, left to propitiate some god. There was enough starlight to see how wind-tossed she was, there at the door of the cave where the full blast struck her.

"What if he doesn't come?" Ellen called back.

"That's my funeral," Medora said, laughing—but meaning it.

When they parted, the awesomeness they had not been able to find in the initiation came to them. They went down the hill silently, buffeted by the wind, weaving their way between the cactus clumps, their hearts tender for their blood sister left behind at the cave.

11 THE DAY of visiting and celebrating was finished, but no one had brought the news to Base Cudlip.

Zoomy was sound asleep on the floor, bent around a corner in a sharper angle than seemed possible to a boy of his shape. Ordinarily, Shel would have sent him scooting up to bed, but he let him sleep where he was as a sign to Base that day was done. It was not late by clock time, but it was two or three years since morning, considering what they'd all been through. Joicey kept rocking to prove that she was wide awake. It was not ladylike, to her mind, for the hostess to fall asleep in the presence of a guest; but Shel could see that she was relying on the dim light where she sat, away from the lamp, to hide the fact that half the time her eyes were closed.

Only Chad was as wide awake as Base Cudlip—and for the same reason. He, too, was waiting to take a girl home. He stood in the doorway between sitting room and dining room, arms raised resting on the lintel over the door. He was a kind of weather vane, standing there. When the wind shook the house, Chad trembled, too.

Base sat by the west windows, where he could keep a lookout for the girls—though what he would be able to see in the pitch blackness, no one knew. What had already gone wrong during the day appeared to have whetted his appetite for further disasters. He's going to be disappointed, Shel thought, if that girl of his hasn't been raped or bit by a rattlesnake.

Shel had been keeping quiet, hoping Base would take the hint and start homeward. Chad would take Base's daughter home when he took Press Cope and the Raunce girl, so there was no excuse for Base's lingering. Still he lingered. The man was a puzzle to Shel, and he occupied his time, while he tried to sit him out, in attempting to unravel the puzzle. Shel had enough bullheadedness of his own to understand Base's wanting his own way. That far he could go with the man. But Base not only wanted his own way; he wanted those who differed from him punished. And since Base was convinced, in his own mind, that a man like Raunce was rotten to the core, he wanted Raunce to prove it to others, by one more rotten act. He wanted to be able to say, I told you so. Poor old Ralph did not have to *do* anything to prove himself wrong. He had got himself in a hundred-percent wrong from the beginning by getting himself born with a brown skin.

Shel thought, The one thing I ought to be able to understand about Base is the way he feels about color. I was born where he was. But I was left standing behind the door when the color craze was handed out. Color, as far as I can figure out, is nothing but looks. And looks, unless you're judging a beauty contest, is nothing to go by. With a man it's acts, not looks, that count. If I can like a man with my eyes closed, I'm not going to stop if I open them and find he's a Mexican. Shel shut his sleepy eyes, pretending this was an experiment he was making. The minute he did so, Base spoke up.

"Shel," he said, "you went out of your way today to make me lose face."

Shel opened his eyes. "I sure didn't mean to, if I did, Base."

"What else did you have in mind? I been sitting here asking myself that question over and over. And that's the only answer I can come up with. If you got a better, I'm more than willing to listen."

"I don't know what you're talking about, Base."

Base snorted. "Don't beat the devil 'round the bush. I march Ralph up to you to teach that greaser to keep his hands off a white boy. I'm fighting your battles for you. What thanks do I get? You light into the boy yourself."

"He had it coming to him."

"That's neither here nor there. Can't you see the kind of figure I cut with Ralph the minute you do that? I march Ralph up to you for daring to lay hands on your boy. What thanks do I get?"

"I wasn't standing up for either one of you. I was standing up for my boy."

"You got a funny way of doing it."

"Don't you spank your kids, Base?"

"Not before greasers, I don't."

"I spank mine when they need it."

The wind swept down about the house with a boom that made Shel hold his breath and hope he'd put his nails in where they'd do the most good.

"Good thing I'm standing here holding things together," Chad said.

Base did not turn away from the window. "What're those girls doing out in weather like this, anyway?"

"It don't hit a person with near the force it hits a two-story house set on top of a rise," Shel said. "The girls more'n likely don't even know it's blowing."

"What's taking their minds off it? That's what I'd like to know."

Shel and Chad exchanged glances. They had girls out there in the wind, too.

"In Kentucky, a girl don't go roaming around in the dark. Except for one reason."

"This ain't Kentucky, Base. Things are different here."

"Girls ain't different."

Shel watched Chad take his hands down from over the door, open and close them, to start up the circulation, he hoped.

"I reckon you know your own daughter, Mr. Cudlip," Chad said.

"What do you mean by that?" Base asked.

Shel saw where Chad was headed, but he let him alone. If it came to a fist fight, he'd be on Chad's side, of course. But he wasn't going to use his sore tongue to help him out.

"I mean what I said," Chad answered. "I reckon you know Medora. But I know my own sister. And I know Press Cope."

"So you've got to know Press Cope well enough to say what she'll do or won't do out at night?"

"I know her well enough not to let you class her with those other girls you mentioned."

Chad had stopped opening and shutting his hands, and Joicey did not have to rock any more to show she was awake.

"What other girls?" Base asked.

"Those others, back in Kentucky, you were speaking of."

Shel waited. Base Cudlip waited, also. And in the silence they all heard the approach of someone whistling.

"That's Ellen," Shel said.

The girls came in, dusty, red-eyed, straggle-haired. It was impossible even for Base to suspect them of having had a rendezvous with boys. No boy in his right mind would look at a one of them. But there were only three of them.

276

As Base took this in, he got to his feet. "Where's Medora?" he demanded.

He looks triumphant, Shel thought. Now if Ralph will knife somebody before morning and Raunce be caught out with a choir singer, Base won't have had such a bad day, after all.

"Where's Medora?" he asked again.

Shel somehow expected Crystal Raunce to have the answer, but it was his own Ellen, out of her natural goodness and concern for a father's worry, who spoke up first.

"Medora went directly home. It was out of her way for her to come on here. Did she know you were going to wait for her?"

Base looked crestfallen. His daughter was safe—but he was wrong. "I'd took for granted she'd know it."

"I'm going to drive Press and Crystal home," Chad said. "Would you like to ride with us?"

Base was in no mood to accept favors from anyone. Especially Chad. "If it's all the same to you, I'll hoof it," he said.

"It's all the same to me," Chad told him without batting an eye.

The two girls knew how dramatic their situation was: both of them in love with the same boy, and both of them being taken home by that boy. They were capable of renunciations of love, declarations of love. Before their ride was finished, lives might be blasted, friendships hallowed, promises betrayed. There was no real silence: only words they did not speak; no real lack of movement: only caresses held back.

Chad knew nothing about this. His sole idea was to get rid of Crystal and be alone with Press.

Crystal sat in the center, between Chad and Press. Press had seen to that, out of irony, out of the shared blood of recent sisterhood, and, most of all, out of an instinct for difficulties. Crystal knew why she was next to Chad. She was there as a gift from Press, not by choice of Chad. Time was passing. She would soon be home and the miraculous chance of riding next to Chad would then be finished. She wanted to be near him and, since Press had arranged it so she could, she did not draw away from him.

They were all three of them hungry for touch. They trembled at the touch of the wind or a wisp of hair. They were ready, by touch, to build up kingdoms and live in them. They were at the age when

277

they possessed a magic which permitted them to use the most fragmentary and fleeting materials for this purpose. The only trouble was, it took a wrong touch to learn a right one, and the magic they possessed could build a prison as easily as a paradise.

Chad knew why Crystal was where she was. Press was running away by putting Crystal there, and he was supposed to run after her. But to pursue Press meant to hurt the human territory that separated them. If he wanted to punish Press, all he had to do was to pretend an interest in Crystal he didn't have. Press deserved punishment, but Crystal didn't. She deserved the truth.

He pulled Chinopsee to a standstill. "You girls get out," he said.

"Is something wrong?" Press asked.

"Yes, there is."

The girls climbed slowly down. They were about a mile from the townsite, on level ground, where the wind had nothing to slow it down but the buggy and themselves.

"What's he going to do?" Crystal asked Press, courteously assuming that Press, as Chad's girl, was the one who would know.

"Make us walk, I guess."

"Now, Press," Chad said, "you climb back in."

Press climbed.

"You're next, Crystal."

When the girls were in, Chad said, "Crystal, I'd be glad to take you out riding sometime, if you'd go. But Press is my girl, and it don't make any sense, us riding around together the way we were."

It didn't, and Crystal knew it. But neither she nor Press could find a word to say.

After Chad let Crystal out at her home, he and Press continued in silence until they reached the Cope place. There Press said, "You shamed Crystal."

"I did not. I shamed you, if you have enough sense to recognize it. But I treated Crystal like a human being. You're the one shamed her."

"How did I? I put her next to you. That's where she wanted to be."

"That's not why you put her there, though. She was just something to separate us. For all you cared, she could've been a sack of barley."

"You made her think you didn't want her next to you."

"I didn't."

"She loves you."

278

"Shut up," said Chad, "and don't you ever say that again, and I didn't hear you this time. That's for her to say."

"Do you want to hear her say it?"

"That's none of your business. I don't want to hear you say it, that's all."

They sat at opposite corners of the buggy trying to see each other's faces. They were experimenting with their power to hurt each other. The extent of that power was a proof of their resources. They didn't care about the wind or the stars. They might have been in hell. In a lull in the wind, they heard Indy Cope's voice.

"I must go in," Press said.

When Press said that, Chad picked up the reins, put one arm around Press, and drove Chinopsee at a lope back toward the townsite. After a quarter-mile, he drove off the road, where they were sheltered from the wind in the lee of a little rise. He did not pretend that he had driven there for that purpose. He wound the reins around the whip, and turned to Press. She moved instantly to him. Both were trembling. Chad had a body that trembled and a mind that was very clear and tender, and the two, the trembling body and the clear mind, did not get in each other's way. In his mind, he was as tender toward Press as a husband or a father. He believed her to be better than anyone else because she was Press. His body trembled, and he let it; in the midst of trembling he was serene. Neither had ever kissed before without separating the mouth from the body in order to accomplish a family politeness. They held back a little, frightened by the risk, and not wishing to squander their riches; but they were not hoarders, either, and they had riches to spare. It was a great wonder to both that what was so natural had been so long postponed. They were both evidently born kissers; they experienced none of the heralded difficulties with arms, noses, hair, tongues. Their kisses had a sweet sound. Kissing was too new for them not to be aware of how they did it. They saw almost at once that love-making was a language. Without words, lips could speak.

The stars they could not name had moved above them. Chad said, "It's time for you to go home now, Press."

Press leaned against him. "Take care of me, Chad."

"I will," Chad said. "That's what I want to do."

"I don't mean support me."

"I know you don't."

279

"Sometimes I do the opposite of what I want to do."

"I know."

"Help me, please help me, Chad. I love you so much."

He held her close to him. Then he headed Chinopsee back into the wind, toward the Cope house.

After everyone had cleared out and Zoomy had been trotted upstairs to bed, Shel came back down to talk to Joicey and Ellen. Joicey was still in her rocking chair; Ellen sat where Base had been sitting, by the window, looking out into the windy darkness.

"You gave Base a big disappointment tonight," he told Ellen.

"How did I?" Ellen asked.

"Telling him Medora had gone home. He had his mind set on the lot of you being up to no good. And here you all turn up, not a bit the worse for wear."

When Ellen did not answer, Shel, in high spirits, said, "Well, you ain't, are you?"

"I don't know, Papa. I'm tired. I'm going to bed."

After she left the room, Shel said to Joicey, "As long as a girl don't know whether or not she's the worse for wear—she ain't."

"There's more than one kind of wear," Joicey said. "Though to hear you men talk, no one would ever know it."

Shel went over to Joicey and gave her his hand. "You've had a hard day, honey. You get on to bed."

"Aren't you coming?"

"I'm going to see how my trees are weathering this wind first."

"Looking at them every minute! You're like a woman with her first baby."

But she got up and took the little night lamp from the side table. "I've got something to show you first, Shel."

She led him to the spare room, for her usual nightcap of prettiness, Shel thought. When he saw that wreath of flowers on the pillow, his heart turned over. The last time he had seen anything like that was back in Kentucky when his mother had been laid out. His eyes ran down the coverlet hunting for the shape of a body beneath the covers.

"My God, Joicey, what's happened?"

"Rosa's expecting a baby."

He didn't get the connection. "But the flowers," he said. "What're they doing here?"

"Rosa," Joicey said. "Rosa put them there."

He still didn't get it. "What for?"

"It was this bed," Joicey reminded him.

Shel whistled. "I'll be damned."

"Don't swear so much," Joicey told him.

"It's a pretty good bed, looks like."

"That's why Rosa put the flowers here."

"A funeral was all that came to my mind. That's the way the bed was fixed when Ma died. Feel me. I'm still sweating."

"Don't talk funerals and births in one breath," Joicey said. "Don't forget we got something out of the bed, too."

"I ain't forgetting it for an instant."

Joicey shut the door on the flowers, and Shel took the lamp out of her hand. "I'll carry this up for you."

"No use you making a trip upstairs for nothing. You've had a long day, too."

"I ain't in a family way."

"You are, too. You're in a family way for five of us now. I'm carrying just the one. You've got the lot of us."

"Don't make me the least queasy," Shel said.

"You go on," Joicey told him. "Those squirrels were terrible, weren't they?"

"They were hot and they weren't tender as pie dough, but they sure stick to the ribs. My stomach's still grinding on them."

Joicey pushed him away and closed the stairway door firmly behind her.

Outside, Shel picked up his hoe on the chance that a basin had sprung a leak, and went down the slope toward his trees. The wind, coming at him from behind, sent him dancing tiptoe down the incline. The air had cooled. The wind was still a desert wind, dry and warm, but there were seeds of coolness in it. It was a sweet sign to him. He was not licked yet. Above the ruckus of the November wind, the stars were blazing like lighthouses above waves. Except for the Big Dipper and the Pole Star, he did not know their names, and was sorry for it. They glittered above him, and he felt like a stranger at a party.

Before he got to the trees, he saw the lights of a car, coming up the road from the south, beaming smokily through the dust. He stopped to watch them. Night travel on the Tract was unusual. When the lights turned in the driveway, he recognized the wheeze of Ben

Jessup's Maxwell. Ben worked down at the pumping plant—though there was no pumping going on there yet—and sometimes Shel thought that Ben was unlucky enough with machinery to account, singlehanded, for all of Sylvester Perkins's setbacks in delivering water.

He walked down the road to meet Ben, holding his hoe horizontally in front of him. Ben chugged on until his headlights touched the hoe handle. Then he got out, turned off his hissing acetylene lights, and joined Shel.

"This is some blow we're having," Ben said. " 'Ideal climate for citrus fruits' . . . We won't have to ship, if we ever get a crop. If these winds come along at the right time, they'll blow the fruit right into Los Angeles."

"Blow like this," Shel said, "and they'll overshoot L.A. and head straight for China. We missed you for supper."

"Had a little car trouble," Ben said. "How'd it go?"

"Can't say that socially it was a hundred-per-cent success. Base Cudlip was on a rampage. First, he'd had a run-in with Raunce's cow. He started over here to get up a lynching party for Raunce and run into Ralph giving Zoomy a tanning for swimming in the ditch. So he brought Ralph along at the end of a buggy whip. Then he got it in his head the girls were all going to get knocked up out in the hills. That car of yours, Ben, makes you miss a lot of fireworks here on the Tract."

Ben laughed. "Ralph's a Mexican. But what's Base got against cows?"

"Having calves. He don't think it looks pretty."

"Did LeRoy leave her out in the back yard?"

"Yep. And Base's wife saw her. He don't want his wife getting any ideas childbearing ain't fun."

"She ought to have the facts firsthand by now. How many Cudlip kids are there?"

"Five or six. Anyway, Base wanted to protect his wife. So he tried to put a tent over her."

"His wife?"

"No, the cow."

"Well, that was standard procedure back in Emporia."

"Kentucky, too. *Not* in a high wind, though."

"Don't sound like you had much time for planting."

282

"You come on down and see for yourself. It's cooled off, don't you think?" Shel asked.

"I don't feel the need of any coat yet."

"You can feel a change, though, can't you?" Shel asked anxiously.

"There's a little freshness somewhere," Ben admitted.

They walked down the slope toward what Shel already thought of as "his grove." The trees were Valencias, but they had a lemony scent that put Shel in mind of the smell of lemonade stands cutting through the muggy heat of a county fair, back home.

"Catch that citrus smell?" Shel, breathing deep, asked Ben.

"Be a wonder if we couldn't, with the trees whipped around the way they are."

Shel preferred not to think of that. "Never knew water could smell so sweet."

"It's the wet ground you're smelling, not the water. Wait till the morning after the first rain."

"I'm waiting," Shel said.

"Well, Shel," Ben said, "you're a lucky man. That's one of the reasons I stopped by."

Shel had an idea what was coming, but he wanted it handed to him a pure gift without any questions on his part. He pinched a single leaf from the tree by which he was standing, and rolled it in his fingers. It broke, crisp and juicy, fully alive and growing.

"You bet on a long shot and won. We reached water today. We've stopped drilling and started casing-in. Syl's going to have water in the pipes when he said he would."

"He's yelled water so often it's hard to believe."

"He's not yelling this. I am."

There was enough starlight to put a shine on the film of water in the tree basin at their feet. Shel squatted down and touched his fingers to it like a man touching wood. He had had so much good luck he was scared. He was about due for a change.

"There ought to be water in your weir box in a couple of weeks. With these trees in the ground, you're really lucky."

Shel knew it. But hearing the word "luck" again made him nervous. He didn't want his luck to get to feeling self-conscious. Or overworked. He changed the subject.

"You had any supper yet?"

"Not yet."

"Better come up to the house. There's a gallon or two of stewed squirrel up there."

"I don't know I'm that hungry."

"Well, I'll get on up to the house, then. Thanks for stopping to tell me about the water. I don't want to say much about it. But if this wind lets up a little—I ought to be able to sleep good tonight."

He took a step up the hill, and Ben said, "Got a minute or two more, Shel?"

"Got the whole night," Shel said, which was half the truth. The other half was that he wanted to spend it in bed.

Ben stood there, his features invisible, without saying any more. "What's on your mind, Ben?"

"Perkins is talking about water assessments again."

"I don't think we need to bank too much on what Perkins says or don't say."

Shel leaned on his hoe handle, closed his eyes, and thought of a song his mother used to sing.

> Only another night to travel,
> Only another night to roam:
> Then home at last, the harbor passed,
> Safe in my Father's home.

The joke on the poor sailor who sang that song was that, though he did not know it, the home he was headed for was heavenly and his father's name was spelled with a capital F. That song used to scare the hell out of me, Shel thought. God playing jokes like that on poor sailors who thought the worst was over. He was more than half asleep and wholly in the past when Ben spoke next.

"I've been intending to speak to you about Ellen."

Shel blinked himself awake in no time. "Speak to me?"

"I want to marry her."

"Marry Ellen?" Shel asked. "Ellen?" he repeated, as if he had half a dozen daughters and wanted to make sure they were talking about the same one.

"Ellen," Ben said solemnly.

Shel's first thought was that Ben was too old, a man his own age. "How old are you, Ben?"

"Twenty-five," Ben said. "I'm plenty old enough to be getting married."

Shel couldn't help grinning, in the dark, where it didn't show. God

284

Almighty, he thought, while I've been thinking of me and Ben as young fellows together, he's been thinking of me as his father-in-law.

"I didn't want to be making plans without first speaking to you."

"What's Ellen think about it?"

"I haven't spoken to Ellen."

Shel was shocked. "What's the use speaking to me if you haven't talked to her? You got any reason for thinking you won't make a good husband?"

"No, sir. Except I want to be a preacher."

"For God's sake, Ben, you don't need to apologize for that. There's good men been preachers."

"Their wives don't have any easy time."

"Oh, Ellen's a born preacher's wife, if it comes to that," Shel said, and tried to rouse himself up to meet the occasion. Love's the subject here, he told himself. But that was the very reason he rebelled. Ben's thoughtfulness went against the grain. It wasn't the nature of love to be thoughtful. Wasn't the nature of mine, anyway, but I can't say I want any of that for Ellen. Ben's doing an honorable thing, speaking to me first. Can't you get cured of your backwoods ways? he asked himself. You still got a hankering for shotguns?

Ben seemed to have got an inkling of what he was feeling. "You don't need to think that a yes or no, either one, from you means I'm going to Ellen and say, 'Your father said I could marry you.' Or, 'Your father said I couldn't marry you.' No matter what you say, I'm going to try to get her to marry me. The minute I saw her come running up ready to claw my eyes out if I picked on Zoomy, I knew I wanted to. Everything I've seen about her since then has made me love her more. I know it's not my place to say this to her own father, but I don't think you folks appreciate her. You're used to her. You don't see her soul. She's all sweetness and goodness, but she's just somebody to help around the house to you. Well, I'm glad it's dark. I can't talk about her without crying. And I warn you, Shel, I'm going to marry her. I hope you like the idea, but if you don't, it's not going to cut any ice with me if Ellen'll say yes. I hope we've got that straight."

Shel said, "You had me worried for a minute there, Ben. I thought you were going to put a ring on me."

"Maybe I should've let Ellen do the speaking to you. Since I don't intend to let anything you say stop me, I don't know what good I've done."

"You got to talk about her. And as I remember my own courting days, that was always a pleasure. So if you ain't done yourself no good, you ain't harmed yourself either. It's up to Ellen."

Ben would have talked all night. Ellen, the wind, striking water, seemed to have gone to his head. Shel got rid of him finally, by saying outright, "Ben, I'm going to bed."

He walked up to the house, sleepy drunk, the wind in his face so strong it was hard to breathe it in. His mind jumped from one thing to another, any one of them on a less crowded day enough to keep him thinking. The new baby, Zoomy, Cudlip, the planting, the wind, the water, the assessments, Ben and Ellen. He felt like it was his duty to think of Ben and Ellen; and, duty aside, his mind circled around the idea of Ellen married, Ellen grown-up, Ellen a wife and mother. No longer his little girl. Wonder what Ben would think if he knew he had an unborn brother-in-law?

Ellen was up when he came back to the house. She had come downstairs in her nightgown and was in the sitting room, seated beside the center table. A young woman whose hand has been asked in marriage, Shel told himself.

"Papa," Ellen said, "I lied to Mr. Cudlip."

Shel, living in the future, tried to take this in. This is the soul of goodness Ben was telling me about, he thought, the tender conscience we don't appreciate.

"Well, don't worry about it," he said. "Not many of us get through a day without a little fibbing."

Ellen gave him a look that reminded him that she was Chad's sister. "Medora didn't go home," she said.

"That's a fair-sized fib," Shel agreed. "Why didn't you tell Base? This is pretty serious."

"We took a vow at the cave that whatever we heard there would be secret."

"You just leave the cave and vows out of this and tell me where Medora is."

"We took a blood vow in the cave to protect each other." Ellen put her head down on the table.

Shel started toward the stairs. "In that case, I better get to bed."

Ellen came running after him and grabbed his arm. "Please, Papa."

"Where is Medora?"

"At the cave."

"Where is the cave?"

286

"It's a secret."

"I'm too tired for this kind of nonsense," Shel said. "If you find you've got something that ain't secret, you can come upstairs and wake me."

He started again toward the stairs, and Ellen continued to cling to his arm. Shel wished Ben had this pure soul married and mopping the linoleum in some parsonage.

"It's up in the hills," Ellen said.

"That's not much help."

"She's meeting Julian Ortiz there."

Then Shel turned without a word, went back to the chair Ellen had vacated, and sat down heavily.

"Why didn't you tell Base Cudlip this, instead of me?"

"Because of the vow we all took. I told you."

"Who's all?"

"Medora, Press, Crystal, and me."

"So you all swore to protect Medora?"

"We all swore to protect each other."

"What have the rest of you got to be protected about? Are you in love with Pete?"

"No," Ellen said, "Tom Mount."

"My God," Shel said wearily. "Have you been meeting him at the cave, too?"

"Of course not. I've never said a word to him in my life since the first day we came to the Tract. It would spoil everything to speak to him."

Shel didn't know what "everything" was, and decided Ellen didn't either. His chief wish was that Ben could be present. After Ben's declaration, he felt Ben ought to be taking some of the responsibility for this and not leaving all the problems to his father-in-law.

"What're you going to do?" Ellen asked.

"Go see Base Cudlip, I reckon. I don't know what else. If Julian had to meet the Cudlip girl, why couldn't he of picked—" Shel started to say, "some decent place," and changed it to, "some less out-of-the-way place?"

"He didn't pick it. Medora did. She don't even know he's coming, for sure."

"You mean she asked him?"

"Yes."

"Don't you girls know you can't go with a Mexican?"

"I don't want to."

"Medora! Medora!" Shel yelled. "Don't *she* know it?"

"No."

"You saw what Base did to Ralph for spanking Zoomy. What do you think he'll do to Julian for making love to Medora?"

"Medora's the one going to make love. She said so."

"I doubt Base'll see much difference."

"How will he know, if you don't tell him?"

"There's two other girls know about this? That right?"

"Yes."

"Well, if they're no better vow-keepers than you are, the news is liable to leak out."

Ellen began to cry, and Shel let her. Silly as a five-year-old. He didn't know what to do. What he needed to do was get some sleep. If he went to Base, Base would, sure as shooting, head for Julian with a shotgun. If he didn't go see Base, Medora was liable to get knocked up. This wasn't the worst thing that could happen to a woman. But if it happened to Medora, and Julian was responsible, Julian would get his neck stretched by Base. Which was one of the worst things that could happen to a man.

"Get dressed, Ellen," he said. "You're going to take me up to that cave."

"Papa, we promised."

"Ellen, if I hear that word out of you once more tonight, I'll switch you and switch you hard. You already broke your promise, and I didn't make any. Don't think I want to take this tramp, but you put your clothes on and show me where that cave is."

Shel still had his broken orange leaf in his hand. He held it to his nose, but it had lost its flavor.


12   OUTSIDE the thick adobe walls, the wind was still blowing. Rosa watched the lacy shadows of the pepper tree move across the wall; but she could not hear the wind that moved the fronds. Pete was already asleep. She could tell by his breathing. And her own eyes were closing.

This was the moment she had been waiting for since they were married, the moment when she could say to Pete, "Pete, we are going to have a baby." She had waited all day; first, until they were home from the Lewises'; then, until they were cleaned up; and now, Pete would have to be waked up and she herself had better get the news out or she'd be asleep, too.

Before she had started a baby, she had imagined that the moment of telling would be quite different. She might faint; Pete might burst into tears. They might hear heavenly voices or have doves light on them. She wouldn't have been surprised at any wonder. Now she was going to have a hard time staying awake. Starting a baby when you didn't have one had seemed a miracle. Once it was started, it seemed as natural to have a baby inside you as a liver.

Pete was, of course, surprised. But he wasn't any more able than she to live up to her dreams about this moment. She might have been announcing babies to him regularly every year since they were married. They lay hand in hand like experienced parents.

After a little while, Rosa said drowsily, "I thanked the bed today."

"You did what?" Pete asked, waking up some.

"Thanked the bed. I put a wreath of flowers on it."

"My God," Pete said. "The Lewis bed?"

"Yes. That's why I went."

"What did Mrs. Lewis think about that?"

"She thought it was sweet. The same day, the same place, she got a baby."

"My God," Pete said again.

"Don't swear so much, Pete. You will mark the baby."

"That is a God-damned remarkable bed."

"Yes," said Rosa. "Stop swearing. I told you it would be so."

"Perhaps it was the weather that day? Perhaps it was good weather for babies?"

"The weather had nothing to do with it."

"Just the bed?"

"Yes."

"Not the husbands?"

"You had to be there, of course."

"Maybe not. Maybe the bed could do it alone."

"Don't be silly. It takes a man."

"I'm glad to hear you still think so."

"I am going to call the baby Peter for you. Do you like that?"

"Yes, I do. I thought maybe you would call it Bed, for the bed. Little Bed Ramos."

Rosa laughed and moved closer to Pete. "The first baby is always named for the father. You know that."

"The second must be Bed, then. The second will be a girl, and it don't matter what you call girls, just so you kiss them."

Pete kissed her, and Rosa could feel that it was already a changed kiss, the kiss of the father for the mother of his children, a kiss full of tender respect and devotion. She had returned it, and Pete was no more a father than he had ever been.

# BOOK III

I    As soon as Sylvester Perkins had water in the pipes, as soon as the sound of water could be heard spilling over the lips of weir boxes and bubbling up in standpipes and trilling along the loamy furrows, then of course the rains began.

"To him that hath," LeRoy said, delighting in Biblical truth even more than in the rain, "shall be given."

There had been a spattering of rain in October, no more than enough to pockmark the dust. At the end of November, there was a shower of heavy drops scarcely marked by anyone except Asa and Ellen. Asa had been lying face down at the bottom of his arroyo watching ants when the shower started, and he noted the million tiny explosions as summer's refuse of shattered leaves and empty seed husks bounced upward when struck by the minute rain hammers. Ellen, walking in the hills, had scarcely noticed the shower, but the scents those sparse drops released were so strong and sweet, she made herself lightheaded trying to breathe them all in.

But it was not until the end of the first week in January that the settlers were awakened in the night by the steady drum of rain on the roof.

At first, they listened skeptically. Then, as it kept up, they began to hope. And finally, as it settled down without a letup, to rejoice. This was it, the rainy season they had been waiting for! They slept and wakened. The very cadence that made them want to stay awake also made them drowsy.

That heavy watery sound on their roofs, the continuous lighter sound of the runoff from their eaves, convinced them that they were over the hump. They had toughed it through the dry spell; they had weathered the big wind; they had managed to pay their unexpected water assessment; they had hung onto their wives through the water-hauling days. The worst was surely past. The year 1917 would be different. Shel Lewis's trees had not only weathered wind and drought, he had a Valencia tree in bloom. Nothing would come of it; there were too many blooms, probably a sign that that particular tree was diseased. To Shel it was a sight to see—and smell—and people drove over to the Lewises' just to sniff the sweetness and to exclaim. It was the beginning of the valley's bloom, which Sylvester Perkins had advertised so prematurely.

Though the settlers had longed for rain, prayed for rain, despaired of rain, though they had scanned skies, tested the wind with wet fingers, and sniffed the air for dampness, they had not, meantime, stopped working. Shel had finished planting his lemons. Milo Tarley and Sid Pridham, ranchers over at the west end of the Tract, had planted five and ten acres, respectively, of Valencias. Others, ready to plant, were holding off until after January, when the threat of frost would be over.

Houses were springing up like toadstools. Tom Mount had all the work he could handle. Asa Brice appeared to be the only resident determined to live and die under canvas. The church was finished and dedication day set. Raunce was getting up even earlier than usual, working on a dedication sermon. Eunice Fry's school had twenty-three pupils enrolled. Automobiles were supplanting horses on the roads. Wendlin Jessup had a new Ford. He said he had been forced to buy one in self-protection. He was losing his rest and wearing out his horses hauling in Ben from his breakdowns. Fight fire with fire, he had decided. Use the Ford to jerk the Maxwell out of the mud. Wendlin either had a better car or was a better mechanic than his son. Or maybe both. Anyway, when he started out anyplace, he arrived.

The war was coming closer. A man had been on the Tract collecting money for Belgian war orphans. Teddy Roosevelt continued to preach intervention. Even Wilson began to speak of preparedness. One of the Pridham boys enlisted in the Canadian army. This made two Tract boys, if you could call young Perkins that, fighting. The Pridhams, as if to balance things, had the second baby born on the Tract, too. They called him Perkins, and Syl gave him a silver mug with just the one word "Perkins" engraved on it.

292

No one had yet died on the Tract, though Mary Jessup was visibly failing.

A truck from an Olinda store started making twice-weekly trips to the Tract, picking up orders and delivering. A chamber of commerce was being talked by forward-looking citizens. The resident Odd Fellows were recruiting members for a local lodge.

Some of this news was in the air. A lot of it came by way of Lute's *Reporter*. The settlers scanned it each week to find out what they had been up to. It was there they read that Ben Jessup had finished his studies, and that as soon as the Elders over at the Rose Park Training School had put their stamp of approval on him, the Society of Friends would record him as a minister. No one doubted he would make the grade. If the Quakers had recorded a fellow like Raunce, sincere Christian that he was, in spite of his crude ideas about cows, Ben could not miss. He was a scholar and a gentleman beside LeRoy.

The Pacific Electric Railway, according to the paper, was going to run a line from Los Angeles to the southeastern boundary of the Tract. Los Angeles would then be only an hour and one dollar and fifteen cents away.

The good old days were passing. The six-months pioneers, the veterans of water-hauling and homemade bread and the first big blow, talked to the newcomers of the golden era they had missed. They talked like sodbusters and Indian fighters, men who had broken the plains and tamed the prairies, not suburban orange growers who could travel to L.A. by electric train in sixty minutes.

The rain put the seal on the change. For a while, with no rain, it had looked as if Perkins had hoodwinked them into settling on a desert. But the rain that had not known how to start did not know how to stop either. It was satisfying in the same way money in the bank is satisfying, but it was not, after a week, very exciting. There was no lightning, no claps of thunder, no cloudbursts; just a steady downpour out of a gray sky that hung about the length of a hoe handle above their heads. A cold, raw wind, right off those snow-crowned golden Sierras, it felt like, blew the rain in their faces when they stepped outside, and people who, up to January, had been complaining about a desert now began to complain about the cold. "It never was this cold back East," they told each other. "Ioway was never like this." "Never felt the cold this way in Ohio." "Sunny Southern California!" "May be southern, but it sure as hell ain't sunny!"

Winter underwear, discarded, it was believed, forever, but fortunately not destroyed, was hauled forth and appreciatively donned. Airtight heaters were kept roaring. Petroleum-soaked timber could be had free in the oil fields, and there was a smell of burning crude oil in the air all that January. The black smoke rose from the chimneys, hovered over the frame houses, and was held there, immovable, by the rain. Those who had been loudest to complain "When's it going to rain?" were the first to ask, "When's it going to let up?"

Ordinarily, in January, the Tract would have been a sea of rippling grasses, of blue stem and volunteer oats, of barley and mustard. But the drought had kept the earth brown, and the heavy rains had then blackened it. The settlers kicked their airtight heaters and looked out of their rain-washed windows onto the drab, sodden fields, and wondered when in hell the rain would let up and the sun shine again. What had Sylvester Perkins done? Sold them a quagmire?

Press and her mother watched Chad, his invitation turned down by Press, drive off through the rain.

"Why wouldn't you go with him?" Indy asked.

"I wanted to help you."

"Help me what?"

"To tell the truth, I didn't want to go riding around in the rain all day."

"All day? It's already afternoon."

"I didn't want to go."

"I should think you'd like to see a real town for a change."

"I'd rather help you, Mama."

Indy did not need help. She was burning with energy. She, who had so often been laid up with ailments, had lost every ache and pain. She, who needed an opponent worthy of her mettle, had only these willing daughters and this devoted husband. Not that she was worthy of their willingness and devotion. But she was worthy of something. Something they knew nothing about. She, either, for that matter. But she was searching.

She had been laying linoleum in the kitchen, a job that was beyond her. She had chosen it for that reason. Chad's arrival had broken the rhythm of the work, and she had no more heart for it. She went into her and Lute's bedroom and closed the door behind her.

The room was cold and damp. The only heat in the house came from the cookstove in the kitchen and the heater in the sitting room.

A bedroom, until the bed is made, she thought, has a sad disreputable look, a look quite different from that of an untidy kitchen or sitting room. This is the way a room looks when somebody has died in it. She took hold of the covers, thrown back to let the bed air, and a memory of twenty years ago stopped her. So that was what it had been!

She went to the rain-streaked window and saw, instead of the sodden earth, the Ohio she had so often watched from the windows of her father's and mother's bedroom in Madison. So that had been the smell! That strange, musky, toadstool smell of the bed which she had wondered about when, as a helpful girl of fifteen, she had put her father's and mother's room to rights. Wondered about, and all these years never recognized; believed it to be the smell of old folks, of falling hair and bad teeth and wrinkling flesh: her father and mother at that time being her and Lute's age now, exactly.

That this smell should take her back to her girlhood! If she had been asked what smells reminded her of her home, there by the heavy snake-round body of the muddy Ohio, she would have said honeysuckle; or the sweet wave of iciness that rose off a newly opened freezer of ice cream; or the scent, early on the morning of the Fourth, of burning punk; or the fruit-basket smell of the pink Sempre Jovenay her mother rubbed into her skin each night. But not this!

Such ignorance seemed a condemnation of her upbringing as a girl, of her experience as a wife, and especially of Lute: that only now should this scent of her father's and mother's bodies be recognized and named!

She lay down on the bed, wrapping the cold sheets of the rainy day about her. She heard Press come in, but she refused to look up. She was not proud of her treatment of Press, but she kept right on, pushing her wickedness up to the fine hairline of Press's ability to take it. When she reached that, she felt some release from her perversity.

"Mother, are you sick?"

"I'm not very well, Press. That's a fact." She took Press's warm hand between her two cold ones.

"You rest, Mother. I'll take care of everything. I knew I shouldn't go with Chad."

So she was left alone: Lute at the newspaper office, Hannah at school, Press in the kitchen. Alone in the prison of Indiana Rose.

At fifteen, she had already been waiting in that prison three years for the one who would free her. She couldn't call out to a passer-by.

It was forbidden. And even if it hadn't been forbidden, she did not know what words to use. How did a girl learn the language of men? She knew a man would free her. From what, to what? She didn't know that. She had signaled constantly. Every dress, gesture, smile was a signal made in self-conscious desperation. The slightest response was dwelt upon. Had he said "yes"? Or if it was "no," had he said it in a particular way? She had thought about such things night after night. Had she failed to recognize a signal, a sign, a beckon?

How could I know, Tom?

She quenched that cry, though in the past weeks it had come to her more and more often.

Lute was the first: the first to kiss me, to say he loved me, to ask me to marry him. I had all those dreams. I couldn't wait to begin to use them. Wait to see if there was a better or different one? Be that cautious? Could I? He was the image of what I'd been taught to expect. He said "love." So did I. How could I turn my back on that? He was the first. What is the power of the first? On a young girl, anyway? I loved being chosen. I didn't love the chooser. I loved being touched. I didn't love the toucher. I loved a man's looks. Lute was a man, but I didn't love Lute. How could I know this before? Or until?

That quick neat business, at least quick, that made us one flesh. I lived for quite a time on those words, "one flesh." I had a marriage in the mind. "Now we are one flesh, now we are one flesh." One day, my flesh, unbidden, spoke up and said, "No, we're not." That was final. So then I endured.

I didn't say a word. I couldn't. Who could hurt a man at so strange a time? I was used. I kept as quiet as a mother with a child. I don't know how long that lasted. Years, I expect. But you must feel. So I hated. Tears ran down my cheeks. I loathed. It was not noticed in the least.

Finally I left my body. What happened to it, after I left it, didn't matter one way or the other. I was a real quitter. This was worse than when I lived in my body and hated.

After I left my body, I marveled that a human being, so divided, could live, could act as one. And in respect of this one matter, I could not. The wound was too deep. Body and spirit took up their abodes in different lands. Or if it was the same land, a land of indifference so deep it was like death and what happened there was not known. Before I left my body, he had not noticed that he did not meet me, and my total absence was not noted either.

Once he said, "It would be better to go to a whore." I thought so myself. Though I doubt the experience would be much different; a difference in pay would be all; a body laid down with the same degree of practiced indifference and professional celerity.

Oh, the long warfare! I was as strong in endurance and stoicism as he in use and blindness. Perhaps, after war, love is too tame. But I have been faithful all my life to some vision of love, never letting what's happened to Lute and me tarnish it. The real love, before which nothing else will matter. Only reach *him,* then let the house fall down, the world molder, the people die.

She felt capable of that indifference and that devotion; her body carried about like a castle, like a palace wreathed and lighted, waiting a true dweller.

Wrapped in the musty sheets, in the cold room, a January rain falling, her daughter deprived of her love, she argued the case against herself and for Lute. What is it you want? she asked herself. Not love pats and romantic speeches and remembered anniversaries. Not feet cleaned before entering, and dirty socks put in the dirty-clothes basket. Not a decent, law-abiding, nondrinking, nongambling, good provider. That wasn't why she was lying here. She was lying here heartsick for something she had never had from Lute. She had never had from Lute the use of all her powers. Something had gone amiss, at least for her, when Lute made love to her; but it wasn't for any betterment here she was longing. I could live like your sister, Lute (though you wouldn't like that), if we could meet in some real way; if you wouldn't be so careful; if no words scared you; if you would talk to me, I could live any way you asked, Lute, if you would really meet me, a live, unsettled man.

She was still there when Lute came in at two o'clock.

"Press says you aren't feeling very well."

"You know Press," she said. "She'd like to make an invalid out of me and run the house herself."

"That don't sound very good, coming from a mother about her daughter."

"It was a joke."

"You're not sick, then?"

Indy got up and walked to the window. "Never felt better," she said. "Something just struck me as I was making the bed and I lay down to think about it. When I was a girl at home, I used to make the folks' bed and I always noticed a musty smell about the covers.

297

I noticed the same thing here this morning and, after all those years, it came to me what that smell was. It was the smell of Papa and . . ."

Lute interrupted her, as she knew he would. "I haven't got much time, Indy. I've asked two men out for supper and I thought I ought to come out and give you a little warning. They don't have to come if you don't feel like doing for them, though."

Indy turned her back to him for a minute. When she turned around, she said, "There's nothing wrong with me but laziness. No, that's not true. I'm not lazy. Oh, Lute. I'm lonesome."

"Lonesome?"

"Blue. I'm so blue, Lute."

Lute came to her and gave each breast a quick little upward bounce in the palm of his hand. "I know what's wrong with you," he said. "You come on back here." He nodded toward the bed. "I haven't got much time, but I've got what will cure your blues."

At those words, Indy felt a distance between her and Lute as impassable as ice fields and glaciers. He was touching her, his hands were on her shoulders, but she would have felt more at home with a rock that did not mistake itself. Cure, cure. But she could no more contradict him than she could go to some preacher who had, all of his life, felt that his sermons and prayers helped people, and say, "No one ever heard a word you said." If there had been one iota of doubt, of wonder, of anxiety, of concern. But this great false building of complacency, inside which he lived—if she broke that, might not exposure to the truth kill him? So she protected him, cried out for him to emerge from, and at the same time kept intact, the false walls behind which he lived.

She hid her face on his shoulder. She could not face him. "I would like to be a better woman, Lute."

"You're good enough for me, Indy."

"I'm not good enough for myself."

"You've got two daughters and a husband who don't want you changed."

"Press hates me."

"Come on," Lute said, "you need the cure."

"Talk to me, Lute. What're we doing here? Where are we heading? Our lives are running through our fingers. What've we got to show for it?"

"More than most. Two daughters. This house. A growing business."

She gave it up. "Who's coming to supper?"

298

"Sylvester Perkins and Tom Mount."

"Why them?"

"They were both down at the office this morning and I asked them."

"Don't ask Tom Mount."

"Why not? I like him. He's baching and I don't know anyone who would appreciate a little home cooking more. What've you got against him?"

"He thinks he's so handsome."

"You're against everybody today. I can tell both men not to come. But I can't very well let Syl come and tell Tom to stay away."

"Why can't you?"

"It wouldn't look right."

"Look right? Who cares about 'look right'?"

"I do."

He did. There had been a time up north, before they'd built, when she'd been at her father's and mother's. Lute was staying in a hotel, and she'd come out to be with him. She arrived at midnight after a sixteen-hour bus trip, sick with her monthlies. Lute had given her the welcome of a man who's been separated from his wife for a couple of weeks; not, under the circumstances, a welcome she wanted, but not one, either, that she objected to or didn't expect. What she had objected to was Lute's hauling her down to the hotel dining room at seven o'clock next morning. It wouldn't look right, he said, her not showing up at breakfast time; his fellow lodgers might get the idea that he'd given her a bad night.

It was mid-January then, too, and she had followed Lute down the stairs, bone-tired, shivering, and cramping. At the time, she hadn't thought much about it. That was the way Lute was. But the memory of that morning had stayed with her, and whenever she heard Lute say, "It wouldn't look right," the resentment not then expressed came again to the surface.

"I can call the whole thing off, if you're so dead set against Tom Mount."

It wouldn't do any good to say, "I'm falling in love with Tom Mount." Lute would laugh at her. He would give her the cure. Lute wouldn't have believed his eyes if he'd seen her in bed with another man. He'd have found an excuse to make it look right: both fainted at the same moment, he'd decide, or been pushed there by some jokester. But that she could have climbed in there of her own free will out of love or desire, Lute could never believe. Why? They were married.

Sometimes Lute was downcast about the two of them, but it never entered his head that either of them would look at anyone else.

She didn't know what that idea made of marriage; or made of them. Yes, she did. It made marriage some kind of a machine and her and Lute little cogs that that machine ran.

If she said to Lute now, "Save me from Tom Mount," he would think she was joking. She could save herself, of course. But she didn't want to be saved by any effort of hers. She wanted to be saved by Lute, which meant that Lute would have to be a different man. She kept asking him to be that different man, showing him what that different man would be. Or maybe not "different," only "real," the Lute beneath the surface of "looks right." It wasn't the "hard night" she had objected to—it hadn't existed—it was Lute's squeamishness at the idea that someone might think it had existed. It wasn't being accommodating now to Lute in the middle of a rainy afternoon; it was the knowledge that Lute, with Press in the house, would never have the nerve to lock the door and proceed with his plan. It wasn't that he didn't have any cure. It was the pretense everywhere. It was Lute's invitation, which he didn't mean; and her refusal, which she did mean, but to protect Lute, not herself.

She knew how to endure and fight. But to pretend! She thought she would rather kill a man and mean it than kiss a man and pretend. Oh, let us break through, Lute. Let's be real. Let's be finished with "looks right." Looks is one thing and right's another and we're mixed up about both. Let's accept our tragedies, if that's what we've got. Let's throw pots and pans at each other if that's what's left to us. But I'm going to have something real, even if it has to be hate.

"Tom Mount's too handsome," she said again. "I don't trust myself around him."

Lute laughed. "Why, Indy, you've never noticed a man's looks in your life."

With words like these, Lute confessed time and again that she was a stranger to him. What Lute met in his life were not real things, but ideas about them he'd picked up—where, she didn't know. At his mother's knee, most likely. And from these ideas he would not budge one dangerous exploratory step. So he lived inside one set of ideas called "husband"; and he put her inside another set called "wife"; and there they were, walled off from each other, guaranteed never to meet or touch, and dying of loneliness and unweddedness and unbliss.

Lute thought the matter of supper was settled. "We'll be here early,"

300

he said. "I don't want to keep Hannah setting around at the office all afternoon after being in school all day. Wear your red dress," he said. "I'd like Syl Perkins to see we're not the peasants he sometimes thinks we are."

Chad was surprised to find himself stopping at the *Reporter* office. When Press had said "I have to help Mother," he had expected to go on home. Then, when he saw Crystal alone behind the rain-blurred windows, he stopped. Why? Vanity? Prove that somebody would have him? Lonesomeness? Kindheartedness? Whatever the reason, he stopped and asked her to go for a ride.

He saw her try to hide her gladness. She answered as if she'd have to give it thought before deciding. "Where are you going?" she asked.

"Anaheim." Switching girls, he switched towns. He had planned to go to Fullerton, but he wouldn't take Crystal to the town he had had in mind for Press.

"Why?"

"It's too wet to work. Why not?"

"Why isn't Press going? Didn't you ask her?"

"I asked her."

"I'm supposed to be working here, not going for rides."

"You don't look very busy."

"I'm not. There's nothing to do."

"You might get some news for the paper in Anaheim."

"We're just interested in local news."

"I might get drunk. That'd be local news."

"They won't sell liquor to you. You're not twenty-one."

"I look twenty-one to saloonkeepers."

Anaheim was nine miles away, but Chinopsee stepped off the miles at a good clip. The rain and cold air made him brisk. The wheels lifted runnels of water, and raindrops, linked together like a fly net, dripped from the buggy top. They had the road to themselves, and felt scorn for weather-bound stay-at-homes. What was a little rain? After brown hills and bleached stubble, the palm trees and orange groves they passed were parklike. The groves seemed arranged in patterns for games or beauty, and to have nothing to do with producing crops. An hour's drive had put them in another land; Borneo could not be any more unlike the Tract than this. The power of a turning wheel! Climb in a buggy, say "Giddap," and without another word you were carried to a foreign country. Big two-story houses behind iron fences and a half-acre's worth of good orange land given over to grass and hydrangeas, just for the looks of it. These people were rolling in money.

"Will the Tract look this way someday?"

"I reckon. Makes me feel like an old prairie dog."

"Wonder what it's like inside these houses?"

"Carpets and sideboards and electric lights and the hired girls peeling potatoes for supper."

"Why, it's only two-thirty now."

"They're forehanded in houses like these."

"How do you know? Did you ever live in a house like that?"

"Nope. But that's the way they live. The potatoes on frying by three p.m. Don't you ever read?"

"I never read anything about potatoes at three p.m."

"Money's the same the world over."

"It would be fun to visit in a place like that."

"You wouldn't have to visit. Your father's a driller. You could have a house like that."

"We never will. My father gives it all to the church."

"That's what a good preacher is supposed to do."

"He's not good."

"You still harping on that cow?"

"There's other things."

He doubted it and let the doubt show.

"He's licentious."

For a minute, Chad was stumped. She means horny. Good thing I do read. Don't she know everybody is, except women? Bet my father is more licentious than your father. Then he had to laugh. Bragging to each other about such things. Bet my father can out . . . Well, he wouldn't think the word, sitting by a nice girl like Crystal.

"It's nothing to laugh at."

He agreed. "It sure isn't. I was laughing at something else."

"What?"

"Oh, that big word of yours."

"That's what the dictionary calls it."

"How'd you know where to find it?"

"I didn't. I had to look."

"Your father's not so bad, or you'd of heard some worse words at home."

"It's what he does, not what he says, I'm talking about."

"Men are all alike. Being a preacher don't change your father from being a man like other men."

"He isn't a man like other men."

"You said he was licentious. That's like other men."

"He praises God all the time. Other men aren't like that."

"Men are the way God made them."

"Some men are more the way God made them than others."

She was always able to make him laugh. He looked at her closely, as if this power might somehow be detected from the outside. She returned his gaze, but there was not a sign of her wit in her eyes.

"You are so good," she said.

"I'm no angel."

"Who would love an angel?"

"Another angel, I guess."

"I'm no angel either."

He wasn't quite sure what this meant, or where it left them. He was startled and took another quick look at Crystal. She was staring straight ahead, but her lips trembled.

"Chad," she said, in a voice so low it seemed like memory's echo inside his head, "I love you."

Now she looked like someone steeling herself to be vaccinated. It came to him that she was extremely brave, and he looked quickly away. But he couldn't think of a word to say.

"I don't expect you to do or say anything," Crystal told him. "I've been trying to tell you for a long time. I don't think it's honorable to go around hiding it. It's not fair to you."

"You don't have to be fair to me," Chad said. "I never did ask it of you."

"It wasn't just to be fair," Crystal admitted. "It might get results."

Chad was silent again.

"What if you wanted to be a mountain climber or a general? But all you did was to sit around and dream of it? You wouldn't get any results that way, would you? Where would Teddy Roosevelt be if he'd lived that way? He'd be an invalid, not a hero. It's the same with love, exactly the same. You mustn't dream it."

"Where did you . . . how did you learn all this?" Chad managed to ask.

"Medora. She is the one who should get the credit. She explained it. I would never have thought of it, except for her."

"Well," Chad said, "Medora's getting results all right, I guess."

"Medora's private affairs are none of our business."

Chad agreed. He was glad to find something they could agree about.

He believed he ought, now, to look at Crystal, once more. It couldn't be very nice for a girl to say what Crystal had said and not get even a straight look from the fellow. Still, he kept staring at Chinopsee's hind end. If he looked squarely at Crystal, she might say it again. And I can't thank her, like she'd given me a pocket handkerchief. I can't kiss her as much as to say, "You didn't win, but here's the booby prize."

Oh, Press, Press, why don't you love me and save me?

"Don't cry for me," Crystal said. "I'll be all right. I feel better already, for having told you."

He wasn't crying for her; he wasn't crying for anyone, but he was glad to see the town. It might take their minds off love. Anaheim had two streets, and both were wet and deserted. But they were streets, and they were paved, and they were lined with stores with plate-glass windows, and behind the plate-glass windows, there were clothes and house furnishings and drugstore medicines and perfumes. After the bare hills of the Tract and the empty streets of the townsite, it was like a fair. Neither owned or had ever owned a raincoat, umbrella, or overshoes; they would get wet, walking, but they expected to. That was the point of rain.

"I see you picked a place near a saloon to stop," Crystal said.

He hadn't noticed it, had only taken the first hitching post his eye lit on. But now that he saw it, he felt like going in for a drink at once. Did his love for Press make poor Press feel the way Crystal's love was making him feel?

Crystal saw a store she wanted to go into, a variety store, with a little of everything: china, saucepans, pictures, books, ink tablets. Chad went in with her, but wandered down the chinaware aisle, alone. He saw a pitcher, for fifteen cents, his mother would like, one she could put the dip in, for puddings. The sight of it, and his anticipation of the pleasure it would give his mother, eased his misery. There was one woman, anyway, who was pleased with what he had to offer and didn't ask for something more or different.

When they got back to the buggy, Crystal said, "I bought something for you. Let's get in out of the rain. I want to give it to you now."

Whatever it was, it was wrapped in fancy paper and tied with ribbons, and he dreaded the minute when he would see it, something he didn't want, and would have to say thanks anyway for. It was fully as bad as he had imagined. *Sonnets from the Portuguese,* bound in limp suede leather, a book that fell across his hand as spineless as a piece of liver. It had cost three dollars—the price mark was still on it —and every poem, he saw at a glance, said, first of all, "I love you," then went on to say that this love was bigger, better, richer, deeper, fuller than any love any woman had ever loved before. Crystal looked at him, her light-blue eyes gone almost violet, asking for praise; or, worse, for love.

He thrust the pitcher toward her. "This is for you," he said. Then he jumped out of the buggy and went into the saloon, book in hand.

When he came back, he felt better. He had had two glasses of Kentucky whisky, and without trying to he had forgotten the book and left it behind on the bar. He had had enough whisky, if he had not needed it to settle his feelings, to make him drunk. As it was, he had come out even, enough whisky to calm his emotions, enough emotion to absorb the whisky. He had never felt more clearheaded. He walked to the buggy with razor precision, rebuking his usual sloppy gait with every step. He jumped in, clean as a jackknife. He picked up the lines without waste motion and started Chinopsee, true as a die, down the road toward the Tract.

The clarity of his thinking made him aware of the similarity between his life and Crystal's. She loved someone who didn't love her. He loved someone who didn't love him. She had a licentious father. So did he. She had given him a gift. He had given her a gift. She had confided in him. He ought to confide in her; the whisky he'd had made many things, which before had been fuzzy to him, absolutely clear. A kindness which he ought to feel for Crystal filled him, and he expressed it.

"One thing you ought not to do is worry about your father. You're a girl and you're probably shocked if he blows his nose without a handkerchief."

"No, I'm not."

"All right," he said, using his clear mind to express his kind heart, "let me ask you some questions. Did your father ever kill anyone?"

"Of course not."

"Did he ever steal?"

"He gives everything away!"

"Lie? Cheat? Have false gods? Dishonor his father and mother?"

"No."

"Does he lust after his neighbor's wife?"

"No, not that I ever noticed."

"You'd notice if he did. Did he ever have a bad disease?"

"I don't know. I don't think so."

"Did he ever have a bastard?"

"A bastard?"

"Didn't you ever look that up in the dictionary?"

"You mean a child born out of wedlock?"

"I do."

"I never heard of it if he did."

"What've you got to complain of?" He didn't give her a chance to answer. "I know a man who got one girl in a family way, then caught a bad disease from another girl so he couldn't marry the first girl. What do you think of that?"

She looked at him with big startled eyes. "I think you're drunk."

"What's that got to do with it?"

"I think you don't know what you're talking about."

"I know what I'm talking about. That's the one thing I do know. I'm that bastard. Or, if I'm not, it's no thanks to my father. He didn't claim me of his own free will. Only when he had the choice of me or both barrels of a double-barreled shotgun. That's the way I got my father. I don't see as you've got anything to complain about. So before you start calling people licentious you better learn the real meaning of that word, hadn't you?"

Chad's conviction that he was able to see truths ordinarily hidden began, after that outburst, to fade. He was no longer above the facts, and their master, but like Crystal their victim and as much in need of kindness and sympathy as she. When she moved closer to him, he put his arm around her.

"Did your folks tell you?" she asked in a low voice.

"Don't be silly."

"How did you find out, then?"

"Everybody else told me."

"Back in Kentucky?"

"Back in Kentucky."

"Well," Crystal said, "nobody knows it here."

"Nobody but me," Chad said, forgetting Crystal. "And I wish it was the other way round. But I can tell you one thing. None of that messing around for me."

"That's why I love you," Crystal said.

"I don't love you," Chad told her, the power of whisky fading but still strong enough to keep him that truthful.

"You told me that once before."

"You told me you loved me once before."

"It doesn't seem the same."

"It's not," he agreed.

"What I meant was, saying it twice," she explained.

"I don't see the difference."

"Kissing somebody twice isn't the same as hitting him twice."

"It's just as twice," he said. He gave her a little hug to show her he knew the difference between the two. She bunched down closer to him than he would have supposed possible. He gave her a little kiss. But his heart wasn't in it.

"This has been a kind of unusual conversation," he observed.

She lay against him, his pitcher in her hands, and didn't say a word. If she was to hold the pitcher outside, she could get it filled with rain water; and in the old days of water-hauling it would have been a worth-while job; but it wasn't worth the effort with water all around them.

"We are heading due east," he said, "through a winter rain, toward some bare hills and the shelter of a few planks and shingles. I don't know why we went and I don't know why we're coming back."

After a while, she said, "I wish Lute would put things like that in the newspaper."

"What I said ain't news. Everybody, almost, says it every day and does it every day."

"I never knew it," Crystal said. "It's news to me."

"You've got a lot to learn."

"I know it," she said humbly.

"I'm not going to be your teacher."

"Oh, that's as clear as the nose on your face."

"When we left town, do you know who I felt sorry for?"

"You?"

"No, you. Now the one I feel sorry for is me."

"You could feel sorry for both of us."

He wasn't going to get them mixed up together in anything, not even sorriness. "You're not in such a bad fix," he said. "D'you know that? You can talk to the person you love. And I can't talk to the person I love."

"Why can't you?"

"Search me."

"But you can talk to me?"

"Have you been asleep?"

"That don't make sense."

"Is sense what we're talking about?"

"I don't know."

"We're talking about love, and sense don't play any part in that. If it did, I'd fall in love with you instead of Press. But I didn't," he said.

"You've got your arm around me."

"If you think that's got anything to do with love, I'll take it away."

"Do you like it there?"

"I'm not suffering," he said.

"Me either," said Crystal.

When they reached the newspaper office, she said, "Come in, Chad. I want to write your name in your book so you'll remember our ride."

He hadn't intended going in with her, but since he'd forgotten the book, he felt he ought to break it to her gently.

They stopped at the door to stamp the mud off their feet.

Inside, he said, "Crystal, I don't have your book. I forgot and left it in the saloon. I appreciate your thoughtfulness in giving it to me, but you can't write in it because I don't have it."

"You really don't love me, do you?"

"Last time I told you, you said I didn't need to tell you that again."

"You never will."

"Never's a long time."

"You don't think you ever will?"

"No."

"Why?"

"Press."

"You didn't buy this pitcher for me either, did you?"

"No."

"Press?"

"No. My mother."

"I don't care who you bought it for, I'm going to keep it. You gave it to me. You better not give things to people if you don't want them to have them."

"I want you to have it."

She looked down into it. "There's some rain water in it. This is

308

probably the only time in my life I'll ever get a pitcher with rain water in it. Thanks. Especially for the rain water."

"You don't need to thank me for the rain water."

"All right, I won't." She tipped the pitcher and poured the few drops on his hand. "Now I haven't got a thing you didn't give me. Have I?"

"No."

"Thanks for the ride," she said.

"Thanks for going."

He and Chinopsee headed home in the slashing rain. The wind had veered, and he took the rain on his face and welcomed it as a misery he could deal with.

Indy had on the red dress when the men arrived at five. She had not intended to put on anything special, but Lute's command—and the irony involved in following it—made it possible. It was still raining, and the men stamped the mud and the water off on the front porch before coming in to warm up and dry off by the heater in the living room. She had not, however, changed her supper menu to impress either Sylvester Perkins or Tom. It was Monday, and though she had not been able to wash, because of the rain, the washday beans had already been simmering on the back of the stove when Lute told her they were having company. She was lifting the dumplings out of the iron kettle when Tom Mount came into the kitchen. He leaned against the wall while she heaped the big, creamy puffs onto a platter.

"How are you, Indy?" he asked.

"I'm all right," she said.

"Getting tired of this rain?"

She gave the platter of dumplings to Press to carry in to the table. Then she looked at Tom. It frightened her to look at him. He endangered her. Without a motion, standing there quietly, he propelled her toward some action.

"I've missed you," he said.

She told him the truth, that she had missed him. As she did so, she knew it was a double act: the truth for Tom, but an example of straightforwardness, to observe and emulate, for Lute. Was every act of hers for the rest of her life going to be two-faced? Never anything in itself, but also some protest or comment to Lute? Was every act of hers, with Tom or anyone else, going to be the dialogue she'd never been able to have with Lute?

"You're changing things for me, Indy."

"Don't let me," she said. "I don't want to."

She did not want him changed for or by her. She thought he lived, more than most men, his own life; had shifted from job to job, from place to place, had known more than one woman, was not committed, was still searching, had fallen into no pattern.

"I'm an old, cold Englishman," he had told her once. "Ugly, quick-witted, and strong." This had made her laugh, and was not perhaps intended to be the truth about himself. But he was interested in the truth about her.

"How do you feel about your husband?" he had once asked her. "You've got some ideas you never mention to Lute, haven't you?"

Tom's questions were not the empty time-fillers of getting acquainted. When she answered them, he listened. Then he questioned the answers. When she was with him for even so short a time as now, doing no more than dishing up beans and dumplings, cutting corn bread and custard pies, these acts had meanings, because he was present, that went quite beyond her wrists. The skin across her cheekbones began to ease in his presence. She acted to some purpose and without lonesomeness. Tom took the big tureen of beans from her, and she followed him into the dining room, carrying two heaped plates of corn bread.

Lute, when she entered the dining room, put his arms across her shoulders, endangering the balance of the plates. "A man don't deserve good looks and good cooking in one and the same package," he told Sylvester Perkins, "but that's what I got."

The caress was offensive to Indy. She took it to be a gesture for others to see and not directed toward her. It made her an accomplice. The whole supper began to appear deceptive, and she felt ashamed to be a part of it. She saw what, to a stranger peering in through the rain-streaked window, it must look like: happy family; pretty daughters; kindness to neighbors.

She would like to make that stranger's vision the true one; but if that were not possible, to accept the realities of this supper. She and Lute separated; Press feverishly fighting something, fighting her, she supposed. Hannah lost in being Hannah. Sylvester Perkins busy pulling the wool over Lute's eyes, hobnobbing with Lute so that Lute would get a sympathetic version of the water assessments and print that version in his paper. And she, no proper person to speak of any man's pulling the wool over Lute's eyes, she, trembling at Lute's table, at the glances of Tom Mount.

Wake up, Lute, wake up! she wanted to cry. But she had wanted to cry that to Lute all of her life. See how things really are! She wanted to make this cry now, not alone for Lute's sake, but for her own. Wake up! Take charge. Make change for me impossible! Lute, Lute. She was frightened. But Lute, who had put Tom and Syl on either side of him at his end of the table, was busy talking water to Sylvester Perkins.

"You got a problem on your hands, Syl," he said, "explaining matters to Cudlip."

"Cudlip's a professional sorehead, I'm afraid. Nothing suits him. Now if Shel Lewis was dissatisfied, that would be a different matter. He carries weight here. I don't think Cudlip does."

"He carries weight when what he says makes sense. Shel isn't dissatisfied with the water assessment because he's had water, he's irrigated. But here's Cudlip, no trees out yet, no water used, and he has to make the same payment Shel does. He's yelling his head off about it; I admit he's always yelling his head off, but at the minute, it being the slack season, he's doing a particularly thorough job."

Sylvester Perkins laughed. "I don't suppose the preacher's cow can calf again so soon? I hate taking the brunt of Cudlip's temper alone."

"What is the explanation?" Tom Mount asked. "As an outsider, not owning land or water stock, can I ask why a man who hasn't used water has to pay the same as a man who has?"

"Sure you can, Tom. If you ride in a streetcar, you don't pay any more than some little woman who weighs under a hundred. Or any less than some big three-hundred-pound buster. Do you?"

"What's the assessment for?" Indy asked.

"Operating expenses, Mrs. Cope. Water don't just gush up, then run into pipes that we picked off trees. Pipes don't go into the ground under their own power. And water don't just end up by itself in a weir box on the very day a rancher happens to be furrowed out for irrigation. Water comes out of a well, and the well has to be dug. That costs money, and once the well is dug, quite a lot of electricity has got to be burned to keep the pumps going, and that costs money. Pipes leak and have got to be repaired, and that means a repair crew. And they don't work for nothing."

"That's something else Cudlip objects to," Tom said. "Mexicans doing that work."

311

"I'm lucky to find anybody for the job. Chinamen or niggers. Does Cudlip know there's a war being fought? Maybe I better resign and let Base run the Water Company. He seems to know so much about it."

No one defended Base. Tom said, "I've been working out at the Ocie Davis place. Ocie thinks the assessment was pretty high."

"Expenses have been pretty high. You haven't heard Shel Lewis complaining, have you?"

Lute said, "Shel's so setup, getting his trees out and through the wind and drought, he's willing to pay through the nose for a while. This won't last long with Shel. It can't. He'll run out of money. And so will others. What'll you do then?"

Indy approved every sensible word. See through him, Lute. Speak up to him, Lute. Reconcile me to you, Lute. Love me, Lute. Don't make me choose something strange. If this supper table's a lie, it's a lie I'm used to. I don't want to leave it. Be a man I can't leave, Lute.

"If there's going to be sides taken in this affair," Syl said, "and there's no reason they should be—I was for the Tract before there was a Tract—you'll find Shel Lewis on my side. You wait and see. He's going to work for me after the first of the month."

"What doing?" Lute asked.

"He'll have charge of the repair crew. Ben Jessup's going to be chief man down at the pumping plant. With your own people running the Water Company, Base Cudlip will have to squawk to his neighbors about his neighbors, if he thinks things are going wrong."

"They going to have any say about assessments?"

"Not until they get elected to the board of directors, they won't. But the minute they are, they will."

"Who elects the directors?"

"Up to now, they've been appointed."

"Who appoints them?"

"Up to now, me. Mrs. Cope, you got any more of this corn bread in the kitchen? I don't know when I've tasted its equal."

Indy went to the kitchen, and Tom followed her. "What can I do to help?"

She had asked Lute to stand up to Perkins, and hadn't he done so? She heard him asking more questions. Now, she said, Lute, why are you in there, talking water with Perkins when Tom Mount's followed me to the kitchen? What did she want of Lute, anyway?

Tom Mount stood there, a big man, dark and quiet. She handed him the plate of corn-bread squares, more conscious of the absence of touch, as he took the plate from her, than of any caress Lute had ever given her in his life.

2     On the last Saturday in January, Opal wakened with the feeling that something was wrong. She lay still, listening. The room was filled with sunlight; the air on her face was fresh and cold. There was not a sound, yet something had awakened her. She sat up and looked out of the window beside her bed. The rains had stopped. It was the silence, after weeks of downpour, that had aroused her.

She dressed quietly, so as not to awaken Eunice, and went outside. The air was clear and delicate, still sharp, but warming up. During the wet, gray days, she had not noticed that the earth had been turning green. Near at hand, she could see that the grass blades were sparse, but across the valley, the foothills looked solidly carpeted. Spring had arrived. The roof was steaming in the sunshine; there was a froth of yellow on a field of mustard down the road, and somewhere a meadow lark sang as if it were already full summer. Life keeps unfolding, she thought, the life inside you and the life outside you. Time and again you think, That's the end, that finishes it, everything's over for me, and find you're fooled. It's not over. Perhaps it's never over.

You marry thinking that's a beginning. Instead, you find that something has ended. But you go on, you outlive that ending. You're widowed. That seems final, but it isn't. You fall in love again. That's what I felt for Tom Mount, she remembered: love. I was going to love him forever, just like Eunice. Eunice has told herself that she'll love Tom Mount until she dies. I don't think you ought to tell yourself too many things. You've got to listen to what things tell you once in a while. It turned out I couldn't love Tom Mount forever. His loving all and sundry may make him like God to Eunice. But I'm just too much of a Protestant to put a ring on my finger like those nuns, and wed a man who doesn't feel anything special for me.

Why don't I sorrow? I was just as much betrayed as Eunice. I don't know why. It's a fresh morning and I've got a fresh heart for it. That's my luck or my tragedy, I don't know which.

She could see the smoke from breakfast cookstoves all over the Tract rising black in the delicate shimmer of the morning air. She thought of the families she knew, cooking their pots of oatmeal mush and turning their brown flapjacks and boiling up their Mapeline syrup. I'm getting like Tom, she thought. I love everybody.

The idea startled her. Is that why I don't mourn? Lost Tom, but didn't lose loving? Or perhaps even learned loving? Oh, all you people, she thought tenderly, all of you, working hard raising your families, trying to make out. Hannah, who feared during the long rain that the Tract was in for another flood and who kept her fears from everyone but me. Hannah, my little daughter. Mary, my sister, dying. Indy, myself. Shel, if you could have come courting me early enough, there was a beginning that would never have ended. Raunce, pray for me, brother. Press, I still don't fathom you. Asa, you and all your pitiful bugs and worms. Poor old Cudlip, snapping and snarling, willing to bite yourself if nothing else is handy.

Without knowing it, she had opened her arms. Pete and Julian, going by on the Water Company repair wagon, returned what they took to be a wave. Opal yelled good morning to them in the Spanish Rosa had taught her, Spanish that was both good morning and a joke for all of them, she as well as the two Mexicans.

If men were going to work, it was later than she had thought. She took one more look: the sky, the color of rinse water, lightly blued, was pale enough so that when she looked upward her gaze went through the blue into colorlessness. Where the sky met the earth, the sky was tinged with green, as if the grass had jumped a boundary. Far off, she heard a hen cackling; a biddy fooled by the unusual sunshine into thinking it was midday and time for egg-laying. That sound hustled her into the house.

At breakfast, over the bowl of dried beef gravy, she said, "What's your plan for the day, Eunice?"

"It's Saturday," Eunice said. "That's enough for me."

"I'm going in to Mary's after I finish up here. You want to go along?"

"No. If I went to the townsite, I'd think I ought to go in and write some seatwork on the board for Monday. My plan for the day is not to catch sight of the school or anything connected with it."

"Suit yourself," Opal said, fishing the last piece of dried beef from

314

the gravy. Eunice left the table and went into the sitting room for another look at the novelty of a rainless day.

"What's Indy Cope going into town this time of the morning for?" Eunice called back to her.

"It's not so early," Opal said. "It's ten."

Opal followed Eunice into the sitting room and stood beside her at the window, watching Indy.

"If she wants to go into the townsite, why doesn't she ride in with her husband?" Eunice asked.

"This kind of weather makes anyone want to walk. Even I walked around the house a couple of times this morning before you were up."

Indy had on a long coat, and her hair was pushed up under a knitted green cap. You couldn't see her face and you couldn't see her figure but there was something about her that made you want to. She walks with a nervous step, like some thin cat that hasn't had a mouse to eat for a month of Sundays, Opal thought.

"Tom Mount ought to tangle with her," she said.

"Don't you care anything about me?" Eunice asked. "Don't you?"

"I do. You know that. But what difference is it to you, whether it's Indy Cope or someone else? It's bound to be someone."

"We've been over all of this before," Eunice said. She went into her room and closed the door behind her.

Opal was finishing the dishes when Eunice came into the kitchen. "I think you're right, Opal. This is the day for a walk."

She wasn't properly dressed for a walk, but Opal was glad to see her bestir herself. "If you end up down by the townsite, come on over to Mary's. I'll be there."

"I just want to walk," Eunice declared.

She wanted to walk, but she wanted to walk in the direction Indy Cope was going. She was not jealous of Indy, but she had to know where she was going. She could bear anything, but she had to know what she had to bear. Base, when he pulled up beside her, had to repeat his question.

"You heading down to the townsite?"

"I might end up down there," she replied cautiously.

"Want a lift?"

"No, thanks just the same. I want to walk."

"Kind of sticky underfoot, ain't it?"

"Not if I stay to one side of the road."

"Determined to foot it, looks like."

"I guess so."

"Well, I reckon you know your plans better than I do."

"Except to walk, I don't have any plan."

It was a lie, and she saw that Base Cudlip knew it. An embarrassed flicker, with some pity in the embarrassment, touched his eyes.

"I'll leave you to it, then," he said, and slapped the reins over his horse's back.

The lie hurt her, and she didn't care for Base's pity either.

The landscape, which had appeared springlike when she set out, was actually wintry, raw, and muddy. The buildings were cheap and ramshackle. The church itself could have been a hardware store. There was no grace or dignity about it. Over on the Raunces' clothesline a miserable wash of faded dresses and bedraggled underwear was whipping about in the sharp breeze that had sprung up. The main street was empty, except for Cudlip's two-wheeled cart and, out in front of the *Reporter* office, Lute Cope's car. Base had been right about the stickiness. Her feet were heavy with mud. A momentary sensation of strangeness took hold of her. Is this where I live? she wondered. Is this my home? Lute's sign and a Tract billboard down at the end of the street could have been in Chinese and she would have been less surprised than to see them in a language she knew.

She went slowly to the back of the church. Wild mustard and baby blue-eyes were growing under the steps to Tom's room. She dragged herself up the steps, and pictured as she did so what she wanted to see when she opened the door. She wanted to see Indy in Tom's arms. Or Indy and Tom lying together on Tom's bed. And she wanted Tom to see her at the very moment that he gave her proof of the life he lived. That was what she had made her long walk for, that was why the landscape had uglied, that was why her heart beat so sickeningly: the anticipation of that proof.

Something she had not thought of occurred to her: Tom might be there by himself. Just Tom, alone, cleaning his room, or fixing himself one of his grass bouquets. She felt, as this possibility came to her, like someone entering an empty theater on an afternoon when a stirring performance has been expected. Blankness and emptiness and disappointment filled her. Just Tom, alone, looking up, saying, "Hello, Eunice." Her heart fell away from the image, empty.

She opened the door on an unoccupied room, closed it, and was by herself. She had not wanted Tom. At a moment when she could choose, she hadn't chosen Tom. She had chosen something more stirring, Tom's guilt. Not Tom, not Tom. She had not wanted Tom. She had wanted spying, and chance-taking, and doubts confirmed, and accusations proved, and the sickness of guilt, and the horror of desired pain. She had wanted desolation, the desolation that was all she knew of love. Tom, waiting, guiltless: her mind in its moment of imagining and choosing had found this image of Tom less satisfying than the torment of seeing him in another woman's arms.

Oh, God, she thought, I have been living in hell and calling it love.

She left Tom's room without a look at the letters and the notebooks and the gifts upon which it had been her wont to feast.

In the Sunday-school room, at the other end of the building, she stood motionless for a long time, then sat on the floor and put her head on one of the small chairs intended for an infants' class.

I did not choose you, Tom. I did not choose you.

The pine boards on which she sat had been stained, and she followed, as if her life depended upon it, the whorl that circled a knothole and sank, finally, deep into that wooden vortex.

3   CRYSTAL pushed aside the orange-box door, sat down at her orange-box desk, and was alone and happy in her orange-box world. It was odd that this could happen in a world less than waist high and from which the Raunce world was fully visible. But it did happen.

One thing, though, her orange boxes could not do; they could not shut out the sound of her father's voice. He was upstairs practicing his dedication-day speech, and if he didn't lower his voice, there would be no need of delivering it on dedication day. His voice boomed inside her head; her ears were filled with all her father's favorite words, love and blessings, faith and thanks.

Her mother, coming into the dining room, paused to listen. "Papa has a fine voice, doesn't he?" she said. "A born preacher's voice."

If she meant loud, Crystal agreed with her. But she was too pleased with her mother's stopping to talk to her, to argue. It was hard to get a word in edgewise with her own mother because her father demanded—and got—all of her mother's attention when he was around. When he wasn't talking to her mother, he was hugging and kissing her. Crystal was sure her mother didn't care for all of the fondling she received. She'd seen her draw away from kisses and squirm out of hugs and pretend not to hear when her father said, "God in heaven, I thank Thee for my sweet wife."

Kiss or pray, Crystal thought, it's all one to him.

"Are you too busy to talk, Crystal?" her mother asked, standing outside the orange-box walls and smiling down at her.

Crystal felt ashamed: her own mother asking if she was too busy to talk, as if they were businessmen who couldn't meet without an appointment.

"Of course I'm not busy, Mama. Sit down."

Her mother sat down, but in the world outside the orange-box domain. No one came inside to sit with Crystal. She conversed with all callers, including her mother, with that barrier between them.

Her mother, who knew nothing of neatness in housework, kept herself neat as a pin. She had a pale-brown almond-shaped face, white, curved-in teeth, and smooth brown hair, which she wore in small, neat scallops about her cheeks.

Her mother faced Crystal like an applicant for a job. Crystal, looking at her mother across her desk, over the top of her walls, knew this, but did not know how to go out to her or to ask her in. Crystal J. Raunce, who had built herself a private world, wanted desperately to escape, to outwit the guard, tunnel under the walls, and become a citizen of the unwalled world. But the Crystal who wanted to escape was guarded by a Crystal who feared the unwalled world and who had set her orange-box foundations deep.

"Don't you have to go over to the newspaper office this afternoon, Crystal?" her mother asked.

"I don't have to, but I planned to go."

"I'm awfully proud of you, Crystal."

"Proud of me? Why, Mama?"

"A writer, working on a newspaper. Sometimes I think I must've marked you before you were born."

Crystal held her breath. Perhaps her mother was about to begin one of her times of remembering, times when she talked about her own mother so that Crystal felt that she had had a life before birth with these two women; had hunted guinea eggs with them, cracked hazelnuts, and polished case knives. Something mysterious happened to her when her mother spoke of her own girlhood in Missouri, something almost frightening. Partly, it was because her mother herself ap-

318

peared to believe that they were recalling the past together; that she was not telling her daughter anything new, but reminding her of happenings they had shared. Partly, it was because this past world in which she lived with her mother and her grandmother was, though unwalled, cozy and safe. It was a world into which her father had not yet entered, where he had never been heard of, even. She was the daughter and granddaughter of these two women by blood and necessity, and her father's daughter only by chance; for her mother might have married almost any man, pretty as she was.

"I saddled you with my own wishes, I expect."

"Did you, Mama?"

"I never had any education to speak of. I married so young. I wanted to go away to Normal, after I finished the eighth grade, like the other girls. But your grandpa would pick up an eighth-grade book and ask me questions until he found one I couldn't answer. Then he'd say, 'Don't make sense, sending you off to Normal when there's things you don't know in eighth-grade books.' So back I'd go to the eighth grade. I went through the eighth grade three times and graduated three times. But Papa could always find something I didn't know, and back I'd go once more. The third time I graduated, I was sixteen. So I got married. There didn't seem any sense spending my life in the eighth grade. Besides, I was in love. But I had a little notebook your grandfather didn't know anything about. It was the color of your blotter."

There was a long silence. Her mother gazed out into the afternoon sunlight, which flaked off the new, hard greenness like sparks from a grindstone. Crystal didn't know whether to speak or keep silent. She spoke, trying to make her words have the sound of a voice heard by her mother inside her own head.

"What was the notebook for?"

"Poetry," her mother said, as if to convince herself. "Rhyming came just as natural to me as breathing in those days."

"I never knew that, Mama."

"Try me on a word."

"A word?"

"A word to rhyme."

"Lute," Crystal said, without thinking.

"Flute," her mother said, promptly. "Flute, scoot, root, toot, mute, salute. No, you can't count that. It ends the same. But you can see for yourself, I have the knack."

"You never told me before."

"I haven't thought of it for years. You know my hand-blown paper-weight? I won it in a newspaper contest for the best poem."

"What was its name?"

"The *Banner Plain-Dealer*."

"The poem's, I mean."

" 'Evening,' " her mother said, smiling out into the bright after-noon. "I called it 'Evening.' I had a special liking for that time of day. When I was young."

"Could you say it for me?"

Her mother shook her head. "Oh, no," and Crystal didn't know whether she had really forgotten it or was only bashful.

"Did you write a lot of poems?"

"Oh, I did. I'd have on my nightgown, ready to blow out my lamp and go to bed. Have a long breath drawn to blow with, even, and a poem would come to me. I'd have to let out my breath easy so's not to put out the light. Then I'd sit there on the edge of my bed half freezing, though I wouldn't feel it until afterward."

"Afterward?"

"After I'd written the poem in the notebook."

"Where's the notebook now?"

"Why, I don't know. I haven't seen it for years. Or thought of it. After I was married, I didn't use it any more."

Crystal didn't ask why. She knew why. Her father had killed the poetry in her mother.

"That notebook was filled with daydreams. After I met your father, there wasn't any more need to be daydreaming."

Any more chance, Crystal told herself. She could clearly see her father throwing that blue notebook away. "Don't waste your time on that stuff, praise God." Then leading his wife by the hand, with all thanks to our Heavenly Father, into a bedroom whose door he wouldn't take the bother to lock.

"So I marked you," her mother went on. "I thought about poems, even though I didn't write them any more."

"Why, Mama, I never wrote a word of poetry in my life."

"Look at that." Her mother pointed to the pencils stuck in a water glass, and the paper, three different sizes, lined up in a neat pyramid, on her orange-box desk.

"There, that's my mark on you, pencils and paper. And lined up in exactly the same old-maid way I had before I met LeRoy. Why, I used to have every pin pointing in the same direction. I'd trim the

320

broom straws because I couldn't bear the looks of anything uneven." Her mother shook her head wonderingly. "It all dropped away from me the minute I was married. But I used to be as much hipped on the subject as you are now. Oh, I marked you all right, even your name. Do you know what your grandma wanted you called? Emma! Emma Jane! Why, I wouldn't call a setting hen Emma Jane. Names were Mama's blind spot. Do you know what she wanted me to call Burleigh? Homer! And she was set on Bernita's being called Jessie. But I said, 'If there's nothing else I can do for my children, I can give them beautiful names.' Why, you'd have been sunk before you started, with a name like Emma Jane."

Crystal hated her name and always had, but she had never loved her mother so much. Her mother had marked her, passed on her daydreams and her neat arrangements, and had saved her from a name that would sink her before she started. What gift could she give her mother? She could give her the whole of herself.

"Mama, I was in love all last fall. But I'm beginning to get over it."

"I never noticed a thing."

"I know you didn't. I've been in love with Chad Lewis."

"Why, petty. That tall, dark boy? The skinny one?"

"He's not skinny."

"Compared with your father . . ."

"He's slender. I told him I loved him and he told me he loved someone else."

"My poor girl. Why, poor petty, you've been bearing it all alone."

"When I told him, I started to get over it. I would've anyway, I expect, as soon as I got to know Mr. Cope."

"Crystal, don't tell me you've fallen in love with a married man old enough to be your father? What kind of a girl are you getting to be?"

"Mama, don't be silly. What I meant was, that as soon as I knew a man like Mr. Cope, I'd see how kiddish Chad was. I admire Mr. Cope, and I know he admires me. We talk politics and put out the paper together. I love him because of his intelligence. I haven't the least desire to kiss him or anything like that. He's almost elderly. He knows how I feel."

"You haven't gone and told him you love him, too, have you?"

"No, I haven't, but I could and he would understand. Mama, there's nothing to worry about."

Her mother had given her a gift of what she truly felt, and she had wanted to pay her back in the same coin, an open heart for an open heart. The trouble was, she didn't know how to put what she felt into words. If she could say to her mother, "I love Mr. Cope like a father," her mother would understand; though she would probably say, "But you have a father." But her feeling for Mr. Cope was nothing like her feeling for her father. It was, she thought, what a girl *should* feel for a father; but she didn't intend to lie about it, to make the telling easy.

"Mama, you told me about your poems and I told you about Mr. Cope. It's the same."

"It don't seem the same."

"It is. You wrote your feelings down, is all the difference. Mr. Cope ran away from home when he was fifteen because his stepfather wasn't a nice man. His mother has a name you would like. Ettiwanda. She's called Etty for short. He was a miner and a stagecoach driver and a sheepherder before he was a newspaperman. The first money he ever earned, he bought a book of etiquette."

Her mother began to smile. "Yes, I see. I remember a pack-peddler back home, the second year I was in the eighth grade. He wasn't an ordinary pack-peddler. He was a professor with a broken heart. He carried a book of poetry with him, and he read my poems. He was the only human being who ever did read them. He told me about himself. He timed his visits when I wouldn't be in school. I used to go down the pike a ways to a place where a log seat had been set up beside a spring branch. I didn't want to have to talk to him with all the folks about. He came once a month, and I just barely managed to live between his visits."

"Yes, yes. That's the way it is. You loved him, didn't you?"

"I guess I thought so."

"And if you'd told him, he would've understood. Wouldn't he?"

"I expect so. I remember he showed me a picture of his wife one day. She was a beautiful woman."

"Like Indy."

"I hope not. She broke the professor's heart. It's funny. I can remember her name and I can't remember the pack-peddler's."

They were deep, deep inside the bubble of past time, with the poems and the notebooks and the beautiful names for children and pack-peddlers with broken hearts.

Crystal breathed her next question carefully. "What was her name, Mama?"

322

But all of her care was wasted. Her father banged the bedroom door shut, upstairs, and came running down the steep stairs, talking as he ran.

"Dolly, you got to help me."

Her father was always too warm, no matter what the weather. Now, in midwinter, he didn't have a shirt on, and there was a sweat patch under each arm of his B.V.D.s. He bent over and snuggled his frowsy unshaved face against her mother's shoulder. "How's my Dolly?" Crystal turned her face so she wouldn't have to see the kissing; but she heard it. Poetry? Her mother had been lucky to be able to keep on with her breathing.

"Dolly, I'm in a fix. I never wrote out a sermon before. It's finished, but I just don't know. It don't sound right to me. You come on over to the church and tell me how it sounds to you. I can't read it and listen to it, both. You come on, too, Crystal. You know more about writing things out than I do. Come on, the two of you, and help me."

"Mama and I were talking. Though you didn't notice it," Crystal told him.

"You two can talk every day of your lives. This may be the only dedication sermon I'll ever preach. Come on, Dolly."

When her mother didn't answer, her father picked her up, bodily. "Want me to carry you over to the church like a Bride of the Lamb?"

"Father, some things are holy," Crystal said.

"Some things are holy? Why, Sis, what ain't? You name one. Not you, not your mama, not even me. Your orange boxes and the church. They're all holy. Ain't that right, Dolly?"

"Put me down, LeRoy. I'll come, but I've got to freshen up a little first."

After her father left, her mother sat down, and they faced each other exactly as before, but her father had ruined everything. The beautiful iridescent bubble of past time in which she and her mother had been living had winked out and left her alone behind her orange boxes.

"I expect I'd better get on over to the church," her mother said. "Your father's right. We can talk any time." She went upstairs to change her dress.

Crystal thought about her mother's girlhood for a long time after her mother had left: saw her lean over the lamp to blow it out, then hold her breath, filled with the idea for a poem; saw her down at the

323

spring branch, waiting for the brokenhearted professor. She became a mother to her own mother, and shed tears for her, because of all that had been and was no more.

There was no one else in the house. It was Saturday, but Burly and Bernie, celebrating the end of the rain, had headed with their lunches for the hills. When there was no one around, her orange-box world, built as a defense, was not very satisfying. Whom did she defy with it? She decided to go to the office.

The afternoon was turning cold. The air was perfectly still, and though it wasn't yet near sundown, there was a strange green-yellow rim around the sky at the horizon. She could hear her father over in the church practicing his dedication sermon. Birds were picking up an early supper, their feathers puffed out against the chill. She had begun in her mind to tell Mr. Cope all she'd been hearing—a poem called "Evening." Destroyed by my father. Emma Jane. His wife looked like your wife. She marked me. Both of us admire fine men. She needs protecting. I have a heart of love. The world is strange and sad. I would like to tell you everything. My mother has my father, but who do I have?

Lute was setting type to the tune of "Swanee River." He had once fancied, or at least his mother had fancied, that he could sing. His mother had seen to it that he had singing as well as piano lessons. Sometimes he sang for Indy, and, though she never said a word, he could feel her waiting for him to finish. Nowadays, he did most of his singing at the office. "Way down upon the Swanee River, far from the old folks at home."

Not the "old folks," but far from mother. Far from the banks of the Feather, from the buttes, far from the blaze of summer, the river thickets, the big single oaks on the slopes of the wheat ranches rising toward the hills. Far from the white house, built eight feet off the ground so that the Feather and the Yuba, overflowing, would have some space to swirl in before they set the Boston rockers and Martha Washington sewing stands afloat. He had watched his mother wrest that house from widowhood and crop failures, from river floods and tule fogs, watched her hang onto it in spite of a philandering second husband. She had married that big-headed prancer; had been, and still was, everything a wife should be to him. But she had never for a minute let her only child doubt that he came first with her.

He and his mother had moved into that white house when he was

324

eight. It was there he had acquired his early taste for a settled domesticity. He was drunk from the beginning on well-mowed lawns and starched white curtains and smoke rising punctually from kitchen flues; delighted with his mother, wearing her little white apron, watering the lawn at four, calling him to supper at six, saying after supper, "How about a little song fest, son?"

With this pattern of pleasant living well established in his mind, he had been able to help Indy, in the first days of their marriage, get settled as a housekeeper. Indy was as brisk and energetic as his mother but she hadn't, naturally, much understanding of the running of a house.

As a boy, he had been a thin, gangling stomach-acher who needed a good deal of special food and attention to keep him well. His looks, if he had any, and his size, had come to him after thirty. With boys his own age, he had been an outsider; he had told himself he didn't care; but except for his mother's assurances that he had something these toughs would never possess, he would have had a very unhappy childhood. She spoke to him of a delicacy and clean-mindedness which, once lost, could never be recovered. His stepfather, that rolling, bigheaded fellow, who carried himself as if his privates were his most valuable part, seemed proof of this.

His stepfather, Steve was his name, and Lute always called him that, would walk into a restaurant, give his order to the waitress in a voice that could be heard across the room, then repay the poor girl for hearing him with a pinch on the bottom and the latest dirty story. His mother had brought Lute up to be clean-minded and clean-spoken; but without the example of Steve, he might not have learned his lesson so well. Indy objected to this day to the low voice he used when ordering in a restaurant. "Don't whisper, Lute," she would urge him. But though he wanted to please Indy, the long-ago habit of pleasing his mother and proving, by contrast, what a boor his stepfather was, was too strong. He simply couldn't be a second Steve, not even to please Indy.

He had heard it said that mothers with only sons opposed their son's marrying. Nothing could have been less true of his mother. She had helped him every step of the way in his courting of Indy. "There's nothing more I hate in this world," his mother used to say, "than a selfish old bachelor, rinsing out his own socks and blowing out the light at night when *he* gets ready. That's not my plan for you, Luther, you may rest assured."

325

She continuously praised Indy to him. Many of Indy's traits that he later learned to appreciate had first been called to his attention by his mother. "Have you complimented Indy on that flattering new shade of powder she's using?" "Luther Cope, I do believe I appreciate this girl more than you."

She couldn't appreciate Indy more than he did. But because she was a woman, she could help him show his appreciation. He had never, before his marriage, picked out a present for Indy without his mother's help. His own taste in presents ran to chocolates, rhinestone lavalieres, and silk stockings. His mother pointed out to him that such presents, impractical and too intimate, insulted the taste, to say nothing of the morals, of a nice girl like Indy. She suggested, instead, warm woolen scarves, table runners, even a set of aluminum saucepans. When he had objected to the saucepans, his mother said, "No gift can be more flattering to a girl than the gift of showing her that you are seriously thinking of your future together." He hadn't any desire to flatter Indy, and when he gave her the saucepans, she hadn't acted flattered either.

"You may think," his mother said, "that you are getting yourself a wife. And of course you are. But what I keep thinking is that you're giving me a daughter."

He told this to Indy, believing it would please her. "You tell your mother," Indy said, "that if she wants a daughter, Steve's the man to give her one." Indy's very ignorance and innocence let her speak in a more forthright way than a more knowing person would have dared. His mother wanted to be called "Mother" by Indy, but Indy refused. "She's not my mother, and I won't call her Mother. I'll be nice to her for your sake, but I can only like her if it turns out that I like her."

As it turned out, she hadn't liked her; but she was, as she had promised, nice to her. Indy had faithfully gone with him to all those family get-togethers, which had, before he was married, formed a large part of his picture of a happy domestic life. But she had never really participated; and had, peculiarly enough, seemed more drawn to his old—he wasn't really old, being some years younger than his wife—reprobate of a stepfather than to others of the family.

Indy didn't understand, and it wasn't a matter a man could very well speak of to his wife, how much she owed to his mother. Since he had no father of his own to tell him about—life—his mother had taken this responsibility upon herself.

Before his wedding, she had told him, "I've brought you up clean-minded and pure as a girl. That's my real wedding present to Indy.

But I owe her one more present. As I say, I've brought you up as nice as a girl, but you aren't a girl, and when you're married, you'll find it out. You'll find you've got certain inclinations a girl knows nothing about."

This was crazy nonsense, of course; his poor little mother, thinking that her son was so pure that he wouldn't have any "inclinations" until he got married. He had already been torn with inclinations for some years. But though she was wrong about men, she was a woman and no doubt knew about women. Indy, at least, had borne out what she had to tell him about women. And it was for Indy's sake his mother had undertaken, what was not easy for her, to warn him that a woman was prepared, out of love for her husband, to endure what was naturally repellent to her. A man, in his turn, ought to make what his wife had to endure as short, delicate, and impersonal as possible. A wife should be able to meet her husband's gaze as frankly afterward as if nothing had happened.

"I've had two husbands," his mother had said, "and I know what I'm talking about."

She *had* known, too. Without this talk from his mother, Indy would have been a painful puzzle to him. That night she had thrown herself at him? What if he had supposed her passionate, not just a romantic girl, making what she thought was a suitably flowery, love-smitten gesture? He would have spoiled his own ideal of marriage and hurt Indy. For whatever else she was, romantic, high-strung, spirited, excitable, stubborn, Indy was one hundred per cent uninterested in sex. He had been absolutely faithful to Indy; had never had another woman before or since his marriage; but he had heard his share of stories—women who took their sex like men—worse than men, in fact; threshing around like beached catfish, unable to live or die. He supposed there were such freaks, but he had no fault to find with Indy's quietness. Occasionally, she cried at such times, and occasionally he felt like tears himself. But that was the nature of the act, with its seeming closeness and real separation. He never spoke of the tears. He had made it a rule of his life not to tamper with some subjects, not only because he felt uncomfortable doing so, but because nothing came of such talks. Indy could worry an idea to tatters. Like most women, he supposed, she liked nothing better than to turn souls inside out: examine, search, dissect, explain, speculate, complain. "Oh, Lute," she would say, "let us get to the bottom of things. Why are you, you? Why am I, I? How did we two happen to get together? Why do we do what we do? Would we have been better off if we had married someone else?" And she would be angry when he refused to go poking around these mysteries. But it takes two to make a quarrel, and when Indy was in one of these dissecting moods, he simply walked away from her, saying, "I'll talk to you again when you're feeling reasonable."

He had, for her sake, cut all of his family roots; he had come away from the Feather and its drifting cottonwood fluff and the houses built to accommodate passing rivers. "Far from the old folks at home." There was nothing he would not do to make Indy happy. "Oh, how my heart is turning, ever." It had meant turning his back on a good business, on his home town, on his own people, on his mother. He had done it. He had given Indy her head, and she had come back to him of her own accord.

Lute stopped his humming when Crystal came in.

"What're you doing here this afternoon?" he asked.

"I thought I'd work on my church article."

Since Crystal had shown him, with her piece about the Lewis planting, what she could do as a reporter, he had given her other special assignments. She had gone over to Pete Ramos's place, spent a day cooking with Rosa, and written an article on "Mexican Food." This had lost Lute Base Cudlip's subscription, but it gained him half a dozen others. Then Asa Brice, seeing that Lute was willing to print something besides "confined to her home," "dainty refreshments were served," and "a good time was had by all," came in and made some suggestions of his own. The *Reporter* had since then carried pieces by Asa on the eyesight of buzzards, trap-door spider silk, tarantula battles, the uses of soapweed, cactus as a food: there seemed to to be no end to Asa's observations and theories. Lute had been skeptical about the success of such writing. The newspaper theory was that what happened to a spider was not news. But settlers on the Tract were ignorant of newspaper theory and curious about the new county where they lived; and everywhere—Lute had had letters from as far east as New York—people were interested in California. About half of his subscribers now lived outside the state. Later, when the Tract was better known to its residents, he might have to change his policy; though if the present trend continued, by that time he might be publishing a magazine instead of a newspaper, with most of the subscribers living elsewhere.

328

Since Crystal's father was a Quaker minister, a piece about Quakers and the new church would, he had supposed, be easy for her to write —and a pleasure to boot. It might have been both, but Crystal had refused to get any of her information from her father. "He doesn't know a thing more about Quakers than I do," Crystal had told him.

"He's the minister," Lute had said mildly, "signed, sealed, and delivered by the brethren over at Rose Park."

"He's not one bit different from what he's always been. He likes to talk about God, and the Quakers let him."

"He does more than talk," Lute had defended him.

"Yes, he does," Crystal had agreed blackly. "I'm going to ask Mary and Wendlin about Quakers, if it's all the same to you."

It had been all the same to Lute. Though he no longer twitted Crystal about Teddy Roosevelt, he still liked to tease her, and he said now, as she came in, "So you came back just to work? I was hoping you'd say you'd come over to keep the old man company."

Crystal was inventive and imaginative when it came to Mexican cookery or the introduction of citriculture in California. But she was very matter-of-fact and intense in personal relations. She told the truth, and she always took for granted that the truth was what others were interested in. She walked over to the counter, and Lute was afraid she was going to take his question personally, contradict that "old man" or apologize for wanting to work instead of wanting to keep him company. He tried to divert her from any such embarrassing declarations with another question.

"How's the article coming?"

Crystal leaned across the counter and gave her whole attention to *that* question. After the ladies of his family, she was nothing to look at; though with her standing as she was, the upper third of her body above the counter and leaning toward him, it was impossible not to notice that she had a well-developed figure for a girl.

"The only trouble with the article is that it's getting too long. One whole paper will be nothing but Quakers. Could we print two or three pieces? Mary and Wendlin remember more every day to tell me."

"Mary and Wendlin, eh? You don't call me Lute."

He regretted this, too, the minute he said it. He was not such a dullard as to have missed the fact that Crystal Raunce had a good deal of admiration for the editor she worked for; nor was he so ignorant of his own feelings as not to know that he enjoyed her admiration. But he wanted it all kept well under the surface.

Today, Crystal was tactful as well as admiring. She said, "Quakers want to be called by their first names," which let him drop the subject right there.

"What do you think about Mary and Wendlin?" he asked.

She leaned still farther toward him, so that the upper part of her body appeared to be resting on the counter like oranges on a tray. He wished she'd move; but he knew the girl well enough to know that when she was carried away by a subject, she forgot that she was anything but words.

"I love Mary and Wendlin, Mr. Cope. I feel honored to be on the same earth with them."

"You sound like your papa."

She was silent for a minute, digesting that. "I'm not like him, but I may have picked up some bad habits from him. I was at the Jessups' all morning."

"Is that why you're so happy?"

She looked at him with astonishment. "Could you tell I was happy?"

"Yes."

"How?"

"Oh, I've got my ways."

"I am happy, but not about the Jessups. I'm happy because of something Mama told me. She marked me with her wishes before my birth. She used to write poetry. You would never guess that in a thousand years, would you?"

"Oh, I don't know. My mother didn't write it. But she used to fill scrapbooks with poems she cut out of magazines and newspapers."

"Did she really?"

"She really did. After supper, I'd sing her a song and she'd read poetry to me."

"That sounds beautiful. My father wouldn't stand for anything like that. Mama never wrote another line after she was married. Except for him, I'd like to start singing and poetry-reading at home."

"He likely wouldn't mind. My stepfather was sure no poetry-lover, but he didn't raise any objections to a little poetry-reading."

"Mama is proud of me. I didn't know that before."

"They're all proud of us, Crystal, and we always disappoint them."

"I'm not going to disappoint mine."

"You'll be a better man than I am, then. My mother was proud of me, too. She worked and saved and had plans galore. She never let anything come between her and me, and she was a bright, good-looking woman who could've had all kinds of life and pleasures if she'd been the selfish kind. Anything she set her hand to, she was good at. She chose me because she loved me. And my reward to her has been to run off in her old age and leave her. I don't sing any more—except here at the office—and I don't suppose she's got anyone to read her poetry-clipping to nowadays."

He hadn't seen so much sorrow and concern in a face since he'd left the banks of the Feather. Tears filled Crystal's eyes, and didn't fall, but stayed there, darkening them. The blood beneath her white skin rose to the surface, and her lips trembled. She started to speak, but couldn't for the trembling. She leaned even farther across the breast-high counter and extended her hands to him. He took them without intending to do so, and his response to their lively clasping warmth was immediate. To feel so in the midst of his talk about his mother made him, in addition to everything else, a hypocrite. Where had his mind been, really, for all his talking of his old mother, alone with her clippings in that riverbank house?

"Oh, Lute," Crystal said, "don't be sad—I love you."

He dropped her hands at once. He retreated, putting the press as well as the counter between them. "Crystal, I've been intending to tell you this for some time. You ought to make an effort to curb that imagination of yours."

His words might as well have been bullets. She couldn't have looked more stricken if he had shot her. She dragged her arms and breasts off the counter. "All right," she said. "I'll try to. Thanks for telling me. If it's all right with you, I'll go home now."

She left the door open behind her, and Lute went over to close it. The office was still sun-warmed, but the air outside had grown solidly cold. Down the street, running for home, was Crystal. An impulse to run after her and explain his words—though what would his explanation be?—formed in his muscles, but he was able to control it. Still, glad as he was to have her leave, he didn't close the door, but continued to gaze after her. He was filled with an unexplained sadness. I seem always to be turning down love, he thought. Then he jeered at himself. How many times have you turned down love? But in a wave of sick understanding, he saw what the affection of a girl like Crystal might have meant to him if he had known how to accept it. He didn't know how, though, and actually he didn't think there was any way. You couldn't compromise with situations like this. You knew that, Mother, he thought.

The doorknob in his hand, as he watched Crystal, had a familiar, remembered feel. That night in his mother's high-and-dry house above the Feather came back to him, the night when he had closed the door behind Indy, running on tiptoe after his warning, out of his room and up the hall to her own. But that hadn't been a refusal of love, had it? He and Indy had been married in a few days.

And Crystal would be back to work on Monday.

And his words to her, if brusque, had been fortunate. He was still standing in the door, fearful lest the heartache that had let him alone for a while might be returning, when Base Cudlip came hustling up to the office. No matter what the facts were, it wouldn't have looked right to an outsider, seeing him and a sixteen-year-old down at the office on a Saturday afternoon holding hands.

"What's on your mind, Base?" he asked. Since the Mexican article, he and Base had not been on the best terms.

"I want you to come on over to the church with me."

"I could stand a little churchgoing, right now," Lute said.

"This is no joking matter."

"I'm not joking."

"Come on, then," Base said, and steered them off the main street. "We're going in the back way," he explained.

Eunice heard the voices and the steps, though she tried not to hear them. She tried to keep her world as small as the pine-knot whirlpool at her feet. She was cold and stiff, and the coldness and stiffness were also a protection. Sensations that shut out other and worse. An idea came into her reluctantly stirring mind, flooded it for one minute with living warmth. What if the steps were Tom's? What if he came running, lifted her in his arms and said, "My darling, the past is past. Come away with me. Marry me. Be my wife."

The warmth receded. Nothing would be changed. Going away with Tom might put them in the midst of other hills, under a bluer or darker sky; but what could change the blackness, the craving for blackness she now had? She would always watch him, always say, "Who now?" She had lived a life of sensation with Tom, and one sensation rather than another had proved stronger in its hold over her. She had set herself the task of loving him, no matter what he did. But she had loved what he did rather than the man: she had loved, without knowing it, the black thickening of her blood as she feared and suspected; she had loved the fierce, triumphant pain of seeing all of her suspicions and fears confirmed.

She was still on the floor, and was still resting her arms and face on the child's chair, when Basil and Lute came in. She lifted her head. Their expressions told her that they could see on her face the marks of her terrible knowledge. She let them stare at her without any apology and without any attempt to hide her face. What they were seeing was the truth.

Base Cudlip spoke first, in a low voice recognizing her disaster. "Where is he?"

"I don't know," she said.

"He was here ten or fifteen minutes ago."

"Maybe. I didn't see him."

Lute Cope spoke to Base as if she weren't present. "I don't believe she's taking in what you're saying." To her, he said, "Eunice, wouldn't you feel better off the floor?"

She let him help her up, and for a second or two, stiff and swaying with lightheadedness, had to hold onto his arm. She saw Base Cudlip's face tighten with disgust—and felt unmoved; she deserved it.

"Miss Fry," Base said, "you lied to me this morning, didn't you?"

"Yes," she said. "I did."

"You knew you were coming to the church, didn't you?"

"Yes."

"You were planning to meet him then, weren't you?"

"I was planning to come here, but I didn't have much hope of meeting him."

"Well, your hopes panned out, didn't they?"

"No."

"One lie a day I'll swallow. But that's my limit. I saw you and him not more than twenty minutes ago in that back room on the bed."

The facts she knew so well still had power to hurt. She looked at Lute, wondering if she ought, for Lute's sake, to say she was the woman. Such a lie could do no more than postpone. "I'm not surprised," she said. "But I was not the woman."

Lute spoke to Base, "Could you have made a mistake?"

"Raunce was all over her, I admit. But I saw her come here to the church after lying to me about it. I saw Raunce come here, and when I looked in the back room, there they were. If it wasn't her, who do you think it was? It looked like her then, and she acts like it was her now."

Eunice stared at the two men. "Raunce? Are you talking about Reverend Raunce?"

"Who do you think?"

Was it possible for people to live so separated from each other? In worlds so secret? They thought she had come to see LeRoy Raunce? That she could love *him*? A preacher, a married man? They had seen her for a year, talked to her, sized her up, and come to that conclusion? Her love and suffering, her damnation and death had been unnoticed? Was it possible they would be able to understand anything she would say?

"Reverend Raunce? I don't know anything about Reverend Raunce. I didn't know you were talking about him."

"Who did you think we were talking about?" Base asked.

She told the truth flatly. "I thought you were talking about Tom Mount."

"You came down here hoping to meet him? You came down to his room?"

She nodded. "Yes."

Base turned to Lute again. "What does that prove? Mount wasn't here; Raunce was. When a woman starts running after men, it's not the cut of his nose she's interested in. To a loose woman one man's about as good as another."

"I wish that were true," Eunice said.

Lute said, "Cudlip, my knowledge of loose women is limited, so I'm not going to dispute you there. But LeRoy's a man I know, and my impression is that he's not aware there's any other woman except his wife on earth."

"I saw him and I'm not blind. Spread-eagled over a woman."

He turned to Eunice accusingly. "What do you mean? Saying no one's been here? You could hear Raunce preaching half a mile away! What was the point of lying about that if you're so innocent? And he's so innocent?"

"I didn't hear him."

"Didn't hear him?"

"I heard something, but I didn't know what it was."

"That hardly seems reasonable, Eunice," Lute said, "he being next door to you here."

"I heard something, but I didn't think what it was."

Cudlip made a motion of anger and disgust. "This is the woman that teaches our children! Let's go see Raunce, Lute. For whatever reason, she's not in full possession of her senses."

Base left the room, but Lute lingered. "Are you all right, Eunice? You look sick."

That kindness determined her. "Please close the door," she said.

Lute didn't do it. Perhaps, she thought, he believes what Base said. Perhaps he thinks that having let two men slip through my fingers, I've become really desperate: to reassure him, she moved a couple of steps farther away.

They both heard Base stomp out of the church. Lute, as if that gave him permission to speak, said, "What can I do for you, Eunice?"

"Take care of Indy," she said.

"I don't know what you mean."

"Don't let what's happened to me happen to her."

"I don't know what's happened to you."

"I'm dead," she said, which she felt was the truth. But she made her request clear. "Don't let Indy fall in love with Tom Mount."

"Eunice, you're letting your imagination run away with you," he said for the second time that day. "You're not dead. And there's not the least danger of Indy's falling in love with Tom Mount. Your jealousy's painting pictures for you. Indy's a married woman. You seem to have forgotten that. She's not going to take Tom Mount away from you."

"She can't take him away from me. He's not mine. I'm not thinking about myself."

"I appreciate your thinking of me."

"I'm thinking of Indy."

"For a married woman, Tom don't have the same attraction he does for a spinster."

"Marriage has nothing to do with it."

"Married or unmarried then, Indy's the last woman in the world to be carried away by some charmer. She's wholesome to the core. I wonder you've failed to notice it."

"She's with Tom Mount now."

"How do you know that? Did you see them?"

"No."

"Did they tell you?"

"No."

"You've got a sick imagination, Eunice. A man's not the rarity to Indy he may be to you. She can go out for a ride to get a breath of fresh air or to talk over the war news with a man, the same as she would with a woman."

"Tom Mount's not interested in fresh air or the war news."

"With the right woman, he might be. Did you ever think of that,

Eunice? A man takes his cue from the woman. Now you go on home and forget all this nonsense about Indy and Tom Mount."

Outside, Base was waiting for Lute. He had the white, drawn look of a man who's been hurt. "I about give you up," he said.

"You had as well," Lute told him. "I find I can't go over to Raunce's with you after all."

"Why not?"

"Something's come up at home."

"Lute, I don't know whether you know it or not, but every time a problem comes up here on the Tract, you're someplace else. You write your editorials. But you don't do a thing to back them up. Lute, you're all wind and no weather."

"Maybe," Lute said, "I am. Maybe you've got my measure, Base."

"Break your measure, then. You've got growing girls. What're you for? Decency or Indecency? Marriage or Whoring? Black or White? You can't be for both."

"I never said I was."

"Come with me to Raunce's, then. I'm not going over there alone. What's said needs a witness."

"I can't go."

"You're weasling."

"I'm not weasling. I think Raunce needs questioning, but I can't go with you."

"Questioning? Well, what question would you suggest asking a preacher you saw on a bed with a woman not his wife? And that bed in a church? Suggest me a question, Lute. 'Were you laying on hands this afternoon, brother?' 'Did you make a new convert?'"

"One thing I don't think," Lute said, "is that this is any time for joking."

Base's face changed. It beseeched Lute now, without any scorn or anger. "Joking? I was trying to reach you, Lute. I was trying to speak to you where you would listen. Rectitude, Lute, what I'm talking about is rectitude."

He spoke the word in all of its syllables, both plainly and softly, the stiffness and inflexibility observed in every consonant, yet his lips and tongue wrapped round that stiffness and inflexibility with so much love the word came out smooth and velvety as a red rose.

"Rectitude, Lute, that's what I'm talking about. Rectitude. I'm far from home, Lute, and that's the reason. For the lack of rectitude I lost

336

my heritage. By rectitude I'll win it all back. Joking? Why, Lute, I'm nearer praying. You do what you're called to do now, Lute. And I'll do the same. But sooner or later we'll meet. Rectitude. In your heart you know it means as much to you as it does to me. Rectitude. That's my religion, Lute. Duty for the sake of right. It's a hard path, Lute, but the only one. You'll walk with me. A man of rectitude. That's all I ask to be called. When my time comes."

Base looked at Lute intently, then turned from him abruptly and headed down the street. Lute watched him pass the Raunces' and continue in the direction of the Jessups'. He envied Base—and admired him. A man who knew right from wrong and was willing to act for the right.

4    MARY often remembered the day she told Asa that dying was nothing more than accepting the idea of death, and of enduring pain. She hadn't changed her mind about it, but when she said it, she'd had a good deal more strength with which to contemplate death and endure pain. And she'd had a good deal less pain, too.

She supposed, since she'd accepted dying as the job ahead of her, each day's gain in weakness was a triumph. She tried not to fight her pain. It was leading her toward her destination. She tried not to fight her sickness by "taking care of herself." When she could be up and around, she was. When she could eat, she did. When the food had to come up, she let it. When the pain made her moan, as later she knew it would make her scream, she wrapped the pillow around her head, pleaded an attack of lumbago, and moaned.

She still had good days, unbelievably sunny plateaus on the dark downward climb. She still discovered food which for a day or two she could eat with pleasure and keep down. Buttermilk and graham crackers were at the minute causing her so little trouble she had her recurring conviction that the doctors had been mistaken.

A curtain parted, a fog lifted, when her pain and weakness momentarily let up. Views, which in better times were commonplace, were then flooded with golden light. Small things were treasures: a letter from Paula; one of old Wendlin's jokes; Ben, preparing for his exami-

337

nation over at Rose Park and asking her to quiz him on the Bible. To-day, she not only felt well but there was sunshine after the long rains. It all seemed sweet enough to justify a lifetime of suffering.

She and Opal were sharing a cup of tea before the hurly-burly of supper getting started: though her tea was buttermilk. She sat in the rocker that had belonged to her mother, in which she had been rocked as a child; and in which she had, in her turn, rocked Paula and Ben. There were some days now when the slightest movement started up her nausea, but this afternoon she was able to rock gently as she sipped. That movement was all that was needed to put Eternity into the room. Death was already there, but the faintly creaking sound of the rocker brought back her mother and the stone farmhouse in Pennsylvania. And here, between the two graves, her mother's and her own, she and Opal were alive and talking.

Opal was eating a slice of the spice cake with penuche icing which she had made that morning at Mary's request, because it was a favorite of Wendlin's. Mary was trying in every way she knew to make Wendlin's last days happy. Last days with her, she meant. And there was nothing egotistical in her recognizing that her death would be a sorrowful loss for Wendlin. For thirty-five years, Wendlin had been telling her that she was his life. And whatever else old Wendlin was, he was no storyteller.

"Opal," she said, "I've been thinking about what's to become of Wendlin after I'm gone."

"If matchmaking is what's on your mind, you can leave me out," Opal said. "I've been wondering if having me bake this cake was the beginning of your campaign to prove to Wendlin that I'd be a good second choice."

"Opal," she said, "you don't have a thing to worry about. I haven't leveled my sights on you. You wouldn't suit Wendlin at all."

"Why?" Opal asked. "I'm finished with marrying, but I'd like to know what's wrong with me."

"There's nothing wrong with you. But Wendlin's never been used to anything but a brokenhearted woman."

If Opal asked her any questions, Mary was willing to answer them, but she didn't intend to volunteer any explanations. Opal remained silent.

"Eunice is the one I have in mind," Mary said.

Opal put down her teacup with a clink. "What makes you think Eunice is brokenhearted?"

338

Personally, Mary thought the reason was that like recognizes like, but she didn't care to bring herself into the conversation again. "It shows on her. I think she set her heart on somebody she couldn't marry when she was a girl."

"What makes you think Wendlin would want a woman with her heart set on someone else?"

"At his age, Wendlin wants respect. Anything stronger would make him uneasy."

Opal stirred her tea a long time, picked up her cup, and put it down without having taken a sip.

"Eunice is a lot younger than Wendlin."

"I know that, but she doesn't act young. In a lot of ways, Opal, you're the youngest of the two. You know that yourself."

"I don't think Eunice feels any pull toward Wendlin."

"Of course not," Mary said. "Wendlin's a married man. And I'm not expecting her to fall in love with him, even after I'm gone—at his age, and a plain, practical old fellow. But he's the best man I ever knew. Being good and turning women's heads don't seem to go together. I know. And turning a woman's head would embarrass Wendlin. It would go against his grain."

"Maybe the idea of a woman's falling in love with Wendlin goes more against your grain, Mary, than you're willing to credit."

Mary protested. "It's Wendlin I'm thinking about. I want someone level headed but young enough to look after him in his old age. Old Wendlin's used to being looked after. Why, he's never ironed a shirt or fried an egg in his life. Shel Lewis was over here the other day. You know Joicey's expecting? Well, Shel gets up every morning nowadays and gets breakfast for the whole family. I tell you, old Wendlin stared at Shel when he heard that as if he was listening to a cruel, inhuman story. Inside a house, Wendlin's as helpless as a baby. He comes in, picks up the *Emporia Gazette*, and is lost to the world till you say 'supper.' He knows where every army's located this minute in Europe. But ask him where his socks are and he's baffled. He needs a strong, steady, solemn girl like Eunice to take care of him."

"Eunice is the one you'll have to convince, not me."

"Eunice is a reasonable girl. She's already gambled and lost. I can tell that. Second choice is all she can expect now. When I'm gone, Opal, I want you to promise me you'll do all you can for this match. That's why I'm telling you this now."

"I don't know what I can do, Mary. Telling Wendlin and Eunice it

339

was your dying wish is not the right way to start a love match."

"I'm not dying at the minute. And I don't want them told. And it don't need to be a love match. Have Wendlin over to supper. Let nature take its course. That's all I ask of you."

"I can have Wendlin over easy enough. But I'm bound to tell you, Mary, I've tried my hand at matchmaking before with Eunice, and nothing came of it. Or at least no wedding."

"God was saving her for Wendlin."

"He like to let her die in the process, if He was."

"I'm not asking any questions about Eunice. I told you I knew she was brokenhearted. It'll make her appreciate Wendlin."

Mary put down her cup. There were times when, without the reminder of pain, she felt death to be very near. Such a moment had come now. Her heart had stopped beating, her lungs had stopped sucking in air, and she hovered in calm consciousness a little above the outworn body of Mary Jessup. Now that old Wendlin was taken care of, what remained to be done?

Mary was still floating free of her body and far removed from all temporal problems when she saw Basil Cudlip, with that walk of his which called every other man lazy, coming toward the house. Curiosity alone brought her back down into her body. I'm not as bad off as I thought, she told herself. Not as finished with life as I supposed, if Cudlip can call me back. Basil still wore the clumping boots with which he had climbed the Kentucky hills; still sported the cap with ear flaps, as if California's mild climate was a rumor in which he did not put any faith.

"Look out the window," Mary said to Opal.

"And they say lightning never strikes twice in the same place. Don't he ever come, except when I'm here?"

"Oh, yes. He's over here haranguing Wendlin, in season and out."

"Do you feel like seeing him?"

"In the best of health, I don't feel like seeing Base. He's always got a chip on his shoulder. But ask him in."

The chip on Base's shoulder wasn't visible this afternoon. He had a mild stricken air. "Mrs. Jessup, I know Wendlin's not home. And I know you've been feeling poorly lately. But something's come up makes me need your help. Do you feel like going over to the Raunces' with me for a short visit?"

"Don't tell me that cow's done something unladylike again, Basil?"

340

Base said, "I'm used to Wendlin's being a cutup, Mrs. Jessup. I thought you might take things a little more seriously."

"Now, Wendlin's as serious as can be underneath his joking, and you know it, Base Cudlip."

"I didn't mean any slight to Wendlin. I reckon I better come right out with it. I caught LeRoy over there in the church with a woman."

"You can catch him there every Sunday with several."

"Well," he said, "you're asking for the tree with the bark on it and I can give it to you that way. The Reverend LeRoy Raunce was in bed with a woman."

"What woman?"

"Eunice Fry."

"It wasn't Eunice," Opal said. "I know that."

"Were you over there?" Base asked.

"No, but I know it wasn't Eunice."

"Was she here with you ladies?"

"No."

"She was at the church. She lied to me this morning about going there. I looked in, just to prove my suspicions, and she was there. Then later I saw Raunce go over. After awhile I looked in again, and the two of them was on the bed together. I got Lute Cope to go over with me. Raunce had cleared out by that time, but if ever I talked with a guilty-looking woman, it was Eunice Fry."

"We're all guilty," Mary told him. "And her guilty looks aside, what did Eunice say?"

"Say? Under the circumstances, what you'd expect. She said it wasn't her!"

"Are you sure it was her?"

"Unless LeRoy keeps a harem over there, who else could it be?"

"Maybe it was his wife."

"LeRoy lives a hundred yards from the church. He don't have to meet his wife—for that purpose—at the church. That don't make sense, does it, Mrs. Jessup?"

"Sense, from what you say, isn't what LeRoy was trying to make."

"Mrs. Jessup, you've got your ideas of what's funny and I've got mine. His wife or a stranger, the church is no place for a preacher to be with a woman."

"He was in Tom Mount's bedroom, I suppose."

"It's a part of the church. You don't need to go with me. Mrs. Tet-

341

ford, here, will go. I thought, for Mrs. Raunce's sake, it would be more delicate to have a woman with me."

Opal said, "I won't go. I don't care anything about delicacy any more."

"Base," Mary asked, "why don't you go get your own wife for this visit?"

"My wife's been protected from ugliness. An ugly happening like this would upset her."

"I'm already upset," Mary admitted. "I'll go with you, Base."

The Raunces were all at home. Mary could see Crystal in the dining room, seated in the midst of some sort of playhouse of orange boxes. Burleigh was astride the ironing board, which was set up in the center of the sitting room, driving his sister, who was on the floor in front of him and hitched up like a horse.

LeRoy closed the door to the dining room, sent Burleigh and Bernita out to play, took down the ironing board, cleared enough newly ironed shirts and B.V.D.s off the chairs to make room for his guests, and smiled his pleasure at the visit.

"Mary, I'm happy to see you're feeling better. Base, I've been praying you'd get over your feelings about that cow. I'm sorry to see your wife isn't with you. Ain't this glorious weather? After all that rain, it was a real tribulation not to be able to get outside today. But I set this day aside to practice on my sermon."

"We've been hearing you," Base said.

"I hope I didn't get to trumpeting too loud? You folks've been church people all your lives. It's still new to me. The glorious gospel, and me publishing it! I forgive myself for getting carried away now and then, and hope you'll do the same. I'll tone it down in time."

Mary half expected Base to drop the matter he had come over about. She tended to credit people with motives as good as her own. She would hate to cut a man down in the midst of his rejoicing. Base evidently had no such compunction.

"Mrs. Raunce," he said, "they say the wife's always the last to know, so this may be news to you. You thought your husband went over to the church to practice his sermon this afternoon, didn't you?"

Mary interrupted Base. "Dolly, Eunice Fry was at the church. Base says your husband was making love to her. Eunice denies it."

"Eunice Fry?" LeRoy had a fit of laughing. "Well, Dolly," he said, "you'll have to share the honor with me. You're no more first than

342

I am. Base, you've got a wonderful faculty for sniffing out sin. But this time you've outsniffed yourself."

"I saw you on the bed in Tom Mount's room with Eunice Fry. That wasn't sniffing. It's seeing."

"It wasn't Eunice," Dolly Raunce said, in a hesitant, choking voice. "I was listening to LeRoy practice, and on our way out—we stopped in there." She reddened as she spoke, but she looked Base in the eye.

"Mrs. Raunce," Base said, "if I was in your husband's shoes, I'd hope my wife would do for me what you're doing for LeRoy. But it's plain to see that the very idea of what we're talking about makes you blush."

Raunce came and stood over Cudlip. "What *are* you talking about, Cudlip?"

Base got to his feet. "There's ladies present, Raunce."

"It's a little late for you to be thinking of the ladies. Anything the Bible can say, Base, you can say. The ladies here have all read that Book. If you've got something Biblical on your mind, Base, you spit it out."

"Raunce, you're not fit to preach the gospel."

"I may not be. But using gospel language don't unfit me. And loving my wife don't unfit me. And scorning dirtmongers don't unfit me. And telling the truth don't unfit me."

"So you're trying to tell us that it was your wife? There may be some excuse for a man sneaking off to meet another woman in church. But your own wife? What's the excuse for that? If you don't respect her, you might at least have some respect for a holy building."

"Holy building! That building's a building, no more holy than any other."

"It's a church. Don't you call a church holy?"

"What's a church, Cudlip?"

"Don't beat the devil around the bush, Raunce. The church, to you, is a building where you preach on Sunday and where on weekdays you——."

"Go on, Base," LeRoy said. "Finish it."

Base remained silent.

"If you won't tell me, I'll tell you," LeRoy went on. "You heard me preach in a tent for pretty near a year. That tent's folded up now, and been sold secondhand. But God wasn't sold with the canvas, and when we pulled up the tent pegs, we didn't uproot God. We're the church, Basil. You and me and Mary and Eunice and Wendlin and

Lizzie. No building's a church. Where we meet don't matter a hoot in the eyes of God. Here's as good a place as any, or an oil derrick, or an outhouse, or a dry-goods store. A building don't make an act holy. It don't take a steeple and a cross to get God's attention. He'll hearken to you wherever you are. Hearts and souls are what interest Him, not buildings."

"There's a time and place for everything."

"I thought we were talking about places? You're entitled to an opinion about places. But time, my time, is none of your business."

"You admit it all, then?"

"All? All? With a mind like yours, Cudlip, all's liable to cover a good deal of ugly territory. You saw me with my wife in Tom Mount's bedroom. Now if anybody's pardon's to be asked, it's Tom's. God don't care about time, and He don't care about buildings, and He made marriages and men and women Himself. But I don't expect the same broadmindedness from humans I get as a gift from God. That was a private room, and I was overstepping my rights to go in there without Tom's permission. I'll ask his pardon. But I don't ask your pardon, and there's nothing I've done this day I need to ask God's pardon for. And what I don't need to ask God to forgive me for, I sure don't need to ask Base Cudlip to forgive. I pray God to forgive you your smutty mind. But there's nothing in my heart but praise for my blessed Saviour, who has made my life so rich in love. Let us pray."

Base slammed his fist down on the center table. "Pray after I've gone, if you want to. But I'm through hearing you pray, in church or out."

He turned to leave, but Dolly Raunce put a hand on his sleeve.

"Mr. Cudlip," she said, "you've stirred up a mulish streak in LeRoy. He won't give you the satisfaction now of telling you the facts. We were in that room but we weren't . . ."

Raunce would not let his wife finish.

"Dolly, some things are private. Some things, we don't have to apologize for."

Mary saw, but no one else, the dining-room door being slowly opened. Crystal Raunce, white-faced and red-eyed, entered the room and walked over to Cudlip.

"I couldn't help overhearing what you said, Mr. Cudlip. Papa's been over at the church all afternoon, but not Mama. She's been here with me. She couldn't do anything like that. I wouldn't put anything past my father, but don't go accusing my mother of licentiousness. She was here talking poetry with me. See that paperweight? She won it for a poem called 'Evening.' While you were watching my father, she and I were talking poetry and finding words to rhyme, and remembering olden times. That's about as far as you can get from what you're talking about, isn't it?"

Cudlip said to Mary, "This puts a different face on matters, wouldn't you agree, Mrs. Jessup?"

5   ON THE Tract that night, people feeding their stock observed the yellow afterglow, smelled the crisp dryness of the air, and went inside to eat fried potatoes and read in their day-old papers that German submarines had sunk another neutral vessel, without any thought of danger closer at hand. Old Silver, at Shel Lewis's, did howl a good deal, but he was old, thin-skinned, and given to complaining. When the deepening cold hit the sockets of his lost teeth and began to penetrate his rib cage, he felt sorry for himself and would not stay in the barn, but came to the back steps, and sat there and howled.

Shel had had a hard day, and neither Silver's howling nor Zoomy's insistence that the dog be let in to sit by the fire did anything to soothe him.

"No, for the last time," he told Zoomy. "I'm not going to have fleas hopping off him onto the carpet and the house smelling like a dog kennel."

"He's cold," Zoomy said.

"Cold," Shel snorted. "He don't know what cold is. And you don't either. There isn't any blizzard blowing, is there? You don't see any icicles, do you? He's not standing in a snowdrift, is he? No, it's a fine, clear evening after a sunny day, and if that hound's getting too old to be comfortable after the sun goes down, he's getting too old to live. I've been thinking that for some time, anyway."

Zoomy knew he had and didn't say another word. But, when Shel wasn't looking, he went out and sat with his arms around the old hound, warming and quieting him.

Shel walked to the west window. Outside, the night was clear as a bell, with the stars shining and his grove, on the slope below the house, like an orchard he'd dreamed. He had time to gaze because they were waiting supper for Chad. Shel was hungry, and he wished the boy would put in an appearance. He had had a long day, and the drop in the temperature had sharpened his appetite.

People generally are not prepared for nature's being a quick-change artist. Yesterday, the Tract had had rain, today sunshine. Tonight a freeze? That was rushing things a little, wasn't it? Their senses had not caught up with the sunshine yet, let alone anything else. In their mind's ears they could still hear the eaves dripping. Besides, there were all those reassuring billboards preaching "Ideal climate for citrus fruit." A freeze could hardly be called ideal. And if a cold snap came, the Tract had a soldier's healthy confidence; amidst the carnage, others might die, but it would be spared. Anaheim, Fullerton, Orange, Santa Ana, Pomona, Monrovia, Riverside, Norwalk, Gardena, Riviera, Puente, Los Nietos, Corona, Azusa, these districts might get it in case of frost, but not the Tract.

Shel, in particular, felt safe. Not only was he on high ground, but having weathered wind and drought, he felt that no more suffering would be required of him. He felt like Job, on the far side of his boils. The worst was over; though there was still a good deal amiss generally.

It was this general plenty that had him upset, and he was taking his irritation out on Zoomy, on Old Silver, on the tardy Chad, and even on blameless Joicey. He had said he was hungry, and Joicey had said, "Let's wait supper a few minutes and see if Chad doesn't come." So, all right. If that's where Joicey's heart was, fine and dandy. It didn't matter that her husband was famished. They'd wait supper, let the pork chops fry to leather, on the chance that her irresponsible son would turn up sometime before midnight.

Chad had a job working on the new road, "the boulevard," it was called. According to Sylvester Perkins, the boulevard would be, in time, the thoroughfare connecting Los Angeles and the Imperial Valley. In fact, Syl expected Los Angeles to suffer a setback as a metropolis after the boulevard was finished.

"I am already figuring on moving my main office to the Tract," he said. "Los Angeles is bound to go downhill. It's an inland city. The harbors are down at San Pedro and Long Beach. L.A. either gets too much water in a wet season, when the Los Angeles River floods, or too little in a dry season, when the river dries up. I wouldn't tell everyone this, but you folks on the Tract had as well know it. We've got the town of the future right here in our midst."

346

So, Sylvester Perkins. But Sylvester Perkins as an expert on the future was not quite the prophet he once had been. The memory of Sylvester Perkins's past prophecies that had not turned out got in the way. Shel, if he had known how to deal with Syl's slipperiness, would either have eaten his supper without waiting for Chad or waited cheerfully, without making himself out to be the starving victim of a heartless wife and thoughtless son.

Joicey came to join him at the window. "There's no need our waiting any longer, Shel. I can dish up right now."

"What're we running here? A cafeteria? No, I'll wait."

"Chad'll surely be here in a minute or two."

"He's probably not coming at all. He's probably out somewhere mooning around with that Cope girl. I swear to God, I'd have too much pride to keep courting a girl who kept giving me the mitten."

Joicey, at that, went back to the kitchen. She had had her fill of what was wrong with the Copes—and Chad—recently.

Shel was mad at all the Copes. Lute had promised to come over that very afternoon and talk with him and Bert Kinsella and Travis Burdg about the latest water assessment. Wendlin hadn't showed up either; but everyone knew there were days when Wendlin couldn't leave Mary. LeRoy, holding down two full-time jobs, had his excuses. Cudlip's absence was mourned by no one. No one had asked him to come, as a matter of fact; but Base was usually so sure he had the answer to everyone else's problem that he had been expected to arrive with a solution for this, which was his own problem. But Lute's absence was not excused.

Shel, though he was beginning to forget how much he had once expected of Lute, still suffered some of the pangs of disappointment. Because he expected more of him, he punished Lute in his mind for what he would not have held against another man. He had promised Burdg and Kinsella that Lute would be present, and Lute's presence would have been the making of the meeting. Shel felt like a small boy who has promised the kids that the best ballplayer in town is his personal friend and will show up and pitch a shutout game for them against their old enemies. He doesn't show up, and the kids, being kind, say, "Well, he probably understood it was another day." Or another game or another place, or someone else asking him to come, Shel thought sourly.

The truth was, he and Chad were in the same boat, both making fools of themselves, both wooing the Copes, who thought themselves better than the hillbilly Lewises. That the Copes might actually think

347

this didn't go against his grain so much as the fact that the idea had occurred to him. He wasn't responsible for what the Copes thought. But for Shel Lewis's thoughts, he was taking high responsibility. And by God, he was finished with that old backwoods chip-on-the-shoulder conviction "They think they're better than we are." If they did, they were either right or wrong: and the opinion either way wasn't worth two hoots in a hot place, except as time proved or contradicted it.

Joicey, who couldn't bear to be on the outs with him for more than a few minutes, came back from the kitchen.

"What did you decide this afternoon about the assessments?"

Joicey was trying to take his mind off the passing of time and his hunger. She didn't know straight up about assessments. Or cars. But he took some of his meanness out on the poor girl. All right, kiddo, he thought, you asked for this, now you stand right there and keep on pretending.

"We decided to go to law," he said.

That shocked her. "You mean sue?" she asked.

Joicey was brought up better than he had been, but for her folks, too, the law had been what you hoped nobody would use against you. If you had trouble, you "took the law in your own hands"; you did this, first, because you didn't have the money it took to "go to law," and, second, because you didn't have much confidence in the law, anyway, especially if you were in trouble with a big bug. Your ideas about the big bugs were such that, except in spiteful, underhanded ways, it never occurred to you to come out in the open and fight them as your equals. It didn't occur to you for the very good reason that you knew damn good and well you weren't their equal.

"Sue is what I mean," he said.

Joicey couldn't have looked more stricken if he'd announced he had double pneumonia. But she surprised him by asking, "Do you think you can win?"

"I think so. It looks like Sylvester Perkins is swindling us, or trying to. It looks like he's bit off more here than he can chew. He under-figured on what it would cost to set up a water system. When we bought our land, we bought stock in a water company. That means we own the pumps, wells, the water, and all that goes to pump and pipe it. As long as we keep up our payments, the water stock belongs to us as much as our ranches do. But Syl got hard pressed for money, and sold water-company stock elsewhere to raise it. That's what we figure, anyway. Well, that got him over one hump. He had the money to finish sinking the wells. Now he's got to have money to pay interest on the stock he sold. To get that, he's had to levy assessments on the stock owners here on the Tract. We expected to pay assessments for running expenses. But men who've never irrigated have been assessed. That's where Syl made his big mistake. That's what roused our suspicions."

He stopped and looked at Joicey. He had forgotten that he was talking to an opponent to make her suffer, and had begun to speak to a wife, to his Joicey, a woman red-cheeked from leaning over a pan of pork chops, five months along, and trying to please her husband.

"Honey, you got an old rascal for a husband. I'm worried and I'm taking it out on you."

Joicey leaned against him. "Where would you get the money to go to law?"

"If everyone on the Tract put what he's paying in assessments into feeing a lawyer, we'd have the money."

"If you sued, could you put a stop to the assessments?"

"We could if we won."

Joicey didn't say anything for a while. Then she looked up at him tremulously. "If you lost, would they put you in jail?"

Shel stared down at his wife. "Going to law don't mean if the other side ain't guilty, we are. If somebody's tried for murder, it don't mean that if he's found innocent, the man who accused him's guilty."

"If I was guilty of murder I'd accuse somebody else."

"Forget murder."

"Well, you were the one who . . ."

"I know I was. I made a mistake. And so far we don't have any proof about Syl."

He had talked himself out of his meanness. He didn't have to pretend to be a man with a selfish wife and an inconsiderate son any longer. "Let's eat," he said. "The smell of those pork chops has been driving me crazy for the past half hour."

"I've been trying to get you to eat for the past half hour," Joicey reminded him.

When Shel had thought, Chad's just as crazy as I am, courting those Copes, he had been absolutely right. The minute Chad finished work on the road, he had headed straight for the Cope ranch. That detour added two miles to his three-mile walk home, but even after a day with the pick and shovel, it was nothing if he could see Press.

He saw her, but that was about all. The girls were alone, Press cooking supper, Hannah doing the chores. Press kissed him, then kicked him out. There was no prettier way to put it. She kicked him out without reason—unless she didn't love him. Her folks weren't home, there was a good supper cooked on the stove, there was no reason for her not asking him to stay—unless she didn't love him. But, also, there was no reason for her throwing her arms around his neck, kissing him, and clinging to him unless she did love him.

"I am worried about Mama," she told him. That was the sole reason she gave him for getting rid of him.

He was willing to stay and worry with her. He knew more about her mother than she did.

He had seen her mother with Tom Mount around noon, headed toward Fullerton in Tom Mount's red car. The coincidences of life are such that there are times when a word overheard or a look intercepted appears as the answer fate is giving us to questions we have been unable, up to this time, to answer in our own lives. We have heard a thousand words and seen a thousand gestures that are self-contained and without bearing on our own lives. Then, one pertinent glance, and we are reinforced in our conviction that we are earth's center and that all of its happenings are calculated to bring us messages.

He had emptied his wheelbarrow of oiled gravel and was facing the old unsurfaced road, which at that point paralleled the new boulevard, when Mount drove by. Press's mother faced Mount, and there was in her face a look Chad could not name, but which summed up the answer to a question he had been asking himself. The question was, What is love? He said he loved Press, and Press said she loved him. What did they mean? He did not know, but this was love's look: waiting, open, listening, ready to become. When Press kicked him out, sent him away because she was worried about her mother, he left her, thinking of the look he had seen on Indy Cope's face. That look was what he wanted from Press. When he got that, kissing wouldn't matter. It would be an addition, but it wouldn't matter.

He didn't linger a second after Press's dismissal, but slanted homeward, not seeing a thing or thinking of a thing but Indy Cope's look. At the Jessups' place he woke up a little. Wendlin was driving into the yard with a load of wood from the oil fields. Wendlin did not glance his way, and Chad, not wishing to talk, passed silently by. He saw Mrs. Jessup watching her husband out of a lamplit window. This was

350

his day for seeing women gazing at men. It was like fording a stream, being for a minute part of something that took no account of him. He envied the Jessups their contented old age. Would Press wait for him like that someday?

The Raunces' house was dark, all gone to bed, or lights out and everybody praying. No telling what that queer family might be up to. Indy Cope had love, the Raunces had God, the Jessups had each other, but he was absolutely alone. He hadn't even the comfort of an enemy. Who was there he could fight? Who was his rival? He didn't know who his rival was. Who separated him from Press? Was it Indy? He would never leave Press. Nor was he going to take her in his arms and say, "I'll show you what I mean by love," because that wasn't what he meant. Or was at least only part of what he meant, and a part he had decided a long time ago he wasn't going to have outside of marriage in that mean woods-colting way he had so much reason to hate.

From horizon to horizon, the world was roofed with stars, and he and one hoot owl were its only occupants. Once again he had broken his heart on Press; but he had discovered that what was broken in the evening would heal in the night. Since there was no rival he could challenge, he challenged the night and space. He challenged the deepening cold. He challenged the hills that lay between himself and home, and conquered them like enemies; the cold went through his clothes like water, but he was warm.

On the back steps at home, he stumbled onto Zoomy and Old Silver, huddled together like sweethearts under one lap robe.

"What're you doing out here?" he asked.

"Keeping Old Silver warm."

"Why don't you take him inside?"

"Papa won't let me."

"You can't spend the night out here."

"I can. The cold makes Silver sick."

"He ought to be put out of his misery."

"He don't have any misery when I'm with him."

"You can't hardly give up your life to that," Chad said, though he knew it was possible.

He took Zoomy and Old Silver out to the barn, and showed Zoomy how to make the old dog a nest in the straw, and cover him with one of the upturned packing cases that had brought their household goods from Kentucky.

351

"He'll get out," Zoomy said.

"No, he won't," Chad said, and put two bags of rolled barley on top of the packing case. "That takes care of Old Silver."

"Papa's mad," Zoomy told him on the way back to the house, repaying favor with favor.

"Too bad about Papa," Chad said.

Their father and mother were eating when they came in. His mother got up from the table. "You boys look cold."

Chad held his hands over the stove. "I think it's going to freeze tonight."

The idea had not occurred to him before, but the minute he heard the words, he believed them. They explained the current of iciness, that river of cold he had been walking through all the way home.

"What's the thermometer say?" his father asked.

"I didn't look."

"Go look," his father said. "It may not matter to you, but the rest of us here have some interest in whether the trees survive or not."

Chad looked and came back. "Thirty-eight," he said.

"What're you talking about freezing for?" his father asked. "I don't know what makes people out here take on so much about the cold. Back home, thirty-eight was considered balmy."

6    THERE was a Mexican eating place called Ortega's, a shack, really, on the east edge of Anaheim. Ortega's was an oasis of bare, sandy ground in the midst of the groves that bordered the town. The lack of growth about the restaurant was emphasized by two great fan palms, which spread their fronds like atolls of green a hundred feet above it.

Tom looked up as he got out of the car, and said, "Gardens in the sky."

Indy, when Tom said that, thought, Gardens in the sky, heavens on earth. But she said nothing. Talk might lessen the horror of something terrible, but one word might cause the dream palace of happiness to tumble down. If it was a dream palace. She didn't want to find out. She put her hand through Tom's arm, and they went into the place without a word.

352

The room was almost as bare as the yard, a half a dozen tables without covering of any kind, four Mexicans at one of the tables, drinking, and, behind a shoulder-high partition, Mr. Ortega, the owner, clanking away at his stove.

"I'll go phone Lute," Tom said when he had seated Indy.

"What're you going to tell him?"

"Oh, that we had a blowout, ran out of gas, broke an axle."

"We didn't," Indy said.

She had said that because her first thought, or her first feeling, *before* she began to think was, It is wrong to lie. But immediately after that, she thought pridefully, And Tom knows it is wrong and he can do it.

Tom smiled down at her. He wasn't perturbed, he wasn't in a hurry, he didn't have anything better to do than to talk to her. He delighted in her when, as now, she was most Indy, foolishly straining gnats and swallowing camels; he saw the foolishness, but didn't ask her to change. He was not comparing her with anyone else.

"Do you want me to tell him the truth?" he asked.

She knew it was not a make-believe question. He would do it; he would accept the responsibilities of the truth, if she would. There was warm color under his olive skin; his blue eyes had deepened, the irises were wide and dark. In his face she saw the happiness she felt. It was very odd, her feelings mirrored on another face: odd and satisfying to see the person she was, inside, come to life outside in the countenance and bearing of another. She felt the joy of a search ended, a search of the kind one struggles through in a long night of dreams, not knowing what one looks for until the treasure is found. She felt that she had been told in her cradle, and only now remembered it, "You will never be happy until you see your own feelings mirrored on another's face."

Now the search was ended: What did she do now? Had that also been whispered to her in her cradle? Was there more to life than what she now had? It didn't seem possible. She wanted to stay where she was, her body still enchanted, yet conscious of her enchanter and able to speak to him. That was the real magic: to be rational and irrational, animal and human, body and soul, wicked and loving, at once; and, above all, to be man and woman, reconciled. All contradictions reconciled. Reconciled? Was that the word? One blotting out the other? No, not contradictions reconciled, for in this moment she could see that there were no contradictions, only that elements which

353

ordinarily were not used had hindered. But used. Not reconciled. All used. All participating. The enchantment was in that, in the addition and multiplication, until she, feeling what she had never before felt, which in itself was more life than she had ever before known, had also Tom beside her to shine it all back, to save her from the terrible loneliness of solitary joy.

There was no real need of speech between them. It was a luxury. They used it as others might use a sudden ability to fly or walk on water: as a pleasure, an excess, a confirmation of endless capabilities, as a sign that they were rich enough to be wasteful.

When Tom had said "Do you want me to tell him the truth?" he knew her answer before he asked the question. She did not want him to tell Lute the truth. She was not ready for that yet.

He stayed beside her smiling, for another minute. He did not touch her. The new touch might arrest the shimmering resplendency of the old, which still enveloped them. Inside the world called real, which they could see more vividly than usual, they still lived, in a world of their own, a delicate world of touch and tenderness.

Tom said, "You want me to lie, then?"

She didn't have to answer. Tom had said the word. He said all words without fear, and by doing so, exempted her. He to be bold and she to exclaim, "Oh, Oh." That was what she had longed for; not the unnatural other way around.

"Yes, I want you to," she said. And added, "Will he believe it?"

"Lute," Tom said, "has been practicing all of his life to believe what he wants to believe. I don't have any reason to think he's going to change this evening. Do you?"

To agree to this seemed a greater infidelity to Lute than any she had yet practiced. Because she had lived as she had, as if she and her body were not one, the straying body's sin was like the wandering away of some pet, valued perhaps, but from which too much had never been expected. But her mind, her reason, her judgment, these constituted, she had always believed, her true self; her body was no more than a wheelbarrow or knapsack to provide them transportation. If with words she passed this judgment upon Lute, then she did betray him. She could not do that. With words, and words alone, she had espoused Lute, and with words she still felt a compulsion to be faithful. Tom seemed to know all about this, too. Both his insight and his incisiveness startled her.

Before he left her to phone, he asked Mr. Ortega to bring her an order of tacos. She could not eat them; she no longer lived in the realm of eaters, people who cut, forked up, and swallowed food. But she was pleased that Tom had thought of them. Lute would never have done so. A platter of food before the regular meal? Nothing ahead of time, out of place, conspicuous. She and Lute would never have been in a Mexican eating place at all; and once there, Lute would have acted as if they weren't. She and Lute had driven by Ortega's many times, and she had suggested stopping. Lute always kept on going. "I have nothing against Mexicans," he would explain. "I'm interested in them. I'll read a book on their eating habits any day. But it stands to reason that the food they've developed suits them better than it does us."

"Why does it?" Indy had asked.

"Otherwise we would've developed it ourselves. There's no patent on mixing cornmeal, meat, and chili together."

"We could just go in and see, perhaps. Not guess."

"All we would do would be to make the Mexicans uncomfortable. And make it necessary for us to down some food that might stick in our craws. But this is your evening," he had told her, the last time she had asked. "I told you we'd go wherever you wanted and do whatever you wanted. If you still want to go to Ortega's, I'll turn around and we'll go back there. I'm yours to command. We can be back there in ten minutes. What do you say? Shall I turn around?" They hadn't, of course, turned around, and she was glad. Lute was necessarily in her mind, but she did not want him also in this room.

As she waited for Tom, she remembered the dining room where she and the young man who had driven her to the Tract that first night had eaten. There had been a Mexican cook there, too. She had forgotten the young man's name, which was strange since she could remember his wife's—Rosalie. But that night when she and the young man reached the tent, she had felt that she couldn't part with him, that she could not bear for their conversation to cease. She had felt then that any sudden word or touch, any unexpected springing up of a night wind or crying of a bird, would have pushed her into saying, "Don't go. Never leave me." There had been in him, also, she knew, the same reluctance to part, and that had made her silence more difficult.

She was glad that she had not spoken, of course, but all of her powers of resistance had perhaps been used up that evening; and all of her powers of receptivity and loving stirred up. Fate had, without her knowing it, been kind to her, saving her for Tom.

355

7    THE MINUTE she got home from the Raunces', Mary took a painkiller. She hated to become dependent upon them, and up to this time she had never taken one until bedtime; but tonight she was determined to call on the Cudlips. She was already in misery, and without the painkiller the trip would be impossible. It hurt her pride to swallow it, but she felt there was something more important at stake than her pride.

Base was set on seeing that LeRoy did not get the call to the ministry at the new church. About that, she and Wendlin might be unable to do a thing to help. But helping LeRoy did not seem very important to her now. Base was the one who needed help. All of her life she had excused herself from trying to understand men like Base. "That man's beyond me," she would tell Wendlin, speaking of some fellow human whose beliefs or practices seemed too outlandish for her to comprehend.

She had tried to help the victims of these men: black men, poor men, the men with outlandish religions. She didn't have a blind spot when it came to them. But she had had a blind spot about their oppressors. She hadn't tried to see what it would be like to stand in *their* shoes. "They're beyond me," she dismissed them. She had treated such persons as bears or polecats. "Beyond my ken," she'd sum them up, taking pride in her miniature ken like a Chinese woman in her tiny feet.

She had bound up the wounds of the afflicted. She had suffered with the wronged and the innocent. But she had shied away from the task of trying to understand the wrongdoers, the despoilers of innocence, the haters, the belittlers.

At the Raunces' that afternoon, a door of insight had been opened for her. She had expected to feel sorry for poor LeRoy, caught in an undignified (to say the very least) act, denounced before his family, threatened with the loss of his pulpit, deserted by his own daughter. But through that door of insight she had seen LeRoy and Base in a different light. She saw that LeRoy was going to require from his congregation, if he ever got one, much love and understanding. But LeRoy could be safely left to God. He had never, as most men have,

356

been evicted from Eden. There he still lived, praising God and loving Eve.

Base, on the other hand, was still beyond her ken. But the insight that had come to her about him was that if she hurried, there might yet be time for her to enlarge her ken. Base needed someone to say, and mean it, "Basil, tell me all about it." Opposition only whetted Base's animosity. The wounds Base would be responsible for in after years, she wouldn't be able to bind; his future victims would have to take care of themselves. But Base's own wound she might help a little. And helping it, help theirs. And hers. Her wound, which had made her refuse all of her life to take the world's evil into her mind, to undergo the pain of understanding it.

She waited for Wendlin to come home, never doubting (why should she? Wendlin had never failed her) that at her word he would clean up from his wood-hauling trip, have a bite of supper, and drive her over to the Cudlips'.

She was standing at the kitchen window when Wendlin drove in with his wagonload of petroleum-soaked timbers. Supper was already cooked and keeping warm on the stove, and she had nothing to do but watch him unhitch. There was a strange, yellow-green afterglow, melancholy and foreboding, which put her in mind of past times, of evenings when she'd watched old Wendlin drive into barnyards in Pennsylvania and Kansas. There was so much of these past times in her watching that she felt uncertain in her mind that time had progressed. The watching now seemed no more than all those earlier watchings prolonged into unendingness. She had been standing at the same window all of her life, never moved from it, while various backgrounds (with Wendlin in them all) slid past her eyes.

In the dusk, Wendlin loomed up more like a statue than any particular man. Seeing him in this impersonal way, she noted with surprise what a fine figure of a man he was. She was so accustomed to thinking of old Wendlin as the man who wasn't Chester that she didn't often catch sight of the actual big-shouldered, fine-headed old fellow. She had never given Wendlin any credit for his good looks. In the first place, his being Wendlin had taken the edge off his looks; in the second place, she had held his good looks, along with his good heart, good mind, and good providing, against him. They gave him too much of an advantage over Chester, who had excelled in none of these.

She often wished Wendlin could have been the man who had jilted

357

her and Chester the man who married her. Wendlin was so easy to live with, she was unable to picture her devotion to him as being as sacrificial as she would have liked. The other way around, if she had married Chester, that born failure and scamp, and had loved Wendlin, and he had jilted her, her long marriage would have been a monument to something else besides good sense and knowing which side her bread was buttered on. She hated that. She wanted marriage as well as love to ask a great deal of her; she wanted to be devoted to Wendlin in spite of something. And she didn't know what she could be devoted to Wendlin in spite of. Except in spite of his not being Chester. She wanted to give her husband something he didn't deserve. This was difficult with Wendlin. There was nothing he didn't deserve; and this reduced marriage to a kind of simple arithmetic. She had wanted a marriage as painful and high-minded as a religion. Religion requires devotion to a God who inflicts pain and sorrow. Wendlin never inflicted pain or sorrow.

It was only by never letting Wendlin oust Chester from her heart that she had been able to keep in her life some of the misery and mystery she felt life needed. She had divided herself up, loved one man and been true to another, and the tension of this self-created drama, which might have been too much for another woman, had kept her vividly alive, always aware of an alternative and with the enhanced consciousness that daily decisions require.

It was only now, leaving life, that she began to worry about Wendlin, to wonder if life with a divided woman might not have been a trial for him. When Wendlin, coming toward the house from the barn, saw her at the kitchen window with the lighted lamps behind her and stopped with his usual look of pleasure and admiration, she went with some of her old speed to the kitchen door. Wendlin was not a very demonstrative man, but he was always a responsive one, and he opened his arms to her now. She leaned her face against his cold mackinaw and touched his cool cheek with her hand.

"You feel frozen," she said.

He took off his coat and went to the stove to warm his hands. "It's not freezing," he said, "but it will before morning, I'm afraid."

"What's the thermometer now?"

The *Emporia Gazette* wasn't Wendlin's only source of news. He would take Willie White's word for some things, but about the weather he was his own prophet. Whenever they had moved, he put up rain gauge, weather vane, and barometer before he set up stoves and beds.

358

No man she knew lived in a world as big as Wendlin's. His need for such a big-sized world sometimes seemed a weakness to her. She had a woman's difficulty convincing herself that there wasn't some virtue in living close to the bone, making do with little. There was none of that in Wendlin. He didn't think he was any less of a man for wanting to know from what quarter the wind was blowing or how Hiram Johnson was voting. Though she still believed she could do without such knowledge, after thirty years with Wendlin such knowledge was her possession, and when other women showed that they didn't know which side the Italians were on or what was the average rainfall in Southern California, she was shocked, forgetting that except for her long years of living in Wendlin's big-sized world, in his rain, wind, and sun-filled world, she would be just such an ignoramus herself.

"It's thirty-eight now and dropping fast," Wendlin said. "It was only forty-five when I left Olinda."

"How low does it have to get to hurt the trees?"

"Nothing under thirty degrees'll do them any good. If it goes to twenty-five or -six, it'll start killing."

"Poor Shel."

"Shel's been forehanded enough to lay in some smudge material. I don't think he's got much to worry about. He's up on high ground, too. It's the groves down in the low places that are liable to be hit hardest."

Mary had recognized a strange thing about her sickness. Disasters, which in her days of good health would have grieved her, now had a kind of curative power. They drew her outside herself; the threat of dangers that could be fought and perhaps conquered cheered her. For all she accepted her sickness, and had to, it was for this very reason monotonous and depressing. A good struggle was what she had always enjoyed.

She put a real supper on the table; she had no patience with women who cooked the same kind of meal for supper they cooked for dinner. She had made dinner's mashed potatoes into crisp-crusted creamy-centered potato cakes; the leftover pot roast was cut up and reheated in brown gravy; there was fresh applesauce, still warm and with a glaze of cinnamon and butter on top. And there was Opal's spice cake to finish with. Except for a few nibbles, she was no longer able to eat real food. But a strange thing had happened recently. Watching Wendlin eat actually seemed to nourish her. If Wendlin was away from

359

home at noon and ate dinner in Placentia or Fullerton, by midafternoon she was weak with hunger. But when she sat at the table with Wendlin, watching him take seconds and listening to him praise her cooking, she rose from the table satisfied.

"My favorite cake," Wendlin said, as she cut him a big wedge of Opal's spice cake. After a bite or two, he said, "Good, but not quite up to your usual standard."

It wasn't generous-hearted of her, but she couldn't resist telling him that Opal had baked it.

"That explains it," Wendlin said. "She hasn't got your touch."

She waited until Wendlin had eaten the last crumb, up to standard or not, before she spoke to him about going to the Cudlips'. First she told him about her afternoon at the Raunces'. When she finished, Wendlin said, "Poor Crystal. I suppose she figured she was saving at least fifty per cent of the family honor, telling that story."

It was Crystal he felt sorry for, and Raunce—not Cudlip. She felt sorry for them, too, but they were not beyond her ken, she didn't have anything to make up to them. But she had a lifetime of neglect to make up to Cudlip, and she needed to see him before it was too late. Too late for her.

"Somebody ought to listen to Base," she said.

"Sounds to me like you spent the afternoon listening to him. I don't know what good any more listening will do."

"It will do me good," Mary said.

That settled it for Wendlin. "I'll have to shave before we go."

"No," Mary said. "Let's not slick up. Let's not go like an Elder in the church and his sweet old wife."

"How shall we go, Mary?"

"Let's go like people trying to stand in Base's shoes."

"You can't jump out of your skin, Mary."

"I don't know whether I can or not. I never tried. I've taken a lot of pride in being myself, Wendlin. I ought to try to understand Base."

"We don't understand ourselves, Mary."

"I understand you, Wendlin."

"You're a couple of jumps ahead of me, then. You don't think this could wait until morning? It's colder outside than you think."

"I don't want to postpone it. I been postponing it all my life."

"All right. We'll be there in a half hour. You think I'd look too slicked-up with a tie on?"

360

He stood in front of the mirror over the sink to put it on. "The Tract's not going to forgive LeRoy," he said.

"Even if it was Dolly with him?"

"They might come nearer forgiving him if it had been someone else. People've got a sneaking liking for lawbreakers."

"You bundled up enough?" Wendlin asked, when they stepped out onto the porch. He lit a match and looked at the thermometer. "Still going down," he said.

She was warmly dressed but the air was colder than she had imagined. There was a new moon, small and transparent at the edges, as if honed sharp for cutting purposes. She had often heard of them, but for the first time in her life she saw stars that looked like diamonds. Under their light and in the clean air, newly rain-washed, the Tract was desolate, barren as a desert. There was lamplight to be seen in a few houses; but these houses were too far apart to do any more than make you feel lonesome, poor pitiful shelters thrown up to shut out the cold and the stars and the stillness. Poor pitiful people inside, too. Unloving, loving their wives and blamed for it, hating their fathers, calling on God, learning to die, spending a lifetime not saying what was on their hearts.

"This cold going to be too much for you?" Wendlin asked, as they drove out of the yard.

"No, I like it." She liked to feel anything that wasn't her pain. She was very busy collecting her last sensations on earth, and rejoiced even in uncomfortable ones. They proved to her that she was still more than her disease. I'm not so bad off, she would think, if I can still complain about a tight shoe. The cold made her eyes water and her temples ache. She thought, This is the way an icy night in January feels, and was glad once more to feel such a thing.

Wendlin sniffed the air. "I smell burning oil. Somebody down on the low ground along the river must've fired up his smudge pots."

She breathed deeply and added that smell, also a new one, to her collection. "How can you tell where it's coming from?"

"That's the direction. And nobody on the Tract's got smudge pots."

She was still unaccustomed to the automobile. She couldn't get used to the idea that Wendlin controlled it. They seemed, rather, to be in a vehicle drawn through the night by some unseen power. If travel in this automatic, mysterious way, with no visible means of locomotion could be true, anything could be true. Nothing hereafter would surprise her. They moved smoothly through the heavy, quiet cold, under the rattlesnake glitter of the diamond-back stars, on their way to do what she had never been willing to attempt before. And she herself growing strange to herself. Only old Wendlin the same, warm and serious and joking.

She moved closer to him, and Wendlin put an arm about her shoulders. "This don't equal buggy riding," he said, "with a horse that could take you home even if you never touched the lines."

"You better slow down, hadn't you, driving with one arm?"

"Maybe I should. But the boys are right. It can be done."

She leaned against Wendlin's solid warmth and watched the black scallops of the hills slide by against the starlit sky. The car appeared to be standing still while the earth wheeled past them its show of hills and fields and distant mountains.

"What do you figure on saying to Base when we get there?" Wendlin asked.

"I don't know," she said. "Except not argue with him."

She closed her eyes and remembered long-ago nights of home-coming, asleep inside the circle of her father's arms and unable to believe that they had already stopped in the driveway beside the upping-block.

Wendlin's slowing up and stopping seemed a part of the daylong interweaving of past and present, and she timeless and dying inside time's flow. She didn't say a word. She let the illusion persist. She could almost smell the heavy-headed phlox that grew beside the driveway in Towanda.

Wendlin took his arm away from her shoulders. "There's a man out here," he said. "There's something wrong with him."

Wendlin had stopped the car. He got out, and the phlox smell and the warm sleepiness went with him.

When she heard Wendlin speak, she had to get out, too. At the back of a car, leaning onto a fender, half-supported by Wendlin, was a man she knew, even though his face was out of shape, swollen, and bleeding.

"Julian," she said, "what happened?"

He seemed unable or reluctant to speak.

"He's been in a fight," she told Wendlin.

"No," Julian said.

"Who did this?"

"Medora's father."

"What did you do?" Wendlin asked.

362

"Nothing. I knocked on his door!"

"That's all?" Wendlin asked.

"We better get him in the car," Mary said.

"No, I'm . . . dirty."

He was bleeding, and he began to vomit. After he had vomited, he slid through Wendlin's arms to the ground. Wendlin knelt beside him.

"We'll have to get him to a doctor," Mary told Wendlin.

"I don't know of any this side of Fullerton. Do you feel like that much of a trip?"

"Of course I do. There's nothing wrong with me."

"I could take you home first."

"It would only waste time."

Together they got him into the back seat, and Mary rode there, holding Julian's head on her lap. Wendlin was driving faster now, and the car had no side curtains. Julian had to be held onto the seat by main force, and the only place she was warm was where his blood seeped through her dress onto her thighs.

"Shall I slow down?" Wendlin asked. "Is it too rough back there?"

For her own sake as well as Julian's, she wanted him to hurry. Her painkiller was wearing off fast.

"Hurry," she said. "Get there as fast as you can."

After a while, Wendlin called back again. "You wanted to understand Base better. Does this help any?"

"No," she said.

"This speaks louder than words, it seems to me."

It did. What it said to her was that she had postponed her visit to Base too long.

8    It took three more warnings, after Chad's report, to undermine Shel's faith in the weather. He had a natural mobility about nature. He didn't think nature had it in for him. Some of the things nature did got in the way of some of the things he wanted to do. But he had foresight, he prepared for these eventualities as best he could, and, having done so, trusted nature the way a man trusts his wife. Not fatuously, but understanding that if she's made up her mind to betray him, suspicions won't provide much protection. Shel didn't intend to

sweat every time the weather cooled off, thinking, This is the end of everything.

Ben arrived with the second warning; but Ben was always eager for any excuse to see Ellen. He was conducting his courtship in a very peculiar way. Shel often wondered what Ellen made of Ben and his visits. He doubted Ellen knew she was being courted. For a man who was convinced he could sin, Ben appeared mighty unwilling to put the matter to any kind of a test.

Ben thought Ellen too sweet and innocent to listen to talk of love and marriage. She was sweet, she was innocent; but a man can talk straight carnality to such a girl and her very sweetness and innocence will change every word he says into an echo of her own romantic dream. Shel knew. He had courted a girl like that. It was the experienced ones who were liable to slap you for a sidewise look. But if Ben was without experience with girls, Shel was without experience with sons-in-law. He didn't suppose it was up to him to give Ben any hints.

Since Shel heard every word Ben said as nothing more than Ben's roundabout way of courting, he wouldn't have paid much attention if Ben had said, "England's surrendered" or "Black Jack Pershing's declared himself the Emperor of Mexico." Ben's about to run out of excuses for coming over here would have been his conclusion at such news. Sooner or later, he's going to have to come right out with it, to say, "I want to see Ellen. I love Ellen."

"I thought I ought to drop in and let you know I had a phone call from Sylvester Perkins," Ben said, staring at Ellen.

Shel felt like teasing Ben a little. "You talking to me?" he asked. "Syl's phoning may be a big thing in your life, Ben, but there's no need for you to make a special trip here to let me know about it."

"This call was for you."

"For me?"

"You as much as anybody. Syl says the forecast is for freezing tonight."

"That relieves me," Shel said. "If Syl says that, we can rest easy. What Syl promises, he don't deliver."

"There's no reason for him to spread word like that if it's not true."

"He's probably trying to get us to pull up stakes and decamp. Then he'll sell our places all over again to another pack of believers."

"He said to warn the ranchers," honest Ben persisted.

"Warn them to do what?" Shel asked. "'Frost free,' he told us. That's why we bought. There's not a smudge pot on the Tract. I've got some brush piled up and I've got the tree trunks wrapped. Besides, it's only thirty-eight."

"It was thirty-five when I came in."

"That won't do no harm."

"Syl says it's been known to drop ten degrees after midnight."

"Did Syl suggest what to do then? What's his plans for after midnight?"

"He didn't speak of that."

"The great white father! If it freezes, he's warned us. If it don't, no harm's done except maybe he scared a few ranchers out of their wits."

Ben, without saying any more, moved his chair closer to Ellen. Now we get to the heart of the matter, Shel thought.

Asa Brice came at eight o'clock. Asa's message did not come from Sylvester Perkins, but from the heavens themselves, from the stars and the color of the moon and the smell of the air and the silence of the earth, and the taste of his own spit and the feel of his own finger tips. Asa was a weather dowser the way some men are water dowsers. And Shel wasn't sold on dowsing in any form. Asa enjoyed talking about the weather, he figured, the way other men talked about women. Asa had tramped over more than once to have a confab about cooking mustard greens, or to report on his attempt to unspin trap-door spider silk.

So when Asa peeled off his coat and announced it was going to freeze, Shel considered it the opinion of a weather bug, who wanted to debate the proposition, the way an atheist wants to debate the existence of God. Nothing either one of them said was going to have much influence on the facts.

"Have you looked at the thermometer recently?" Asa asked.

"Not the last minute or so."

"It's thirty-two now."

"That's a good stopping place," Shel said.

"I've kept a ten-year record," Asa said. "There's never been a time when it's reached freezing this early in the night and stopped there."

He had brought his statistics with him. They were supposed to prove his case. Shel found them reassuring. They translated bad weather and loss of crops and personal failure into history, and figures. He and Asa settled down to talk about record-breaking cold spells like men living on a star. The death of a few Valencias at the edge of a range of Western foothills of no more than passing planetary interest; cold, and its effect on citrus groves, their hobby, and what happened tonight would be a dot on a graph, not Shelby Lewis's personal survival or failure.

The stove roared and finally grew rosy around the mid-section. Ben had moved still nearer Ellen, and Shel wondered if before the evening was over he might not advance to hand holding. Chad sat, his chair reared back on two legs, leaning against the wall, and to all appearances asleep. Ordinarily, Shel was against this backwoods way of sitting, believing it went with a hound's scratching under the table, and an occasional squirt of tobacco juice in the general direction of the stove. Tonight, the boy looked so tired he let him rest as he was. Zoomy, every now and then, tiptoed outside to see if Old Silver was still surviving. Though he left the room on tiptoe, he always returned at a thundering gallop. Shel let this pass, too. Joicey made a big pitcher of cocoa, thickened a little, and beat to a froth. She served it with molasses cookies.

Shel, drinking his cupful, said, "This is the best wake I ever attended."

Asa, a stickler for facts, said, "The wake will be tomorrow night, Shel. This is just the deathbed scene."

It was a grisly joke, but nothing fazed Shel until Pete's arrival. It was eleven o'clock then. Joicey and Zoomy had gone upstairs to bed; Chad's eyes were closed; Ben was talking to Ellen in such a low voice Shel couldn't do more than catch enough words to know that the weather wasn't the topic.

Pete brought the fourth warning, and the minute he stepped inside the door and before he had said a word, Shel knew what lay ahead. Ben and Asa were both lonesome bachelors: Ben a would-be lover, and Asa a confirmed weather bug. Both served their own pleasures by coming. Pete had no need to make an eight-mile ride by horseback for the pleasure of hand holding; and if he had any interest in the weather it was news to Shel. Before Pete had spoken a word, and in the midst of his thinking that Pete in a knitted green stocking cap looked as peculiar as an Eskimo with a palm fan, Shel had accepted his doom.

"The trees are done for," he said. He meant it as a statement but he couldn't keep the rising inflection of a question out of his voice.

"Maybe not," Pete said. "You're in a good spot. You've got smudge stuff ready. A wind might come up."

"It's going to freeze?"

"It's freezing now."

366

"I overreached myself."

"Don't give up yet," Pete said.

"What can we do?"

"First of all, let's cover up the trees that have the best chance of pulling through."

"Cover them with what?"

"Anything, sheets, towels. I got a bundle of stuff out on my horse that Rosa sent."

Shel was convinced that there was no use trying to save anything. He had set himself up too high and he would now have his lesson.

But even so, his moment of giving in without fighting had passed. His fate would have to prove itself every inch of the way. He did not intend to make it any gifts. If he was destroyed, let the blood be on fate's head; he wasn't going to co-operate.

He went upstairs to tell Joicey. He held the lamp over the bed, and Joicey opened her eyes slowly. He saw he didn't have to tell her. She read his face the way he had read Pete's. She reached up a hand to him.

It was worse than losing money. It was not like a crop failure. It was more like a death in the family. Oh, not that he wouldn't kill every tree on the Tract to save any human being whatever. But the prospect of those trees dying hit him like the coming death of any young and promising thing, colts or calves. And it went beyond that. The youth that was dying with them was his own. When morning came, if he looked out on trees blackened and drooping as if hit by a fire, the young Shel Lewis, the Shel Lewis who had believed that the world was on his side would be done for.

He was tied up with that grove; he had planted himself with every tree. It had been a sign to him that he was finished with being a renter and a hired hand, finished with being moved around to suit the needs of someone else, his only merit in his muscles, and valuable only as a guide to plows and harrows. When his grove went, the Shel Lewis who had never doubted that he could swing it, who believed in his own luck and in the co-operation of some force outside himself, was done for. Bad and good, loving and unloving, ugly and handsome are not so separated as lucky and unlucky. Shel felt cold around the heart. Those miserable ones for whom nothing ever went right, whose stores burned down, whose wives had female diseases, whose children whined, who were themselves stricken with kidney disease, beaten in horse trades, burdened with cows that scoured and tobacco that mildewed, who got sick on good whisky, broke wind in company and were constipated in private, this was the common run of mankind, and after tomorrow morning he, who had lived in his pride of being above such men, would be right down in their midst.

He, who had always been able to give Joicey more than himself, had been able to give her the world's weight, thrown in the direction he was going, was asking her now for any rags and tags she could scare up to wrap around his doomed trees. It was as silly as bandaging soldiers before they went into battle, as if the knowledge of death could deflect bullets and be its own cure.

"Well, Joicey," he said, "here you are, right where they warned you you'd be. Married to old Jud Lewis's son, from the Plum River District, the son like his old man, always ready to move on to where the prospects are brighter and the work lighter."

"Shut up that kind of talk," Joicey said.

She was too worried to take time to put on wrapper or slippers. She worked in her nightgown, stripping the beds. She roused up Zoomy, to get his sheets, and hushed his protests by telling him he could get in bed with her. She emptied the drawers and finally gave Shel the wrapper she should have been wearing.

"Don't tear things up if you don't have to, but if it will save the trees, go ahead."

"The trees are already goners."

"Why not come to bed, then?"

He could not explain it. He could not admit to himself that he hoped. He could not spend the night on tenterhooks. By saying good-by to everything now, he could get through the night's work, and perhaps achieve a miracle. But he could not work and hope together.

9    PRESS didn't know that the weather was freezing. She was filled with the warmth of self-denial and sacrifice. She had sent Chad away when she had wanted him to stay, and she was flushed now with the work of preparing a good supper, which would be ready to dish up the minute her mother stepped in the door. She was preparing her winter evening specialties: corn fritters, baked pork chops, cole slaw, and gingerbread.

In a single minute, she passed from the fear that her mother would arrive before the cooking was done to an apprehensive impatience about her delay. What can be keeping her? Has she had an accident? Supper will be ruined. She worked like a child, immersed in the moment, and when the moment's work was finished, there was no more world for a while unless the next act happened as planned.

She opened the back door to listen for the sound of an automobile, to look for the beams of a headlight. The night was silent. There was nothing to be seen but the flashing stars and the dark curves of the hills against the gray sky. She went into the sitting room, where Hannah sat by the stove reading *The Five Little Peppers*. Press remembered the time when what happened to Polly and Jasper and Joel mattered more to her than her own fate. She read over Hannah's shoulder, and had no more feeling about the Pepper children than about ants in the wood box. Back in the kitchen, she looked at the supper she had prepared and was convinced that at the very minute she was cooking it, her mother, pinned under an auto, had been gasping her last in some ditch.

Love and guilt, love and guilt; out of that combination come the most intense feelings: the guilt unconscious, the love premeditated, the heart pulled two ways at once, stretched thin until it quivers with responses which that healthy muscle ordinarily never feels.

Press was making it up to her mother. Making up what? She didn't know. If she knew, she could do something about it, be freed from having to make it up in roundabout ways, sacrifice Chad and herself, bend over hot stoves, protect her father, listen at doorways when her mother had sick headaches to discover if she still breathed. She didn't send Chad away for her own pleasure. If she hadn't liked him, if he had been some poor ugly boy she pitied, he would be sitting here by the stove at this minute. She sent Chad away because it hurt her so much to do so. The pain was her gift to someone. The pain was the proof that what she was doing was right. What caused her to suffer could not be wrong. She had a debt of suffering to pay. To whom? To her mother. Why? Chad was so much younger than her mother. She would have years of time in which to make it up to *him,* after her mother was dead. After she had made it up to her mother. Made up what? It was a circle, and she broke out of it to look in the oven.

Her mother might be dead now. She was never away from home at suppertime. Standing by the stove, turning corn fritters, she acted out in her mind the tragedy of the accident in which her mother had perished. She was her mother dying, she was herself, receiving the news. She was her mother's substitute, caring for the house and Hannah and her father. No words entered her mind. She kept these events wordless, but lived through them, shuddered in the ditch, cried at the grave, presided with tender competence at the table for Hannah and her father. She and her father faced each other at the ends of the table in the father's and mother's places.

The dream was finished in a minute. It had not been in words, and no words left their tracks to give her clues as to who was guilty, who had been wronged. She woke up from it as from a dream, with only the heaviness of "Who have I wronged? What retribution must I make?" more pressing than usual.

Her father arrived without her mother, just as she had dreamed it.

"I don't know what could please me more, Press, than to be welcomed home this way," he said. "I've had a hard day. You roll back the years. You make me feel like a boy coming home to supper."

This was undoubtedly what she had willed, but because she *had* willed it, she felt guilt. "Where is Mama? I'm worried to death about her. I'm afraid something's happened."

"Don't get so wrought up, Press. Don't cross your bridges until you come to them. There's nothing to worry about. Your mother went for a ride with Tom Mount. I've just been talking to Tom on the phone. They had a little gear trouble. I've warned Tom a dozen times about that car of his. I told them to have supper while they were waiting for it to be fixed. Tom said your mother had refused to eat until she got home, but that didn't make any sense. I'll feel a lot better eating this good food knowing your mother's not going hungry."

But her father was not very interested in the food after all. He talked; he asked Hannah about *The Five Little Peppers*. He asked her several questions about Miss Fry's teaching. Did the children like her? Was she thorough? Was she ever absent from class? Had the Reverend Raunce ever visited the class? Had Tom Mount? He talked about the freezing weather, and the war, and he asked Press if she had found Crystal Raunce a little on the flighty side. He did not eat, but he talked steadily.

"I couldn't be enjoying myself like this," he said, "if I didn't know your mother was having for herself, thanks to you, Press, a little vacation from cooking and dishwashing."

But the talkative spurt died down before Hannah had finished her gingerbread, and her father got up from the table without excusing

370

himself and went in to sit by the fire. He was still there when Press finished her kitchen work. Hannah, with school tomorrow, had been sent to bed. Her father had a paper in his hand, but his eyes were on the flames that could be seen through the isinglass insets in the stove door. There was no sound at all but the steady sigh of the well-drawing stove in the quiet of the windless night.

They had started a checker game when Tom and Indy came in. Lute had at the sound of their approach risen, knocking checkers left and right.

Indy let Tom, who was all charm and affability, do the greeting and talking. She had thought she might return with guilt, or with pity or with hatred. There was none of this. Some light, some yellowness of light, as if she herself were the wick, the oil, the flame of a burning lamp, shone over the room. The room was transformed. She saw Lute and Press more clearly because, aware of herself as she had never been before, she had a less wavering place from which to do her viewing. It made those she looked at clearer. She was filled with a kind of burning gaiety, with the wonder of the extraordinary joke that she discovered had been played upon her all her life. She was not the person they thought. Or she thought. This new person had no apologies to make, for the apologetic happenings had been before her time.

Tom had said, "Let's tell no one about us yet." He had said, "We must be married."

She looked at Lute from behind the power of a secret. He thought she was one woman and she was another. She might have been wearing one of the invisible coats of the fairy tales. She had escaped the person she had been, the pattern she had assumed. But nothing she could do would ever persuade Lute that she had changed. She was experiencing already the pleasures of living a double life; not simple multiplication, but the irony of seeing one thing accepted as another. She did not know why this should be—unless vanity and cruelty in human beings feed on seeing others taken in by what they themselves see through.

Tom left. He made his graceful, thoughtful, sincere farewells. Press was busy making amends for something; without tact, thinking that every situation centered upon her and was to be judged in the eyes of God solely on what Press Cope did or did not do, she fussed and bustled.

371

Lute said, "Don't you have some reading to do, Press?" And Press left the room. Always offering, always refused.

So husband and wife faced each other, and beyond the room in which they stood was the bed where, Indy knew, Lute thought something could be proved. Some cure wrought. There he would find an answer to the question he would not put in words. There husbands and wives met; there the marriage pattern provided an impersonal way of acting.

She wished Lute were her friend, so that she could tell him the truth. Not the truth of "I want to marry Tom Mount," but the truth of her discovery. All along, she had been the woman she was with Tom. She had been—as a woman—like a child who doesn't learn to read until his sixteenth year. She had been without a language; she, who could speak, had lived with deafness; she, who could sing, had had no voice; she, who could pray, had received no answers.

"I didn't feel like eating with you gone," Lute said. She made him hot chocolate and she sat with him by the fire while he drank it.

Where was the guilt? If Lute had been hurt, then she would have knelt at his feet. But what had Lute lost? Nothing! Everything he valued was here beside him, and to her there had been added wonder. When she married Tom, that would hurt Lute, but that time wasn't come yet.

She went into the bedroom with Lute and into the bed with him; still herself, inside the effulgence that surrounded and protected her. The double life upon which she was embarked was possible because she now had two bodies. The one long trained to disappear entered the bed with Lute. The one from which she died for a few minutes, and which after a little use she reclaimed. The impersonal, the unaffected body, the body which, while used, suspended its own living to be more useful more quickly.

She put her arms about his neck, never more gentle.

"What are you doing?" she asked, like an ignorant and dumfounded bride.

A minute later she was out of bed.

It was not a question Lute could ever have answered, and certainly not now, with Indy invisible in the dark room, her teeth chattering with cold, gasping, half crying.

"Are you sick?" he asked.

She was sick. A double life was possible only for one who was not alive, and could be cut up like any bar of soap or piece of ribbon. The

372

living can't live double. Double, triple, quadruple lives might have been possible, lived as she had been living with Lute. But now that she was alive, she would have to live single.

She took the comfort from the foot of the bed. "Lute," she said, "I don't feel well. I'm going to the spare room."

10   Nothing short of an invasion by Germans or Mexicans could have suited Chad more than the threat of the freeze. He had been longing for an opponent, and now he had one. Suicide had never entered his head, but something just this side of suicide suited him to a T. He wanted something to absorb him so deeply that he could hear Press's name like a far-off sleepy echo.

Shel, Ben, and Asa went to wrapping trees. Pete took Chad with him to the uncleared land adjoining Shel's to gather up sagebrush, cactus, greasewood, whatever they could lay their hands on that was green enough to slow down the burning of Shel's oil-soaked wood.

"A fire burning in a field next the trees, if it's warm enough to do any good to the trees in the center of the grove, will burn down the outside rows. What we've got to do is to get enough green stuff to get a big smoke going and pray for enough wind to move it through the trees."

Chad grubbed, hacked, and sawed to forget Press. But he contradicted himself. He wanted her to see him grubbing, hacking, and sawing to forget her. All of his prodigality of effort, his speed, the flourish with which he threw what he had loosened from the earth onto the wagon was for Press's eyes and Press's admiration. He might want to forget Press, but until the actual minute of extinction, he couldn't chop down a mesquite except in a manner calculated to impress her.

Pete believed the boy to be in a frenzy to save trees. Doubting this could be done, he thought there wasn't much sense in killing themselves at a hopeless job. There was not much sense, even if it wasn't hopeless. Live trees and dead men, particularly if he was one of them, weren't Pete's idea of a rational world.

"You better take it easy," he told Chad. "It's a long time till morning."

Chad had already sweated away the tiredness of his day's work. He hung his jacket over the tail gate, and took a minute to look out over the Tract. The valley below was gray under the starlight, and the three houses still lighted floated like ships in a lonesome sea. There were no smudge fires yet on the Tract, but the horizon to the west and south was lighted by a murky glow where smudge pots were already burning. The hard, cold air was heavy with their smell.

Pete and Chad had started back to the grove with their wagon filled when Pete said, "Do you know a girl named Medora Cudlip?"

"She's a friend of my sister's. She goes with a friend of yours."

"I know that," Pete said. "I guess they're together tonight. Julian wasn't home tonight when I went over to his place. What kind of a girl is she?"

"She's pretty," Chad said.

"Is she pretty wild? That's what I want to know."

"I don't know anything about that. Her father don't like her going with . . ."

He had hesitated before saying "Mexican," but Pete came right out with the dirty word. "He don't like her going with a Mexican. Well, I don't like Julian going with her. She'll get him in trouble. She's been running after him. She is bad for him."

"Why is she bad for him?"

"Her father may shoot him. That is always bad for a man."

Chad didn't want to joke. If Pete knew what made one girl bad for a man, and another not, he'd like to know.

"Except for her father—would she be bad for him?"

"Yes. She spoke first. She acted like a man. What can go right for them now?"

Chad didn't feel convinced. This was perhaps a Mexican idea. A man could speak first and nothing go right.

The grove, when they got back to it, looked like a rag bag; it looked like a bunch of bigheads come down with the mumps. Under the starlight, the white tablecloths and petticoats gave the trees from a distance the appearance of being in bloom—or snow-laden. The trees looked peculiar, ridiculous, poulticed, and bandaged. They looked like cats dressed up in sunbonnets or old hens wearing shawls. Nothing natural is improved by clothing. Or if it is, dish towels and nightgowns aren't the right style for orange trees. Chad felt ashamed, as if he had seen an unnatural act, a dog set to walking on two legs or a bitch making love to a gander.

374

When they reached the others, Shel said, "Pete, you're the boss here tonight. You take charge."

"I'm no expert on smudging," Pete said.

"You know more about it than any of the rest of us."

That was true, and it was an act of intelligence to put him in charge; and Shel, though he felt he was finished before he started, didn't intend to give the other side, the side of fate and freeze, a chance to say afterward, "If he had used his head, he needn't have lost his trees." He was going to use his head *and* lose his trees. The outcome tomorrow morning would be the same whether he put Zoomy or Pete in charge. He could open up a chicken and let the kinks in the entrails tell him when to light his fires, and the result, when daylight came, would be just the same: dead trees.

Pete thought he had a chance. He wasn't fighting against any conviction that he was a born no-good and had bitten off more than he could chew. He was fighting the cold, and he was fighting for his friend. Pete was man enough to be tender about men. He didn't want to live with Shel or Julian. Another man around the house would have been harder to bear than living with his horse. But outside the house, he would die for Shel or Julian as soon he would for Rosa. Oh, if Rosa was in danger, he'd save her before Shel or Julian. But he'd try to save the three of them. Shel and Julian made him more man, more human being. He added their lives to his own. He would do for them what he would do for himself. Julian's girl and Shel's trees were his girl and his trees. Or at least their worries about their trees and girls were his worries.

Asa was the only one present enough different from Pete to understand all this. Pete's nature revealed itself to him in the way that water gives away secrets to fire that additional water never discovers. Asa was like Pete in many ways. He would work as hard as Pete. He knew less about smudging than Pete, but more about the effect of cold on vegetation than Pete would ever know. He knew more reasons for admiring Shel than Pete would recognize if they were named, numbered, and written down like a laundry list. The world Pete took for granted, the loamy hills wheeling under the turning stars while five men with old petticoats and pinpricks of fire fought the cold which could freeze them all into druid circles of stone, made Asa heavy and somber with love. But his love had to be expressed in words in those notebooks of his; and the need to do this caused him to separate him-

375

self from the scene before him, a scene before his eyes, yes, but of which Pete was a part.

Did it always have to be this way? Did knowledge, conscious knowledge, always separate? Or was it only his unremitting itch to set it down? Could it be set down only by the man who separated himself from it? Pete did not want to record it. Asa was going to do everything Pete did that night: light as many fires, carry as many armfuls of sage and greasewood, get as cold, hungry, sleepy, discouraged. But he was never going to experience the night and the cold and the tree-saving as Pete did. That was his tragedy, a personal and selfish one. Pete's tragedy was his friend's danger. Asa wanted to be where love and knowledge were not in conflict—and perhaps that place could be found only in the heart of a man who had the capacity to reconcile them. If Asa had believed in prayer, he would have prayed, Make me like this Mexican.

Though he knew well enough that if he made this prayer and it was granted, he would begin at once to rid himself of God's gift, work himself out of Pete's simple state and back to the tragedy of separation, of observing and recording. He would reclaim his fate in spite of God.

Ben was simple enough to pray. He was as uncomfortable working without praying as he was praying without working. Martha and Mary lived in him simultaneously, and he was able at one and the same time to sit at the Lord's feet and keep his eye on the cooking. He did not walk in at heaven's gate with Raunce's confidence, but there was nothing in his theology which persuaded him that God might not hearken to a request that the orange trees of a well-meaning man like Shel Lewis be spared.

Pete's praying had been done at Rosa's side on Sunday morning, and he was now free to concentrate on the problem of when to get his smudge going—a big problem, requiring much thought. Start too soon and have all the fuel used up by three or four in the morning when the temperature took its final plunge, and all their work would be useless, and the grove, which might otherwise have been saved, lost. Start too late after the trees were already damaged and the result would be the same.

About one-thirty, with the temperature standing at a point where damage began, he had some help from nature in making his decision. A little wind sprang up from the south. He could fire only from the southwest and north sides of the ranch. Shel's house, with the lemons

376

Pete had decided from the first not to try to save, was on the eastern edge of his property. On the south, the road that would in time be a part of the boulevard separated Shel's place from that of an absentee owner. Here on the road, smudge material was piled, and with the wind springing up to carry the smoke, Pete knew the time had come to light. The wind would not only carry the smoke, but it would tend to steady and raise the temperature.

With the fires burning, with the green stuff keeping the flame down, with the wind moving the warm smoke into the orchard, Shel began in spite of everything to hope. He began to hope without knowing he had done so. A scene had formed in his mind. It was daylight, and he and Joicey sat at the breakfast table, looking out over their undamaged grove circled by a horizon black with smudge smoke. Shel once again was an uncommon man, a man who faced Joicey heroically with luck on his side, a man who had the world traveling in his direction. His mind pictured himself sitting at that breakfast table with pride, a thousand fallen on every side, but Shel Lewis, a man of foresight, energy, and wisdom, preserved unharmed.

He quenched that vision. He was done for, his grove finished; he would not get drunk on hope. He pinched from the tree next him a spray of leaves the size of his palm, and inhaled deeply its sweet tang. He smoothed the thick, glossy leaves between thumb and forefinger. He could have put them to his lips. The scent carried him back to a rare Christmas orange in Kentucky, which had smelled to a ten-year-old like the gifts of all the Magi. The smell carried him forward to the grove he was never going to have, lit with oranges like candles, and glinting with irrigation water like silver spangles.

Good-by to all that. He shook the vision from his mind. He watched the smoke, white and steamy from the green stuff, black where the oil-soaked wood was burning, drift slowly northward up the tree rows.

He walked toward the center of the grove, to see how far the smoke was carrying. Pete joined him, took a thermometer from his pocket, and hung it in a tree.

"There's not much hope of saving the center," he warned Shel.

"I got no hope for any part of it," Shel said. He put the spray in his pocket, embarrassed to have Pete see him carrying it around like a lock of hair cut from the head of a dead sweetheart. "I'm finished. I bit off more than I could chew."

"Maybe so," Pete said. "But we still got a little chance."

He took down the thermometer and looked at it by the light of his lantern. "Not much hope here," he admitted, and Shel, though he had given up hope, would not ask him how hopeless it was.

The wind lasted about an hour, then it ceased completely. The night was without movement, as still as a wedge of iron, and the thermometer, which had held steady while that little breath came in off the ocean, began once again to drop. Pete lit his fires on the north and west sides. There was no use holding back anything for the killing frosts of early morning. The killing frosts were here.

"If I had enough stuff to keep the fires going all night on the south side, I might save the outside rows there," he told Shel. He was fighting his war like a good commander, retreating where he had to, doubling his strength where he thought he had a chance to hold.

Asa and Chad brought down another load of smoke producer, but the green stuff was valueless without burnable material underneath, and the burnable material was getting low. It was then Chad remembered the load of wood he had seen Wendlin hauling into his yard at dusk. It was probably still there on the wagon. Ben said he could get it to them in an hour. He was back with it at four o'clock, the thermometer standing then at twenty-five. Pete had stopped firing everywhere except along the south road. The thermometer went to twenty-four, and the best the fires could do was to lift the temperature at the depth of the second row to twenty-six.

Pete walked out to meet Chad, who was bringing down another load of green stuff from the hillside. "No use unloading it," he said.

That told the story. The five men gathered around the fires that were doing the trees no good and warmed themselves. Shel asked them to come up to the house for some coffee. But it was over. No one wanted to see the orchard by daylight. Best thing to do now was to sleep and forget it; Shel understood this and let them depart without urging, Asa on his motorcycle, Ben in Wendlin's wagon, Pete astride his horse. Chad alone remained with his father.

"Go on to bed," Shel told him. "There's nothing more to be done."

Chad climbed to the seat of the still-loaded wagon like an old man and sat huddled there for so long without clucking up Chinopsee and Diamond that Shel thought the boy had fallen asleep. But finally he slapped the reins over their backs and went up the hill toward the house.

378

11  MARY opened her eyes and looked at the clock. It looked like three. Wendlin was in the rocker by the bed, the lamp was turned low, and the door to the kitchen was opened so that there was heat in the room. She had a hot-water bottle at her side and there were warm bricks wrapped in flannel at her feet. She had not been asleep. She had been, it seemed, away, and was now returned. It was impossible to bear more than you could bear. Sweating, screaming, vomiting, moaning, calling upon God. She had been fully resolved to leave God out of this, at least to the extent of petition or accusation; death and pain were a part of life, and, having accepted life, she thought it unseemly to accuse God, at the last, of unfairness or to ask Him to change life's conditions. But she had called upon Him. She could hear His name in the room. Her throat was raw from speaking it. She was not, after all, good at enduring pain or even good at enduring pain's lesser symptoms: the nasty sweat, the foul vomit, finger tips and upper lip numb, the body thrashing and twisting to escape what it could not escape because it was a part of the body. The idea of death she now not only accepted but remembered as a promise. Death was the final going away when pain became too great, too long. It was what she had heard it called, but never understood before: a release.

Wendlin saw that she had come back, and he reached a hand to her. She was perfectly clearheaded, without pain, and even, at the minute, without fear of pain. She knew where she was. She was returned like an explorer who has succeeded in climbing something insurmountable or traversing something impassable, only to discover that the effort was not worth it. But not lamenting it. Chalking it up to experience. She felt as she had after childbirth; though knowledge was all she had now to show for her pain. She felt coquettish, gay. She would like to make a joke. It was ridiculous for a woman who had been making the racket she had all night long to feel as she did now. Anyone but old Wendlin, who had bathed her and held basins for her and changed sheets, and brought pain tablets and rubbed her with camphor, would have believed she had been putting on a show of suffering.

"Are you easier?"

379

She pressed his hand. The rawness in her throat was real. She had to try twice before she had a voice. "Old Wendlin," she said.

She had thought of Wendlin this way all of her life, but had never before so spoken to him. It seemed the most natural thing. She had less strength now to keep up the barrier between thought and action. She was worn down so thin that what was in her mind showed through.

"Your old Wendlin," he said.

"You were good to me last night."

"I'm not much of a nurse."

"I don't want better." When she was dead, she would miss Wendlin. Wendlin had been her life.

"I have not been a very good wife."

Old Wendlin smoothed her hand between his. "Mary, you're wandering again."

"Was I out of my mind last night?"

"When you thought you weren't a good wife, you were."

"Chester," she said. "Did I talk about Chester?"

"The sewing-machine agent?"

"Is that what he is?"

"When he isn't in jail. Didn't you know?"

"I've never seen or heard from him since we left Towanda."

"I shouldn't have told you."

"No, I thought he might be worse."

"Nothing worse than running off with a little of the sewing-machine money now and then, that I've heard of."

To her amazement, Mary laughed. After such a night, and at this hour, and talking with Wendlin about Chester. As long as it lasted, life was surprising.

"I loved him, not you," Mary said, in plain amazement, like the man who, safely down, gazes back at the summit that it was silly to have climbed. "It breaks my heart."

"You loved me," Wendlin said.

"Did I, all along?"

"Yes."

"How do you know?"

"You never did an unloving thing. Not a thing you did was unloving. Never once, Mary, did you turn from me. Do you think I could live with a woman who didn't love me? What kind of a man do you think I am? Why, Mary, you couldn't for the life of you kiss someone you didn't love."

"I wish I could've told you 'I loved you,' if I did."

"You told me. Every time you put your arms around my neck. Every time you lectured me about the *Gazette*."

Old Wendlin had tears in his eyes. They rolled down his cheeks. That calm, stouthearted old fellow, shedding tears for her.

"I am like Cudlip?" she asked finally.

"Not that I've ever noticed."

"My actions speak louder than my words?"

"Everybody's do."

"Why didn't you tell me 'Forget Chester'?"

"People don't forget to order. I thought maybe you needed to remember him. Maybe it made what happened easier to bear."

"Why, what do you think happened?"

"Nothing. Except he skipped the country the day before you two were to be married."

"Loving him all my life would make that worse, wouldn't it, not easier to bear?"

"It would make it easier for you to hate him. Skipped off and left you to mourn him all your days."

"I didn't really mourn him very much, did I?"

"If there was ever any high jinks going on, Mary, any cornhusking or sledding or forensic society or taffy-pulling or missionary meeting, you were its center."

"I didn't want to forgive him?"

"There wasn't anything to forgive him for, if you saw he'd done you a good turn by skipping off with that widow."

"She was a lot older and uglier than me."

"There wasn't anything to forgive him for, if his leaving you let you marry a better man."

"Is that what you've thought all your life—that you were a better man?"

"Yes."

"Why didn't it give you the big head?"

"You never gave me a chance to get one."

"I guess I loved myself? I loved the idea of a woman faithful all her life to her wrongdoer? I haven't been a very good Christian."

"It's not easy for a woman to be a Christian."

381

It was a new idea to her. "I hope God feels that way."

"He will."

"I am going to die, Wendlin. I am dying." She gave it to him as news but was not surprised when he accepted it like an old story.

"I know, Mary." He bent his head, and she felt his tears on her hand.

"It's too bad we had to wait until now to talk."

"I've never been much of a talker," Wendlin said.

"I like to talk," Mary said. "I would like to have said, 'I love you.' Since I did, it would have been more straightforward to have said so."

"You said it all the time."

"Wendlin, do you remember how I used to make milk toast with poached eggs when we'd been up late?"

"Yes."

"And how good it was?"

"Yes, Mary."

"Could you fix us some now?"

"Could you eat some?"

"Maybe no more than a bite. But I'd like us to eat together."

She must have been wrong about everything. Old Wendlin could cook, too. There wasn't a thing the matter with the milk toast or the poached eggs. The hot milk, yellow with butter and flecked with pepper, had the remembered taste of nights long ago.

After they had eaten, Mary said, "I think if I had another pill, I might sleep a little now."

Wendlin gave her the tablet, then sat again by the bedside with her hand in his.

"I picked out a brokenhearted second wife for you because that was what you were used to. But if I haven't been brokenhearted, she won't fill the bill, will she?"

She was getting sleepy, beginning once again not to be present. Before she left, there was something she wanted to say. "I love you, Wendlin." But it was hard to break the long habit of silence.

Wendlin sat perhaps an hour. Then he went out onto the back porch to have a look at the weather. There was scarcely any dilution yet of night's darkness. The stars were all aglitter and the cold was solid. Wendlin knew by long experience that it was below freezing, but he lit a match to see the thermometer—twenty-four degrees. Off to the east, in the direction of Shel Lewis's, there was a smoke-laced blaze. He judged that what he saw was Shel's attempt to save his grove. In every direction except the north, where the foothills had to weather the night and the cold without anyone's help, there was the sooty glow of smudge pots. What was happening was as destructive as a flood or a fire, and man had fewer ways to fight it. The cold could not be dammed or sandbagged; you could not backfire or quench it with water. You lit your little fires, but the little fires could only lessen, not extinguish the cold. Cold was nearer death itself than any other destructive element. It was without visible movement, or color. There was no distracting uproar, no crackle of flames, no pounding of waves. The cold was. It did not have to do anything. It was the negation of all, the end.

He went back into the house heavyhearted and stood by Mary's bed. The woman, lying high on her pillows, her mouth slightly open, breathing heavily in her drugged sleep, was still his yellow-haired Towanda Mary. He thought her sleeping, but when he took her hand, she spoke.

"That widow, did Chester stick to her?"

"No, Mary. The older Chester got, the younger and prettier the widows got."

"I'm glad I came to my senses before it was too late."

Nevertheless, it was late. Wendlin turned down the lamp, and in the soft half-light watched her sleep. It was too late for so many things, too late for much he had missed. And she, too, he supposed. It was cold in the bedroom in spite of the fire he had kept going all night long in the kitchen. He was dead tired, but not sleepy. He put a quilt around his shoulders, settled deeper into his chair, and slept.

Mary opened her eyes once more. Poor old Wendlin, she thought, but she went back to sleep without worrying, long accustomed to Wendlin's care.

Wendlin woke at his usual hour of six. He woke out of a dream he could not remember but which for a second kept him happy. Then he came back to the cold lamp-lighted room and last night's pain apparent on Mary's sleeping face.

Her age was not apparent to him. To him, she was still his high-spirited, opinionated, loving, brokenhearted girl. What should he have done? How could he have managed better?

If Chester had run away with Mary instead of the widow, and if after three months he had abandoned Mary, as he had the widow, Mary would not have persisted in her lifelong idealization of that scamp. She would have loved her husband when she married him; and known it. *She would have loved me,* Wendlin thought, *and known it.*

Yes, but would he, that boy of twenty-one, brought up with Mary's own ideas about chastity and one love for a lifetime, would he have recognized in this "fallen woman," this girl who had run away with a Singer sewing-machine agent and been abandoned by him, his Mary, the one woman for him? Probably not. He would have heard the phrase "ran away with a man" and never have looked closely enough to discover that it was Mary, his Mary, they were talking about.

Mary had saved herself from any such escapade. She had not "fallen." But at what price had she saved herself? And at what price had he had his untouched girl?

Their life together was ending. And by whatever means, and perhaps no other would have served, they had had a life together. And whatever the price, he would have spent his life nowhere but with this girl. But oh, the waste, the waste. The waste of life which was our only gift.

Old Wendlin, the jokester, put his face in his hands and cried.

Alone with my dead, Shel thought. Something held him to his trees. He decided, since there was so little night left, to make a night of it. He had a fire to sit by and a bucket to sit on. And if his fire began to get low, why, he had a whole grove of dead trees he could dig up for firewood. He had overreached himself, gone out too far, aimed too high, bitten off more than he could chew, tried to sit in the seats of the mighty. Now he was down where he belonged and about as low as he could get: galvanized bucket, dying fire, dead trees, head over heels in debt, the world and he traveling in opposite directions at last.

He hadn't been content to get hold of a few acres of bottom land along the Spring Branch Creek. Oh, no, not Shel Lewis. Shel Lewis was bound for California. Well, he got to California, and, once there, was he content to land himself a good job, work in a packing house, plow another man's land? Oh, no, not Shel Lewis. Shel Lewis had to have the best; he had to have himself an orange grove and he had to have it sooner than anyone else. Shel Lewis didn't live by the laws that bound other people. No water? Shel Lewis didn't let that stop him. High winds? No money? Winter? A strong man wasn't stopped by such things, and Shel Lewis was a strong man. Now he was paying for that pride.

He built up his fire and half dozed. In his waking moments he thought, Pa moved on at times like this. But where do you move on to, when you owe as much as I do, and the Pacific Ocean is the next county? He went to sleep thinking he was the man they'd had in mind when they said, Between the devil and the deep blue sea.

He opened his eyes, with Joicey looking down at him.

"How can you go to sleep on a bucket?" she asked severely, as if that were the night's worst happening.

He got up stiffly, rubbing his numb behind. There was no need to say a word. The ruin lay all around; the rag-bag orchard, where it wasn't bandaged, was already visibly dying. Last night's glossy upright leaves were already darkening and drooping. To the west and south, the sky was black with the smoke of the night's smudging; his own trees, ringed around by the charred remainders of the fires Pete had lit and by the bigger circle of the smoky horizon, looked like the center of a world-wide conflagration.

They stood side by side without speaking or touching. Shel took the still-unwilted sprig, all that was left of his green grove, from his pocket, looked down at it, touched it, smelled it.

Joicey said, "Do you want to go home, Shel?"

"Yes, I could stand some hot coffee."

"I don't mean the house. Back home. Kentucky."

"Are you still calling that home? For God's sake, no. Turn tail and run? We're lucky to be shut of those backwoods."

"What can we do now?"

"Do?" He didn't know when the idea had come to him. While he dozed on that bucket, maybe. It was so fresh and strong in its newness for him that he felt put-out with Joicey because she couldn't see his plan without his having to explain it.

"We're going to plant this place to potatoes. It's the right time to plant, and the whole family can help. You and Ellen can cut, Zoomy and me'll plant. Everybody out here's so orange crazy nothing to eat's been planted on the whole Tract—with the exception of Asa's little gully. Potatoes will sell like hot cakes. It's what I ought to've done in the first place. We'll make enough money to replant."

Chad came out of the house and started down the hill toward them. "Take Chinopsee," Shel yelled up to him. "Ride to work this morning."

Chad stopped beside them. Tiredness and sleeplessness, when they leave their mark, show more on a young face than on an old. The old face is already smudged and broken. A few new scars amidst the damage of the years don't show; but Chad's nineteen-year-old face looked hurt; he was dark under the eyes, and pale-lipped.

385

"You better stay home today," his mother told him. "You don't look very well."

"I'm all right," Chad said. "I'm still cold from being up all night. The walk will warm me up. All I need is a good day's work to warm me up and a good night's sleep to rest me."

He left them with his usual ground-covering, deceptively slow-looking gait.

"Well," said Shel, watching him, "I ain't got that kind of stamina any more."

"Where will you get the money for the seed potatoes?" Joicey asked.

"Borrow of Chad, I reckon, if the worst comes to the worst. And I reckon it has. I'll plant White Roses and Burbanks. If Asa's right, and he's got figures to prove he is, this freeze will last three days. After that we'll have about a week of moderating weather. Then rain. I'll have my seed potatoes in the ground in time to profit by that rain."

Joicey was wearing one of his old coats and she had a purple toboggan cap of Zoomy's on her head. "If I had anything left to save, I'd leave you down here for a scarecrow," Shel said, looking at her.

They started together up the slope through the ruined trees. The sky, over Old Saddle Back, was a translucent saffron streaked with rose. The sun was as cheerful as ever. It had a clear conscience about the night's happenings. It had an alibi. The killing had taken place during its proved absence.

Joicey said, "Shel, I was afraid you'd be half crazy if your trees were hurt."

"I was," Shel said. "I was half crazy until I seen you this morning. I was ready to give up. I was finished. I don't know why I'm not now."

"Maybe this outfit scared you back into your senses."

He didn't think it was seeing Joicey that had scared him back into his senses, put potatoes in his mind, and taken failure out of it. He searched his mind to find the cause for the change. The cause was too much a part of his mind for another part of it to recognize it. What he was trying to discover and name was his thirty-year habit of not giving up when pushed in a corner. Character is nothing but habit. Strong when habit is strong.

"Don't start whistling till we're out of the woods," he advised, "and remember we're not out yet by a long shot."

"I don't mind being in the woods with you."

"I mind, I sure as hell mind. And you couldn't hire me to whistle.

386

Though I keep telling myself I ain't lost a thing but money. And that nothing's dead but trees."

Joicey put her arm through his.

"I hope to God you don't mark the baby with that rig you've got on," he told her.

Before they got to the house, he threw his orange leaves away.

12   I T W A S about four-thirty when Pete rode into his own yard. He was bone-tired, his eyes burned, and his hands and face were numb. The house was lit up, but that didn't surprise him. Rosa would be expecting him and have something warm for him to eat and drink. He supposed he could have worked on through the day, but he was glad it wasn't necessary. Part of his tiredness was actually sadness for Shel. He would like to get into bed and forget Shel's frozen grove. That was his one idea, as he put up his horse: swallow something hot, get into the warm bed, and forget all about poor old Shel.

When he opened the front door he saw Medora Cudlip. His first thought was to turn tail and run. He didn't have any love for that girl at the best of times, and four o'clock in the morning after the night he'd been through was scarcely the best.

"She wants to see you," Rosa said, her voice indicating exactly how selfish, stupid, and crazy she thought the girl.

Pete wished Rosa hadn't spoken in that voice, because he did not want to feel sorry for any more people that night. He considered Medora a fast, brassy girl who deserved every misfortune she brought upon herself, and he didn't want any harsh words spoken to her that might disturb this conviction. Whatever her reason was for being here, he wanted to say, "It's none of my business. You brought it on yourself." But Rosa, by glaring at her, and Medora, by sitting there so straight, meek, and silent, endangered his feeling of justified indifference.

He went to Rosa and put a hand on her shoulder; but Rosa stayed rigid under his touch.

"*She* is waiting to see you," Rosa reminded him.

Medora said, "I didn't come to see you. I came over to see if Julian

387

was home. When he wasn't, I remembered you were his best friend."

"Best friend!" Rosa said.

"I'm his friend," Pete agreed.

"Julian's told me how you took care of him since he was a baby."

"Took care of him!" Rosa said. "They are the same age."

"I'm two years older."

"What's two years?" Rosa asked him.

"At three and one, quite a lot."

"It's nothing, now. If he is big enough to go around getting girls in trouble, he is big enough to look after himself."

"I'm not in any trouble, but Julian is."

"Her father beat him up," Rosa said. "I don't blame him."

"What did Julian do?" Pete asked Medora.

"Nothing. He knocked on the door and asked for me. Then my father turned on him and began to hit him."

"Why didn't you help him?"

"I couldn't. I was locked up."

"How did you get here, if you were locked up?"

"I slid down sheets from upstairs. I wanted to see if Julian was hurt. I couldn't find him, and he isn't home."

Rosa said to Pete, "You are not going to go hunting for him. Let his family hunt for him. Let her hunt for him. You have been working all night. She got Julian in trouble. Let her get him out of trouble. This is not your business."

Julian was his business, not Medora; though he had some admiration for the stern-looking girl running around barefooted on a freezing night. But if she had been running barefooted for anyone else, she could keep right on running, and he would go to bed. He had an admiration for her, but it was the admiration he would give a man, not the tenderness he would give a woman, or even the tenderness he gave Julian, his friend. He was vulnerable where Julian was concerned because of that tenderness. Two years' difference meant nothing now, but at three he had lugged Julian around, and at ten had been a father in knickerbockers to the undersized eight-year-old.

Such tenderness happens. It takes hold of us for reasons we do not understand, and it is perhaps because we do not understand it that we are never free from it. Pete had been overcome by tenderness for Julian as some boys are overcome by tenderness for a puppy. Every year, boys risk their lives for their pets, jump into rivers after them, sprint onto railroad tracks for them; sometimes too late to save

388

either themselves or their pets. No one is surprised by this. Such devotion is accepted as a part of boy nature. The devotion dies ordinarily as the boy hardens into manhood and the puppy becomes a broken-toothed old dog. And this surprises no one either. But Pete did not harden into manhood, and Julian did not decay into canine senility. The tenderness Pete had felt lugging the fat little Julian around as a baby did not cease when Julian grew up to be a religious dandy, a deceptively tough little fellow. The two young men were very different. Pete did a good many things Julian couldn't or wouldn't do, and Julian did a good many things Pete couldn't or wouldn't do: play the piano, for instance, follow church rule exactly, and, before Pete was married, stay away from the girls. But Julian continued to delight Pete; he continued to feel the old protective tenderness for the younger, smaller man. There was a bond between them Pete could not sever without wounding himself. He had been late to sire a child, but with Julian he had an early experience of fatherhood.

"If you were locked up, how did you know about all this?" Pete asked.

"I could hear it."

"What did you come here for?" Rosa asked, getting to the point. "You will get us all in trouble. It is none of our business that you fall in love with Julian and hang around him and never give him a moment's peace. That's what you do, isn't it?" she demanded.

"No. He came to see me tonight without my asking him or even knowing he was coming."

"But at first," Rosa persisted, "you ran after him, didn't you?"

"Yes."

"He wouldn't be hurt tonight—maybe dead—except for you, would he?"

"No."

"You go on home," Rosa said. "You go right home and stay there. The next thing, you will have your father beating up my husband. Get Julian killed if you want to. That's your business. But not Pete."

"He won't have such an easy time with me," Pete said.

"He won't fight fair, will he?" Rosa asked.

"No," Medora said.

"Go home. You ought never have come. Don't mix us in it."

"Julian is your husband's friend."

Rosa turned to Pete. "I never said anything against Julian before, did I?"

389

"No, you never did, Rosa."

"He is your friend, maybe. I am not sure. But she is not. She got Julian in trouble. She will get us in trouble. She is mixing in where she doesn't belong. Make her go home. You can't find Julian in the dark." She turned again to Medora. "While your father was killing Julian, my husband was helping a white man. Why wasn't your father doing that? Why wasn't he over there working for his own people? Now you come to get Pete to help you after he's been working all night. Aren't you ashamed? Isn't harming one man enough for you?"

Rosa stood, and the baby she was carrying inside her was almost visible, as if she held it cradled in her arms.

Rosa is small-boned, and the baby, Pete thought, must take after me. Probably its feet are already bigger than Rosa's. Rosa, who had wanted the baby so much, never asks to be babied because of the baby. Instead, she acts as if a woman carrying a baby was of a proved strength and could endure for two. She looks tired but she won't mention it. She will fight Medora because she thinks Medora is wrong but she won't ask me to stay home because of her condition.

"Let's go to bed," Rosa said to Pete, in a quiet, private way, as if Medora were not present.

"Do you want her to spend the night here?" Pete asked.

"No, loan her your horse."

"It would be better if her father never knew she was here."

"It's not our business if her father whips her for running after boys."

"Better for us, I mean."

"How can you keep him from knowing?"

"Can you get back into the house the way you got out?" Pete asked Medora.

"If I get there before daylight," Medora answered.

"You are going to go?" Rosa asked Pete.

"You know I have to."

"I don't know that, but I know you are going."

"Julian would go look for me."

"I wouldn't be so sure of that."

"I have to go anyway."

"You will kill yourself after working all night."

"Kill, kill. Now, Rosa, you know I don't die that easy."

"I know it. I never said it. But don't mix us up in it, Pete. It's between them."

390

He took her in his arms, and this time she leaned against him, though because of the baby she had to turn sidewise to do so comfortably.

"I'll be home in time for breakfast. If Julian's on the Tract, it won't take much time to find him as soon as it's daylight. You go back to bed now and get the bed warm for me."

Rosa didn't turn her lips away from his kiss, but for the first time in her life she wouldn't tell him good-by.

"You wait here until I saddle," he told Medora.

When Pete left the room, Rosa said, "I should've locked you up when you came, the way your father did, so Pete would never know you were here."

"I would've screamed."

"I know you would."

"What else could I do?" Medora asked. "I love him. You would do the same for Pete."

"Pete is my husband. Julian is not your husband. Or ever will be," she added spitefully and to cause pain. "It is not right to take a strong, good man away because your father is bad and your sweetheart is weak."

"Julian is not weak."

"If he is not weak, why must Pete always take care of him?"

Rosa didn't wait for an answer, but went back into the bedroom and closed the door behind her.

She thought, as she heard Pete lead the horse to the house, If I went out now, threw my arms around his neck, and sobbed, he would stay. The front door opened, and she heard Pete say to Medora, "Come on."

She stayed where she was. As she listened, the horse went down the first hill slowly and up the next at a gallop. She thought, Medora would have sobbed. And if I had, I wouldn't be alone now.

The Anaheim Sanitarium had formerly been the twenty-room plaster-and-cement mansion of a German-born sugar-beet baron. Nothing on the exterior of the building, with the exception of the black-and-gold sanitarium sign, had been changed since the days of Oscar Sidenstricker. The same tub-sized urns, filled with trailing nasturtiums, occupied the twin halves of a lawn bisected at its exact center by a cement walk. The same stained-glass panels, filled with stained-glass lilies, occupied the top quarter of the windows and the whole of the front door. Black-and-red-striped awnings, perhaps not the old ones but of the same color and design as the old ones, covered the side windows.

These domestic details affected patients in different ways. Some enjoyed going there for an operation because the sanitarium was so homelike. Others, for the same reason, distrusted it. Domesticity, they feared, might be carried right into the operating room, the incision made with a bread knife and closed with a turkey skewer.

All this was nothing either to Julian, who had been unconscious when Wendlin brought him in, or to Pete, when he finally found him the next morning.

Julian, with head bandaged and face so swollen that eyes, nose, and mouth were without separating boundaries, was half sitting in his bed when Pete came into his room. He had already been shoved down onto his pillows a half-dozen times that morning by a nurse who explained to him that if he had a fractured skull, sitting up might kill him. Julian believed that death, his own death, would warn him before warning some strange nurse. He had received no such warning, and pulled himself up, though the effort made his head throb, each time she left the room. Except for a tendency to be dizzy when he moved, he felt all right. Pete's expression showed him that he didn't look all right.

"What's the matter, Pete?"

"Jesus," Pete said, "he really hit you, didn't he? Can you see?"

"Sure I can see. Why not?"

"Your eyes."

"I can see."

Pete's face, as he looked at Julian's bruises, swelled with anger. "I think I better go have a little visit with this Cudlip," he said.

"Stay away," Julian said. "Let him alone. How did you find out I was over there?"

"Medora. She came out to our place."

"She was locked up. I heard her yelling."

"She got loose."

"She didn't know I was here."

"She knew I would find you."

"Let's go home," Julian said. "My clothes are in that closet."

"Julian," Pete said, "what're you going to do about this girl? Her father'll kill you both before he lets her marry a Mexican. Why're you so crazy about her?"

"Crazy about her? Who said I was crazy about her?"

392

"A man must be crazy about a girl to get himself beat up for her."

"I got beat up because she's crazy about me."

"What were you going to see her for?"

"I wasn't going there to see her. I was going there to see her folks."

"She thinks you were coming there to ask them to let you marry her."

"I don't know what makes her think that. I've never mentioned marriage to her. I didn't see her last night and I didn't want to. I heard her yelling, though, and that was enough. You ought to hear her yell. My God, even if I had been going there to ask her to marry me, after I heard that yelling I would've run."

"Looks like you should've run anyway."

"I wasn't planning on marrying her, so her yelling didn't bother me any. She screaming. Her father hitting me." Julian smiled, stopped that because it hurt, shook his head at the fix he was in, and stopped that because it hurt even more.

"If you didn't want to marry her, what was the fight about?"

"It wasn't any fight. But what it was about was my being a Mexican. Mr. Cudlip don't like my being a Mexican."

Pete's arrival didn't please Julian. It didn't surprise him either. And it did solve one thing. He wanted to get out of the place, and while he felt like sitting up, he didn't feel like a ten-mile walk.

Pete came closer to the bed, leaned over, and stared at Julian. Julian recognized that look. He had seen it a thousand times in the days when Pete had heard him teased about his piano lessons, his churchgoing, or his clothes. Nobody teased him twice when Pete was around. No one had ever laid a hand on him, because, before that happened, Pete would have to be licked. And no one could lick Pete. Sometimes Julian thought that sooner or later he would have to fight Pete himself. He would get the beating of his life, if Pete could be persuaded to fight, but he didn't know any other way he could demonstrate that Pete's protection was nothing he had ever asked for or enjoyed.

Julian wasn't—and he knew it—all that Pete thought of him. Who could be?

He didn't know, though, how far Pete went beyond all *his* estimates of Pete. He considered Pete a good, solid fellow, easygoing, not the brightest or most energetic man in the world, but, since his marriage, improving, holding down steady jobs, showing up at Mass every Sunday, keeping his eyes off the girls while there, and, as far as he knew, staying home nights.

393

Tenderness enhances and magnifies the object it envelops. It adds the heart of the observer to the dimensions of the observed. A parent needs tenderness in order to put up with a child, and a child needs indifference in order to endure this tenderness. David was a king and Absolom was his son. He was also old King David's pet. It is a tragedy to be a human pet. Someone is bound to suffer. If a pet is any good, he outgrows his dependence. The old dog never disappoints the master who has petted him. He is more dependent in his age than he was as a puppy. But the human pet, growing up, appears to betray his protector. The protector, if what he has valued has been his own feeling of power and generosity, not the growth and development of the pet, will feel bereft, and will struggle to castrate his darling.

"What's he care, if you don't want to marry Medora? Does he know you don't want to?"

"He knows. That's why I went there. I got that much said. 'Keep your daughter home. Teach her to keep her hands off me.'"

"Did you say that to him?"

"Well, he hit me before I finished. But he heard enough to know what I meant."

"My God," Pete said. "No wonder he beat you up."

"Why? I went there to tell him we both want the same thing. He don't want his daughter mixed up with a Mexican. I don't want it. He don't want it. So why can't we work together? I will help him. He can help me. I can go to church and make an act of contrition. But this will not help his daughter if she throws her arms around my neck once too often."

"Has she already thrown her arms around your neck once too often?"

"I hope not."

"She loves you," he told Julian.

"You're too softhearted."

"She said last night she loved you. She ran five miles barefooted in the middle of the night to get help for you."

"She's crazy about me," Julian admitted.

"She's very pretty."

"I have to choose."

"Even if a pretty one chooses you, you won't have her?"

"No."

"Why?"

Julian thought for a while without answering. The one who was

394

asking that question had been a chooser: had stuffed him with tortillas when he wasn't hungry, tickled him when he didn't want to laugh, lugged him around when he wanted to walk, protected him when he wanted to fight, wiped away his tears when he wanted to cry. He didn't want anything handed to him, not even the best thing in the world. He didn't have to choose the worst; he would try not to; but he would rather have his own worst than somebody else's best.

"I choose," he told Pete.

"If you loved her, you could run away with her. She'd go with you."

"I choose," Julian repeated.

"After what you said, her father's going to take it out on you anyway if you stick around here."

"I can take care of myself. If I have a chance."

Pete looked at Julian, bandaged, swollen, and defiant. Why, the little gamecock, he thought. I'll look after him. Julian, the little fool. To go to Cudlip and ask him to see that his daughter stayed home and kept her hands to herself. A Mexican to ask that! In what had been Oscar Sidenstricker's own bedroom, chosen by Oscar because of the palm trees and the cross visible from the window, Pete felt the tenderness, the responsibility. Perhaps it was the night without sleep, or the hard light on the palm fronds, or the rhythmic lift and fall of the curtains that intensified the feeling. He experienced it as a state in which Julian was only incidental, one of the persons, but only one, for whom he would give himself.

Julian, the little gamecock, shoved himself farther upward on his pillows, as if resisting the sacrifice—if that was what it was. But the net of tenderness was thrown over him. The two were bound together, bound to their past and to their future.

# BOOK IV

I   C H A D, who had hoped to work himself into a state where he wouldn't care what Press did, almost overshot the mark. After the freeze in January, he kept on with the road job in spite of a cold that settled on his lungs. He didn't complain, and in the midst of all their other troubles, Joicey never thought of him as being seriously sick until one night, taking him an onion poultice for his chest, she found him white-faced against the pillows, his eyes bright and hard with fever. When she bent over him, he grabbed her hands, kissed them, and called her "Press."

She and Shel had carried him out of his tent and into the spare room. The doctor who came out next morning from Anaheim gave them the news: pneumonia, a touch-and-go case.

It was touch, not go. Chad had wanted a little vacation from his agony over Press, but he had no intention of dying until he and Press had lived their long and happy life together. He was as sure of that life before death as others were of life after death. He had been given that revelation on the night when the two had stood together by the horses. He believed that what is true for a minute is true forever. The truth does not change, but people weaken in their strength to live by it. He himself felt capable of hanging on until Press was also ready to live in the truth of that moment of revelation. He hoped he could do so without getting grabby and spoiling his and Press's life together with any of his father's looseness.

He was in bed from mid-January until mid-February. The first and only thing he had asked for, as he began to regain his strength, was a calendar. Joicey had hung the Perkins Investment Company's big oversized calendar on the wall beside him. She had at the same time put the mantel clock from the sitting room on his dresser. Anyone interested in keeping track of the days and weeks would also, she thought, be interested in keeping track of the hours and minutes. Chad wasn't. He didn't feel ready yet for anything as concentrated and busy as a clock. The calendar gave him unmoving pools of quiet in which to rest. He spent hours looking at the calendar. It was time past and time to come, divided into neat little boxes, and the boxes named and numbered. He would look at a box ahead, say, February 25, 1917, and think, Inside that box, I and everyone else on earth, minus a few who will die before then and plus a few who will be born, will have our lives. Inside that box, each of my acts and feelings for that twenty-four hours awaits me. And because he was sick, there was not much he could do to prepare for or to control those acts which waited for him to become their center.

The doctor still called him sick, though he was without an ache or pain. But he was content to follow the doctor's orders. "Lie still, eat, don't worry." What did the doctor think he had to worry about? A burden to his father? And his kiss-and-run girl, usually running? He wasn't worrying about either. Time was up there on the calendar, ahead of him and behind him, but he himself lay suspended, floating outside of time. His sickness, like a telescope turned wrong end to, made everything visible but remote, too small and too far away to care about.

His family, as if knowing about and fearing this remoteness, came to his bedside to bring him the life-sized news of the day. The news each brought was different.

Ellen brought him the news of spring. She brought him the outdoors for which she thought, mistakenly, he yearned. She brought him the arroyos where the wild tobacco was leafing out, the leaves blue green and needle-shaped like the wings of newly hatched dragonflies. She brought him the sycamores at the heads of the big canyons with buds like glassy drops of water. She brought him the masters of spring, the elderberry bushes that made all other greens look yellow or blue. She filled his sick room with all of spring's swollen progress: mustard and wild radish in bloom, grass lengthening toward waving. The true flowers were not yet in full bloom, but Ellen swore that facing a southeast wind she could smell the flower tide moving their way. You could believe, she told him, that nature was jealous. Nature had killed everything that man had planted and had prospered everything else. She told him about the birds: road runners whimpering; wild

398

doves cooing at dusk like summer waterfalls; meadow larks, sweet as canaries and ten times as loud. The meadow larks were not news; he could hear them outside his windows. But he didn't tell Ellen. He let her talk; he floated in time, and what floated with him, birds or words, didn't matter. It didn't matter, he didn't care. Spring had come, the grove was frozen, and spring flowed over it as indifferently as water over a dead body. Or over his live body. Live, but not caring about the world's spring, waiting for its own seasons.

Ben came, sat by his bedside, and tried not to take advantage of Chad in his weakened condition with prayers and Bible readings. He stuck to the news, like an honorable man, refusing to strike an opponent who is down. Chad recognized this chivalry, though it wasn't necessary. News about the Huns seemed about as remote as news about the Hittites. Medora and Bathsheba were all one to him. But Ben was determined to forswear heavenly matters for his friend's sake.

Julian had been beaten up by Base Cudlip and might lose the sight of an eye. Medora had been jilted, if a girl who has never been engaged can be said to be jilted. Julian's pride evidently would not allow him to keep company with a girl whose father had half put out his eye. Ships were being sunk in the Atlantic like flies. The Huns were torturing the Belgians, cutting off the hands of the boys and the breasts of the women. If this kept up, Ben didn't know how long he would be able to hang onto his convictions about not fighting. The Reverend Raunce had been accused of making love to some woman in the church. Raunce said it was his wife, and Crystal said it wasn't. A sad mess, whatever was the truth. And in any case, Raunce was not going to be asked to be the pastor. Ben was, if and when the Rose Park Elders approved him and the Yearly Meeting recorded him. The Tract was banding together to sue Sylvester Perkins. The live citrus trees left on the Tract could be counted. School was closed. Eunice Fry had resigned. His mother was growing weaker every day.

Ben was a faithful visitor and a conscientious reporter. In the midst of his recitals, Chad had only one interest. Press. How is my girl? Ben never mentioned her. Why? She had come when he was sickest, knelt by his bedside, cried his pillow wet with tears, and whispered alternately, over and over, "Don't die" and "I love you." He had no intention of dying. He knew she loved him. When he got well, he would begin again his efforts to lead her back into the moment they had shared. But where was she now? Ben didn't say, and Chad wouldn't ask. In one of those numbered boxes on the calendar they would meet.

Most of the time, he was alone. He took deep breaths of the raw smell of seed potatoes, newly cut and bleeding their milky starch. He inhaled the sun-warmed scent of the creosote-stained redwood planks. The top quilt on his bed was pieced in a star design. Each star was made up of God knows how many pieces, and each piece was of a different color and design. The designs were a tanglewood maze of leaves and flowers and stars and branches. When he got tired of calendar quiet and of cataloging smells, he took up quilt-gazing. He didn't need a world a minute bigger than his room, an inch wider than his calendar, or an iota sweeter than his own breath. But he was the only one who knew this.

Zoomy was neither Ellen nor Ben. Spring didn't interest him, and chivalry didn't affect him. He made no effort to bring Chad what he thought Chad might want. All of Zoomy's news was news about Zoomy. Or Old Silver. He didn't really differentiate between the two.

"Old Silver is sick," he told Chad.

"He's never been very healthy."

"He's sicker. I think he's got pneumonia."

"What makes you think that?"

"He acts like you."

Chad didn't ask how Old Silver acted. He didn't care to see his actions mirrored in an old hound. Zoomy told him anyway. "He wheezes. His eyes are full of matter. His hair's like broomstraw. He stinks."

"That's me all right," Chad agreed.

"Since he's got a human disease, nothing but human medicine will likely save him," Zoomy said, looking at the bottles on Chad's bed table.

"Take them all," Chad said.

"What if you die without them?" Zoomy asked, and Chad saw that Zoomy was willing to risk it.

"Take them," Chad said, and Zoomy's eyes filled with tears but he accepted the sacrifice.

Shel came most often at suppertime and sat by lamplight for a few minutes. He looked older than Chad had ever seen him. High time, Chad thought. All those high spirits, that singing and whistling, the overconfidence, a new pack of children started with one bunch almost grown! Let him settle down, act like a middle-aged man instead of a young buck.

Shel came in often because he felt guilty about the boy. He didn't like, and never had liked, the boy's looks. Chad was a throwback in looks to his own father, a living picture always before his eyes of what he was trying to run away from. Give Chad a straggly black mustache and a quid and he'd be the spitting image of that old slab-sided, black-haired petticoat chaser. Telling himself that, looks aside, Chad was nothing like old Jud Lewis didn't do a thing to quiet the instinctive dislike he felt when he saw his son's face, a dislike that persisted even now, the boy just back from the jaws of death. It was bad enough to carry a resentment against your father around for a lifetime, let alone saddling it onto your son. Shel made himself sit by Chad's bedside when he wanted to be elsewhere, because of that guilt. And because of the guilt of having let the boy go back to work the next day, after that punishing night in the grove. And because of the guilt of thinking, when Chad first took to his bed, not of the boy but of the money he'd lose by his sickness. And because of the guilt of his lack of sympathy for Chad in his unsuccessful suit of Press Cope.

Guilt doesn't make a good bedside companion. Shel was trying to make himself, not Chad, feel better; he was trying to cure something in himself. Chad, who heard the talk of his other visitors like the sound of bees or rain, heard every word his father said. He wished he would dry up and leave.

"Poor old Silver's on his last legs," Shel said, when he saw that Chad's eyes had closed. He wanted to rouse him up. With his eyes closed and his big death-pinched nose lifted upward, Shel was reminded of Rosa's wreath on that bed and the thoughts it had given him.

"You been hearing Silver at night?" Shel asked. "He was old when we got him. I wouldn't care to guess how old he is now. He ain't got no teeth to speak of, can't even eat cornmeal mush if there's lumps in it. I'm going to put him out of his misery. I don't see any help for it. It'll be painless. I've got chloroform. The old dog'll never know what hit him. The druggist told me how to go about it. You soak a rag in chloroform, put the rag in a flour sack, put the flour sack in a paper bag, then you put the paper bag over the dog's head and tie it around the dog's neck. Last of all you put the dog under a box. That's the end of his suffering. I thought I'd better tell you about it. That dog's strong point's always been howling. He might howl a little, but it won't be because he's suffering."

"Dog," "dog," instead of "Old Silver," Chad thought. Now that he's

401

going to kill him, he don't want it to be any dog in particular. Not Old Silver, just some nameless, sick hound.

His father, leaving, said, "I didn't want you to worry if you heard anything." Chad thought, Worry is something I've gotten over.

But when he heard, after everyone else had gone to bed, the sounds his father had warned him about, he was immediately wide awake and listening. The sounds weren't loud. How could they be? Even so practiced a howler as Old Silver wasn't able to perform very well tied up in two bags, under a box, and half chloroformed. Far away, in another world and of no concern to me, Chad told himself. A good thing really, as his father had said, for the dog to be put out of his misery. But the next series of strangled whimpers set him to trembling. The time of his separation from the world had ended. Had Old Silver's dying cries ended it? Had it ended by itself? At any rate, it was gone; and with it had gone his floating world of quilt patterns and potato smells, of secondhand reports of spring and sin, of time someplace ahead in a neat pigeonhole on the sheets of a calendar.

When he got out of bed, he understood better why he had been so content to stay there. He couldn't walk. There was no use trying. He made it out of the house and to the box, but only by crawling; and he couldn't do that without occasional rests. The night was soft and warm, the sky clouded. In the moments in which he rested, he saw stars appear and disappear as clouds moved across the sky. When he reached the box, he lay across it for a while, unable to start the work of lifting it without resting. Old Silver knew he was there, or knew someone was there. His howls quieted and changed. The box was one of Shel's packing cases, made to stand the two-thousand-mile trip from Kentucky to California. Even after rest, Chad found he couldn't budge it. He got onto his hands and knees, and from that position was able to push an arm, then a shoulder under the edge of the box. Finally, shifting the weight of the box onto his back, he reached the dog. For a while, he believed that instead of rescuing the dog, he would have to spend the night under the packing case himself. Old Silver wouldn't or couldn't move, and Chad couldn't hold the box up and haul the dog out at the same time.

He was at last able to claw the old hound free of his chloroform-soaked rag, and with that in his hand, he struggled free of the box. Old Silver was still imprisoned, but in a cell now, not a coffin.

Chad crawled slowly back to the house. Because he was so weak, he had the sensation of making his way through a heavy surf or through deep grass. After he was in bed and his trembling had stopped, he began to think of Press. Not as someone far away whom he had known a long time ago. As Press, his living girl. His vacation from life was over.

It was raining when he opened his eyes, but it was Zoomy, not the rain, who had awakened him. Zoomy was not making a sound, just standing there at the foot of the bed, willing him to wake up.

"Silver's better," he said, when Chad opened his eyes. "It was your medicine cured him."

"I'm glad to hear it."

"I knew human medicine would cure him."

"What's Pa say now?"

"About putting him out of his misery?"

"Is he still determined to do it?"

"No. He was going to, if Silver wasn't better this morning. But he's a lot better. Now he says he'll let nature take its course."

Zoomy set the two bottles, both still a quarter full, on the table by Chad's bed.

"I don't need them any more," Chad told him.

"You might have a setback," Zoomy reminded him.

"That's not my plan."

Zoomy, the business of his visit over so far as Chad knew, continued to stare at him pensively. "You still look sick," he said.

"Appearances are deceiving."

"I'll pray for you this morning."

"Pray without ceasing," Chad said.

The resurrection of the night before had made a truth-teller out of Zoomy. "I couldn't pray without ceasing," he said. "Could you?"

"Never tried it yet."

"I meant I'd pray in church this morning."

The Lewises were by no means regular churchgoers. Chad looked out the window, where the eaves were still dripping from the last shower.

"Kind of rainy for church, isn't it?"

"Papa's doing it for the Reverend Raunce. The church is being dedicated."

"You go on," Chad said, "and dedicate it. And pray for me. I'm still not out of the woods."

403

2 THE thoughtful California rain, which had fallen intermittently during the night, eased off toward daylight, and by ten had stopped altogether. The rain was also thoughtful enough not to scare people into thinking, when so much more was needed, that it had finished for good. The sky was still overcast, and, below the general grayness, darker clouds were moving north and east behind a fresh, wet-smelling wind. But even a thoughtful California rain cannot tell a Sunday from a weekday, and this was a Sunday and the daytime letup helped no one. Rain or shine the children would have played outside, and rain or shine their parents would have gone to church to hear LeRoy Raunce preach his dedicatory-and-farewell sermon.

There had been some question about letting LeRoy preach this sermon. True, he had been invited to do so and had written and practiced—as a good many of them had heard—such a sermon. But the invitation had been issued before LeRoy's trouble and at a time when the congregation expected that LeRoy would become its first minister. Since LeRoy had been rejected as their minister on the grounds that he had defiled the church, it was not suitable, in the opinion of many, that he occupy the pulpit on dedication Sunday. He was permitted to do so because the very people who had voted against offering LeRoy the pastorship were the most insistent on his preaching.

They were insistent, in the first place, because they did not suppose he would have the gall to accept the invitation; and, in the second place, because they believed they showed themselves, by offering the invitation, to be tolerant, forgiving men.

LeRoy accepted the invitation and blasted their hopes of being able to have their cake and not eat it. They had it and now they would have to eat it. They had asked for a sermon and now they would have to attend church and listen to it. They now pinned their hopes on the expectation that an exposed woman chaser (even if the woman *was* his own wife) could say nothing from the pulpit from which he was being ousted which would not sound pretty silly.

Those who had voted for LeRoy's being retained as their minister planned to hear what LeRoy had to say as much for their own sake as out of loyalty to him. During the year of his preaching, they had grown accustomed to walking out of his tent on Sundays into a world that his words had altered. In LeRoy's world, all the furnishings from pebbles to people were rare gifts, objects of wonder which they had only a few years to enjoy and contemplate. For these listeners, LeRoy's sermons and personality provided a magic strong enough to cause them, after listening to him, to experience life for a few days in far more direct and vivid fashion than was customary. By Thursday or Friday, as they began to slip back into their own drab patterns of seeing and understanding, they began also to be impatient for Sunday and another of LeRoy's renewing sermons. They believed as they listened to him that the world he preached was the real one. They remembered, or thought they could remember, a world like that. They had once jumped, had they not, out of bed each morning to just such wonders? They had formerly, it seemed to them, gone to bed each night thankful for these wonders and sorry for all hatefulness and hoping that God would bless everyone everywhere. It was with such childlike hearts they left LeRoy's tent on Sundays, and it was to regain such hearts that they were going to listen to his last sermon.

Eunice, who had no hope of regaining a childlike heart, and who had not voted against LeRoy, was going to listen to him preach his last sermon because she felt guilty. She felt responsible for LeRoy's trouble. It was her lie to Base and her presence in the church that had aroused Base's suspicions.

It was an odd thing that the outside world, which had never punished her and Tom, was punishing, because of them, this innocent man, whose only crime was that he loved his wife. Tom, who had loved so many wives not his own, had never to her knowledge lost a job or been publicly denounced because of his promiscuity. The guilty know how to cover their tracks. Or they involve themselves with other guilty ones who dare make no accusations, and for this reason there is no need for track-covering. The guilty have an instinct for self-preservation, but the innocent are open to their enemies.

That day when she had been hunting Tom, and when Indy had found him, they, the three guilty ones, had gone scot-free, while poor LeRoy, come to the church to practice his praise, had been punished, deprived of his pulpit, denounced by his daughter. Eunice intended for at least one hour to take her mind off Tom Mount and to employ that hour asking God to undo the harm she had done LeRoy Raunce.

405

She had given up her school for the simple reason that she had found teaching impossible. She could no longer rouse herself to impart such knowledge as c a t spells cat, $2 + 4 = 6$, and, "In 1492 Columbus sailed the ocean blue." She had lost her belief in the importance of these facts. She herself knew them well, and how had they helped her? Something else was needed, though what, she didn't know. She would find herself staring at her children, no more able to communicate with them than if they had been stones—or flowers. And the children stared back, locked in her dehumanizing gaze. It was no way to teach school. Besides, she felt a compulsion to share LeRoy's fate of joblessness. And in addition to everything else, Cudlip intended to have her fired soon, no matter what she felt.

By nine, she was dressed for church. She told Opal she would walk, taking a roundabout way. Out of work, she had discovered once again the exercise of her Colorado days. She tramped the hills and, like many a woodchopper and walker before her, found that fatigue was an antidote to sorrow; found that when muscles ache, the mind, as if out of sympathy for its brute partner, lets up with the memories and the accusations. She had heard this a thousand times, but it was a remedy she had to walk her way into, stupid as a patient who can take the doctor's word for nothing.

After a tramp of ten or twelve miles, she would find that she had, without knowing when, stopped remembering her terrible past with Tom and dreaming of her impossible future with him. By hard work and sweat, she had been able to trade her painful memories and hopeless dreams for the anticipation of a good rest and a hot bath.

In addition to helping her sorrow, she had walked herself into all kinds of knowledge. She understood as never before the pleasures of hunters and athletes. As she sat in Opal's sitting room after a day in the hills, she wondered if love-making itself might be in some respects no more than a form of exercise. She remembered evenings following afternoons of love-making in which she had experienced just such sensations of tranquillity.

Tom and love-making were things she tried not to think of, particularly during the two hours after her long hard walks. If she became self-congratulatory, conscious of her respite from pain, if she said, "You have lost Tom, but you are not really suffering so much now, are you?" she fell into a black, despairing misery. What was the purpose of the grace she was experiencing, except that she be able to share it with a companion? Except that she be able to face someone

406

whose beatitudes flooded to meet hers? Sorrow alone, she thought, is easier to bear than joy alone. If you see a man alone in a room, shedding tears, that sight, though sorrowful, is understandable. But if he is alone jumping for joy, the sight will embarrass you. Joy without a compulsion to share it is both sorrowful and unnatural.

She had been taught to live by reason, and she had reached a spot where reason could not help her. Reason, which told her that this man was a liar, a man incapable of loving one person, incapable of repaying a debt, also told her that only with him had she ever experienced happiness. Should she condemn him because he was less limited than she? Because he could be happy with any woman? Or at least any number of women? Reason told her, Throw away such labels: liar, adulterer, thief. What do they mean? reason asked her. You love a man. But reason also told her, Those are the names for his acts, and such acts kill you. Reason replied to that. Without Tom, you had as well be dead. Reason told her that with Tom her pain was so great she could not see the world. And reason told her that without Tom there was no world. When she cried out, "I love Tom," reason never contradicted her. But when she tried to discover the reason why, if this was so, she had to suffer so much, reason answered, You suffer because you love him.

She was dying of reason, on a rack, with reason pulling her first one direction, then another.

And Tom had never repudiated her. If she would take him as he was, he was hers. She could at any minute (if he didn't happen to be with another woman; "Give me a few hours' notice, sweetheart" was his only request) go to him, and he would take her in his arms and say, "If it isn't my dark Irish gypsy, come back to her proper home."

Tom had never repudiated her, and she had said, in her heart, to Tom, "Not my will, but thine." Why, then, having taken that vow, had she repudiated it? Why had she longed more passionately that day in church for evidences of Tom's unfaithfulness than for Tom himself?

Had she hoped that enough evidence, finally, would free her? If so, it had been a fruitless hope. The more the evidence, the more she struggled like some latter-day Job to be faithful in spite of all her afflictions.

She was in need of a miracle and was without hope of getting one. Tom was her life's miracle, and here she was, out to forget her life's miracle, to walk it to death, silence all of its contradictory answers.

407

The morning was warm, gray, and blustery. Her skirts slapped around her legs. She could taste the water in the air and feel under the sparse grass all of spring waiting for the sun. Already there were glints of color: yellow violets, baby blue-eyes, blue teakettle stems, flaming-red Indian paintbrushes, orange-yellow California poppies. She knew the names; she recognized the colors; they might have been names in a book and colors on a chart for all they meant to her.

As she passed Asa Brice's tent on the opposite side of the arroyo, he hailed her.

"If you'll wait five minutes for me, I'd like to walk with you. Come on in," he urged. "I have to shave, but it won't take me but a second."

He did his shaving at a wash bench outside the tent and called to her through the canvas as she waited for him inside.

The two had often met in the past weeks. Asa had espoused nature with as much passion as Eunice had espoused Tom Mount; and nature had never been unfaithful to him, or at least no more unfaithful than was natural. If anyone was unfaithful in their relationship, it was he. He had somehow expected of nature more than nature gave to him. Repetitions of experience did not get him any nearer that mystery at the heart of nature that had, in the first place, elicited his passion. Lately, he was constantly turning to persons, hopeful of finding in them the answers nature denied him. He had not been very successful with them either. Ben had disappointed him; Tom revolted him. He knew that one of his friends had said that he would as soon think of taking hold of the limb of a tree as of taking Asa Brice by the arm; and since trees no longer satisfied him, Asa was trying to become less treelike himself. Even when you get to the heartwood in a tree, he thought, what you have to deal with is still wooden.

Asa believed marriage to be the poetry of life, woman a fellow human being, and love the only portent of what, if anything, lay beyond the stars. Falling in love was not a state he aspired to, but he was eager to love. He was eager to have his heart touched; he was eager to feel again the ardor he had once known as an inspector of snow-storms and an observer of woodchucks; but he was also eager to know that ardor for a being more responsive than they: such were his hopes and intentions, but they did not make conversation any easier, and Eunice was as out of practice as he with trivialities. Passion may be self-consuming, but it isn't trivial and it isn't talkative.

Being a man, Asa was more able than Eunice to speak of what

408

did not interest him; and he had also made up his mind to take some pains in order to get to know her.

"I don't know why more women," he said with pauses between phrases to accommodate, Eunice supposed, the shaving of some critical area, "don't take walks."

The answer to that was "Not very many of them are broken-hearted." If she had said that, they might have had a chance. But she could not expose her wound. She wanted Asa's love as much as he wanted hers, but she was unable to give him the whole of herself. If Asa had come in from his shaving and made love to her there on his narrow thinly mattressed cot, she thought she might have been able to give him the whole of her body—and by that means work slowly toward mind and heart: the mind and heart that later might be Asa's, but which were still too taken up with Tom to be bestowed on any other man.

She liked to look at Asa. He came in from his shaving, his face pink under his unfaded summer tan, and stood before her finishing his drying and patting. He was a shorter, ruddier, craggier man than Tom, a tree that would gnarl rather than rot. He was a big-nosed, commanding fellow, for all his shortness. What did Tom have that Asa lacked? Asa's angularity was more masculine than Tom's long, soft, tomcat silkiness; but Asa's masculinity was less concentrated than Tom's; it pervaded his mind and imagination as well as his body.

You have no right, Eunice rebuked herself, to ask this man to teach you that Tom is not the only man in the world. But she had more right than she knew. Asa was asking her, Teach me that there is more in the world than trees.

"Do I look all right for church?" Asa asked, putting on a tie.

He looked well-razored, whetted and honed like a hunting knife.

"You look fine," Eunice told him.

Asa had intended suggesting that they spend the time before church walking, but it struck him that one of the distinguishing marks of the nontree was that it was found indoors. He pulled up a chair. "We've got three-quarters of an hour," he said. "No use starting yet."

Three-quarters of an hour. The words frightened them both. It was too long a time for any conversation either felt able to manage, and too little time for the rescue operation each longed for.

Asa was determined that this should not be a conversation about centipedes or sunsets; Eunice was determined not to speak of Tom

Mount; and neither was interested in anything other than the impersonal force each was struggling to suppress and overcome.

Eunice's case was more desperate and ambiguous. The impersonal force that had mastered her looked like a person, spoke with the intimacies of a person, but was in fact so much a force and so little a person that it no more conveyed any of those rasping irritations and contradictions that are a part of the highly individualized even when they love than spring or wintertime or tide. Like the wind, Tom accommodated himself to any crevice or corner; like the sea, he was at home in any cave or abyss; like flame, he could lick up anything flammable. The wind is said to complain, the sea to moan, a fire to race. These actions are attributed to nature by human complainers, moaners, racers, who see themselves mirrored everywhere. Tom, like nature itself, was free of these faults; he took his own sweet time and smiled even while he destroyed.

Asa was better informed about nature—and, in some ways, about Tom—than Eunice. He knew that nature was impersonal, and until lately he had believed that this impersonality suited him. Why should he want nature to be personal? He did not like to hear his own footsteps and took care not to leave a track behind him. He had accepted for himself Keats's saying "The wind is my wife, the stars my children." But recently the wind, which he had espoused and which he knew to be ungrieving, grieved him. Overhead, the stars, his children, blazing in the winter sky, left his heart empty. He was ready to be delighted by any show of humanness in Eunice, silly or gossipy, but having to do with men and women. When Eunice, breaking all her own resolves, unable in the room that had known Tom's voice and presence, not to speak of him, said, "How long did Tom Mount live here?" he was pleased. Such confidential, womanly talk domesticated his tent and made him a man instead of a naturalist. He did not care for Tom Mount, but he had never made it a habit to speak only of what he approved.

"About two weeks, as I remember," he answered.

"Why did he leave?"

"I asked him to."

Eunice looked up, amazed. Tom was the prize, the rejecting, not the rejected. Turning the matter over in her own mind, she answered her own question, "How could anyone want to get rid of Tom?," without asking it.

410

"Tom's a pretty big man to try to coop up in a tent this size" was her answer, and she gave it to Asa.

"I've cooped up bigger," Asa said flatly.

"I expect after living alone, it's hard to get used to a pardner?"

"A pardner," Asa repeated, as if that was the strangest or nastiest word he had ever had in his mouth. "A pardner was the last thing I wanted. Tom as a pardner, anyway."

"What did Tom want?"

"A roof over his head was his chief interest, at the moment. Or one of them anyway."

"A single man in a new territory like this is at a disadvantage. No boardinghouses or anything."

She had forgotten that she was speaking to a single man, and Asa was too tactful to remind her that he himself felt at no disadvantage.

"Tom seems to make out pretty well. First the church and now the parsonage."

"I don't know how the Raunces find room to put him up."

"LeRoy can put people up in his heart," Asa said. "He's not dependent on floor space."

"What do you think of LeRoy, Asa? Did you vote for him?"

"I'm no churchgoer, so I didn't have a vote. But I would've voted to keep him."

"Do you think he's a good preacher?"

"He's a good man. That's more unusual."

"Do you think he was in the church with some other woman?'

"Other than his wife? No."

"Do you think he was making love to his wife in the church?"

"I hope so."

"I don't see how LeRoy can bear to have Tom living at his place after all this. The man who caused it all."

"Caused it all? You can't blame Mount because his bedroom was handy."

"I can blame him," Eunice said.

"I don't see how."

"Asa, I was looking for Tom that day when Base saw me go into the church."

"Is that Tom's fault?"

"Yes, he wants women to look for him."

"Most men want that."

"You don't."

"I do. It's a lack in me that you don't think so."

"It's not a lack. You wouldn't want women phoning you, writing you, giving you gifts, eating their hearts out for you, would you? It would make you ashamed of yourself, wouldn't it?"

"I have a high regard for love."

"That's what I'm saying. That's what I've been telling you."

Asa did not reply. After some minutes of silence, he said, "Did you tell Base why you were going to the church?"

"Of course I told him."

Eunice rose and turned her back on Asa. She thought that she might be unable to keep from crying. How Tom had loved her tears, not tears that blamed him or that were shed for any overt purpose (and she had never shed such tears), but Tom had never been more tender with her than when she had cried. "Don't hold back, sweetheart," he would urge. "A woman who can't cry can't do anything else." Though she saw that Tom did not dislike her tears, she was ashamed, at first, to cry. "I'm so noisy," she would apologize, trying to quiet her sobs. "You're quiet compared to a lot of women," he had told her, holding her in his arms and looking sympathetically at her shuddering body and drawn face. "Why, once I made the acquaintance of a woman on a train for no other reason than that I had never in my life seen anyone so broken up with crying. Give way to it, girl."

For a time after hearing about the woman on the train, she had felt that she disappointed Tom with her naturally quiet weeping. He would never have been drawn to her seeing her crying furtively into a handkerchief. But she couldn't bring herself, even though she knew that Tom would like it, to make her crying noisier.

For a minute, hearing some movement of Asa behind her, she believed that he knew how she felt and was going to comfort her, would put a hand on her arm, or even his arm about her shoulders. She both hoped he would and wondered if she could endure it.

But she did not turn to face him, and although Asa had taken a step toward her and had extended a tentative hand, he needed more encouragement from her than a turned back.

"We have time," Asa said, when she still could not speak nor face him, "for a little look at Reservoir Hill on the way to church. Flowers came out there earlier than anyplace else."

There was no talk at all outside. The flowers excused them both. Asa was busy, stooping to examine details not even visible to Eunice.

412

Occasionally, he wrote in a notebook. He did look up once, seemingly surprised to find her standing beside him. "I keep track of the first flowers of the season and where I find them," he explained. "It makes an interesting record over the years. Unless I'm mistaken, this is the earliest I've ever seen a sego lily."

He took a little magnifying glass from his pocket, round, and hinged in a weathered brown leather case, knelt and held the glass over a pale flower. Eunice watched him for a while as he prodded around the leaves and took notes, but finally she lost interest and turned from him to gaze at the churchyard on the floor of the valley a half-mile away. A few people had already arrived. Instantly, she wondered if one of them was Tom, and tried to pick him out. Some intuition would make it possible, she believed, for her to know him even at this distance; seeing a man and a woman walk a little apart from the others, she immediately thought, That's Tom. The pain she felt on seeing the couple was her proof. The church bell, LeRoy's final gift to the church, rang at ten-thirty, though neither Asa, looking at his sego lily, nor Eunice, watching the couple she believed to be Tom and Indy, heard it. There was a clock in the sky for Asa, and he knew without listening to bells when to start down the slope toward the church.

When they arrived, they were greeted with smiles. They were a suitable couple. Asa was an odd fellow, and any woman who teaches was thought to be a little queer. Match them up and avoid spoiling two good couples. The smiles Asa and Eunice received were only for them; but smiles were general that morning; so many people felt guilty. They felt guilty because they were about to enter a church that would not be standing except for the efforts of one man. They had been summoned to the church by a bell that was the gift of one man. They were about to listen to the loving, praise-God sermon of this man. And this was the man they had kicked out. They smiled because they wanted to convince themselves that they had done the right thing. They smiled because a congregation that had rid itself of a proved lecher *should* smile. They smiled and began to feel self-congratulatory. A man creased his face with a smile, inquired of himself, "What have I got to be so happy about?," answered himself, "This is the last I'll have to listen to Raunce," and believed his own lie.

Base Cudlip and his wife did not smile. They were not happy, and did not try to convince themselves that they were. In their opinion, LeRoy had stayed too long and he should never have been permitted to deliver this final sermon. Clemency for the wicked is a betrayal of the virtuous. The Cudlips had betrayed virtue, no smiling matter.

The Wendlin Jessups smiled occasionally. They had been LeRoy's chief supporters. People had believed that the selection of Ben Jessup as LeRoy's successor would reconcile his parents to LeRoy's dismissal. It did nothing of the kind. Mary Jessup was known to have said that she was disappointed in Ben's choice of a profession. She loved God and believed in goodness, but in her opinion a man who made the love of God and a show of goodness his paying profession got more and more professional and less and less loving and good. Nevertheless, in spite of the fact that the Jessups, or at least Mary, did not want LeRoy to lose his job, or Ben to get it, their sympathies appeared to be less with LeRoy than with those who had ousted him, and especially with Cudlip.

Base saw Mary's benevolent glance turned in his direction and tried not to catch her eye. He had spent an acutely miserable evening with that woman, and since then he had avoided her. She and Wendlin had come over, after his run-in with that Mexican who had been fooling around with Medora, and for two hours Mary Jessup had treated him to all the loving forbearance of an old mother telling her condemned son good-by at the foot of the gallows. Not a hint of condemnation; though except for the Jessups finding him, the Mexican might have died. Nothing but openness, nothing but understanding. He became nakeder and nakeder before them; threw off, unwilling and unforced, all the layers that protected him.

There had not been a subject he could bring up that Mary Jessup would not listen to. A word here, a look there, and she had led him on to saying things he hadn't known to be true until he said them, which, as soon as he heard them, he wished weren't true. She let him choose his own subjects. He chose those he had convictions about, which ought to have showed him to be a man willing to exert himself night and day for the welfare of his community: Raunce, Sylvester Perkins, the freeze, the assessment, the war, the Mexicans, his daughter, her daughter.

The sweat had stood out in the hollows of her temples, her upper lip had trembled, her eyes under her lids could be seen to be throbbing. Still she listened. And still he talked, until finally he was as defenseless as that small boy who long ago had needed no defense, protected as he had been in his grandfather's home.

Mary Jessup herself had saved him from whatever he might have

414

been mesmerized into saying next. She had appeared to be on the verge of some kind of a breakdown or seizure. Wendlin had gone to his wife, then asked Base for a glass of water. Base had done better than that. He had provided a drink that was half whisky. This had eased her, but after a sip or two, she said to her husband, "I have waited too long."

She had apologized to him then, as if by her departure she were breaking up a party. He himself had never had a guest he was more eager to speed. Now, seeing a greeting in her eyes, he turned away hastily, pretending that Sylvester Perkins's "How are you, Basil?" was a question demanding a full and immediate answer.

Mary's smile, now that she had grown so thin, was a terrible thing to see. Exposed teeth, with pink flesh framing them, mean merriment; but with the jaw and cheekbones scarcely veiled with yellow skin, they mean death. Mary knew nothing about this; and when, with the help of luck and drugs, she was able to rise above her pain, she was able also to rise above the earth, to brood down upon it in a state of beneficent power, understanding, and humor. She and old Wendlin, though she never thought of him thus any more, had traded places. She had become the jokester. A jokester needs to see two things at once, appearance and reality. Wendlin, who had seen this vision for years, had lost it. Nowadays he saw one thing only: Mary dying. Mary in the midst of death saw life: this gave her the jokester's double-barreled vision.

She was holding onto Wendlin's arm, not so much for support as out of a tipsy humorous delight in the peculiar world; a humor and delight she wanted Wendlin to share with her. She had loved him all along! And Wendlin had been smart enough to know it. The minute Wendlin had said to her, "What did you ever do to me that was unloving?," she had known the truth. She had maintained, in her mind, a wife's fidelity to old Chester; but to Wendlin she had cleaved like a lover. Time and again she could have caught Chester, who had proved to be a marrying widower, between wives, and have become the wife he had refused to make her in the beginning. Old Chester had got less choosy as time went on. She hadn't turned to Chester because, she had told herself, it was her duty to stick to Wendlin. Duty! She was so glad she had been taught to do her duty. It had been her duty to stick to Wendlin and it had been her duty to make it up to him for not loving him, and so, with dignity and pride, she had been able to enjoy the whole of her marriage to darling Wendlin.

If there were more time, she thought, I would give way to remorse. But there is too little time, and besides, I'm not sure the whole thing wasn't laughable.

She indicated by a pressure on Wendlin's arm that Base was ignoring them. She and Wendlin were so close nowadays that few words were necessary. One word would suffice to put them in a past scene: the firefly Kansas dusk; a ride out of town to "stir up a little breeze," after a close thundery day; the women in white dresses on the porches; the Victrolas playing "Three Little Blackberries" in the living room; men watering their lawns while the children played beckons wanted. One word and they were in the past, heading west out of Emporia into the clear apricot sky. One word and, from the back seat, Paula once more called, "Hurry, Papa, let's catch up with the light."

Oh, Paula! There is nothing better than to have a daughter and to love her. She is on your side forever. She sees the things that hurt you. She understands what is important in a way no man is ever able to understand. Most people thought she was lucky to have a daughter who chose to be a foreign missionary. Those people had never heard the one-year-old Paula say as she watched a snowstorm, "Look at all the pretty flowers." Now Paula was saying to Chinese girls, "Basketball practice at ten tomorrow." Was that a choice to rejoice in? No, but it was Paula's choice. She and Wendlin marveled at their children, preacher-to-be and missionary-already-established, not knowing whether to take these professions as a sign that they had brought their children up better or worse than they'd known. Surprised at their choices, but more content on the whole, Mary thought, than if they'd chosen burglary and streetwalking.

But Mary, who could smile at her children's professions, and who could see the comical aspects of her lifelong illusion about old Chester Bannister without remorse, felt sick with remorse every time she thought of Basil Cudlip. She had tried again this morning to reach him, but he had turned his back on her. She knew that she would never have another chance; and she knew that whatever he was, or would do from now on, was her responsibility, too. Of all her sins, the only one that still bothered her was that of saying about Base, "He's beyond me." No human being should say that about another. It may prove, finally, to be true; but the declaration before the proof invites the sin.

She could not bear to look at his resistant back and his brown, thin neck, still boyishly corded.

416

"Let's go speak to the Lewises," she said to Wendlin.

She took Joicey's hand in hers. Mary had never been a hand-holder before her sickness. Now she never spoke to anyone without taking his hand. She had noticed the change in herself, and had asked herself, What am I doing? Saying good-by? It wasn't that, but, rather, in the short time left her on Earth, there had come the desire not to limit herself, the desire to touch, to see, and to hear simultaneously. Without letting go of Joicey's hand, she also took Asa's. "Asa, what's a bug lover like you doing here?"

"LeRoy's a natural phenomenon, too, Mary."

When Mary, by taking Asa's hand, freed Eunice from paying any more attention to him, Eunice turned toward Ellen Lewis, and saw that she was gazing at the Raunces' house. When she, too, faced in that direction, she saw why. Tom Mount and Crystal Raunce were coming out of the Raunce yard, Crystal talking and Tom listening, his whole body conveying that interest and absorption Eunice knew so well.

"How I envy Crystal," Ellen said. "And you, too," she added.

"Why me?"

"You know Mr. Mount. He's your friend. You knew him back in Colorado."

"Yes, I did."

"Was he just as popular there as he is here?"

"I think so."

"Once, you said you thought I'd make a good teacher. Well, if I would, it's partly Mr. Mount's influence on me."

"How has he influenced you?"

"He makes me want to be worthy of him. Whenever I do anything, I think, 'Would you want Mr. Mount to see you doing that?'"

"What makes you think Mr. Mount is interested in what you do?"

"Oh, I don't think so, Miss Fry. He doesn't know I'm alive. But look at him now with Crystal. He cares about people's minds and souls. You can tell that by watching him, can't you? Anybody might want to be with Press or Medora, they're so beautiful. But Crystal's plain. A handsome man like Mr. Mount has to be kind to talk to Crystal like that. He has to be the soul of thoughtfulness and unselfishness."

Eunice said nothing. She was wholly absorbed in the approach of Tom and Crystal.

"Did you ever know anyone handsomer?" Ellen asked.

417

"No," Eunice said, "I never did."

"I just love his walk, don't you?"

"Yes."

Tom, as he came nearer, stopped talking to Crystal and turned upon Eunice all that old doting warmth, that warmth without contradiction. He was wholly what he did, as an animal is. Nothing of Tom was left over when he acted. Tom could plan and calculate as an animal couldn't; she knew that; but the minute he began to move, to act, the shadow of the calculator was excluded. He had the animal's inability to put himself in the place of another. The cat, chasing a mouse, does not remember what it has suffered a few minutes ago with a dog and take pity on the mouse. Tom willed one thing. He had an animal purity of heart which gave every glance of his a pristine quality. Eunice could remember such glances as he was giving Crystal turned toward her; but for Tom himself, these were obviously the first fond looks he had ever bent upon a woman.

Ellen couldn't endure the excitement of having him so near. "Excuse me," she said to Eunice. "I think Mama wants me."

"I'm big, ugly, and harmless," Tom called after her, but Ellen didn't turn or speak.

He held out both hands to Eunice. "Eunice," he said, "has it come to this? I have to go to church to catch sight of you? I hear you've given up the school. I hear you and Asa are bird watching together. How are you? I've missed you. It's good to see you."

He continued to hold her hands, but he didn't forget Crystal. "Eunice and I are old neighbors," he explained. "We knew each other before the Tract was ever thought of. And almost before you were."

With the touch of Tom's hands, Eunice was back in her prison, back in her narrow world which was Tom. The true churchyard, the real and cheerless people disappeared. In the beginning, she thought, Tom was a world vaster and richer than any I knew. He still is. Why can't I live there? Because I can't live there with Tom's other women.

She saw one of them, and said, "There's Indy Cope signaling to you."

She didn't know whether Indy had been signaling or not. She had, at least, been looking in Tom's direction. She gave Tom his chance to say, "Let her signal."

He didn't take it. He never would. He let go her hands. "I've been wanting to see Indy. Thanks for telling me."

He turned to leave, but he forgot no one. "Remember, you promised to sit with me in church," he reminded Crystal. To Eunice he said, "Let's go for a ride together sometime, Eunice." He didn't even forget Ellen, gazing her full from the safe distance of her mother's side. "Told you I was harmless," he called.

When he reached Indy and Lute, he saw that he needed to do something quickly. Indy's face was a dead giveaway. It wasn't that he didn't welcome that look, that he didn't feed on it. But the more it gave to him, the more he had better try to get it hooded. If Lute, who was beside her, turned to her and saw her watching another man with that gone look, there would be trouble. Or there ought to be.

He addressed Lute first. This was a little obvious and he wasn't proud of it. But it should be a lesson to Indy. He had told Indy time and again, "Neither one of us has a thing against Lute. He's a fine man. Let's not cause him any undue suffering. What we have is so fine and rich we ought not to begrudge him a crumb or two. We know what we have and that it's right for us. With this knowledge we can walk right through any situation, calm."

Indy was far from calm, but it didn't matter. Lute didn't have a glance for her. If Indy wasn't a model wife, Lute appeared to be determined never to become aware of it. Tom's advice to Indy on calmness and the sharing of crumbs might have been, to judge from Lute's bearing, his doctrine, too. "Tom's a fine man," he might have said. "Let's not cause him any undue suffering. We know what we have and with this knowledge we can walk through any situation, calm."

He certainly appeared calm, and when Tom, thinking that he might be overdoing it, ignoring Indy completely, began to speak to her, it was Lute who drew the conversation back to himself. Not, it appeared, out of jealousy or anger, but because as a newspaperman he wanted to know Tom's reaction to the latest news. Tom often forgot that husbands weren't one-hundred-per-cent uxorious and that a wife who was at the moment occupying his mind continuously hadn't the same intense hold on her husband of twenty years.

"What do you think of the Zimmerman note, Tom?" Lute asked.

First, Tom took in the fact that Lute was speaking as citizen and editor, not as husband. When he had digested this, he considered the question itself. There had been a lot of notes passed back and forth between Wilson and Lansing, and the Germans, and he supposed this was one of them, but he was damned if he knew which one or what was so special about it. With a woman, he was accustomed, when ignorant, to bluff. He had to prove his manhood with them, and one

419

of the proofs was to show them that he knew more than they did. With another man, this wasn't necessary. He could admit with another man that he was an ignoramus, and the other man would be charmed with Tom's honesty and with his own ability to provide the information. So, since he couldn't play both roles at once, he chose under the circumstances to charm Lute rather than to impress Indy.

"Lute," he said, "sitting up on a ridgepole shingling, I can see quite a distance, but I can't hear a thing but the wind and my own hammer. This is the first time I've heard the word Zimmerman. Who in the hell or what in the hell is Zimmerman?"

It worked with Lute as it did with other men. Lute laughed a little, then said, "Tom, if everyone was as honest as you, a lot of time spent beating around the bush could be saved."

"The time you've saved beating around the bush will have to be spent educating me, so it evens out in the long run, I'm afraid."

"Maybe so. Zimmerman's sent a note to the German minister in Mexico. 'Tell the Mexicans we will finance a Mexican strike against the United States,' that's the gist of it."

"What've the Mexicans got against us?" This was putting it on a little thick. Tom knew about the Alamo, but that seemed too long ago for thoughts of revenge still to be bothering the Mexicans.

Indy, sensitive to Tom's ignorance, and eager to share all of his misfortunes, said, "Yes, Lute, why would Mexico want to fight us?"

"Indy, I know you're no historian, but I think Tom's pulling my leg."

"A little," Tom admitted. "I remember the Alamo."

"The Mexicans also remember New Mexico and California and Texas. That's why Germany is saying to them 'We'll help you get back what the United States stole from you.' Now what do you think of the Zimmerman note?"

"I think the Germans are getting desperate."

"Maybe so. But what's that to the Mexicans, if the Germans will help them? Help's help. What's behind it don't matter. The Mexicans hate us, and the Germans are saying 'We're on your side.'"

Tom himself didn't hate anyone. He couldn't comprehend that kind of hard focusing upon a single object. He made an effort, imaginatively, to understand all those handsome liquid-eyed people wanting to kill persons like himself in order to get back some stretches of earth most of them had never seen. He couldn't do it.

420

"I can't believe they hate us enough to fight us."

Lute snorted. "They hated us enough to massacre eighteen Americans less than a year ago in New Mexico. And they didn't have any Germans egging them on then either. And what do you think Black Jack Pershing's been doing down in Mexico? Sight-seeing? They hate us for that, too."

"That killing last year in New Mexico. A thing like that can boil up anyplace."

"You should talk to Base Cudlip. He thinks we ought to take some precautions about the Mexicans here on the Tract."

"Base afraid Ralph's going to cut his throat?"

"Ralph's got some reason to, after the way Base treated him. But that's not what he's afraid of. He thinks they might blow up the reservoir."

Tom couldn't help laughing. "I can see Pete and Rosa wasting a night climbing up Reservoir Hill with an armload of dynamite."

"Pete and Rosa aren't the only Mexicans here."

"Base is hipped on setting people right. Now that he's taken care of LeRoy, he's got to find something else to work on."

Lute put a hand on Indy's shoulder. He could feel her camisole and petticoat straps under her light coat and, without thinking what he was doing, he moved them up and down a little, feeling the lift of her breasts as he did so. He stared at Tom. Mount was a hard man to pin down. He was woman-like in his constant ricochet off the real issue into something personal. Lute could understand a man who believed the Zimmerman note wouldn't incite the Mexicans to war, but he couldn't understand a man who didn't hate the Germans for making the try. Or hate the Mexicans for that massacre last year. Unless, like Wendlin Jessup, he was a Quaker set against all violence. And Tom wasn't.

While Lute stood there, fiddling with Indy's shoulder straps and trying to make out the kind of a man he had to deal with, Sylvester Perkins hailed him.

"Howdy, Lute," he called. "How're you making out?"

"I can't complain," Lute said. "These are fine times for newspapermen, if for nobody else."

Syl shook hands all around, talked about the weather, the war, and even the Zimmerman note, then he said, "I've been looking for Shel Lewis. Any of you seen him?"

421

"He was here awhile back," Lute said.

"I saw him standing behind the church as I came over," Tom told him. "Maybe he's still there."

Shel was still there, brooding on the difference between the dedication Sunday he had anticipated and the one he was experiencing. He had expected to be there as a successful rancher listening to LeRoy, the newly elected preacher. He had himself failed, and he had failed LeRoy.

With his back to the church, he faced his own ranch, invisible in the gray, shapeless clouds that topped the hills north and east. But he could see his dead grove as clearly as though he stood in the midst of it. And he could see that potato patch of his, alive enough, but more suitable for the kitchen garden of an old Irish biddy than the entire ranching operation of a Western orange grower.

He felt heartsore. Not alone about his ranching failure. That had wiped him out; he was in debt for his dead trees, and behind in payments on both land and water. But that was the smallest part of his failure. Through his mulishness in getting his trees planted before anyone else, he had worked Chad into what might easily have been his deathbed. Chad was mending, but his face on the pillow that morning had reminded him of Rosa's wreath. He had knocked on wood, standing at the foot of Chad's bed. Chad had asked him what for. "For good luck," he had answered. "I'd like a little good luck for a change."

Good luck or good sense, he thought. A man's got to have one or the other, and I've been without either recently. Jesus, Jesus. First I pick a crook like Perkins as a man to trust. Next I pick Lute Cope, who's got a paralysis of some kind, as a leader. Then I turn thumbs down on LeRoy, because he don't fit a hillbilly's notion of a close-mouthed, starch-fronted deacon. And even when I find out different, I lack the gumption or the git-up to get out and work for him. I let a man like Base Cudlip, drowning in his own bile, have the say-so.

He had on no overcoat and was glad of it. He wished the wind was colder, wetter, stronger. He'd like to be buffeted by something he could stand up to, have a chance to fight something besides himself and his mistakes, endure something besides his own dumbness.

He tried to tell himself he didn't have any troubles a little money wouldn't cure, but it was a lie. All money could do was get him out of debt. It wouldn't settle a thing between himself and Perkins or between himself and Cudlip; it wouldn't restore his faith in Lute or give LeRoy back his pulpit. It wouldn't lift Chad off his sickbed or restore Joicey's faith in her husband.

He walked to the corner of the church, planning to rub salt on his wounds by looking at his family, the ones who were having to pay for that biggity gamble of his. There was Ellen, gazing at Tom Mount. Joicey was hand in hand with Mary Jessup. In his twenty years of knowing Joicey, he had experienced more than one kind of love for her: the love of his first courting days, when she never left his mind for a minute, night or day; the love of early marriage, the impassioned, never-satisfied satisfaction of loving her. Joicey had never been a postponer in love, a bargainer, a woman who endures love-making; she took it like a Christmas-tree gift and was only sorry Christmas didn't come every day in the year.

Thinking these thoughts and watching Joicey fling the warmth of her living around Mary Jessup's fading life, he was surprised at the life that rose in him. Sunday in a churchyard and a middle-aged has-been watching his wife heavy with child. And the old Adam as strong in him as ever. Well, you can't keep a good man down, he thought, and was heartened by the sign.

Sylvester Perkins had to call a couple of times before Shel heard him. Syl was wearing a long-haired green fedora beaded with moisture. His little brown eyes looked out from under its brim with the good humor of some forest animal sheltering under a fern.

"Howdy, Shel," Syl said. "I've been looking for you. What're you doing back here? You gone sour on your neighbors?"

"Some of them," Shel said, giving Syl the chance to use all the truth he had the capacity for. "But mostly I've gone sour on myself."

"The freeze?" Syl said. "That was an act of God and nothing to blame yourself for."

"God didn't put my trees in the ground at a fool time."

"We all make mistakes."

"Some of us can afford them."

"Shel, there's something I wanted to talk to you about. I hear you're hard pressed for money."

"Hard pressed? I'm flat broke."

Syl started to say something, but Shel stopped him. "No sympathy from you, please. When a rattler strikes you, his crying afterward don't mean a thing."

423

"In the first place," Syl said, "I haven't got any tears. In the second, though it's a matter of opinion, I suppose, I've never thought of myself as a rattler."

" 'Frost-free,' " Shel quoted, starting from the rattler's beginning.

"This is the first freeze this section's had in a quarter-century. And as you said yourself, the trees were planted at a fool time."

"All right," Shel said. "Forget the freeze. What about the assessments? By God, there's something crooked going on in the Perkins Investment Company. Something's being put over on us."

"Shel, that's what I've been hunting you for. I've got some things I want to talk over with you."

"It's mutual," Shel said. "But this ain't the time or the place."

"I know that. I want you to come into my office some time this week. There's a lot I've got to say to you."

"With my team, that'll take two days out of my week. I don't have that much time to waste."

"I'll send my car out after you."

"You really want to see me, don't you?"

"That's what I'm trying to tell you. What day'd suit you best?"

"It's all one to me."

"What about Friday?"

"That's as good as any."

"Somebody'll pick you up around one and bring you back by bedtime. I'd like to take you out to supper. Ever been to Good Fellows Grotto?"

"Never been anyplace, never seen anything," Shel said, unwilling to put any foot but his worst forward with Syl.

"I tell you what," Syl said, "we'll make it an evening. . . . We'll . . ."

Shel shushed him. "Here's LeRoy," he said.

LeRoy was late for preaching because he'd been lost in prayer. LeRoy's congregation did not usually wait outside the church for him. And usually LeRoy did not keep them waiting. Why he was doing so this morning no one knew. Not for reasons of making a showy entrance, all eyes upon him. No one thought that; that would take some calculation, and LeRoy had amply proved that he was the last man to calculate the effects of his actions. A man, calculating effects, could never have brought himself, in the circumstances, to preach this farewell sermon at all. Instead, he would be out of town, saving his face. He was late, his enemies believed, because he could not find his suspenders, or because he had not been able to leave bed and wife at a reasonable hour. Those who were not his enemies believed that LeRoy had been praying.

LeRoy advanced with his wife by his side. His congregation made way for him as it would have for a man bound for the gallows or a throne. There was a come-and-go light as clouds of varying thickness passed across the sun. The wind that blew in their faces smelled of spring as well as rain. No man ever looked less like Jesus than LeRoy. He was more godlike than that. If he had had a big beard to hide his knobby, red face, and a flowing white robe to hide his heavy thighs, the resemblance might have been striking. Instead, he had shaved himself so close his face was redder than usual, and he had unearthed somewhere and was gallantly flaunting an outfit more suited to a Negro minstrel than a Quaker preacher. It was the most un-Quakerly garb in the world. Or the most Quakerly, depending upon how you looked at it, and at Quakers. If a Quaker was a man who tailored his coat to fit his heart, instead of the fashion, that opulent, encompassing, pearl-buttoned outfit of LeRoy's made him a true member of the Religious Society of Friends.

In any case, it won him some stares. The getup impressed his enemies. They thought they might have made a mistake in firing him. He looked every inch a preacher, and in that rig all of his inches were displayed. He looked the equal, this morning, of the handsome James Whitcomb Brougher, pastor of the Baptist Emmanuel Church of the Open Door in Los Angeles.

Those who were for LeRoy loved him in spite of his costume. He had bought it, or rented it, they figured, in honor of his installation as pastor, and in honor of them all. He had thought to grace the pulpit on dedication day. When he had discovered that dedication was also dismissal day, he was too big-souled to belittle the event by wearing less than his best.

He looked like the late Gladstone, roughed up a bit, and with a fiercer spark of life lit in him. He looked like a younger Grover Cleveland, fined down in the belly and shorn of Grover's walrus equipment. He looked most of all like the Manassa Mauler, if the Mauler had been a family man with God's power in his heart instead of his fists. He was not looking merry this morning, but you could not say he looked sour or put out or disappointed either. The truth was, he looked like a man in the midst of life and conscious of it. He looked like a man blown on at the minute by a threatening wind and stand-

425

ing up to it. He looked like a man living his life. He took them all in as he passed, their common circumstances and peculiar sorrows. Also their particular joys. He was a big enough man for that job. He could do that and not lose himself.

Under his arm he carried a roll of lined white paper, the sermon he had been practicing that afternoon when his own eloquence had so overcome him he could not wait until he got his wife home and to bed. No one, unless it was Cudlip, any longer believed that it had been any other woman. LeRoy might have had a better chance if they had. A man with a woman not his wife is in desperate need of some out-of-the-way place for his love-making. A little lapse in a Sunday-school room can maybe be excused in his case. What's the excuse for a man with his own wife? Nothing but greed and poor management and a lack of regard for the sensibilities of others. If LeRoy had been with another woman, say, that big down-in-the-mouth schoolmarm Base had accused, the men at least would have banded together to save him. But his wife! That didn't bring out any charity in them. A vicarious adventure is one thing; an untidy marriage is another. They were looking forward to his sermon though. Powerful piece of preaching it must be, considering the effect it had already had on LeRoy.

It came to them, looking at that roll of composition sheets, that LeRoy might have switched sermons on them. LeRoy did not usually write down his sermons. He opened his mouth and the word of God came bubbling forth like spring water. This message, written after he had found out that he was fired, might be all hell-fire and brimstone, nothing to make any wife look like a sweetheart.

Dolly walked beside LeRoy, taking two steps to his one, not touching him, blown along by his side like a leaf caught up in the draft of a passing auto. If she thought that walk was a trial or a comedown, her face did not show it. Nothing was to be seen there but her contentment in being by LeRoy's side. The congregation let them enter the church, let them walk past the Sunday-school room where LeRoy had met his downfall. Then silently his flock fell in behind him.

Silently, except for Mary Jessup, who had too little time left for her to enjoy the luxury of postponement. What she had to say had better be said the moment it came to her. The next minute might find her beyond words. She whispered to Opal, who, with Wendlin, was helping her with the steps, which had become difficult.

"Opal, I was completely wrong about Eunice."

Opal did not know what her friend was talking about.

426

"Wrong about Eunice and Wendlin," Mary explained in a voice loud enough to worry Opal. Eunice's name was mixed up with enough men already without dragging the blameless Wendlin into the lot.

"Eunice wouldn't be right for him at all. That brokenheartedness of mine was all a dream."

In perfect happiness, laboring up the steps, Mary smiled her dreadful smile. Opal held Mary's arm closely, but could not, because they were now in the church, ask for further explanations. "My brokenheartedness was all a dream." The words echoed in her mind during the sermon.

It was a peculiar sermon and a peculiar meeting; also a peculiar meeting place: a bare room, a platform at one end, and plain sash windows lining the walls. The windows had never been properly cleaned. They were smudged with putty, splashed with the red-brown mixture with which the walls had been stained, and smeared now with the teardrops of last night's rain.

Mary whispered, "Stained-glass windows," and Wendlin nodded.

Through the north windows, in spite of the stain, LeRoy's cow and its calf could be seen, pleasantly bucolic and no affront in their present state to anyone's sensibilities. The calf, in spite of its difficult birth, was growing into a fine heifer. Beyond the cow and calf, the Tract sloped up toward the foothills, whose tops this morning were covered by gray rain clouds.

On the opposite side of the building, the stained-glass windows gave on to the sodden townsite, Asa's weather-beaten tent, and, rising above the tent, Reservoir Hill.

In the past, LeRoy had been flanked on the platform by Elders of the church: Wendlin or Base or a couple of the Du Pau brothers. This morning he was alone, whether by his own choice or by the choice of those now running the church, no one except those running the church knew. The pulpit was a mere washstand arrangement of pine boards, built by Tom Mount, and looking as if it should hold a washbowl and pitcher instead of Holy Writ. LeRoy sat behind it, but he loomed above and over it. He made furniture of it.

No one was able to fathom LeRoy's feelings by his face. Not that he was now, any more than at other times, impassive or stony-faced. LeRoy dead in his coffin was going to provide a bigger shock than most men. The change would be more noticeable. LeRoy was a strong argument for the presence of something beneath the flesh. No one had ever accused LeRoy of being a mental giant. What looked out

427

from those eyes, deep-set under their prize-fighter ridges, and what illuminated those knobby cheekbones must be spirit. And might be soul. Flesh did not have that effect on the observer. Nor did the mind, even if LeRoy had been thought to have one.

Whatever name it was given, it jumped the two-foot platform with ease, came down and dwelt amongst them. The Prince Albert, if *that* was the name for his outfit, was no barrier. The pine washstand might as well not have been there. Nor Holy Writ. LeRoy was in their midst. He warmed them like sunshine. He stirred the sap inside them. They were all dangerously unprotected. It had happened before. This was one of the reasons LeRoy was being deprived of that platform and taken away from that pulpit. He had too much power. A saint might have been trusted with that power; and they might have trusted their own nakedness before a saint. But LeRoy was no saint. It would have built up his arrogance to stay here and see his power demonstrated three times a week, once on Wednesdays and twice on Sundays. They had to depose him for his own good. Maybe it was his own wife in the Sunday-school room, this time. Encourage him a little and he'd be looking for new countries to conquer. Somebody else's wife in the choir loft. That was only human nature, and human nature was nothing LeRoy had ever conquered. A man of God ought to make up his mind which he was for, body or soul. LeRoy never had. Right here in the pulpit, with soul turned on full force, body was far from being extinguished. That shad-belly coat of his made it impossible for anyone to miss the massive heft of his shoulders or the whittled shaft of his waist.

The service usually began with singing. All their music was buried inside them this morning. Some of the muscles at the backs of their throats necessary for vocalizing had slackened and dried. LeRoy knew this. He rose, his ruled composition sheets in his hand. He was a long-waisted man, and the pulpit was no more protection to him than a wooden apron. It made him an Adam with lumber instead of leaf. He looked down at his ruled sheets as at something he was surprised to see. Then he put them down on the slanted top of Tom's pulpit. They were a part of the past. What did he, or they, have to do with that? He opened his mouth and made them all Jonahs. They heard no words but the thundering whisper of their own unspoken replies.

Mary answered LeRoy with her whole life, a life sweeter than she had known. She thanked God for this last time, surely it would be the last, when she was able to worship with the seekers. She expected

428

to die into the Light; but there had been times in the past when a band of them had been able to pull down Light from heaven, to fill a bare room with radiance. She experienced once more in life a foretaste of death's glories. She looked at all the dear ones, and had no longing for angels. I'm a worldly woman, she thought. And why not? The world is God's. She took her farewell fill of worldly faces. The faces were open and yearning. The worshipers were living in their own best images of themselves.

Zoomy was refusing to sell something. "Take it," he said, "it's a gift." Base stayed his punishing hand. Asa said, "There is a Presence beyond the Particular." Eunice thanked God. So did Opal, though for a different reason. Lute was a husband, and the woman beside him was his wife. Joicey carried her baby *and* Shel. She was given that strength. Sylvester Perkins was exactly where Zoomy was. Louella was undivided. Ellen forgot Tom Mount. Indy didn't. She believed him to be the cause of her openness now to God. She believed that loving him, she was learning to love God. Medora made no such distinctions between Julian and God. Press was able to make up everything to her mother without denying Chad. Shel was indebted to nobody. He was alive and the center of life. Crystal resisted. She was Crystal, sitting by Tom Mount, the man who thought buzzards were hawks.

Tom knew this. Like Mary, he looked about, but for a different reason. He was not saying farewell to faces; more like harvesting them against a famine. He was a real miser of persons. He liked to keep a good supply on hand, even though there were some he might never get around to using. His feeling for experience was much the same, and this was a new one. A silent meeting. LeRoy had opened his mouth, and, though no word had come forth, LeRoy himself and none of his congregation appeared to be aware of the lack. Tom was. He looked at all the drowned faces. All except Crystal's. He was content. Opal friendly, Eunice faithful, Indy passionate. The past and the present. What about the future? He slid a hand down toward Crystal's. He let it lie lightly against her long, freckled, spatulate fingers, a strangely ungirlish hand. She didn't pull it away. He took it wholly into his own, looked down at her, and saw those hawks forgiven. He had a power that was not dependent upon sermons or silence. He felt safe with Indy now. He was insured even if she had told Lute, as she said she had, that she wanted to end her marriage.

3    Two weeks after he issued the invitation, Sylvester Perkins sent his car to the Tract to pick up Shel. As Shel rode toward Los Angeles, he instructed himself as to how he should act when he met Syl. First of all, he wanted to hide his mistrust and dislike. If Syl suspected how much trouble was brewing out on the Tract, he might try to cover up his misdeeds. He would get set for the possibility of a lawsuit. Better let him keep right on with his shenanigans. Let him believe that we've never noticed the third-rate pipe, that we expected the assessments, that we're pleased not to be represented on the Water Company board of directors. Let him believe that roads torn up because of leaks suit us to a T. Let him think we're too dumb to notice that the irrigation water is delivered on irregular schedules. And even if it would be a good thing for Syl to know how we feel about these things, nobody's deputized you personally, Shel Lewis, to tell him. So keep your mouth shut, Shel. This is a trip for listening, not talking.

Shel had another inclination that he was determined to fight. He had seen men all of his life; the more they failed, the bigger they talked. You could always tell which man had the most on the grocer's books. He was the one down at the store who claimed he couldn't drink anything but a high-priced special brand of coffee. The man with the big bank balance could drink anything. That was the way he'd built up his big balance. No, he wasn't going into Syl's office head up and tail over the dashboard. He was short on dollars, and he'd got that way by being short on sense. There wasn't any legal way a man could mint himself a few new dollars. But there was no law against a man's working himself up a fresh supply of common sense.

He had never been in Sylvester Perkins's office, or any like it, before, and he was impressed. He told himself that all those files, adding machines, and typewriters were no more than the plows, harrows, and manure spreaders of a farm. Not a tenth as much steel in any one of them as in a medium-sized harrow. And the secretaries and bookkeepers were no more than a farm's hired hands. There was one difference, however, he couldn't shut his eyes to. The crop Syl cultivated was money. He sowed it with a typewriter, cultivated it with a secretary, harvested it with an adding machine, and stored it in a steel cabinet. Shel's operations were small potatoes for a surety beside these.

430

A secretary with ratted blond cootie-catchers hurried to greet him. "Mr. Lewis!" she exclaimed.

Shel was taken aback. The woman sounded provoked. Though the sign on the door said, "Enter," perhaps he should have knocked first. Nothing of the kind. The secretary was Miss Trubody, and she was eager to greet him, that was all.

"Mr. Perkins has been expecting you. He was too busy at lunchtime to eat. He's stepped out now for a sandwich, but he asked me to make his apologies and to tell you he'd be back in a few minutes. He wants you to wait in his office."

Shel thought he *was* in Sylvester Perkins's office. He saw his mistake when Miss Trubody took him into the next room. That outer office had been no more than the tool shed on a ranch. Naturally, the boss didn't hang out there, though he didn't know what room on a ranch could be likened to the one into which he had been ushered. It gave him the same tiptoey feeling he got in a church. The secretary handed him a *Literary Digest* in the same way ushers hand out hymn books. She put him in a black leather chair buttoned full of dimples, then tiptoed away as if the room's holiness wasn't something he had imagined. He waited until she closed the door, then he got up and began to examine the room.

He had known, he didn't know how, that there were offices like this: offices with rugs on the floor, pictures on the wall, the desk not an office desk but a big library table topped off with flowers and pictures. When he went closer to the table, he was surprised to see, left out so that anyone who cared might examine them, several stacks of typewritten sheets, some covered with columns of figures, others with writing. There were two flat wicker baskets filled with letters, one marked "Incoming," the other "Outgoing," both open for any visitor's investigation. Syl's carelessness with the facts of his business, particularly when his business was suspiciously shady, didn't impress Shel favorably. He himself, who had nothing to hide, wouldn't think of leaving his papers lying open to the curiosity of strangers. If Syl was a crook, he wasn't a very careful one.

There was something else on Syl's desk he didn't care for: a picture of Syl's wife, her plump shoulders only semicovered by gauze. He liked a woman with her clothes off all right, but if he had had a picture of Joicey like that, he wouldn't have stuck it out in public for any passer-by to stare at. Why had Syl done that? He squinted down at poor half-naked Louella, her shoulders shining through the gauze like plump curved moons and her curled hair lit up by lamps, like a cloud in a line storm. He felt sorry for her. That wasn't the way to use a wife, put up her picture in a public place. He would as soon have thought of tacking Joicey's picture between the plow handles. Louella's picture made him forget Syl's business papers, which it was his duty, perhaps, to investigate. He turned his back on the desk. He felt as guilty looking at that picture as he would have felt staring through a keyhole at Louella in her bedroom. And the fact that Syl had invited him in to take a peek only made matters worse.

Walking away from the desk, he walked smack into another picture. This one hung on the wall that Syl, seated at his desk, would face. He supposed it was Syl's son, a boy in uniform. A canopy of Allied flags had been arranged over the picture, and two gold basketballs dangled from the flags' crossed staves. If Louella in her picture had been decked out like an angel, this boy had been set up under a shrine like a saint or hero. Louella embarrassed him. This boy broke his heart. Take him down, take him down, he told Syl silently. Give the boy some privacy. He couldn't understand *why* Syl had Louella's picture on his desk. He couldn't understand *how* he could bear this boy's picture looking at him all day long. The boy's eyes caught his and held them like the eyes of someone on a departing train, anxious to keep the folks at home in sight as long as possible. But it wasn't the folks at home this boy was saying good-by to, it was the world. Chad at his sickest had never had such a look. And it's not the uniform that gives me the idea, either, Shel thought. That look has been there a long time; the boy ran off to Canada to put on his uniform and get his license to be killed so that his eyes and the facts would match. He and the boy said good-by a long time. Finally, he went to the window and the mountains.

There was a picture full of hellos instead of good-bys. There was his country; the snow peaks and a blue sky big enough to hold them, and the foothills, sloping up in green waves to meet them. If he was Sylvester Perkins, he'd take the angel off his desk and the farewell off his wall, and when he had a few minutes free from defrauding the customers, he'd look out the window at the Sierra Madres.

If you were Sylvester Perkins, he told himself, that's what you'd do. What do you do when you're Shel Lewis? You ever lift your own eyes to the mountains? You seen anything recently higher than a hill of potatoes? He didn't kid himself that a big sky and a row of mountains was anything his family could live on. The baby that was coming

432

couldn't be wrapped up in a view; Joicey had had her try at feeding them on ground squirrels; Zoomy couldn't stock his store with cactus apples and horned toads; Ellen, if Ben ever got around to marriage, couldn't say "I do" in trap-door spider silk. He had a hard row to hoe ahead of him; but he needn't forget, as he'd done the past months, *where* that hoeing was being done: under those mountains, in his own country.

He was still at the window when Syl came in. Shel heard the door close, but didn't turn around. Syl had asked him here. If he had something to say, let him say it. Syl came up beside him and turned the gazing into a duet. When Syl finally spoke, he might have been talking to himself. Shel heard him but he didn't know that he was actually being spoken to.

"A man comes out here," Syl said, "because he likes the country. Likes its looks, that is. It was a March day, just like this, when I stepped off the train in the old S.P. depot. I didn't have an idea in the world then that I wouldn't be catching the train back to Colusa the next day. L.A. wasn't anything then—a ramshackle collection of ramshackle buildings. But those mountains were there just the same then as they are this afternoon, white-topped with a couple of feathers drifting over them. And the ocean was down there—the air was clear enough those days you could see it. And we had rivers then. The Los Angeles, the San Gabriel, the Santa Ana. Before the irrigating began, those rivers were as pretty little streams as you'd ever want to see, and in the rainy season they could really get up and hump. Too much so, sometimes. But I didn't know that, that March morning. All I knew was that I wasn't ever going to catch that train back to Colusa. We'd had a cold, wet winter up north. When it wasn't raining, it was freezing, and sometimes it was doing both. I'd stepped out of that train from the north into air soft and warm as new milk. There were sweet peas blooming, and you know how they smell. Somebody had trained a mess of them up over the back wall of the freight platform. One of the Mexicans, I suppose. Anyway, it didn't take me thirty minutes to know I didn't want to stop looking at those mountains or stop feeling that air or stop smelling those sweet peas. I got a job next day with a draying company. From that I went into sand and gravel, and from sand and gravel I progressed, if you want to call it that, to real estate a little more tacked down.

"Well, Shel, I didn't intend to bore you with my life story. But when I saw you looking at those mountains, you put me in mind of myself

433

when I first landed here. Not many people really look at them. You pull up stakes and leave home because you like the looks of those mountains. Settle down here to be with them, and your first look proves to be your last. After that, you're too busy. I first saw this valley twenty-eight years ago. I'd lived in California since I was six, but my folks had settled up in the grain country north of Sacramento, and Southern California was as new to me as to any out-and-out Easterner. My folks were from Nebraska. They were fed up with Nebraska. So what do they do when they get to California? Why, hunt up what looks most like Nebraska. I was too young to be hit by this Nebraska-or-nothing fever, so when I came down to L.A., nursemaiding a couple of horses, it didn't take me long to discover that life didn't have to end with Nebraska—or something that looked like it."

Shel didn't know what to say to this. He didn't want to start agreeing with Sylvester Perkins, even about the mountains. On the other hand, he didn't know how to contradict him.

"Come on over and sit down," Syl said. "I didn't bring you all the way in here to tell you the story of my life, as I said before."

Syl put him in the same big chair again, sat down behind his desk, and looked at Louella for a few seconds.

"It was good of you to take the time to come in," he said finally. "I understand you're pretty busy nowadays."

"I've put in five acres of potatoes," Shel said.

"How're they coming?"

"All right. The trouble is, the weeds and bugs are coming along a little faster."

"How much do you expect to make on them?"

"If prices hold up and the weather stays good, I ought to clear around a thousand."

"That's not bad."

"For a man as much in debt as I am, it don't mean much."

"How much in debt are you?"

Shel had no intention of making these figures public. "More than I care to remember," he said.

Syl didn't press him. "You had poor luck with your trees."

"What I had," Shel told him, "was poor sense, planting them when I did. And poor help from the man who sold me the land," he added.

"You mean me?"

"Who else sold me land?"

"I wanted you to succeed as much as you did yourself. More, maybe."

434

"No, you didn't. There'd have been water in them pipes on schedule if you had."

"Shel, you keep talking like it was to my benefit to see you go under. I'm selling citrus land. Those dead trees of yours don't do me any good with prospective customers."

"My dead trees can be explained easy. 'Damn fool planted in the middle of winter.' That's all you need to say. No, my dead grove's not going to sink you."

"What is going to sink me?"

For a second, Shel thought he'd give himself the pleasure of telling Syl. But he decided the price for the pleasure might be too high.

"Nothing, maybe. Some men appear to be born unsinkable."

"Not me. I'm liable to go under any time. Shel, haven't we beat about the bush long enough? You've stopped work to come in here to talk to me. I've done the same thing to talk to you. Don't you have any notion what I've got to say?"

"Going to foreclose?"

"When that's got to be done, I'm not the one who brings the news. Shel, you don't think I'm so blind I don't know what's afoot out there on the Tract, do you?"

"Maybe I'm the blind one."

"I thought we decided to stop beating around the bush? But you only know half the story. You only know the way things have worked out for you."

Syl looked at Louella and, as far as Shel could make out, began to address himself to her. The conversation was between the two of them, and Shel invited now to listen as he had been invited before to look. He began his listening with disbelief. The longer he listened, the more he began to feel that he might be hearing the truth. Though he didn't believe for a minute that Syl's purpose in telling the truth—if that was what he was doing—was just to get the facts straight. He had begun his listening bolt upright, not taking a thing off Sylvester Perkins, not even the comfort of his chair. He still didn't like Syl's little brown eyes, his hair with its wig-straight part and neatness, but as Syl explained to Louella how it was that "his people" had come to the point of suing him, Shel found himself leaning back and thinking "poor bastard" as often as he thought "dirty thief." And yet Syl was a dirty thief.

He began to weigh as well as to listen. Syl's troubles seemed to have started where his had, in believing in his luck. Things at first had gone too well for him. Nothing failed until he began to believe that

435

nothing could fail. And back of this belief, which Syl was explaining to Louella, was Louella herself, who was chiefly responsible for his belief in his luck. He had never gotten over the wonder of her looking at a plain fellow like himself in the first place. And her continuing love and belief had been an outright miracle.

He had tried to hide his own self-doubts and weaknesses from her. She believed him to be a strong, capable man, a man of foresight and business ability. It was his determination to be the man Louella thought him that was responsible for his success. He had never let her see his weak, uncertain side. By hiding his weaknesses and uncertainties, he had finally overcome them. He had become the man he had at first pretended to be, the man Louella admired. And finally he had come to believe that as long as Louella did approve, his success was guaranteed. He wasn't excusing himself or blaming Louella. He was, in fact, giving her the credit for all he had achieved and taking all the blame for his present predicament. She had never wavered in her belief in him, but in looking back over the facts, he now saw that she had never shared his enthusiasm for the Tract.

In the beginning, nothing had been misrepresented. He would make money on the Tract. Certainly he had planned to do that. He wasn't a socialist or a charitable organization. But it was his plan that every man on the Tract make money, and every man had been convinced that he would, otherwise there would have been no buyers. But money-making had been, for him, less than half of it. All those things that had drawn him originally to Southern California, the Tract owners were going to have as a bonus. The flowers, the milk-soft air, the mountains, the sea. Those were his gifts to the Tract owners. He never saw a kid out in the Tract chasing a tumbleweed, or a housewife watering a geranium, but his heart melted with pleasure.

"Seen her carrying the water in a bucket from a barrel, too, I reckon. That sight melt your heart with pleasure?"

"I don't think a little pioneering ever hurt anybody. But that water-hauling was never my intention. I had every reason to believe I could deliver water when promised. How was I to know the war was coming? Or what it would do? I'm no prophet. I laid my plans for conditions as they were. And under those conditions there wouldn't have been a bobble. But prices went up. The government was bidding against me for steel. I couldn't get workers. We had hard luck with our drilling. The engineers miscalculated about the water level. The Tract sold faster than anybody had foreseen, and the demand for wa-

436

ter came earlier. People piled out there at a rate that was unbelievable. Well, this is all an old story to you. You know all about these matters. You were there."

"Yeh, I know all that. If that's all you've got to tell me, this has been a wild-goose chase."

"I ran short of money. That's where the real trouble started," Syl told Louella.

"Lack of money can be troublesome all right," Shel agreed.

If Syl heard him, he gave no sign. He still looked at Louella. "The real trouble started with the way I tried to raise it," he confessed.

"Stealing money's always risky," Shel said.

"There wasn't any question of stealing involved."

"What's your name for it?"

"I had an obligation to every family on the Tract. Every man there was depending on me. I'm not the kind to disappoint others easily."

"When it came to assessments, you sure didn't let us down, did you?"

"No man on the Tract did more to force my hand than you, Shel."

"So I'm responsible for your crookedness?"

"Why don't you wait until you know what you're talking about before you start calling names, Shel?"

"I'm waiting."

"To continue the drilling, pipe-buying, and so forth, I had to have more money."

"Those pipes oughtn't to have cost you much. There's a dozen leaks every day."

"They were the best I could get—or afford."

"I'm still waiting."

"I sold bonds to raise the money. I bonded the Water Company."

"We're the Water Company. The stockholders are the ranchers on the Tract. We bought water stock with our land."

"Up till just recently, I owned the majority of the water stock. I controlled it."

"So you did sell bonds? You mean our water stock ain't clear? That there's an indebtedness against it?"

"As of now, yes."

"We paid money for mortgaged property? That's what you're telling me, ain't it? Property we thought was clear was mortgaged. And now we're having to pay your interest on the mortgage? That's what the assessments are for?"

"Prices kept going up. Shel, I had no choice. I did it for the Tract."

437

"You did it for the Tract! You did it to the Tract."

"The debts were undertaken for you. None of you could've swung it by yourselves."

"Did we ever have a chance? Were we ever asked?"

"There wasn't time for that, and I did it for you. Without me, where would you be? No roads, no water, no homes."

"And no debts. You robbed Peter to pay Paul."

"I took the risk. Every cent of money I took in I put right back in the Tract. Louella and I have never lived closer to the bone in our lives. With a little more time, we'll all of us be in the clear."

"Those people you sold the bonds to. You've cheated them, too. What're they going to get out of your deal?"

"They're getting a good rate of interest."

"As long as we're willing to pay it. What're you going to do when we stop?"

"I'm keeping track of everything. You'll all be repaid."

"You bet we will."

Syl disregarded that. "The land you paid three hundred dollars an acre for will be worth a thousand an acre in five years. I still own a thousand acres out there. In five years, I can repay everything."

"Is that what you're asking for? Five years' time?"

"I'm not asking anything. I'm telling you what the situation is and showing you a better way and a cheaper way to get your money back than by going to law."

"There might be some people who wouldn't want to wait five years. Or couldn't."

"If they knew what they'd save by waiting, they would."

"Maybe they'd rather go broke on their own than to be handed prosperity by you."

"They're not fools."

"You ain't, so far, been a man to build up anybody's trust. Even if everything panned out as you say it will, what guarantee have we got you'd ever pay off the bonds yourself and repay us the interest we've paid on them?"

"I'm willing to put written guarantees in your hands."

"Whose hands?"

"Yours."

"You're in no position to go before a lawyer with this."

"I know that. That wouldn't invalidate any document I'd sign."

"I think we'd better go to law."

438

"Did it ever occur to you, Shel, you might not win?"

"No, it never did. We got an open-and-shut case."

"Have you read your contracts recently?"

"No."

"You better do that before you start any suits. There's nothing there says that the Water Company in which you own shares is guaranteed to be debt-free."

Shel felt his face begin to burn. Syl had stopped telling his story to Louella and was dealing directly with him now. "You planned from the first to fleece us?"

"No. But I knew what I was doing when I sold those bonds."

"Our understanding was that those water shares were unencumbered."

"The law's not interested in understandings, Shel."

"The fact that you're willing to repay us shows you admit responsibility."

"I admit concern. That's got nothing to do with legal responsibility. I want the best for the Tract. I always have and I'm still fighting for it. That's why I asked you here today, Shel. I can see what's best for the Tract. But I can't swing it by myself. And even if I could, the Tract ought to be represented. It ought to have a vote equal to mine. That's what I'm asking you to do. Represent the Tract."

"Don't you think the Tract might want to choose its own representative?"

"It has. Don't think I went at this blind. And what good would it do me to have someone the Tract opposed?"

"What good will it do you in any case? That's a little point that hasn't been made clear to me yet. What good will it do you? And, particularly, what good will it do me? I'm free to admit, Syl, I ain't got your missionary spirit. According to you, all you want to do is rescue the Tract. I'm a selfish man beside you, Syl. All I want to do is rescue Shel Lewis and family. We've sunk twice already. Once more and we're done for. Show me how to rescue Shel Lewis and I'll listen to you."

Syl went back to Louella. He let Shel overhear him again. He was making a proposal to Shel, and Shel knew it, but he did it like a suitor with so much delicacy he can't bring himself to speak directly to the girl. I'm being wooed like Ellen, Shel thought. Louella's the go-between. Syl don't want me without Louella's approval.

"Shel Lewis can help us all," Syl was telling Louella. "First of all, he ought to represent the Tract on the Water Company's board of directors. We need the benefit of Tract views, and the ranchers need the assurance their views are being listened to. Shel's trusted out there. I've been at pains to find out. Sure, he went off half cocked, planting when he did. But the ranchers don't hold that against him. He was working for them and against me when he did that, and they knew it."

Syl looked up at Shel, but Shel didn't say a word. Until Syl got around to putting the question to him direct, he didn't intend to say yea, nay, or kiss my ass. Syl saw that. He had some more to tell Louella.

"The Water Company's grown so," he told her, "it's reached the place there's got to be a resident superintendent. There's got to be someone on the spot in charge. I've known this for some time. Irrigation schedules, pipe repairs, reservoir upkeep. We're going to need a new reservoir over on the north side of the Tract, a new booster-pump station. The pumps have to be looked after. The assessments have to be collected. All these jobs ought to be under the control of one man. Not farmed out the way they are now. It would be a big job, and a big paying job, two hundred and fifty a month, at least. Not including a car and car expenses. Shel Lewis is the man for the job. Everybody will stand to profit if he will accept it, Shel, the ranchers, the bond owners. You and me, Louella.

"There's been talk about a lawsuit. That won't help anybody, no matter who wins. Shel, as superintendent of the Water Company and member of the board of directors, could put an end to that talk. He could get everybody to pulling together for the good of the Tract. That's what I'm primarily interested in, not Shel, not myself. I had a dream about that land and its people. I saw people leading good lives there in a beautiful place. It's a hard dream to give up."

When Syl stopped speaking, Shel found himself waiting to hear what Louella would say. Syl appeared to be doing the same thing. Finally, when Syl did take his eyes off his wife, it wasn't to look at Shel. He shifted his gaze from his wife to his son. Syl had made his confession to them and his proposition to him at the same time. While he was saying to Shel, "Here's a chance to save yourself, Shel," and saying, "Shel, help me save my family," he was also saying, "Family, forgive me."

The two men sat in silence. The room was darkening, the spring day drawing to a close. The silence was more noticeable because there

440

were so many people in the room: the families of both, the families they had sprung from as well as those they had established, their fathers and mothers as well as their children and wives; the soldier's fellow fighters were in there with them; all the men and women on the Tract were present. Shel saw what was being offered him, all right, and saw even more clearly what the offer could mean to him. That was enough to wrestle with, more than enough, without being required to see also what his acceptance or refusal could mean to Sylvester Perkins. He rammed himself back into one corner of the big, soft chair, trying to increase the distance between himself and Syl.

Without any right or wrong to it, just as a checker problem or as a situation involving human beings he didn't know, was there any possibility that one of these human beings (Shel Lewis) would be able to do what the other human being (Sylvester Perkins) had suggested? The brain has no morals. Or his didn't. It went right at the problem suggested, testing acts and words for their usefulness in "swinging it," as Syl had called it, in "holding the community together." The mind bypassed the painful part, which was the necessity of deciding right and wrong, and helped itself ahead of time to the pleasures of the game. It tested its powers. If there was absolutely no chance of accomplishing what Syl had proposed, there was no problem. If a man says to you, "Fly to the moon," there's no use wasting time on "yes" or "no." It can't be done. Could this be done? Legal or illegal, proposed by a crook or by a well-meaning man who had overreached himself, could it be done? Could it be done by Shel Lewis? Overlooking the fact that Syl, in spite of his love for the Tract, was going to be the chief gainer, could it be done? Did the people have the confidence in him Syl claimed? Could he run the irrigation system? Lower costs? Improve service? Make the people swallow the assessments? Make Syl keep his promise about the reimbursements?

He kept his mind off the money. He considered the job that had been offered him in the impersonal way of a man sizing up a boulder and wondering, "Can I lift it?" No purpose in it. Just as a test of power.

Syl, without a word, left his desk and went to the window. His movement lost him his anonymity in Shel's mind, and lost Shel his own. What had been proposed to him was no game. Knowledge of his own predicament closed down upon him, and added to it was the weight of his knowledge of Syl's predicament. He turned to look at Syl leaning against the window sill, a man still in love with those

441

mountaintops: the white now turned to pink and the blue to lavender as the sun set; Syl still feeding on his precious peaks. Shel tried
to remember that those mountains were Syl's bait, that he used them
on his letterheads to hook customers, that Syl's response to them was
less heartfelt than dollar-centered. He tried to find again the uncom-
plicated distrust and hatred he'd had for Syl when he entered this
room. He couldn't find them. They had disappeared. He looked at
Syl, thinking that on a March morning, twenty-eight years ago, Syl
had, by deciding not to return to Colusa, been preparing this afternoon for a ten-year-old kid back in Jackson County, Kentucky. My
God, my God, he thought, how tangled together we are in our suffering and pleasure. Spitting, singing, sneezing, sleeping, no act is private.

The sun was down. The mountain snow had turned gray white, and
below the snow the flanks of the mountains were a hard spring blue.

"Shel," Syl said, "I didn't have any lunch to speak of. You ever been
to Good Fellows Grotto?"

"I never had a meal in Los Angeles," Shel said. "Out on the Tract, if
we're going to get caught away from home at mealtime, we take a
bag of crackers and cheese."

"You like fish?"

Shel liked whatever was put on the table, and he didn't want to
give himself the airs of a man accustomed to any choice in the matter.

"I eat fish."

"Let's go, then," Syl said.

Shel had never been in a place like the Grotto. Fish swimming in
the window, thick red carpet on the floor, lamps with shades made up
of pieces of glass of all different colors glued together so that they
looked (he supposed), with the light shining through them, like
stained-glass windows in a church. Syl might be a scamp out on the
Tract, but he was a hero in the Grotto. The waiters came to him as
if the evening would have been spoiled if he hadn't put in an appearance. They were put at "Syl's" table and drank "Syl's" whisky and ate
"Syl's" fish. Not another word was said by either of "Syl's" proposal.
They talked for five hours.

It was eleven o'clock when Shel got back into Syl's car and the
driver headed eastward toward the Tract.

4    PRESS, helping her mother with the supper dishes, could see Hannah through the windows over the sink, solemnly jogging up and down the driveway. Hannah's desire to improve herself, to develop wind and increase endurance, was no doubt an evidence of spring; but Hannah herself, jolting past and breathing hard, oblivious to the evening songs of meadow larks and to the western sky, flushed with wild flower colors, was not springlike. Press couldn't help hearing her, but she turned away from the window so she wouldn't have to look at her.

Spring was a poemlike time, Press thought, with more meaning than was visible. Much was visible, but something was being said beyond the facts of wild flowers and tender evening colors, which the eyes could see. Beyond the soft sweet air, which the skin could feel. But what was it? The house was filled with flowers. Hannah, with no school to attend, tramped the hills and returned at dusk, flower-laden. Every vase and bowl was filled. The house smelled bosky. The yellow violets were the sweetest, but even the flowers no one was ever drawn to sink his face in, Indian paintbrush and teakettle stems, had a smell of sky and water, of air and earth.

It was warm enough to keep the outside doors wide open, even after supper. Spring days were perfect and of exactly the right length. Summer days were too long. You got feverish with all that light, and tired with all the running around, for it seemed weak and lazy to stop until a star came out to excuse you. Winter days were too short, dark at five and the foothills bleak and bare, and a cold wind blowing. March days, ending at six-thirty with apricot skies and a soft wind off the ocean, a little blade-sized blower with only strength enough to move the grass at your feet, provided exactly as much day as a human being could stand. As much as she could stand, anyway.

Press, polishing a glass, walked to the kitchen door. The sky was flocked with opal clouds. March days are the standard length, she thought; everything else is too short or too long. In March, you love the light as long as it lasts, and welcome the dark when it comes. But there is a moment just now, when the two balance, which is painful. If one comes, the other must go. A golden day and the meadow lark's

443

song, which is a cry of "Oh, never stop"; then day's ending, sadder in spring than at any other time because spring itself is only a moment's greenness before the sun says, "Green end, brown come."

There were times when a voice inside Press spoke to her saying, Remember. This happened most often when she was with her mother. She had been obsessed as long she could remember by the threat of her mother's death. Like Hannah, she, too, was practicing endurance, the endurance of the time when her mother would be no more. The voice that said Remember, also told her how to remember: in absence, teach the eye to see. She stored up pictures. She watched her mother in the dishwashing twilight hour of spring, rainbow lights on the dishpan of Fels Naphtha suds and her mother's wedding ring clinking a sundown tune against the china she washed. There her mother stood, alive, alive, and Press struggled to put her thus into her mind forever. She had rescued her mother in this manner time and again from the grave. It was nothing that could be done once and for all. The more her mind turned toward Chad, the more she required of herself this rescue of her mother. This was no more than fair, since long after her mother was dead, she would have years for Chad. She dried dishes with the least part of herself; for the most part, she took stock of all that was mortal in her mother.

She had something to make up to her mother—and she didn't know what it was. She had tried and tried to make it up, whatever it was, in ways that were beyond her. She required of herself what only a lover could do, find Indy Cope adorable in every respect. Press asked of herself this feeling for her mother, when it was for her father it would have been easy; her father, who never irritated her, never rubbed her the wrong way, who was always right. She never once thought of her father's dying, never once chided herself for loving him less than she should.

She kept all of her sensibilities exposed in order to register, even to the degree of pain, all that her mother was. Recently, there had seemed less need to do this. She had been excused for some reason from the obligation to love her mother so intensely. She did not know why. Still, though it did not come to her in these words, she asked herself, What is my crime against my mother? Whatever it was, it had come to seem smaller, to require less sacrifice from her.

Indy's ring finger on her right hand had been injured when she was a girl, in a corn sheller. The finger itself was slightly misshapen at the tip, and the nail was divided like a harelip down the middle. Once,

444

when Press had remarked on it, her father had said, "Do you know your mother never let me see that finger until after we were married?"

"I wanted to be perfect for him," her mother had explained.

Press was still uncertain what had been in her mother's voice as she said those words. She often wondered about it. Sorrow? Irony? Amazement? For a long time, Press had required of herself that she also live through the disappointments of this vanished girl who had wanted to bring perfection to her husband. Why did she think there were disappointments? Press did not know the answer to that question either. But this evening, she had a certain freedom; she was able to see that damaged finger as her mother wiped the ledge between sink and window without saying to herself "Remember, remember," without the conviction that if she did not get the sight of that finger by heart, like some password, her failure would sooner or later be the cause of pain or death. Not her pain or death, her mother's; when she could no longer remember that marred finger which her mother had kept hidden, her mother would die.

Why was she excused these memorizings tonight? Where had the loss gone which she had been required to make up? Where was the wrong she only could undo, and undo only by offering her mother her own life? Not that her mother had ever said she was wronged, or had ever asked for her life.

Press put her polished and repolished glass in the cupboard and picked up another. "I wish Hannah wouldn't do that," she said.

"Do what?" her mother asked, absently.

"Run up and down that way."

"Why?"

"It's such a beautiful evening. Such a beautiful evening of spring," Press explained.

Indy had given up trying to speak to her daughter in any direct way. Press loved her to death, or pretended to, but it would have been as easy to speak to someone from the other side of the grave. She had given up, in the past months, trying to discover what the trouble was. She connected it in some way with Lute, this impenetrable devotion of her daughter.

Lute had not come home for supper. Alone in the house, they dawdled away the twilight; they knew what they were missing by not being outside, still they let all that mottled gold slide away while they polished the stove, mopped the Congoleum, and set the table for breakfast. It was finally full dark, day's longed-for and dreaded end,

445

but because darkness had come gradually, uninterrupted by lamplight, they scarcely knew it. Press finished the table setting by feel alone. The two women had nothing to say to each other, but neither left the kitchen. How can two women be closer than mother and daughter? Or more separated?

Indy got a glass of water, and sat by the table sipping it. Press stood by the window watching the stars come out and reporting the happenings of the night.

"Hannah's nowhere to be seen," she said, though it was nothing to worry about, and she knew it.

"Now there's a car coming," she reported later.

"It must be your father, finally," Indy said.

They listened to the car come into the driveway and stop. They listened to footsteps that they recognized as Lute's. The darkness kept them silent, imposed a kind of dare upon them: perhaps you can live without speech as well as without light. Neither spoke. The darkness and the sound of Lute's footsteps coming nearer proposed another dare: perhaps you only think it is Lute. All cars sound alike. Perhaps a murderer is walking toward you. First, he met and murdered Hannah when she threatened to scream. Now, with bloody hands, he is coming nearer and nearer to you. I dare you to imagine that, the dark and dragging footsteps said. Press accepted the dare. She imagined what the dark and the slow footsteps suggested. You will die because you would rather die than scream and discover that you have no one to fear but your own father, she thought. You would rather die, she told herself, than live to discover that you have made a fearful mistake. That is how silly you are. She had not breathed for a long time; her heart no longer beat in her chest, but in her ears. It kept time to the footsteps. The footsteps ceased. The murderer spoke, and he *was* her own father.

"Why are you sitting here in the dark?" he asked.

Press opened her eyes, which she didn't know she had squeezed shut. She waited for her mother to speak. She didn't want to seem to be taking her mother's place. Only after her mother didn't answer, she said, "We like the dark, Papa."

"I don't like the dark," Lute said. "Light a lamp."

Press got the matches.

"Have you eaten, Lute?" Indy asked.

"No."

"I'll get you something."

"Don't take the trouble. I couldn't swallow."

He went through the kitchen into the sitting room.

"Bring the lamp in here," he called to Press.

She carried it in to him, leaving her mother alone in the dark. Her father was stretched out on the sofa, his head lifted at an uncomfortable angle by one of the wooden arms. She stood beside him holding the lamp, forgetting to put it down. His face was hard and gray, his eyes red-rimmed; his lips trembled.

"Are you sick, Papa?"

"No, I'm all right. Put the lamp on the table."

When she had done so, her father called, "Indy."

Her mother came into the room and stopped by the center table, where the lamp was.

"I know all about him, Indy. I've unearthed everything. You ought to know, too."

Her mother didn't say a word.

"You picked a fine one. I don't know that I've got the heart to tell you, or the stomach either."

"Tell me what you're talking about."

"You know what I'm talking about. What do you think I'm talking about? And who? Do you think you can tell me, 'I want to marry Tom Mount,' and have me let it go at that? I don't know what our marriage has meant to you, Indy. Nothing, I guess. But it meant too much to me to let it end with you saying, 'Excuse me, I've finished.' If it's finished, you're going to know what you're finishing it for. You're going to know that while you've been eating your heart out for that man, he's been blocking it out night after night with a half-dozen women."

Press heard these words in the same way she had heard words in dreams that were on the surface meaningless, but that nevertheless carried beneath the surface the threat of a meaning that was unbearable. She wanted, as in a dream, to move, but as in a dream stood rooted, incapable of motion. She made some sound, and her father, who had apparently forgotten her, took his eyes off her mother and said without expression, as if she were a part of some dream of *his,* "Leave the room, Press."

Her mother's undreaming voice had the urgency of here and now. "Stay where you are, Press. Listen to what your father has to say."

"What I have to say is not for a girl's ears," her father said. "Let alone your daughter."

447

"It's the truth, isn't it? Isn't it, Lute? I can count on that, can't I?"

"It's the truth, Indy."

"Let Press hear it, then. Let her know what the truth is. I'll feel better if she knows the whole story."

"You'll feel better? Maybe you should stop thinking about how you feel and think how I'll feel. Or how Press'll feel."

"Press'll feel better. I don't know what's been the matter with her. I don't know what it is she's been making up to me. I don't know why she's been tied to me hand and foot. Press, you've hung on my every breath. Why? It's not natural."

Her mother looked at her beseechingly, but Press couldn't answer her question. She couldn't because she didn't know the answer. Her mother went on. "You listen to your father now. This is the woman I am. No one for you to sacrifice yourself for."

"It's not you I'm going to talk about," Lute said. "What I've got to say has to do with Tom Mount."

"You can't talk about him without talking about me, can you?"

"I can talk about him and talk less about you than you might think."

Her father no longer looked at either of them. He stared straight ahead of him, not into space, but as if he saw someone, invisible to her or her mother.

"How did you find out—all these things?" her mother asked.

"I had some help."

"Detectives? You hired detectives?"

"Don't act so shocked. You don't have any right to act so shocked. I could've done it by myself. He never took any trouble to hide his tracks. He picked out women like you, who would hide them for him. Women who would lose their jobs or their church work or the respect of their old parents. Or their husbands. Or their daughters. They covered up for him. That's the man you preferred to me. That's the man you were willing to sacrifice me for. You were nothing to him. One more feather in his cap. One name in a book with dozens of others. Oh, believe me, Indy, you were nothing to him."

"He asked me to marry him."

"Words. Words are cheap. Especially to Tom Mount. He can ask anybody anything."

"You don't think—he meant it?"

"How could he? He's married. He wouldn't have asked you, if he hadn't been."

Press said, under her breath, because she could not manage her full voice, "You don't have to say that, even if it is the truth," but neither her father nor her mother heard her.

Her mother took one step forward, so that she could put a hand onto the center table. But she took it off immediately, as if to remind herself that there was no support she could depend upon.

"He doesn't live with his wife." These words were not a question as her mother said them, but her eyes and face contradicted the words.

"What makes you think he doesn't? When you come home to me, where do you think he goes? Do you think he's so much better than you?"

"Yes, I thought so."

"Better than me, too, I suppose?"

There was no answer to that.

"Where do you think he was this last weekend?"

Press thought, Don't make her answer that. Don't make her. You're right, you've got the upper hand, you've suffered. Don't make her suffer more than she has to now.

"Where?" her father insisted, continuing to look straight ahead at the invisible presence to whom he was telling these things. "Where?"

"I don't know," her mother answered him. "I don't know."

"With his wife," Lute said. "In Los Angeles with his wife."

"Does—she know about me?"

"She knows about you—and a dozen others."

"Why did she let him stay then?"

"She knows what he's good for, I guess."

"Doesn't she love him?"

"Love him? How can she love him? Things got too hot for him in Colorado. He lost his job. So he remembers he's got a wife in California. He always remembers her when he is down on his luck."

"That's what she told you?"

"That's what she told me."

"Perhaps she . . ."

He wouldn't let her finish. "Perhaps, after being married to him for twenty years, she doesn't know him as well as you do? Is that what you're going to say? Perhaps when he knocks on her door and says, 'Jenny . . .'"

Now it was her mother who interrupted. "Is that her name?"

Her father was momentarily distracted from his concentration on the invisible. He turned to her mother, his face contorted. "Anything he touches interests you? His neglected wife? His . . ."

449

Press said, "Don't, please. Please."

Her father replied sharply, "I told you to leave. I'm doing this for your mother's good." He faced away from Indy, but continued to talk to her. "Her name is Jenny, if that's of interest to you. He knocked on the door and said, 'Jenny, here's your poor old Tom out in left field again.' So she took him in. And I can't blame him for wanting to get back to her. She's a nice-looking woman."

There was silence. A moth went round and round the lamp chimney. No one will speak, Press thought, until it stops—or dies. It didn't stop or die, and her father said, "His wife called it a second honeymoon. You've been associating with Tom Mount. I don't suppose there's any need mincing words with you. Blocking it out all night, those were his wife's words."

"Press," Indy said. "Press is here."

"You were the one who wanted her to stay."

"Does . . . his wife . . . hate me?"

"Hate you? What's she got to hate you for? You don't take him away from her. You just take him away from some of your rivals. No, you weren't any surprise to her. I was, though."

Indy said nothing. She put her hand over her mouth.

"She's been expecting some husband to shoot Tom for a long time. She was beginning to lose her respect for husbands until I showed up. She said she didn't like to think that the only kind of women Tom could find were women whose husbands didn't care enough about them to shoot Tom over. His running around with women like that didn't do anything to increase her self-esteem. I gave her pride a little boost."

"You didn't think about shooting him?" Indy whispered.

"I thought about it. Yes."

Her mother gasped for breath like someone who'd been running— or sobbing. There was another long silence. The moth did what moths are never supposed to do: it left the light of the lamp and flew through the open door into the dark kitchen.

"Is she going to divorce him?"

"You go ask her. He was there last weekend."

"But she knows all about him?"

"She knows. Don't think that I understand it. She's been two-timed —ten-timed for twenty years. But there she is when he comes home, ready like the others with whatever he wants. Money . . ."

450

"I never gave him any money."

"Well, if you had, you would've had plenty of company right here on the Tract."

"Here?" Indy spoke the word as if it had been choked from her lips.

"Right here. Friends of yours. Opal. Eunice."

"He asked me first. I come first. I always did. He said I had only to give him thirty minutes' notice and he'd break any other date he had. He couldn't just sit in that Sunday-school room waiting for me."

"He didn't anyway, did he?"

"I didn't want him to."

"You really love him, don't you? 'He asked me first.' There's real fidelity for you. Why, this man'll dip himself into any woman who passes by. It don't have to be a woman. He'll rub himself against any sex. Sex, sex. He don't care what shape it takes. There's been a hundred women in his life. There'll be another hundred if he doesn't meet up with a hunting accident. Tom Mount! Tomcat. He'll run after anything in heat. He's not as decent as a tomcat. Eunice gave him her life's savings. That's how he got to California in the first place. You've got Eunice to thank for that. He took her money to come to his wife. That's how he repaid Eunice. And his wife took care of him. And he repaid her by taking up with you. And you loved him."

"I still do."

"Well, he doesn't love you. Only last night he told . . ."

"Don't!" It was Press, not Indy, who screamed that. "Stop it."

Once again her father turned his head so that he spoke to someone visible, or at least looked at someone visible. He looked at her, his daughter.

"Stop what?" he asked, as if he didn't really know.

"Stop torturing Mama."

"Torture?" he asked. "What do you know about torture? Who do you think's been tortured?"

Her father again faced away from her toward the unseen person to whom he spoke.

Her mother looked steadily at her father. She was still standing, still unmoving, still not touching anything. She had rolled her kitchen apron upward around her arms, and she leaned forward into it, as if the apron were a sling that supported her, held her together. There

451

were red spots on her cheeks, but her mouth had no color at all and had completely lost its shape as a mouth. It was a long, thin, white line that cut her face into two parts.

Her father went on speaking. He seemed to have forgotten the interruption. Press didn't interrupt again. There was a change in her listening. Let him say all he would. She was collecting evidence; she had to catch every word. And though her father used words she had never heard before, their meanings were terribly clear to her. For the first time in her life, her feeling for her mother was for her mother's sake. She didn't know why this was so. She wanted to help her mother in order to make her mother feel better, not in order to make herself feel better. For the first time in her life, she had nothing to make up to her mother. Her father continued to speak and she continued to listen. She didn't stand aside from the occasion, trying to memorialize it, trying to make some payment required of her in return for something she had done that was wrong. She listened like a learner, like a child being taught a lesson, though she didn't know what the lesson was.

Finally, her father stopped. Perhaps he had stopped speaking some time ago and it was the clock's striking that called her attention to it. It was nine-thirty. They had been in that room three hours, her father lying there staring at the wall and speaking and she and her mother standing, listening.

When the clock finished its chime for the half-hour, her mother said, "Lute, I'll leave."

"No, no." Her father sat up and turned to face her mother. "No, Indy, you mustn't say that or think it."

"You don't love me. I had better go back home."

Her father got up and ran to her mother, knelt and clasped her around her knees. Her mother swayed a little, but didn't unwrap her arms from her apron.

"Never leave me, Indy. Never leave me."

"You don't want me here, after what's happened."

"Indy, don't reproach yourself. What happened to you has happened to me. The only difference is that you never knew. You're no more guilty than I am. Don't speak of leaving me. Put it out of your mind; I'll tell you everything."

"Press," her mother said, looking at her sidewise over her father, who still knelt with his face covered in her mother's skirts, "Go on outside. You should never have heard what you have."

452

Press didn't move, and her mother, held as she was, couldn't take Press by the arm and shove her out.

Her mother spoke to her father. "Lute, let me go. I've heard more than enough. I don't want to know any more."

"You listened about him, now listen about me," her father said.

"I didn't have much choice."

"I had to tell you. You had to know what kind of a man Mount was. But don't leave me, Indy, never leave me. I don't hold anything against you. I've done everything you've done. You remember the summer your mother was sick and you went home? The summer after Hannah was born? That was the summer she came to the house as soon as you left. I'd always had an eye out for her."

"Don't tell me. I don't want to hear."

"You've got to hear. You've got to listen. Gertrude Armsbury? You remember her? You hadn't been out of the house for thirty minutes before she was over, and I was making love to her. Something crazy hits us sometimes, Indy. We aren't responsible for what we do. We have to accept it in each other. I accept it in you. Thirty minutes and I was eating her up. We're equals, Indy. Equals."

Press felt goose pimples rising along her arms at her father's play acting. Couldn't her mother see that his face had gone all slippery and guileful and calculating as he made up that story to catch her and hold her, out of her pity and admiration? Pity for his weakness, admiration for his honesty?

She had been home with her father that summer. She had seen how he had been with Mrs. Armsbury: stand-offish, as he was with every woman. Mrs. Armsbury had never been at their house, and when she went to the Armsburys' to play, her father would stay outside and call to her rather than risk going in. "Eat her up!" Why, her father thought women were poison. He was afraid of them. She could see that now. A man pretending to be good is bad enough, but her father pretending to be wicked was ridiculous and disgusting. He acted as if he felt this himself. He sank his face deeply into her mother's skirts. He trembled and butted at her like a sick lamb nursing. Her mother had to unfold her arms and steady herself with a hand on the table.

For the first time in her life, Press felt a distance which she had not willed separate her from her parents. She knew her father was lying and she knew why. He was saying, "Indy, we are two bad ones together. We ought to cling together. I won't cast any stones because I'm guilty, too." But he had cast stones. Stones and slime and mud.

He had thrown his fill. Now that he had separated her from that man, he had to pretend that they were in the same boat, he had to make himself out to be as low as he thought her to be. He went on doing that, his face so deep in her mother's skirts his words were muffled. But his words were still of the same kind, full of fake suffering and fake guilt. It was none of it true. All he was suffering was fear that she would leave him. He needed her mercy and pity to make her stay. "Forgive me as I forgive you," he was saying. He was calling upon her for appreciation of his generosity. "I gave up this woman, though I thought I would never get over it, because it was my duty. And thank God I did. I would never have been happy with her. And she did her duty and married that Burden boy, and it's been an ideal marriage. Each doing the right thing and repaid ten times over in the long run. Let it be a lesson to us now."

The clock struck ten. Her father kept on talking. Her mother believed every word he said. She had put a hand on his head. For the first time in her life, Press was looking through her mother's eyes at her father. She saw a different man. Why was she able to do this? Why were she and her mother no longer enemies? How had she stopped wronging her mother? She didn't know, she didn't know. But she was free as a bird to go. She was happy to leave the fallen to her mother. And she had better run, she had better run fast, she had better make sure of her escape. Her mother had made her listen, and what she had heard was the tables turning. She ran behind them out through the kitchen into the spring night under the spring stars, their light soft and sweet as flower honey, so that she stuck out her tongue to taste it. She was crying and running and escaping, and she knew where she was going.

5   Chad, while his father was eating fried oysters and drinking whisky at Good Fellows Grotto, was in bed. He had been there since three o'clock. When his father left for Los Angeles, he decided that the time had come for him and not his body to call the tune. If he continued each day to ask his body what it felt like doing, the answer might be forever, Nothing. He had given his body every choice, fed it, rested it, offered it all the sleep it would take. His body had not co-operated

by giving him health. He decided to finish with coddling his body. It had had its chance, and had done nothing with it. From now on, he would do what he wanted to do, and his body could suffer along as best it could. Its opinion wouldn't be asked again.

That didn't stop his body from offering an opinion. It had an opinion for every movement he made as he dressed. "The hell with you," he told it, sick at his stomach and trembling. He intended to go out and help with weeding and spraying the potato patch. Everyone had been out there, even his mother, now too big to bend over. He didn't suppose he would be able to make much pigweed fly, but a beginning had to be made somewhere; and he believed that he could at least fire Zoomy and Ellen into a little more efficient effort.

So he thought. But out in the potato patch he learned a thing or two. He learned who was boss, mind or body. The mind can say, Work, Endure, Hasten, and the body does exactly what it damn pleases. But let the body say, Suffer, Faint, Collapse, and the mind winks out like a candle. At two-thirty exactly, as he stooped over a potato plant and looked at a red ladybug with black spots, the ladybug suddenly became invisible. I'm going blind, he thought. That showed how much his mind understood, let alone controlled, events. He was fainting.

His body, which had taken charge then, had continued in charge for the rest of the day. The mind with its noonday vows had not been heard from since two-thirty. He had gone back to the spare room and to the spare bed, and while the weeds grew through the long warm afternoon, there he lay. It wasn't until everyone else was in bed, except his father, who wasn't home yet, that old king mind began to stir again. By body's kind permission, no doubt; or perhaps body itself had whispered the message. His belief was that mind had suggested that a little food would do him good. On whoever's orders, he got out of bed and went slowly and carefully out to the cooler. He got a crock of milk, then broke bread into the milk. He ate all of it, his largest meal since he'd been sick.

On the way back to the spare room, he passed the sitting room, sat down in a rocking chair, and, just for the hell of it, rocked. It gave him an odd feeling: rocking was for women, for daylight and conversation. He explored the future, tried out in his imagination being an old sleepless man, rocking the night away while remembering his vigorous past. He tried, but did not succeed in, imagining himself a woman rocking a child. He remembered his own identity, an invalid whose nighttime adventure it was to rock. The reality was so ridiculous he went slowly back to his room.

He made it, with no more spells of blindness, but he was trembling when he got there. He leaned against the sill of his opened window, and the fresh air steadied him. He looked south toward the ocean and toward Press. There was a lopsided moon, and the hills, where the moonlight did not reach the bottoms of the arroyos, were furrowed with shadows. Under that moon and under the pale spring stars—stars playing second fiddle to the moon, like girls with an old woman—slept his girl. His girl? His girl? If Press was his girl, any girl might be his; for she was his only because he said so.

Shall I give her up? Forget her? Put her out of my mind? That was old king mind himself speaking again, the old dictator who never learned. Unseated that very afternoon, overthrown, here he was once again proposing that life be lived on his terms. Old big mouth. Old papal bull. Old wind and no weather. He had about as much chance of putting Press out of his mind as he'd had of weeding potatoes on the same orders. Weed potatoes. Stop loving Press. Old king mind sure knew what was best. Know-what-is-best, Do-what-is-best: those two are not even stepbrothers. What kind of a girl would old king mind pick out for him? Would the old king care what she looked like? Would he want to touch her? Would he choose her by an examination? Pick out the girl with the highest grades in kindness, good sense, and dependability? Press would be right down at the bottom of the list when it came to grades in kindness, good sense, and dependability. Good sense? She was as crazy as they came, kind as a tiger, dependable as a coyote. And he loved her. The hell with the old king, the old dictator. He was putting it to a vote. What was the sense of a war to make the world safe for democracy if you didn't practice democracy at home? He was putting it to a vote. Mind and heart and liver and lights and tongue and eyes and lips and balls and kidneys and guts and body and soul, let them all ballot. He was putting it to a vote. Press won. What he wanted, body and soul, mind had better learn to like. He loved Press Cope. He loved her craziness and the clear whites of her eyes and the way she stood, legs spraddled a little when she was mad at him, divided in her mind whether to run or hit him; whether to hit him first, then run.

He didn't know how it was with other men. With them one girl was perhaps as good as another. And two perhaps better than one. His

456

own father had found it that way. How it was with others didn't matter. Why ask? He would never be able to give his whole heart to anyone else. Even if she were first on the old king's list and Press last, still he would be with that examination winner as Press was with him: faithful to someone out of sight. He would be faithful to Press.

Faithful to someone out of sight. The reality behind those words took the sweetness out of the air and dried up the soft spring stars. He was in love with her, stuck with her, saddled with her, crazy about her. But why in hell couldn't he have fallen for someone like Medora, someone willing to tramp right over Mama and Papa to get the man she loved? Why do I have to be the one who is loved (for Press loved him) and tramped on, while Mama is cherished?

He went to bed speculating about Medora; and if he had to dream of girls, why couldn't he dream of someone willing, like Medora? But it was Press he always dreamed of, Press calling his name, trying to wake him. But that was the last thing he intended to do. Wake up, and she wouldn't be there.

"Wake up, Chad, wake up," she kept whispering, contrary, and as true to herself in dreams as in life. Wake up and lose her! Keep on dreaming. He was wide awake with his eyes closed, and she was still whispering, her lips on his ear, "Chad, wake up."

Awake or asleep, he was putty in her hands. He opened his eyes and there she was.

"Press," he said, "Press."

"Be quiet. You'll wake everyone." She leaned closer, so that her breasts rested against him.

"Is something the matter, Press?"

"No. Everything's all right. I love you. I'm never going to leave you. Never again."

She sat on the edge of the bed and turned sidewise so that she could put her hands under his shoulders and her face on his. He was awake but the kissing was like a dream. She had come without a coat, and her skin was warm and her dress a little damp with dew and she smelled like roses or talcum powder.

"I'm not shaved, Press, or cleaned up. I've been sick. I'm a mess."

"I love you. I'm never going to leave you."

He didn't want her to leave him; he didn't want to say words to put such an idea into her head.

"I don't want you to ever leave me." He whispered his words into

457

her ear, he touched her ear with his lips, he tantalized his lips with her hair. "I've wanted you to come for a long time. You know that. But you wouldn't."

"I hate my father," she said, not as if she really hated him, but in wonder.

This made less sense as an explanation of her coming than the "I love my mother," she had always before used as an excuse.

"I don't want to be mixed up with your family," Chad told her. "I don't want you to come here because of them, loving *or* hating, any more than I wanted you to stay away because of them."

"I'm not mixed up with them any more. Something happened."

"What?"

"I don't know. But you're the only person I'm mixed up with now. I know that. Can't you tell it? Don't you believe me?"

He said nothing.

She got off the bed, bent down, whispering, with her lips against his cheek. "I am. I am. Make it so I can't ever leave you."

She straightened up, stretched herself into a birdlike shape, with her elbows sticking out like wings behind her. He saw that she was unbuttoning her dress. Once it was off, everything else came off in a flash. She talked all the time, like someone whistling in the dark.

"Love me, Chad, please love me. Please don't ever stop loving me. I always did love you. You know that, don't you? It was just that I had this other duty to Mama and now I don't have it any more. I am so happy, Chad. I had to come to be with you the minute I could. The minute I knew, I came. I ran all the way. We'll never be parted again, will we?"

For a second, she was naked in the moonlight, no girl at all with her clothes off: a tall woman, broad and narrow, black and white, her body branching upward above him like a tree covered with snow and touched with shadows.

She turned back the covers and slipped under them. She lay beside him lightly and confidently, kissing him, touching his knuckles with the tip of her fingers, touching his feet very delicately with hers and smiling, for he could feel her lips curving against his cheek, as if feet were a joke.

What could he say to her? She was sure of him and of herself. She was loving him. Didn't he want her love? Who was he? Old king mind himself, saying, "Wait until we're married," or "I'm not in A-1 health tonight"? Or, "This is the way my father got in bed." He could say all these things truthfully, and they were all reasonable. But this was Press's body speaking to him, and Press's body didn't know a thing about reason or his father's history or his own day's record. If he said any of these things, if he suggested postponement, Press might understand with her mind. But her body wouldn't understand. Her body might never forgive him, and he couldn't risk that. She his wife, but her body, for the rest of their lives, his enemy.

He knew better, after his day's experience, than to try to instruct his own body in any way. Besides, he was wholly filled with tenderness for Press. He had too many things to say to her to tell himself anything. He raised himself on one elbow and slid his arm under her head and lifted her into the cradle between his shoulder and his lips.

"What are you whispering?" she asked. "What do you keep whispering?"

"I don't know," he answered, and he really didn't. "I am trying to tell you," he said, "what I keep whispering." His mind had no words for what his body was feeling, but he kept on whispering, trying to make everything known to her in every way at once.

6   O n  t h e way home from Los Angeles, Shel sat up front with the driver. He didn't like the idea of sitting alone in the back seat like a lord mayor in his coach, and he hoped the driver, a young fellow named Seaman, would help him keep his mind off Sylvester Perkins and his proposals. When the time came, he would make a decision. Meanwhile, he'd enjoy the ride through the spring night. Seaman was eager to talk, but Shel found he couldn't keep his mind on what the boy had to say.

"I guess I'm too sleepy for talk," he excused himself finally. "Or had too much to drink."

He wasn't sleepy and he'd had exactly the right amount to drink. But above the valley, the snow peaks glistened in the moonlight and out in Orange County the valencias were blooming. Snow on the mountains, bloom in the valley; soft darkness, deep sweetness, peaks alive in the starshine and lights blown out in the ranch houses. Syl loved these, too. He really did. He used them as bait for buyers, he made money off them, but he loved them for themselves. This doesn't

459

excuse me, Shel thought. I should've been out of his office one minute after I saw what he was up to—in spite of the fact he loves mountains. Instead, I spent a long evening eating his oysters and drinking his whisky.

Out near the Tract, the smell of the wells was stronger than the smell of blossoms. Seaman dodged a skunk and was unable to dodge a jack rabbit.

"I'm glad to see you give animals a chance," Shel said. "Some drivers go out of their way to hit them."

"You notice it was the stinker I missed," Seaman said.

It was ten of twelve when Seaman left him in the yard at home. Shel took off his shoes in the kitchen so's not to wake Joicey. He was halfway up the stairs, shoes in one hand, lamp in the other, when the thought came to him that Chad might be lying sleepless, wondering how the trip had gone.

The day's happenings had humbled and upset him. He had looked at two pictures. He had seen yes and no and life and death and right and wrong so close together he wasn't sure where one left off and the other began. He had seen the good intentions and the fatal results. He had seen that a man in middle life might wake up after industrious building and find that the name of the house he inhabited was hell, not heaven. We're all to be pitied, he thought wearily. Me, too. I don't deny myself pity.

He came back down the stairs and leaned against the door to Chad's room. The boy don't like me, he thought. Somehow I ain't the cut he admires. That's the worst thing a parent has to swallow, not his kid's meanness. He don't like me, and there's been things about him rubbed me the wrong way. His feelings don't excuse mine. If your child don't cotton to you, you can't shame him into a change of heart. You live with it. You try to do better. Or at least, you ought to. Anyway, I haven't driven him off to the trenches yet.

He opened the door slowly, his mind occupied with the Chad of the past, the baby who was not yet a person, only the premium from his and Joicey's first love-making. Somehow a distance had come between them. He knew what he had to fight in Chad's face and stance, but what Chad had against him was Chad's secret. You think what you please of me, Chad, he thought, and I'll hold true to you in spite of it.

Deep in his thoughts, he lifted his lamp without knowing he did so and looked at Chad's bed without knowing he looked. The knowledge of what he saw there, the words for it, arrived a few years after his

460

seeing. What he saw was a boy and girl in bed. The recognition of that boy and that girl came traveling slowly toward him; he saw it coming, watched it, knew it would arrive, knew that he could not escape its arrival, but for an endless time, it was knowledge on its way to him. The boy was Chad and the girl was Press Cope. He saw that, but he didn't know it. It was an arrow flying, destined for him, coming, coming. Then it penetrated.

Chad and Press Cope were in bed together.

He took a step nearer the bed and lowered the lamp so that its light fell directly on their faces. If he only imagined he saw them, he was imagining, too, the rhythm of their breathing, the position of Press's hand on Chad's chest, and the intermingling of two shades of black hair. He was imagining bloomers and garters and stockings on the floor. He was imagining the shadows of their long eyelashes on their white cheeks.

He stared for a long time, thinking, I've already seen so much today. I'm not willing to taper off. I've got to be astounded by one more sight, before I go to bed: a neighbor girl in my sick boy's bed, for my nightcap.

The arrow went deeper; he knew that what he saw was real. He felt he ought to cry out, "We come to California to get away from all this woods-colting!" It was no dream, but he behaved like a man caught in a very bad dream. His tongue was useless; it hung down in the dry pit of his mouth, slack as a string. All of his energy was drained off in his eyes' looking.

His minute-ago resolution to forgive Chad everything was the most remote fact of his life. The sight he saw made him sick. This was no way to start; this was what he had been trying to live down; this was Chad, all right, who always managed to do everything the wrong way or the wrong time, or both.

When his energy came back, he would haul them both out of that bed; though he knew well enough how he would find them. They would be shamefaced, but they had something to be shamefaced about. Let Chad learn that if he had to beget bastards, home wasn't the place for it. And if he had to choose home, not his mother's spare room. Everything in his son that had ever gone against the grain was concentrated now in that thin white face, half hidden in a girl's black hair.

He was moving to free his hands by setting the lamp on the bureau when he heard Joicey's whispering voice, "Come on out of here."

He turned, unstartled. Joicey wandering, uncomfortable with heartburn or aching legs or painful breasts, was no uncommon sight these nights; and certainly she was the best sight of the past twelve hours. He started to speak, but she put her fingers on her lips, shook her head, and held his arm firmly. He let her pull him out of the room and close the door silently.

They then stood, lamp between, at the foot of the stairs.

"Come to bed," she whispered.

Her calmness before what they had seen seemed nasty. "Did you arrange that?" he asked. "You're so willing to leave them."

"Don't throw that up at me."

Her brown eyes were as black as water under ice. He wasn't throwing anything up at her and she knew it.

"Did you know they were there?"

"No."

"Do you want to leave them there?"

"Yes."

"Why?"

"Come upstairs and I'll tell you."

"We'll wake the children."

"Better them than these."

"I won't have those innocent . . ."

"Don't yell and they won't hear a word."

"I'm not yelling."

"Whisper."

She took the lamp out of his hand and went up the stairs ahead of him. Slowly, because she was so big, and because she was always careful with a lamp. Upstairs, she put the lamp on the washstand, turned it low, and got into bed as if this was any other night's bedtime.

He felt that their going to bed together consented to that bedding together downstairs, condoned it, said, "Everybody does it. Why make a fuss about when and where?" The spring air which, before midnight, had been soft and sweet with blossoming, came into the attic sharp and raw. He was postponing a decision about Syl. Could he postpone this, too? Say, "Later, later," to every problem? "Later, later," while bastards grew and men were robbed?

"Get undressed and get under the covers," Joicey said. "You're shaking."

"I've got something to shake about."

"I'm not denying it," she said. "But the grippe won't help matters."

"I'm not cold."

"I am," she said. "Get in bed."

462

He undressed slowly. He had to. His fingers were half numb. He fumbled with buttons, and his tie tightened up like a hangman's knot when he tried to loosen it.

"Bend over," Joicey told him. She loosened the tie and slid it over his head.

He sat on the edge of the bed in his underwear and shirt. "I can't sleep. There's no use going to bed."

"I don't want you to sleep. I want to talk to you. And I'm cold. Get under the covers and warm the bed."

He left his socks on to show that, though he was putting the covers over him, he was not going to bed. He braced his back against the bed's headboard, refusing to lie down.

"Like breeds like," he said.

"I hope so."

"You don't mean that. You don't want him like me. You don't want her going through what you went through."

"What did I go through, Shel Lewis? Since you know all about it, you tell me."

"Hell—if you loved me. In a family way, and me too sick from running with another girl to marry you. That was hell, wasn't it?"

"No."

"Why not?"

"It evened things out a little."

"Evened what things?"

"It put a little wrong on your side."

"What was wrong on your side? Now don't tell me, 'Tolling you to me.' You tolled me all right, but that's every girl's business. That's what she was born for. We were too intimate that once, and I admit you didn't run or holler. But if you think your giving in that once balances my running with that other girl when I loved you, and getting the dose I got, you're crazy."

"It was then I was crazy. Crazy about you."

Shel said nothing. When Joicey had acted like she was crazy about him, that had been fine, but he didn't like to hear her say so. He felt it hurt her pride.

"She was, too."

"She was, too, what?"

"Cora was crazy about you."

"Don't talk about her. If there's any person I hate on this earth—it's that woman."

"She wanted to marry you, too."

"I hadn't put her in any family way. Thank God."

"You hadn't put me either."

Shel turned and stared down at her. Her face, plump with pregnancy, was nearer the face of the girl who had carried Chad than it had been for a long time. She was lying there on her pillow smiling, not at him, but back into the past.

"Chad's mine," he said. "I know he is. He's rotten with all my faults."

"Oh, he's yours, all right."

"What're you talking about then?"

"I didn't know I was in a family way when I sent Papa to make you marry me."

"It was a trick?"

"Yes."

"You might've got me killed."

"Papa wasn't going to kill you before he got you married to me."

"After that, you didn't care?"

"Afterward I thought I could soften him up. And you."

"You might've gotten your father killed."

"He thought he had something against you. But what did you have against him?"

"I don't like a man pushing a gun against my head and telling me what I've got to do."

"Well, you didn't do it."

"I never had any intention of doing a thing but marry you from the minute I laid eyes on you. But I didn't have any intention of dancing to any such tune as your father was piping either. Not to that instrument he was piping on, anyway. I was going to marry you because I wanted to, not because some old fool told me to with a gun to my head."

"He was protecting my honor."

"You chose a poor way to get it protected."

"I didn't know much about men then. How mulish they are. How they'll bite off their noses to spite their faces."

"I like to did, with what I caught."

"Was it just to spite me?"

"It was to spite you. Though I reckon that's not the whole story. I wasn't going to be drove, not by a man like your father. But you having to wait for me the time you did was nothing I planned. I didn't get the clap to spite you. I wasn't that mad at you. I wasn't even that mad at your father."

464

Shel had forgotten for the minute the two downstairs. Zoomy, turning in his bed, reminded him. "Why are you telling me this now?" he asked. "You think Press is fixing it so Lute Cope will be over here with a gun to make Chad marry her?"

"I don't know anything about what Press is fixing to do. Except that they've been in love."

"You think being in love's all the excuse they need? If it was Ben who'd crawled into Ellen's bed, would you think that was right?"

"I don't think it's right."

"Do you think we ought to shut our eyes to what's not right?"

He was thinking of Syl and asking a two-edged question and he knew it, and knew she didn't.

"Sometimes I guess I do. If there's nothing we can do to help, only make a fuss. If the damage has been done, rousting them out now will only shame them."

"Chad's been pretty sick. Maybe no damage has been done."

"I hope not," Joicey said.

The possible second meaning of this came to Shel tardily.

"Hope not what?" he asked.

"Hope he's not been too sick."

Shel looked down at his wife again. She wasn't smiling now. She knew how serious a thing she'd said.

"That don't sound like the hope of a very good mother."

"I'm not thinking how I sound. I'm thinking of them. He wouldn't ever forgive himself. If he was too sick," she explained. "And she wouldn't forgive him either."

"All right," Shel said, finally, "that's your hope for them. What's your plan for us?"

"Nothing."

"What do you plan to say to them when you see them in the morning?"

"She won't be here. And we won't say anything to Chad."

"You think she'll walk home in the dark? It's a good four miles."

"She got over here in the dark."

"It's easier to make a trip to than away from."

"I didn't say it wasn't easier."

Shel slid down into the bed so that his head rested on the pillow. Joicey put her feet on his, but quickly withdrew them. "You've gone to bed with your socks on."

"I didn't decide to go to bed until now," he defended himself. But he sat up and took them off. Joicey was silent; he thought she had

465

gone to sleep, but she was only giving them a little pause before changing the subject.

"What happened in Los Angeles today?"

With those two downstairs he didn't feel like talking about Los Angeles. Besides, he didn't know what had happened.

"I don't know, Joicey. And I'm too tired to say another word."

He said a few more, though. The quiet lasted only a few minutes before he heard Zoomy thud out of his bed and come stumbling toward them.

"I can't sleep a wink," Zoomy said.

"You can sleep now," Joicey told him. "We're all through talking. We're going to be quiet."

"It's the quiet that keeps me awake."

"You get right on back to bed," Shel ordered. "We've got something else to do besides talk you to sleep. What are you, anyway? A baby?"

"No."

"Get, then, and don't let me hear another word out of you."

After Zoomy left, Shel slept for two minutes; then, as often happened when he was dead tired, opened his eyes in a dry wakefulness.

"I'd be easier in my mind," he said, "if Chad was still sleeping in his tent."

"It's no worse their being in the house than out there."

"At least they wouldn't be in that damn bed out there."

"Bed?" Joicey asked, then caught on. She was the one who was shocked now. "It's nothing to joke about," she said.

"I don't know what else to do about them, since you won't let me go down there and roust them out."

"Pray," Joicey told him. "You could pray for them."

"Joking's my way of praying," Shel said.

"What's the connection?" Joicey asked.

He couldn't tell her, but the minute he'd said those words, he knew he'd heard a truth.

When Shel didn't speak, Joicey said, "The one thing in it all that we can' be thankful for is that Chad never knew. Moving clear away from your folks and mine was the best thing we ever did. Chad's the kind who would've taken it to heart."

Shel still didn't answer, but she went on. "He's the kind would've held it against us, if he'd known."

Listening to the pauses between Shel's incoming and outgoing breaths, she knew he was asleep. She hearkened to his breathing and

466

to the air whose slightest movement around their two-story hilltop house could be heard. Inside her, her baby moved, not gently, like the air, but suddenly, like a sleeper in the morning hours. Downstairs, a grandson was perhaps already started. A grandson. Oh, the web of life, the ties and strands, the knittings-together. She lay midway between her parents and her grandchildren, and inside her lay the link to both. The baby—he must be a boy—kicked to hurt. "Sleep, baby, sleep." She hummed the tune in her mind and heard her mother's voice singing it. "Thy father is guarding the sheep." She had sent her father without a thought for him on that gun-cocking mission, lying to him as easily as a bird sings, not caring at all how she hurt him, just so he bring Shel home to her. And her father had departed, for all he let her see any qualms or hurts, as easily as a bird sings. Not a word from him of "Never darken my doorway again." A tiger couldn't have been more hardhearted about a meal he wanted than she had been about getting Shel. "Bring me what I want," she told her father, and he'd set off without a word of reproach to do so. And he still lived for her letters, he wrote her; and if that was his life, it was a meager one, for there was never time to write him properly. She figured out the difference in time and imagined him sleeping his widower's sleep in the grayness of morning already come to Kentucky, and thinking, wakeful as old men are, of his only child.

With life in her and life being got by her son, she thought of her father and death. When she was young, she had often thought of death as girls do, but romantically and tragically, as something that threatened her alone: threatened her in her youth with consumption or drowning or being kicked in the head by a runaway horse. If she could avoid these misfortunes by luck and smart planning, and she could, for she was smart and lucky, death could be defeated. That was the way it had seemed to her as a girl—death often on her mind, but in the guise of a personal enemy she could wrestle with and best.

She no longer thought of death as an enemy, Joyce Matthew's personal enemy, a fearful challenge to be fought and conquered, but as a place. It was a place they were all going. That was death, the place that waited, and there was no way of fighting it. In seventy-five short years, everyone in this house, even the unborn, would likely have gone there. This house Shel had built for them would have fallen down; there would be nothing left to tell of the babies made and born here, of the love and work, the tears and the laughing; all lost, gone to dust in the Santa Ana's blowing.

Oh, Papa, she thought, Papa. People, when they die, say "Papa" or

467

"Mama," and those by the bedside think it's Papa or Mama in heaven being seen and spoken to. I don't suppose that's true, Joicey thought. We talk to Papa and Mama all of our lives, and when we're old and sick, we don't take the pains any longer to pretend. We speak to them right out loud and let the listeners gape.

Shel moved closer to her. She put an arm across him. If she forgot her father, it was because she remembered Shel. If she was a good wife, that, too, was a gift from her father. Husband, son, grandson, father. The wind strengthened, and the sharp corners of the house cut it with a thinner sound. Into the dead grove, over the growing potatoes, west and east, upstairs and downstairs, grandsire and grandson, and the dark land waiting for all. "Sleep, baby, sleep." She could hear her mother sing, in her voice breathy as a boiling kettle. And her daughter slept.

7  THE FIRST time Press awakened she wished she were dead. She felt disgust for herself and Chad. No wonder mothers told their girls it was a fate worse than death. She would surely rather die than have that happen again. She didn't blame Chad. It was her fault, and she had ruined everything for both of them. She could not imagine facing anyone in broad daylight after behavior of that kind: anyone, let alone Chad, whom she respected. She had wanted to separate herself from her family and to seal herself to Chad, and what she had done was to separate herself from everyone. She was alone in the world now, and before Chad woke she would be gone. She didn't blame him at all. What else could he do? He was no doubt lying there as unhappy as she was. It is a blackness we can never live down. I would gladly have my hands cut off, if it could never have happened. He put that part of himself inside me. *That* part. It was remarkable as well as terrible. He acted as if he were out of his mind. I have heard it said you never know a man until you marry him, and I can see that it is the absolute truth. I could never have dreamed this of Chad, that he could make those sounds or say those words. Perhaps the experience will kill me. I think that it might. But it was an experience. It had to happen with someone, sooner or later, I suppose, and I'm glad it was Chad. It was bad, but it would have been worse with anyone else. He'll

468

be as ashamed as I am. He'll understand. He'll want to keep it a secret as much as I do. It's the price I had to pay to get free. Papa's a terrible man. I don't have a thing to make up to Mama any more. Chad hurt me. But he was sorry. He cried. I felt his tears on my cheeks. It was a terrible thing, but I would have been disgraced if he had refused. I can live this down. Why is it easier to live down some terrible thing you asked for and got than some terrible thing you asked for and were refused? It was disgusting, but he wanted me. He didn't sound happy, but perhaps he was. Perhaps he will remember me kindly. I will leave in a few minutes. I will go to Los Angeles and get work. I don't suppose I'll look the same again, but in a big city it will never be noticed. I will never marry. I will have an understanding now of fallen girls. Perhaps I will be the guiding angel of a rescue mission. I will never see Chad again. I will send him a card each year on the anniversary of this night to show him that I have never forgotten. If that is marriage, I understand better why the church must bind men and women together. No one could stand that except as a religious duty.

The second time Press awakened, she thought, I am glad I had the self-control not to yell or cry or complain. It was I who asked. It was a terrible thing, so silly, as well as nasty, but since that was what I wanted, what chance did Chad have? He was very strong; he kissed me, held me close, and told me he was sorry to hurt me. It is not his fault that this is the way men and women are made. I do not see why. It is a revolting way. I never imagined anything like it. It is a good thing to have that behind me. It has to be done sometime; without it your life hasn't started. You aren't legally married until it happens. A man can divorce you if it doesn't happen. You are not a wife unless it happens, and when it has happened you are called a common-law wife, preacher or no preacher. So I am a wife already, and the worst is over. I am glad I did it without thinking or without knowing what was to come. If I had known, I wouldn't have had the courage. Fools rush in where angels fear to tread. We are one flesh now, though that is hard to believe. If he were to do it again, I might realize it more. It probably cannot happen at once. The chief thing is the strangeness, that he could get so big and could go inside me. Inside me. He is the only human being in the world who has been inside me. I didn't have to urge him. He longed for me. "Night after night I have longed for you. You come to me like a dream." He acted as if I were a blessing. I must stay far away from him on the bed. I must be careful not to touch him, especially there. It might happen again.

The third time she awakened, she moved without knowing it closer to Chad, and thought: In the midst of it all, there was, for one second, a very strange feeling. It was not like any feeling I ever had before. Perhaps I imagined it.

The fourth time Press awakened, she looked into Chad's opened eyes. It was the beginning of day, the very beginning. At first she looked into Chad's eyes as if gazing into gray light. Then she saw that the light was Chad's smiling. His mouth smiled, too. His whole face ached, with tenderness. She could tell because her own face ached in the same way. Every thought of the act left her. There was only Chad, looking at her from under his dark crooked eyebrows. She could trust his face. She had only to look into his face and all their acts were justified. The windows were open, and air like sweet, cool water flowed across them. It had no scent she could name. It smelled like morning air, but she had never smelled a fragrance like it.

"What are you doing?" Chad whispered.

"Breathing."

"I never knew anyone could breathe so quiet. I can't hear you at all. But I can feel you."

He put his hand at the base of her throat. She wanted to breathe even more quietly, to impress him, but thought this would be showing off. She must not disappoint him by pretending to be something she wasn't.

"I will always love you," she said.

It was the beginning of her farewell message, before she left him. He did not know this. He thought she was speaking out of a backward, not a forward, look. His hand, light and warm, touched her between her breasts.

"I am going to Los Angeles today," she told him quickly.

"Los Angeles," he repeated without surprise. "No, it's Santa Ana."

"Santa Ana?"

"Santa Ana's the county seat. We have to get our license at the county seat. It's the law."

She knew what he meant. She was only wondering, not asking a question. But she repeated his words, "Our license."

"We can't get married without it."

"When are we going to be married?"

"Today. This is our wedding day."

"Was last night our wedding night?"

"It was mine. Was it yours?"

470

She could remember what she had thought in the moments of her earlier wakening, but these thoughts now seemed to her a child's imaginings in the dark. He put his fingers between her fingers, and she had a feeling of games and innocence. This was the way you held hands for go in and out the windows and drop the handkerchief.

"Will I go with you to Santa Ana?"

"You have to. They won't give a man by himself a license."

"How do you know so much about marrying?"

"I've been planning to get married."

"I'm afraid to see your folks."

"Me, too. We'll leave before they're up."

"Maybe you shouldn't go. You've been sick."

"I'm well now."

His hand, which was still between her breasts, moved softly, and her flesh waited with longing for its arrival.

"We will never be parted again."

She couldn't speak. In the silence there was a soundless roaring which was the movement of her heart. The feeling for which she had no name had begun again and was spreading. The feeling was without any sound, but she waited for a sound like that of a breaking wave. She waited for the sound of its toppling. The wave would fall and break into creaminess, as it had on the beach when she had watched her mother, only now she wouldn't call out to her father or be frightened for her mother. It was happening to her, which made all the difference.

8    HALF ASLEEP, Joicey groped toward Shel's warm body. The night had cooled, and she had been roused by a feeling of chilliness. When her hand touched the edge of the mattress at Shel's side of the bed, she awakened completely. Shel was not in the bed.

"Shel," she said in a low voice.

Shel answered from the west window.

"What're you up for, Shel?"

There was no reply, but she heard the sound of a vehicle being turned in the yard below, the scrape of a wheel being cramped, then the clap of hoofs after the turn was made. It was still barely daylight. She sat up in bed and began the slow process, which her size required, of getting up. Before she had her feet on the floor, Shel was at her side. When she was standing, he pulled the top quilt from the bed and draped it around her shoulders like a shawl.

"If you've got any old shoes," he whispered, "or rice, now's the time to bring them forth."

From the west window she looked down on those two early risers, Chad and Press, with Chinopsee hitched to the buggy, already halfway down the lane which led through the potatoes. Chinopsee was trying, in the brisk air, to start off at a lope, and Chad, with one arm around Press, was not succeeding in holding him in very well.

"Oh, I do hope he's dressed warm," Joicey said.

"He can't get very cold as long as Press stays that close to him."

"Don't joke. He's not well yet."

"You weren't worrying about his health last night."

"There were more important things to worry about last night—but this morning there's no reason for him not to be dressed warm. I wish he'd worn your overcoat."

"A man don't like to get married wearing his father's castoffs."

"You think he's getting married today?" The idea had come to Joicey, too, but Chad married was an idea that could stand considerable talking about.

"Chad never was one to do things halfway."

"That's a long drive to Santa Ana for a boy just out of a sickbed."

"If Chad pulled through the night, he'll likely pull through the day."

At the bottom of the slope, the buggy turned south. Shel and Joicey stood to one side of the window, and not a minute too soon, for Chad turned and gazed upward in their direction.

"Oh, I wish we could wave to him," Joicey said. "I wish we could tell him we love him and wish him well."

"We can't," Shel told her, "and you know it. The best present we can give Chad is for him to think we never knew they were in that bed last night."

"God bless you, God bless you," Joicey said. She kissed her hands and held them toward the departing couple. There were tears on her cheeks. "Oh, Shel, I hope they're one-tenth as happy as we've been."

"They ought to be ten times as happy. Chad's giving his girl ten times as good a start as I gave you."

The buggy turned west again as it left the Lewis ranch and headed down the main road toward the townsite.

472

"There goes my last hope of getting us out of debt," Shel said. The boy'll need all he can make to set them up at housekeeping without loaning us anything."

"I was hoping," Joicey said, "Mr. Perkins might've had something in mind for you that would help us out."

"Oh, he did, all right," Shel said. "He had something in mind for me. He sure did."

"A job?"

"A job."

"Good paying?"

"Very good paying."

"A job you could do?"

"Yes. I think so. I been thinking about it all night. It's a job I could swing, I think."

There wasn't any use asking the next question. Joicey knew that. Something in Shel's voice had answered it already. Still, she asked it. "But you aren't going to take it?"

"No, I'm not, Joicey. It'd put us on Easy Street, but I'm going to say no."

"Why?"

"It's not honest. Or it's only about half honest, anyway. I had myself kidded for a while last night I could take it. But I can't."

The buggy, which had been out of sight at the bottom of a wash, climbed a hill. The sun, which Shel and Joicey couldn't see from the west window, was already up, and Chad and Press traveled in morning light, wheels flashing and black leather shining.

"There they go," Joicey said.

"You get back in bed," Shel told her, "and I'll go downstairs, get the fire started and the coffee on."

"No," Joicey said, wrapping the quilt more tightly around her. "It's warmer under this than it would be back in bed."

They watched the buggy until it disappeared behind the last hill.

"There goes our boy," Joicey said.

Shel gave the baby under the quilt a soft pat. "We're not bereft yet," he said. "There's a new crop coming on."

They went downstairs together to cook breakfast for themselves and for the children who still remained under their roof.

# BOOK V

I   L UTE AND I NDY had nothing but a sheet over them, and didn't need that. The calendar said spring but the sun said summer. Yesterday's sun, that was. Today's sun wasn't up yet. Lute lay on his back, wide awake. Summer in a dry land, the true summer of July and August, has the look of fall anyplace else, a brown and dying look. In a dry land, only a summery day in April has an Eastern summer's look, some green to go with the warmth, and a little moisture left from winter's rains to temper the heat.

The spring month and the summer warmth were contradictory, but nothing suits the human condition better. Early snow, late blooming, wise children, innocent old people, that's what we're all hungry for. A true April of rain, of alternating bright sun and cold wind, would have gone unnoticed on the Tract. But the Tract had had a crumpled gold sunset, and a twilight sky of broken opals. Doves had cried down by the Anaheim lake. The air was sweet with the muggy fragrance of wild flowers. April and summer. They contradict each other. April is not summer. Yet it *is* April and it *is* summer. Sparks fly in the mind as the opposed facts rub against each other, one truth denying the other.

It is like Indy and sex, Lute thought. *They* don't go together. They are contradictory. But I have seen them reconciled.

Indy, to judge by her breathing, was still asleep. Because of the heat, he supposed, she was far from him on the other side of the bed. But she had been close to him earlier. To whom had he once said, "Sex don't mean a thing to Indy"? Or had someone said it to him? Whoever had said it, and he certainly had once believed it, had been

475

wrong. He would be the first to admit that the means by which he had reached this knowledge were not pretty ones. He had said to himself, in the nights when his imagination had pictured Indy and Tom Mount together, If that's what she wants, if that's what she likes to feel, she'll take it from me and she'll feel it with me. And she had taken it from him and she had felt it with him. He had given her only one other choice: Run away. Decamp. Pull your freight. Tom Mount had nothing to offer her other than that, had he? Home, marriage, security, intellectual companionship? Nothing. An itinerant jack-of-all-trades whose only steady line of work was in bed with women. And if that was what Indy wanted, he could give it to her. He insisted on giving it to her. Why hadn't she told him before? If he had formerly been selfish, he had now reversed himself. He thought only of Indy. It took a little patience on his part, but he owed her that, and with patience no woman could be more responsive. He sometimes feared for her. He had, he saw, changed his mind completely about women and sex. As a young man, he had believed that there was no connection for women between love-making and love. He now believed that one *was* the other. Indy, trembling in his arms, was Indy loving him.

He was a lucky man. As a husband, his lately lost wife newly ardent. He was lucky as an editor, with more news than he could print. If he could get out a paper twice a day, the people would read it. There was no longer any room for the lives of ants or the eating habits of Mexicans. How many ships sunk in the Atlantic? How many lives lost at the front? How many warnings given the Germans? How many days until we are in it? And on the Tract itself, without any help from the trenches or from Woodrow Wilson, writing notes in Washington, D. C., there was enough news to fill the paper. "Will we get our money back from the Investment Company?" "Will Sylvester Perkins be ruined?" "Should Shel Lewis have taken the job?" "Were we fools to sue?"

As the darkness thinned, Lute turned to face Indy. She was, he saw, truly sleeping. The idea of waking her came to him, the idea of exercising that new-found power of his. He faced her, this thought in mind, like an enemy, like an opponent. He was aware of the capitulation he could command in the attack which he called love.

In the half dark, Indy was plainly a woman but not plainly Indy. Memory had to provide the outlines that gave her an identity, that made her the Indy he had once known. Lying there, remembering the

476

face he could not see, he was surprised, the lucky husband and editor, by tears on his face.

It was in the middle of this unexpected act, for crying is an act, his wife, whose face he couldn't see, sleeping beside him in the morning darkness, that he imagined that he heard someone crying, "War, war," in a loud voice.

He did not hear the voice again and he believed himself to be dreaming. But if it had been a dream, Indy had also dreamed it. She sat up in bed saying, "Lute, someone shouted 'war.' "

They both listened, and there was nothing more to be heard. Even the birds that usually twittered at this hour were silent—as if they, too, were listening to hear again that which had interrupted them. Then out of the windless morning grayness, a voice they did not dream called, "Lute, Lute!"

There was no mistaking that sour, soft voice. Lute ran to the window. "What's the trouble, Base?" There were footsteps as Base came from the back of the house. "War," he said, even before he came in sight. "War's broken out."

"Broken out," he said, as if speaking of a wild animal, usually caged.

"How do you know?" Lute whispered, and wondered why he did so. As if Base knew a terrible secret which ought to be hushed up.

"My brother in Los Angeles." Base, who had been shouting, now also whispered. The war was still too new and strange to be spoken of in an ordinary voice.

"It's not six yet," Lute objected.

"The papers will be signed this afternoon. My brother's son is in Washington. It's all settled but the signing." He made the war sound like marriage or the purchase of a car. Something not legal without a license or a bill of sale.

"Go around to the kitchen," Lute whispered. "The door's unlocked. I'll make us some coffee."

As he dressed, his mind whispered, "War, war." The biggest action of all. Every minute filled. Every nerve strained. Every thought employed. All for the best of reasons, all to save the country. "I am saved," he told himself.

Indy, still sitting up in bed, her hair somber in the morning grayness with none of the lights sunshine put in it, said, "What did you say, Lute?"

He knew what he had said, and because he did, couldn't repeat the

477

words. A terrible truth had made itself known to him. Saved, saved. Saved by *blood*.

"I didn't understand what you said, Lute," Indy repeated.

He didn't intend her to understand. He didn't want to understand himself. Saved? Saved by death? Who was going to die to save him? How could bloodshed save a man? Yet, "I am saved." Those were the words that had come to him when he had heard with terrible joy Base's cry of "War."

When he didn't answer, Indy said, "War is a terrible thing."

"It had to come," Lute told her.

She didn't ask why. She did not believe it; she was a woman, and though she had not managed her own life well, she believed that life could be managed, that we make of it what we want. The minute Lute left the room, she got up, went to the window where he had stood, and whispered to herself the words he had said, "I am saved."

But she was not saved. A woman has to die for herself. War is not her salvation. Men, who need saving, wage it. It is not real, she thought. It is an artificial, made-up thing, though the suffering it causes is real. She dressed by the window. The foothills were already changed. In mornings of peace, they had not appeared to be waiting for terrible happenings.

The two men, by the time she got to the kitchen, were already half through their coffee. They paid no attention to her. Women were not serious enough for war. She leaned against the sink with her own cup of coffee while they sat at the table. For the first time, she saw that there was a certain likeness between Lute and Base. Perhaps not a true likeness of bone and color—which would last—but only a passing likeness based on the feelings and opinions they now shared. Their voices were very low, throbbing with secrets. She had not heard these notes for a long time in Lute's voice. He no longer spoke to her often. His conversations with her were carnal. Both men ignored her, but by their whispers they justified her eavesdropping, they gave her the status of a spy.

"After the rally," Base was saying, "we ought to have a meeting of the volunteers."

"I can't bring myself to believe," Lute said, "that any of the Mexicans around here have got it in for us enough—or this country—to do any harm."

"I can believe it. And even if they haven't, a guard at the reservoir won't do any harm."

478

"It's preparedness, I suppose. Foresight."

"It's more than that. It gets people into the right frame of mind. It brings the war home to them. It gives them someone to fight. The war's six thousand miles away from the Tract. How d'you expect people here to get excited about that? They need something to protect *here* and somebody to fight *here*. We've got the reservoir and we've got the Mexicans. They'll put the war right here on our doorstep. They'll put us in the middle of it."

"We can't *use* them."

"The hell we can't."

"I suppose in any case we'd have to organize some kind of a home guard?"

"We'll be required to. And to do what? Shoot jack rabbits? Hunt coyotes? Don't be a fool. The reservoir's our weak point, and we got every reason to be suspicious of the Mexicans. Lute, did you ever look in the eyes of one of those fellows? Well, I have. D'you know what's there? Hate. Pure hate. They're not far removed from the red Indian. They'd as soon scalp you as not. Except, compared with a Mexican, the Indian was an honorable fighter. The Mexican's a skulker. He'll knife you in the back."

They finished their coffee. Lute, before leaving, said, "Indy, I'll be back to take you to the rally. Don't expect me for supper, but be ready by seven at the latest."

He didn't kiss her good-by. He no longer laid hands on her in public. After the men were gone, she had another cup of coffee, still standing at the sink. Then, leaving the table uncleared and the dishes unwashed, she, Indy, the ardent housekeeper of former days, went to Press's unoccupied room. It now seemed to her that Press was her greatest loss. Not Tom. The Tom she had known had not existed at all. The true Tom, the Tom who lived in Lute's words, she did not know.

So she had lost no one except Press. Lute she would never be able to lose. They were bound together. Something in their upbringing or natures made it impossible for either of them to progress beyond any first encounter. It made no difference what either was or did. It was as much a fatality as that of having a mad woman for a mother. She was your mother, and nothing you wished or hoped or prayed could change it.

But Press! She looked into her daughter's pretty room, saw the things Press, living in her two-room shanty, no longer had: window seat with cretonne curtains and cushions; white desk with chair to match; a dressing table with cut-glass candlesticks. A wastepaper basket covered with cretonne. Oh, my daughter, I have driven you from your home. You couldn't stay where I was.

The room was exactly as Press had left it. The same dress over a chair back, the same withered flowers. Press had not come home for as much as a hairbrush. She had always known that, back of Press's feverish care for her, back of her incessant fussing over her, Press was making up something to her. Making up what? I wasn't the mother Press wanted or needed somehow. And the more she felt that, the harder she worked to hide it from me. Oh, Press, come back, come back. Feel what you want to. Hide nothing. You don't have to love me or make it up to me for not loving me. All those hours Lute talked, I thought it was Tom I was losing. Or Lute. Instead, it was my daughter Press.

The people who have enough sorrow, she thought, don't need war. And, as an afterthought, added, Or the people who have enough love.

2  WAR WAS declared on April 6, 1917. The calendar called that day spring, but on the Tract it felt like summer, bright sun, sweet flowers, a soft, balmy wind. No one the night before had closed a window or locked a door. The beneficent weather put trust in their hearts. If the weather was with them, who could be against them? Then in the midst of this trust came the word "war," and hearts unusually open to earth's beauties had to take in death, too.

People stopped doing everything else that day. Of course, a man furrowed out to irrigate, did not let his water run wild. But he did neglect it. Nothing except "being in the war" seemed worth doing. The trouble was, no one knew how to "be in the war." Something they had only read about, but never seen, was turning out to be real. It had as well have been an approach of dragons. They had to drop everything in their effort to imagine "war."

Some few on the Tract instinctively understood "war." Wendlin was one. Base was another. Some of the women on the Tract practiced the feel of being widows. Some liked it. Some knew they would prefer to die themselves. Young men practiced being hit by shrapnel. They held out their hands imagining holding bayonets and hand grenades.

The dream of war was best for young girls. For them, it was all sacrifice; greatly loving and heroically dying, they sank to rest, by all their country's wishes blest.

Ellen died a dozen heroic deaths during that first day. She was told to spit on the American flag, refused, and was tortured. Tom Mount looked on with pity and admiration. It gave him the courage to face *his* ordeal. She reached Chad in prison, freed him in the face of a hail of bullets. As she died, the admiring Boche said, "And they told us these Americans were cowards! If their girls are like this, God pity us when their men arrive."

No human blood, outside an occasional fist fight, had, to anyone's knowledge, ever been spilled on the Tract. Mountain lions had once been killed there, pigs and cows butchered, a couple of horses with broken legs shot. But men had not killed each other there. The Indians were peaceful; the Spaniards interested in their barley ranches. It was left to these orange growers, these ranchers and churchmen, to fight a war; to envisage by seven o'clock that evening, when the rally would take place, *killing*.

Though the rally was not to begin until seven, people had begun to drift into the townsite by noon. War! Each man, to believe it, needed to hear that word in another's mouth. When he said to himself, "We're in the war," his words did not carry conviction. He needed to hear another man, a known truthteller, say the words. It was for that reason they congregated. The townsite in itself offered them no comfort, no reassurance. The wild growth had been beaten down and nothing new had been planted to replace it. The rest of the Tract was rich with flowers and grasses: carpets of baby blue-eyes; sunshiny streaks of yellow poppies; smoldering veins of Indian paintbrush. On the townsite a war had already been waged by man against nature, and man had won. Nature was in ruins. Man had celebrated his victory by building raw, sharp-cornered buildings, with front yards of packed earth and gardens of frayed cactus and trampled sage.

But it was a center, a meeting place. There was the school, the church, the grocery store. There you learned, prayed, bought Suetene, Fels Naphtha, dried beans, kerosene, soda crackers, canned tomatoes. There you went on the day the war broke out to learn about fighting. There some few prayed. There everyone ate.

By dusk, the shelves in Sam McFadden's grocery were empty of all edibles that could be eaten out of hand, and people were starting on food that could not be so eaten: canned peas and the like. Whatever else the war should prove to be, it was evident from the first hours that fighting was a hungry business. Stomachs growled just imagining it. Whatever war would bring to other men, Sam McFadden saw that it would bring business to grocers.

The people who were not on the townsite by late afternoon could be accounted for. Wendlin Jessup's wife was dying. LeRoy Raunce was working the swing shift at the fields. Ben Jessup had his job down at the pumping plant by the river. Shel Lewis was working on the road.

Shel's daughter was there, though; and LeRoy's, and Base's. Base and Lute, Sam McFadden, Oscar Wheatland, and other of the Tract's leading citizens were having a prerally meeting in the schoolhouse, planning, so it was said, community defense.

"Community defense" was a harder idea to take in than war. Most had at least read about war; Bunker Hill, Gettysburg, Shiloh; they could sing songs about war, "Tenting Tonight," "Columbia, the Gem of the Ocean," but no one had ever read a word or sung a song about "community defense." Who were they to defend the Tract *from?* The Germans might want it, but only as a part of the United States. Even the Germans, once they saw it, might wonder if it was worth fighting for. The idea tickled them; the Germans arriving on the Tract, goose-stepping high to avoid cactus and rattlesnakes; taking one good look, and goose-stepping out of there at the double. The idea of community defense had been put in their heads by Base Cudlip, who had made a little preliminary speech from the schoolhouse steps. Mainly, he told them to stick around until seven, when the big rally would start. But somewhere he had brought up community defense, and, along with it, a hint as to whom they would need to defend the community against—Mexicans.

This was an even harder idea to take in—especially after Pete and Rosa Ramos arrived. Rosa looked as if she might produce her baby as a part of the rally program, and Pete talked about enlisting. If he enlisted, they could not very well protect the community against him. In the first place, he would be someplace else. And in the second, as a soldier he would be an official defender himself. Somebody suggested that Pete's enlistment talk was a cover-up for other plans. "Who's most likely to stab you in the back? The man who says he hates you or the man who says he dotes on you?" "The man who says he hates you." Maybe. But Pete's enlistment talk was thought by most to be the result of high spirits—some of it under Pete's belt; some, the result of what he knew was under his wife's belt. All the Mexicans liked children, and Pete and Rosa had been childless for a good many years. Half of Pete's talk of enlisting was banter directed toward Rosa. "This war didn't come along a minute too soon. Now I've got a good excuse not to be home when the crying and bawling starts. Rosa will be walking the floor at nights with the baby. But I'll be in Paris with those French babies. Oh man!"

He held Rosa's arm while he said it, and Rosa smiled. Unless she was in on the plot, too? The war was only about two hours old, and already people had learned something about it. In war you did not take anybody's word at face value. You had your suspicions. They let big Pete laugh and little Rosa smile, and they laughed and smiled in return; but they were not taken in. They had started to protect their community.

Somewhere between four and five, when the spring afternoon ended and the spring evening began, the people filled with sardines and soda crackers, their dry throats moistened with canned tomatoes and soda pop, began to sing. The day that had begun in peace was ending in war. People had shadows the size and shape of peaked tombstones. Blueness, fold on fold, enveloped the foothills. The stomp of oil wells deep inside the earth was felt. Meadow larks and blackbirds were suddenly quiet, then, as if resisting the oncoming night, sang loudly. Raunce's cow bawled to be milked. Old Saddle Back was rosy above the valley's shadows. The April summer evening, the first of the war, came down with melancholy softness and beauty.

Crystal, who was plain, had a voice that could pick up a song and make every note a barb to enter the heart and hurt it; barbs so beautiful that the heart would not for a minute forego the pain. She did not use it often, because her father, considering it a gift of God, insisted that she use it in God's praise, singing "Brighten the Corner," and "Throw Out the Lifeline." Crystal liked these songs, but she did not like to sing for any cause. She sang now, not for the war, but because in the act of singing she was distracted from her own troubles. She could not feel sorry for herself, singing of prisoners far from home and young men dying on the battlefield.

She stopped singing when people began to depend on her to give them the pitch and to carry the tune. She went to the back of the church (the people were gathered in the street between the school and the church) and sat on the steps there. She had felt guilty about leav-

483

ing the singers leaderless; but if they missed her, it could not be told by their singing. Another leader had taken her place, and they were singing "There's a Long, Long Trail A-Winding." Voices rose and fell; the color on Old Saddle Back mounted, intensified, faded. The step on which she sat was still warm with the day's heat. Lizards still played in Tom Mount's neglected garden. She was not like Ellen. She did not imagine herself a heroine in the war. She had almost forgotten her Old Roughrider, though earlier in the day she had for a moment thought, "Teddy, this is your chance."

She closed her eyes and wished she could close her ears.

She opened them when Tom Mount spoke to her. He was almost the only person she could stand, who did not shame her with the memory of some stupidity or of some offer of love refused.

He said, "I hope you don't mind my following you? These steps used to be mine, you know."

He sat down without being asked. "How're you making out nowadays at the Raunces' without me around?"

"We miss you," she said.

"I miss the Raunces."

"Why did you leave?"

"It was too much work for your mother, keeping a boarder."

"Papa told you to leave."

"You're mistaken, Crystal. Your father never did anything of the kind. I left for two reasons, to be out near that new house I was working on and to spare your mother extra work. Why should your father ask me to leave?"

When she did not answer, he put his hands on either side of her face, then turned her face so that he could look into her eyes. "If you're going to lie, look me in the eye while you do it."

He took his hands away the minute she did look at him. "The first time I ever saw you, you lied to me," she said. Then she added, "I can lie to anyone. But you're almost the only person I can tell the truth to."

"Is that true, Crystal?"

"It is the truth that I can tell you the truth," she said steadily, looking at him. Tears came into his eyes. "That is the best thing anyone ever told me," he said. The tears did not fall. She saw him make the effort to hold them back. "I'm not ashamed to be crying," he told her. "I don't trust people who can't cry."

"You ought to trust me a lot, then."

484

"I do trust you a lot. Why do you cry?"

"I am a failure."

He smiled. "It's pretty early in life for you to say that, isn't it?"

"I'm a failure now. I can't rejoice now because I'll be a success at forty, can I?"

"No. But you might smile through your tears, remembering it."

"Do you believe it?"

"I know it."

She could not help smiling at that, and when she did, he said, "But you don't have to stop crying either. You can cry for me. I'm a failure at forty."

"You're not forty."

"I'm thirty-six. I thought you were going to say, 'You're not a failure.'"

"Maybe you are. I don't know you well enough to say. Why do you think you are?"

"You tell me why you are, first. You're younger. It'll be a shorter story."

"I did something to help my mother. It made her despise me."

"You did it to hurt your father, too, didn't you?"

"Yes."

"Why? He's a good man."

"He's not good to my mother."

"I lived at your house, remember. I never saw any signs of his not being good to her. Or of her thinking he wasn't good."

"He treats her like a beast."

"Oh. This isn't something you imagine?"

"I saw it."

"By beast, you mean animal?"

"A bad animal. I never saw any animals act that way. I never saw one animal try to make another ashamed. Or try to hurt them in that way."

"So that's why you hate your father?"

"There are other reasons. He's a hypocrite, too."

"How does this make you a failure? You're not responsible for what your father does."

"I'm like him."

"Are you a beast, too?"

"No, of course not. I couldn't be. I'm not a man."

"Only men are the beasts?"

485

"You ought to know," she said. "You're a man."

"We're all beasts, men and women."

"I'm not."

"How're you like your father, then?"

"I can't keep my mouth shut. Whatever I feel, I say. I'm not quite as bad yet," she admitted. "I don't say it in a pulpit. That's the only difference. Look how I'm talking to you. That's my father all over again. My mother would die rather than talk to you like this."

"I expect you *are* more like your father."

"My mother was a poet until he ruined her."

"She would rather be a wife and mother than a poet."

"I wouldn't."

"I feel sorry for you."

"I don't want your pity. Everybody pities me."

"Name one."

"Chad. Chad Lewis. I told him I loved him."

"Did you?"

"I said I did."

"I mean, did you love him?"

"Yes."

"What've you got to be sorry about, then? People like to know they're loved."

"They don't. It embarrasses them. It embarrassed Chad so much he got drunk. I told Lute I loved him, too. What I meant was I honored him. I made him sick. He has never given me a straight look since."

"But you still work for him?"

"I work there, but he won't look at me since I said that, or let me explain. He says, 'Let's not speak of that, please.'"

"You were unlucky," Tom said. "Chad's a kid, and he was in love with someone else. Lute don't know what love is and never will. The whole idea scares him to death. He probably turned tail and ran when he heard you speak the word."

"He turned tail all right."

"I bet he did. I can just see him. You're unlucky and lucky both. Do you love Chad now?"

"No, not now. It went away when I said it."

"That's the trouble with love. It goes away when you say it. That's why your father's a remarkable man. He can say it and not lose it. But you're lucky it went away when you said it to Chad. It would've gone away sooner or later."

486

"Am I lucky Lute won't look at me?"

"Luckiest of all. I feel sorry for anyone Lute's ever looked at."

"His wife?"

"I feel very sorry for Indy Cope."

"I honored him because he seemed the opposite of my father."

"You're right there. He's the opposite of your father. That's where you're unlucky. You're too young to appreciate your father."

"You think I will someday?"

"I hope you will. I hope you'll live that long and be that lucky."

"I'll never forget, no matter how long I live."

"Not forget, maybe. But understand."

"No, I don't want to."

"Don't be like Lute," he said. He picked up her hand, laid it in the palm of his opposite hand; but he let it lie there untouched. "Or like me."

The conversation was now getting beyond her. She was able to produce sentences that appeared to be related to those she had heard, but she did not know what "Don't be like me" meant, and she was afraid to ask. She was afraid to enter someone else's life. She had asked Chad and Lute to enter hers and had been cast down when they didn't. Here now was Mr. Tom Mount asking her to enter his. She knew this. She looked down at her hand, lying in the center of his callused carpenter's palm. Her hand, without her willing it, had drawn itself together. It was closed as if against some threat.

Tom Mount looked down at her hand. "Are you afraid?"

"No."

He closed his fingers slowly around hers. "Now you are caught," he said.

"Not if I don't want to be," she told him. As she opened her fingers, he opened his.

"You know me very well."

Once again she didn't understand him, and was afraid to ask for explanations.

He unloosened his cage of fingers. It was perfectly safe for him to do so because her hand no longer required a cage. It stayed willingly where it was.

"We have talked the sun down," he said.

The singing had stopped. "We have silenced the music," she told him.

Somebody shouted, "To hell with the Huns!"

487

"We haven't stopped the war, though," he observed.

How long could it go on, Crystal wondered. How long could they, each adding to the other's thought, build higher and higher? She forgot about hands, his and hers, touching or apart. They were building with something nearer themselves. He takes what I say, she thought, as if he had said it himself. My words are as real to him as his own. Her father wanted to give her God. Her mother would give herself to her daughter, past times as well as present. Oh, but Tom Mount gave her something more precious, something she had been wanting for a long time: he gave her herself. He sat there giving her Crystal; he reflected Crystal as the moon does the sun, and she felt that he made her harsh light gentle.

The flowers Tom Mount had planted about his doorstep were petunias. In the warm dusk they were very sweet and still shaken by the movements of late-working bees. Some, gone too deep in the flowers, were mad at honey and trying to kick the treasury down. On the other side of the church was the war. But on their side, there was nothing but honeybees and light the color of barley stubble and long fields stretching without a stop, south to the river and east to the mountains. The promise of her life opened up before her.

Her hand was still on Tom Mount's when she saw Indy Cope come around the corner of the church. Mrs. Cope was walking slowly, watching the last of the light on Old Saddle Back. She stopped, not noticing them, and folded her arms on her breast. She stood in profile to them, and Crystal examined her face. She had always believed her to be beautiful. She looked like Sarah Bernhardt, a woman capable of feelings of such variety, range, and depth as she herself, Crystal, could scarcely imagine. Imagining what that woman might feel, Crystal began to tremble. She started to take her hand away from Tom Mount's, but he closed his fingers, and she was ashamed, because she had made, by not wanting Mrs. Cope to see, something shameful of something natural.

Mrs. Cope was turning away without seeing them at all. Tom Mount called, "Indy, I must talk to you."

Mrs. Cope turned, looked at them, but did not speak. Tom Mount went to her. He put a hand on her still-folded arms. "I've been looking for you, Indy. I must talk to you."

Mrs. Cope said, "I'm not stopping you, Tom."

"I can't talk to you here. Let's drive out to the Santa Ana Canyon.

488

Let's go down by the river someplace. We need a little quiet to talk in."

"No, Tom. I'm not going away from here. Talk to me here."

"You were told a lot about me."

"Yes, I was. I listened for three hours."

"You believed it all?"

"It sounded like the truth to me."

"Did you want to believe it?"

"Want to believe it? I thought what I heard would kill me. I'd like to think it was all a bad dream. I'd like to hear every word denied."

"I can't do that," Tom Mount said. "But what's past is past."

"Yes," Indy Cope said. "I feel that, too."

"I could tell you bad things about your own past."

"I know you could. I can tell myself even more."

"Do you want to go on with that? That's the question. Not what our past has been, but what our future's going to be?"

"It's going to be some more of our past."

"Why? It don't have to be. Come with me."

"Come with you?"

"Marry me."

"From all I hear, you're not marriageable."

"Neither are you. We both could be."

"No, I never could do it."

"You talk like a woman in prison."

"I am."

"It's a prison you built yourself."

"It doesn't matter who built it, if you're locked inside."

"I've got the key that will let you out. You were outside for a while. Didn't you like it?"

"I loved it."

"Come out again. It's not any better back in there now, is it?"

"It's worse. A thousand times worse."

"Come on out."

"No, I had my chance. I'm back in, and the key's lost."

"You're the first woman I ever proposed to."

"You picked a safe one for it." She had been facing Tom Mount and also facing Crystal. Now she turned to face the street and the war makers.

"You're not going?" Tom Mount asked.

489

"I'm looking for Press. The Lewises said that they expected her and Chad tonight. She's the one person I want to find."

"I'm here. You've found me. You don't need anyone else."

Mrs. Cope turned again and looked at Tom Mount. She used her eyes on his face the way blind people are said to use their hands. She felt it. "But who are you, Tom?" she asked.

He did not answer, and she went back the way she had come, never having once unfolded her arms. Tom Mount watched her go. Crystal thought that she had been completely forgotten. But he came back to her as if there had never been an interruption. He sat down, leaned against the door of his former home, took her hand, and said, "I told you I was a failure."

She was too tactful to recognize the possibility of truth in that statement by denying it. She was not sure what she had just heard. She had, like a good girl, tried not to hear anything, but sound flows into the ears in spite of the strongest resolutions. Something had been asked, something had been refused. She was sure of nothing except that if there was to be any more talking, Mr. Mount should do it. She watched a night moth, big as a hummingbird and with the tongue of a snake, drink a supper of petunia honey. An odd thing had happened. Her hand, the hand that lay on Tom Mount's hand, was tingling with life. It seemed to her that if her hand should be severed from her body, it would be her hand, not her body, that would live.

The singing had died down. Most people had brought picnic suppers with them, and Crystal supposed they had stopped their singing to eat. Though the silence was not complete. Someone with an accordion was playing "Marching Through Georgia," and someone else was making up a song as he went along to match this war to that old tune. "Bring the good old bayonet, boys . . . te tum, te tum, te tum. . . . Hurrah, Hurrah, we'll sing the jubilee, While we are marching through Ger-man-ee."

She had not looked at Tom Mount since Indy Cope had left. Now she decided to make her world larger than a hand. He looked thoughtful, neither sick nor sad, and if he was a failure, it did not in any way show on him.

"Well, we were interrupted, weren't we?" he asked, as if he knew by her quickened pulse that she was looking at him. And no sooner had he said that than they were interrupted again. Ellen Lewis, calling "Crystal, Crystal," came running around the corner of the church. Ellen stopped in her tracks, as if a man and girl touching was a forbidden sight. She was already preparing not to have seen them when Crystal, her lesson learned about shame, called, "Ellen, here I am."

"Excuse me," Ellen said, "but all the girls are here. There's time for a club meeting before the rally starts if we hurry."

"You go on and have your meeting," Tom told Crystal. "I'll be waiting right here when you've finished."

"You mustn't wait for me," Crystal protested.

"Who says I mustn't? The Kaiser?"

"I didn't mean it like an order."

"Thanks for telling me. I want to wait. You go on now, with my friend Ellen."

When they were out of earshot, Ellen said without a trace of envy in her voice, "I envy you, Crystal, knowing Mr. Mount so well."

"I don't know him so well," Crystal answered, understanding exactly what Ellen meant, and understanding also that Ellen could never say, "But you were holding hands."

"The rally's been postponed till eight," Ellen explained, "and it's only six-thirty now. There's plenty of time for a meeting."

"What are we meeting for?" Crystal asked.

It was an unfair question. The only answer, "Because it would be fun," was beneath consideration. "Press suggested it," Ellen said.

"Is Press here?"

"I told you we're all here. It's the first time all of us have been together since the initiation."

"Where are we meeting?"

"We haven't decided."

Ellen and Crystal walked through the crowd. For people coming out of lamplit houses, it was already night. For those who had been outside since sundown, it appeared to be still light. If it was not light, they had all learned miraculously to see in the dark. The schedule of events for the rally, printed in a hurry by Lute, had been tacked by the front door of the schoolhouse. The girls stopped to look it over. "Bugle call by Orin Quigley. 'Star-Spangled Banner' led by Crystal Raunce."

"I won't do it," Crystal said.

"You're the only one can go that high."

"Prayer by Benjamin Jessup."

"He won't do it either," Crystal said. "He won't pray for war, I know."

There were enough events planned to keep them all rallying half the night: speeches, calls for enlistments, appeals for money, organization of a home guard, of a Red Cross chapter, of a Corps of Victory Gardeners, of a club to study military tactics. And between the speeches and the appeals and the formations, there was to be singing.

"A singing army is never defeated," Crystal said.

"Is that a known fact?" Ellen asked.

"I have no idea. I read it someplace."

The crowd, finishing up its supper, was quieter than it had been. Crystal said, "This is scarcely like the night before Waterloo."

Ellen asked humbly, "What is the difference?"

"There was revelry that night."

There was certainly no revelry. The Tract, which had been too busy fighting its own battles with Sylvester Perkins to worry about Europe, was trying now in a single evening to anticipate wounds and bullets, losses and hatreds. In the moments in which they were able to do so, sudden silences, like a thickening of night's darkness, would settle upon the crowd. Though the air on the skin was as warm as summer, there was no summer for the ear, no summer sounds of katydids and locusts, cicadas and crickets. War had come overnight, but a real summer has to ripen. A war can be thought up, anyone can declare it, and death can be instant. But no amount of thought has ever produced a katydid, life cannot be declared, and summer takes a little time.

Crystal and Ellen went past the war talkers, through the summer air and the sudden silences, hunting their blood sisters. There were places to rally on the townsite, but places to be private were harder to find. Church, newspaper office, school, store: even if these places had been empty, they did not suit the girls. And tonight they were not empty. The four of them settled down, finally, on the lot next to the schoolhouse. It was recognizable as a lot because stakes topped with rags still white enough to be seen in the dark marked the boundary lines. These stakes gave the girls the sense of being in some particular place, contained by something, not homeless under the stars. They clustered together in the center of the staked lot; imaginatively making room for the chairs and sofas and bookcases that would naturally line the walls of a house. They had grown away from the natural cave of their beginnings. They linked arms, trying to overcome the shyness of having vowed so much, hoping, like old married couples, by a calculated act to restore the lost uncalculated passion.

The war was a help. It pushed them closer. It gave them sensations

492

of precariousness and sacrifice. It was their substitute passion. Their minds, anticipating losses, valued present treasure. Still, they recognized that time and experience had separated them.

"The cave seems years away," Press said.

Ellen counted on her fingers like somebody calculating marriages and births. "It's been five months."

"Five months exactly," Medora agreed.

The girls went back to what had joined them, hoping in its memory to be joined again. "The wonderful wind that night," Press said.

"You stood at the cave like Ariadne, when we left you," Crystal said.

This was news to Medora. "Like what?"

"A sacrifice."

Medora made her old snort of defiance. "There wasn't any sacrifice."

"Medora," Ellen said, "I've never told a soul before, but Papa and I went up to the cave that night hunting for you."

"You didn't find me, did you?"

"No."

"Why did you come?"

"To rescue you."

"Rescue me from what?" Medora asked coldly.

"Julian," Ellen answered, hesitantly.

It seemed that might be the end of any conversation, but, after a minute, Medora said, "Julian never came."

Crystal and Ellen suffered for themselves as much as for Medora. If Medora had failed, how could they expect to succeed? Her confession subtracted from their powers.

"I thought you said . . ." Crystal began, but Medora interrupted her. "It didn't work with Julian."

"It didn't work with Chad either," Crystal said.

"When I said it to Chad, it worked," Press boasted.

"Chad already loved you," Crystal reminded her.

"I told him something he hadn't told me," Press insisted.

"Since the cave," Crystal asked, "has everyone followed Medora's advice?"

"Not Ellen, I bet," Medora said.

"How did you know?" Ellen asked.

"It shows on you."

"I'm in love."

"Tom Mount! Don't tell us any more about that."

"No," Press said unexpectedly. "Shut up about Tom Mount. He's a philanderer."

"How do you know, Press?" Medora asked.

"You forget I'm a married woman," Press said, as if marriage made all kinds of knowledge, hidden to girls, available to matrons.

"I like him," Crystal said.

"That's all right," Medora said. "Like him. Have a love affair with him. Then we'll listen to you. But not Ellen. She's dreaming. Who wants to hear what Ellen dreams?"

"I'm eighteen," Ellen protested.

Press put her arm around her blood sister, who now by law as well as ritual was her sister. "Let's not fight. There's enough of that without us doing it."

Medora said, "It is easy for you to talk, Miss Beauty. You're lucky."

Press repeated Medora's words. "It is easy for me to talk. I am the luckiest girl in the world."

"You like marriage?" Medora asked in a new and broken voice.

"Marriage?" Press asked scornfully. "I don't know anything about marriage. I love Chad. And I love to be with him. Is that marriage?"

"It's yours," Medora said, once more the oracle, "and you like it."

"Since the cave," Crystal began again, still bent on history and assessment, "a lot has happened to us. Press is married."

"That's my story," Press said, "and I'm proud of it."

"My story," said Medora, "is that I'm not married. But I tried. And I'm proud of it."

"I," Ellen began, but once again Medora shut her up: "We're talking about real things."

"This is real."

"Excuse me," Medora said with overdone humility. "I didn't understand. You have now transferred your dream affections to Asa Brice."

"I have had a proposal," Ellen said with dignity. "That is real, isn't it?"

"Jesus," Medora said. "Oh boy! I'll say it's real. You listened to me at the cave, Ellen. Now I'll listen to you. What's your system?"

"System? I don't have any system."

"Did you accept?"

"The proposal wasn't made to me. It was made to my father."

Medora said "Jesus" again. Then she asked, "Are they haggling over the size of the dowry?"

494

That finished Ellen's confidences. "I shouldn't have mentioned it. Except we promised . . ."

"And you were the first to break the promise."

"Let's not fight," Crystal urged.

"Crystal," Medora said, "you've asked everyone the story of his life. What's yours?"

"I followed your advice, Medora. I told two men I loved them. That was the truth. You won't catch me doing that again. I lied about something else to help somebody I loved. I won't do that again either."

"If you won't lie and you won't tell the truth," Miss Character asked, "what's left? Will you take a vow of silence?"

"Hell, no," Medora said. "She'll do what everyone else does. Mix 'em up. A pinch of truth and a cupful of lies. That's what's expected."

"Don't," Press said. "Let's not talk this way."

Medora ignored her. "Well, Crystal, I can say this for you. You may've struck out, but you sure went to bat."

"Let's stop this," Press cried. "This is the first night of the war. People are going to be killed. Let's be happy now while we can. Let's be happy in spite of it."

"You be happy in spite of it," Medora said. "You be happy for all of us."

Press accepted the charge. "I am. I will be. My story is just beginning. Chad and I are going to have a baby."

The girls, even Crystal, even Medora, were silent.

Ellen spoke first. "Have you been married long enough to have a baby, Press?"

Press laughed, a long, clear, ringing laugh, and they could hear people listening, and hear them thinking, This may be the last laugh we'll hear till peace comes again. When she stopped laughing, Press said, "Exactly long enough, Ellen. It doesn't take but a minute to start a baby."

"And a man," said Medora.

"That goes without saying," Press said.

"Not to Miss Character."

The silence of the girls now matched one of those deeper silences, the warm night empty of summer sounds, the people holding their breaths as if at any moment a shot might ring out. In the midst of this deep, empty, listening silence, Medora spoke, and, strangely for Medora, with hesitation. "When do you expect your baby, Press?"

"In six months. It will be an October baby." Press said this with pride, as if any other month would be second best.

She was prepared, the girls saw, to talk on this subject all night. The *idea* of having a baby interested Ellen and Crystal, but not the details of pregnancy, morning sickness and food fancies and an expanding waistline. They, however, were as polite with her as they would have been with another invalid determined to share his symptoms. Only Medora, who had the gall to say "shut up" when what she was hearing did not interest her, appeared to be truly interested in the subject. They were saved from Press's pregnancy, finally, by Press's catching sight of her mother.

Indiana Rose Cope was leaning against the schoolhouse next the rally program notice. The other girls had seen her for some time, but Press had been too busy with her baby to notice anything else. Then she, too, saw her and was suddenly gone, stepping over boundary lines as if they did not exist.

Press had not seen her mother since her marriage. In the old days, before listening to her father that night, she would have been compelled to look in on her mother every day, to treat her, as she had all of her life, like an invalid under sentence of death. She had lost that compulsion. She no longer had nightmares of her mother drowning, believing that she was dying because her daughter delayed coming to her. She no longer dreamed she ran the house for her father, her mother's adequate substitute. It was not that a home and husband of her own had freed her of these dreams and nightmares. She had her own home and her own husband because she had been freed from them and she was returning to her mother for the same reason.

Her mother did not lift a hand toward her, nor say a word. She waited, leaving the whole choice of reunion to her. Press understood this. Her proud, outrageous mother, who had put up with all those hot cloths for headaches and ill-intentioned cups of tea and wakings out of sound sleep to be asked if she wanted anything. She had never once, Press saw, accepted her mother's love. She had needed, for whatever reason, to prove that she, Press, had loved, loved, loved a mother who did not love her. Her conscience had required her to suffer for those dreams. In order to achieve the required pain, she had been willing that her mother suffer some, too. What a roundabout, counterfeit way of living. Everything standing for something else. Here was

Indiana Rose Cope, who happened to be her mother and was a real woman.

"Mama," she said.

Her mother neither cried nor smiled, but there was enough light to see that her face, watching her daughter, grew tender. "Press," she said.

Press held out both her hands. "Mama, I'm so glad to see you. I've been lonesome for you."

Her mother took her hands. For the first time in her life, Press was aware of their unique feel and shape and of the strength with which they clasped hers.

"Press, you looked so happy over there talking to the girls. I've been watching you."

"I am happy, Mama."

"I'm glad you finally waked up to Chad. He's a fine boy."

"You always knew that, didn't you?"

"Yes, and I don't know how I did. I'm not a very good judge."

Press didn't answer, couldn't answer. She was remembering the last time she'd seen her mother.

"Everything your father said that night was true, Press. Perhaps I shouldn't be talking to you. Tom Mount asked me to go away with him tonight. I told him I wouldn't. I wanted you to know."

"Go with him, Mama, if you want to."

"Don't you care about your father any more?"

"I don't care whether you stay with him or not any more."

"I used to be a little jealous of you and your father, Press. That's another thing I have to be ashamed of, besides everything else. You two seemed so close."

"He oughtn't to have encouraged me."

"It was only natural."

"Don't stand up for him. After all he said that night and shamed you."

"All he said was true. I was in love with Tom Mount. I expect I still am."

"That makes it worse."

"I told you I wasn't going with him."

"Worse about Papa, I mean."

Her mother didn't understand her, and Press couldn't explain. She couldn't say to her mother, as if they were two women, unrelated and

497

of the same age, If you had a man like Chad, you couldn't see Tom Mount for dust. Tom Mount! Beside Chad, he had a womanly sponginess; he didn't want what was his only; he wanted whatever he could get. There were two subjects she and her mother would never be able to talk about, Tom Mount and her father. Or not for a long time, anyway. Press changed the subject completely.

"Mama, I'm going to have a baby."

Before her mother could do more than squeeze her hands, her father came around the corner of the schoolhouse. Press would have confessed murder to him before she confessed the baby. He made her feel bashful about the best thing in her life. He said hello to her as calmly as if they were not separated by three months, a marriage, an expected baby, and a terrible conversation. What he was interested in was getting his wife into the schoolhouse. "You and me, Base and his wife, and a few others are to sit up front. We ought to be in there now. It won't look right, our straggling in there late." Indy, without a word, went with him.

When they went inside, Asa and Chad came to her. Press put her arm through Chad's. "I was afraid you'd forgotten me."

"I stayed away because I thought you'd like to be alone with your folks."

"That's true," Asa said. "He's been too busy watching you to hear a word I've said."

When hard up, Asa would work for a week on the road, and he and Chad had become friends—or at least friendly. "If I spend enough time with him," Chad had told Press, "I'll never miss my lack of schooling. I can learn more from him in an hour than I learned in school in a week." Press was proud when Chad talked like this. She believed him to be already a master of knowledge. A little more wisdom, and she wouldn't be able to understand two sentences out of three when he spoke; what she wanted was to learn as much as she could and still to be ignorant beside Chad. She made it possible for Chad to be with Asa oftener by asking Asa to supper occasionally. The first time Asa came, she had worked all day to provide a company supper, something out of the ordinary: everything molded or creamed or artificially colored. The creamed chicken was served in saw-toothed pastry cups. The gelatine salad was molded to look like a melon. For the dessert, which was called Ambrosia in the cookbook, she had scalloped orange halves for containers.

Asa had taken one look at the supper table and said, "How much time did all this gingerbread work cost you, Press?"

498

"Cost me?" she had answered. "Nothing. I've got all the time in the world."

"No, you haven't," Asa had said. "You've got barely enough time to live your life in. And not any to waste on ruining the looks of an orange, hacking it up this way. Or in spoiling a cabbage, jellying it up into that soggy mound."

Such talk ought by rights to have broken a hostess's heart. From Asa, such talk had made Press feel fine. He cared for her life more than for his own supper. She believed every word he said. She would never scallop, saw-tooth, or mold again.

She took Asa's arm now as well as Chad's. "We'd better go in if we want to get seats," she said.

"I'm not going in," Asa told her.

Press was astonished. "Are you against the war?"

"I'm against affairs like this to celebrate the beginning of a war."

"It's not a celebration," Press objected.

"What is it then? What's your name for a rally?"

"Why're you here," Chad asked, "if you're against such a meeting?"

"I'm here to watch," Asa said.

"Like an ant fight?" Press chided him.

"Since I'm one of the ants, I feel a little more concerned with this fight."

"Do you think it's right," Press asked, "to watch something you think is wrong and not say a word?"

"I haven't taken any vow not to say a word."

"But will anybody listen to you if you do? A man on the side lines?" Chad asked.

"A man on the side lines is about the only one with much chance to see what's happening."

"If Chad has to go to war," Press said, "I won't like it, some man who could fight standing on the side lines telling me what he sees."

"What that man sees, Press, may be of more help to your son than your husband's fighting."

"Son," Press repeated, the war gone completely out of her mind. "My son." No one had used these words to her before. She and Chad talked about "the baby," but, "your son." And how did Asa know? Did parenthood show on her and Chad? Shine out from them? Was there a change not visible to them, but visible to other eyes?

"How did you know, Asa?"

"I didn't," Asa said, abashed. "I was talking about the future."

Press was embarrassed, and she embarrassed Asa. In confusion

499

and out of consideration for both of them and against his better judgment, Asa went in to the rally with them.

The schoolhouse was crowded, the windows few, the night warm, the people heated. Asa had a fine nose, made more sensitive by living in the open. He was able to smell what others missed, the stench of fears and hatreds, passions and prejudices. He did not care for what he smelled now. He did not care for the red faces up front, faces swollen with new powers and private passions, powers and passions curbed in peacetime but released and justified now, because of the war. Ant fights: the ants, when they fought, did not have preliminary pow-wows, with those who would not share the carnage taking the limelight. The ants did not believe that there was a god who loved red ants more than black ants and supplicate him, in the name of one who had died without lifting a hand, to make their killing effective. There was nothing like that with the ants.

There were plenty of words tonight, words to hide the one word: Death. Didn't Lute Cope, his mouth full of newspaper words, know the word he was hiding? Base Cudlip knew that word. With Lute speaking, and Base sitting a little behind him, dark and hot, his face pulled together like a fist, Asa had the feeling that Lute was no more than the mouth of the cannon. All the firepower lay behind him, in Base.

Kill. Kill. I might do that, Asa thought. I don't stand with Wendlin on this. But I'm against preparing myself for that action with a minstrel-show performance. He looked around the room; he examined faces. He was the only person, evidently, who felt this. The entire Tract, with a few understandable absences, was present: Sylvester Perkins, the first man on the Tract to say the word "war" in a public meeting, should have been there. He was a prophet without honor in his own country. Syl was made for occasions like this, Asa thought, and it is an irony of fate that he is now fighting the people he should be heartening for the fray.

Everyone else was present, carried away, happy to be experiencing any strong feeling, even though that feeling was rooted in the threat of death. For someone else, of course. The crowd was pagan, worse than pagan because it hid from itself the source of its joy. The Aztecs celebrated with their victims present. But the Aztecs knew what they were celebrating, and they knew who was going to die. Someone else. They knew why the blood ran heavier and warmer in their own veins. It was because another's blood was to flow.

Who would be the sacrifices here? What victims would the Tract offer up? Chad Lewis? Pete Ramos? Ben Jessup? Asa Brice? There was a victim amongst them, of this Asa felt sure. And the crowd felt this, too, otherwise there was no accounting for its deep, trembling joy. They anticipated death. The prospect of life caused no such exquisite expectancy. Take away impending death, send someone into the room to say the declaration of war had been a hoax, and the emotion which lifted and united them would vanish. Though there was enough life-to-be in the room, if people were capable of rejoicing in life, to set them all to jubileeing. If birth meant anything to the crowd, Joicey Lewis and Rosa Ramos both looked so near to being two that they might provide that doubling miracle before the evening was over. To say nothing of those in the room who, like Press, still carried their heroes secretly. But such a miracle would not be enough to move the crowd—as it was moved. The crowd felt itself increased by endings, not by beginnings. It was death that united them and gave them a more intense sense of life, not life itself. It was victims they wanted, not babies; except as babies were needed to keep up the supply of victims.

Leaning against the wall listening to the songs and speeches, Asa asked himself, Is there nothing that will bind you to your fellow men? Don't you love your country? Aren't you a patriot? Have you forgotten the Minute Men, the bloody footprints at Valley Forge, Pickett's Charge, Custer's Last Stand, the Alamo, San Juan Hill? Have you forgotten the *Maine*? The blameless dead, the deathless fighting men? I remember them, he told himself, but this crowd does not remember them. I see men, muscles knotted with undelivered blows, who are tired of refraining. I see women who do not love, in desperate need of emotion. I see girls who believe that they have discovered the sacrifice for which they imagine they were born. I see little boys who expect war to provide them the pleasures of frog killing and cat mauling, multiplied by as many times as men are larger than cats and frogs. I see men who believe that Bull Run freed us, and Chancellorsville united us, and the Alamo saved us. Lute thinks that. He thinks that to save himself the trouble of thinking. I'm no Wendlin. I'm not even a Raunce. Strike me and I'm likely to strike back. But I consider that my weakness. And I'm not going to celebrate my weaknesses nor call my stupidity patriotism.

Stop singing, he told the crowd. Get down on your knees. Eat out your hearts. Shed tears. Study logic. Emulate the Man you name your-

501

selves after and call Master. Take no thought of the morrow. Love your enemy. Turn your cheek. Take all you have and give to the poor. Do unto others as you would be done by. Love one another. Try that, at least, if loving your enemy is beyond you.

Press, who stood next to him, whispered, "Asa, you're talking to yourself."

He couldn't silence his thoughts, but he did clamp teeth and lips together and silence his talking. He survived the singing of "Onward Christian Soldiers" and "Bring the Good Old Bugle, Boys." He survived two solos, "The Marseillaise" and "Columbia, the Gem of the Ocean." He survived a collection of money for the home guard, a flag drill, and a speech by some newly arrived fire-eater on the Tract. But he did not survive a recitation by a Cudlip child. When she reached the lines

> A man is dying in no-man's land,
> Before he goes, he asks for your hand,

Asa departed the rally.

He was glad to escape, but he was no happier outside than he had been inside. He was not sure where the greater sickness lay, in himself, unable by love or war to feel himself united with his neighbors, or in his neighbors, united by the cause and in the manner they were. He looked up at the stars, winter's constellations setting in the west, summer's constellations marching up the eastern sky. They had the power to calm and ease, but to take that calm and ease on the first night of so many men's deaths seemed ignoble. Endure the pain, he told himself, star love is too easy. The stars ask nothing of you. He defended himself against his own abuse. "I ask a good deal of myself. What? In God's name, what? Tell me quickly," his suffering self demanded. "To know, to understand." It was a barren defense. He got no comfort out of it. He took what comfort he could get from the stars.

He walked up the townsite's main street. When he headed north, he saw the Jessups' house, lamps lit in every room. Each day they told him, "Mary can't live through another night." Each morning Mary was still alive. She stayed alive by virtue of no one's prayers, certainly not her own. No one could wish that her life, as she now lived it, should continue. The townsite on occasion heard her screams. She was a strong woman, and death was having a struggle with her. Asa visited her often. There were hours when death itself became weary of the struggle, and Mary was left to herself, weak, weary, but untormented and perfectly rational. She knew what she had suffered and would suffer again. In these hours Asa looked down on a face yellow and broken as some old winter-rotted pumpkin. The face was not Mary, but behind the face, in these hours, Mary was. This survival, this persistence in the midst of pain and wreckage of the individual, moved Asa more than any other fact he had yet encountered. Death played with Mary like some old broken-whiskered grimalkin playing with a mouse, and when there was any letup in that cat-and-mouse game, Mary looked up at Asa, undaunted. The humor Mary had taken over from Wendlin, a gift Wendlin gave her when her need was greater than his, rose, phoenix-like. Asa had a sensitive ear for words. When Mary used them for his pleasure, united opposites in that marriage which is humor's passion, he wished that he, too, might die. He could not endure the pain of seeing so much life be slowly buried alive.

There were no screams tonight, and Asa was glad, for his own sake as well as Mary's. The mingling of sounds, Mary's agony and the rally makers' heartiness, would be intolerable. He walked back toward the schoolhouse, where there was a speech in progress, a voice he did not recognize, the man's individuality lost in the conventional ups and downs of the soapbox haranguer. Asa listened, unable to make out words, the rising and falling voice as impersonal and universal as war. The sound lifted the hairs at the back of his neck. As he listened, a woman, followed by a man, ran out of the building. The woman, either because she did not care where she went or because she recognized Asa, made straight for him. Asa, when he saw who it was, held out his arms to catch or steady, whatever was needed. Rosa Ramos was in no condition, it seemed to him, to run—let alone fall.

"Is she sick?" Asa asked Pete when he arrived.

Pete laughed. "Sick? She is mad."

"You should be mad, too." She appealed to Asa. "If somebody said you would blow up the reservoir, what would you do?"

"He didn't say I would blow it up."

"He looked at you."

"Let him look. Looks don't do any harm."

"You know what he was thinking."

"Let him think. Let him spend his nights tramping around the reservoir. What do I care? I won't be there. I will think of him in my bed. Maybe I'll be in the army, killing Germans while he goes round the reservoir hunting me. Cudlip will be a big fool."

Rosa changed her tack. "You will not be in the army."

"Tell Mr. Wilson," Pete said.

"Mr. Wilson will not want you. You will be a father."

"Having a baby may slow you down some, Rosa. But not me. I am as good as ever. The baby has not made me big, fat, and bad-tempered."

Rosa slapped his arm, but she also laughed. "I am fat, but I am not bad-tempered or slowed down."

Pete said, "Talking the way you do, you'll make Asa glad to be a bachelor."

"No," Asa said. "She makes me sorry to be a bachelor."

Rosa had only started to glory in that admission when Wendlin joined them.

"Is Mary worse?" Asa asked. The question was dishonestly worded. By "worse" his question meant dead, but worse for Mary meant a continuation of life as she was.

"No," Wendlin said. "She's having one of her easy spells. She heard the singing. She knows what it means. She wanted me to come over and say a few words. She asked me to do it," he said earnestly. "I'm no speaker. I've got convictions, but Mary was accustomed to do the speaking for us. But I told her I'd come."

Asa, who had had enough of the rally, returned to it with Wendlin for Mary's sake.

"Don't expect any fireworks," Wendlin warned. "I'll do well to manage a couple of sentences."

After Asa and Wendlin left them, Rosa said to Pete, "When they talk about fighting Mexicans, I have had enough of their rally."

"The Mexicans are talking about fighting them," Pete reminded her.

"That is different," Rosa said, "and we do not ask them to come to our rally."

"They didn't ask us either."

"They ask you to fight, though, for them. You said so yourself. You fight for them and they fight you. What sense does that make?"

"It doesn't make sense," Pete admitted. "Let's go home."

They were at their buggy when Medora called to them. "Wait. Don't go. I want to talk to you."

Her first words, when she caught up with them, were apologetic. "I'm sorry to bother you all the time. I didn't want to. But when I saw you were leaving, I had to see you."

Rosa said, "You want us to try to get Julian back for you, don't you? Well, we can't, because we don't know where Julian is. And we don't want to know."

"No," Medora said. "That's not what I want."

"What do you want then?" Rosa asked. "You want something about Julian. Don't you?"

"I want to find out where he is, is all."

"You want us to go tell him you're going to have a baby, don't you?"

Medora was silent for a long time. Rosa finally said, "You are going to have one, aren't you? Don't lie. I can tell."

"I didn't think it showed yet," Medora said, at last.

"It doesn't show. But you can't fool me. How far along are you?"

"Five months," Medora said.

Rosa was scornful. "At three months everyone could tell that I was going to have a baby. What's the matter with your baby?"

"It was different with you," Medora said.

"I was married," Rosa agreed.

"You wanted people to know. I don't."

"How do you keep it from showing? Do you lace?"

"I lace and I don't eat."

"That's not very good for the baby, is it?"

"No."

"What you really want," Rosa insisted, "is for us to go get Julian, bring him back, and make him marry you, isn't it?"

"No. He won't marry me. He said he wouldn't."

"You asked him?" Rosa was more shocked by this than by the expected baby. "You asked him to marry you?"

"Yes."

"Before or after the baby was started?"

"Before. He doesn't know about the baby."

"Now you want us to tell him, don't you?" Rosa said again.

"No, I don't want you to tell him anything. All I wanted was news of him."

"What are you going to do?" Pete asked.

"Go away someplace and get a job. The war will make lots of jobs."

"Go away someplace," Rosa agreed. "That's the best thing you can do. You have caused enough trouble here. You and your father."

"Medora," Pete said, "I'm sorry this happened."

Rosa hurried to explain Pete's words. "We are sorry for you, but not one thing more. Your father thinks Pete will blow up his reservoir. Well, your father had better think more about his daughter and less about my husband."

Medora made no reply to this. "If you get any news of Julian, will you let me know? I'll give you my address when I leave so you can write to me. He said he might join the army, and if he did that, something might happen to him and I would never know it."

She walked away from them a few steps, then stopped. "You are the only friends I have." Her voice scarcely carried.

"I am not your friend," Rosa said in a strong voice, "and you are not my friend."

"Pete helped me once," Medora said, "when I was in trouble. He acted like a friend to me and Julian."

"You are in trouble again. But Pete is not going to help you or help Julian again. He has his own family to think about now."

Asa had been unable, much as he hated the rally, to let Wendlin make that effort for Mary, alone. But he couldn't bring himself to go inside the building again either. He stood in the doorway while Wendlin walked down front; a man the size and shape of one who has endured, his big shoulders heavy and still unstooped, his thick hair snowy in the lamplight.

Lute, who had been on his feet when Wendlin entered the room, looked a little uneasy when Wendlin asked for three or four minutes' time to speak. But he answered heartily enough. "Take all the time you want, Wendlin. This is a free country. Every man can have his say. That's what we're fighting this war for. Now I know you're going to tell us we oughtn't to fight at all. But, Wendlin, that's what we're fighting for—your right to tell us we oughtn't to fight."

The crowd laughed, then clapped. Lute looked surprised and pleased. Then he said, "Wendlin, the floor's all yours."

Wendlin had the floor, but he didn't know what to do with it. Asa supposed he had been exaggerating, some at least, when he had said, "I'm no speaker." It appeared to be the literal truth. Wendlin stood in front of the crowd mute, a one-man silent meeting, for the crowd was far from silent, fidgeting, whispering, wondering if the strain of his wife's long sickness might not have affected Wendlin's wits.

Then, through Wendlin's silence and above the whispering and restless movements of the crowd, they all heard a long, pain-racked shriek, the cry of a woman who did not want to cry out, who resisted, but

506

who was mastered by her agony. All the whispering and shuffling stopped. They all recognized that voice. Wendlin lifted his head and shut his eyes. Asa, watching, expected him to leave the room. Instead, Wendlin opened his eyes and began slowly to speak.

"I think everybody here knows," he said, "that my wife has been sick. She is dying. She has been dying for six months. I'm with her most of the time and would be tonight, except she asked me to come over here.

"I never had any idea it was possible for a person to suffer the way she has. She was a fine, strong woman, as most of you will remember. She enjoyed work and she enjoyed pleasure. She was glad to have it get light in the morning and sorry to see it get dark at night. There weren't enough hours in the day for her to get through her plans for herself and for others. It isn't easy to see a woman like that not yet old—" Wendlin smiled—"not yet old by the way I reckon old, anyway, laid low before her time, doomed and suffering. I tell you it is very hard to bear. If I was the cause of her suffering, if I was the one who had taken away the life and the work she enjoyed, and the one who caused her suffering, I don't think I could bear it.

"But that is what you are all going to have to bear in this war. Boys young enough to be Mary's sons, and a lot more anxious than she was, even, to be up early living their lives, are going to have to suffer the way she is suffering and finally lose their lives. You won't hear them scream or see them suffer. But they will scream and they will suffer. And you'll be the ones who caused the screaming and the suffering. You won't see the work they wanted to do and had to leave undone, but their families will, and the world will.

"I wouldn't want that on my conscience. I'd think twice, if I was you, before deciding that differences between countries can be settled only by putting some boy through what Mary's going through tonight. And maybe no good come of the fighting and suffering either. All to no purpose.

"But if you are set on it, you ought at least to remember that war is dying and suffering. You ought to keep that in mind. And not raise the kind of hullabaloo over it you been raising here tonight. In the face of what's to come, it don't sound hardly Christian."

Wendlin stopped speaking and gazed earnestly at his audience. They were as quiet now as he had been, and in the silence Asa hurriedly left the rally.

The rally was over, but Wendlin must have lingered to talk to some-one. Opal was in the bedroom with Mary. In the sitting room were Asa, Eunice, and Paula Jessup, who had been home from China a week.

They all, even Paula, felt like interlopers in that room that mirrored Mary so faithfully. She would want them to be there, still, it was like reading a diary in the absence of its owner. Even Paula, who had known those rockers and fern stands and table scarves since childhood, sat in their midst like a stranger.

She had no one to blame but herself for being there at all. Both Ben and her father had taken pains to let her know that there was nothing "she could do" at home. "Your mother does not want you to know that she is sick," her father wrote. "She wants you to keep on with your work and to remember her as she was before she lost her health."

When she had read Ben's phrase "There is nothing you can do for your mother," she had raged. That sounded like Ben, and perhaps like most men, convinced that unless something was "done," meetings were useless. She was not coming home to "do" anything for her mother. Her father could hire better nurses than she would ever be. She was coming home to "be," not to "do"; to kneel by her mother's bedside, to look into her eyes, to mirror her mother's smile, to be her mother's only daughter and eldest child. She was coming home to re-vive for her mother and herself those past moments when each, fully aware of the other, had doubled the amount of life each possessed.

So she had no one to blame but herself for being here—and she didn't blame herself. She had failed of her purpose in returning, but that was a fact she could never have learned if she had stayed in China. There, she would have longed to come home, and her longing would have made her useless in her work. It had been necessary to return, to sleep on the pillow shams embroidered by her mother, to eat the apricot jam put up by her mother, to walk through rooms, in the house she had never seen, that duplicated so exactly those in the old home in Emporia that she could have made her way safely blindfolded. It had been necessary for her to return and to do these things; to dis-cover, even in the midst of the familiar and unchanged, that she had changed, that she could only "do" for her mother, that she could no longer "be."

Her discovery had nothing to do with any alteration in her mother. Her mother had changed, of course. Physically, except for brow and nose, the mother she had known had disappeared. But that disappearance did not matter. From out of her faded and sunken, but clear, eyes, her mother in those moments when she was free of pain looked as much herself as she ever had. Her mother gazed and gazed; she endlessly searched her daughter's face hoping to find, behind the missionary who had returned, the girl who had left. The girl was not there. And in those moments the returned missionary could offer nothing but good works. "Mother, may I rub your back?" "Plump up your pillows?" "Give you a sip of water?"

Where had the girl her mother searched for gone? How could she have lost herself without knowing it? It had naturally taken a hardening of will to set out for China, to put the Pacific between herself and her family. A homesick girl, faltering, irresolute, she had implored God to strengthen her will, to keep her purpose firm. She had beseeched Him to give her the strength to put first things first. Morning and night, she had prayed that, having set her hand to the plow, she would have the courage to keep it there. And God had answered her prayer. It was true that while making her prayer she had supposed the Pacific to be as recrossable as the Mississippi, and home, when once again she set her face in that direction, immediately reclaimable.

Perhaps they once were. But not now, for Paula Jessup. The mother was dying; but the girl who had left her mother was already dead. The girl's death, if the missionary were to live, had possibly been necessary. That girl could never have ministered to the dead and dying, never have taken care of the newborn, never have given doubters firm answers. The missionary, a person able to deal with mysteries professionally, had taken the girl's place.

In spite of what Ben had written her, there was much that she could do for her mother. She had a steadfast tirelessness which others, more centered than she in the pathetic death of the flesh, could not match. Mrs. Tetford, for all of her good will and devotion, would soon need nursing herself.

Paula often saw in her mother's faded eyes knowledge of the change in her daughter. With that smile which was now more a reflection of the heart's feeling than any movement of the flesh, Mary accepted the ministrations of the missionary. And Paula was too honest to pretend it was not so. By making every old Chinese woman her mother, she had lost her own mother. She who is a daughter to all cannot be a daughter to one. She who chooses eternity cannot also have time. But her mother, who would have eternity soon enough, was not crossing any celestial bridges before she came to them. She still valued the

509

world she was in and talked to Wendlin and Ben about it. "What's the temperature this morning?" she would ask Wendlin, in her slow, broken voice. "How's Ellen?" she would whisper to Ben. But of her missionary daughter, she asked for no news of this world. The heart, Paula thought, once weaned from particulars, can never find or give satisfaction in them again.

Her conviction that this was a good as well as necessary change for the heart preparing itself for eternity was shared, Paula believed, by the two with whom she sat. It was that, she thought, which made her feel so easy with them, strangers of a week's acquaintance. She knew little about them and cared to know little. She no longer lived in what was transient and personal. Asa, she understood, was a truck gardener and naturalist. Eunice, she had gathered from a whispered word or two of her mother's, was a woman disappointed in love.

Mrs. Tetford, when her mother had screamed, though she knew well enough the sound was that of a woman drugged who did not know that she had screamed, came out of the sickroom crying.

Paula had spoken to her reassuringly. "God knows the preparation each of us needs for eternity, Mrs. Tetford."

Opal had looked at her uncomprehendingly, then without a word had returned to Mary's room and closed the door.

When the door closed, Asa had said, "Mary is my last hold on life."

"Your last hold on mortal life," Paula agreed.

After a declaration of war and the prospect of so many deaths, Asa was in no mood to belittle mortal life, not even his own, and certainly not Mary's.

"What other life is there?" Asa asked. "I'm mortal. Mary is mortal. I don't know about any other life."

Paula did not let herself be influenced by the anger and pain in Asa's voice. "I understand you're something of an amateur astronomer. What do the stars say to you when you gaze at night into God's firmament, Mr. Brice?"

"Nothing," Asa declared. "They say nothing to me except that they are distant and blazing and speechless. And not one fact that I can learn about them reconciles me for a minute to a harder fact, that we are alive beneath them and cannot communicate our loneliness. One world at a time, Miss Jessup, one world at a time. Until I can open my heart to one person here, what heart have I got to take into eternity with me? That stone in my chest? Add that stone to God's firmament of light? Your mother was more to me than any star. More than any sun. I learned more about God in five minutes with her than in twenty-five years of stargazing. One cry of hers outweighs a million light-years. I would put out every star to save her pain."

"You must reconcile yourself to God's plan, Mr. Brice," Paula said. Asa jumped to his feet. "I am not reconciled," he shouted. "I am not reconciled to pain. I am not reconciled to the leaden life we lead. I am not reconciled to loneliness. I am not reconciled to your mother's death."

"I'm afraid," Paula said quietly, without condemnation, "that you are thinking more of yourself than of my mother."

"I am. I am." Asa clenched his hands to his forehead. "Your mother takes life into the grave with her. What do I take when I go? Back to earth with me will go the little knowledge of earth I've been able to pick up. What a gift! Carrying coals to Newcastle. That is my life. You ask me about God's firmament, Miss Jessup, and the stars in it. That is eternity, if you like, and when I go into it, all I'm going to be able to say to the shining stars is, 'Stars, I have noticed that you shine.' That is my life. And it's not enough. It is no answer to pain and death. To balance them, there must be something else."

"There is something else," Paula said. "There is God."

"You may be right, but God's existence doesn't excuse me for not living."

Asa took his hands from his forehead, started toward Mary's room, stopped himself, turned, and ran out of the room as if in search for whatever it was he could not name but knew he must find to counter-balance pain and death.

After he left, the room was very still. Paula turned to Eunice. "He seems beside himself."

Eunice left the house without a word to Paula. She found Asa standing a few feet from the house, and went to him at once. She put her hand on his arm. He was trembling and wet with sweat. He was shuddering like an animal who has been frightened. Eunice put both arms around him and said his name, "Asa." Though his shuddering did not cease, it became less convulsive. She took her arms away from him. Without either speaking a word, and without either—as far as Eunice could tell—choosing a direction, without touching, they walked together away from Mary dying, and from the schoolhouse, where a few settlers still remained, celebrating the declaration of war.

3    A T T W O, Ben was on his way. It was customary after a morning session at Rose Park for staff and candidates to have lunch together, and this Ben had endured more like a Christian martyr, he was afraid, than a Christian. He had pleaded the unreliability of his car as an excuse to make an early start home, and no one looking at his car had doubted that an early start was needed. Now his car, like some child disparaged and hurt, was out to prove him a liar. It floated like a leaf; it flew across ruts and ridges. Perhaps his father was right; the trouble he had with his car was not so much the car's fault as his own. Certainly now, with his mind not on it, the poor little car, though it moved with a loose-jointed hump and clatter, was covering the ground. Every time he gave the countryside a look, they were someplace else.

He was not like his father; the world did not touch his senses acutely. He knew hot from cold, and rain from drought, and wind from calm. But he only knew them, he did not feel them. He was not like his mother either, who, though as blind to wind and weather as he, had lived her life believing that each moment put something to trial. And even now, when most men would be, he supposed, furiously angry, furiously disappointed, he was calmly angry and calmly disappointed. If he could have chosen his nature, he would have chosen another kind, been a daredevil, a wild man of God, an extremist. Even a ranter like Raunce. Such was not his nature; he knew it, and every time he tried to disguise it with some false flourish of act or word, the attempted deception made him uneasy. He would have to move through his life, himself; reconcile himself to his own lack of fire. And yet, though he knew this and knew, too, that as a result he would never set the world on fire, he thought there was, years away, an old Ben Jessup he would not hate, waiting for him.

When he went through Whittier, he remembered that it was May Day. Little kids already home from school were out delivering May baskets, homemade baskets of paper pasted together and stuffed with the big, bright flowers little kids pick. In La Habra, two boys were driving a billy goat hitched to an express wagon, and the billy goat, in honor of the day, wore a necklace of black-eyed daisies. Out past Randolph, where the heavy petroleum scent of the oil fields began, he thought of Raunce. If his mother were not sick, if his father were not wholly taken up by her sickness, he would naturally go home. None of this being true, it was Raunce he thought of and Raunce he wanted to see.

LeRoy, working swing shift, left for Olinda around fifteen or twenty minutes of four. If he could catch LeRoy before he left for work, Le-Roy would take the time to talk to him. When Ben turned off the boulevard onto the townsite's main street, he was relieved to see Le-Roy's car down at the end of the street. LeRoy himself, when Ben pulled up in front of his house, was on the front porch crowded into a frayed wicker rocker like a big, overgrown nestling in a ramshackle nest. On the steps below him, Crystal, in such a pretty dress that Ben had to give her a second look, was talking to her father.

"Howdy, Parson," LeRoy addressed Ben, smiling. But he spoke with a question in his voice, and Ben shook his head and said, "No, LeRoy."

"Well, then, we are the very two who ought to meet," LeRoy said. "We are the two halves needed to make a whole."

What he meant was that he, LeRoy, was a recorded minister without a pulpit; and that he, Ben, was a man with a pulpit offered him for which he could not qualify. Ben looked up at LeRoy. The late sun was shining on his red, knobbed cheekbones; his blue eyes under his red, frizzled eyebrows were kind; but Ben, for all that he recognized the kindness and believed that LeRoy, cast out by the church, had set an example of Christian love for the Tract, knew that LeRoy shared the beliefs of the men who had just put an end to his own aspirations. LeRoy was a dyed-in-the-wool Rose Park product, believing in the second birth, and that this made men incapable of sin. LeRoy thought himself to have been thus born again, and thus incapable of sin. There was no use rehashing these matters with him.

"There's other churches," LeRoy reminded him. "You're not finished as a preacher because of what happened this morning. The Baptists and Presbyterians are great believers in sin."

"They are also great believers in matters I don't hold with," Ben said.

"Maybe you'll have to start your own church," LeRoy said. "The way George Fox did."

"George Fox started one that suits me to a T," said Ben.

"George believed he couldn't sin."

"Maybe he couldn't," Ben said. "And I don't say you can either. But nobody can tell me I can't."

"Nobody is telling you," LeRoy said. "All they're saying is, In the true shepherd, the old Adam must be dead."

Ben said nothing. LeRoy's rocker creaked a little. The wind touched the blue four-o'clocks trained up cord strings at one end of the porch like notes on a zither. Crystal leaned back on the porch railing, the low sun putting color into her pale cheeks.

"Well, no use our going over it again, I reckon, Ben. But I'm sore-hearted for you. It's a real sorrow to be forbidden to preach the gospel."

"LeRoy," Ben asked, "don't you ever feel like fighting the church here for throwing you out of the pulpit? Particularly since except for you they might not've had a pulpit to throw you out of?"

"Fight?" LeRoy asked. "How would I fight the church?"

"D'you think what they did was right?"

"They've got the right to decide who they want to preach. I know that. Maybe they were wrong, but they got the right to be wrong."

"Well," Ben said, "it's too bad it's not the other way around. Since I'm the one who believes in sinning, I'm the one who ought've been caught in the Sunday-school room. It would fit our beliefs better. As it is, we're both out. You don't act right and I don't believe right."

LeRoy rocked away without speaking, but Crystal flashed to her feet. "Papa acted all right," she said. "I lied about him when I said it wasn't Mama. I didn't know what I was talking about, and I don't have much respect for all you people who couldn't see it. I knew it was Mama all the time. Papa had been preaching about God's goodness and glory, and he was filled with love and on the way out he stopped to tell my mother he loved her. What's wrong with that? She wanted him to. It's only the people jealous of love and who don't have any who want to punish those who do."

Ben didn't feel able to summon up any reply to this. Besides, he wasn't given a chance. LeRoy stopped rocking, looked at his daughter, then rose to his feet. "Praise God," he said. "Crystal, you don't know how that lie of yours has hurt me."

Crystal ran up the steps to where her father stood. It was the kind of reconciliation that asks an onlooker to be gone. Ben saw this, turned his back on them, and walked down the pebble-marked path to his car.

514

Ellen was irrigating the potatoes. Outdoors she was the man of the family, indoors the woman of the family. With Chad married and living in Placentia, with Shel doing road work like any hired hand, with her mother so near her time, there was no one else for it. Ellen was glad. Nothing made her happier than to get up early, cook the breakfast, set the bread to rise, and put the house to rights. She supposed such feelings of pleasure about work were nothing really to be proud of. Press and Medora, she felt sure, had no such tingling delight in looking back through the kitchen door into a room as shining as soap and water could make it, and in seeing there a pan of bread curving upward under a covering of white cloth. She was commonplace, she supposed, unstirred by the passions of poets and lovers.

Her daydream love for Tom Mount was her only reassurance. A girl who could feel what she felt for Tom, who could keep that feeling alive for so long without help, was no mere drudge. Other girls needed words and kisses. Her feelings were strong enough to thrive on an occasional sight of that big, dark man's slow smile and swinging, body-conscious walk. She thought about him as she stood on the slope below the house, watching the smooth flow of the water in the irrigation ditches. Shel had furrowed out for her before he went to work, but all of the connecting up and caring for the water had been left to her.

Now, at the close of the afternoon, she had a breathing spell. There were no break-throughs anywhere that needed repairing. She leaned on her hoe and thought that the acres of potatoes, patterned with ribbons of water and decorated with the green bouquets of potato plants, looked like a pretty wallpaper. Prettier, because the ribbons on a wallpaper do not sparkle red and silver, and wallpaper bouquets do not have white blossoms quivering like white butterflies above the green.

Daybreak was a fine time, but fierce as well as beautiful, with all the determination and anxiety about the work to come. Evening was radiant with its own light and with the contentment of work accomplished. The sounds and sights of evening were suited to its quiet joy. Doves, gray and soft-feathered, cried in their peaceful, haunting way off by the Anaheim lake; up on the slopes of the foothills, where the sunlight was still warm, meadow larks bade the day farewell. Their song, so much more cheerful than the cu-cu-rooing of the mournful doves, came nearer to breaking Ellen's heart. Why, she wondered? Why should a song so clear and happy make her uneasy? Because, she thought, the doves are prepared for sorrow. Death and hard times will

515

not surprise them. But the larks have never heard of such things. They sing at sundown as if the dark would not stop their singing. They are like drowning men who do not know that they cannot live beneath the water and sink into darkness with happy smiles.

Spring's green had already vanished from the hills. They were clear brown like moles, gray brown like elephants, yellow brown like lions, purple brown like a black horse shagged over with his winter hair. Only at the bottoms of the canyons were there threads of green to show where the winter water had been. Now, at sundown, the brown hills were drowning in blue; though there was not enough of it yet to reach the hilltops. There at the top was the land the larks still sang of, sunny as daybreak. The sun itself was red as autumn. If the larks at nightfall had never heard of night, the May sun had never heard of spring. The derricks of the oil wells latticed it over with their laddering crosspieces like fire screens in front of a fire.

The evening was rich and sad, beautiful and disturbing, peaceful and forlorn. The day dying, that was one thing. The work done, the house behind her waiting clear as a pool, dark already spreading in it. Supper on the banked fire, keeping warm. That was *her* world, but evening was so various, so multicolored, because it brought to her mind other worlds upon which her setting sun was rising, or shining in its full midday splendor, or gone altogether. Across the potato plants, she saw foreign ports and morning light on green water, and the masts of ships rocked by the water. She saw, over great stretches of snow and forest, the full noon of a blazing midday. She saw the afternoon pause where the sun shone down in its leisure, its journey three-fourths done. She saw on the far everlasting places of the earth, prairie and steppe, tundra and pampas, this lingering light. She saw the deep of night and the sun long set in many cities; she knew the pitch black of desolate streets and empty parks.

She thought about the mystery of knowledge and the power of the imagination. She, barefooted, one of her father's old neckties looped around her waist for a belt and her dress tucked up under it so that it wouldn't get wet and muddy, held the world in her mind. The water, moving downhill in one of Shel's furrows, across a handful of gravel, whispered in her ear. Behind her, the day and its work; around her, the rich world's curiosities; ahead, the days to come, with their strangeness and trouble.

She had no feeling of easy sorrow, of dove-sweet mournfulness or of bread always rising under a pure-white towel. The birds sang, the wa-

516

ter lipped its singing flutter over gravel, the sun turned brown to rose and blue to purple. These were facts, and, with the work done, she indulged herself with them. They were real, but not the real world. The real world opposed you. The water had resisted being put into ditches, and once in, tried to break out. It preferred wasting itself in gopher holes to watering potatoes. The beautiful brown hills, sinking deeper in folds of blue, were barren. No crops grew there. When the eyes had harvested them, their usefulness was ended. She knew all this, because if it were not so, how would she ever have learned that she had the power to put the reluctant water into the furrow that needed it, or to set the dough where the warmth would double its size? There was a spotted potato bug on the potato plant at her feet whose only sin was to want what the Lewises wanted. This one she would let escape. But she had the power and the will to kill what was beautiful if it asked too much. Knowing that she could do these things, she leaned more arrogantly on her hoe.

She was accepting the beauty and not refusing the pain, each in its way enhancing the other, when she saw Ben Jessup's car turn into the lane leading to the house. She untied the necktie that held her skirts up, put her hoe across her shoulder, and walked down to meet him. When he saw her coming, he stopped his car and started on foot to meet her. It was as if, she thought, he had said, While you walk, I won't ride. She couldn't help liking that. She knew that Ben had told her father he wanted to marry her, but information received in this roundabout way, while interesting, was interesting in the same way as Dickens's report of David Copperfield's feeling for Dora. She was curious about the outcome of this story, but not impatient. Would Ben marry Ellen? She was waiting for time to write the story's next installment.

Her sundown mood of looking was still upon her, and she watched Ben climb the slope with the same eyes that had looked at potato bugs and oil rigs and brown hills: as if he were something to see. To her surprise, he was. Nice-shaped heads were important to her, and Ben had one. His brown hair sprang up lively from a side part, and this was a time when pompadours were fashionable. His eyes were either hazel or brown, not sparkling like her father's, but very steady and intent. His face was rather narrow, with a straight nose. When Ben laughed, there was at the height of the merriment a look at the corners of his mouth like crying.

When he reached her, he took her hands. "Ellen," he said, "they've turned me down. They don't think I'm fit to be a preacher. I'll tend a pump for the rest of my life. You don't have to marry me."

"Marry you," Ellen repeated. "You've never asked me. How could I marry anyone who didn't ask me?"

Ben stared at her. "Why, I don't know," he said distractedly. Then he took her in his arms. He moved his hands across her shoulders and down her shoulder blades, and he spanned her waist and felt out the flare of her hips below her waist and brought his hands back to her cheeks and her hair.

"I have asked you," he said, finally. "You know that. I spoke to your father in so many words, but I've been here since then, dozens of times, imploring you. You know that, Ellen. Don't you?"

"No," she said. "You never said the words."

"What words? Said what words?"

"Marry me. You never said that to me."

"Marry me," Ben said. "Marry me, marry me, marry me. I'll say it a week. You don't have to say yes. But don't you ever tell me again, Ellen Lewis, that I didn't ask you. You've been asked. You've been begged and beseeched. I love you."

"How did you ever think you could be a preacher if you couldn't speak up, even to the girl you loved?"

"I don't know."

"I don't know how you could talk to people about loving God if you couldn't talk to one girl about loving her."

"Maybe I couldn't."

"Why do you want to marry me?"

"Because I love you. Because you're so beautiful and sweet. Because I never saw anyone so loving and honest. Because you're Ellen. I want to marry you most of all because you're Ellen. I want to spend my life looking at you and kissing you and taking care of you." He picked up her hoe, which she had leaned against a tree, and gave it a far toss. "You'll never hoe again."

Ellen knew this was untrue, but she saw that he believed it and would himself hoe twelve hours a day to make it true. He held her to him again and gave her his first kiss, but followed it so soon with his second and third that she lost count. His kisses were soft and firm. There was enough space between them to give her time to think, Oh, has he stopped? But he never had. His hands at the small of her back seemed to touch her lips when he kissed her, and where his hands were, she could feel his kisses.

518

She pulled away from him. "Is something wrong?" he asked.

"I wanted to see you, is all." There was still enough light for that. She saw that his mouth was changed with the kissing and there was a look in his eyes that she could not name but that made her feel tender and compassionate.

"How do I look, Ellen?" he whispered.

"You look like my husband," she whispered.

He did not kiss her then, but pressed his face to her face and to her breasts.

"I feel like your husband," he said.

Ellen had spoken in surprise and wonder. How could Ben Jessup look like her husband when she had been in love with Tom Mount? Had been. What had her love for Tom Mount been, if the minute Ben Jessup touched her, he looked like her husband? Her dream love for Tom Mount had been, she thought, a place in which she had lived, waiting for the touch that would awaken her. Who knows what dreams the sleeping beauty dreamed while waiting for that first kiss? Perhaps they were not of the prince who kissed her at all, but of another, darker man. But dreaming of him, she had prepared herself for love; dreaming, she had been content to wait. What would have happened if she had been kissed by the man she dreamed of? What if flesh and dreams could meet? Ellen did not ask herself this question. Tenderly, lovingly, she put her arms about Ben's neck. She possessed in full measure woman's great gift of reality. She lived where she was, and loved the man she kissed.

4    THE LOS ANGELES *Herald,* an evening paper, was ordinarily delivered at the Perkins' residence around five o'clock. A boy on a wheel would take it out of his canvas bag and skim it onto the walk, or sometimes, when he was especially energetic, smack it against the front door. Louella usually heard it arrive and reckoned the day's official ending with the sound of the paper sliding along the cement walk or thumping against the door. But the paper always lay where the boy threw it until Perk came home.

On May the fourteenth, for the first time in her life, Louella was anxious for the paper to arrive. She had come downstairs a little after four and was waiting in the front hall on the ladder-back chair that faced the mahogany drop-leaf table and the Duncan Phyfe mirror hanging above it. She had watched the room itself when she first came downstairs. The front door, heavy and of oak, had three rectangular pieces of glass set in its upper half, and through these she could see the glossy leaves of the clematis vine that dangled across it from the gable of the house. The shadows of these leaves, moving in the late afternoon air, shifted across the buff plaster of the wall at her right and reminded her of the alternating sparkle of dark and light as a creamy surf breaks toward evening on dark, wet sand. In the midst of the ebb and flow of this dark and light, she found herself looking into her own eyes. She had been doing so for several minutes before it came to her that she was scrutinizing herself. No, not herself, not the outward Louella, but the Louella who lived behind the disguises of marcelled hair, rouged cheeks, and corseted body. This outer shell, this Louella rigged in foulard and crocheted collars and cross-strap pumps, wavered, it seemed to her, as inside the shell her true self swelled and throbbed with the anticipation of release. If she watched closely enough, the transformation might take place before her eyes. And she had better watch closely, otherwise her true self might be a person she would not recognize. What would she look like? Louella knew only one thing for sure about the appearance of the real, the true Louella. She would look like a woman who had never known Perk. She would be the girl Perk had never met or married, though grown older, of course. This girl who had never married Perk was no stranger to Louella, for in spite of outward compliance, she had always been true to her. But her visible shape and demeanor, freed from disguise, what would that be? Louella's face reflected in the mirror showed no smile, yet inside someone smiled, contemplating the day's news which would permit her to make her declaration and to live in her freedom.

Though she waited for the paper, she knew what that news would be. It was news she might have had earlier by calling Perk. It was news she might have had firsthand by being present in the court. But after twenty years of waiting, she had the power to say no to short cuts. She did not want to hurry the climax. It had been a lifetime gamble, and now, as she was about to win, she would have the satisfaction of seeing the hands spread out, not rob the resplendent, anticipated moment of its power by any preliminary peeks or tip-offs from cronies. She had played with an ordinary, unmarked deck, learning the game as she went along, and banking everything on her knowledge of her opponent.

The paper arrived a half-hour early, and was delivered with an unusually sharp smack against the front door. This early arrival on the only afternoon she had ever waited for it caused Louella's heart, in spite of the fact that she was sure of the news it contained, to lurch with solemn and sickening anticipation. "Sylvester Perkins Convicted of Fraud." She *saw* those words, and with them saw her life come at last into balance. "He is a fraud." She had said those words over and over again to herself, in public, as Perk was applauded, or complimented, or kowtowed to. She had said in the privacy of her bedroom, "He is a fraud." She had said them on the day when Perk talked Lloyd into enlisting—"Your father is a fraud." But she was not a cocksure person. This had been her opinion; but she was only one woman. She put her life at the center of this teeter-totter about the nature of Perk, and on the day that the weight of outside opinion balanced her own, she would be free. She had never dreamed that this evidence would not arrive piecemeal, or that when it arrived it would be summed up in her own word, "Fraud."

Though she had come downstairs, in her eagerness to read that word, she now delayed going outside to pick up the paper that would contain it. The idea suggested itself to her of not looking at the paper at all, of leaving it where it was until Perk came home. Let him see it lying there against the door. She knew exactly what his interpretation of this would be. He would never doubt for a moment that it had been left there because she could not bear to have the news, whatever it was, except from his lips. The last act of her life with Perk had as well be like all the others, filled with irony and knowledge of power. She saw herself listening as Perk told, once again, a story with which she was not only familiar, but whose meaning for her was a meaning he could not even guess.

While she had been thinking of this, envisaging Perk's arrival, she had forgotten the reflected self who sat opposite her. She looked up from her vision of the fraudulent Perk and his naïve reporting, and there was a new Louella, or at least a Louella she had not seen before, sitting watchful, listening, but on the outside of what was happening, unmoved by it. Was this the Louella beneath the crocheting and under the foulard, whose prison she would soon be unlocking? This marble woman? She could not say, for as she looked, the accustomed image returned.

521

She would not ordinarily have been in her and Perk's room when Perk came home from work. But she went there now because she wanted an interval between his arrival in the driveway and the moment when she faced him and heard from his own lips the confirmation of all her own long-held and unspoken convictions. She wanted to hear him climb the stairs. She had waited a long time for this moment and she would not at the very end hasten or skimp it.

She sat in an armchair, prettily upholstered in flowered cretonne, by the front windows. The windows were too high to see from when she was seated, and she leaned back content to wait and perfectly relaxed. But deep inside the exterior calm a knot of exquisite tension awaited the release that only Perk's appearance could provide.

Either he came sooner than usual or time had been passing more quickly than she had realized. It seemed to her that she had no more than seated herself before she heard Perk's car slow down in front of the house, then turn into the driveway. She heard his footsteps along the walk at the side of the house, she heard the pause as he stooped to pick up the paper, the steps on the front porch, the opening and closing of the front door. Then there was a pause as he listened, she knew, for some sound of *her* in the house.

When he heard nothing, he called, "Louella, where are you?"

"I'm upstairs," she called back. "In our room."

He came up the stairs at his usual gait, neither slow nor hurried, and there was nothing to be learned from that. But what was there, anyway, that she didn't know? He entered the room, the paper folded in his hand.

"You're not usually up here at this hour of the day," he said.

"No," she agreed. "Not usually."

There was not a sign on his face that gave away the news. He had been, since the onset of his troubles, since Shel Lewis's refusal to work for him and since the filing of the suit against him by the Tract, steadfastly serious and absorbed. Not downcast, not complaining; hopeful, even, energetic, but knowing that for the first time in his life, his luck had turned against him. His face now showed no more than this.

The paper was folded with one corner tucked in to hold it shut. Perk unfolded it slowly, straightened it carefully, and handed it to her. He handed it to her so that the headline was quite clear before she touched the paper.

SYLVESTER PERKINS CONVICTED OF FRAUD.

"Fraud," she repeated, without any intention of doing so. "Fraud. You are convicted of fraud."

She put the paper on the floor without reading any further. Perk seated himself in the chair that faced hers.

"You know what that means?" he said.

She did. He had told her. It meant bankruptcy. It meant that Sylvester Perkins was not only publicly declared dishonest, but impoverished, ruined, wiped out. All he owned would have to be sold to repay ranchers and bondholders.

"Yes," she said, speaking with a double meaning, "I know exactly what it means."

Perk looked across her to the picture of Lloyd on her dressing table. "He will die, too," he said.

Louella had never doubted this, but she was surprised that Perk knew it, also. Perk had sent Lloyd to his death, but this was one of the many things she knew about Perk that she had kept to herself.

"Yes," Louella said. "I expect he will. He was never cut out for soldiering."

"I am responsible," Perk said.

Louella said nothing. Whatever else she asked for, she did not ask for her son's death as further proof of Perk's fraudulence. There was enough proof without that. Twelve unprejudiced men had said that very afternoon, "Louella, you were right, all along." Perk sat, as he always did, legs uncrossed, knees wide apart. His own hair imitated a toupee better than any toupee ever imitated hair. His full jowls made his small eyes and small mouth smaller. He wore black lisle socks. He was fresh-colored and had neatly cut and cleaned nails.

"What are you going to do, Louella?" Perk asked.

This was the moment she had waited for, but she had not expected Perk to anticipate it.

"What had you expected?" she asked.

"Nothing," Perk said. "I haven't let myself expect anything."

She had said to herself, when she had played with this moment in her imagination: I am going to leave. Everything I have believed about you has been proved true. You are, as I knew all along, a fraud. Now that this is no longer simply an opinion of mine, I shall go. I am free.

She faced Perk saying nothing. She was silent because if she said those words now, she would not, as always before, be able to remain. She had been forced all of a sudden into a present that *was* the future she had imagined, the future that had proved (as this minute had proved) Perk fraudulent. The leave-taking had necessarily been an imaginary act. What her imagination had pictured was leave-taking, repudiation, truthtelling. What her body had practiced had been staying, vindicating, lying. Wrapped in, solaced by the unpracticed, imaginary act, she had carefully, cell by cell, habit by habit, built a stayer. She moved in painful, awkward agony on the bright-colored chintz chair, in the clear afternoon light, as this fact came to her.

"Always with me in my troubles," Perk said.

She heard his voice with surprise and understood his words slowly. Where would she go? Why go? Where else would she find this ironic, godlike power? "You know not what you say" practiced at the level of real estate and double beds.

He said again, "I didn't expect anything, Louella, but I knew that when I found my Louella waiting, so sweet in her silks and satins, nothing else would matter."

"Stop soft-soaping me that way, you old fraud," Louella said in a broken voice.

Perk looked at her, ready to laugh or cry.

"Perk, you poor old fraud," Louella murmured again, and Perk threw back his head and laughed Perk's famous laugh. But there were tears in his eyes, too.

"Oh, God," he said, "not many men are blessed with a wife like my Louella."

He came to her, and since the idea of going on his knees was in his mind as he came, it almost seemed to Louella that he came on his knees. He put his head in her lap, and misfortune had made it no softer or cooler or lighter. But because of the misfortune, and perhaps to hide his tears, he burrowed against her thighs so that her knees parted a little. She put her hand on his hair, she with her thoughts about it, and Perk said, "My precious pet."

She could not unlock her prison door because she was in no prison; there was no door, no bar, no bolt, no key, and hence no escape. There was no true Louella incarcerated. She was the true Louella. There had been no gamble and no game, only the double-dealer's foregone outcome.

"You poor old fraud. You poor old fraud."

Her words were for herself. Perk was a fraud only by bad luck and good intentions. His acts were fraudulent; she was fraud itself. Her tears dropped onto Perk's cheek.

524

"Don't cry, my pet," he said. "I don't deserve it."

She couldn't stop. Nor could she say, "I'm crying for myself, Perk. I'm the fraud." Her tears continued to fall, true but false, even her body's secretions serving her in double-dealing.

5    W E   D O N ' T need you for a while," Dr. Heilman told Pete. "You go take a walk."

The idea startled Pete. He had never "taken" a walk in his life. He sometimes, if necessary, walked, but he would no more think of taking a walk for the sake of walking than he would think of chewing for the pleasure of working his jaws up and down when he did not have anything to eat.

"I don't want to go anyplace, Doc," Pete said.

Dr. Heilman, who had been roused from sleep at four, who had arrived from Anaheim at four-thirty, and who had delivered Pete's wife of a twelve-pound boy at six, felt no call to handle Pete with kid gloves. Pete was a damn lucky fellow. His wife had babies like a cat has kittens, and his son was a fine, healthy buster.

"I don't care what you do or where you go. But get out of the house for thirty minutes. You're in the way."

"I haven't seen Rosa."

"She don't want to see you."

Pete was alarmed. "Is there something wrong you haven't told me, Doc?"

"Yes. You're a big nuisance. I've got half the town in here now."

"Throw them out," Pete said. "They're nothing but aunts and uncles. I'm the husband."

"I'm throwing you all out," Doc Heilman said. "You're the first, is all."

Doc slammed the door, and Pete went out into his yard, which was where he wanted to be anyway. At least he wanted to be alone for a while, to say to himself, "I am a father. Rosa is a mother. We have a son." Otherwise, he would go in unchanged to see Rosa. Having the baby had made Rosa a mother. Nothing yet had made him a father, certainly not the sight of that solemn, red creature with its great shock of black hair. "Here's Pete, Junior, your son and heir," Doc had said, and held up something that looked like a slippery fish in a wig. While Rosa rested, he would try to think himself into fatherhood and be able to go back to her, if not a full-grown papa, at least acting so much like one she would never know the difference.

Everything about the birth (except the looks of what had been born) pleased him. He had said that he didn't care whether the baby was a boy or a girl. And he still believed that he didn't care in the way Rosa did. If Rosa had had a girl, she would have felt that she had not done her work properly, had presented him with something incomplete, a shirt without a tail. But a girl would have been all right with him. First a girl, then a boy. There was nothing wrong with a family that started like that, for he had no idea, now that they had the hang of it, that they would stop with one. And even if they hadn't got the hang of it, that crazy bed of the Lewises' would turn the trick again, according to Rosa. Thinking of the bed, he thought of Joicey Lewis. She was in that bed now, he supposed. She wasn't having Rosa's easy time. Doc Heilman had spent most of yesterday with her, but Joicey's pains had let up with nothing to show for them. The Doc was heading for the Lewises' again as soon as he finished with Rosa. "It was real thoughtful of you two women to have your birthday parties at the same time," he had told Rosa. Pete had smiled, hearing that, and exchanged looks with Rosa. He didn't suppose thought ever had so little to do with a happening.

A girl would have been all right with him; still, he knew that as soon as the Doc let him see Rosa again that he would head down the hill with the news, "It's a boy!" If they'd had a girl, he wouldn't have told the news that way. He would have said, "It's here," or "I'm a papa," and let the girl news come out later, a fact, but unimportant.

Why? What made the difference? He didn't know. Because the boy, born a Ramos, would stay a Ramos? Because a daughter would end up being a Yorba or a Padilla or a Sepulveda and produce Yorbas, Padillas, Sepulvedas instead of Ramoses? Did his son bring him closer to his own father? Did his son in a way resurrect that good old man from his grave? Did his son tie him to all who had gone before? For the first time, Pete felt the continuity of life, felt himself to be the living element in a family line that stretched back to vanished beginnings and forward to hidden continuations. He himself was no longer the end, the jumping-off place.

He was pleased that the boy had been born at six in the morning. That was a good hour—to start a day or a life. Afternoon was a lazy

526

time, all right for a girl maybe, but he didn't know that he would have much respect for a boy who put in his appearance at that hour. Night also had its place; but a night baby might be headed for dark deeds and trouble. Six o'clock: six o'clock on a summery May morning! It was the hour and the month and the weather he would have chosen for his own beginning, and, in a way, it seemed that his son in arriving at that hour had paid a compliment to his father's judgment.

He was pleased with the weather. It was weather he especially liked, already warm and with none of those startling alternations of ballooning white clouds and hard blue sky. But not a settled day either. A come-and-go day, a summery day with a sky full of little fall-colored clouds, floating like flecks of butter in a churn full of cream. Some of the clouds were brassy. Others were touched with pink. In places they looked smudged with smoke. There were enough of them to cut down on the sun's light, but the heat came through as if they weren't there. Later, there would be sundogs burning against the clouds. He had always loved such days, sweet to touch and smell as well as see. There was a threat in such days, or at least a mystery. They were filled with contradictions. Cloudy but warm. Summery but fall-colored, the sun hidden but felt. Shadows grainy and broken. Sudden breezes. Breezes that tossed one bush and left the others around it unmoved. Birds high in the air, hardly to be seen, but practicing ventriloquism, so that their songs rang in your ear. Birds of the fields coming in to roost in the dooryard. Two crows in the fig tree and a butcher bird on the clothesline. It was the kind of a day that made a man narrow his eyes and listen and wait.

Pete walked over to the hydrant in the clump of oleanders. It was the kind of day that made him sweat without stirring; he took off his shirt, picked up the soap from the sardine can on the ground, and had a complete and lathery wash. He was walking about the yard, shirt still off, drying, when Dr. Heilman called him.

"You can see your wife and kid now, Pete."

Pete pulled his shirt back on. He had the feeling that this was a solemn occasion and that he ought to be dressed properly for it. Dr. Heilman shooed out of the bedroom the women he had not been able to shoo out of the house, so that Pete could be alone with his wife and son.

Outside, Pete had been able to produce some suitable thoughts about fatherhood, but inside with Rosa and the baby, he lost them. Rosa looked well. No one would ever have guessed that she had not just wakened after a full night's rest. She showed none of the tiredness of childbirth—and none of its satisfactions either. Pete had expected a madonna on the pillows, somebody with a holy, worn-out smile and a faint light shining just above her black braids. Her eyes would be fixed with wonder on her pink cherub. Rosa wasn't smiling, her baby was neither pink nor a cherub, and it was Pete whom Rosa was looking at. Pete found any baby in bed with Rosa strange—particularly this one. If this baby was a link between Pete and his father, handsome old Domingo Ramos, there was nothing in the baby's appearance to show it. Except maybe that wild bush of black hair. Pete had never seen a baby with hair like that. The baby's head took up as much room on its pillow as Rosa's. And for all of its twelve pounds, the baby wasn't fat, not a dimple to be seen, and a hand less babyish than Rosa's. A big, bony, solemn, red face. He would as soon think of chucking Father O'Flaherty under the chin.

He went around to Rosa's side of the bed, dropped to his knees where he couldn't see the baby, took Rosa's hand, and held it to his cheek.

"How do you feel, honey?" he asked.

"I feel all right," Rosa said. "It is nothing to have a baby. Not for me, anyway."

"That's good," Pete said. "We'll have a lot of them."

"Have you seen him?" Rosa asked.

Pete nodded.

"How does he look to you?"

"He looks fine. A big, healthy baby."

"Do you like him?"

"Of course I like him. He's our son."

"Pete?" Rosa said.

"Yes, honey."

"I don't feel like a mother. That baby's a stranger to me. I was more used to him inside. I don't feel like he belongs to me. Do you think it was because he came out so fast? That I didn't have time to get used to him? He could be anybody's baby."

Pete put one arm under Rosa's pillow and lifted her up and cradled her. "You're tired, honey," he said.

She stayed in his arms but she shook her head. "I don't even like him as much as other people's babies, Pete."

"You will," Pete said.

528

"He's so ugly."

"Don't say that," Pete said. "He looks like my father."

"Your father was a handsome man."

"Like me," Pete said.

Rosa smiled a little. Then she was sober again. "I don't think I'm going to like him. I think that's the reason God wouldn't let me have a baby. He knew I wouldn't like my own baby. I worked against God's will, having him."

"You'll have to nurse it," Pete told her. "That's what the doctor told me. It's just anyone's baby till you do that. When you nurse him, he'll be your baby, and you'll love him. That's the way it is, according to Doc."

Rosa was quiet for a while thinking about this. Then she said, "How are *you* ever going to get to love him?"

"A father," Pete said, "loves his son from the beginning."

Rosa looked at him with wonder and respect. "Is that the way you feel right now?"

"That's the way I feel right now," Pete said.

"What did you think when you first saw him?" Rosa persisted. "Did you think he was cute?"

"I thought," Pete said, "that's the cutest baby I ever saw."

"Did you really, Pete?"

"I really did. I thought, That's the damnedest cutest little baby I ever laid eyes on."

"Don't swear," Rosa said, and Pete knew she was already feeling better about the baby.

"Well, you asked me, and that's what I thought."

"Your father wasn't cute," she said suspiciously. "You said he looked like your father."

"He was cute when he was a baby."

"And when I nurse it, I'll love it?"

"That's what Doc says."

"It's funny, isn't it, that the father loves the baby sooner than its own mother?"

"Maybe the mother loves it longer."

The baby, on the other side of Rosa, made a sound. Pete reached across Rosa and lifted the big, shaggy-haired fellow up so that they could both see him. The baby at that minute opened his black eyes and gazed, or seemed to his parents to gaze, straight at them; even straight into them, as if he'd been listening. Pete thought, I'm damned glad I said what I did. I'm glad I praised him. As the baby gazed, there was a flicker across his face, not a smile exactly, but more a look of humorous recognition and acceptance. As if he knew they were his parents, knew what their doubts had been, and loved them in spite of it.

When Pete finally put the baby back on its pillow, Rosa turned to him and said, as if answering a question, "I'll always love you the most, Pete."

6    J u l i a n was in bed and, until Pete came in, had been asleep.

"What the hell!" Pete said. "That boy of mine was up at six, and you're still here in bed."

Julian had been awake half the night. He opened his eyes now, mad. Here was Pete, as always, looking down at him, making him out to be lazy or irresponsible or disappointing. He'd had a boy and had come over to boast about it.

"So it's a boy," Julian said.

"You don't think we'd start out with anything else?"

"People have," Julian said.

"I'm not people," Pete said. "I been trying to teach you that all my life."

"That's one thing we agree on. You're always trying to teach me something." But you couldn't dent Pete, couldn't insult him. Not this morning, anyway. Loved everybody, couldn't be convinced everybody didn't love him. Big, handsome Pete Ramos of the town of Ramos.

"You're feeling mean this morning," Pete said, in the jolly way he'd greet a pet dog. Pat him on the head, give him a bone. Kid him out of it. "Don't you want to know the baby's name? Or how much he weighed?"

"No," Julian said.

Pete thought all this surliness was a game, one person to say no, another to say yes. It suited him perfectly. It provided the seesaw he wanted to ride. He thought it was all done for his pleasure.

"I'll tell you, then," Pete said. "Pete, Junior. He weighed twelve pounds. Not an ounce of fat on him."

"Look like a skeleton?"

"No, he looks like my father."

"Another woman chaser, eh?"

Julian shut his eyes. Those were unfortunate words. He wished he could take them back. He didn't want to get started on that again. He tried to get back to the baby.

"How's Rosa?" he asked.

"She's fine. We've been looking at the baby together. You start it together, you look at it together. If I had to do without one of them, I'd keep on starting them and give up looking at them. But it makes a nice finish."

"Finish?" Julian asked. "Finish? That's no finish. That's a beginning. You'll have that kid on your back for twenty years."

"Whose kid are we talking about?"

"Mine," Julian said. "That's what you've been talking to me about for the past couple of days."

"I've stopped," Pete said. "I've got no more to say."

"I haven't," Julian said. "I've been listening to you. Now you listen to me. I let you talk me into coming back here. I thought I was talked into marrying that girl. I'm not. You come over here now, talking about your kid and how great it is to see it. And you want me to believe that's the way it will be when I see mine. I'm not going to see mine. You asked Rosa to marry you and you wanted that kid. I never asked Medora to marry me; I never even asked her to look at me. She ran after me. She threw herself at me. She got this kid in order to make me marry her. I don't love her. I told her I didn't. I told her to let me alone. I told her I hated her whole family. If I had a kid who looked like Cudlip, I'd strangle it. There's no use talking church to me. I've been to church a hundred times to your once. The church don't say, Marry every girl that throws herself on you and gets knocked up in order to tie you down. The church says, Marry one woman and stick to her. It don't say, Marry the woman who sticks to you. When I marry, I'm going to marry a wife, not some girl with hot pants who throws it at you. What kind of a wife is that? And nothing you can say is going to make me change my mind."

"I never said you ought to marry her."

"You went to an awful lot of trouble to hunt me up. Why?"

"I thought you'd want to know that Medora was going to have a baby. I never said the word 'marry.'"

"No, you didn't say 'marry.' But you made Medora out to be some kind of a suffering saint. Saint? Hell, I don't even know if the baby's mine."

531

"I can't swear my baby's mine, for that matter. Who can?"

"Don't try any more persuading. It won't work. I thought about this all night. When you came to see me, sure, I want to do what big, handsome Pete wants me to do. That's what I've been doing all my life. Please Pete. Pete knows best, Pete'll be disappointed if he can't take charge. Up to the time you found me, everything was settled. I hated that girl and I sure as hell wasn't going to marry anyone I hated. Then you come. Then you think that what's good for you is good for me. You're going to have a baby. I'm going to have a baby. You're going to look at your kid. I'm going to look at my kid. So I come back with you. I do what I've been doing all my life. In the night, I thought it over. How many lives does Pete need to lead, I asked myself? He's leading his. Isn't that enough? He's running his own life to suit himself. He married a girl to suit himself and had a kid to suit himself. How about me? This is a free country, isn't it? Can't I pick out my own wife and arrange for my own wedding and have the kid I want to have? The answer is no. Pete's got to do that for you. That's what he's been doing all his life and that's the way Pete's going to keep it. The hell it is. You got one life. Go lead it. You don't get mine. You got your own little boy now. You don't need me any more. Pick out his wife for him."

Julian had succeeded in firing himself up with his own words, and this had been his intention. He believed what he was saying, and had believed it for a long time. But the long silence he had kept made it necessary now for him to overspeak in order to speak at all. Hearing his case overstated, he believed the overstatements. He burned with anger. He had no compunction. His anger and the feeling of power that speaking up to Pete gave him were also useful for another purpose: they covered up whatever blame or doubt he had about deserting Medora. It was Pete who was actually forcing him to turn his back on Medora. If he didn't, he would be in for a lifetime of jumping whenever Pete cracked the whip. He asked himself how he had been able to put up with it as long as he had. There Pete stood at the foot of the bed, a big Mexican among small Mexicans; handsome, as athletes are, with their long muscles and calm, fatigued smiles; friendly with everybody brown, white, or black, Indian, Mexican, Spanish, American. Julian was able, roused by his own eloquence and his long-unspoken resentments, to see Pete's bigness as tyranny, his handsomeness as vanity, his friendliness as a two-faced effort to get whatever he wanted. What he saw convinced him that he had two reasons for clearing out: he needed to escape Pete as much as he needed to escape Medora. In fact, he needed to escape Pete more than he needed to escape Medora. Medora was only giving him an unwanted baby. Pete was making a baby of him. The thought of his long years of submission and the feel of his present defiance and coming escape flushed his face with blood.

Pete, evidently, was able to read his face. "When are you leaving, Julian?" he asked.

"Tomorrow," Julian said. "Unless you tell Cudlip I'm here and get me thrown in jail."

"Do you think I'd do that?" Pete asked.

"Sure," Julian said, "if you decided it was for my own good."

Pete didn't say a word. He just stood there and looked. Finally he said, "Good luck, Julian," and walked out of the room.

When he left the Ortiz house, Pete walked slowly up the hill toward his own place. His talk with Julian had put him out of the mood of spreading the news about his son. Something he had believed in, which, except for his feeling for Rosa, had been the happiest part of his life, had done worse than die. It had never lived—so it couldn't die. It had disappeared like a mirage. His heart was heavier than it would have been at a death. Death let you cry until finally you had some ease. He couldn't cry about this. How could a man cry about a friendship that had never existed? How could he shed tears over his blind foolishness?

He had loved Julian, been proud of Julian, boasted about him to his other friends. When people had said to him, "You and Julian are as different as night and day. How do you get on so well?," his answer had been that their difference was the reason for their getting on so well. They were friends *because* of their differences, and each admired in the other what he himself didn't possess or couldn't do. "Julian can play the piano," he would say. "I'd knock a piano down if I touched it. Julian is as smart as the teachers. Half the time in high school they were going to kick me out. Not Julian. Geometry, Latin, history. I tell you, the teachers asked him for the answers. Dance? Go to church? Did you ever see such a nifty dresser?" He would shut up, finally, feeling embarrassed at opening his heart so freely.

But that was what he had felt, and he had never doubted that Julian felt for him the same pride and tenderness. And all the time he had been doting on Julian and praising him, Julian had been resenting and enduring him. A darkness had come down and blotted out the golden light of his boyhood. A self-scrutinizing devil had taken the place of his natural spontaneity.

He made a long trip out of the short walk that separated his place from Julian's. He had run down that slope ten thousand times, he supposed, in full confidence that Julian was waiting as eager to see him as he was to see Julian. Had he always—or usually—been the one to make that trip? Would he ever make it again? Was he climbing up this slope for the last time? And why *had* he chosen Julian for a friend? Because he was younger, smaller, and could be bossed? No, by God, no. His admiration was genuine. He had been mistaken in thinking that Julian's feelings were the same as his. But he wasn't for that reason going back on what he himself had felt for that cocky little high-stepping bantam! The tenderness and pride for Julian were still there. They hadn't disappeared. He wouldn't make any effort to deny or falsify them, simply because Julian resented them. He would keep them to himself. And maybe Julian had been right. "You've got a son to teach, now."

Though he talked sensibly to himself all the way up the hill, he was sore-hearted, heavy with loss and disappointment. And even shame. To have persisted where he wasn't wanted. And guilt. If it hadn't been for me, he thought, Julian might have endured Medora. But after my throwing myself at him, another one like me was more than he could put up with. Was a baby going to be born without a father because of his blindness?

When he saw that Doctor Heilman's car was still in the driveway at his place, an idea came to him. He would ride over to the Lewises' with him and talk to Shel. He had started down the hill toward Julian's with a chestful of happiness and a headful of talk. Most of the happiness had been drained off, but he still felt the pressure of the untapped talk—more of it now, if anything, than before he'd seen Julian—and Shel was the man he wanted to spill it to.

Things were going better with Joicey. Another hour, Doctor Heilman said, and it should be all over. Shel and Pete, with this news, went out to the weir box and stretched themselves along its rim. A little water, spilling over the lip of the weir, made a rainy sound. If they were quiet enough, barn swallows darted down for skimming drinks. A morning breeze, seaward from the warming earth, moved the brassy clouds across the sky. It was after ten. The potato plants were green

534

and glossy, and white butterflies hovered above the white blossoms. Maybe they thought they were looking into mirrors. It was warm, but too sultry for the shimmer of heat waves. Because of this, the foothills looked rounder and more solid than usual. The fleece of clouds moving seaward mottled the hills brown moleskin, stippled their velvet so that it was easy to believe that the shifting shades of brown were caused by movements below the moleskin instead of above it.

Pete was smoking hand-rolled cigarettes; Shel was chewing. Shel didn't let himself do this often. It was a habit he had picked up at ten from his father and had given up on the day he married Joicey. But he was never without a plug, and a couple or three times a year he took a chaw. He would rinse his mouth out with black coffee before he saw Joicey, but after last night and the day before, he felt he deserved some forbidden refreshment. Not that what he'd gone through could hold the feeblest candle to what Joicey had suffered—and was suffering. He listened, not only with the ear but with the entire side of his body nearest the house, for a sound from the spare room.

"When Joicey had Chad," he told Pete, "I hardly turned a hair. Women having babies seemed to be the naturalest thing in the world to me then, and I didn't doubt Joicey would be as good at it as the next one. Since then, I've learned a thing or two. It may be natural, but it's sure not easy. I take each one harder. If Joicey was to have three or four more, I likely couldn't stand it."

Pete, stretched out, supported by one elbow and with one knee drawn up, looked at Shel in surprise.

"You don't get used to it?" he asked.

"You don't get used to it," Shel said. "It gets harder for your wife as she gets older. And you love her more—and you're not as crazy to have the fourth or fifth kid as you were the first or second."

"You love her more?" Pete asked, as if that was a little hard to believe.

"If you love her, you do," Shel said.

"That don't make it so good," Pete said. "Harder for her and you care more."

Shel spat and looked across the water at Pete, wondering at the chance, though he supposed it wasn't chance, that had made this Mexican instead of Lute his closest friend on the Tract. Closest for me, he thought, though maybe not for Pete.

"Whatever happened to your friend Julian?" he asked.

535

Pete, who was making a cigarette, looked up quickly from his work, but finished the job and put the cigarette in his mouth before answering. "He left without leaving any word."

"Any idea why?"

"He didn't tell me anything."

"You've known him since you're kids?"

"He lived next door to us."

"Must be nice to be near somebody you've known all your life."

Pete lit his cigarette. "It could be," he said.

Shel, feeling that he had gotten onto a subject Pete didn't want to talk about, changed to something else. "They say," he said, making a motion with his head toward the house, "that a criminal always returns to the scene of his crime."

Pete didn't get it, and was about, Shel saw, to ask for an explanation. Then the meaning came to him and he smiled.

"Nine months ago," Pete said, "I sure as hell felt like a criminal, Rosa and me in your bed."

"That was a busy day," Shel said. "Busy bed, too," he added.

"Rosa thinks it was all the bed. She don't give me any credit. Might be. It was the bed's first try and it sure wasn't mine."

"It worked for my son and his wife, too," Shel said. "They're expecting."

"Yeh? How's it feel, going to be a grandfather?"

"Damn queer. You look forward to being a father. But I never heard of anybody looking forward to being a grandfather. But you 'bout as well start thinking about it, Pete. Once you get a son, you're as good as a grandfather."

"I ain't used to my son, yet."

"They're not much to begin with."

"Mine is," Pete said.

"Yeh?" Shel said, smiling. "You got an unusual one?"

"I reckon I have," Pete said, taking Shel's question straight. "He weighed twelve pounds, and that's all bone and muscle. No fat. He needs a haircut right now."

"How about a shave?" Shel asked.

Pete got that, but he went right on. "I picked him up just before I come over here, and you know what, Shel? He looked at Rosa and me and he recognized us. Not many babies can do that the first day, can they?"

"No," Shel said. "That's pretty unusual."

"At first, he could've been anybody's baby. Bigger and stronger than most—but anybody's. And all that hair looked pretty wild. A hairy baby. Hair's not what you think of first when you think of babies. But after that look he gave me—he took me, so I took him."

" 'Til death do us part," Shel said.

"Don't talk like that," Pete said. "This kid'll live to be ninety. I tell you, Shel, that look did something to me. I ain't the same. I feel sorry for the man who don't get that look."

"You pay for it, too," Shel said. "Don't matter what they do, you ache for them. Shit in your pocket, and you never blame them. The dear sweet little shitter, you say. But this is something you don't know anything about."

"I know about it," Pete said. "I learned when he looked at me."

Shel looked across at Pete. Pete was smoking in a Mexican's way, cigarette pasted on his lip and hanging downward. Smoke, in spite of the fact that it didn't look to Shel as if he could get any of it inside, was drifting out of the other corner of his mouth. Pete's face had closed up again, as it had when Shel asked him about Julian. Shel kept quiet.

"Shel, you want a girl or a boy?" Pete asked.

"Girl," Shel said. "If we could choose, we'd take a girl."

A boy was what they got. Zoomy brought them the news, though he had screamed it to them before he reached them. "It's a boy," he yelled, and the screen door, slamming behind him, was like a pistol shot celebrating the birth.

Shel spat out his quid, and the two men got off the weir box. "We got twins, I guess, Pete. You and me."

They shook hands, smiling. "What're you going to name him?" Pete asked.

"Joicey was set on his being a Junior if it was a boy."

"That's what mine is. Junior."

"One bed, one birthday, and the same name," Shel said. "This'll be a day you and me won't soon forget, Pete."

"This day each year, we'll have a big fiesta," Pete said.

"One year tamales, the next year beefsteak."

They shook hands again. Pete went over to Doc's car to wait for his ride home, and Shel went in to see his new son.

7   THE SPRING day, warm as summer, colored like fall, had ended, leaving everyone dissatisfied. The sky had worn clouds like chain mail all day. Through the chinks, the body of the blue giant who wore it could be seen.

"Cloud up or clear off," the Back-Easterners said.

In Ioway or Missoury, such a day of brassy clouds and sultry airs would by midafternoon have produced thunderheads, sheet lightning, and a sluicing downfall of water. By sundown the sky, washed clean as a newly opened bluet, would have been filled with the pale, clear light of a resolved day's ending. The fireworks smell of lightning would linger, but only as the seasoning, the spices added to the big rich smell of the wet earth: the big earth, rich as a fruitcake, containing every animal and vegetable that had flourished since time's beginning; every tadpole, deer, skunk cabbage, and rose; every Indian, Spaniard, Mexican, Yankee; every trapper, gold digger, and barley rancher whose body had gone back to earth; every one of these, water-soaked and sun-warmed, would have had its place in the column of incense rising from the rain-drenched Tract. And breathing that scent, sweet and rotting, fresh and humid, filled with death and promising renewal, the people would have received an ease that the burnished, rainless, but still-threatening sunset denied them.

It had felt like rain but there had been no rain, and there could be no rain (unless the climate of the West Coast went topsy-turvy) until October or November. By tomorrow, the clouds would have blown away. For six months, the peerless, empty sky would hang above them. The dry Santa Anas would lift their columns of dust and send their tumbleweeds, like empty rib cages, rolling across the hills to shatter in fence corners and pile up in empty arroyos. For people accustomed to ten changes of weather in a day, six months of sunshine was a monotonous prospect. They felt the hardships of waiting. They felt the weight in their bones of all that dependability. Shine, shine. It made them mad at the sun. Blow, blow. To hell with the sweet sea wind. They had to take it all on their skins, the whole dint of perfection. Rain and sleet, hurricanes and blizzards can be fought. For these, there are storm cellars and raincoats and base-burners and felt-lined

538

boots. How do you fight flowers and sunshine? Where's the umbrella against brilliant stars and clear skies? A man can shovel snow, but he looks silly smashing tumbleweeds. He can be put in an asylum for shaking his fist at a bougainvillaea. How can you go down a storm cellar (that does not exist) when the sweet air blows up each evening off the blue Pacific? It was like living in heaven before you were prepared for it. The men on the Tract felt restless and itchy. The weather had bogged down into a six months' dreamless sleep. They themselves would have to provide the action. Nor were they helped that evening by the news from the Western Front. Men were dying. Men were also being born, two on the Tract that very day. But the news from the trenches reached them daily, while their own news had only a weekly publishing. That day's news was only of death, the death of their own men at the hands of the Germans. The news made them want to strike a blow. But against whom? Their muscles were clotted with unused fury.

After the sun went down, the warmest days on the Tract cooled: except this one day. The sun set; the air continued warm; the still-clouded sky weighed like an extra and unwanted blanket on their beds, a blanket they could not get rid of. People stepped to their bedroom windows to cool off and have a look at the sky. The blue giant had disappeared. The moon shone through the chinks like light from a smoky lantern.

Because of the color of the sky, the fruitless weather, the unavenged deaths, Lute practiced his dark arts early and with violence. He had a victim, and her unresisting presence tempted him. Would she never raise a hand against him? He needed an opponent. Would she not volunteer? If what she suffered from was love, you could not tell it by listening. And this power to violate, he had always had; and this power to suffer had always been hers. Those sounds had always been in the back of her throat, and these wild movements had always been in the muscles of her buttocks and belly. And that these sounds and movements should be the sounds and movements made by Indy, the girl he had married and the woman who had been a mother, made the violation more terrible and more appealing. As terrible and unthinkable (except that he thought it) as incest.

He could never have enough of it and he was never satisfied. His hunger had nothing to do with numbers. It was something he did to another, and he was unchanged by the action. It was like a death blow that does not kill. She cried, her movements were agonized, but she was always able to cry again and to move again. Afterward, he felt contrition and guilt for the shameful act, and in his desire to forget his shame, with another act he replaced old shame and contrition with new. Act, act. Only in action did his mind have some ease. Did he love or punish? Did he love and punish? Did he say to Indy, If this is what you want, have your fill, take it, until it kills you. Speak up, beg mercy. But she said nothing: Neither stop, begin, hurry, don't stop, never again, forever. Not a word. He could not force her to shape her sounds into words. She would not say his name. She would not say any name. In her mindless moments, he had thought she might speak another name. Why did he want that? Where was he trying to force her? Into a region where the only differences were those of function, male and female, infinite rapacity and infinite receptivity?

They lay under the unnecessary blanket. Lute felt the weight of the chain mail sky above them. By reason and logic he could defend himself. Logic told him, This is what she wants, this is what she left home for, this is what she doesn't have to leave home for again. All true. But logic did not erase the memory of his latest crime. Only the action in another crime did that; only action promised at its heart a mindless moment of quiet. But he could not find this quiet in bed with Indy. Sometimes there was promise of quiet in his thoughts of revenge. Tom Mount was the man responsible for this nighttime of horror. Why not punish him? Kill him. Geld him. Jail him. Denounce him. Lute knew he would never do any of these things. All done, every one of them, the offender dead, gelded, imprisoned, denounced, how would he, lying here dry, burning, spent, desiring, be helped? How would he, his shame published abroad, a betrayed husband still cherishing his guilty wife, be easier? Yet there was a cleansing act for which he longed, an immersing act, an absorbing act, an act that did not have to be repeated.

Indy had developed the power of sleep. When Lute clasped her, she was scarcely awake; when he released her, she was instantly unconscious. Everything that happened to her happened to her in her sleep. She had bad dreams of pleasure and slept more deeply and forgot them. And had worse dreams of pain and wakened to what was called love. And slept through that. Her body's center was no more than a tooth or a strand of hair. The tooth hurt sometimes; the strand of hair was tossed or wind-blown or coiled tight. She slept.

She heard the voices, even recognized Lute's and Base's voices. She understood the words and told herself she had the power to sleep, though Lute confer with devils and call up all the powers of hell. That was no new thing. She had slept through such conferences and had wrestled with such powers. He wanted one thing only of her. That was her only life, and where that didn't happen she had no real existence. Lute knew that. He didn't bother to lower his voice or hide his intentions. He was talking before a sleeper, a woman whose world contained nothing but what he gave her.

After he left, she didn't disappoint him. She slept. But in her sleep, it must have been, she heard the conversation with the ears of her long-ago presleeping self. She woke up instantly, got out of bed, washed, and dressed. Hannah was sleeping soundly. They had taken Lute's car, but Base's horse, still hitched to the buggy, was in the barn lot. She had not driven a horse for ten years, had never felt safe with one, had supposed Base's horse would be balky and vicious or perhaps a runaway bolter. Still, she climbed in, took the reins, and drove out of the yard. Under the mottled sky the road was not very plain. The horse, to her relief, was as much of a mind to go to the townsite as she.

Whom could she rouse up? She didn't know many people, and her mind turned to those she did. They were the ones who should decide. She would pass Asa's tent. If Tom was living in the Reynolds' house while he carpentered on it, she would awaken him. Wendlin and Ben. Raunce, of course. That ought to be enough.

He said to her, "I have never made love to a girl before. I had no idea they were so sweet."

"They aren't," Crystal said. "Only me."

With Tom she had this magic power of repartee. She could say nothing wrong. Every word fitted; every idea pleased them both. They were lying on a pile of redwood shavings, pushed together for this purpose by Tom, in a corner of what was to be a bedroom in the Reynolds' house. Tom chose the bedroom because, he said, "I don't hold with making love in any old place that's handy, kitchen or dining room or back porch." Then he thought of her father. "I'm sorry I said that," he told her.

541

It didn't matter in the least. No one had to defend her father to her any more. She tried not to forget the reasons she had had for hating him. But she *was* forgetting them, because the girl who had hated and misjudged was disappearing. The rafters of the Reynolds' house framed the stars for her. She gazed upward, thinking, Stars ought always to be framed this way—no more than can be caught between two rafters and a ridgepole.

"A skyful of stars is just too much," she said.

"We'll take a few out," Tom said.

"I mean to look at."

Tom smoothed her hair back; he traced with his gentle touch the shape of her face. "I was always afraid to love a girl."

"Why?" she asked dreamily, lying on his arm gazing at the stars, scarcely hearing him. She never paid much attention to what Tom said. She listened, she was pleased to hear his voice, but she labeled most of his answers "more hawk talk about buzzards." That's what *he* thinks, she would tell herself, smiling a fond, hidden smile. He told her many truths which she did not believe, and he, discovering this, almost never lied to her. A lie was unnecessary. She took it all as the truth of a fairy tale, which she loved but didn't believe in.

"Why?" he answered her question. "Girls have everything. I was afraid to put myself forward to anyone who hadn't lost something. I courted cripples. They were happy for a look. They would dry my feet with their hair. Times were stormy for them, and I was a port."

"You weren't very brave, were you?" she asked, listening to the thud of his heart, like an oil well in a distant field, pounding away under her ear.

"I wasn't brave at all. I was way out in left field. Why would a girl look at an old, cold Englishman like me?"

She knew he was speaking to be contradicted, but she thought he *was* old. She didn't know whether or not he was English. Probably not. But he wasn't cold. She never lied to him, though there were questions she didn't answer, and statements she ignored. She misunderstood his use of "cold," put her hand on the big, well-fleshed arch of his chest, and said, "You are always warm, burning warm. We would never need a stove."

"When are you going to marry me?" he asked. He asked all women to marry him, and was prepared to marry without complaint the first one who, in spite of everything, held him to it. She would be the one fate intended for him.

542

Crystal, who did not lie to him or believe, very often, his truths, said, "I am married to you." Which was as much as to say, politely, I'm as married to you as I'll ever be. Which in turn was a way of saying, This is a marriage that can be dissolved by our leaving each other. It did not say, but she thought, This will be soon. This is real love, but a play marriage. They would make a ridiculous married couple, and she understood that while lovers may make a ridiculous pair, married people had better be suited to each other. He would be taken for her father, and that would be fun for a little while; but not fun, only funny, when she was thirty. She knew that she didn't love him as she had loved Chad, to say nothing of Lute and Teddy Roosevelt.

"You're too smart for me," Tom would tell her, which he didn't believe, and she did. He was neither her hero, as Teddy and Lute had been, nor her equal, as Chad was. But she loved him dearly. She could talk to him by the hour, be touched by him by the hour; she would have risked her life for him gladly; he had reconciled her to the world; he had, by choosing her in his tender and overpowering way, healed the wounds given her by Chad and Lute and her father. She would remember him on her deathbed. She moved her cheek against his warm flesh with some of a child's content in being close to its mother —a content she had not often known, because her parents, in being so taken up with each other, had partially orphaned their children. But though he was dear, though she ran toward him as toward all she had ever loved, books and flowers and her mother's memories, she believed him in many ways ridiculous. She possessed, in truth, all that he had feared in young girls except beauty; her lack of beauty had disarmed him. And she was a cripple, too, because of Lute and Chad; but neither knew this, and by the time the idea occurred to her, she was healed.

She thought him ridiculous, and was mother instead of child because of it, loving him because of his weaknesses. His crazy sayings, which saved him the trouble of being newly alive to fit a new occasion. The dye he used on his hair and which rubbed off on her blouse. That was ridiculous and unnecessary. He was handsomer than anyone already, and no one would think him young whatever the color of his hair. The pride he had in being liked, in making conquests, even of cats and dogs. His persistence in airing his false hawk knowledge. His vanity, which he hid under various of his patented sayings, hoping to be contradicted and proved wrong. His esteem for his body and what it could do.

"Wouldn't you like to have this for your very own?" Such questions had overcome Eunice. Eunice had almost fainted. Crystal said, "Don't I already?" and he had to laugh.

"Why do they tell girls loving is so terrible?" she asked him.

"Making love, you mean?"

"Yes."

"I didn't know they did."

"Well, they do."

"I never did."

"Don't joke. Why do they?"

"I think it is, for some people."

"People I know?"

"Yes."

"Not my father!"

"Don't be so suspicious. Not your father."

"Who?"

"Forget it."

"I think it would be a good thing if we didn't know a thing about it at all. If no one ever said a word to us, then, one day, we discovered it."

"Who you planning on making this discovery with?"

"Boys," she said, not tactful enough to have said "men."

"What if no one told the boys either?"

Crystal smoothed his hair and kissed his eyelids. "Boys are so dirty and curious, they'd find out for themselves."

"I was curious but not dirty," he said.

This was true, and she believed it to be true.

"Why can't we learn from words?"

"I don't know what you mean."

"Even if someone had told me, 'It's not dirty, it's beautiful and natural and holy,' what would I have known?"

"Nothing," he admitted. Then added, "Nothing is true from the outside."

Crystal thought about this a while. "Nothing's true from the outside, but once inside, where you've got to be to know, perhaps you'll be caught and have to stay there forever."

"Perhaps," Tom agreed. "There are people like that, I expect."

"Not you?"

"No."

"Why not?"

"I don't know. But not you either."

544

Crystal continued to run her fingers through his hair, which, if dyed, was heavy and silky. She touched his eyelids with her finger tips, liking the surprise of hard muscle beneath the soft folds of skin.

"That's not hawk knowledge, is it?" she asked.

"Hawk knowledge," he repeated. "What kind of talk is that?"

She had used these words so often to herself when she was with Tom that she had forgotten that she had never said them aloud before. He wasn't hurt when she explained them.

"I told you," he said, when she had finished, "that I used to be afraid of girls and now you see why. I like old ladies who have been out of school a long time and with poor eyesight. I like to be smarter than a girl."

"Mister," she said, "you will have to get up early."

He laughed and pulled her closer to him. "I don't want to get up at all," he said.

She kissed him many times, only stopping because she was breathless.

"I love you," she said, when she was able to breathe and speak at the same time.

"My darling," Tom said. "My precious Irish gypsy."

Indy stopped first of all at Asa's. In the mottle of shifting starlight it was hard to see anything substantial enough to knock on. She called and called and called. The tent was silent, thin and empty as an old snail shell. She was fearful, and she took out her fear on Asa. Why doesn't he stay home, she demanded, where he can be of some use, instead of roaming around stargazing? "Asa, Asa," she called, but there was no reply, though the canvas, in a sudden current of air, moved a little as if it, at least, had heard.

She drove on toward the townsite. Tom's car was parked in front of the unfinished Reynolds' house, and she slowed the horse. He's in there, she thought, he's in there. She was as sure as though he had touched her, but she could not bring herself to stop, to go inside, or to call to him. She was afraid of what she might see or hear.

Lights were burning in all the rooms at the Jessups', and she knew what this meant. Mary was suffering—perhaps dying. Nevertheless, she knocked and went in. Wendlin was alone in the sitting room, not reading, not sleeping, slumped in a rocker, his hand over his mouth, his eyes on the door to Mary's room. From behind this closed door came the terrible groans of a sufferer, drugged until identity has been

545

lost—but not pain. It seemed inhuman to Indy to speak in the presence of such pain, inhuman for people to continue their usual lives while it went on.

Wendlin straightened himself when she came in, and took his hand away from his mouth. "Is something wrong, Mrs. Cope?" he asked.

It wasn't so late that a call, before she had spoken a word, should suggest that something was wrong, so her fears must show in her face. She told him as quickly as she could.

When she finished, Wendlin asked, "Did you hear Base say in so many words that he intended to kill Julian?"

She tried to remember what, exactly, she had heard. "I don't think he ever said that. I can't remember that he said 'kill.' But he said, 'Get your gun.' He told Lute to do that. Why would he say that, if he didn't intend to use it?"

"Perhaps it was only to be a threat." There was a movement, a change of color at the back of Wendlin's tired eyes, as though humor or a memory of humor stirred somewhere deep in his mind. "Lute's gun was maybe intended to be the bouquet for a shotgun wedding," he suggested.

Indy could not respond even to humor's shadow. "No," she said, "there was no talk of weddings."

"Did Lute put up any arguments when Base asked him to get his gun?"

"I was half asleep. I tried not to wake up. If Lute argued with him, I didn't hear him. But when I woke up, when the words came back to me, I looked to see if the gun was still there. It was gone."

"Did they say they were going to Julian's?"

"I can't remember. But where else would they be going when they talked about him?"

"You said they talked about the reservoir, too?"

"Base did. But he's been doing that for a long time."

"Maybe he saw someone up there tonight. Maybe he was getting some guards together."

Indy held her head in her hands, then she looked up at Wendlin. "I don't think so. I was so sleepy and so tired, I tried not to hear. But it was Medora they talked about most." She shut her eyes and could hear again the sounds of Base's voice. "Base sounded terrible," she told Wendlin. "He sounded like a man—out of his mind. I hated to bother you. But I didn't know who else to come to. I stopped at Asa's.

546

He wasn't there. I remembered that LeRoy is working swing shift. You and Ben were the only others I knew—and trusted."

"Ben isn't here," Wendlin said. "He's at the Lewises'. He's going to marry their girl, you know."

"What should I have done?" Indy asked. "I had to come, didn't I?"

Old Wendlin stood up; he shoved himself up out of the chair as if his own weight were a great burden.

"You did right, you had to come," he said. "Don't worry yourself about that. I guess I better try to find some help and head right over to Julian's place. I don't think he's been home for a month or two, but I'll be easier in my mind to go see."

"It's a terrible time to take you away from your wife."

"I wouldn't go if I could help her," Wendlin said. "Not even to save Julian's neck, I'm afraid. You wait here. I'll be right back."

He went into his wife's room, and a woman Indy had never met but knew to be Wendlin's daughter came out. "I'm Paula Jessup," she said, "and you're Mrs. Cope, the editor's wife."

Indy looked at Paula with admiration—and with envy, thinking, This is the woman I might have been, a missionary, a woman who knows right from wrong, a woman of principle. *She* wouldn't have been sleeping when those words were said. She would've heard, argued, protested. She would've been here hours ago.

"How is your mother tonight?" Indy asked.

"Weaker. We pray for her release. We think every night will be her last. She is suffering because of her own vitality."

We all are, Indy thought. But she said nothing. She had no right to. She had never yet groaned as Mary Jessup was groaning.

"I'm sorry to bother your father," she said. "But I didn't have anyone else to turn to."

"It'll do him good to get away from the house," Paula said. "There's nothing he can do here."

When Wendlin came out of the bedroom, Indy saw that he had been crying and envied him because of his long, happy married life. Wendlin, as he put on his coat—he had lost track of the weather and didn't know that the evening was warm—spoke to his daughter. "Paula, if your mother should regain consciousness, I want you to tell her one thing—without fail. Tell her, 'Father's with Base.'"

Paula objected. "Father, she might be dying. That's not your last message for her, is it?"

Wendlin fronted his grown-up missionary daughter as if she were still a little girl. "'Father's with Base.' Nothing else unless there's time."

"Will she care about that?" Paula persisted.

"If she's able to care about anything, she'll care about that. If there's more time, tell her 'Father always knew you loved him.'"

"You mean you always loved her, don't you?" Paula asked, plainly believing her father to be confused by sorrow and weariness.

"She knows that," Wendlin answered shortly. "Don't tell me what you think I ought to say, Paula. I know what Mary wants to hear. Have you got it straight, now? What she wants, not what you think's best."

"Yes, Father."

"I'll be back as soon as I can, and I wouldn't go at all except that it's what your mother would want me to do."

Wendlin's car, usually so dependable, was hard to start and he drove slowly, humoring it. When he saw Tom Mount's car parked in front of the partially completed Reynolds' place, he pulled up.

"It looks like Tom Mount's staying here nights," he said. "We may need all the help we can get. I don't like to ask you to go call him, but I think I better save my strength for the driving. I'm tireder than I thought."

Indy walked slowly, in spite of the need for hurry, to the Reynolds' house, paused in front of it, pulled herself by means of the studding—she didn't see the orange box that served as a step—up onto the floor boards. She stopped there because she heard, someplace in one of the rooms, voices murmuring. She could go no farther. She knew that somewhere in the house in which she stood Tom Mount lay with a woman in his arms. Her mind—or was it her heart—ached with pain. Who was it? Eunice again? Mrs. Reynolds? Someone she didn't know? There was no use speculating. It could be anyone. But what of it? she asked herself. He doesn't exist for you. You refused to go with him. But the pain was real. She could not move forward. She could not call out. She could not, by any act of will, make herself walk toward Tom and the woman he held to him under the clouded stars of the warm May night.

She did speak his name aloud, but under her breath, "Tom, Tom Mount. Wendlin's looking for you. He needs you. It may be life or death, Tom. Somebody may be dying while you make love. Some-

548

one *is* dying," she whispered to herself, clasping herself again as she had on the night Lute had talked and talked.

There was no answer to her whispers. All the murmurings and rustlings had ceased. The house was silent. Overhead, stars and clouds still alternated, and Indy stood in the roofless house under the shifting light like a dead woman in the ribwork of a ship sunk in tidal waters.

"Tom," she said once more, this time loudly enough to be heard. Still there was no answer.

She went back to Wendlin. "I called him," she said, "and there was no answer."

"Perhaps it is just as well," Wendlin told her. "We don't want to go out to Julian's like an army. I'll get Ben and Shel. That's likely enough." But Ben wasn't at the Lewises'. He and Ellen were out courting, "at last," Shel said.

Wendlin told Shel why they were there, and Shel told him and Indy what they didn't know, that Joicey had had her baby. "Shelby Lewis, Junior, weight nine pounds. I don't know, with Ellen gone, whether I ought to leave Joicey or not," he said. "Joicey had a hard time, and Zoomy's not much of a nurse."

"I'll stay with Joicey," Indy said.

"I wouldn't urge you," Wendlin said to Shel, "and maybe there's no occasion to. The last I heard of Julian, he was down in San Diego. But I don't like the idea of Base's wandering around with a gun. I saw what he did to Julian once without a gun."

From the bedroom, Joicey, in a strengthless voice, called, "Shel."

Shel went to the door of her room. "Yes, honey?"

"You go on and go," Joicey said. "All I need's a little rest."

Before they left the house, Shel said to Wendlin, "If Base's got a gun, how about me getting mine?"

"I don't know about Base," Indy told him. "But Lute has his, I know."

"I'm not anxious to meet an armed man empty-handed," Shel said.

"Leave your gun at home," Wendlin said. "We aren't going out gunning for Base, or Lute either, Shel."

Shel hesitated, then said, "I reckon not if you say not, Wendlin."

Peter Ramos, Junior, on the first evening of his life on earth, slept with his father and mother. At ten o'clock, he was sleeping soundly;

his father, whenever his mother was silent for a few minutes, also slept. This was not often, for Rosa was wide awake, talkative, and merry.

"This is the best and happiest night of all our lives," she told both of them. When Pete didn't answer, she prodded him with her elbow. "Isn't it, Pete?"

Pete fooled her. She had expected him to say yes, after which she would catch him in his pretense by saying, "Yes, what, Pete?" Instead, he repeated, "This is the best and happiest night of our lives."

But she didn't want parrot talk either. She wanted Pete to think carefully and give her a serious answer, even if he disagreed with her. "Do you really believe that, Pete?"

She got her serious answer. "Who can say if this is the happiest night? We don't know what's to come."

"You mean, maybe there will be nights to come so much better than this that tonight will be nothing beside them?"

"That could be."

"What could be better?"

Pete didn't answer, and Rosa was quiet, trying to imagine what could be better than the first night she had her sleeping son on one side of her and Pete on the other. She thought she had never known before this hour what love meant. She was suffused with tenderness. She had not supposed that having a baby would make her love Pete more. Would this keep on? Ten more babies and ten times as much love? She started to ask Pete this question, for she was not a person who enjoyed having thoughts she did not share. But Pete was plainly asleep now, and the motherliness which had been increasing in her all day reached out to him. She looked down at the big, sweet mouth, and the black lashes on the brown cheeks. She felt a pity for him she had never experienced before, a compassion because he would not have the baby near him as she would, and because he had to live and work in a man's hard world; though she felt, in her motherhood, shrewder than either her son or her husband, and more capable, for their sakes, of being ruthless.

But she was the one who had been in labor, who had brought forth the child. While they, who had been nothing but onlookers, were worn out, sleeping and resting, she stayed awake and thought and planned. They had not in their veins her enduring blood. Women of her mother's people had had babies on horseback. I could do that, she

550

thought, if I had to. She had slept most of the day, and it was a hardship for her to lie still and be silent now. What she wanted was not to have a baby on horseback, but to wear a beautiful dress and go to a big party. She would hold Little Pete in her arms, and Big Pete, in a white silk shirt and a red silk necktie, would put his arms about both of them, and, with the baby cradled between them, they would waltz, whirling and dipping until all of their friends stopped their own dancing to watch and admire this beautiful, everlasting dance for three.

She lay quietly for a long time, imagining this dance; and could not, when it ended, resist leaning over and kissing Pete.

"Rosa," he asked, but without opening his eyes, "do you want something?"

She was surprised by her own answer. "I'm starving to death," she said pitifully. But it was the truth.

Pete kept his eyes closed. When she saw his indifference, all of Rosa's motherly compassion left her. She was again the girl who had danced, merry, coquettish—hungry and highhanded.

"Pete," she said in a loud, outraged voice.

"I'm right here; I can hear you."

"I can't talk to you when you keep your eyes shut."

"Prove it," he told her, but his eyelids twitched.

She was astounded. Was the glory of being a new mother finished so soon?

She spoke very mournfully. "I need something to eat. I am beginning to feel faint."

"You ate a big supper," Pete, his eyes still closed, reminded her unsympathetically.

"It all went to make milk. There is nothing left for me. I am totally empty."

Pete opened his eyes, yawned until his jaws cracked. "What do you want?" he asked good-naturedly, but without concern.

Rosa considered. Pete was no cook, and she was truly starving, both hungry and thirsty.

"Canned tomatoes and crackers," she said.

Pete, at that, sat up in bed. "That's all past," he reminded her. "All that wanting crazy stuff to eat. After the baby is born, you don't feel that way any more."

"There is nothing crazy about tomatoes and crackers and they are

551

easy to get. Pete, we can have a party right here in bed. It will be the first time the three of us have eaten together. It will be a big celebration. Like a wedding supper. It will be a sacrament."

Pete yawned again, and tears came to his eyes.

Rosa had no honor for his tears. She was scornful. "How can you sleep at a time like this, Pete?" She took his hand, kissed it, and placed his arm across her breasts. "I am so hungry and so happy. All my wishes have come true. We have our big baby. You will not go to war. We will have four sons and two daughters. I love you. You are a good man and make beautiful babies. The bed had nothing to do with it. Put the tomatoes in a dish. The can poisons them. Bring the new baby spoon for the baby."

"Baby spoon," Pete exclaimed. "What do you want a baby spoon for?"

"To feed the baby, of course."

"A baby can't eat tomatoes."

"He can. And a crumb of cracker. It is our first meal together. Do you think I would leave him out? He will always remember it."

"Rosa," Pete said, "I am going to call Dr. Heilman. I think you are out of your head."

Rosa laughed. "Call him. Tell him. Out of my head! There is nothing wrong with me but health. You are the sick one, eyes closing. I thank God the boy has a strong mother. Otherwise, he will be a sissy like his papa."

Pete laughed and kissed her. "I wish to God I was married to a sissy, not someone who wants to stay awake all night and eat meals."

"The boy and I," Rosa said, "are not sissies. You will have to learn to be a man."

"It is not a man's work to get tomatoes," Pete said, but nevertheless he went to the kitchen and returned with the tomatoes, as advised, in a bowl, crackers on a plate, and three spoons—one of them the new baby spoon.

He put the tray on the bed, looked at it with pride, then said, "I forgot the dishes for the tomatoes."

"Let them go," Rosa said, as he started for them. "We are not strangers, to need to eat separate."

So the three of them ate from the single bowl, and Pete, eating the salty crackers and juicy tomatoes, woke up completely and found that he, too, was hungry and that Rosa had hit upon a fine combination. He did not say a word, either, when Rosa put a cracker crumb followed by a sip of tomato juice in the baby's mouth. Pete knew what she was up to, and the baby, once again opening his black eyes wide, appeared also to know. Rosa crossed herself, and Pete kept his peace while she fed him and herself as she had the baby. But when that ritual was over, it was the party again, and the headstrong coquette ate as heartily as any girl after a long evening of dancing.

When the food was finished, Pete lifted the baby nearer Rosa's edge of the bed. "Isn't he beautiful?" Rosa asked. "Most babies are bald. They look like old men. They do not have a beautiful head of hair like our baby."

"You didn't think he was beautiful this morning," Pete said.

"You must never mention that again," Rosa told him, "or think it. The doctor gave me a drug. I wasn't in my right mind."

"He didn't give me a drug," Pete confessed.

"You didn't think the baby was beautiful?"

"I thought he looked like a big, black spider."

Rosa clucked her tongue. "Your own son. And with no excuse of a drug."

Pete sat down on the bed, and held Rosa against him. "You are beautiful. And I have no drug."

A car went slowly by, and stopped down the street.

"Somebody looking for Julian," Pete said.

"Julian?" Rosa asked. "Is he home?"

"He don't have to be home for people to look for him, does he? He's a popular boy."

"Boy! You have your own boy now. Forget Julian."

"I have," Pete said. "No more looking after Julian. He didn't like it, anyway." He moved backward and forward, gently rocking Rosa. "I've got my own boy now, and my own girl."

"We are happy," Rosa said.

She knew Pete was, without his saying it. She could feel it in the way he rocked her in his arms and in the way he was careful not to scratch her face with his tomorrow's beard, already strong and rough.

"Rosa," Pete began, but a woman down the road screamed, and he stopped to listen. There were no more sounds, but Rosa could hear Pete's heart pounding faster and faster. Both of them held their breaths, listening. Pete had begun to breathe once again when the screams started once more, and this time there was no letup. They went on and on, up and up. Pete took his arms away from Rosa and stood up.

553

"Where are you going?" Rosa asked sharply.

"To the front room, where I can hear better. Somebody's been hurt."

She heard him cross the front room and open the front door. When he did that, she could hear, beside the unceasing screams, men's voices.

"Pete," she cried, "Pete! Don't leave me."

"I haven't left you," he called, but she knew he had moved out into the yard.

She got out of bed, and discovered that it was one thing to lie in bed dreaming of dancing and another to take, standing up, a single step. She held onto the bed, unable to breathe or to see properly.

"Help me, Pete. Help me," she called.

But her voice was drowned out by another voice from down the road, calling the same thing. "Pete, Pete. Help me, Pete. Help." She knew that voice and that cry. It was Julian.

She pulled herself, trembling and sweating, to the front door. By the time she got there, Pete was already running down the road. "Julian," he called, "Julian, I'm coming."

Rosa reached the gate to their front yard and clung there, as another car, its lights illuminating for her the car down the street and what was going on there, approached. She had heard Pete cursing and now she could see him fighting, pushing one man down, and struggling to pull another out of the car. As the second car stopped, its lights blazing full on Pete, a shot was fired, and her dear husband whirled, turned toward her and his home, took two steps in their direction, then lifting his arms as if he saw her and said farewell, he fell, face downward, his arms stretched as near her as he could get them.

She could not run, but she did. She reached him before his heart stopped beating. She fell forward, knowing that she had reached him and aware of the feel of his warm flesh. But that was the last thing she did know.

8    M A R Y and Pete died the same night. They were buried on the same afternoon two days later, Pete from St. Joseph's in Yorba, Mary from the preacherless Quaker church on the townsite.

Shel wanted to go to both funerals. He wanted to say good-by to Pete, get on his knees by Pete's coffin and say, "Pete, forgive me. Pete,

554

this is a mistake. You ought not to be dead. You're dead because we messed things up some way. You're dead without any reason, except that you stood by your friend and we didn't stand by you." But he went to Mary's funeral, not Pete's—for several reasons. Pete was surrounded in death by his family and Rosa's; and when the Ramoses and the Padillas of Orange and Los Angeles and Riverside counties congregated, there wasn't room for outsiders. Wendlin, on the other hand, except for neighbors, had only his son and daughter to keep him company at Mary's grave. And with Ben and Ellen soon to be married, Shel was beginning to feel related to the Jessups. Still, his chief reason for going to Mary's funeral was Pete. He didn't think he'd be able to sit through a service for Pete without making a show of himself, of his grief and his anger. Jump up, maybe, in the midst of the mumbo jumbo of Pete's church, foreign languages and bells ringing and people bending their knees and crossing themselves on signal, and yell, "What're you sitting here mumbling about? The man who murdered Pete is over in Santa Ana, safe and sound. Why don't you do something about him? You're not helping Pete any, sitting here listening to your bells, and crooking your knees."

But how would anything they could do to Cudlip help Pete? Pete was gone, clear beyond them all, lost to them all, and a bell rung in church or a shot fired at a county jail were, alike, happenings in a world he had left forever. So Shel went to Mary's funeral.

He and Ellen, leaving Zoomy to look after Joicey, went together. They started in good time, and Shel drove slowly toward the church. It was only mid-May, but summer's unstained days had already arrived. There were no clouds except those kicked up by Diamond. Dust settled on both of them, but neither he nor Ellen said a word. Two, today, *were* dust, and this was no time to complain about what those two would count a blessing: a ride along a dusty road under the cloudless sky of a May afternoon.

"I'm sorry you aren't going to have Mary for a mother-in-law," Shel said. "She was a fine woman."

Ellen nodded. Then she asked, "Will they hang Mr. Cudlip?"

"No," Shel said, "I don't suppose so."

"He murdered Pete," Ellen protested. "I thought they hung men for murder."

"Mr. Cudlip claims he shot in self-defense."

"Self-defense? All Pete was trying to do was to save his friend. You said so yourself."

"The friend Pete was trying to save had put Mr. Cudlip's daughter in a family way." Sorrow—and Ellen's approaching marriage—kept Shel from mincing words.

"That wasn't Pete's fault."

"No, it wasn't. But Mr. Cudlip says Pete was interfering with justice."

"Justice!" Ellen's voice filled with outrage. "Justice is the law, not Mr. Cudlip. Ben says there's no justification for a man's drawing a gun against an unarmed man."

Shel's face muscles were too heavy with sorrow to permit a smile, but he knew that in better times he would have smiled at Ellen's already quoting Ben to him as a fount of wisdom.

"Base says," he told her, "that he thought Pete was armed."

"Why did he? Did he see any gun?"

"Gun? No, he didn't see any gun. But he thought Pete had a knife. He thought Pete was coming at him with a knife."

"Knives? What did he think Pete was? A bandit? People don't carry knives any more."

"Mexicans do."

"Do they?" For all that Ben was the new authority, Ellen was still ready to take her father's word for some things.

"It don't matter whether they do or don't. That's the reputation they've got."

"Is that why Pete was killed? For a reputation Mexicans have?"

"No," Shel said. "I reckon Pete was killed chiefly because he *was* a Mexican. If it had been me or Wendlin trying to save Julian, Base would've thought twice before shooting."

"Save him? Why did Pete have to save Julian?"

"Base was going to carve him up."

"Carve him up? Is that what they were going to do?" Ellen didn't know what she was talking about, though she thought she did, envisaging a scene where Julian was hacked at with knives instead of beaten with fists; and Shel didn't set her right. "Julian's mother said that's what they were threatening."

"Was Mr. Cope going to help carve him up?"

"He was there, so I guess the idea was agreeable to him."

"Is that why Mr. Cope's in jail?"

"I don't know any other reason for him being there."

The church was in sight before Ellen spoke again. "Papa, do you think Julian did right to yell for Pete to come help him?"

556

"Right or wrong likely didn't play any part in it. Julian likely yelled 'help' the way you yell 'ouch' when your hand hits a hot stove. I don't suppose he had any chance to decide."

"Pete had a chance. Do you think he did right leaving wife and newborn baby the minute somebody yelled 'help'?"

"Julian wasn't somebody. And I ran off and left my wife and newborn baby, too."

"Ben says that he thinks *he* is as guilty as anyone. If he hadn't stayed out so late that night with me, he'd have been home when Mrs. Cope came for help. And I'm guilty, too. I didn't want to go home. We were spooning," she said. "Perhaps Pete's dead because I wanted to spoon."

"We're all guilty," Shel said. "You can't single out any one person. Base is guilty. He fired the shot. And Medora's guilty. She got the baby. And did you ever think what might've happened if you'd told the truth a little sooner, that night you and I went to the cave?"

"No," Ellen answered slowly. "No, I never once thought of that."

"Well don't," Shel said. "No good can come of it. It's past. Let's think of Mary for a change. It's her funeral we're going to."

But he couldn't take his own advice. Inside the church he was surrounded by the culprits, the men and women who had killed Pete. And there was very little in that building to remind him of Mary, or that this was her funeral. By Mary's own request her coffin had been placed at the back of the room. And the pulpit, which usually stood on the platform at the front of the room had been removed, stored for the afternoon in Mount's former bedroom. The vacant pulpit, it had been felt, would be an unhappy reminder of what had happened, first to LeRoy, then to Mary's own son. Better, by keeping the pulpit out of sight, keep people's minds off the fact that they were a congregation without a preacher.

Shel himself had asked Wendlin, the day after Mary's death, if he wouldn't like LeRoy to preach a funeral sermon. He knew that Mary and Wendlin had held out against those who wanted to oust LeRoy; and he was prepared, if Wendlin wanted the sermon, to put LeRoy in the pulpit for that one occasion, if he had to do it by force. But Wendlin had said no. He and Mary had both been brought up in silent meetings and he thought that Mary would like, on her last trip to church, to go back to the old days, to rest with her friends, and before God, in silence. Anyone could speak who felt moved to do so. He hoped LeRoy might have a few words to say. But he didn't care for anything planned.

Shel was a little shocked. A funeral without sermon, song, reading of scripture, prayer, eulogy, or testimony, struck him as being scarcely human. He'd seen his kids bury dead birds more ceremoniously.

Wendlin, recognizing Shel's feeling, had said, "Shel, it don't take a sermon to bring God down to us."

Maybe not. But a sermon at the very least occupied your mind while you were in church, even if the chief use you made of your mind was to contradict every other word the preacher was saying. Without the sermon, without the sight even of Mary's casket, Shel had nothing to keep his mind from its examination of Pete's death.

He had asked himself continuously since Pete's death, "If I had arrived five minutes sooner—and with a gun—would Pete still be alive? Did *I* kill Pete Ramos?"

He had also asked Wendlin this question. "Pete might be alive," Wendlin had said, "but it's more likely that another gun would have lost lives, not saved them."

"I can't say I'd mourn any, if one of the lives lost had been Cudlip's."

"And you in jail now. That'd be a great help to your wife and children, wouldn't it? No, I thank God you didn't have a gun."

Shel had said no more to Wendlin about it. Wendlin had enough sorrow on his heart without having to listen to him ask, "Would Pete be alive if we had gotten there earlier? If we'd had a gun?"

Pete was dead. He was a good man and he was dead. He was dead because he was a good man. That's why I have to ask myself these questions, Shel thought. When a good man is killed, you have to ask why? And who? Who killed Pete? Ellen lying? Ben out late spooning? Medora chasing Julian? Was it Lute, encouraging Base, going with him? Was it Indy Cope, too sleepy to get up out of her bed and go spread the news? Was it Asa, moth chasing or stargazing? Tom Mount, what were you up to that night? Indy Cope called to you at the Reynolds' house. What kept you from hearing her? You had a car; you could have been there in short order. Raunce, if you'd stayed away from your wife that afternoon in the church, you'd have been a full-fledged preacher now, home nights and not out in the oil field. Raunce killed you, Pete. And you were killed by Sylvester Perkins, who opened up the Tract to Mexican-haters like Cudlip. And you were killed by Julian, who called on you for help. And Woodrow Wilson killed you, Pete, declaring war and stirring up the Mexican-haters. And I killed you. Somewhere along the way, I killed you, Pete.

Shel's mind whirled around in dry and painful circles, hunting a murderer. Well, Mary, he thought, you at least were guiltless. You, on your deathbed, escape my charges. You had no hand in it.

Someone, while he had been thinking of Pete, had risen to his—or maybe her—feet, and spoken; he didn't know what. But Biblical language echoed in his ears. The room was silent again, and he went back to his questions. Why did Base . . . Why did . . . But his questioning was stopped. In the silence, a voice spoke inside his own head. "You are launching into a history of the human race. You will end with Cain, or not even there—his father. You are turned in the wrong direction."

In the midst of culprits, in the midst of the silence, Shel listened. He contradicted no one. There was no one to contradict. In the silence, he stopped saying, "We have killed a good man." He heard instead, "Don't let him die in vain." The silence cast these words toward him time and again in the way the surf casts up the same strand of seaweed. The shore can do nothing about these poundings. But a man can. He can throw the words silence gives him back into the silence.

"Do not let him die in vain," Shel said.

As he remained standing, it came to Shel that this was Mary's funeral, not Pete's, and he added, "I have not forgotten Mary Jessup. I speak for her, too."

He sat down abashed, and the silence that enveloped him was again wordless, though various others spoke. The windows were all open, and whatever sounds or scents there were outside the church came freely in: the dry earth and withered grass smell of a warm day in an arid country, and the soft, everlasting clickings of insects, and the faint whisper of the sea wind around the solitary building.

It was Ellen who told him it was time to go. "Papa," she said, "people are leaving."

In the churchyard, the enormity of what he had done came over him. He went over to Wendlin and Ben.

"Wendlin," he said, "I can't account for what I just did. I want to apologize. I had no right. . . ."

But Wendlin wouldn't let him continue, though he was too broken up to say much. "You spoke better than you knew." He attempted a few words, then said, "Some other time, Shel, I'll talk to you."

The people were trying not to be hypocrites. They knew that tomorrow they would eat, laugh, and make love. They knew also that they were brokenhearted now. In Mary's death, they lost their own

559

mothers all over again. They faced the paltriness of their own lives, the short span, the meanness and the meagerness. But, sobbing now, they remembered tomorrow, and tried to make today's sorrow square with tomorrow's forgetfulness. Their voices were subdued, their eyes red-rimmed, but they spoke of the world they would continue to live in. Mary had passed beyond, but they hadn't—the war, their suit against Perkins, Cudlip's crime, Shel's baby.

"What're you calling your baby, Shel?" Eunice asked him.

"Peter Ramos, Junior."

Shel felt the consternation amongst his listeners—some of which he shared. The idea had come to him with the question.

Mrs. Reynolds, on whose home Tom Mount was working, said, "I thought that was the name of the Ramos baby."

"No," Shel said, "the Ramos baby, since its father's been killed, is no longer Junior. There were supposed to be two Pete Ramoses in the world. My baby's younger than Pete's and Rosa's so it'll be the Junior. I haven't talked to Rosa about it yet, but I hope she won't have any objections. That's the name I'd like my boy to have."

Ellen said, "Mama was counting on a Shelby, Junior."

Shel put his hand on her shoulder. "You and Ben'll have to take care of that, I reckon, Ellen."

Ellen was going to the graveyard with Ben and Wendlin. Shel, because Joicey was alone with Zoomy and the baby, didn't think he ought to be away from her long enough for that journey. He could see that Ellen, leaving him for Ben and Wendlin, felt homesick. She had always before gone home with her own folks.

"Tell Mama I don't like to be away now, when she needs me."

"She'll understand," Shel said. "She'd want you to go with Mary. Mary took a great liking to your mother from the very first."

Shel waited until the hearse, followed by a half-dozen cars, pulled out of the barren churchyard. Then, feeling lonesome himself, he got into the buggy and started Diamond homeward. He drove slowly because he felt himself to be leaving so much behind. Mary, of course. His own two, married and marrying. Pete, most of all—except perhaps for the Shel Lewis who had arrived on the Tract nine months ago. That cocksure fellow he was also leaving behind, that man who had picked Lute Cope for a friend and who had thought LeRoy a laughingstock. The man who had felt honored when Tom Mount had stopped, in his flashy red car, at about this very spot, to greet him; who had believed that his family was completed, that Pete Ramos was his hired man, Sylvester Perkins his benefactor, Chad his enemy, religion his hindrance, and himself a big-time citrus grower. All gone. Past history. The nine months that had made a son for him had also made him a different man. Better or worse? He wouldn't care to say. Road-worker, potato cropper, speaker in church, his best friend a dead Mexican. If he'd learned one thing in the past nine months, it was that there were more answers in the world than he could squeeze out of his own gray matter.

On the last rise before the hill on which their house stood, Zoomy had made a rock pile which he used as a lookout to scan the road east for Indian war parties or Confederate outriders. The rock pile was occupied now, and Shel slapped the reins across Diamond's rump, afraid that Zoomy had come down to meet him with bad news. Nearer, he saw that the lookout wasn't Zoomy, and when he arrived, he spoke more out of his irritation for the scare than relief.

"Asa, what're you doing out here?"

Asa showed his surprise at Shel's tone but replied calmly. "Watching the sun go down."

"Why here?"

"I don't know why here," Asa said. "I started walking, and when I stopped, this is where I was. Am I trespassing?"

Shel apologized. "You gave me a scare," he said. "I thought you were Zoomy, come out to meet me with bad news. How'd you get out here so fast, anyway?"

Asa shrugged. 'I wasn't in any mood to loiter."

"Mary Jessup was a special friend of yours, wasn't she?" Shel said.

"She was my friend."

"I'm sorry you lost her."

"It wasn't an experience I would've missed."

Shel was taken aback. What did that mean? There was no answer on Asa's face. His stance, on top of the rock pile, was Indian, his face hard and expressionless. He didn't look at Shel but at the bright snake bends of the Santa Ana, lucent as quicksilver under the low sun.

"Pete was my friend," Shel said, "but I feel his death was an experience I could just as easy do without."

Asa turned away from the Santa Ana's quicksilver. "You can't do without anything that has happened," Asa said. "You don't have that choice. The only choice you've got is what you'll do with the happen-

561

ing. Whether or not you'll experience it or let it pass you by. Mary died outside my wanting or not wanting. But her death was her last act, and it isn't an experience I would've missed."

Shel, the man who had learned to listen a little, listened now.

"It was her last act as a live woman, and I was close enough to her to take it in. When she was alive, we spoke of small things, lemonade, the need of a haircut, the war news. The talk obscured her. Now it is finished, and her death has completed her."

Asa paused, and Shel bit his big tongue, preventing himself any questions.

"Now she speaks to me out of her wholeness," Asa said. "She doesn't have to shape herself to meet me with small answers. Now I see her. If she had outlived me—I would've missed her. I thought about death a good deal as a boy. I thought it was a personal encounter, a hand-to-hand struggle between Asa Brice and the grim reaper. With Asa Brice winning. There aren't any winners, Shel."

Asa stepped off the rock pile, and Shel was surprised once again to see how short Asa was, a little fellow of few inches as a yardstick measures. The sun had gone down; the river had lost its sheen. But the light that had left the water was now on the foothills, bringing to life their wrinkled old lion pelts.

"Death's not personal even though persons die. It's no hand-to-hand struggle. It's a place we're all going. Some of us are already well on our way. Mary was gone. Oh, I would fail her now, and myself, if the experience of her going was something I could do without."

Shel, who had had no reply to this, said when Asa appeared to have finished, "Asa, why don't you come on home with me for supper? We're missing two at the table tonight. We'd enjoy your company."

Asa shook his head. "It's kind of you. I appreciate the invitation. But not tonight."

Shel didn't press him. The invitation had been sincere; still, Asa's possible loneliness by himself in that tent of his, after the day of burying, had been more on Shel's mind than his own pleasure.

"Suit yourself, Asa," he said, "but remember the latchstring's always out for you. You don't need to stand on ceremony or wait for formal invitations. Just put in an appearance any time."

Asa said, "Thanks," but nothing more; and Shel gave Diamond, barn-bound and eager for his evening barley, his head. They traveled eastward at a good clip, through the saffron afterlight and under an evening sky that, for all it was star high and world wide, curved over

Shel's head with home familiarity. The brown hills whose curves he knew by heart went with him to the north. Old Saddle Back got bigger for his benefit as he approached it. Absorbed, he did not hear Asa's first shouts, but when finally he did, the earlier ones of which he had been unconscious still echoed in his ears. Asa was jogging toward him, but Shel turned the buggy around and drove back to meet him.

"I know you're anxious to get home," Asa apologized, when they met, "but there's something I ought to have told you—the reason I couldn't have supper with you."

"You don't owe me any excuses for not coming," Shel assured him.

"I'm not making excuses," Asa said. "But I wanted you to know the reason I couldn't come. I'm having supper tonight with Eunice."

"Who you have supper with is your own business, Asa. There's no call for you to tell me about it."

"You may not have any call to listen, Shel, but I've got a call to let it be known. I'm through trying to protect myself and live to myself. I'm throwing my lot in with the human race. I'm winding up my career as ant watcher and bird expert. I'm going to ask Eunice to marry me tonight."

"Congratulations," Shel said because he didn't know what else to say.

"You can congratulate me on coming back here and telling you my intentions. But so far as Eunice goes, there's nothing yet for congratulations. She may turn me down. But I don't intend to try to hide the fact I asked her. I'd like it known. I'm living in the open. I'm dependent on people. I'm ready to admit I can't make a go of it alone."

Shel was moved. Asa was no easy babbler. He didn't wear his heart on his sleeve by nature. He was voluntarily putting it there, because he thought a sleeve so decorated made a better gift for a friend. Shel reached a hand out to Asa's shoulder, felt Asa flinch under it, then steady.

"Eunice is a fine girl, Asa. I wish you luck."

Asa lifted his chin and narrowed his eyes like a real courting man. "One thing I have got is patience," he said. "Those years with the ants weren't all wasted. If she turns me down tonight, I'll try again tomorrow."

The two shook hands, and Asa said, "Well, she's expecting me," and turned westward with his long, ground-eating, short-legged stride.

Shel watched him for quite a spell. The lamps had been lit in his own home and he imagined Zoomy, aproned like a plump grandma, getting supper while Joicey, with Peter Ramos, Junior, by her side, directed his operations from her bed in the spare room. It came to him that Joicey didn't know that the baby *was* Peter Ramos, Junior. He'd better get home and break the news to her. He took one last look at Asa, bigger at a distance than near up, climbing a hill toward Eunice and the human race. Shel swung Diamond round away from Asa. Two of us, he thought, heading in opposite directions toward the same thing. This hasn't been the best day in the world, but I'm alive, ain't I? I'm learning. I've got plenty of cause to praise.

ALBERTSON COLLEGE OF IDAHO
PS3545.E8315.S6
South of the Angels.

3 5556 00045464 5

WITHDRAWN